Mikhail Sholokhov
Quiet Flows the Don

a novel in two volumes

volume one

translated by Robert Daglish

Raduga

Collets

Translation from the Russian

English translation © Raduga Publishers 1984

First unabridged English edition 1984
as part of Mikhail Sholokhov's collected
works in eight volumes.

First unabridged separate English edition 1988

Raduga Publishers, *119859 Moscow, 17 Zubovsky Blvd., USSR*
Collets, *Denington Estate, Wellingborough, Northants, U.K.*

Printed in the Union of Soviet Socialist Republics

ISBN 0569-08956-5

CONTENTS

TRANSLATOR'S INTRODUCTION

Nearly fifty years have elapsed since Sholokhov's novel first appeared in English. Life has changed enormously since then. War has shaken the world to its foundations. New states have emerged, others collapsed. In personal life, too, our attitudes have changed; even our language differs from that of the thirties, particularly with regard to what can and cannot be said in print. And yet the enormous canvas Sholokhov painted to describe the impact of the Russian Revolution on the lives of ordinary people has lost none of its freshness, none of its intense emotional appeal. On the contrary, when we turn again to its pages we constantly stumble on something, a flash of insight, a note of compassion or irony, that we had either forgotten or never noticed before. I have yet to meet a Russian who after re-reading *Quiet Flows the Don* did not tell me that it was like reading a new novel.

This feeling seems to have been shared by literary scholars. In the USSR the list of Sholokhov researchers is naturally long, the most interesting for the translator being F. A. Abramov and V. V. Gura (life and work), S. N. Semanov (historical sources) and K. E. Priima (textology and world impact). In the West too, the last fifteen years have seen the appearance of at least three important studies in English. In his *Critical Introduction* Professor D. H. Steward of Michigan[1] gives strong literary and historical reasons for regarding Sholokhov as the Homer of modern times. Professor Brian Murphy (Coleraine) is currently completing the most detailed line-by-line commentary on the various Russian editions of *Quiet Flows the Don* yet to appear in any language.[2]

---

[1] D. H. Stewart, *Sholokhov. A Critical Introduction*, Ann Arbor, 1967.

[2] A. B. Murphy in association with M. Duncan, V. Svoboda and V. P. Butt, 'An Introduction and Commentary to *Tikhiy Don*', New Zealand Slavonic Journal, 1975-1982.

And Professor Herman Ermolaev (Princeton) has combined biography and linguistic study[3] with an examination of conflicting views of Sholokhov's art that leads him to the conclusion that Sholokhov has a unique place in literature.

When Stephen Garry produced the first English translation of the novel, fascism was on the march in Europe. Even in England and America publishers were not much interested in putting out a first novel about the Russian Revolution by a young writer who had only just achieved recognition in his own country. But Garry persisted, and the first two books, in abridged form, were eventually published in 1934. It says much for both the quality of the original and the skill of the translator that even in this form the novel won immediate acclaim and became a best-seller in Britain and the US.

But the cutting had been severe. Professor Stewart has told us that it amounts to 25 per cent of the original text.[4] To cite only a few examples. Much important historical background is obliterated by the omission of the chapter describing the suicide of General Kaledin (we also lose the artistic counterpoint between that scene and the story of Pantelei's very differently expressed grief); also missing are episodes connected with General Kornilov's abortive attempt to overthrow the Kerensky government, the British and French intervention during the Civil War, and the documentation of General Krasnov's collaboration with the Germans. On a more intimate level the omission of Timofei's diary leaves the story of Liza Mokhova only half completed, whereas Sholokhov by introducing a young Cossack's notes on his life with Liza in Moscow and at the front in 1914 showed great skill in bringing this story-line to a highly meaningful, anti-war conclusion and in adding further gradations of colour to the picture of the Cossack middle-class intelligentsia, which otherwise might have appeared rather cursory.

In short, when I considered Raduga Publishers proposal to produce a collected edition of Sholokhov's works in English, I found there were ample grounds for making a new translation of his finest novel. The only question was, could I accomplish it?

In the spring of 1980, when I had done about a year's work on my new version, Sholokhov invited me to spend a few days with him on the Don, to see the country and discuss any problems that I might have. I had seen Sholokhov only once, over the heads of the world press at a press conference he gave after receiving one of his many awards. I had been to the Don country before, when Sergei Gerasimov had been shooting his film of *Quiet Flows the Don*. But that had been on the Donets, the little Don, not the great river itself.

After so many years of work on Sholokhov's other novels and stories it was like a homecoming. A rapid drive from the station of Millerovo on the Moscow-Rostov main line took me some 130 kilometres through rolling farm lands to the banks of the Don. The road followed fairly closely the route of the old Hetman's Highway, the track that the Cossack horsemen and Ukrainian settlers used when this land was mainly steppe. Though most of it has now come under the plough, the characteristic features remain—the ravines and gullies, the wooded dells, the sandy summits and

[3] Herman Ermolaev, *Mikhail Sholokhov and His Art*, Princeton University Press, 1982.
[4] D. H. Stewart, *Op cit.*, p. 204.

chalky headlands. Tractors and cultivators are often to be seen, but with its thatched and white-washed cottages nestling among the poplar groves the countryside still has that air of peace for which the river has long been famous. And despite the pesticides and weed-killers that come with modern agriculture, the traditional steppeland flowers and grasses—the wormwood, sweet clover, wild thyme and feathergrass—are still to be found on the hillsides.

Vyoshenskaya, or Vyoshki, as the local people call their district centre, appears suddenly as the road sweeps down to the river.

It was here that Sholokhov began writing his epic in 1925 and he was still living here, in a spacious house overlooking the Don, in 1980. I found him in far from good health, but through a two-hour dinner with his family and the local people who were to be my guides he drank to toasts, made his quiet jokes and never stopped asking me gently probing questions about myself and my work, in which I felt a warm and friendly interest. When I confessed to having a Russian wife, he chuckled and rhymed in the local dialect, 'You're like a Cossack—where you ride you take a bride.'

Only that morning, I learned later, he had had an article I had written about translating *Quiet Flows the Don* read to him in Russian by a local teacher of English, Nadezhda Kuznetsova, who is the daughter of Timofei Mrykhin, Sholokhov's first tutor. It was Mrykhin who encouraged Mikhail's early interest in literature. Sholokhov's father, who had sacrificed Cossack status for love, had been constantly moving from place to place, and he asked Mrykhin to make good the consequent gaps in his son's education, a task he must have performed very well indeed.

It was not long before I felt so much at home that I was able to ask Sholokhov about the editions and was delighted to learn that he still regards the first edition of the novel, despite the misprints and occasional slips, as his favourite. 'But,' he added, in reply to my next question, 'if you translate from that you'll have a lot more problems with dialect. And didn't you just say yourself that Cossack dialect cannot be conveyed in English?'

The Don Cossacks speak a specific South Russian dialect, and their speech differs in various parts of the Don country. As recently as 1975, the Rostov University compilers of the Russian Don Dialects Dictionary (over 14,000 words) could claim that notable variations of speech were to be found in Don villages only three kilometres apart. These are the dialects that Sholokhov has known since childhood and that he filters for the nuggets with which his dialogue and even his descriptive prose are studded.

This special lilt or accent cannot be conveyed in English, any more than the splendid Russian translations of Burns can reproduce his Scotticisms. It can only be hinted at occasionally, as I have done when I make an old woman call Khristonya 'my bonnie', for instance. But this does not mean that all the 'colour of saying', to borrow a phrase from Dylan Thomas, is lost in translation. The speech of Sholokhov's Cossack characters abounds in imagery and comparisons that have almost as much impact in English as in Russian; their earthy humour, the epithets they hurl at each other, their heroic or bawdy songs have meaning enough to engage us without being uttered in a specific accent, and I ask the reader's indulgence for attempting them all. The trick here is to maintain the colloquial level at the right moments without sliding into a vulgar, urbanised slang.

The fabric of Sholokhov's narrative is rich with metaphor and simile and presents a tremendous challenge to the translator. Though Russian with its flexible word-order is a little more suited to this style than modern English, I have tried whenever possible to reproduce the atmosphere-creating passages (far too exact in their descriptions of nature to be called 'pathetic fallacy') in something like the form of the original. I have even tried to use English words in the same unusual way in which Sholokhov uses the Russian, when, for instance, he speaks of smoke 'rearing' from a chimney or the 'bruised' sky that hangs over Aksinya at the time of her elopement from her brutal husband. I see all this not as mere ornament but as one of the subtle ways in which Sholokhov expresses his philosophy of life.

I had begun my translation using the latest, 1975 edition of the novel, but this gave rise to a problem. In 1953, *Quiet Flows the Don* had been subjected to considerable editorial revision in Russian. Three years later Sholokhov himself restored the text almost to its original form. But he did not restore part of the argument between Bunchuk and his fellow officers at the front in 1916, or the short chapter describing Bunchuk and Anna's life together, or the brief altercation between Podtyolkov and Krivoshlykov over taking Podtyolkov's mistress Zina with them on the ill-fated expedition into Whiteheld territory; several descriptive strokes, such as Veniamin's habit of eating the food his master spat out, also went by the board.

It may well be that Sholokhov thought the editors had a point in shortening the officers' argument. The idea of Bunchuk being able to quote from Lenin and Marx at such length in so hostile an environment does perhaps strain artistic credibility. He may also have felt that Bunchuk's sweeping denunciation of false patriotism could be sacrificed since it was already implicit in the one quotation from Lenin he had retained and in the pamphlet that Listnitsky finds in the trenches the next day. In his commentary Professor Murphy reports that Sholokhov felt the character of Bunchuk was beginning to overshadow that of his main character Grigory and this may have been responsible for his decision not to restore the description of Anna and Bunchuk's life together in the early days of the Civil War. But whatever consideration decided the fate of these few unrestored pages (not more than six in all), I could not help feeling it would be a pity if in presenting a new, complete translation I did not give the reader the chance of judging them for himself. I put my thoughts into a letter to Sholokhov and he responded with a letter to Raduga Publishers giving his consent to my using the earliest editions[5] (1928 for the first two volumes and

[5] For this, 2nd edition of the new translation the 1939 Russian edition was compared with the Russian edition of 1933. Besides Sholokhov's own footnote (see pp. 340-41, Book Three), the only essential change revealed in the Russian edition was that the passage regarding Trotsky's visit to the Red front had not been included in 1933. However, in deference to Sholokhov's preference for the 1939 edition and in view of its historical interest, the passage has been allowed to remain in the present edition of the translation.

With all due respect to Mr. Svoboda's opinion (*Irish Slavonic Studies*) the red commander Mironov does *not* play "a prominent part" in the narrative. Neither he nor his actions are described in any detail. His name has therefore been restored not mechanically but in such a way that the reader will at least know on which side he and his men were fighting.

1939 for the last two) in view of 'the interest that continues to this day among American and English readers and scholars in the early editions of the novel'. I have therefore based my version on the 1928 Moskovsky Rabochy and 1939 Rostov-on-Don editions of the Russian original, while retaining corrections to some dates and names made in later editions.

But translation is not just a matter of selecting editions. It is a long battle for the sound and weight of every word, or rather for sounds and meanings. To give only one example—the problem of the title. *The Quiet Don* is a literal and, up to a point, accurate rendering of the Russian title, but it is flat and also rather ambiguous (what kind of 'don'?). On the other hand the old double title (*And Quiet Flows the Don* and *The Don Flows Home to the Sea*) puts too much stress on the idea of the eternity of nature as opposed to the ways of man. This element does exist in Sholokhov's writing but he does not lean on it so heavily. His title is more enigmatic, perhaps even ironical, and certainly broader in its associations. The near synonyms of 'quiet'—'gentle', 'peaceful', 'silent'— offer no solution. They are narrower than 'quiet'. But the word 'flows', though not in the Russian, is valuable in English. It is dynamic like the book itself and leaves the reader in no doubt that we are talking about a river.

It would seem then that the snag in the old title is the little word 'and'. If we eliminate that, we reduce the deterministic element. But is this version less poetic? Perhaps, if one equates the poetic with the elegiac, but not otherwise. Sholokhov, I am sure, did not want his title to sound elegiac, but rather stimulating and ironic, underlining a contrast between the traditional Cossack way of life and what was to come.

Some students of translation maintain that local terms should not be translated but only transliterated. At one time it was thought that Lev Tolstoy's stories about peasants could not be properly rendered without the use of the word *izba*—the Russian peasant's log house. If this were so, the translator of Sholokhov would have to pepper his text with such localisms as *kuren* (house), *bashlyk* (hood), *shashka* (sabre), *cherkesska* (long tunic-like coat), *khutor* (village), *stanitsa* (district and district centre), and many other purely Cossack terms, along with all the names for the ranks of the Don Cossack Army, which, though subordinate to the Imperial High Command, retained its own system up to the rank of Lieutenant-Colonel.

I have used some of these terms at points where they have a special significance in the story, but on the whole my feeling has been that with the novel's descriptive passages providing so much local colour, the reader would prefer to know, for instance, that at home and for work in the fields Cossacks wore over their white woolen socks flat-heeled leather shoes or sometimes cut-down riding boots (it was the leg that wore out first) than to be left wondering if the mysterious *chirik* is a moccasin, a sandal, or some kind of sock.

Another problem was that of names. While I was on the Don I asked Sholokhov why he sometimes gave quite different characters one and the same second name. 'Ah,' he said, 'but that's what life's like down here.' It turns out that Cossack country is rather like Wales. There may even be as many Koshevois as there are Williamses and Evanses across the marches. The two Kudinovs, Pavel and Semyon, that appear in the novel are, in fact, historical personages.

Like any other Russian writer, Sholokhov often uses the very flexible and expressive diminutive forms of names. Some translators believe one should anglicise all Russian names—Gregory for Grigory, Michael for Mikhail, and so on. But would one do this with a French or German novel—Peter for Pierre, John for Johann? Why should one preserve a special ignorance with regard to Russian names, so many of which are derived from the Greek? My policy has been to retain the author's forms and even some of his nicknames, in the hope that the reader will catch the implications. 'Grishka' is short for Grigory, and 'Grisha' is an even more affectionate form. 'Mishka' is short for Mikhail, and Sholokhov nearly always refers authorially to Mikhail Koshevoi as 'Mishka'. 'Dunyashka' is short for 'Yevdokiya'; the Melekhovs' youngest daughter is also sometimes 'Dunya'. We never learn the first name of Grigory's mother, 'Ilyinichna' is her patronymic, and this is a very common way for middle-aged women to be addressed in the country, although mature people are usually referred to in formal conversation by their first name and patronymic, and Sholokhov keeps this form of address for Grigory's father—Pantelei Prokofievich Melekhov. For readability, however, I have usually shortened this to Pantelei, retaining the patronymic only where it seems necessary in dialogue to convey formality.

Those three days I spent down on the Don were a wonderful experience. I felt the magic of Sholokhov's humorous, brave and kindly personality. It was a distillation of what I have experienced in the years while his ideas and characters have been passing through my brain. Their sorrows, their joys, the grandeur of their country and the total absence of pettiness in the description of their lives have left a deep impression that has, I believe, contributed much to my own personal happiness. I hope this translation will, at least in part, repay that debt.

In conclusion I should like to thank Professor Murphy and his colleagues for showing me their commentaries, and to express special gratitude to my bilingual Russian editors Raissa Bobrova and Alexandra Bouianovskaya, who checked the whole translation for accuracy and made many invaluable suggestions.

Robert Daglish

THE MAIN CHARACTERS

The Mélekhovs
    Panteléi Prokófievich Mélekhov, a Cossack
    Ilyínichna, his wife
    Pyotr, 'Petró', his elder son
    Grigóry, 'Gríshka' or 'Grísha', his younger son
    Yevdokíya, 'Dunyáshka', his daughter
    Dárya, wife of Petro.

The Astákhovs

    Stepan Astákhov, a Cossack
    Aksínya, his wife

The Kórshunovs
    Mirón Grigórievich Kórshunov, a Cossack
    Lukínichna, his wife
    Dmítry, 'Mítka', his son
    Natálya, his daughter
    Grisháka, his father

The Mókhovs
    Sergéi Platónovich Mókhov, a merchant, owner of a shop and mill
    Yelizavéta Mókhova, 'Líza', his daughter
    Vladímir, his son
    Anna, their stepmother

The Listnítskys
    Nikolái Alekséyevich Listnítsky, a retired general, master of Yagodnoye estate
    Yevgény Nikoláyevich Listnítsky, his son, an officer in the Russian Army

Other People of Tatarsky Village
    Mikhaíl Koshevói, 'Míshka', a friend of Grigory's
    Khrisánf Tókin, 'Khristónya', a Cossack guardsman
    Ivan Alekseyevich Kotlyaróv ⎤
    Knave   ⎬   employees at
    Davýdka   ⎦   Mokhov's mill
    Anikéi, a neighbour of the Melekhovs
    Prókhor Zýkov, regimental comrade of Grigory, later his orderly
    Osip Davýdovich Stókman, a newcomer and revolutionary

At the Front
    Ilyá Bunchúk, a volunteer in the 1914 war, later officer and revolutionary
    Ánna Pogúdko, a member of his machine-gun squad, revolutionary
    Major Kalmykóv, an officer in Bunchuk's regiment, joined Kornilov conspiracy
    Uryúpin, 'Curly', a Cossack in Grigory's troop
    Fyódor Podtyólkov, Chairman of the Don Military Revolutionary Committee
    Mikhaíl Krivoshlýkov, Secretary of the Committee
    Yákov Yefímovich Fomín, deserter in 1915, later an insurgent

,

BOOK ONE

Not by the plough is our fair land furrowed...
It is furrowed by horses' hoofs,
And sown is our fair land with Cossack heads.
Adorned is our quiet Don with young widows,
Beflowered is our father, the quiet Don, with orphans,
Full are the waves of the quiet Don with fathers'
                                        and mothers' tears.

———————————

Oh thou, our father, quiet Don!
Why dost thou, the quiet Don, so sludgy flow?
How could I, the quiet Don, but sludgy flow!
From my depths the cold springs rise,
Amid me the white fish leap.
                        Old Cossack songs

PART ONE

I

The Melekhov farm stood on the very edge of the village. The gate of the cattle yard faced north, towards the Don. A steep path dropped fifty feet between moss-greened chalky boulders, and there was the beach. A pearly sprinkling of shells, a grey jagged fringe of wave-kissed shingle, and then the burnished, steel-blue rip of the mainstream, seething in the wind. To the east, beyond the wattle fences of the threshing floors ran the Hetman's Highway, with its grizzled fringe of wormwood and hardy brown, hoof-hammered plantains; a little shrine stood at the fork of the road and beyond lay the steppe, wrapped in a shimmering haze. To the south was the chalky hump of a hill. To the west, a track crossing the square and running out to the riverside meadows.

During the last but one campaign against the Turks, the Cossack Prokofy Melekhov had returned to the village, bringing with him a wife from the Turkish lands—a little woman wrapped from head to foot in a shawl. She kept her face covered and seldom showed her wild yearning eyes. The silken shawl bore the scent of strange aromatic perfumes and its colourful patterns fed the Cossack women's envy. The captive Turkish woman held herself aloof from Prokofy's family and old Melekhov soon gave his son his portion. So deep was the offence that to the end of his days he never set foot in his son's house.

Prokofy was not long in making a place for himself. Carpenters built him a sturdy log house, he himself fenced off a yard for the animals, and by autumn he was able to take his bowed foreign wife to her new home. As he walked with her behind a wagon carrying all their belongings, the whole village, young and old, came out to watch. The men chuckled quietly into their beards, the women shouted stridently to one another, and a horde of unwashed children ran catcalling after Prokofy. But with his long Cossack coat unbuttoned he walked on slowly, like a ploughman in a fresh furrow, gripping his wife's frail wrist in his dark hand and holding his head with its thick straw-coloured forelock proud and high. Only the swell and ripple of his jaw muscles and the sweat breaking out between his motionless, rock-like brows betrayed any emotion.

After that he was seldom seen in the village and never came to the village meetings. He lived a lone-wolf existence in his far-out house overlooking the Don. Strange tales were told about him in the village. Herdboys grazing the calves on the outskirts said they had seen Prokofy of an evening, when the sunset faded, carry his wife in his arms all the way to the Tatar burial mound. He would set her down on the very top with her back against the ancient pitted stone and sit down beside her, and they would sit there together, gazing out over the steppe until the last gleams of sunset died. Then Prokofy would wrap his wife in his coat and carry her back home. The village was lost in conjecture as to the explanation of such outlandish behaviour and gossip among the women rose to such a pitch that they had no patience for their usual pastime of searching each other's heads for lice. All manner of things were said about Prokofy's wife. Some would have it that she was beautiful beyond belief and others, quite the contrary. The matter was settled after the most venturesome of the women, the grass-widow Mavra, slipped into Prokofy's house on the pretext of asking for some fresh leaven. Prokofy went down to the cellar for the leaven and Mavra had time to discover that in picking his Turkish woman Prokofy could not have done worse if he had tried.

Soon Mavra with flushed cheeks and kerchief all awry was holding forth to a crowd of women in a by-lane.

'What could he have seen in her, my dears? Call that a woman! Why, there's nothing to her, back or front. It's not decent. Our girls have far more flesh on them.

Her waist's so thin you could pull her apart like a wasp. And those great dark eyes that she shoots about like the devil—God forgive me. I believe she's near her time too, honestly I do!'

'Near her time,' the women gasped.

'Must be! I ought to know, I've raised three myself.'

'Is she pretty?'

'Pretty? Yellow. And her eyes are muddy. She doesn't find life much to her liking in a foreign land, I'll be bound. And you know what, girls? She goes about in Prokofy's trousers!'

'No?!' the women gave one concerted gasp of fright.

'I saw her myself—in trousers, but without the side stripes. She must have got hold of his everyday ones. She had on a long blouse, and under that were the trousers, tucked into socks. When I saw that, my blood ran cold.'

The word went round the village that Prokofy's wife was a witch. Astakhov's daughter-in-law (the Astakhovs also lived on the outskirts, not far from Prokofy) vowed that on the second day of Whitsuntide, before dawn, she had seen Prokofy's wife, bareheaded and barefooted, milking a cow in their yard. After that the cow had lost its milk, its udder had shrivelled to the size of a child's fist, and soon the animal had died.

That year a murrain struck the cattle. Every day the watering place on the sandbar running out into the Don from the cattle pens was strewn with the carcasses of cows and their young. The infection spread to the horses. The herds on the stanitsa* grazing lands began to melt away. And it was then that the black rumour crept through the lanes and streets.

After holding a meeting to consider the matter the Cossacks went to Prokofy's house.

The master came out on to his porch and bowed.

'What good purpose brings you here, respected elders?'

The crowd advancing on the porch remained dumbly silent.

At length a tipsy old fellow gave the first shout: 'Fetch out your witch! We'll deal with her!'

Prokofy dashed into the house, but they caught him in the inner porch. A burly gunner, nicknamed Strut,

---

* *Stanitsa*—in Cossack territory, the centre of the smallest administrative area and the area itself, which comprised several villages. The word is derived from *stan*—camp.—*Tr.*

battered Prokofy's head against the wall, and told him, 'Don't make a row! It's no use! We won't touch you but we're going to trample your woman into the ground. Better to finish her than have the whole village die without cattle. And you keep quiet or I'll knock the wall down with your head!'

'Drag the bitch out into the yard!' came the shout from the steps.

A man of Prokofy's own regiment wound the Turkish woman's hair round one hand, clamped the other over her screaming mouth, dragged her at a run across the porch and flung her at the feet of the crowd. A high-pitched cry pierced the roar of voices.

Prokofy threw off half a dozen Cossacks, dashed into his front room and snatched a sabre from the wall. The Cossacks backed out of the porch, jostling one another. With the glittering sword whirling and whistling above his head, Prokofy ran down the steps. The crowd recoiled and scattered across the yard.

Prokofy caught up with the heavy-footed Strut at the barn and with a slanting stroke cleft him from the left shoulder to the waist. The other Cossacks, who had been tearing stakes out of the fence, bolted across the threshing floor into the steppe.

Half an hour later the crowd felt bold enough to approach the farm again. Two scouts entered the porch nervously. Prokofy's wife lay on the kitchen threshold in a pool of blood, her head thrown back awkwardly, her bitten tongue writhing between bared teeth. Prokofy, his head shaking and eyes set in a fixed stare, was wrapping a sheepskin round a squealing ball of flesh—the prematurely born child.

* * *

Prokofy's wife died the same evening. His mother took in the child out of pity.

They plastered it with steamed bran mash, fed it on mare's milk and a month later, satisfied that the dark Turkish-looking baby boy would live, took him to church to be christened. He was named after his grandfather, Pantelei. Prokofy returned from penal servitude twelve years later. With his clipped tawny-grey beard and ordinary Russian clothes he no longer looked like a Cossack. He took his son and set to work on his farm.

Pantelei grew up into a black-haired swarthy man of ungovernable temperament. He took after his mother in face and lithe figure.

Prokofy married him to a Cossack girl, his neighbour's daughter.

And from that time on Turkish blood mingled with that of the Cossack and the village acquired its breed of hook-nosed savagely handsome Melekhov Cossacks or, as they were commonly called, 'Turks'.

After burying his father, Pantelei got his teeth into the work of improving the farm. He put a new roof on the house, added to his farm an acre or more of vacant land, and built new sheds and a barn with a sheet-iron roof. On the owner's instructions the roof-maker cut a pair of cockerels out of the left-overs and fixed them to the roof of the barn. Their jaunty appearance brightened the Melekhov farmstead and gave it an air of self-content and good living.

As the years slid by, Pantelei Prokofievich grew gnarled and craggy; his shoulders broadened and began to stoop, but he still looked a sturdy old man. He was lean, walked with a limp (he had broken his left leg during the races at an imperial review of troops), and wore a silver half-moon ear-ring in his left ear. The raven hue of his beard and hair did not fade even in old age. In anger he would go berserk, and it was probably this that had prematurely aged his buxom wife, whose once beautiful face was now a web of wrinkles.

Petro, his elder, married son, resembled his mother. He was stocky and snub-nosed with a rebellious shock of corn-coloured hair and brown eyes; but the younger, Grigory, took after his father. He was half a head taller than Petro, though six years younger, had the same hawk nose, the same fierce eyes, like blue-tinted almonds in their slanting slits, the same sharp cheekbones strapped with brown ruddy skin. Grigory also had his father's slight stoop, and even their smiles harboured the same hint of savagery.

There was also Dunyashka—her father's favourite—a long-armed large-eyed girl in her teens, and Petro's wife Darya, with their baby, and that was the whole Melekhov family.

II

Only a few stars still glimmered in the ash-grey morning sky. A light breeze was blowing from under heavy clouds. The mist reared high over the Don, flattened itself against a chalky headland and slithered down into the ravines like a grey headless serpent. The left bank of the river, the great tracts of sand, the backwaters, the bulrush thickets and dew-drenched trees were ablaze in the cold frenzied light of dawn. Below the horizon the sun smouldered and would not rise.

In the Melekhov household the first to shake off sleep was Pantelei. He walked out on to the porch, buttoning the collar of his embroidered shirt. The grassy yard was paved with dewy silver. While he was letting the animals out into the lane Darya ran past in only her shift to milk the cows. The dew spurted like beestings over the calves of her bare white legs and a smoky trail appeared in her wake.

Pantelei watched the flattened grass rise again and went into the front room.

The window was wide open and the petals of a cherry-tree that had shed its blossom lay deathly pink on the sill. Grigory was sleeping face downward, one arm outstretched.

'Grigory, want to come fishing?'

'What's that?' the lad asked in a whisper and swung his legs over the edge of the bed.

'Let's go for the morning rise.'

With a snuffling yawn Grigory reached for his everyday trousers, pulled them on and tucked them into white socks, and was a long time easing his foot into a flat-heeled leather shoe, the back of which had curled under.

'Did Mum boil the bait?' he asked huskily, following his father into the porch.

'She did. Go down to the boat. I won't be a minute.'

The old man filled a clay pot with steaming fragrant rye, thriftily swept up the fallen grains into his palm and, limping on his left leg, made his way down the cliff path. Grigory was sitting hunched in the boat.

'Where shall we head for?'

'Black Ravine. We'll try by that snag where we fished t'other day.'

The stern of the boat scraped the beach as it took the water and shot away from the bank. The current rocked it and tried to pull it sideways. Grigory steered with an oar, but did not row.

'Better row a bit, eh?'

'When we get into the middle.'

The boat cut across the fast water and headed for the left bank. The crowing of the village cocks reached them faintly across the river. They moored with the side of the boat scraping a black craggy cliff that hung over the water as if a great chip had been taken out of the hillside. About ten yards from the bank the splayed branches of a sunken elm rose out of the water. Brown flecks of foam were spinning round it.

'Reel out the line while I spread the bait,' Pantelei whispered, and thrust his hand into the steaming mouth of the pot.

The rye sprinkled crisply over the water, like a warning 'hist!' Grigory threaded a few swollen grains on to his hook and smiled.

'Come and get caught, all you fish, big 'uns and little 'uns!'

The line fell into the water in loops, tautened, then slackened again as the sinker touched bottom. Grigory steadied the butt of the rod with his foot and felt for his tobacco pouch, trying not to move.

'We won't get anything today, Dad... Moon's on the wane.'

'Bring any matches?'

'Uh-huh.'

'Give me a light.'

The old man lighted up and glanced at the sun, now snagged behind the sunken tree.

'Carp bite at different times. Even with a waning moon.'

'A little one's having a nibble,' Grigory breathed. Even as he spoke the water washed away from the side of the boat and a three-foot carp that looked as if it were moulded of red copper leapt with a moan, lashing the water twice with its curved, feathery tail. Heavy drops of spray sprinkled over the boat.

'Now you'll see!' Pantelei wiped his wet beard with his sleeve.

Two carp leaped simultaneously among the grasping bare branches of the sunken elm; a third, a little smaller, leapt again and again by the cliff, spinning in the air.

Grigory chewed impatiently at the sodden end of his cigarette. The pallid sun had climbed half way up an oak. Pantelei had used up all the ground bait and with pursed lips was staring stolidly at the motionless tip of the rod.

Grigory spat out the fag-end and watched its rapid flight angrily. Inwardly he was cursing his father for waking him so early. The tobacco he had smoked on an empty stomach had left a taste like singed bristle in his mouth. He was reaching down to scoop up some water, when the end of the rod that was sticking out about a foot above the water jerked feebly and began to dip.

'Strike!' the old man exclaimed.

Grigory started up and grabbed the rod, but it plunged into the water, bending like the hoop of a barrel. It was as if the springy willow were being dragged down by a powerful winch.

'Hold him!' the old man groaned, kicking the boat away from the bank.

Grigory struggled to raise the rod but the stout line snapped with a dry crack and he staggered back, almost losing his balance.

'There's a bull for you!' his father muttered, fumbling with a hook and some fresh bait.

Laughing excitedly, Grigory tied on a new length of line and made a cast. As soon as the sinker touched bottom, the tip of the rod went down.

'There he is, the devil!' Grigory grunted as he battled to bring up the fish which had plunged away towards the fast water.

The line swished away across the surface, raising a curved green wave. Pantelei gripped the handle of the bailer with his stubby fingers.

'Get him up on top! Keep the line tight or he'll saw it in two!'

'The hell he will!'

A big yellowish-red carp rose to the surface, threshed the water into foam, then ducked its blunt, broad-browed head and again plunged into the depths.

'My arm's going numb... No, you don't!'

'Hold him, Grishka!'

'I am holding him!'

'Don't let him get under the boat! Watch out!'

Recovering his breath, Grigory played the carp, which was now lying on its side, closer to the boat. The old man leaned over with the bailer, but the fish summoned a last burst of strength and dived again.

'Get his head up! Make him swallow some air. That'll quieten him down.'

Grigory again played the exhausted fish to the boat. It drifted open-mouthed into the rough gunwale and lay with its orange-gold fins glittering.

'His fighting days are over!' Pantelei grunted, scooping up the fish with the bailer.

They sat for another half an hour. The play of the carp subsided.

'Reel in, Grishka. Looks as if we've got the last one. It's no good waiting for more.'

They gathered their tackle. Grigory pushed off from the bank. Soon they were half the way home. Grigory could see from his father's face that he had something to say, but the old man sat staring silently at the little farmsteads scattered across the lower slopes of the hill.

'Now, look here, Grigory...' he began hesitantly, fingering the strings of the sack that lay at his feet. 'I've noticed you're up to something—with Aksinya Astakhova.'

Grigory flushed darkly and turned away. The collar of his shirt cut into his muscular sunburnt neck, leaving a white line.

'You just look out, my lad,' the old man continued on a harsh, angry note, 'I'll be talking different to you yet. Stepan's our neighbour and I won't have you fooling around with his woman. It could get you into trouble. So I'm warning you beforehand: if I see any more of it, I'll thrash the life out of you!'

Pantelei bunched his gnarled fingers and watched with narrowed eyes as the blood drained from his son's face.

'It's just talk,' Grigory muttered thickly, and looked at the bluish bridge of his father's nose.

'Enough of that.'

'People will say anything.'

'Hold your tongue, you son-of-a-bitch!'

Grigory put his weight to the oars. The boat shot forward in long leaps. The water under the stern whooped and whirligigged away.

There was silence between them until they reached the little wooden pier. As they swung in towards the bank, the father uttered a reminder.

'Mind you don't forget, or I'll put a stop to your going out in the evening. You won't move a step outside the yard. Remember that!'

Grigory made no reply. As he tied up the boat, he asked, 'Shall I give the fish to the women?'

'Sell it to the merchants,' the old man said more gently. 'It'll buy you some 'baccy.'

Biting his lips, Grigory followed his father up the path. 'Nothing doing, Dad! I'm going out tonight even if you hobble me,' he thought, eyes gnawing fiercely at the back of his father's head.

At home he carefully washed off the sand that had dried on the carp's scales and threaded a twig through its gills.

As he came out of the gate he bumped into his old friend Mitka Korshunov, a lad of his own age. Mitka came up toying with the end of his silver-studded belt. His round impudent eyes glistened yellowishly in their narrow slits. The pupils stood upright, like a cat's, making his glance shifty and elusive.

'Where're you going with your fish?'

'Caught it today. To the merchants'.'

'The Mokhovs?'

'That's right.'

Mitka measured the carp with his eye.

'Fifteen pounds?'

'Fifteen and a half. I weighed it.'

'Take me with you. I'll do the haggling.'

'Come on, then.'

'What do I get out of it?'

'We'll settle that later. Why waste our breath now!'

The streets were full of people coming home from church.

The three Shamil brothers were striding down the road together.

The eldest, one-armed Alexei, was in the middle. The tight collar of his uniform held his sinewy neck very straight, the thin curly blade of his beard stuck out challengingly, and his left eye had a nervous tick. Some time ago, during shooting practice, Alexei's rifle had blown up in his hands and a piece of the breech had disfigured him. Since then his eye had winked in season and out of season, and a blue scar ran across his cheek and buried itself in his curly hair. His left arm had been torn off at the elbow, but he could still roll a cigarette faultlessly with one hand; he would press the pouch to his bulging stove-door of a chest, tear off a strip of paper just the right size with his teeth, groove it, scoop up the tobacco and roll the cigarette with an almost imperceptible movement of the fingers. Before you could look twice, a winking Alexei would be chewing at his *tsigarka* and asking for a light.

One-armed though he was, he was the finest fist-fighter in the village. There seemed to be nothing special about his fist—no bigger than wild pumpkin. But one day during ploughing time he happened to get cross with his bullock and, having no whip to hand, gave it a punch on the head. The bullock sank down in the furrow, blood oozing from its ears and only just managed to recover. The two other brothers—Martin and Prokhor—were like Alexei. They were just as stocky and had the girth of an oak in their shoulders, only each had two arms.

Grigory greeted the Shamils as he passed, but Mitka turned his head away till his neck cracked. During the fisticuffs at Shrovetide, Alexei Shamil had shown no regard for Mitka's young teeth and dealt him a swinging blow in the mouth. Mitka had spat out two good molars on the blue-grey ice scarred by the lads' iron-shod heels.

As he came up to them, Alexei winked five times in quick succession.

'Sell us your monster!'

'You can buy it.'

'How much do you want?'

'A pair of oxen with a wife thrown in.'

Alexei screwed up his eyes and brandished his stump.

'You're a card, you are! Haw-haw! A wife thrown in! And will you take the brats as well?'

'Keep them for breeding, or the Shamils will be dying out soon,' Grigory quipped.

In the square a crowd had gathered round the low wall of the churchyard. The churchwarden was holding a goose above his head. 'Fifty kopecks! Going! Any more offers?'

The goose craned its neck and looked down disdainfully with a beady eye.

In another group close by, a grey-haired old fellow, his chest bedecked with crosses and medals, was waving his arms.

'Our Grandad Grishaka's bragging about the Turkish war,' Mitka said, nodding in that direction. 'Let's go and listen.'

'The carp will swell and stink us out while we're listening.'

'It'll weigh more if it swells. That's good for us.'

On the square beyond the fire-brigade's shed, where the butts on some water carts with broken shafts were getting warped in the sunshine, loomed the green roof of the Mokhovs' house. As he walked past the shed, Grigory spat and held his nose. An old man appeared from behind a water butt, fastening his trousers and holding the buckle of his belt in his teeth.

'Couldn't you wait?' Mitka asked sarcastically.

The old fellow fastened his last button and took the buckle out of his mouth.

'What's that to you?'

'You ought to have your nose rubbed in it! And your beard! Yes, your beard! So it would take your old woman a week to get you clean.'

'I'll rub your nose for you, you bugger!' the old man retorted huffily.

Mitka halted, screwing up his cat-like eyes as though the sun were too bright for them.

'Just listen to His Highness! Scat, you young bastard! Keep off me or I'll take my belt to you!'

Grigory was still chuckling as he walked up to the porch of the Mokhovs' house. Wild vines clung to the wooden railings like intricate carving. Indolent shadows dappled the porch.

'Look at that, Mitka! That's how some folk live.'

'Even the door-handle's got gold on it.' Mitka opened the door on to the veranda a little way and gave a snigger. 'What if we were to get that old fellow squatting in here.'

'Who is it?' came a call from the veranda.

With ebbing courage Grigory entered first. The carp's tail swept the painted floorboards.

'Who do you want to see?'

A girl in a wicker rocking-chair, holding a bowl of strawberries. Grigory stared dumbly at the pink heart-shape of her full lips with a berry enclosed between them. The girl inclined her head and surveyed the visitors.

Mitka came to Grigory's rescue. He coughed.

'Want to buy some fish?'

'Fish? I'll go and tell them.'

She rocked the chair forward and stood up; the embroidered slippers on her bare feet flopped on the floorboards. The sun shone through her white dress and Mitka saw the vague outlines of shapely legs and the broad flowing lace of her underskirt. What surprised him most was the satiny whiteness of her bared calves with only a touch of milky yellow on the small rounded heels.

He nudged Grigory.

'What a skirt, eh! It's like glass! You can see right through it.'

The girl returned and sat down lightly in her chair.

'Go through to the kitchen.'

Grigory tiptoed into the house. Mitka planted his feet apart and narrowed his eyes at the white thread of the parting that divided the girl's hair into two golden semi-circles. She surveyed him with mischievous, restless eyes.

'Are you from the village?'

'Yes.'

'What family?'

'Korshunov.'

'What's your first name?'

'Dmitry.'

She examined the pink tips of her toe-nails and suddenly tucked her feet away out of sight.

'Which of you catches fish?'

'Grigory, my mate.'

'Do you fish?'

'Yes, when I feel like it.'

'With a fishing rod?'

'Ay, sometimes.'

'I'd like to do some fishing too,' she said after a pause.

'All right. We can go if you want to.'

'How could it be arranged? No, I mean it.'

'You'll have to get up real early.'

'I can do that, but I'll have to be woken.'

'I can wake you. But what about your father?'

'What about him?'

Mitka laughed.

'He might take me for a thief and set the dogs on me.'

'Nonsense! I sleep alone in the corner room. There's the window.' She pointed. 'If you come for me, knock on the pane and I'll get up.'

The sound of voices from the kitchen varied between Grigory's timid tones and the thick tar of the cook's.

Mitka fell silent, toying with the tarnished silver of his Cossack belt.

'Are you married?' the girl asked, with a hint of a smile.

'Why?'

'I just wondered.'

'No, I'm not married.'

Mitka suddenly blushed and she, smiling coquettishly and toying with the stalk of a hot-house strawberry that had fallen to the floor, asked, 'Well, Dmitry, do the girls like you?'

'Some do, some don't.'

'Really... And why have you got eyes like a cat's?'

'Like a cat's?' Mitka was utterly taken aback.

'Yes, just like a cat's.'

'From my mother, I suppose. Couldn't be anything to do with me.'

'And why is it, Dmitry, that they don't marry you off?'

Mitka recovered from his momentary confusion and, sensing the barely perceptible mockery in her voice, let his green eyes flare for a moment.

'Cock's not big enough yet—for a hen.'

She raised her brows in astonishment, flushed and stood up.

There was a sound of footsteps coming on to the porch. Her brief laughter-hiding smile stung Mitka like a nettle. The master of the house, Sergei Platonovich Mokhov, padded on to the veranda in his capacious kid-leather boots and carried his corpulent figure with some dignity past the retreating Mitka.

'Do you wish to see me?' he asked, without turning his head.

'They brought some fish, Daddy.'

Grigory appeared without his carp.

III

Grigory came home from his evening-out after first cock-crow. A smell of sour hops and the dry aromatic scent of wild thyme met him in the porch.

He tiptoed into the front room, undressed, carefully folded his striped going-out trousers, crossed himself, and got into bed. On the floor lay a drowsy golden pool of moonlight, criss-crossed by the shadows of the window frame. Silver-fronted ikons gleamed faintly beneath the embroidered towels in the corner. Disturbed flies droned round the shelf above the bed.

He was almost asleep when his brother's baby began to cry in the kitchen.

The cradle creaked like an ungreased wagon wheel. Darya muttered in a sleepy voice, 'Hush, you little brat! Won't you ever give me any sleep or peace?' And she began to sing softly.

> *Oh, magic piper,*
> *Where have you been?*
> *I've been watching the horses.*
> *And what have you seen?*
> *A horse with a saddle,*
> *With a fringe all of gold...*

As he dozed off, lulled by the steady creaking, Grigory remembered, 'Tomorrow Petro will be going off to camp. Darya will be left with the baby... So we'll be mowing without him.'

He dug his head into the hot pillow but the song seeped through persistently.

> *And where is your horse?*
> *It stands at the gate.*
> *And where is the gate?*
> *Washed away by the flood.*

Grigory was startled out of his sleep by a lusty neighing. He recognised it as that of Petro's army mount.

With sleep-weakened fingers he fumbled at the buttons of his shirt and was again nearly lulled to sleep by the undertow of the song.

> *And where are the geese?*
> *They've gone into the reeds.*
> *And where are the reeds?*
> *The girls have mown them.*
> *And where are the girls?*
> *Married and gone away.*
> *And where are the Cossacks?*
> *They've gone to the war...*

Dazed by sleep, Grigory made his way to the stable and led Petro's horse out into the lane. A cobweb tickled his cheek and his drowsiness suddenly vanished.

A rippling road of moonlight that no one had ever ridden lay aslant the Don. A mist hung over the river and above it the stars were strewn like millet across the sky. The horse trod warily behind him. The path down to the water was treacherous. From the far bank came the quacking of ducks and in the muddy shallows near the bank a sheat-fish leapt and flopped as it hunted for fry.

Grigory lingered at the water's edge. A dank, insipid odour of decay rose from the bank. Pellets of water dripped from the horse's lips. There was a sweet void in

Grigory's heart. It was good to have no thoughts. On the way back he glanced towards the east. The blue murk had cleared.

By the stable he ran into his mother.

'Is that you, Grisha?'

'Who did you think?'

'Been watering the horse?'

'Yes,' he replied shortly.

His mother, leaning backwards with an apronful of dung bricks for the stove, shuffled away on her bare flabby feet.

'You'd better go and wake the Astakhovs. Stepan said he'd be leaving with our Petro.'

The cool air put a quivering spring in Grigory's body. His skin prickled with gooseflesh. He bounded up the three steps on to the Astakhovs' echoing porch. The door was unlocked. Stepan was sleeping on a mat spread on the kitchen floor with his wife's head resting in the crook of his arm.

In the thinning darkness Grigory saw Aksinya's shift rucked up above the knees, and her legs, white as birch-bark and parted unashamedly. He stared for a second, mouth dry, iron pounding in his head.

His eyes roved furtively, and in a husky voice that was not his own he asked, 'Anyone here? Time to get up!'

Aksinya gave a little gasp as she awoke.

'Oh, who's that? Who is it?' her hand groped feverishly to pull down the shirt. There was a spot of dribble on the pillow; a woman sleeps soundly at dawn.

'It's me. Mother said to wake you.'

'We'll be up right away... There's no room in here... We're sleeping on the floor because of the fleas. Stepan, get up. D'you hear?'

From her voice Grigory realised that she was embarrassed, and slipped out quickly.

* * *

About thirty Cossacks were leaving the village to attend the May training camp. The place of assembly was the parade ground. Just before seven o'clock wagons with tent-cloth covers and Cossacks, mounted or on foot, in their linen summer shirts and loaded with equipment, began making their way to the parade ground.

Petro was standing on the porch, hurriedly sewing up a

broken rein. Pantelei was stumping about round the horse. As he tipped more oats into the trough he shouted, 'Dunya, have you packed his rusks yet? Did you salt the fatback properly?'

A blossom-pink Dunyashka darted like a swallow across the yard between the house and the outdoor kitchen, laughing and waving aside her father's shouts.

'You mind your own business, Dad. I'll pack up brother's stuff so it won't stir all the way to Cherkassk.'

'Hasn't he had enough?' Petro inquired, nodding at the horse as he wetted the thread with his tongue.

'He's still chewing,' his father replied with dignity, feeling the saddle cloth with his horny palm. A crumb or a blade of grass stuck to a saddlecloth could draw blood from a horse's back in a single march.

'Give him a drink when he's done eating, Dad.'

'Grigory will take him down to the Don... Hi, Grigory, take the horse down.'

The tall lean Don stallion with a white blaze on its forehead responded spiritedly. Grigory led it out of the gate. With the barest touch of his left hand on the withers he was astride the horse's back and off they went at a round trot. He tried to rein in at the slope but the horse broke into a canter. As he leaned back almost flat on the horse's crupper, Grigory saw a woman going down the slope with her pails. He swung off the path and, leaping past his own dust, plunged into the water.

Aksinya came swinging down the slope and let rip at Grigory while she was still at a distance.

'You mad devil! You nearly rode me down! Just you wait, I'll tell your father how you ride!'

'Now neighbour, don't be cross. You're seeing your husband off to camp today. I might come in useful on your farm.'

'You! Why the devil should I need you!'

'You'll be asking me yourself when the mowing starts,' Grigory laughed. Standing on the wooden pier, Aksinya skilfully scooped water into one of the pails on her yoke and, holding her billowing skirt tight between her knees, looked up at Grigory.

'Well, is your Stepan ready yet?' Grigory asked.
'What's that to you?'
'That's a woman... Can't I ask?'
'Yes, he is. What of it?'
'So you'll be a grass-widow now?'
'Yes, I shall.'

The horse lifted its lips from the water, munched the drips noisily and, looking across the river, stamped its forefoot in the shallows. Aksinya filled her other pail, lifted the yoke on to her shoulders and went off up the hill with a light swinging stride. Grigory started his horse after her. The wind billowed her skirt and played with the fine downy curls on the nape of her neck. A small silk-embroidered cap blazed above the heavy knot of hair and the pink blouse tucked into her skirt lay smooth and taut over her sheer back and plump shoulders. As she leaned forward to climb the slope, the groove of her spine showed up clearly under the blouse, Grigory noticed the brownish sweat-faded circles under the arms; his eyes followed every movement. He felt an urge to speak to her again.

'You'll be missing your husband, I reckon. Won't you?'

Aksinya turned her head without stopping, and smiled.

'Of course, I will. You get married yourself,' her voice faltered as she caught her breath, 'get married yourself, then you'll find out whether people miss their dearie or not.'

Grigory spurred his horse and looked into her eyes as he came up with her.

'But some women are right glad when they've seen off their husbands. Our Darya gets real plump without Petro.'

Aksinya's nostrils twitched as she took a deep breath; straightening her hair, she said, 'A husband's no snake but he sucks your blood. Shall we see you married soon?'

'I don't know what Dad thinks. After I've done my army service, most likely.'

'You're too young yet, don't marry.'

'Why not?'

'It dries you up.' She looked at him from under lowered brows and smiled faintly with tight lips. Grigory noticed they were shamelessly avid, puffy.

Combing the horse's mane with his fingers, he said, 'I don't want to marry. Someone will love me without that.'

'Have you spotted someone then?'

'Why should I? You'll be seeing off Stepan—'

'Don't try that on with me!'

'Will you hit me for it?'

'I'll let Stepan know.'

'I'll show your Stepan—'

'Mind you don't end up in tears, brave man.'

'Don't scare me, Aksinya!'

'I'm not scaring you. Your place is with the girls. Let them hem your hankies for you. But keep your eyes off me.'

'Like hell I will.'

'Well, look then.'

Aksinya smiled conciliatorily and stepped off the path to pass the horse. Grigory turned it sideways, barring her way.

'Let me pass, Grisha!'

'I won't.'

'Don't fool about, I've got to pack up for my husband.'

Grigory, smiling, urged on his horse and it advanced on Aksinya, driving her towards the cliff.

'Let me by, you devil! There are people about. What will they think, if they see?'

She cast a frightened glance around her and walked past frowning and without looking back.

Petro was still on the porch, saying good-bye to the family. Grigory saddled his horse. With one hand on his sabre to steady it, his brother hurried down the steps and took the reins.

Sensing the road ahead, the horse stamped restlessly and foamed at the mouth as its teeth chased the bit. With one foot in the stirrup and a hand on the pommel Petro said to his father, 'Don't overwork the Baldies, Dad! Come autumn, we'll sell them. We've got to buy a horse for Grigory. But don't sell the steppe grass. You know yourself what the hay'll be like in the meadow this year.'

'Well, God be with ye! Good luck,' the old man said, making the sign of the cross.

With habitual ease Petro swung his well-knit body into the saddle and straightened the back folds of his belted shirt. The horse walked to the gate. The hilt of the sabre glinted dully in the sun as it swayed in time with the horse's stride.

Darya followed with the baby in her arms. The mother stood in the middle of the yard, wiping her eyes with her sleeve and the red tip of her nose with the corner of her apron.

'Brother dear! The pies! He's forgotten the pies!.. The potato pies!..'

Dunyashka went leaping towards the gate like a young goat.

'What're you bawling about, you fool!' Grigory snapped crossly.

'He's left his pies behind!' Dunyashka moaned, leaning on the gate, and the tears streamed down her hot cheeks, and from her cheeks on to her blouse.

Shading her eyes with her hand, Darya watched her husband's white shirt through a curtain of dust. Pantelei, who had been tugging at a loose gatepost, looked up at Grigory. 'Mend this gate, lad. You'd better put in a new post.' And after a little thought he added, as though giving out a piece of news, 'Petro has gone away.'

Through the wattle fence Grigory saw Stepan making ready for the journey. Aksinya, now dressed more smartly, in a green woollen skirt, brought him his horse. Stepan said something to her, smiling. Unhurriedly, with an air of possession he kissed his wife and let his hand linger on her shoulder. Blackened by sun and work, it lay like a lump of charred wood on her white blouse. Stepan was standing with his back to Grigory and through the fence Grigory could see his firm, smartly trimmed neck, his broad, slightly sloping shoulders and, when he bent towards his wife, the curled tip of his reddish-brown moustache.

Aksinya laughed at something and shook her head. The big black stallion lurched slightly as it took the rider's weight on the stirrup. Stepan rode out of the gate at a brisk walk, sitting like a rock in the saddle. Aksinya kept pace with him, holding his stirrup and looking up into his eyes lovingly and hungrily, like a dog.

Grigory's eyes followed them to the turn in a long unblinking stare.

IV

Towards evening a storm began to gather. A brownish thundercloud loomed over the village. The wind-ruffled Don flung fast choppy waves at its banks. Beyond the water meadows rainless lightning set the sky ablaze and occasional thunder rolled heavily across the earth. Just beneath the stormcloud a kite was circling, pursued by cawing ravens. Breathing down cool air, the cloud moved along the Don from the west. The sky grew threateningly black beyond the meadowland, and the steppe waited in expectant silence. In the village, shutters were being closed with a clatter, old women were hurrying home from evensong, crossing themselves, a grey swaying pillar of dust rose over the parade ground and the earth, heavy with the heat of spring, was already being sown with the first seeds of rain.

Dunyashka, plaits flying, scorched across the yard and banged the door of the hen-house, then stood in the middle of the yard, nostrils aflare, like a horse at a hurdle. Children were prancing about in the street. The neighbours' eight-year-old Mishka with his father's peaked cap, far too big for him, flopped over his eyes, kept spinning round, squatting on one leg and piping at the top of his voice:

> Rain, rain hard and good,
> Then we'll go into the wood,
> And to God we will pray,
> And Lord Jesus obey.

Dunyashka looked enviously at Mishka's bare, chapped feet frantically stamping the ground. She, too, wanted to dance in the rain and get her hair wet so that it would grow thick and curly; she wanted to do as Mishka's chum was doing, stand on her head in the roadside dust at the risk of toppling over into the thorn bushes. But her mother's face appeared at the window, lips flapping angrily. And with a sigh she ran into the house. The rain came down fast and full-kernelled. Thunder burst just above the roof and splinters of sound scattered beyond the Don.

In the inner porch her father and a sweating Grigory were dragging a rolled-up net out of the side-room.

'Some twine and a needle, quick!' Grigory shouted to her.

They lighted a lamp in the kitchen. While Darya sat down to mend the net, the old woman nursed the baby and grumbled.

'You were ever a one for mad capers, old man. Why don't we go to bed? Oil gets dearer every day and you burn it. What fish can you catch now? Where the plague are you off to? And you might get yourself drowned. All hell's let loose outside. Just look at those flashes! Oh, Lord, Jesus Christ, Holy Mother...'

For an instant the kitchen was blindingly blue and quiet, and only the rain could be heard scraping the shutters; then the thunder crashed again. Dunyashka squealed and buried her face in the net. Darya waved little signs of the cross at the windows and door.

The old woman made terrible eyes at the cat that was fawning at her feet.

'Dunyashka! Chase her away, the... Holy Mother, forgive me, sinner that I am. Dunyashka, throw that cat out of the house at once. Shooh, you unclean spirit! May you...'

Grigory dropped the pole of the net and stood shaking with silent laughter.

'What are you all squawking about? Shut up!' Pantelei shouted. 'Come on, you women, hurry up with that mending! I told you only the other day to see to the net.'

'What fish will you catch now,' his wife started off again.

'Hold your tongue if you don't understand! This is just the time for the sterlet. They make for the bank now because they're afraid of the storm. The water must be real muddy. Now then, Dunyashka, out you go and see if you can hear the water rising in the gully.'

Dunyashka edged unwillingly towards the door.

'Who d'you expect to wade for you? Darya can't go, she'll catch a cold on her chest,' the old woman persisted.

'There's Grishka and me. We'll call Aksinya for the other net, and one of the other women.'

Dunyashka ran in, flushed and panting. Raindrops hung quivering from her wet lashes. She smelled of the damp black earth.

'The gully's a-roaring something terrible!'

'Will you come and wade with us?'

'Who else will go?'

'We'll call some of the women.'

'I'll go!'

'Put on your coat then and belt off to Aksinya. If she'll come, let her call Malashka Frolova!'

'That one won't catch cold,' Grigory said with a grin. 'She's as fat as a hog.'

'Take some dry hay, Grisha dear,' his mother advised him. 'Put it next your heart or you'll catch a chill.'

'Yes, fetch some hay, Grigory. The old woman speaks true.'

Dunyashka was soon back, and the women with her. Aksinya, in a tattered jacket belted with rope and a blue underskirt, looked shorter and thinner. Exchanging pleasantries with Darya, she took off her kerchief, tightened the knot of her hair and, as she covered her head again, stared at Grigory coldly. The stout

Malashka was tying up her stockings on the threshold.

'Got your sacks ready?' she croaked hoarsely. 'Sure to God we'll make a good haul today.'

They went out into the yard. The rain was still beating down on the sodden earth. The puddles were foaming and sending torrents down to the Don.

Grigory led the way. He was in strangely high spirits.

'Mind your step, Dad, there's a ditch here.'

'Isn't it dark!'

'Hang on to me, Aksinya, girl, together we sail and end up in gaol,' Malashka chuckled hoarsely.

'Look, Grigory, isn't that the Maidannikovs' pier?'

'Ah, that's it.'

'This is where we'll begin,' Pantelei shouted through the buffeting wind.

'Can't hear you, uncle!' Malashka shouted.

'Wade in and good luck to you... I'll take the deep side. The deep side, I said... Malashka, you deaf devil, where are you pulling to? I'll take the deep side!.. Grigory! Let Aksinya haul from the bank!'

The wind moaned over the roaring river, tearing the slanting sheet of rain to shreds. Feeling his way with his feet, Grigory waded in. The clinging cold rose to his chest and locked itself round his heart like an iron hoop. The waves lashed his face and tightly closed eyes like a whip. The net ballooned out and pulled him towards the deep. His stockinged feet slithered on the sandy bottom. The pole of the net was being wrenched out of his hands... Deeper, deeper. A sudden drop and he lost his footing. The current swept him towards the middle, sucking him down. Using his right arm, he struck out for the bank, frightened as never before by the black shifting depths, and it was a joy when his foot touched the unsteady bottom. A fish struck his knee.

'Go out deeper!' his father's voice called from the sticky darkness.

The net heeled and again slid into the depths. Again the current tore the ground from under him and he was swimming with his head thrown back, spitting water.

'Aksinya, you all right?'

'All right, so far.'

'Rain's stopping, isn't it?'

'The little one is, but there's a big one just coming.'

'Not so loud. Father will tell me off if he hears.'

'Scared of your father, huh?'

For a minute they hauled in silence. Like a thick dough, the water bound every movement.

'Grisha, I think there's a tree under water here. We'll have to go round it.'

There was a great splash, as though a chunk of rock had fallen from the cliff-face, and Grigory was flung far out into the stream.

'O-o-o-oh!' came Aksinya's cry from somewhere near the bank.

Terrified, he fought clear of the waves and swam towards her cry.

'Aksinya!'

Only the wind and the sound of rushing water.

'Aksinya!' he shouted, cold with fear.

'Hulloo! Grigory!' his father's muffled voice reached him from afar.

Grigory struck out wildly. Something sticky clung to his feet.

He made a grab. It was the net.

'Grisha, where are you?' came Aksinya's tearful voice.

'Why didn't you answer?' he yelled angrily, crawling out on to the bank.

They squatted down, shivering, to untangle the net. The moon sailed out from a rent in the clouds. From beyond the meadows came a restrained mutter of thunder. The ground was glistening with unabsorbed moisture. The rain-washed sky was stern and clear.

Grigory watched Aksinya as he shook out the net. Her face was a chalky white but her red, slightly out-turned lips were ready to laugh.

'When it threw me out on the bank,' she related, still panting a little, 'I lost my head, I did that! I was frightened to death! I thought you were drowned.'

Their hands touched. Aksinya tried to push hers up the sleeve of his shirt.

'How warm it is in your sleeve,' she said plaintively. 'I'm that frozen. My body's all aching.'

'Here's the place where that darn sheat-fish broke through!'

Grigory held up the net, revealing a hole in the middle about three feet across.

Someone was running towards them from the sandbar. Grigory saw that it was Dunyashka. From a distance he shouted, 'Have you got the twine?'

'Right here.'

She ran up, flushed and panting.

'What are you sitting here for? Dad says you're to come to where we are. We've caught a whole sack of sterlet there!' There was unconcealed triumph in her voice.

Aksinya sewed up the hole in the net, her teeth chattering. They ran all the way to the sandbar to warm themselves.

Pantelei Prokofievich was rolling himself a cigarette with fingers that the water had left furrowed and puffy like a drowned man's. Hopping from one foot to another, he boasted, 'In our first haul we got eight. And the next time...' he paused, lighted the cigarette and pointed silently at the sack with his foot.

Aksinya peeped curiously inside. A harsh rustle rose from the sack, where the hardy sterlet were still writhing.

'Where did you get to?'

'A sheat-fish holed the net.'

'Did you mend it?'

'As well as we could.'

'Well, we'll try again, just knee deep, and then go home. Wade in, Grishka. What are you jibbing at?'

Grigory waded in, his legs numb. Aksinya was shivering so much that he could feel it through the net.

'Stop shaking!'

'I wish I could, but I can't catch my breath.'

'Come on then... Let's get out and damn the fish!'

At that moment a big carp leapt across the net. Grigory quickened his stride and pulled the net round, hauling on the pole. Aksinya, bending almost double, ran out on to the bank. The water swished back down the sand and the fish lay there quivering.

'Shall we go back across the meadow?'

'It's quicker through the wood. Hi you, over there, how much longer will you be?'

'Go on, we'll catch you up. We're washing the net.'

Aksinya, frowning, wrung out her skirt, heaved the sack of fish on to her shoulder and set off almost at a run. Grigory carried the net. After some two hundred yards Aksinya began to cry out.

'Oh, I haven't the strength! My legs are numb with cold.'

'There's an old haystack. Couldn't you get warm in there?'

'Oh, yes. Or I'll be dead before we get home.'

Grigory pulled off the crown of the stack and dug a hole in the middle. The warm smell of rotting hay hit his nostrils.

'Get down right into the middle. It's like a stove in here.'

Aksinya dropped the sack and dug herself in, up to the neck.

'Oh, that's lovely!'

Shivering with cold, Grigory lay down beside her. Aksinya's hair gave off a tender, exciting smell. She was lying with her head thrown back, breathing steadily, her mouth half open.

'Your hair smells of stramony. D'you know it? It's a white flower,' Grigory whispered, leaning over her.

She said nothing. Her gaze was misty and far away, fixed on the bearded moon.

Grigory freed his hand from his pocket and suddenly drew her head towards him. She pulled back fiercely and half rose.

'Let go!'

'Quiet!'

'Let me go or I'll shout!'

'Wait, Aksinya...'

'Uncle Pantelei!..'

'Lost, are you?' Pantelei responded from the hawthorn bushes near by.

Grigory clenched his teeth and jumped down from the stack.

'What's all the noise about? Did you get lost?' the old man asked as he came up.

Aksinya stood by the stack, straightening the kerchief that had fallen back off her head. Her clothes were steaming.

'Not lost, but I thought I'd get frozen.'

'Bah, woman! Here's a haystack. Get warm in that.'

Aksinya smiled as she reached down for the sack.

V

It was sixty versts to the village of Setrakov, where the training camp was to be held. Petro Melekhov and Stepan Astakhov were riding in the same wagon. There were three other Cossacks from their village with them: Fedot Bodovskov, a young fellow, pock-marked and with a dash of Kalmyk in him, Khrisanf Tokin, commonly called Khristonya, a second-line reservist in the Ataman's Regiment of Life Guards, and gunner Ivan Tomilin, who would be going on to Persianovka. After the first stop for feeding they had harnessed Khristonya's 15-hand stallion and Stepan's black to the shafts. The other three horses, still saddled, were walking behind. Khristonya, huge and, like all guardsmen, a bit thick in the head, was driving. He sat with his great back arched like a wheel, blocking the light out of the wagon, and kept frightening the horses with his deep booming voice. Under the new tarpaulin cover Petro, Stepan and gunner Tomilin lay on their backs smoking. Fedot Bodovskov was walking behind; evidently he found it no effort to stump along the dusty road on his bandy Kalmyk legs.

Khristonya's wagon was at the head of the column. It was followed by seven or eight others with saddled or unsaddled horses tethered behind.

The road echoed with the men's laughter and shouts, their lingering songs, the snorting of the horses, and the jingle of empty stirrups.

With a bag of rye rusks under his head Petro lay full length, twirling the long yellow wisps of his moustache.

'Stepan!'

'Eh?'

'What about a song?'

'It's too hot. My throat's as dry as a bone.'

'No taverns in the villages round here. No use waiting for that.'

'All right, sing up then. But you're no singer. Your Grishka, he's the one! It comes out of him like a silver thread, not just a voice. We used to sing ourselves hoarse of an evening.'

Stepan threw back his head, cleared his throat and began in a low resonant voice:

> *Oh, a fine glowing sunrise*
> *Came up early in the sky...*

Tomilin put his hand to his cheek woman-fashion and picked up the tune in a wailing falsetto. Smiling through the tip of his moustache, Petro watched the knotted veins at the broadchested gunner's temples going blue with strain.

> *Young was she, the pretty wench*
> *And late she went to fetch the water...*

Stepan, who was lying with his head towards Khristonya, turned on one arm and his taut handsome neck flushed pink.

'Khristonya, help us out!'

The lad, he guessed her reason.
Saddled up his chestnut mare...

Stepan's bulging eyes turned their smiling glance on Petro. Petro flicked the moustache out of his mouth and joined in.

Khristonya opened his enormous bearded jaws and his bellow shook the tarpaulin cover of the wagon.

He saddled up his chestnut mare,
Rode out to catch the pretty wench...

Khristonya tucked a massive bare foot under him and waited for Stepan to begin again. Stepan, eyes closed, sweating face in shadow, coaxed the song along, now lowering his voice to a whisper, now pitching it up to a metallic clang:

Oh, allow me, pretty wench,
My horse to water in the stream...

And once again Khristonya's bass pounded in like the thunder of the tocsin. Voices from the other wagons took up the song. The wheels clattered on their iron rims, the horses sneezed in the dust, and the powerful rolling song poured like floodwater over the road. A white-winged lapwing soared up from the withered brown reeds of an almost dry steppeland pond. It flew crying towards a hollow and, turning its emerald eye to look at the line of canvas-covered wagons, at the horses raising the thick velvety dust with their hooves, and at the men striding along the roadside in their white dust-grimed shirts. The lapwing dropped into the hollow, plunged its black breast amid the parched grass and animal tracks and could no longer see what was happening on the road. There the wagons were still rattling by and the horses, sweating under their saddles, were plodding on as unwillingly as ever; but the Cossacks in their dust-grimed shirts had run from their own wagons to the leader, gathered round it and were roaring with laughter.

Stepan, standing at his full height, holding to the tarpaulin cover with one hand and beating time with the other, swept through the song at a cracking pace:

Oh, don't sit down by me,
Oh, don't sit down by me,

People will say you're in love with me,
You're in love with me,
And you come to me,
You're in love with me
And come to me,
But I'm not one of the common run...

Dozens of rough voices caught the words in flight and boomed them out over the roadside dust:

I'm not one of the common run,
The common run—
I'm brigand born
And brigand bred,
And I'm in love with a prince's son.

Fedot Bodovskov whistled; the horses bucked, trying to shake off the traces; Petro poked his head out of the tent, laughing and waving his cap; Stepan with a dazzling grin on his face, wriggled his shoulders playfully; a hill of dust rolled along the road; Khristonya in his long unbelted shirt, his hair matted and bathed in sweat, did a Cossack dance, squatting and whirling round like a flywheel, frowning and moaning, and leaving the monster splayed imprints of his bare feet in the grey silken dust.

VI

They stopped for the night near a heavy-browed burial mound with a bald sandy yellow top.

A stormcloud was coming up from the west, rain seeping from its black wing. They watered the horses at a pond. Dreary willow-trees stood hump-backed over the dam. Lightning cast crooked reflections in water covered with stagnant greenery and a scaly skin of tired waves. The wind sprinkled a grudging pittance of raindrops into the earth's swarthy palms.

The hobbled horses were left to graze and three men were posted as sentries. The others kindled fires and hung the cooking pots on the wagon shafts.

Khristonya did the cooking. While he stirred the pot, he told the Cossacks sitting round him one of his yarns.

'...A real high mound it was, something like this one.

And I says to my father, rest his soul, "Won't the Ataman* rap us over the knuckles for gutting this burial mound without any permission, so to speak?" '

'What's he making up now?' asked Stepan, coming back from the horses.

'I'm telling 'em how me and my dad, may his soul rest in heaven, went looking for treasure.'

'Where did you look for it?'

'Ah, chum, that was t'other side of Fetis's Ravine. You know it, don't you—the Merkulov Mound...'

'Well, go on...' Stepan squatted on his haunches, put a hot ember on his palm and kept it rolling about while he lit his cigarette, sucking noisily.

'Well, as I was saying. My dad says, "Come on, Khristan, let's dig up Merkulov Mound." He'd heard from Grandad, you see, that there was treasure buried there. And treasure, o'course, don't come everybody's way. Dad, he promised God, if you give me that treasure, he says, I'll build a beautiful church. So we decided to do it and off we went. The land there is stanitsa land, so the only trouble was the ataman. It was getting late by the time we arrived. We waited until dusk fell, hobbled the mare, o'course, and climbed up to the top with our spades. We set to right on its top-knot. Dug a hole about five foot deep, and that earth, mind you, was like solid rock, all hard and stringy from age. I was in a muck sweat. And Dad, he kept muttering prayers, but you know what, lads, my tummy was a-rumbling something awful... You know what the grub's like in summer: sour milk and kvass... It gets a cross-grip on your stomach, there's death in your eyes—and that's that! My old father, heaven rest his soul, says to me, "Pooh," he says. "What a stinker you are, Khristonya! Here am I saying prayers and you can't hold your food; the air's not fit to breathe. Get down from this mound, drat ye, he says, or I'll split your head with my shovel. You'll make the treasure vanish into the ground with your stink." So I lay down at the

---

* *Ataman* was the title the Cossacks of tsarist Russia gave to their elected leaders at all levels. The Don Cossack Army was led by the *Army Ataman*, the stanitsas were in the charge of *stanitsa atamans*, and any irregular detachment of Cossacks taking the field would elect its own *Campaign Ataman*. In the broad sense, the word simply meant 'chief'. There were also *Vice Atamans*. When the Don Cossacks finally lost their independence in 1723, the title of Ataman of all Cossack Armies was assumed by the heir to the throne and the Army Ataman became the Vice Army Ataman, or Vice Ataman.

bottom of the mound with an awful ache in my tum and a stitch in my side, and my dad—a tough old devil he was—goes on digging by himself until he comes to a stone slab. Then he calls me and I takes a crow-bar under that there slab... And believe me, lads, it was a moonlit night, and under that slab there was something shining bright...'

'You're making it all up, Khristonya!' Petro burst out, grinning and tugging at his moustache.

'Making it up! You go and stuff yourself!' Khristonya hitched up his baggy trousers and surveyed his listeners. 'No, o'course, I'm not making it up! It's the honest truth of God!'

'Come on, then, let's hear the end of it.'

'Well, lads, there it was shining. So I had a look and—it was charcoal. There must have been about thirty bushels of it. So Dad says, "In you go, Khristan, and dig it out." So in I went and went on digging that damn stuff. Kept me busy till daybreak, it did. And in the morning I look up and there he is.'

'Who?' asked Tomilin, who was lying on a horse-cloth.

'Why, the ataman, o'course. Driving along in his carriage. "Who gave you permission, you so-and-sos?" What could we say? So he picks us up, o'course, and takes us off to the stanitsa. Year before last we were summoned to appear in court, but Dad, he guessed it would happen and died in time. So we sent in a paper to say he was no longer among the living.'

Khristonya lifted the pot of steaming porridge off the hook and went to the wagon for the spoons.

'What about the church, eh? Your father promised to build a church and never built one?' Stepan asked when Khristonya came back with the spoons.

'You're a fool, Stepan. Why should he build anything in return for charcoal?'

'He should've done once he promised.'

'It wasn't for charcoal, he promised, but for treasure.'

The roar of laughter shook the flames of the campfire. Khristonya lifted his simple head from the pot and, without quite grasping what it was all about, drowned the other voices with a huge guffaw.

VII

Aksinya had been given in marriage to Stepan at the age of seventeen. She came from the village of Dubrovka, from the dry sandy lands on the far side of the Don.

A year before her marriage in autumn she was out ploughing with her father some eight versts from the village. During the night her father, an old man of fifty, tied her hands with a hobbling thong and raped her.

'I'll kill you if you breathe a word, but if you keep quiet I'll fit you out with a plush jacket and gaiter-boots with galoshes. So, remember, I'll kill you if there's any—' he promised her.

That night Aksinya ran home to the village in nothing but her torn shift, threw herself at her mother's feet, and sobbed out the whole story. Her mother and elder brother, an Ataman Life Guard, just back from service, harnessed horses to a wagon, put Aksinya in it and set out for the camp. Over eight versts her brother nearly drove the horses to death. They found the father by the camp. He was drunk and lying asleep on a coat spread out on the ground; beside him lay an empty vodka bottle. Before Aksinya's eyes, her brother unhitched the swingle-tree from the wagon, kicked his sleeping father into a sitting position, asked him a brief question, and then hit the old man between the eyes with the iron-tipped bar. He and his mother went on beating him for about an hour and a half. The aged mother, who had always been an obedient wife, tore at her half-crazed husband's hair in a frenzy; the brother used his feet. Aksinya lay under the wagon with her head wrapped up, shaking but not uttering a word. At daybreak they brought the old man home. He was moaning plaintively and his eyes roamed the front room in search of Aksinya, who had hidden away in a corner. Blood and pus seeped on to the pillow from his torn ear. He died that evening. People were told he had killed himself by falling from a cart when drunk.

A year later the matchmakers arrived in a smart-looking wagon to ask Aksinya's hand in marriage. She liked the tall Stepan with his powerful neck and hand-some figure and the wedding was fixed for the autumn, some time after Intercession. The day came on the eve of winter with a light frost and merry crackle of ice. The young couple were joined in wedlock and Aksinya was installed as the young mistress of the Astakhov home. Her mother-in-law, a tall old woman, doubled up by some painful women's disease, wakened Aksinya early on the very next day after the wedding, took her to the kitchen and, fiddling aimlessly with the pot-holders, said, 'Now listen to me, my dear daughter-in-law, we didn't take you in for love games and lying abed. Go and milk the cow and then get busy at the stove with the cooking. I'm old and feeble, so you must take over the household; it'll be all yours now.'

That day in the barn Stepan gave his young wife a calculated and terrible beating. He struck her on the belly, breasts and back, so that no mark would be seen. And after that he began taking his pleasure on the side, with the grass-widows who were out for a good time while their husbands were away. He went out almost every night, leaving Aksinya locked in the barn or the front room.

For about a year and a half he would not forgive her the insult to his manly pride, not until a child was born. After that his resentment abated, but he showed little affection and seldom spent the night at home.

The large farm with all its livestock kept Aksinya hard at work. Stepan took things easy, preferring to comb his forelock and go off to his friends for a smoke, a game of cards and gossip about the affairs of the village: it was Aksinya who had to clean the cattle pens and run the household. Her mother-in-law was a poor help. After fussing about for a while, she would fall on to her bed and stare up at the ceiling, drawing her pale yellow lips thin as thread while her eyes grew animal-like with pain. With a groan she would pull her knees up to her chest. At such moments her face with its ugly black birthmarks would be bathed in sweat, tears would well in her eyes and roll rapidly down her cheeks, and Aksinya would leave her work and crouch in a corner, watching her mother-in-law's face with terror and pity.

A year and a half later the old woman died. In the morning Aksinya felt the first pangs of labour, and at noon, one hour before the baby came, her mother-in-law dropped dead by the door of the old stable. The midwife, who had run out of the house to warn the tipsy Stepan not to go in while Aksinya was still in labour, found the mother-in-law lying on the ground with her legs drawn up to her chest.

Aksinya grew attached to her husband after the birth of the child but she had no love for him, only a woman's embittered pity, and habit. The child died before it was a year old. Life swung back on to its old course. And when Grigory Melekhov entered her life and began making advances to her, Aksinya realised with horror that she felt drawn towards this dark affectionate lad. He pursued her with the persistence of a young bull. And it was this persistence that frightened Aksinya. She saw he had no fear of Stepan, an inner sense told her that he would not give up and, without consciously desiring it, indeed resisting with all her strength, she found herself dressing more smartly even on week days. Deceiving herself, she tried to be seen by him as often as she could and basked happily in the warmth of his dark impassioned glances. At dawn when she woke up and went out to milk the cows she would smile in unaccountable anticipation of joy to come. But what was it? 'Oh yes, it's Grigory. Grisha...' She was frightened by the engulfing power of this new feeling, and her thoughts moved gropingly, cautiously, as one might cross the porous ice of the Don in March.

After Stepan went off to camp, she decided to see as little of Grigory as possible. And after the drag-net fishing the decision took even firmer root.

VIII

Two days before Whitsunday the village folk divided up the meadow land. Pantelei attended the share-out. He came back at dinner-time, kicked off his boots with a grunt and, scratching his tired feet with gusto, said, 'We've got the strip near Red Ravine. The grass isn't so mighty good there. The top end borders on the wood and some of it's as bare as a bone. There's quitch in it too.'

'When do we start mowing?' Grigory asked.

'After the holiday.'

'Are you taking Darya then?' his wife asked with a frown.

Pantelei waved his hand as much as to say, don't bother me, woman.

'We will if we have to. Give us our meal. What are you standing there with your arms flapping for?'

The old woman banged the stove-door and lifted out the warmed-up cabbage soup. At table Pantelei had much to tell about the dividing up of the meadow and the wily ataman, who had almost succeeded in cheating the whole assembly.

'He was up to his tricks last year too,' Darya put in. 'When they'd given out the strips he kept trying to get Malashka Frolova to swap with him.'

'Ay, he's a regular scoundrel,' Pantelei said munching.

'But who will do the raking and stacking, Dad?' Dunyashka asked timidly.

'What will you be doing then?'

'I couldn't manage on my own, Dad.'

'We'll get Aksinya Astakhova to come along. Stepan asked me to mow for him when he left. We must oblige him.'

The next morning Mitka Korshunov rode up to the Melekhov house on his white-stockinged stallion. It was drizzling and there was a haze over the village. Mitka reached down without dismounting, unfastened the gate and rode into the yard. He was hailed from the porch by Ilyinichna.

'What are you riding in here for, trouble-maker?' she asked with visible displeasure. She had no affection for the reckless, quarrelsome Mitka.

'What's eating you, Ilyinichna?' Mitka queried, tethering his horse to the railings. 'I've come to see Grisha. Where is he?'

'Asleep in the shed. What's the matter with you? Can't you walk any more?'

Mitka took offence. 'You're always poking your nose into everything, Gran!' And he stumped off towards the shed flourishing and smacking a smart riding-whip against his patent leather boot.

Grigory was sleeping in a wagon from which the front wheels had been unhitched. Mitka closed his left eye as though taking aim and gave him a good flick with the whip.

'Get up, muzhik!'

For Mitka 'muzhik' was the most abusive word he could use. Grigory came up like a spring.

'What the...?'

'You've done enough napping?'

'Don't fool around, Mitka, or I'll get angry...'

'Up you get, there's something on.'

'What?'

Mitka sat down on the front edge of the wagon, flicked the dried mud off his boots with his whip, and said, 'It riles me, Grishka.'

'What does?'

'Well, look!' Mitka swore at great length. 'The way he shows off just because he's a lieutenant.'

In his irritation he ground out the words through clenched teeth and his legs twitched. Grigory raised himself on an elbow.

47

'What are you on about?'

Gripping the sleeve of Grigory's shirt, Mitka went on more quietly.

'Saddle up right away and let's ride down to the meadow. I'll show him! That's what I told him, "Come on, Your Honour, let's have a trial." "All right, he says, bring all your friends along. I'll beat you all because, he says, my mare's mother won prizes at the officers' races in Petersburg." Well, his mare and its mother can go to bloody hell for all I care, but I won't let him beat the stallion!'

Grigory pulled on his clothes hurriedly while Mitka followed him about, stuttering with fury.

'This lieutenant, he comes to pay a visit to Mokhov, the merchant. Wait a minute now, what's his name? Ay, that's right, Listnitsky. Big beefy feller, all serious like. Wears glasses. Well, let him! Glasses or not, I'm not going to let him get past the stallion!'

Chuckling to himself, Grigory saddled the old mare that had been kept for breeding and, using the threshing-floor gate—so that his father wouldn't see—rode out into the steppe. They took the slope down to the meadows. The horses' hooves munched the mire noisily. By a withered poplar the other riders were waiting for them: Lieutenant Listnitsky on a splendid lean filly and about seven of the village boys on their mounts.

'Where do we start from?' the lieutenant asked Mitka, straightening his pince-nez and admiring the powerful chest muscles of Mitka's stallion.

'From the poplar to Tsar's Pond.'

'And where is Tsar's Pond?' the lieutenant peered short-sightedly.

'Over there, Your Honour, just by the wood.'

They lined up the horses. The lieutenant raised the whip above his head. His shoulder-strap bulged.

'When I say three, off you go! Ready? One, two—three!'

The first away was the lieutenant, leaning forward over the pommel and holding his cap with his hand. He gained a full second's lead over the others. Mitka, his face pale with dismay, rose in his stirrups and, so it seemed to Grigory, was a desperately long time in bringing his raised whip down on the horse's crupper.

It was about three versts from the poplar to Tsar's Pond. In half the distance Mitka's stallion, stretched straight as an arrow, overtook the lieutenant's filly.

Grigory was in no mood for racing. Left behind at the beginning, he rode at an easy canter, curiously watching the broken chain of riders as it drew away from him.

Near Tsar's Pond there was a sandy bank thrown up by the spring floods. Its yellow camel-like hump was covered with a stunted growth of sharp-leaved wild garlic. Grigory saw the lieutenant and Mitka shoot up the bank together and disappear down the other side, and the others follow them one by one. When he rode up to the pond the sweating horses were already standing in a bunch and the dismounted riders were grouped around the lieutenant. Mitka was glistening with restrained joy. Triumph surged through his every movement. Contrary to expectations, the lieutenant seemed not in the least put out; leaning against a tree, smoking, he pointed his little finger at the filly, which looked as if it had just been bathed.

'That was after a ride of one hundred and fifty versts. I only arrived from the station yesterday. You would never have passed me if she had been fresher, Korshunov.'

'Mebbe not,' Mitka conceded graciously.

'There's not a faster horse than his stallion in the whole district,' a freckled lad who had come in last said with envy.

'He's a grand horse.' Mitka, his hand still trembling with excitement, patted the stallion's neck and glanced at Grigory with a broad smile on his face.

The two separated from the others, preferring the hill to the road. The lieutenant took his leave of them rather coldly, raised two fingers to the peak of his cap and turned away.

As they rode home along the lane, Grigory saw Aksinya coming towards them. She was whittling a twig as she walked; at the sight of Grigory she bent her head even lower.

'What are you ashamed of or are we riding naked?' Mitka shouted, and with a wink began a soulful ditty, '*My guelder-rose. Ah, my bitter little guelder-rose!..*'

Grigory rode on looking straight ahead and had almost passed Aksinya when he suddenly lashed the meekly walking mare with his whip. The mare sank back on its haunches and kicked, showering Aksinya with mud.

'Ee-ee, you stupid devil!'

Grigory swung round and rode the excited horse towards her.

'Why don't you say hullo?'

'You're not worth it!'

'That's why I muddied you—don't be so proud!'

'Let me pass!' Aksinya cried, waving her arms in the horse's face. 'What are you trampling me for with your horse?'

'It's a mare not a horse.'

'Let me pass all the same!'

'What are you angry about, Aksinya? Surely not because of the other day, in the meadow?'

Grigory caught her glance and held it. She was about to say something, but in the corner of one dark eye a tear suddenly appeared and her lips trembled pitifully. She swallowed hard and whispered, 'Let me alone, Grigory... I'm not angry, I'm—' And off she went.

The surprised Grigory caught up with Mitka at the gate.

'Will you be coming out this evening?' Mitka asked.

'No.'

'Why not? Or did she invite you for the night?'

Grigory rubbed his forehead and made no reply.

IX

All that remained of Whitsuntide in the village was the dry thyme scattered over the floors, the dust of crumpled leaf-sprays and the wrinkled, withered greenery of the oak and ash branches that had been cut to decorate the gates and porches.

After Whitsun came the mowing. From early morning the water meadow blossomed with gay peasant skirts, brightly embroidered aprons, and coloured kerchiefs. The whole village came out to mow. Mowers and rakers were all in festive attire. It was an ancient custom. From the Don to the distant alder thickets the ravaged meadow stirred and sighed under the scythes.

The Melekhovs were a little behindhand. They came out to mow when nearly half the village were in the meadows.

'Too long abed, Pantelei Prokofievich!' the sweating mowers called out.

'It's not my fault, it's the women!' the old man replied with a crusty laugh, and hurried the oxen with a raw-hide whip.

'Good health to you, mess-mate! You're late, man, you're late...' A tall Cossack in a straw hat shook his head as he sharpened his scythe by the roadside.

'Will the grass dry out?'

'You'll be in time if you get a move on. It'll be too dry otherwise. Where's your strip?'

'Near Red Ravine.'

'Well, whip up your plodders, or you won't get there today.'

Aksinya was sitting at the back of the hay wagon, her head and face wrapped up against the sun. From the narrow slit left for her eyes she watched Grigory opposite her with stern indifference. Darya, also muffled and smartly dressed, sat feeding her sleeping baby from her long, blue-veined breast, her legs dangling through the ribs of the wagon. Dunyashka was bouncing about on the side, happily surveying the meadow and the people they met on the road. Her merry face with a touch of sunburn and freckles at the bridge of the nose seemed to be saying: 'I am merry and happy because the day with its cloudless blue sky is merry and happy; because my heart is full of the same blue peacefulness and purity. Life is a joy for me and I want nothing more.' Pantelei pulled his shirt cuff over his hand and wiped the sweat that was streaming from under the peak of his cap. Dark wet patches showed on the calico clinging to his bent back. The sun streamed through a grey fuzz of clouds, spreading a fan of tinted rays over the distant silvery hills on the far side of the Don, the steppe, the water meadows and the village.

The day began to swelter. Small wind-plucked clouds crept along languidly, lagging behind Pantelei's ambling oxen. He himself had difficulty in lifting the whip and waved it as if in doubt whether to strike the beasts' knobbly backs or not. Apparently aware of this, they kept to the same slow pace, feeling their way forward with their cloven hooves and swinging their tails. A dusty golden-orange gadfly was circling over them.

The meadow glowed with the light-green patches that had been mown near the village threshing floors; where the grass had not yet been scythed, the wind ruffled its silky black sheen.

At length Pantelei waved his whip decisively. 'There's our strip.'

'Do we start from the wood?' Grigory asked.

'We can start from here. This is the place where I made our mark.'

Grigory unharnessed the fidgety oxen. The old man, his ear-ring glinting, went off to look for the mark—a stake driven into the ground at the edge of the strip.

'Bring the scythes!' he shouted a moment later, waving his hand.

Grigory walked away from the cart, leaving a wavy trail in the grass behind him. His father made the sign of the cross towards the thin white pea-pod of the distant bell-tower and took his scythe. His hooked nose shone as if it had just been varnished and the hollows of his cheeks were filmed with perspiration. He gave a smile that exposed a row of innumerable white closely set teeth, lifted the scythe and turned his deeply lined neck to the right. A seven-foot semicircle of severed grass dropped at his feet.

Grigory followed him with half-closed eyes, swathing the grass with his scythe. Ahead there was a scattered rainbow of women's aprons, but his eyes sought only one, a white one with an embroidered hem; then after a quick look back at Aksinya, he would again get in step with his father and swing his scythe.

Thoughts of Aksinya pursued him relentlessly; behind those half-closed eyes he would kiss her and whisper all the passionate and tender words that came to his tongue, then he would throw it all aside and stride on—one, two, three; memory offered fragments of recall: 'We sat in a wet haystack ... a grasshopper was chirping in a hollow ... there was a moon over the meadow ... and drops falling from a bush into a puddle, just like this ... one, two, three... And how good it was, how good!'

A peal of laughter came from the camp. Grigory looked round: Aksinya was bending forward and saying something to Darya, who was lying under the wagon; Darya waved her arms and the two women laughed again. Dunyashka was sitting on the wagon-shaft, singing in a thin, high-pitched voice.

'I'll go as far as that bush, then sharpen my scythe,' Grigory told himself, and at that moment he felt the scythe pass through something sluggishly resistant. He bent down to look and from under his feet a little wild duckling limped away squeaking into the grass. Near the hole where the nest had been another was lying cut in two by the scythe, while the rest scattered through the grass tweeting. Grigory placed the severed bird on his palm. A yellowish brown ball, only hatched from the egg a few days before, it still retained a living warmth in its fluff. A pink bubble of blood on the flat open beak, the tiny bead of the eye squinting cunningly, the legs still warm and quivering.

With a sudden feeling of intense pity Grigory gazed at the little dead thing lying on his hand.

'What have you found, Grisha?'

Dunyashka came running and skipping towards him over the mown grass, her tightly woven plaits dancing on her breasts. With a frown Grigory dropped the duckling and swung his scythe angrily.

They ate a hasty dinner. The whole meal consisted of fat bacon and the Cossack's standby—skimmed milk curds.

'No use going home,' Pantelei said while they were eating. 'Let the oxen graze in the wood and we'll finish mowing tomorrow, before the sun takes the dew.'

After dinner the women started raking. The mown grass wilted and began to dry, giving off a pungent, over-powering aroma.

It was dusk by the time they stopped mowing. Aksinya raked the remaining rows and went back to the camp to cook the porridge. All day she had been making spiteful fun of Grigory and throwing him hate-filled glances, as though taking revenge for some great and unforgettable offence. Grigory, gloomy and listless, drove the oxen down to the Don to water them. His father watched him and Aksinya all the time.

With a surly look at Grigory he said: 'Have your supper and then go out to watch the oxen. And see they don't get at the grass. You can take my coat.'

Darya put the baby to bed under the wagon and went to the thickets with Dunyashka for brushwood.

A waning moon was drifting across the black in-accessible sky. A snowstorm of moths was fluttering over the fire. The supper things were laid out on a thick cloth spread beside it. In the smoky cooking-pot the porridge was simmering. Darya wiped the spoons with the hem of her petticoat and shouted to Grigory, 'Come to supper!'

Grigory appeared out of the darkness with a coat over his shoulders and came up to the fire.

'Why are you so glum?' Darya asked with a smile.

'I've got a crick in my back. It must be going to rain,' Grigory tried to counter with a joke.

'He don't want to watch the oxen, that's why,' Du-nyashka smiled as she sat down beside her brother and tried to talk to him, but it was no use.

Pantelei supped his porridge zealously, crunching the uncooked grains of millet with his teeth. Aksinya ate without raising her eyes, smiling wanly at Darya's jokes.

A restless flush was burning her cheeks.

Grigory rose first and went off to watch the oxen.

'Mind they don't go trampling other people's grass!' his father shouted after him, whereupon a lump of unswallowed porridge stuck in his throat and set him coughing violently.

Dunyashka puffed up her cheeks and swelled with laughter. The fire was burning out and the smouldering embers swathed the folk sitting round it in the honey fragrance of scorched leaves.

* * *

At midnight Grigory crept up to the camp and halted at a distance of about ten paces. Pantelei was snoring sonorously in the wagon. A golden peacock's eye of flame was peeping out of the ashes of the undoused fire.

A grey muffled figure broke away from the wagon and zigzagged slowly towards Grigory. With two or three paces still to go, it stopped. Yes, it was Aksinya. Grigory's heart gave two resonant drum-like beats; bending low, he stepped forward with his coat thrown open and folded the obedient burning body to his own. Her knees sagged under her, she was shaking in every limb, her teeth were chattering. Grigory swept her up into his arms, just as a wolf shoulders the sheep it has killed, and went off panting and stumbling in the skirts of the unbuttoned coat.

'Oh, Grisha... Grisha, darling!.. Your father...'

'Keep quiet!'

Struggling to free herself, gasping in the sour smell of sheep's wool from the coat, choking with the bitterness of remorse, Aksinya said with a moan that was almost a shout:

'Let me go. What's the use now... I'll come myself!'

X

Not flushed like the gentle tulip of the steppes but rabid as the thorn apple, as the roadside stramony is the flower of a woman's love that comes late.

After the mowing, a great change came over Aksinya. It was as if she had been marked out, branded on the face. The women met her with malicious sneers and shook their heads as they passed, the girls envied her, but she held her happy, shameless head proud and high.

Soon everyone knew about Grishka's affair. At first they spoke of it in whispers—believing and unbelieving—but after the village herdsman, Snubnosed Kuzka, had seen them at dawn lying amid the young corn by the windmill, under the moon, the rumour spread like a wave breaking muddily on the shore.

It came eventually to the ears of Pantelei. One Sunday he happened to visit Mokhov's shop. There were so many people no one could move, but when he entered they seemed to give way and with grins all over their faces. He squeezed through to the cloth counter. The owner himself, Sergei Platonovich, came to serve him.

'It's a long time since we saw you here, Prokofievich.'

'I've had a lot to do. The farm work's too much for me.'

'Too much for you? How come? With strapping sons like yours?'

'Sons—huh! Petro's away at camp. All the work's on Grishka and me.'

Sergei Platonovich divided his thick gingery beard in two and shot a meaningful glance at the jostling crowd of Cossacks.

'You've been keeping very quiet lately, old man?'

'What about?'

'What about? You're planning to marry off your son, but you don't say a word about it.'

'What son?'

'Your Grigory isn't married, is he?'

'I hadn't thought of marrying him off yet.'

'But I've heard you're taking Stepan Astakhov's Aksinya as a daughter-in-law.'

'What? With her husband living? Why, you must be joking, Platonovich?'

'No joking at all. That's what I've heard people say.'

Pantelei smoothed out the length of material that lay on the counter, turned sharply and limped to the door. He made straight for home. He stumped along with his head down like a bull, knotty fingers bunched into a fist; his limp was even more noticeable. As he passed the Astakhovs' yard, he glanced over the fence: Aksinya, dressed up and looking much younger, was walking towards the house with an empty pail, hips swinging.

'Hi, wait a minute!'

Pantelei charged through the gate like the devil himself. Aksinya stood waiting for him. They went into the house. The earthen floor was well swept and sprinkled with reddish loam, on a bench in the front corner there were some pies just out of the oven. From the main room came a smell of long-packed clothes and, for some reason, anise apples.

A piebald cat with a big head tried to rub against Pantelei's legs. It arched its back and nudged his boots in friendly fashion. The old man sent it flying into the bench, and with eyes levelled on Aksinya's brows shouted:

'What do you mean by it? Eh? Your husband barely out of the house and you go off on the loose! I'll have Grigory's blood for this, and I'll write a letter to your Stepan!.. I'll tell him... You whore! You haven't been thrashed enough... From this day on, don't you dare set foot in my yard again. Carrying on with a young lad! Stepan will come back and I'll be—'

Aksinya listened with narrowed eyes. And all of a sudden she shamelessly swept up her skirts, bathed Pantelei in the aroma of petticoats, then came at him with her breasts thrust out, mimicking and snarling.

'Are you my father-in-law then? Eh? Are you?.. How dare you teach me? Go and teach your own fat-bottomed one! Give orders in your own yard! I don't give a damn for you, you limping devil!'

'Now wait a minute, you fool!'

'No waiting for you! Go back to where you came from! And if I want your Grishka, I'll have him, bones and all, and won't answer to anyone for it!.. So there! Put that in your pipe! I love Grishka! So what about it? Will you strike me? Will you write to my husband? Write to the Vice Ataman if you like, but Grishka's mine! Mine! Mine! I own him and I'll go on owning him!'

Aksinya advanced upon the intimidated Pantelei, breast forward and quivering like a netted bustard under her tight blouse, scorched him with the flame of her dark eyes, and poured out a stream of words, each more terrible and shameless than the last. Eyebrows twitching, Pantelei retreated to the entrance, groped for the stick he had left in the corner and, waving his arms, pushed open the door with his back. Aksinya drove him out of the porch, panting and raging.

'For all the luckless life I've led I'll have the loving of him! And after that you can kill me! Grisha's mine! Mine!'

Pantelei spluttered something into his beard and hobbled off home.

He found Grigory in the front room. Without saying a word he brought his stick down on his son's back. Grigory twisted away and grabbed his father's arm.

'What was that for, Dad?'

'For a good reason, you son-of-a-bitch!'

'For what?'

'Don't wrong our neighbour! Don't disgrace your father! Don't run loose, you young cur!' Pantelei croaked, dragging Grigory around the room in his efforts to recover the stick.

'I'll take no hidings from you!' Grigory grunted huskily and, clenching his jaws, snatched the stick away. Up came his knee and the stick broke with a crack.

Pantelei swung his fist at his son's neck.

'I'll have you thrashed before the whole village! You seed of the devil! You cursed son!' He danced in for a second blow. 'I'll marry you off to Marfushka the simpleton! I'll geld you!' The noise brought the mother to the room.

'Prokofievich! Cool down a bit! Stoppit!'

But the old man was beside himself; he hit out at his wife, knocked over the table with the sewing machine on it and charged out into the yard, leaving a trail of destruction behind him. Before Grigory could pull off his shirt, which had lost its sleeve in the tussle, the door swung open with a violent crack and Pantelei again towered like a stormcloud on the threshold.

'Marry off the son-of-a-bitch!' He stamped his foot like a horse and drove his eyes into Grigory's muscular back. 'I'll marry him off! I'll go match-making tomorrow. That I should have lived to be laughed at on account of my own son!'

'Let me change my shirt, you can marry me afterwards.'

'I'll marry you all right! To a half-wit!' He slammed the door and his footsteps clattered down the porch steps and died away.

XI

The tarpaulin-covered wagons were drawn up in rows outside the village of Setrakov. A small town, white-roofed and neat, with straight streets and a small parade ground in the middle, patrolled by a sentry, had grown up at astonishing speed.

The camps were leading the usual monotonous life that they led every year in the month of May. In the morning the troop of Cossacks that had been guarding the grazing horses would round them up and bring them back to camp. Then came the grooming, the saddling, the roll-call and the forming up. The loud-voiced Lieutenant-Colonel Popov, the staff officer in charge of the camps, shouted instructions in his usual rasping tone; the sergeants bellowed orders at the young Cossacks they were drilling. On the hill attacks were launched and the 'enemy' was cunningly outflanked and encircled. Buckshot was used for target shooting. The younger Cossacks eagerly competed in cut-and-thrust swordsmanship; the older ones got out of it whenever they could.

Voices grew hoarse from the heat and vodka, but a fragrant exciting wind flowed over the long lines of covered wagons, the susliks whistled from afar, and the steppe beckoned men away from the fug and smoke of the whitewashed huts.

A week before they were due to leave camp Andrei Tomilin, the brother of gunner Ivan, had a visit from his wife. She brought with her some sweet home-made buns, all kinds of goodies, and a heap of village news.

The next day she left early, taking with her greetings and instructions from the Cossacks to their families. Only Stepan Astakhov sent no message. The day before, he had fallen ill and tried to cure himself with vodka. So he saw nothing of Tomilin's wife or of anything else in the world. He absented himself from training; at his request a *feldsher* applied a dozen leeches to his chest. Stepan sat in nothing but his undershirt by the wheel of his wagon, the white cover of his peaked cap collecting grease from the hub. With a pouting lower lip, he watched the leeches sucking at the massive domes of his chest and gradually swelling with the dark blood.

The regiment *feldsher* stood beside him pulling at a cigarette and filtering the smoke through his widely spaced teeth.

'Feel any better?'

'Easier on the chest. Seems to be more room for my heart.'

'Leeches are a great cure!'

Tomilin came up to them and winked.

'Stepan, I'd like a word with you.'

'Speak then.'

'Come with me for a minute.'

Stepan got up with a grunt and walked away with Tomilin.

'Well, what is it?'

'My wife's been here, she's only just left.'

'Ah.'

'They're talking about your woman in the village.'

'What?'

'It's not good what they're saying.'

'What are they saying?'

'That she's carrying on with Grishka Melekhov... Openly.'

Turning pale, Stepan tore the leeches off his chest and crushed them with his heel. Having ground the last of them into the dirt, he buttoned his shirt collar, then, as though frightened of what he had done, unbuttoned it again. His white lips quivered restlessly, broke into a foolish grin, then pursed again in a blue wad. To Tomilin he seemed to be chewing at something hard that would not yield to his teeth. Gradually the colour came back into his face and the lips froze into petrified immobility. Stepan took off his cap, smeared the spot of cart grease over the white cover and said loudly, 'Thanks for the news.'

'I thought I'd better warn you. I'm sorry. That's how things are at home.'

Tomilin slapped his trouser-leg regretfully and walked away to his horse. A hum of voices spread through the camps. The Cossacks had just ridden in from their sabre exercises. Stepan stood for a minute, examining the black spot on his cap with stern concentration. A dying, half-crushed leech crawled on to his boot.

XII

There was a week and a half to go before the Cossacks returned from camp.

Aksinya was lost in the frenzy of her late and bitter love. Despite his father's threats Grigory was still going off secretly to her at night and returning only at dawn.

In two weeks he had exhausted himself like an over-ridden horse. From sleepless nights the brown skin over his high cheekbones was tinged with blue and his dark, drained eyes gazed wearily from their sunken sockets. Aksinya went about with her face uncovered and the deep hollows under her eyes were a funereal black; her swollen, slightly out-turned avid lips laughed restlessly and defiantly.

So unusual and obvious was their mad trysting, so frenziedly did they burn with the same shameless fire, regardless of convention or secrecy, daily growing thinner and darker in the face, that people found it embarrassing to look at them when they met.

Grigory's friends, who had at first been inclined to make fun of him about the affair, now fell silent at his approach and felt awkward in his company. The women, though secretly envious, condemned Aksinya and gloated in expectation of Stepan's return. Consumed by an insatiable curiosity, they spun conjecture upon conjecture about the outcome.

If Grigory had associated with the soldier's wife Aksinya with at least a pretence of secrecy, and if the soldier's wife Aksinya had lived with Grigory without letting it be seen and at the same time not refusing others, there would have been nothing unusual about it, nothing to offend the eye. The village would have talked and stopped talking. But these two lived together with scarcely any pretence. The bond between them was something big and bore no resemblance to a passing affair, so the people of the village decided that it was criminal and immoral, and the village crouched and waited in a hot little fever of expectation—Stepan's return would untie the knot.

Over the bed in the main room hung a string of empty black and white cotton reels. They were there for decoration. Flies spent the night on them and cobwebs joined them to the ceiling. Grigory was lying with his head on Aksinya's bare cool arm, looking up at the ceiling and the little chain of cotton reels. With the rough, work-hardened fingers of her free hand Aksinya was toying with Grigory's curls, which were as stiff as horsehair. Her fingers smelled of fresh milk; when Grigory turned his head and thrust his nose under her arm, the sharp sweetish smell of woman's sweat struck his nostrils like the fumes of fermenting hops.

Besides the painted wooden bed with its carved knobs there was a large iron-bound chest that stood by the door. It contained Aksinya's dowry and best clothes. In the front corner there was a table covered with oilcloth that portrayed General Skobelev galloping towards an array of tasseled banners lowered in submission before him; there were two chairs, and, above them, ikons with garish paper haloes. One of the flyblown photographs on the wall showed a group of Cossacks with heavy forelocks, puffed-out chests, watch-chains, and broad double-edged sabres drawn from their sheaths. This was Stepan with his regimental comrades while on active service. A uniform of Stepan's hung carelessly on a hanger. The moon gazing through the window was distrustfully fingering the two white sergeant's stripes on the shoulder-strap.

With a sigh Aksinya kissed Grigory just above the bridge of the nose, at the fork of his eyebrows.

'Grisha, darling...'

'What's worrying you?'

'We've only nine days left.'

'That's a long time yet.'

'What will I do then, Grisha?'

'How should I know?'

Aksinya held back her sigh and again smoothed and sorted out Grisha's tangled forelock.

'Stepan will kill me.' It could have been either a question or a statement.

Grigory said nothing. He was sleepy. With an effort he forced his eyelids apart and looked up into the glittering blue blackness of Aksinya's eyes.

'You'll give me up when my husband comes back, won't you? You'll be afraid?'

'Why should I be afraid of him? You're his wife; you're the one that should be afraid.'

'I'm not afraid while I'm with you, but when I start thinking about it during the day, it makes me shiver.'

Grigory yawned and rolled his head from side to side.

'Stepan coming back—that's nothing. It's my Dad; he wants to marry me off.'

He smiled and was about to say something else, but he felt Aksinya's arm suddenly go limp under his head and sink away into the pillow, then tremble and grow firm again, recovering its former position.

'Who have they sent the matchmakers to?' she asked hoarsely.

'They're only going to. Mother says it might be to the Korshunovs, to their Natalya.'

'Natalya... Natalya's a pretty girl... Real pretty. Well, marry her. I saw her the other day in church... She was so smart.'

Aksinya spoke quickly, but the lifeless, colourless words fell apart, making no impression.

'I've no use for her looks. I'd rather marry you.'

Aksinya jerked her arm from under his head and looked away dry-eyed at the window. Outside the night was a cold yellow. A heavy shadow from the barn lay across the yard. The grasshoppers were chirping. Down by the Don the bitterns were booming; the deep gloomy sounds crept stealthily through the single window into the room.

'Grisha!'

'Thought of something?'

She seized his unyielding, uncaressing hands and pressed them to her breast, to her deathly cold cheeks, and gave a cry that was almost a moan.

'Why did you latch on to me like that, curse you? What shall I do now!.. Oh, Grisha! You're breaking my heart! It's all up with me... How shall I answer Stepan when he comes? Who will stand up for me?'

He still said nothing. She looked tragically at his handsome gristled nose, at the eyes hidden in shadow, at the mute lips. And suddenly the dam of restraint was broken: frantically she kissed his face, neck, hands, the harsh curly black hair on his chest. She whispered in little gasps between her kisses and Grigory felt her shivering.

'Grisha, sweetheart ... dearest ... let's go away from here. My darling! Let's give up everything and get away. I'd leave my husband and everything if only I could have you. We'll go to the mines, far away. I'll love you so much and care for you... I've got an uncle at the Paramonov mines, he's a guard there. He'll help us... Grisha! Say something, just a word.'

Grigory jerked up his left eyebrow and thought. And suddenly he opened his burning, un-Russian eyes. They were laughing. The mockery in them was blinding.

'What a fool you are, Aksinya! You talk a lot, but there's nothing worth listening to. How could I leave the farm? And besides, this year I'm due for service. It wouldn't work... I'm not shifting off the land. Out here in the steppe there's something to breathe. But there? Last winter I went to the station with my father; I thought I'd die. Those railway engines roaring and the air all thick with coal smoke. I don't know how anyone can live there. Maybe they've got used to the stink.' Grigory spat and repeated, 'I won't go anywhere away from the village.'

The window darkened as a cloud floated across the moon. The cold yellow light flooding the yard grew dimmer, the shadows thinned and there was no telling whether the dark shape by the fence was last year's faggots or just tall old weeds.

The room darkened too, Stepan's sergeant's stripes on the Cossack uniform hanging by the window lost their shine, and in the grey, stagnant gloom Grigory did not see Aksinya's shoulders quiver or the head clasped between her hands jerking on the pillow.

XIII

Since the day when Tomilin's wife had visited the camp, Stepan had been looking badly off colour. His eyebrows were drooping and a deep, harsh furrow ran diagonally across his forehead. He seldom spoke to his comrades, flared up and quarreled over trifles, had a row with Sergeant-Major Pleshakov for no reason at all, and would hardly look at Petro Melekhov. The rein of their former friendship was broken. In his sullen pent-up fury Stepan was as dangerous as a runaway horse. They went home enemies.

Something was bound to happen that brought the vague hostility between them to a head. On the journey back, the five of them drove together as before. Petro's horse was in harness with Stepan's. Khristonya rode his own. Andrei Tomilin had caught a fever and lay shivering in the wagon under a greatcoat. Fedot Bodovskov was too lazy to drive, so Petro had taken the reins. Stepan was walking beside the wagon, slashing the purple heads of the roadside thistle with his whip. It began to rain. The sticky black soil gathered like tar on the wagon wheels. The sky, swaddled in clouds, had the bluish-grey hue of autumn. Night fell. They kept a look out for the lights of a village but there was no sign of any. Petro used his whip generously on the horses. And all of a sudden Stepan shouted from the darkness.

'What's the idea? You go easy on your own horse and never take your whip off mine?'

'Use your eyes. I whip the one that's not pulling.'

'Mind I don't harness you. Turks, they're good at pulling...'

Petro dropped the reins.

'D'you want to get something?'

'Keep your seat.'

'Then you'd better keep quiet.'

'What are you pitching into him for?' Khristonya boomed, riding up to Stepan.

Stepan said nothing. His face was invisible in the darkness. For half an hour they rode on in silence. The mud swished under the wheels. The rain sifted down, beating a drowsy rhythm on the tarpaulin cover of the wagon. Petro let the reins fall loose and smoked. He was turning over in his mind all the jibes he would fire at Stepan if there was a fresh flare-up. He was riled. He wanted to lash out at that creep Stepan, make a laughing stock of him.

'Move over. Let me get inside.' Stepan pushed Petro lightly and jumped on to the step.

At that moment the wagon jerked to a halt. The horses stamped and slithered in the mud, sparks flew from their shoes. The swingle-tree gave a thud.

'Whoa-a-a!' Petro shouted, jumping down.

'What's happened?' Stepan called anxiously.

Khristonya galloped up.

'Had a breakdown, have you?'

'Show a light.'

'Who's got the matches?'

'Stepan, throw us the matches!'

The horse in front was struggling and snorting. Someone struck a match. An orange ring of light, then darkness again. With trembling fingers Petro felt the back of the horse that had fallen. He tugged at the bridle.

'Hiyup!'

The horse gasped and rolled over on its side; the central shaft gave a loud crack. Stepan ran up and lit a bunch of matches. His horse was lying with its head thrown back. One leg was buried to the knee in a marmot burrow.

Khristonya dithered about, unhitching the traces.

'Get his leg free!'

'Unharness Petro's horse! Quick about it!'

'Whoa, you ruffian! Whoa-a-ah!'

'He's kicking, the devil. Stand back!'

With difficulty they hoisted Stepan's horse to its feet. Petro, muddy from head to foot, held it by the bridle. Khristonya crawled in the mud, feeling the lifelessly raised foreleg.

'Must be broken,' he declared in his deep voice.

Fedot Bodovskov slapped the horse's quivering back.

'Try to lead him. Maybe he'll walk?'

Petro pulled at the halter. The horse jumped forward without stepping on its left foreleg, and neighed. Tomilin pushed his arms into the sleeves of the greatcoat and stumped about despairingly.

'Now we're stuck! It's the end of that horse!'

This seemed to be what Stepan, silent up to now, had been awaiting for. Pushing Khristonya aside, he flung himself at Petro. The blow was aimed at his head but missed and hit his shoulder. They grappled and fell down in the mud. There was a tearing sound as someone's shirt was ripped. Stepan got Petro's head under his knee and battered him. Khristonya dragged them apart, swearing.

'What was that for?' Petro shouted, spitting out blood.

'Drive properly, you snake! Don't go off the road!'

Petro tried to break out of Khristonya's grip.

'Now then! No nonsense!' Khristonya boomed, pinning Petro to the wagon with one hand.

They paired up Fedot's short but sturdy horse with Petro's.

'You take mine!' Khristonya ordered Stepan.

He climbed into the wagon with Petro.

At midnight they drove into the village of Gnilovskoy, and halted at the first house. Khristonya went to see if they would put them up for the night. Ignoring the dog that came snapping at the skirts of his greatcoat, he squelched his way up to the window, opened the shutter and scratched on the windowpane.

'Anyone at home?'

Only the patter of rain and the dog's barking.

'Master! Good folk! Let us in for the night for Christ's sake. Eh? Troopers from camp. How many? Five of us. Uh-huh, Christ save you. Drive in!' he shouted, turning towards the gate.

As Fedot led in the horses, he tripped over a pig's trough that had been left in the middle of the yard, and swore. They tethered the horses under the lean-to of the barn. Tomilin, his teeth chattering, went into the house. Petro and Khristonya stayed in the wagon.

At dawn they made ready for the road. Stepan came out of the cottage followed by a very old, hunch-backed little woman. Khristonya, who was harnessing the horses, expressed his sympathy for her.

'Oho, Granny, what a hump they've given you! Must be handy for bowing down in church. You only have to bend a bit further and there's the floor.'

'Ah, Guardsman dear. It's handy for me to bow down, and you'd make a handy post to hang dogs on. We all come in handy for something,' the old soul smiled severely, astonishing Khristonya with a row of small, closely spaced teeth, quite unworn.

'What a toothy one you are, just like a pike. Couldn't you give me a dozen. I'm still a young man and got nothing to chew with.'

'But what should I have left, my dear?'

'We'll give you some horse's teeth, Gran. You'll be dead soon anyway and they don't judge you by your teeth in t'other world; the saints aren't Gypsies, you know.'

'Grind on, organ-grinder,' Tomilin grinned as he climbed into the wagon.

The old woman followed Stepan to the barn.

'Which one is it?'

'The black,' Stepan sighed.

The old woman laid her stick on the ground and with a mannish, confidently strong movement lifted the horse's injured leg. With her thin twisted fingers she felt the knee-joint for some time. The horse laid its ears flat, bared the brown upper edges of its teeth, and squatted back on its haunches in pain.

'There's no break here, my Cossack. Leave him with me and I'll look after him.'

'Will it be any good, Granny?'

'Any good? Who can tell, my bonny... It should be.'

Stepan put the matter aside with a wave of the hand and strode to the wagon.

'Will ye leave him or not?' the old woman called, watching him with puckered eyes.

'Let him stay.'

'She'll cure him all right. You left him with three legs and by the time you come for him he won't have any. That's a fine vet you've found—bent double herself,' Khristonya declared, laughing.

XIV

'...I'm pining for him, Granny dear. I'm pining away, I can see it myself. I can't take in my skirts quick enough—they get bigger everyday. And when I see him go past our yard, my heart beats so fast... I could fall to the ground and kiss his footprints... Perhaps he's put a spell on me?..

Help me, Granny! They're going to marry him off... Help me, dear soul! I'll give you anything it costs. I'll give you my last shirt. Only help me!'

Granny Drozdikha's light-coloured eyes looked at Aksinya from a lacework of wrinkles and she shook her head to the beat of the bitter words.

'Whose lad is it?'

'Pantelei Melekhov's.'

'The Turk's?'

'Yes.'

The old woman munched with her sunken mouth and was slow to answer.

'Come tomorrow early, young woman. At the very crack of day you must come. And we'll go down to the Don, to the water. And there we will wash away your yearning. Bring a pinch of salt with you from home. Remember that.'

Aksinya muffled her face in a light yellow shawl and went out through the gate.

Her dark figure was sucked up by the night. The dry crunch of the cut-down riding boots she was wearing died away. From somewhere on the edge of the village came the sound of brawling and songs.

At daybreak, after a sleepless night, she was back at Drozdikha's window.

'Granny!'

'Who is it?'

'It's me, Granny. Get up.'

'I'll be dressed right away.'

They walked down the lane towards the Don. By the pier the front wheels of a wagon lay abandoned in the water. The sand at the water's edge was prickly as ice. A damp, chill mist was drifting up from the river.

Drozdikha took Aksinya's hand in her bony fingers and drew her towards the water.

'Did you bring the salt? Give it to me. Make the sign to the east.'

Aksinya crossed herself and stared fiercely at the happy flush of dawn.

'Scoop up a handful of water and drink,' Drozdikha commanded.

Aksinya drank deeply, wetting the sleeves of her blouse. The old crone spread her arms like a black spider over the lazily flowing water, squatted on her haunches and began to whisper:

'Cold springs rising from the deep... Suffering flesh...

Wild beast at the heart... Yearning's fever... And by the holy cross ... purest and holiest... Make Grigory, slave of God...' Snatches of the prayer reached Aksinya.

Drozdikha sprinkled some of the salt on the damp sand at her feet, some on the water, and the rest into Aksinya's bosom.

'Throw some water over your shoulder. Be quick!'

Aksinya did as she was told, and stared resentfully at Drozdikha's brown cheeks.

'Is that all?'

'Go off now, my dear, and sleep for a while. That is all.'

Aksinya ran home panting. In the yard the cows were lowing. Darya Melekhova, her face flushed and sleepy under her fine arched brows, was driving her cows out to join the herd. She turned with a smile as Aksinya ran past.

'Had a good night, neighbour!'

'Thank God.'

'Where've you been a-wandering so early?'

'I had to go and see about something.'

The church bells rang for the morning service, their bronze voices brittle on the morning air. A cowherd was cracking his whip in the lane.

Aksinya hurriedly drove out the cows and carried the milk into the porch to strain it. With her sleeves rolled up to the elbow she wiped her hands on her apron; her head was full of other thoughts as she splashed the milk into the foaming strainer.

A clatter of wheels came from the street, followed by the neighing of horses. Aksinya put down the pail and went to the window.

Stepan was walking towards the gate, one hand steadying his cap. Other Cossacks were riding away towards the square. Aksinya crumpled her apron between her fingers and sank down on a bench. Footsteps coming up to the porch... Footsteps through the inner porch... Footsteps at the very door.

Stepan stood on the threshold, gaunt and estranged.

'Well?'

Shrinking in every fibre of her big, firm body, Aksinya came up to him.

'Beat me!' she said slowly and turned her head away.

'Well, Aksinya?'

'Yes, I've sinned, I'm not hiding it. Beat me, Stepan!'

She drew her head into her shoulders and stood facing

him, protecting only her belly with her hands. The dark-ringed eyes stared unblinkingly from the blank fear-distorted face. Stepan lurched sideways and stepped past her. She caught the smell of male sweat and bitter road-side wormwood from his unwashed shirt. He lay down on the bed without taking off his cap and, when he had been lying there a while, nudged off his sword-belt with a movement of his shoulder. His reddish-brown moustache, always so jauntily twirled, drooped limply. Aksinya looked sideways at him, not turning her head. Occasionally she shivered. Stepan lifted his feet on to the end of the bed. The mud began to drip slowly off his boots. He stared up at the ceiling, toying with his leather sword-knot.

'Breakfast not ready yet?'

'No.'

'Then get me something to eat.'

He supped milk from a bowl, licking his moustache. He chewed each lump of bread slowly, the muscles of his cheeks rippling under the pink skin. Aksinya stood by the stove. In a fever of terror she watched her husband's small, gristly ears working up and down as he ate.

At last Stepan rose from the table and crossed himself.

'Well, tell us all about it, m'dear.'

Aksinya bent forward to clear the table and said nothing.

'Tell me how you waited faithfully for your husband, how you guarded your husband's honour. Well?'

A terrible blow on the head tore the ground from under Aksinya's feet and flung her to the threshold. Her back struck the doorpost and a gasp broke from her throat.

That deft head-blow of Stepan's was powerful enough to fell not just a weak, unhardened woman, but stalwart, rugged men of the Ataman's Life Guards. Either it was fear that helped Aksinya or her woman's power of survival, but she lay still for a while and recovered her breath, then dragged herself to her knees.

Stepan was standing in the middle of the room, lighting a cigarette and did not see Aksinya struggling to her feet. When he tossed his pouch on the table, she was already out of the house, slamming the door behind her. He gave chase.

Streaming blood, Aksinya ran like the wind towards the fence dividing their yard from the Melekhovs'. Stepan caught her before she reached it. His dark brown hand swooped on her head like a hawk. Her hair bunched between his clenched fingers. He flung her to the ground, into the ashes that she had emptied by the fence every day after making up the stove.

What was there to wonder at if a husband, hands clasped behind his back, happened to be putting the boot into his own wife? One-armed Alexei Shamil walked past, took a look, blinked once or twice and parted his tufty little beard in a smile. It was obvious enough to him why Stepan should be dealing so affectionately with his lawfully wedded spouse.

Shamil would have waited to see (surely, anyone would have been curious) whether he would beat her to death or not, but he had too much self-respect for that. After all, he was not just a nosy woman.

Anyone looking at Stepan from a distance might have thought the fellow was doing a Cossack dance. So it seemed to Grigory when he glanced out of the front-room window and saw Stepan jigging up and down. But he looked again—and dashed out of the house. He ran to the fence on his toes with numb fists lifted to his chest; Petro clumped after him in his boots.

Grigory cleared the high fence like a bird and, still going full tilt, clobbered Stepan from behind. Stepan staggered, turned round and came at Grigory like a bear.

The Melekhov brothers fought desperately, pecking at their adversary as a vulture pecks carrion. Time and again Grigory went down under the leaden impact of Stepan's flailing fists. He was rather a lightweight against the big man's mature strength. But the stocky, agile Petro bent under the blows like a reed in the wind and kept his feet.

With only one glittering eye open (the other had swollen and was the colour of an unripe plum) Stepan retreated towards the porch.

They were separated by Khristonya, who had come to Petro for a bridle.

'Break it up!' He swung his huge pincer-like arms. 'Break it up, or I'll have you before the ataman!'

Thriftily spitting out some blood and half a tooth into his hand, Petro said hoarsely, 'Let's go, Grishka. Wait till we get him in a corner.'

'Mind I don't get my hands on you!' the bruised and battered Stepan threatened from the porch.

'All right!'

'I'll beat the guts out of you without any "all right"!'

'Are you kidding?'

Stepan came down from the porch fast and Grigory darted forward to meet him, but Khristonya hustled him towards the gate.

'Just you start again and I'll shake the life out of you, like a puppy!'

From that day on the enmity between the Melekhovs and Stepan Astakhov was tight as a Kalmyk knot.

It was a knot that Grigory Melekhov was destined to untie two years later in East Prussia, near the town of Stallupönen.

XV

'Tell Petro to harness the mare and his own horse.'

Grigory went out into the yard. Petro was wheeling a wagon out of the shed.

'Dad says we're to harness up the mare and yours.'

'We know that without him telling us,' Petro responded, guiding the shaft.

Their father, as solemn as a sexton during service, was supping the last of his cabbage soup and sweating profusely.

Dunyashka surveyed Grigory knowingly and hid her girlish laugh-smile somewhere in the shady cool of her curling eyelashes. Ilyinichna, a portly figure in her best pale-yellow shawl, maternal anxiety lurking at the corners of her lips, glanced at Grigory and turned to the old man.

'Surely you've stuffed yourself by now, Prokofievich. Anyone would think you were starving.'

'She won't even give me time to eat. What a pest the woman is!'

Petro poked his long wheaten-yellow moustache round the door.

'If it please you, the carriage is ready.'

Dunyashka giggled and covered her face with her sleeve.

Darya passed through the kitchen and arched her fine brows as she surveyed the prospective bridegroom.

The matchmaker was Ilyinichna's cousin, widowed Aunt Vasilissa, a woman of the world. She was the first to perch herself on the wagon, turning her round, pebble-like head this way and that and displaying her crooked black teeth under the hem of her lips as she laughed.

'Don't open your mouth too wide while you're there, Vasilissa,' Pantelei warned her. 'You might spoil the whole thing with those teeth of yours. They look like a lot of drunks, some leaning this way and some t'other.'

'It's not me that's to be betrothed, cousin. I'm not asking anyone's hand.'

'That may be so, but don't laugh. Those black choppers... They're enough to turn your stomach.'

Vasilissa took offence. Meanwhile Petro had opened the gate wide. Grigory sorted out the redolent leather reins and climbed on to the box. Pantelei and Ilyinichna, seated side by side at the back of the wagon, suddenly looked for all the world like a young couple.

'Whip 'em up!' Petro shouted, letting go the halter.

'Play, would you, you devil!' Grigory bit his lip and lashed the horse as it flattened its ears nervously.

Both horses strained at the traces and dashed away at a good pace.

'Careful! You'll hit the gatepost!' Darya squealed, but the wagon swung round sharply and, bouncing over the ruts, clattered away along the street.

Leaning to one side, Grigory urged on Petro's army mount, which was proving troublesome in harness. Pantelei clutched at his beard, as though afraid the wind might snatch it away.

'Give the mare one!' he wheezed, rolling his eyes and leaning forward to Grigory's back.

With the lace sleeve of her blouse Ilyinichna wiped a windblown tear and blinked at her son's billowing blue sateen shirt. The Cossacks they met on the road stepped back and stared after them as they passed. Dogs charged out of yards and darted under the horses' feet. Their barking was drowned by the rumble of the newly rimmed wheels.

Grigory spared neither the whip nor the horses and in ten minutes the village lay behind them and the orchards of the farms on the other side of it were flashing by in a whirl of greenery. Soon the Korshunovs' large house loomed up behind a board fence. Grigory reined in and the wagon, breaking off its iron refrain, halted at the painted and delicately carved gate.

Grigory stayed with the horses while Pantelei limped up to the porch. The poppy-red Ilyinichna and Vasilissa, her lips inexorably sealed, followed him with a rustle of skirts. The old man, afraid of losing the courage he had stored up on the road, was in a hurry. He tripped over the threshold of the porch, bruised his lame leg and, frowning with pain, stumped furiously up the remaining well scrubbed steps.

He entered the house almost at the same time as Ilyinichna. As it was not to his advantage to stand beside his wife—she was a good seven inches taller—he took another step forward, lifted one foot like a cockerel and, doffing his cap, made the sign of the cross at the black, smudgily painted ikon.

'Good health to you all!'

'Praise the Lord,' the master of the house, a rather short, elderly-looking Cossack with a freckled face, replied, rising from a bench.

'Well, here we are, Miron Grigorievich!'

'Guests are always welcome. Maria, give them something to sit on.'

His elderly flat-chested wife made a show of dusting the stools as she moved them forward for the guests. Pantelei sat down on the edge of one, mopping his wet swarthy forehead with a handkerchief.

'We've come to see you on business,' he began without beating about the bush.

At this point in his speech Ilyinichna and Vasilissa tucked up their skirts and also seated themselves.

'Oh! What kind of business?' their host said with a smile.

Grigory came in. His eyes darted round the room.

'I hope you had a good night.'

'Praise the Lord,' the mistress of the house responded in a sing-song voice.

'Praise the Lord,' the master affirmed after her. A brown flush broke through his freckles. He had only at this moment guessed the reason for the visit. 'Have their horses brought into the yard and give them some hay,' he said to his wife.

She went out for a moment.

'We have a little matter to discuss with you,' Pantelei continued. He stirred the wavy black tar of his beard and tugged at his ear-ring in his excitement. 'You've got a girl of marriageable age; we've got a lad... Could we come to an agreement by any chance? I'd like to know if you're thinking of marrying her off just now or not. Perhaps we could become kinsmen?'

'Well, I don't know--' the master of the house scratched his balding pate. 'To be honest, we weren't thinking of giving her away this autumn. There's a lot of work to be done at home and she's a bit young yet, you know. She's only just passed her eighteenth spring. Isn't she, Maria?'

'That's right.'

'So now she's in full bloom! Why hold on to her? Or aren't there enough old maids already?' Vasilissa put in, fidgeting on her stool (she was being pricked by the besom she had stolen from the porch and tucked away under her blouse; tradition had it that matchmakers who stole the bride's besom would never be refused).

'We had some matchmakers here in early spring. Our girl won't be left on the shelf. We can't grumble, thank the Lord, she's good at everything, whether it be on the farm or in the house.'

'If a good man turns up, why not marry her?' Pantelei managed to say amid the women's chatter.

'Why not?' the master of the house scratched his head again. 'We can marry her off at any time.'

Pantelei thought he was being refused and grew heated.

'Well, it's up to you, of course... A young man, who wants to marry is like a holy beggar, he can ask anywhere. If you're looking for a bridegroom of merchant's rank or something, then it's quite a different matter. We're sorry we bothered you.'

At this point the matchmaking might have come to a sudden end. Pantelei was snorting and turning as red as beetroot juice and the girl's mother was squawking like a brood-hen at the shadow of a hovering kite, but just at the right moment Vasilissa stepped in and mended matters with her soft and soothing patter.

'What's all this, my dears! Now we're about it, we must decide as custom demands and for the happiness of the children. Take Natalya now—you'd go a very long way to find another girl like her! She's a good hand at everything—sewing or housework. And as for her looks—you good folk have seen for yourselves!' Her arms described a pleasantly rounded figure as she turned to Pantelei and the sulky Ilyinichna. 'And the young man is a bridegroom in a thousand. It makes my heart bleed to look at him, he's so much like my late husband Donyushka. And what a hard-working family! Prokofievich is well known for his good works—you could search the whole district to find another like him. So shall we give our word on it or are we enemies of our children's future?'

The matchmaker's cooing voice flowed like treacle into Pantelei's ears. Plucking black curly hairs out of his nostril with thumb and forefinger, he listened and thought to himself, 'What a tongue she has, the old witch! Like knitting a stocking! Loops on the stitches before you know what it's all about. Some women can floor a

Cossack with their patter. A magpie in a skirt, she is!'
And he sat listening in admiration as the matchmaker
sang the praises of the bride and her whole family, going
back five generations.

'Stands to reason, we don't wish our child any harm.'

'What we were saying was that mebbe it's too early
yet,' the master of the house said appeasingly, his face
breaking into a smile.

'It's not too early! Honest to God, it's not!' Pantelei
urged.

'We'll have to part one day, be it early or late,' the
mistress said with a little sob that could have been
affected or sincere.

'Call in your daughter, Miron Grigorievich, let's have
a look at her.'

'Natalya!'

The girl appeared in the doorway, her brown fingers
fussing with the hem of her apron.

'Come right in! You needn't be shy,' her mother
encouraged her, smiling through a blur of tears.

Grigory, who was sitting beside a heavy chest painted
with faded blue flowers, turned to look at her.

Bold grey eyes under the black dust-cloud of a crocheted scarf. A small pink dimple on her taut cheek was
quivering with embarrassment and a lurking smile. Grigory shifted his glance to her hands: they were large and
calloused. Under the green blouse encasing a firm well-
fed body, the small, girlishly hard breasts fanned upward
in wistful innocence, and the sharp little nipples stuck
out like buttons.

In one minute Grigory's eyes took in all of her—from
her head to her long beautiful legs. He inspected her as
a horse-dealer inspects a young mare before making his
purchase. She's good, he thought, and turned his eyes to
meet hers, which were looking straight at him. Their
guileless, slightly embarrassed, honest look seemed to say,
'Here I am, all of me, just as I am. Judge me as you will,'
'You're fine,' Grigory answered with his eyes and smile.

'Go along now,' said the host waving her out.

As she closed the door behind her, Natalya looked
back at Grigory, hiding neither her smile nor her curiosity.

'Well, Pantelei Prokofievich,' Miron began, exchanging
a glance with his wife, 'you consider the matter and we'll
consider it ourselves, in the family. And after that we'll
decide whether to become kinsmen or not.'

As he walked down from the porch, Pantelei promised,

'We'll drive over next Sunday.'

But as he walked with him to the gate his host deliberately made no reply, pretending not to hear.

XVI

Only after being told about Aksinya by Tomilin had Stepan realised with misery and hatred in his heart that, despite the rotten life they had led together, despite the old insult to his pride, he loved her with an oppressive hate-filled love.

At night he had lain in the wagon with a greatcoat over him, hands behind his head, eyes sealed under their blue lids, and thought of how he would return home, how his wife would receive him, and it was as though he had a hairy tarantula at work in his breast instead of a heart. He devised thousands of ways of taking his revenge and his teeth felt as if they were clogged with heavy grains of sand. He had spilled out some of his anger in the fight with Petro and come home exhausted. So Aksinya had got off lightly.

From that day on an invisible corpse haunted the Astakhovs' house. Aksinya went about on tip-toe and spoke in a whisper, but in her eyes, sprinkled with the ashes of fear, an ember of the great fire that Grigory had lighted still smouldered.

Stepan felt this rather than saw it. And it rankled. At night, when the flock of flies over the stove fell asleep and Aksinya, lips trembling, had made up the bed, Stepan would clamp his black rough hand over her mouth and beat her. He would question her shamelessly about the details of her affair with Grigory. Aksinya would writhe and gasp for breath on the hard bed that smelled of sheepskin. When he grew tired of tormenting her soft dough-like body, Stepan would grope over her face in search of tears. But Aksinya's cheeks would be as dry as fire and the only movement was that of her jaws working under his fingers.

'Will you tell?'

'No!'

'I'll kill you!'

'Kill me then! Kill me, for Christ's sake... It'll end this torture... This is no life.'

Gritting his teeth, Stepan would twist the thin sweat-cooled skin on his wife's breast.

Aksinya winced and moaned.

'What? Does it hurt?' Stepan would ask jocularly.
'Yes.'

'Do you think it didn't hurt me?'

He would not fall asleep until late at night. In his sleep he would squeeze and stretch his dark fingers with their puffy joints. Aksinya would raise herself on her elbow and gaze into her husband's face, changed and handsome in sleep, then drop her head on to the pillow and whisper to herself.

She saw scarcely anything of Grigory. They did meet once by the Don. Grigory had been watering the oxen and was walking back up the slope, waving a thin red switch and looking down at his feet. Aksinya was walking towards him. As soon as she saw him she felt the yoke go cold under her hands and the blood fling fire into her temples.

Afterwards, when she recalled the encounter, she had to force herself to believe that it had really happened. Grigory did not see her until they were almost level. The persistent creaking of the pails made him raise his head; then his eyebrows jerked up and he smiled foolishly. Aksinya walked on, staring over his head at the green, breathing waves of the Don, and across them, to the crest of the sandbar.

Colour stormed into her face, squeezing tears from her eyes.

'Aksinya!'

She went on a few paces and stopped, shrinking as if from a blow. Grigory lashed a lagging piebald ox viciously with his switch and said, without turning his head, 'When will Stepan go out to reap the rye?'

'Right now ... he's harnessing up.'

'When you've seen him off, come to our sunflower patch by the meadow. I'll be there.'

Pails creaking, Aksinya walked on down to the river. Foam fringed the bank like frilly yellow lace on the green hem of the waves. White fisher gulls were swooping and mewing over the water.

A silvery rain of small fish was flitting about the surface. On the far side, beyond the white streak of the sandbar, the crowns of ancient poplars, grizzled by the wind, stood majestic and stern. As she was drawing water, Aksinya dropped one of her pails. She pulled up her skirt with her left hand and waded in up to her knees. The water tickled her legs where the garters had rubbed them, and for the first time since Stepan's return she laughed, softly and uncertainly.

She looked back at Grigory; still waving the switch, as though to drive away the gadflies, he was slowly climbing the slope.

Aksinya's tear-misted gaze caressed his strong confidently striding legs. His broad trousers tucked into white woollen socks had red stripes down the sides. The loose cloth from a tear in the dirty shirt was fluttering at the shoulder blade and a triangle of bare brown flesh showed through the rent. Aksinya's eyes kissed that tiny bit of the beloved body that had once belonged to her, and tears fell on to her pale smiling lips.

She put down the pails on the sand and, as she hooked them on to the yoke, she noticed the imprint of Grigory's pointed boot. She looked round furtively; there was no one about, only some children bathing from a distant pier. She bent down and covered the footprint with her hand, then heaved the yoke on to her shoulders and, smiling to herself, hurried home.

The sun was curtained with a muslin haze. Somewhere beneath the curly-coated flock of white clouds lay the deep blue cool of the meadows, but over the village, over the scorching iron roofs, over the deserted dusty streets, over the withered yellow grass in the yards there hung a sultry stillness.

Aksinya came up to the porch with her pails, swaying and splashing water over the cracked earth. Stepan in a broad-brimmed straw hat was harnessing horses to a reaper. He looked at Aksinya as he adjusted the breechband on the drowsy mare.

'Fill up the water cask.'

Aksinya poured water into the cask, burning her hands on the riveted iron hoops.

'You need some ice. The water will get warm,' she said, looking at her husband's sweating back.

'Go and get some from the Melekhovs... No, don't go there!' Stepan shouted, remembering.

Aksinya went to close the side-gate she had left open. Stepan lowered his eyes and grabbed his whip.

'Where're you off to?'

'To shut the gate.'

'Come back, you sly bitch. I told you not to go!'

She hastened back to the porch and tried to hang up the yoke, but her hands were shaking and it fell with a clatter down the steps.

Stepan tossed a tarpaulin coat on the front seat, perched himself on it and shook out the reins.

'Open the gate.'

As she pulled open the double gate Aksinya screwed up her courage to ask, 'When will you be back?'

'This evening. I told Anikei I'd reap with him. Take him some food. He'll be coming out to the fields as soon as he gets back from the blacksmith's.'

The small wheels of the reaper squeaked as they churned through the velvety grey dust round the gate. Aksinya went into the house, stood with her hands clasped to her heart, then put on a kerchief and ran down to the Don.

What if he comes back? What will happen then? The searing thought stopped her, as though she had seen a chasm at her feet. She looked round for a moment, then ran even faster along the slopes above the Don to the water meadow.

Wattle fences. Vegetable patches. A yellow glare of sunflowers gazing up into the eye of the sun. Green potato tops with pale flowers. And there were the Shamil women, late with weeding their potatoes. Bent backs in pink blouses, hoes rising and falling over the grey tillage. Aksinya reached the Melekhovs' vegetable garden without stopping for breath. She glanced round, slipped the wattle hasp off the gate-post and opened the gate. Along a well trodden path she made her way to the green stockade of sunflower stalks, bent down and crept right in among them, staining her face with the golden pollen, then gathered up her skirt and sat down on the weed-woven ground.

She listened; the stillness made her ears ring. Somewhere above her a solitary bumble-bee was buzzing. The hollow, bristly stems of the sunflowers sucked the earth in silence.

For perhaps half an hour she sat there, wondering anxiously whether he would come or not. She had got up to go and tucked her hair under her kerchief when the gate creaked heavily. Footsteps.

'Aksinya!'

'I'm here.'

'Ah, so you came.'

Grigory rustled through the leaves and sat down beside her. For a moment they were silent.

'What's that on your cheek?'

Aksinya rubbed the yellow sweet-smelling pollen with her sleeve.

'Must be from the sunflowers.'

'And there's some more, just by your eye.'

She wiped it off. Their eyes met, and in answer to Grigory's mute question she broke into tears.

'I can't stand it... It'll be the end of me, Grisha.'

'What does he do?'

Aksinya tugged fiercely at the collar of her blouse: the pink, girlishly firm breasts tumbled out all in bluish-red bruises.

'Don't you know? He beats me every day! He's sucking the blood out of me! And you're a fine one. You make a mess like a dog, then run away... You're all—' With shaking fingers she buttoned her blouse and glanced up at Grigory as he turned his head away—had she offended him?

'So you're looking for someone to blame?' he drawled, biting a blade of grass.

His calm voice stung Aksinya like a whip.

'And aren't you to blame?' she cried hotly.

'A dog can't mount an unwilling bitch.'

Aksinya covered her face with her hands. The insult had struck home like a powerful, well-timed blow.

Grigory looked at her sideways, frowning. A tear was seeping out between her first and middle fingers.

A crooked dusty ray shone through the pellucid droplet and dried its damp trace on the skin.

Grigory hated the sight of tears. He grew restless, fiercely brushed a brown ant off his trouser-leg, and sent another brief glance at Aksinya. She was still sitting as before, except that not one but three tear drops were rolling down the back of her hand.

'Why are you crying? Did I hurt you? Aksinya! Wait... I've got something to tell you.'

Aksinya wrenched her hands away from her wet face.

'I came for advice... Why are you like this to me? It's bad enough as it is.'

She's down and I kicked her. Grigory flushed scarlet at the thought.

'Aksinya, love... It just slipped out. Don't take it hard.'

'I didn't come to pester you... You needn't be afraid of that!'

At that moment she really believed she had not come to impose herself on Grigory; but while running along the Don to the meadow she had thought, without being clearly aware of it, 'I'll talk him out of it! He mustn't marry. Who else will I ever have in life?!' And at the thought of

Stepan she had tossed her head spiritedly, as if to drive him away.

'So this is the end of our love?' Grigory said, and rolled over on his stomach, resting on his elbows and spitting out the petals of the bindweed flower that he had been chewing while they talked.

'The end? How could it be?' she exclaimed in fright, trying to look into his eyes.

Only the prominent bluish whites showed as he averted his glance.

The dry, exhausted earth smelled of dust and sun. The wind rustled the green sunflower leaves. For a minute the sun was dimmed by the curly hump of a cloud, and a shadow passed like a billow of smoke over the village, over Aksinya's drooping head, and over the pink cup of a bindweed flower.

Grigory gave a sigh that was like the cough of a horse, turned over on his back and dug his shoulder blades into the hot ground.

'You see, Aksinya,' he said, bringing out the words slowly, 'I feel kind of sick, somewhere up here, in my chest. So I've been thinking—'

The creak of a wagon floated over the vegetable patch.

'Gee-up, Baldy! Gee-up!..'

The shout seemed so loud to Aksinya that she threw herself flat on the ground. Grigory raised his head and whispered, 'Take off your kerchief. The white shows up... Someone might see.'

Aksinya threw off her kerchief. The hot wind streaming through the sunflowers stirred the ringlets of golden fluff on her neck. The creak of the wagon died away in the distance.

'What I've been thinking is this,' Grigory resumed with more life in his voice. 'You can't bring back the past, so why look for someone to blame? We've got to go on living somehow—'

Aksinya listened guardedly and waited, breaking a stalk she had taken from an ant.

She looked into Grigory's face and caught the dry, anxious gleam in his eyes.

'—What I've been thinking is let's put an end to—'

Aksinya swayed sideways. Her fingers clutched at the tough bindweed. With dilated nostrils she waited for the rest of the phrase. A fire of fear and impatience scorched her face and dried her mouth. She thought Grigory would say, '...put an end to Stepan', but he licked his dry lips

81

vexedly (they wouldn't move), and said, 'Let's put an end to the whole thing. Huh?'

Aksinya stood up and walked away to the gate, thrusting the nodding yellow tops of the sunflowers aside with her breast.

'Aksinya!' Grigory called in a low voice.

The gate creaked heavily in reply.

XVII

After the rye, which still had to be carted to the threshing floors, came the wheat. On the loamy ground and on the hillocks the leaves curled and turned yellow and the used-up stems began to wither.

The harvest promised to be a good one. The ears were firm, the grain full and heavy.

After talking it over with his wife, Pantelei decided that if the match with the Korshunovs was agreed upon they should put off the wedding until the last church festival in August.

They had not yet called on the Korshunovs for an answer; now there was reaping to be done, now a festival to be prepared for.

They drove out for the reaping on a Friday with three horses. Pantelei stayed behind, shaping a new strut for the wagon he needed for bringing in the grain. Petro and Grigory went out with the reaper.

Grigory walked beside the machine, holding the front seat, where his brother was perched; his face was sullen. The muscles were twitching from jaw to cheekbones. Petro knew this was a sure sign that his brother was in a dangerous mood and ready for any mad, unthinking action, but he went on teasing him, chuckling into his long wheat-coloured moustache.

'She told me so, honestly she did!'

'All right then, let her,' Grigory grunted, biting the tip of his moustache.

' "I was just going away from the vegetable garden," she says, "and what do I hear? Voices from the Melekhovs' sunflowers." '

'Chuck it, Petro.'

'Oh, ay ... voices! "And so," she says, "I peeped over the fence." '

Grigory started blinking rapidly.

'Will you stop? Or not?'

'What's wrong with you? Let me finish!'

'Careful, Petro, or we'll have a fight,' Grigory threatened, dropping behind.

Petro twitched his eyebrows and swung round so that he was sitting with his back to the horses and facing Grigory.

' "Yes, I peeped over the fence," she says, "and there they were, the pair of them, lying in each other's arms." "Who were they?" I asks. "Aksinya Astakhova and your brother," she says. "Well," I says—'

Grigory seized the handle of a short fork lying at the back of the reaper and charged at Petro. His brother dropped the reins, jumped off his seat and dodged away in front of the horses.

'Oho! You devil! You're mad! Oho! Look at him!'

Snarling like a wolf, Grigory hurled the fork. Petro dropped on to his hands and knees, and it flashed over his head, burying its prongs a good two inches deep in the dry flint-like ground and giving out a vibrant hum.

Petro's face darkened as he seized the scared horses by the bridle.

'You might have killed me, you swine!'

'I would have!'

'You're a fool! A mad devil! You take after your father's tribe, you crazy hillsman!'

Grigory pulled out the fork and followed the reaper as it moved on.

Petro beckoned him over.

'Come here. Give me that fork.'

He passed the reins over to his left hand, took the fork by one of the whitened prongs, and brought the handle down hard on Grigory's unsuspecting back.

'Pity I couldn't get a pull in it!' he said regretfully, watching Grigory spring aside.

A minute later they looked into each other's eyes as they lighted their cigarettes and roared with laughter.

Khristonya's wife, who was riding on a load of sheaves along another track, saw Grigory throw the fork at his brother. She stood up on top of the load to see what would happen next, but the reaper and horses were in the way. As soon as she reached the lane, she shouted to her neighbour, 'Klimovna! Run and tell Pantelei the Turk that his sons are fighting with pitchforks along by the Tatar Mound. That Grishka—you know what a madcap he is—he stabbed Petro in the side with a fork, then the other one hit him back and the blood is flowing something terrible!'

Petro had grown tired of bawling at the fretting horses and all he could do was whistle loudly. Grigory with one dust-blackened foot on the cross-bar was tossing the swathes off the reaper. The horses, their backs bloodied by flies, swung their tails and pulled jerkily at the traces.

All the way to the blue rim of the horizon there were people moving to and fro across the steppe. The knives of the reapers chopped and chuttered and the swathes of reaped corn lay in banks across the steppe. The marmots on their burrows mimicked the drivers with their whistling.

'Another couple of lengths and we'll have a smoke!' Petro shouted through the swishing of the reaper sails and the clatter of the chain drive.

Grigory merely nodded. He could scarcely part his dry, chapped lips. Panting for breath, he shifted his grip up the fork handle to make it easier to toss the heavy swathes of wheat. His chest itched and bitter sweat poured down from under his hat, stinging his eyes like soap. They stopped the horses, drank some water, and smoked.

'Someone's galloping along the highway,' Petro said, shading his eyes with his hand.

Grigory stared and raised his brows in astonishment. 'It's Dad.'

'You're crazy! What could he gallop on? All our horses are pulling the reaper.'

'It's him.'

'You're seeing things, Grishka!'

'Honestly, it is!'

A minute later the horse going at full gallop and its rider came clearly into view.

'Dad it is!' Petro stood gazing in scared astonishment.

'Something must have happened at home,' Grigory voiced the thought that was in both their minds.

While he was still some two hundred yards away, Pantelei reined in his horse to a trot.

'I'll tan the hide off the pair of you... You young bastards!' he roared long before he reached them, and swung a long leather huntsman's whip over his head.

'What's up with him?' Petro was so astounded that he stuffed half his golden moustache into his mouth.

'Get behind the reaper! Honest to God, he's going to use that whip. He'll have the hide off us before we sort this one out,' Grigory said chuckling, and took the precaution of retiring behind the reaper.

The foam-flecked horse came bounding over the stubble at a slow canter. Pantelei rode up, legs dangling (he was riding bare back) and whip swinging above his head.

'What have you been doing out here, you devil's brood?!'

'Reaping—' Petro spread his arms and glanced apprehensively at the whip.

'Who's been stabbing who with a pitchfork? What were you fighting about?'

Grigory turned his back on his father and began counting the wind-scattered clouds under his breath.

'What pitchfork? What are you talking about? Who's been fighting?' Petro blinked at his father and shifted his feet nervously.

'That woman—drat her—came running in and shouting, "Your boys are stabbing each other with pitchforks!" How about that?' Pantelei shook his head frantically, dropped the reins and dismounted from the panting horse. 'So I grabbed Fedka Syomishkin's horse and galloped out here. Well?'

'But who told you this?'

'A woman!'

'That woman's a liar! She must have been asleep on the wagon and dreamt it.'

'That blasted hag!' Pantelei screeched, tearing his beard. 'That crone Klimovna! God almighty! I'll thrash that bitch!' he stamped about, limping on his lame left leg.

Grigory stared at his feet, shaking with silent laughter, Petro stroked his perspiring head and kept his eyes on his father.

After stamping around for a bit, Pantelei quietened down, climbed on to the reaper, drove it up and down the field a few times and, still swearing, mounted his horse. He trotted out on to the highway, overtook two loaded wagons, and rode off in a cloud of dust to the village. The whip with its finely plaited lash and smart tassel lay forgotten in a furrow. Petro fingered it, and shook his head.

'We were in for a rough time, lad. Call this a whip? It's not a whip, boy, it's a crippler—you could cut off a man's head with it!'

XVIII

The Korshunovs were reputed to be the richest family in the village. Fourteen pairs of oxen, a drove of horses, mares from the Provalsk stud, fifteen cows, a fine herd of grazing cattle, and a flock of several hundred sheep. And apart from that there was plenty to delight the eye. The house was every bit as good as the Mokhovs'—six rooms with an iron roof and weather-boarded walls; outbuildings roofed with fresh new tiles; four acres of orchard and vegetable garden. What more could a man want? There had been good reason for Pantelei's timidity and secret reluctance on his first matchmaking visit. The Korshunovs could obviously find a better match for their daughter than Grigory. Pantelei feared a refusal and had no wish to go and pay his respects to the self-willed Korshunov; but Ilyinichna kept at him, like rust on iron, and in the end broke the old man's resistance. Secretly cursing Grigory, Ilyinichna and the world at large, he agreed to go.

They decided to wait until Sunday. Meanwhile under the green-painted roof of the Korshunovs' spacious house the family was quietly at war with itself. After the matchmakers' departure the girl had answered in reply to her mother's question, 'I love Grishka and I won't marry anyone else!'

'A fine husband you've picked, you ninny,' her father remonstrated. 'He's as dark as a Gypsy and that's about all that can be said for him. Is that the best husband I can find you, my sweet?'

'I don't want anyone else, Daddy.' Natalya flushed, and gave way to tears. 'I won't marry anyone else and they needn't come to ask my hand. I'd rather go to the Ust-Medveditsa nunnery.'

'He's a gallivanter, a woman-chaser, he runs after soldiers' wives,' her father declared, using his trump-card. 'The whole village is talking about him.'

'I don't care!'

'Then I care even less. It'll be a load off my shoulders if that's the way things are.'

Natalya—the eldest daughter—was her father's favourite, so he made no attempt to force her choice.

The previous autumn a party of matchmakers—very rich Old Believer Cossacks—had come from as far away as the River Tsutskan; and there had been others, from the Khopyor and the Chir,* but these suitors had failed to please Natalya and the matchmakers' blandishments had been wasted.

In his heart Miron Grigorievich liked Grigory for his

---

* Left- and right-bank tributaries of the Don.—*Ed*.

Cossack daring and his love of the land and the working of it. The old man had noticed him among the common run of Cossack lads sometime ago, when Grigory had won first prize for trick riding at the races; but it seemed a pity to marry his daughter to a man of scant fortune and doubtful reputation.

'He's a hard-working lad and handsome in the face,' Lukinichna would whisper in his ear at night, stroking her husband's freckled ginger-haired arm. 'And Natalya, to be sure, is real gone on him... Proper taken with him she is!'

Miron would turn his back to his wife's cold bony breast and mutter crossly, 'Oh, stop pestering me! Marry her off to Pasha the Simpleton, for all I care! God never gave you much brains! "He's handsome in the face..."' he mimicked. 'Do you expect to reap a harvest off his face?'

'It's not the harvest I'm thinking about.'

'What does his face matter to you? If only he was the right kind of person. To be honest, it goes against the grain to give my daughter away to the Turks. I prefer our own kind...' Miron said with some pride, heaving about on the bed.

'They're a hard-working family and they live quite well,' his wife went on whispering as she cuddled up to her husband's sturdy back and stroked his hand soothingly.

'Keep off me, will you! Haven't you got enough room there. Why are you stroking me like a cow in calf! Do what you like with Natalya! Marry her to a whore if you want to!'

'You must be good to your own child. Never mind about riches,' Lukinichna hissed into her husband's hairy ear.

He gave a sudden kick and turned his face to the wall, then began to snore as if he were asleep.

The matchmakers' second visit took them by surprise. They drove up after service in a tarantass. Ilyinichna nearly overturned the vehicle as she put her foot on the step to climb out: but Pantelei hopped down from the seat like a young cockerel and, although he had made his feet tingle painfully, stumped off gallantly towards the house.

'Here they come! The devil must have brought 'em!' Miron gasped, looking out of the window.

'Good gracious and I haven't changed my skirt since I did the cooking!' Lukinichna cried.

'You'll do as you are! They're not asking for your hand! Who needs you, you horse itch!'

'You always were a ruffian and you've gone right off the handle in your old age.'

'Now then, keep a rein on your tongue, woman!'

'You might put on a clean shirt, your hump's showing through the back! Aren't you ashamed? You old devil!' his wife scolded, inspecting him from all sides as the matchmakers crossed the yard.

'They'll know me as I am, I guess. They wouldn't turn away even if I was in sackcloth.'

'Good health to you!' Pantelei crowed, stumbling over the threshold and, embarrassed by the power of his own voice, crossed himself yet again in front of the ikon.

'Good morning,' Miron responded, looking daggers at the matchmakers.

'God has sent us some fair weather.'

'It's holding, praise be.'

'It'll give people time to bring in the corn.'

'Ay, that's so.'

'Ay.'

'Ahem.'

'Well, Miron Grigorievich, we've come to ask what you've decided among yourselves and whether we'll agree upon the match or not.'

'Please, come in. Do sit down,' Lukinichna invited them, bowing and sweeping the brick-scrubbed floor with her long, gathered skirt.

'Don't go to any trouble, please.'

Ilyinichna sat down amid a rustle of poplin. Miron rested his elbow on the table that had been spread with fresh oilcloth, and said nothing. The oilcloth gave off an unpleasant smell of wet rubber and something else; long-dead tsars and tsaritsas stared pompously from the fancy-bordered corners and the centre was taken up by a fly-blown portrait of the Emperor Nicholas and the spinster ladies of the royal family in their white hats.

Miron broke the silence.

'Well... We've decided to consent. We'll become kinsmen if we can agree on the dowry.'

At this point Ilyinichna from somewhere in the hidden recesses of her lustring blouse with its puffed sleeves produced a tall loaf of white bread and smacked it down on the table.

Pantelei was about to cross himself, but in the act of doing so his gnarled, calloused fingers suddenly bunched into a different shape: the big black, heavy-nailed thumb, quite by chance and against its master's will slipped between the first and middle fingers, and this shameless combination dived furtively into the blue uniform coat and drew out a red-topped bottle, gripping it firmly by the neck.

'Now, dear kinsmen, let's pray to God and drink a glass and talk about our children and the terms.'

Blinking sentimentally, Pantelei surveyed his prospective kinsman's freckled face and tenderly smacked the bottom of the bottle with a hand as broad as a horse's hoof.

Within an hour the two of them were sitting so close that the tar-black curls of Melekhov's beard were groping among the straight ginger braids of Korshunov's. Pantelei, his breath sweetly laden with the aroma of salted cucumbers, set about his work of persuasion.

'My dear kinsman,' he began in a resounding whisper, 'My dear old friend!' And suddenly he raised his voice to a shout, 'Kinsman!' he roared, exposing his black and blunted molars. 'Your demands are too mighty far beyond my means! Just think, old chum, what you're doing to me! Gaiters and galoshes—one; a Don fur-coat—two; two woollen dresses—three; and a silken shawl—four. Why, that's ruination!'

Pantelei flung his arms wide, the seams of his Cossack Life Guards uniform stretched with a tearing sound and released several small puffs of dust. Miron lowered his head and stared at the oilcloth through pools of vodka and cucumber brine. He read the fancifully penned inscription at the top, 'The Rulers of All Russia', then his eyes wandered lower: 'His Imperial Majesty, the Emperor Nicholas...' The rest was obscured by a piece of potato peel. He peered at the illustration: the sovereign's face was invisible under the empty bottle of vodka. Blinking reverently, Miron tried to make out the shape of the rich white-belted uniform, but it was heavily spattered with slippery cucumber seeds. Surrounded by her insipidly similar daughters, the Empress looked out complacently from under her broad-brimmed hat. Miron felt so hurt that he wanted to weep. 'You're looking mighty proud just now, like a goose out of a basket,' he thought, 'but the time will come when you'll have to marry off your daughters. And then I'll look at you ... that's when you'll put your ears back, I reckon.'

Pantelei was still buzzing in his ear, like a big black

bumble-bee. He looked up blearily and listened.

'For us to provide such finery—gaiters and galoshes and a Don fur-coat—for your daughter—and now she's as good as my daughter—for yours and my daughter, we'll have to take cattle off the farm and sell 'em.'

'You grudge that?' Miron thumped the table with his fist.

'It's not that I grudge it—'

'Do you or don't you?'

'Now wait a bit, kinsman—'

'If you grudge it, then to hell with it.'

Miron swept his sweaty hand across the table and dashed the glasses to the floor.

'But your own daughter will have to work all the harder to make up for it!'

'Well, let her! But you make the payment, or the deal is off!'

'Sell our cattle...' Pantelei shook his head and his ear-ring glittered grudgingly.

'There must be payment! She's got chestfuls of clothes of her own, but you've got to show your respect for me, if you've taken a liking to her! That's our Cossack custom. It was like that in the old days, and that's what we ought to stand by.'

'I will show respect!'

'Show it then.'

'I will!'

'And as for working hard, let the young ones do that. We had to work hard and we live no worse than other folk, darn it all, so let them work for their living.' The two fathers' beards wove a colourful pattern, like the twigs of a wattle fence. Pantelei helped the kiss down with a mushy, juiceless cucumber, and was moved to tears by a multitude of mixed feelings.

Their wives sat on the family chest with their arms round each other, deafening themselves with their chatter. Ilyinichna was as red as a cherry, while her new kinswoman was beginning to look green from the vodka, like a late woodland pear, nipped by the frost.

'...She's a fine child, you won't find another like her! If you want a girl that's obedient and respectful, she's one that'll never get out of hand. She's afraid to say a word against anyone.'

'Ah, my dear,' Ilyinichna interrupted, hand under her cheek, 'the number of times I've told him, the scoundrel! The other Sunday evening he was about to go out, putting some tobacco in his pouch, and I says to him, "When are you going to give her up, you bad lot? How much longer shall I have to bear such shame with old age coming on? That Stepan, you know, he could break your neck in a twinkling!"'

From the kitchen Natalya's brother Mitka was peeping through the crack above the door into the best room, while Natalya's two younger sisters whispered below.

Natalya was sitting on a couch in the corner, drying her tears with the narrow sleeve of her blouse. She was frightened by the new life that loomed on the threshold and oppressed by a sense of the unknown.

In the best room they were finishing the third bottle of vodka; they had decided that the wedding should take place early in August.

XIX

The Korshunov home was in a flurry of preparations for the wedding. Some last pieces of underwear were hastily being made up for the bride. Natalya spent her evenings, knitting her fiancé the traditional scarf and gloves out of smoky-grey goats' wool.

Her mother Lukinichna bent her back over the sewing-machine till dusk, helping the dress-maker who had been called in from the stanitsa.

Mitka would come in with his father and the farm hands from the fields and, without washing or taking the heavy field shoes off his sore feet, would go straight to Natalya in the best room and sit down beside her. He took a delight in teasing his sister.

'Knitting, eh?' he would ask briefly with a wink at the fluffy folds of the scarf.

'Yes, I am. What about it?'

'Knit away then, you fool, and instead of thanking you he'll punch you in the face.'

'What ever for?'

'For nothing at all. I know Grisha, we're old pals. He's a real dog—he'll bite you and never say why.'

'Don't tell such stories. As if I knew nothing about him.'

'I know him better. We went to school together.'

With a feigned sigh Mitka bent forward, examining his hands, which were scratched and sore from using the pitchfork.

'You'll end up badly with him, Natalya! Better stay on here and become an old maid. What do you see in him? Eh? He's so ugly it don't do to come near him on a horse, and he's a bit funny in the head. Look closer and you'll see. He's a bad egg!'

Natalya's face was a pitiful sight as she bent over the scarf, swallowing tears of vexation.

'But the main trouble is that's he's got a sweetheart,' Mitka went on mercilessly. 'What are you bawling for? You're a fool, Natalya. Refuse him! I'll saddle up and ride over right away to tell them not to come any more.'

It was Grandad Grishaka who came to the girl's rescue. He would enter the best room, testing the soundness of the floor with his knobbly stick and stroking the yellow flax of his matted beard.

'What are you doing here, young scamp?' he would ask, poking Mitka with his stick.

'I just came in to see how she was, Grandpa,' Mitka would explain.

'To see how she was, eh? Well, I'm telling you, you scamp, to leave this room at once. Now then, quick march!'

The old man waved his stick and advanced on Mitka, walking unsteadily on his withered, reed-like legs.

Grandad Grishaka had been treading this earth for sixty-nine years. He had taken part in the campaign against the Turks in 1877. At one time he had been orderly to General Gurko, but had fallen out of favour and been sent back to his regiment. For distinguished service at Plevna and Roshich he had been decorated with two St. George Crosses and a medal of St. George. He had been in the same regiment as Prokofy Melekhov. Now he was living out his last days with his son. He enjoyed the general respect of the village for the mental clarity he had kept into old age, and for his incorruptible honesty and hospitality, and was spending the brief remains of his life in reminiscence.

In summer he would sit on the coping round the house from sunrise till sunset, drawing on the ground with his stick, and with bowed head meditate upon the vague images, scattered ideas, and dull reflections of memory that came to him from the murk of oblivion.

The cracked peak of his faded Cossack cap cast a black shadow on the dark lids of his closed eyes; it deepened the lines in his cheeks and gave the grey beard a bluish tinge. Black, sluggish blood flowed in those fingers locked over the stick, in the wrists, in the bulging black veins.

Every year his blood grew colder. He would complain to his favourite grand-daughter Natalya. 'Even these woollen socks don't keep my feet warm any longer. Won't you crochet a pair for me, my child.'

'But it's mid-summer, Grandad!' Natalya would say laughing, and sit down beside him on the coping, looking at his big wrinkled yellow ear.

'So it may be, my little girl, but my blood is as cold as the soil deep underground.'

Natalya looked at the net of veins on the old man's hand and remembered how, when she was only a little girl and they had been digging a well in the yard, she had taken handfuls of damp clay out of the bucket and moulded it into clumsy dolls and cows with crumbly horns. She recalled the sensation of touching that lifeless icy soil from so far down and gazed fearfully at the brown, clay-coloured patches on her grandfather's hands.

It was as though a brownish-blue loam flowed through Grandad's veins instead of bright red blood.

'Are you afraid of dying, Grandad?' she asked.

Grandad Grishaka twisted his thin, scraggy neck as if to free it from the high collar of his shabby uniform, and twitched his greenish grey whiskers.

'I'm waiting for death as I would for a cherished guest, my dear. It's time... I've had my life and served the tsars and drunk my vodka,' he added, smiling with a mouth full of white teeth and a quivering of the wrinkles round his eyes.

Natalya fondled his hands and went away, but he sat there hunched and scratching at the earth with his worn stick. His uniform was grey and darned in several places but the red tabs on his stiff high collar laughed youthfully and challengingly.

He received the news that Natalya was to be betrothed with outward composure, although inwardly he was sad and resentful. It was Natalya who gave him the best tit-bits at table. It was Natalya who washed his shirts, darned and knitted his stockings, and mended his trousers and shirts. So for two days after hearing the news Grandad Grishaka gave her stern looks.

'The Melekhovs are fine Cossacks. The late Prokofy was a real brave one. But what about his grandsons? Eh?'

'His grandsons aren't bad either,' Miron replied evasively.

'Grishka is a disrespectful young scoundrel. I passed

him coming home from church the other day and the scalawag didn't even say good morning. Old folk don't get much respect nowadays.'

'He's an affectionate lad,' Lukinichna put in a word for her future son-in-law.

'Eh? Affectionate, you say? Well, let's hope so. If he's to Natalya's liking...'

Grandad Grishaka took almost no part in the making of the marriage deal. He came out of his room for a minute, sat down at the table and downed a glass of vodka with some difficulty. The vodka warmed him a little, but, feeling that it had gone to his head, he walked out.

For two days he glanced in silence at Natalya's anxiously happy face, munching and twitching the tufts of his greenish white moustache, then he softened.

'Natalya!' he called one day.

Natalya came up to him.

'I expect you're glad, grand-daughter, eh?'

'I don't know myself, Grandad,' Natalya confessed.

'Don't you know?.. You're a fine one... Well, God bless you...' And then unable to restrain his annoyance and regret he reproached her, 'Couldn't you have waited till I'm gone, you wicked girl... It'll be a rotten life without you.'

Mitka had overheard their conversation from the kitchen.

'You may live another hundred years, Grandad. How do you expect her to wait that long? You're a tough old bird.'

Grandad Grishaka went black in the face and almost choked. He banged on the floor with his stick and stamped his feet.

'Be quiet, you scamp! Go away! Get out! You, evil spirit! You were eavesdropping, you devil!'

Mitka scuttled out into the yard chuckling, while the old man raged and scolded and his legs in their short woollen stockings trembled at the knees.

Natalya's two younger sisters, Marishka, a girl of twelve, and Gripka, a lively little minx aged eight, impatiently awaited the day of the wedding.

The labourers who lived permanently on the Korshunov farm also expressed a restrained satisfaction. They were expecting lavish feasting and a couple of days off during the celebrations. One of them, as tall as a well-sweep, a Ukrainian from Boguchar with the outlandish name of Het-Baba, went on the bottle about twice a year.

During these bouts he would spend all his wages and sell everything to buy drink. The familiar urge had been nagging him for some time, but he had been saving it up for the wedding.

The second worker, a dark puny Cossack from Migulinskaya, whose name was Mikhei, had only recently come to live at the Korshunovs'. He had lost his own home in a fire and hired himself out as a farm-hand. Having struck up a friendship with Hetko (Het-Baba's nickname), he too would take to the bottle from time to time. He was a passionate lover of horses; when tipsy, he would weep and, smearing the tears over his sharp browless face, would pester Miron.

'Master! Dear old friend! When you marry off your daughter, let Mikhei drive in the procession, I'll drive those horses so they'll make a real show! I could drive them through fire and never scorch a single hair. I used to have horses myself. Ech!..'

The gloomy and unsociable Hetko for some reason became attached to Mikhei and would tease him constantly with one and the same joke.

'Mikhei, d'you hear me? What stanitsa are you from?' he would ask, rubbing his long arms that hung down almost to his knees. Then changing his voice he would answer his own question, 'Migulinskaya.' 'Then why are you so skinny?' ' 'Cos we're all like that out there.'

He would guffaw hoarsely at this repeated joke and slap his long lean legs and Mikhei would stare with hate-filled eyes at Hetko's shaven face and quivering Adam's apple, and call him a 'hooting bog-owl' and a 'festering scab'.

The date of the wedding was fixed for the first day in September when meat could be eaten. There were three weeks to go. During Assumption Grigory rode over to see his betrothed. He sat at the round table in the best room, nibbled seeds and nuts with Natalya and her girl-friends and rode away. Natalya saw him off. Under the overhang of the shed, where his horse, equipped with a smart new saddle, was feeding from a trough, she slipped her hand into her bosom and, blushing and gazing at Grigory with love-sick eyes, gave him a soft little bundle that still retained the warmth of her innocent breast. Grigory took the gift and dazzled her with the whiteness of his wolfish teeth.

'What is it?'

'You'll see ... a tobacco pouch. I embroidered it myself.'

Grigory hesitantly took her in his arms to kiss her, but she held him off, bent supply backwards and shot a frightened glance at the windows.

'They'll see!'

'Let them!'

'I'd be ashamed—'

'That's because it's your first,' Grigory explained.

She held the bridle. Grigory, frowning, felt with his foot for the notched stirrup iron, seated himself comfortably in the saddle and rode across the yard. Natalya opened the gate and stood watching him, shading her eyes with her hand. He sat his horse in Kalmyk style, leaning slightly to the left and swinging his whip jauntily.

'Eleven days to go,' Natalya counted in her head, then drew a quick breath and laughed.

XX

The green sharp-leaved wheat sprouts and begins to grow; in a month and a half a rook can walk in it and not be seen; the wheat sucks the juices of the earth and the ears burgeon; it flowers and the ears are coated with golden pollen; and gradually the grain swells with sweet and fragrant milk. The farmer comes out into the steppe and his heart overflows with joy. But from somewhere, who knows where, a herd of cattle roams in among the corn; they trample the heavy ears and stamp them into the ground. Where they have rolled, the corn lies in flattened patches. It is a monstrous and bitter sight.

And so it was with Aksinya. Her love in all the golden bloom of its ripening had been trampled by Grigory's heavy raw-hide shoe. He had sullied and destroyed it and it was all over.

When she returned from the Melekhovs' sunflower patch, Aksinya's heart was as empty and desolate as an abandoned threshing floor overgrown with goosefoot and weeds.

As she walked home she bit at the corners of her kerchief and her throat was tight with the scream that she could not utter. She entered the inner porch and threw herself on the floor, choking in the tears, the torment, the black nothingness that flooded over her. And then it passed. Only somewhere at the very bottom of her heart a lingering poignant ache remained.

For the trampled wheat rises again. The dew and the

sun lift up the stem that has been crushed into the ground; at first it droops like a man crippled by some unbearable burden, but then it straightens up and lifts its head and the day is as bright as before and it sways in the same wind.

At night, while frenziedly caressing her husband, Aksinya thought of Grigory, and the hatred in her soul was mingled with great love. In her thoughts the woman was planning fresh dishonour; she had decided to take Grigory away from lucky Natalya Korshunova, who had tasted neither the grief nor the joy of love. Night after night the thoughts would race through her head as she stared dry-eyed into the darkness. Stepan's handsome head with its long curly forelock rested heavily on her right arm. His mouth was half open and his dark hand, forgotten on his wife's breast, would stir its iron, toil-scarred fingers. Aksinya thought, calculated and thought again. Only one thing was firm in her mind: she would win Grigory away from them all, deluge him in love and possess him as before.

And the ache at the bottom of her heart, like the sting left by a bee, pricked the festering wound.

This was at night. During the day Aksinya buried her thoughts in household chores and farm work. If she happened to meet Grigory somewhere, she would turn pale and carry her beautiful yearning body past him, staring a shameless invitation into the black savagery of his eyes.

After the encounter Grigory would feel the undertow of that yearning. He would lose his temper for no reason, vent his fury on Dunyashka and his mother, and often he would take his sabre out into the back yard and with clenched jaws and sweat streaming down his face slash at thick willow branches stuck into the ground. In a week he cut a large pile. Pantelei, his ear-ring glittering and yellow eyeballs flashing, scolded and swore.

'Look at the heap he's chopped, the rotten devil. There was enough wood there for two fences! Think you're a trick rider or something, drat your eyes. Go out and practice your tricks on the bushes. Just wait, my lad, when you're called up you'll have plenty of sabering to do! It won't take them long to break in the likes of you!'

XXI

For the wedding train that was to fetch the bride they fitted out four wagons, each drawn by two horses. A festively dressed crowd assembled in the Melekhov yard.

Petro, the best man, in a black jacket and broad light-blue trousers with red stripes down the sides, two white kerchiefs tied round his left arm, maintained a firm smile under his corn-coloured moustache. His place was beside the bridegroom.

'Don't get scared, Grishka! Keep your pecker up! What are you looking so down in the mouth for?'

Round the wagons all was hubbub and confusion.

'Where's the best man? It's time to leave.'

'Cousin!'

'Eh?'

'Cousin, you go in the second wagon. D'you hear me?'

'Have you put seats in the wagons?'

'You won't fall to bits without them. You're well covered!'

Darya, in a raspberry-coloured woollen skirt, as supple and slender as a willow branch, arched her pencilled eyebrows and nudged Petro.

'It's time we were off, tell Father. They must be getting impatient over there.'

After a whispered consultation with his father, who had limped up from somewhere, Petro called out his intructions.

'Take your seats! Five and the bridegroom on my wagon. Anikei, you're the driver!'

They took their places. Crimson-faced and solemn, Ilyinichna swung the gate open. The four wagons dashed off down the street, trying to overtake one another.

Petro was sitting beside Grigory. Facing them sat Darya, waving a lace handkerchief. Voices that had burst into song broke off at the bumps and pot-holes. The red bands of Cossack caps, blue and black uniforms and jackets, sleeves in white armlets, a scattered rainbow of women's shawls and coloured skirts. Muslin scarves of dust floating out behind every wagon. They were off to fetch the bride.

Anikei, a neighbour of the Melekhovs, Grigory's second cousin, had the reins. Leaning over till he nearly fell off the box, he whooped and cracked his whip and the sweating horses strained at the traces and flung themselves into full gallop.

'Whip 'em up! Lay it on!' Petro bawled.

The eunuch-like Anikei winked at Grigory, wrinkling his bare womanish face into a thin smile, and laid on with the whip.

'Make way!' boomed a voice from the side as they were passed by Ilya Ozhogin, the bridegroom's uncle on his mother's side. Behind him Grigory noticed Dunyashka's happy face and bobbing brown cheeks.

'Oh no, wait a minute!' Anikei shouted, leaping to his feet and letting out a piercing whistle.

The horses went into a mad gallop.

'You'll fall!' Darya squealed, leaning forward and clasping Anikei's patent-leather boots.

'Hold tight!' Uncle Ilya boomed from the side. His voice was lost in the droning roar of the wheels.

The other two wagons, crammed with colourful clamorous humanity, were flying along just behind. The horses in their red, blue and pale-green cloths, with paper flowers and ribbons woven into their manes and forelocks, and with their bells tinkling, careered along the bumpy road, scattering flecks of foam, and the cloths on their wet frothy backs flapped and rippled in the wind.

At the Korshunovs' gate a gang of children was waiting for the procession. They saw the dust on the road and scampered into the yard.

'They're coming!'

'At the gallop!'

'We've seen them!'

In a trice Hetko was surrounded.

'What are you flocking round me for? Shoo, you fiendish sparrows! You'll deafen me with your chirping!'

'Ukrainian greaser! Let's come and tease yer! Tufty!..* Tufty!.. Tufty Tar-barrel!..' the children teased, hopping about round Hetko's broad, sack-like trousers.

Peering down as though trying to see into a well, Hetko surveyed the wildly excited children and scratched his long taut belly, smiling condescendingly.

The wagons rolled into the yard amid a hubbub of voices. Petro led Grigory to the porch. The other arrivals trailed after them.

The door from the porch into the kitchen was locked. Petro knocked.

'Lord Jesus Christ, have mercy upon us.'

---

* The disparaging name for a Ukrainian was *khokhol* (tuft), referring to the way they wore their hair.

'Amen,' came the response from behind the door.

Petro knocked again and repeated the words three times to the same muffled response.

'May we come in?'

'You are welcome.'

The door was flung open. The chief bridesmaid—Natalya's god-mother—a handsome widow, greeted Petro with a bow and a sardonic raspberry-lipped smile.

'Drink this, friend, and may you have good health!'

She held out a glass of cloudy kvass that had not fermented properly. Petro smoothed his moustache, drained the glass and gave a throaty cough amid general restrained laughter.

'Well, my dear bridesmaid, that was fine refreshment! Wait a bit, my brambleberry. I'll give you an even better treat. Just you wait!'

'I beg your pardon,' the bridesmaid bowed, and gave Petro another refined and subtle smile.

While the best man and the chief bridesmaid were engaged in repartee, the bridegroom's relatives were each offered three glasses of vodka, as had been agreed upon.

Natalya, already dressed in her wedding gown and veil, was being guarded at the table by Marishka with a rolling-pin in her outstretched hand and Gripka, who was defiantly shaking a sieve.

Perspiring and tipsy from the vodka, Petro bowed and presented each of them with a fifty-kopeck piece in a glass. The bridesmaid winked to Marishka and the sister banged the table with her rolling-pin.

'Not enough! We won't sell you the bride!'

Once again Petro gave them a few chinking silver coins in a wine-glass.

'We won't give her up!' the sisters raged, nudging the demurely seated Natalya.

'But why not! I've paid more than enough already!'

'Let her go, girls,' a smiling Miron commanded and squeezed his way forward to the table. His ginger hair, smarmed down with boiled butter, smelled of sweat and damp manure.

The relatives and family of the bride rose to make room for him at the table.

Petro pushed one corner of a kerchief into Grigory's hand, jumped on to a bench and guided him to the end of the table where the bride sat under the ikons. Natalya took the other corner of the kerchief in a damp nervous hand.

At the table the guests were already chewing hard, tearing boiled chickens apart and wiping their hands on their hair. Anikei was gnawing a breast-bone and yellow fat was rolling down his beardless chin.

With inward regret Grigory looked at his and Natalya's spoons, tied together with a napkin, and at the steaming bowl of chicken broth and noodles in the centre of the table. He was hungry and could feel his stomach rumbling.

Darya was sitting beside Uncle Ilya, who was probably whispering indecent remarks to her as he gnawed at a rib of mutton with his massive teeth. She was blushing and laughing, eyes half-closed, brows twitching.

The feast was long and thorough. The tarry smell of the men's sweat mingled with the pungent spice of the women's. The skirts, frock-coats and shawls that had been kept in chests reeked of moth-balls and a stale sweetness—like old women's tattered finery brought out for a special occasion.

Grigory glanced sideways at Natalya. And for the first time he noticed that her upper lip was rather thick and drooped over the lower, like the peak of a cap. He also noticed that on her right cheek, just below the cheekbone there was a brown birthmark, with two golden hairs sticking out of it, and this for some reason made him feel sick. He remembered Aksinya's finely moulded neck with its fluffy curls and suddenly he felt as if someone had sprinkled a handful of prickly hayseed down the back of his shirt on to his sweating back. He shivered and stared in utter misery at the chewing, guzzling, gobbling faces round the table.

When they rose from the table, someone leaned forward belching the smell of stewed fruit and fresh wheat bread over him, and slipped a handful of millet into the top of his boot—to protect the bridegroom from an evil eye. All the way back the millet scratched his foot and the tight collar of his shirt constricted his throat, and, utterly depressed by the marriage rites, he muttered curses under his breath in a cold and desperate fury.

XXII

After their rest at the Korshunovs' the horses used up their last strength on the return journey to the Melekhov farm. Their breech-bands were dripping with foam. The tipsy drivers whipped them on ruthlessly.

The wagons were met by the old folk. Pantelei, his black and silver-grey beard glistening, stood holding the ikon. Ilyinichna was at his side, her thin lips stonily set.

Grigory and Natalya came forward to receive their blessing out of a shower of hops and handfuls of wheat-seed scattered by the guests. As he blessed them, Pantelei Prokofievich shed a tear, then became nervous and upset at having shown such weakness in public.

Bride and bridegroom entered the house. Red in the face from vodka, the drive and the hot sunshine, Darya darted out on to the porch and pounced on Dunyashka as she ran across from the outdoor kitchen.

'Where's Petro?'

'I haven't seen him.'

'Someone's got to fetch the priest and he's disappeared, the pig.'

Petro, who had taken too much vodka, was lying moaning on a dismantled wagon. Darya fastened on to him like a kite.

'Guzzled yourself sick, you useless dummy! You've got to fetch the priest! Get up!'

'Go to blazes! I don't take orders from you! Who d'you think you are!' he observed reasonably, scrabbling at the ground and raking up a heap of fowl droppings and bits of straw.

Darya, weeping, thrust two fingers into her husband's mouth, pressed his gabbling tongue and helped him to relieve himself. Then she tipped a tub of well water over the astonished Petro's head, rubbed him dry with a horse-cloth that happened to be lying near by, and marched him off to the priest.

One hour later Grigory was standing in church beside Natalya, who looked very pretty in the glow of candles. Squeezing a wax candle-stem in his hand, he gazed at the wall of whispering onlookers with unseeing eyes, and repeated over and over again in his mind the one obsessive phrase, 'You've had your fun... You've had your fun.' Behind him the puffy-faced Petro was coughing, somewhere in the crowd he glimpsed Dunyashka's eyes, familiar and yet unfamiliar faces; the discordant chanting of the choir and the long-drawn appeals of the deacon came to him as if from afar. Grigory was gripped by indifference. He walked round the lectern, treading on the worn-down heels of the nasal-voiced Father Vissarion, stopped when Petro surreptitiously tugged at the hem of his jacket, gazed at the quivering pig-tails of light, and fought the somnolent bemusement that had taken possession of him.

'Exchange your rings,' said Father Vissarion, glancing tepidly into Grigory's eyes.

They did so. 'Will it end soon?' Grigory asked with a glance at Petro. Petro's lips twitched in a faint smile and he said, 'Yes, soon.' Grigory kissed his wife's wet tasteless lips three times, the church was filled with the stench of extinguished candles, and there was a stamping of feet as the crowd at the back pushed towards the exit.

Gripping Natalya's big rough hand, Grigory walked out on to the church steps. Someone crammed his cap on his head. A warm wormwood-scented breeze was blowing from the south. Cool air rose from the steppe. Somewhere across the Don blue lightning flashed. Rain was on the way. And from beyond the white churchyard wall, mingling with the babble of voices, came the gentle and inviting tinkle of harness bells, as the horses shifted restively from one foot to another.

XXIII

The Korshunovs arrived after the bride and bridegroom had been carted off to church. Several times Pantelei had gone outside the gate to look down the street, but the grey road between occasional clumps of thornbushes was still deserted. He shifted his gaze to the Don. The woods had begun to yellow and the ripe tasselled bulrushes were bowing wearily over the small lake on the far side, over the sedge.

The mournful blue drowsiness of early autumn mingled with the twilight and shrouded the village, the Don, the chalky bluffs, the woods on the far side melting in a lilac haze, and the steppe beyond. The sharp top of the shrine at the fork where the road joined the highway showed clearly against the sky.

A barely audible rumble of wheels and barking of dogs reached the old man's ears. Two wagons careered off the square into the lane. In the first sat Miron and Lukinichna, swaying in the back seat. Grandad Grishaka sat facing them in a clean uniform adorned with St. George crosses and medals. The wagon was driven by Mitka, who lounged on the box, not even showing the wildly galloping well-fed raven-black horses the whip that he had tucked under the seat. The second wagon was driven by Mikhei, who was leaning back and trying desperately to rein in his horses. His sharp-featured browless face was flushed purple and the sweat was pouring from under the cracked peak of his cap.

Pantelei threw open the gate and the wagons drove into the yard one after the other.

Ilyinichna floated down from the porch like a mother goose, sweeping the farmyard mud off the steps with the hem of her skirt.

'Welcome to you, dear kinsmen! This is a great honour to our humble dwelling!' And she inclined her portly figure in a bow.

Pantelei put his head on one side and spread his arms wide.

'Glad to see you, dear kinsmen! Please, come in.' He ordered the horses to be unharnessed and came up to his new kinsman.

Miron was brushing the dust off his trousers with his hand. They embraced and walked together to the porch. Old Grishaka, badly shaken up by the wild ride, dropped behind.

'Come in, dear kinsman, come in!' Ilyinichna pressed him.

'Thank you kindly... Just a minute, I'm coming.'

'We've been waiting and waiting for you. Do come in. I'll bring a besom to brush your uniform. The dust is terrible these days, you can hardly breathe.'

'Yes, it's dry weather... That's why it's so dusty. Please, don't trouble, kinswoman, I won't be a minute—' And Grandad Grishaka, bowing to his unperceptive kinswoman, backed away to the shed and disappeared behind the painted side of a winnower.

'Pestering the old man like that, you stupid cow!' Pantelei exploded as he met his wife on the porch. 'He has his old man's needs, and she... Lord above, what a stupid creature!'

'How was I to know?' Ilyinichna looked embarrassed.

'You ought to be able to tell. But that's enough. Go and look after the bride's mother.'

By this time the tables were noisy with the tipsy chatter of the drunken guests. The bride's mother and father were seated in the best room. The young couple soon arrived from the church. As he poured out vodka from a large bottle, Pantelei shed a tear.

'Well, kinsfolk, here's to our children. May everything go well for them, as we have agreed ... and may they live

104

all their lives in happiness and good health.'

A pot-bellied glass was filled for Grandad Grishaka and pressed upon him so fervently that only half of it went into his mouth amid the thickets of greenish beard, while the other trickled down the high collar of his uniform. Everyone drank and clinked glasses, or simply drank. The hubbub was worthy of a fairground. A distant relative of the Korshunovs, Nikifor Koloveidin, an old guardsman of the Ataman's regiment, who was sitting at the far end of the table, raised his hand with the fingers spread out and roared, 'It's bitter!'

'Yes, it's bitter! Bi-tt-er!' the cry was taken up by the rest of the table.

'Oh, how bitter!' came the response from the packed kitchen.

Frowning, Grigory kissed his wife's insipid lips and cast a hunted look around him.

Red faces. Bleary-eyed, bawdy looks and grins. Mouths chewing with gusto, lips dribbling drunkenly on the embroidered tablecloths. In short, the feasting was in full swing.

Nikifor Koloveidin opened his gap-toothed mouth and raised his hand again.

'It's bitter!'

Three golden squiggles—his long-service stripes—wrinkled on the sleeve of his light-blue guardsman's uniform.

'Bitter! Bi-tter!'

Grigory stared with hatred into Koloveidin's mouth. As he uttered the word 'bitter', the wet crimson tongue protruded through the gap between his teeth.

'Kiss, blast you,' Petro hissed, twitching the vodka-soaked moustache that hung from his lip like pig-tails.

In the kitchen Darya, tipsy and pink-faced, struck up a song. Other voices picked up the tune and tossed it into the front room.

> Here's the river, here's the ferry
> Here's a boatman to meet us...

The voices mingled and soon Khristonya's booming bass joined in, catching up with the others and making the windowpanes rattle:

> If someone will treat us,
> We'll drink till we're merry.

105

From the bedroom came a steady wailing of women's voices:

> I lost and I squandered
> A voice clear and merry.

And then an elderly man's voice, rattling like a loose hoop on a barrel, came to their assistance:

> Oh, I lost and I squandered
> A voice clear and merry,
> While in the orchards I wandered
> 'Mid the prickly guelder berry.

'What a time we're having, good folk!'

'Try the roast mutton.'

'Keep your paws to yourself—can't you see my husband's looking!'

'Bi-tter!'

'Look at the way the best man's carrying on with the chief bridesmaid. He's a fast worker!'

'Oh, no, don't palm off your mutton chops on us... Mebbe I like sterlet better... It's nice and rich!'

'Proshka, old mate, let's have one for the road.'

'Lights a fire under your ribs, eh!'

'Semyon Gordeich!'

'Eh?'

'Semyon Gordeich!'

'Oh, get stuffed!'

The kitchen floor began to sag and sway, heels clattered, a glass fell with a crash that was immediately drowned in the general uproar. Grigory glanced over the heads of the guests towards the kitchen; there the women were doing a round-dance to the accompaniment of whoops and squeals. They wobbled their plump behinds (there were no thin ones, for each was wearing five or six skirts), waved their lace handkerchiefs, and worked their elbows in the dance.

The sound of an accordion broke in peremptorily. The player struck up a Cossack jig with accompanying runs in the bass.

'Make a circle! A circle!'

'Make way, ladies!' Petro begged, pushing his way between the women's damply warm bellies.

Grigory livened up and winked at Natalya.

'Petro's going to let 'em have it, you just watch!'

'Who's he with?'

'Can't you see? With your mother.'

Lukinichna planted her hands on her hips, a kerchief in her left hand.

'Off you go, then. Or else I'll start!'

Petro danced up to her with very short steps, cut a splendid figure, and returned to his place. Lukinichna gathered up her skirts as though to step over a puddle, tapped with the toe of her shoe, and to a chorus of approval went round in a circle, strutting like a man.

The accordion-player dashed off in the lower register and this swept Petro into action. With a whoop he came down in a squatting position and began flinging his legs out and smacking the tops of his boots, all the while holding one tip of his moustache between his teeth. His legs shot out this way and that in a series of figures too fast to follow, his damp forelock shaking with every bound.

The people crowding round the door hid Petro from Grigory's view. He could hear only a tattoo of iron-tipped heels that was like the crackle of burning pineboards, and the wild urgings of the drunken guests.

In the end Miron did a dance with Ilyinichna, performing his steps in a serious businesslike fashion, just as he did everything.

Pantelei climbed on to a stool, swung his lame leg and clicked his tongue. His lips and even his ear-ring danced instead of his legs.

Skilled dancers and those who could scarcely bend their knees vied with each other.

All received shouts of advice and encouragement.

'Don't let us down.'

'Put some zip into it! Wow!'

'He's light-footed, but his backside's in the way.'

'Go it, faster!'

'Our side's winning.'

'Hot it up, or I'll—'

'Out of breath, you old crow? Dance or I'll give you one with a bottle!'

The tipsy Grandad Grishaka had one arm round the broad back of his neighbour and was buzzing like a mosquito in his ear.

'What year did you take the oath?'

His neighbour, rugged as an ancient oak, waved him aside and rumbled, 'Thirty-nine, son.'

'What year? Eh?' Grandad Grishaka cupped his hand round a wrinkled ear.

'Thirty-nine, I told you.'

'What were you?'

'Sergeant-major of Baklanov's Regiment, Maxim Bogatiryov. And I was born ... I was born in the village of Krasny Yar.'

'Are you related to the Melekhovs?'

'What?'

'Are you related, I say?'

'Uh-huh, I'm their grandfather.'

'And you were in Baklanov's Regiment?'

The old man stared at Grandad Grishaka with time-dulled eyes, rolling an unchewed morsel over his bare gums, and nodded.

'So you took part in the Caucasian campaign?'

'I served with the late Baklanov himself, God rest his soul. We subdued the Caucasus... We had a rare breed of Cossacks in our regiment. They only took men of Guards height, but as broad as one of your present-day Cossacks is tall. That's the kind of people we had in those days, son... One day, in the village of Chelenjiysky His Excellency, our late General, was pleased to strike me with his whip...'

'And I was in the Turkish campaign... Eh? Yes, I was.' Grandad Grishaka puffed out his withered chest, making his St. George crosses jingle.

'We occupied that village at dawn and at noon the bugler sounded the alarm—'

'And we too served the white tsar. There was a battle at Roshich and our regiment, the Twelfth Don Cossacks', fought their Janissaries—'

'...And the bugler sounds the alarm,' the Baklanov man continued, paying no heed to Grandad Grishaka.

'Their Janissaries are something like our Ataman guardsmen. Ay, that they are,' Grandad Grishaka began to lose his temper and waved his arm crossly. 'They serve their tsar and on their heads they wear white sacks. Eh? They have white sacks on their heads.'

'So I says to my mess-mate, "Looks as if we're going to retreat, Timosha, so get that there rug down off the wall. And we'll take it away with us."'

'I've got two Georges! I was decorated for gallantry in action!.. I took a Turkish major prisoner, took him alive...'

Grandad Grishaka wept and thumped his bony fist on the Baklanov man's resounding bear-like back; but the latter, dipping a piece of chicken in some cherry jelly instead of in the horse-radish sauce, stared lifelessly at the soup-soaked tablecloth, and muttered with sunken lips, 'That's the sin the devil tempted me into, son...' The old man's eyes gazed stolidly at the white creases in the tablecloth, as though it were not a tablecloth soaked in vodka and noodle soup, but the dazzling snow-white folds of the Caucasian mountains. 'Before that I never stole a thing in my life... We'd take a Circassian village and there'd be property in the houses, but I wouldn't so much as look at it... It's the devil that makes you take other people's stuff... But here, if you please... That rug caught my eye ... with its tassels... That'll make a fine horse-cloth, I thought—'

'We've seen plenty o'that kind of thing. We've served in foreign lands too.' Grandad Grishaka tried to look into his neighbour's eyes, but the deep sockets were overgrown like ravines with the grey tufts of eyebrows and beard, and those prickly thickets were impassable.

He tried a trick; hoping to attract his neighbour's attention to the high point in his story, he started without any preliminaries right in the middle.

'So the order comes from Major Tersintsev: "In troop columns, at the gallop—forward!"'

The Baklanov man lifted his head like a war-horse at the sound of the bugle; thumping his gnarled fist on the table, he whispered, 'Lances at the ready, swords drawn, Baklanov men!..' His voice suddenly grew stronger, the dim eyes shone and blazed with the fire that age had not quite extinguished. 'Good fellows, the Baklanov men!' he roared, exposing his bare yellow gums. 'Into the attack—forward!'

With a clear youthful gaze he looked at Grandad Grishaka, not bothering to wipe the tears from his chin with the stained sleeve of his long uniform coat.

Grandad Grishaka also sprang into life.

'He gave us the command and waved his sword. So off we galloped. And the Janissaries were formed up like this,' he drew a rectangle on the tablecloth with his finger. 'And they were shooting at us like mad. We charged them twice, but they drove us back. And then, all of a sudden, from the woods on the flank their cavalry comes at us. So we swung our right wing, reformed our ranks, and charged. Down they went under us. Can any cavalry stand up against the Cossacks? Never. They galloped away to the wood, howling... And then in front of me I saw one of their officers galloping on a brown horse. Dashing young officer he was, black drooping moustache, looked round at me and pulled his pistol out of its holster. The holster was fastened to the saddle, you see... He fired once and missed. I spurred on my horse and overtook him. And I was going to cut him down but changed my mind... After all, he's a human being. So with my right hand I got a grip round his waist and, out of the saddle he comes like a cork. Bit my arm like a madman he did, but I took him prisoner just the same.'

Grandad Grishaka looked triumphantly at his neighbour. The old soldier's huge angular head had dropped on to his chest and he was snoring peacefully amid the hubbub.

PART TWO

I

Sergei Platonovich Mokhov could trace his ancestry far back into the past.

In the reign of Peter I, a royal barge bound for Azov had been on its way down the Don with a cargo of biscuit and gunpowder. The Cossacks of the little 'brigand' town of Chigonaki on the upper reaches of the river, near the mouth of the Khopyor, attacked the barge at night, slaughtered the sleepy guards, pillaged the biscuit and gunpowder, and scuttled the barge.

The tsar ordered troops out from Voronezh. They burnt down the town and inflicted a crushing defeat on the Cossacks who had taken part in the plunder. Major Yakirka and with him forty other Cossack prisoners were hung on a floating gallows and the little fairground with its swinging bodies was sent downstream to strike terror into the hearts of the rebellious stanitsas of the lower Don.

Some ten years later the place where the hearths of Chigonaki had smoked was resettled by Cossacks from other parts and by those who had survived the sacking. The stanitsa grew up again and surrounded itself with ramparts. And it was in those days that Nikita Mokhov, a fellow of peasant stock, arrived from Voronezh to be an eye and ear for the tsar. He traded in various odds and ends that were of use to Cossacks, such as knife hafts, tobacco and flints; he bought and sold stolen goods, and twice a year he travelled to Voronezh ostensibly to replenish his stocks, but actually to report that the stanitsa was calm and the Cossacks were not plotting any fresh mischief.

From this Nikita Mokhov the merchant family of Mokhov was descended. It put down deep roots in Cossack soil, scattered its seed abundantly and grew into the stanitsa like roadside weed—just try to pull it up. The family reverently preserved the half-rotten letter of instruction given to their ancestor by the governor of Voronezh when he was sent to the rebellious stanitsa. The letter might have survived until this day had it not been for the great fire in the time of Sergei Platonovich's grandfather, when it was burnt along with the wooden casket in which it had been kept behind the ikon. The grandfather, who had squandered one fortune at cards, was only just beginning to get back on to his feet again when the fire took everything, and Sergei Platonovich had to make a fresh start. After burying his paralysed father, he began his business on a shoe-string, buying up pig's bristle and goat's wool. For about five years he lived a hand-to-mouth existence, swindling and squeezing every kopeck he could out of the Cossacks of the surrounding villages. And then all of a sudden he grew, and instead of 'pedlar Sergei' became 'Sergei Platonovich', opened a little drapery stall, married the daughter of a half-mad priest, and with the bride's not inconsiderable dowry started a proper shop. Sergei Platonovich chose a good moment to go into textiles. On the instructions of the Cossack Army Government, whole villages were moving across the river from the left bank, where the land was hard and barren, to the right bank. The young stanitsa of Krasnokutskaya spread rapidly and was soon fringed with new buildings; new Cossack villages sprang up on the borders of former estates, on the rivers Chir, Chornaya and Frolovka, over steppeland ravines and gullies, and side by side with Ukrainian settlements. To buy the goods they needed they had to travel fifty versts or more, but suddenly here, right on the doorstep, was a shop with its fresh pinewood shelves stuffed with pleasant-smelling fabrics of all descriptions. Sergei Platonovich expanded his business with the zest of a man playing a full-size accordion. Besides textiles he sold everything that a simple farming community might need: saddlery and harness, salt, kerosene, haberdashery. Of late he had begun to supply farm machinery. Reapers, seed-drills, harrows, ploughs, winnowers, sorting machines from the Aksai factory stood in neat rows beside the shop, whose green shutters kept it cool even in summer. There is no counting the money in another man's purse but the astute Sergei Platonovich evidently did well out of his business. After three years he opened a grain elevator and, when his first wife died, started building a steam flour-mill.

His small brown fist with its sparse shiny-black hairs took a firm grip on the village of Tatarsky and the surrounding hamlets. There was scarcely a farm that had not given Sergei Platonovich a green slip with an orange border promising to pay for a reaper, for a daughter's dowry (time for the girl to be married but wheat prices were low at the Paramonov elevator, so 'Give us a loan, Platonovich!'), and for all kinds of other things. He had nine men working for him at the mill, seven in the shop, and another four servants at home. That made twenty mouths that would eat only at the merchant's pleasure. From his first wife he had two children: a daughter Liza, and a boy, two years younger, the puny and scrofulous Vladimir. Anna Ivanovna, his second wife, a spare, sharp-nosed matron, was barren. All her belated, pent-up maternal love and accumulated bitterness (she had not married until she was nearly thirty-five) were poured out on the children that had been left to her. But the stepmother's nervous temperament was a poor aid to the children's upbringing and their father paid no more attention to them than to the stableman Nikita or the cook. Business and travel devoured all his leisure. Now he was in Moscow, now in Nizhny, now at Uryupinskaya or various stanitsa fairs. The children grew up without any proper supervision. Their stepmother, not endowed with sensitivity, made no attempt to share their inner lives; there was no time, with such a large household to look after. Brother and sister grew up complete strangers to each other, so different in character that they seemed to be scarcely of the same family. Vladimir was secretive, inert, with a constant frown, and serious beyond his years. Liza, who kept company with the maid and the cook, a dissolute, hard-boiled woman, soon learned about the seamy side of life. The women awakened an unhealthy curiosity in her while she was still only a shy and gawky adolescent and, left to her own devices, she grew up like a bush of wild spurge in the forest.

The unhurrying years flowed by.

113

The old grew older and the young grew like young fields of corn.

Looking at his daughter over tea one evening, Sergei Platonovich was quite astonished to see that Liza, who had just finished high school, already had the makings of a good-looking girl. He nearly dropped the saucer of amber-coloured tea that he was holding. Wasn't she the very image of her mother? Lord, what a likeness! 'Now, then, Liza, turn your head, girl!' How had he failed to notice the striking resemblance between Liza and her mother that had been there since she was a child?

...Vladimir Mokhov, now in his fifth year at high school, narrow-shouldered, with a sickly yellow complexion, was crossing the steam-mill yard. He and his sister had recently come home for the summer holidays and as usual he had gone straight to look at the mill, mingle with the flour-sprinkled crowd, and listen to the steady rumble of rollers and cog-wheels and the swish of revolving belts. It fed his self-esteem to hear the respectful whispers of the mill's Cossack customers, 'That's the owner's son and heir...'

Making his way carefully round the piles of ox dung and wagons scattered across the yard, he reached the gate, then remembered that he had not visited the engine-room. He went back.

Near the red oil-tank at the entrance to the engine-room the rollerman Timofei, the scalesman, nicknamed Knave, and Timofei's assistant, a young white-toothed lad called Davydka, were plodding about with their trousers rolled up to the knees, puddling clay in a large pit.

'Ah, the master!' Knave greeted him derisively.

'Good afternoon.'

'Good afternoon, Vladimir Sergeyevich!'

'What are you doing?'

'Puddling clay,' Davydka replied with an ugly smile, dragging his feet laboriously out of the clinging mire, which smelled of dung. 'Your Dad grudges a ruble to hire women for the job, so he makes us do it. He's an old skinflint, your father is!' he added, squelching round the pit.

Vladimir flushed. He felt an unconquerable dislike of the constantly smiling Davydka, his sneering tone, and even his white teeth.

'A skinflint?'

'Yes. He's terrible mean. He'd eat his own shit,' Davydka explained simply, and smiled.

114

Knave and Timofei chuckled approvingly. Vladimir felt the sting of the insult. He surveyed Davydka coldly. 'Are you dissatisfied with your work?'

'Climb in here and do some puddling, then you'll know. What fool would be satisfied? Your father ought to try it; it'd get his big belly down a bit!'

Davydka plodded round the pit, rolling from side to side and lifting his legs high. His smile was quite cheerful now and unmalicious. With a sense of pleasant anticipation Vladimir flipped through his thoughts and found the right answer.

'Very well,' he said, timing his words carefully, 'I will tell Father that you are dissatisfied with your work.'

He glanced sideways at Davydka's face and was astonished at the impression he had made. Davydka's lips were trembling in a forced smile, the two others were frowning. For a minute all three puddled the thickening clay in silence. At length Davydka dragged his eyes away from his muddy feet and said in a tone both wheedling and resentful, 'I was only joking, Vladimir... It was just a bit of fun.'

'I will tell Father what you said.'

Feeling that tears of resentment for himself, for his father, and for Davydka's pitiful smile were welling into his eyes, Vladimir walked on past the oil-tank.

'Vladimir! Vladimir Sergeyevich!' Davydka cried out in fright, and climbed out of the pit, pushing down his trousers over his muddy legs.

Vladimir halted. Davydka ran up to him, panting.

'Don't tell your father. I was only teasing. Forgive me, fool that I am. I didn't mean any harm, honestly! It was just teasing.'

'All right. I won't tell him!' Vladimir almost shouted the words, and walked away frowning to the gate.

Pity for Davydka had won. With a sense of relief he strode along by the white fence. The jovial sound of a hammer reached his ears from the forge tucked away in the corner of the mill yard. One blow, a muffled thud, on the iron, then twice, with a bounce, on the ringing anvil.

'Why did you have to needle him?' Knave's muttering bass reached his ears. 'Don't touch it and it won't stink.'

The swine! Vladimir felt a fresh surge of anger. So that's the way he talks... Shall I tell Father or not? He looked back, caught a glimpse of Davydka's former white-toothed smile and made up his mind. I will tell!

A horse with a wagon behind it was tethered to a post

outside the shop. Children were amusing themselves, shooing a grey cloud of twittering sparrows off the roof of the fire brigade's shed. From the veranda came the fruity baritone of the student Boyaryshkin, and another voice—strained and husky.

Vladimir climbed the steps to the porch. The wild vine that had spread riotously over the porch and terrace and hung in foamy green bunches from the blue-painted carving of the eaves stirred as he passed.

Boyaryshkin was shaking his shaven violet-coloured head as he talked to Balanda, the schoolmaster, a young man but already bearded.

'When I read him, despite my being the son of a Cossack farmer and having a quite natural grudge against all the privileged classes, I find myself feeling devilishly sorry for this moribund section of society. I practically become an aristocrat and landowner myself. I admire their ideal of a woman, feel concern for their interests—the devil knows what! That's genius for you, my dear fellow! It can make you change your faith.'

Balanda twisted the tassel of his silk sash, smiled ironically, and studied the red embroidered patterns on the hem of his shirt. Liza was lounging in an armchair, evidently not in the least interested in the conversation. With eyes that always seemed either to have lost something or to be looking for something she occasionally cast a bored glance at Boyaryshkin's violet-coloured, razor-scratched head.

Vladimir walked past with a bow and knocked at the door of his father's study. Sergei Platonovich was sitting on a cool leather-upholstered couch, turning the pages of the June issue of *Russkoye Bogatstvo*. A knife with a yellowed bone handle was lying on the floor.

'What is it?'

Vladimir drew his head into his shoulders and nervously straightened his shirt.

'When I was coming back from the mill,' he began hesitantly, but then he remembered Davydka's dazzling smile and, noticing his father's corpulence under the tight tussore waistcoat, went on resolutely, 'I heard . Davydka saying—'

Sergei Platonovich listened attentively. 'We'll sack him. Now go away.' And with a groan he bent down to pick up the knife.

Evening gatherings of the local intelligentsia were a frequent occurrence at the Mokhovs'. There was Boyaryshkin, a student of the Moscow Technical College; the emaciated schoolmaster Balanda, eaten up by his enormous self-esteem and tuberculosis; his mistress, the teacher Marfa Gerasimovna, a plump and still youthful spinster, whose petticoat was always showing; the post-master, an eccentric, rather fusty bachelor, who smelled of sealing wax and cheap scent. The young lieutenant Yevgeny Listnitsky would also come over occasionally from his estate, where he was staying with his father, a landowner and aristocrat. They would drink tea on the veranda, carry on aimless discussions, and when the limp thread of conversation finally snapped, one of the guests would start the expensive inlaid cabinet gramophone.

Occasionally, at festival time Sergei Platonovich liked to make a splash. He would give a party and treat his guests to expensive wines, fresh sturgeon caviar, specially ordered from Bataisk, and other delicacies. Otherwise he lived parsimoniously. His only indulgence was books. Sergei Platonovich loved reading and getting to the bottom of everything with his own tenacious, creeper-like brain.

His partner Yemelyan Konstantinovich Atyopin, a fair-haired man with a pointed beard and eyes hidden in mysterious slits, seldom visited him. He was married to a former nun of the Ust-Medveditsa convent. In fifteen years of married life he and his wife had begotten eight children and he spent most of his time at home. Atyopin had worked his way up from regimental clerk, and from his humble beginnings he brought to his family the fusty atmosphere of boot-licking and ingratiation. In his presence the children went about on tip-toe and talked in whispers. After washing in the morning, they would form up in the dining room under a huge black, coffin-like wall clock with their mother behind them, and as soon as their father's dry cough reached them from the bedroom, they would begin a discordant, tuneless chant of 'Lord, Save Thy People' and then 'Our Father'.

By the time they had said the prayer, their father would be dressed and would make his appearance, crinkling the slits of his colourless eyes and holding out his hairless fleshy hand like an archbishop. The children would come forward in turn and kiss it. Then he would kiss his wife on the cheek and say in his lisping voice: 'Have you made the thea, dear?'

'Yes, Yemelyan Konstantinovich.'

'Pour me a throng cup.'

Atyopin kept the shop's accounts. He covered page after page of debit and credit columns with his clerkishly ornate handwriting, read the *Stock Exchange News*, needlessly fixing a gold pince-nez on his knobbly nose, and treated the staff politely.

'Ivan Petrovich, kindly therve this gentleman. He wants thome Taurida cotton.'

His wife called him Yemelyan Konstantinovich, his children—Pappy, and the shop assistants—Lispy.

The two village priests—Father Vissarion and the Reverend Father Pankraty—were not on friendly terms with Sergei Platonovich; they had an old grudge against him. Nor were they on very good terms with each other. Father Pankraty, a self-righteous tale-bearer, was adept at harming his neighbour, and the widowed Father Vissarion, who lived with his Ukrainian housekeeper, a man of jovial temperament despite his syphilitically nasal voice, disliked his reverend colleague for his excessive pride and captious character and kept away from him.

All of them, except the schoolmaster Balanda, owned their own houses. Mokhov's solid residence, faced with match-board and painted blue, adorned the square. Opposite it and well to the fore stood the shop with its double doors and faded signboard, 'S. P. Mokhov and Y. K. Atyopin'.

Adjoining the shop was a long low shed with a cellar, and about fifty yards further on rose a low brick wall enclosing the church, and then the church itself with a cupola that looked like a ripe green onion. Beyond the church were the whitewashed, institutionally stern walls of the school and two smart-looking houses: one, painted light-blue and with a fence of the same colour, belonging to Father Pankraty, and a brown-painted house (to be different from the other) with a carved fence and wide balcony, belonging to Father Vissarion. Atyopin's absurdly narrow two-storey house ran from one corner to the next, and beyond it were the post-office, the thatched or sheet-iron roofs of the Cossack farmsteads, and the sloping back of the mill with its rusty tin weathercocks on the roof.

They kept themselves to themselves, shut off from the rest of the world behind their bolted double shutters. If they were not going out in the evening, they would shoot the bolts and let the watch-dogs loose in the yards, and the only sound to be heard across the silent village came from the chattering wooden tongue of the night watchman's rattle.

II

At the end of August Mitka Korshunov happened to meet Liza Mokhova down by the Don. He had only just rowed across from the far side and as he hitched his boat to a stump he noticed a light, brightly painted skiff skimming the water. The skiff had come from somewhere near the hill and was heading for the pier. Boyaryshkin was at the oars. His shaven head was glistening with sweat and little sprigs of swollen veins were showing at his temples.

Mitka did not recognise Liza at once. She was wearing a straw hat that cast a bluish shadow over her eyes. Her bare sunburnt arms were pressing a cluster of yellow water-lilies to her breast.

'Korshunov!' she exclaimed, shaking her head at Mitka. 'So you lied to me.'

'Lied to you?'

'Don't you remember? You promised to take me fishing?'

Boyaryshkin let go of the oars and straightened his back. The skiff shot up the bank, grinding over the chalky beach.

'Don't you remember?' Liza laughed, jumping out.

'Haven't had the time. Too much work to do,' Mitka explained, and suddenly stopped breathing as the girl approached him.

'No, that is impossible! I resign, Yelizaveta Sergeyevna. You've had all you'll get out of me! Think of the distance we've covered over this damned river. My hands are all in blisters. Give me dry land any day!'

Boyaryshkin planted his big bare feet firmly on the rough chalky shingle and mopped his brow with the top of his crumpled student's cap. Without answering him, Liza went up to Mitka and held out her hand. He took it awkwardly.

'When shall we go fishing?' she asked, tossing her head and frowning slightly.

'Tomorrow, if you like. We've done with the threshing now.'

'Will you let me down again?'

'Not likely!'

'Will you come early?'

'Before it's light.'

'I'll be expecting you.'

'I'll come. Honest, I will.'

'You haven't forgotten which window to knock at?'

119

Mitka smiled. 'I'll find it.'

'I'll probably be leaving soon. I should like to do some fishing.'

Mitka toyed silently with the rusty key that he used for padlocking his boat, and stared at her lips.

'Are you coming?' Boyaryshkin asked, studying a pearly shell that he had picked up.

'In a minute.'

She was silent for a moment, then, smiling at something, she asked, 'There's been a wedding in your family, hasn't there?'

'My sister's.'

'And whom did she marry?' Before he could answer, she gave him a strange fleeting smile. 'Be sure you come!' And once again, as it had done the first time, on the veranda of Mokhov's house, her smile stung Mitka like a nettle.

His eyes followed the girl down to the boat.

Boyaryshkin squatted to push off; Liza looked smilingly over his head and nodded good-bye to Mitka, who was still toying with the key.

When they were about ten yards from the bank, Boyaryshkin asked quietly, 'Who's that young tough?'

'Someone I know.'

'Oh, so it's an affair of the heart?'

This much Mitka heard above the creak of the rowlocks, but he missed her reply. He saw Boyaryshkin bend to the oars and lean back laughing, but Liza's face was invisible; she was sitting with her back to him. The lilac ribbon flowing from her hat on to a bare sloping shoulder trembled in the feeble breeze and teased Mitka's misty gaze as it melted into the distance.

Mitka, who rarely went fishing with rod and line, had never made such careful preparations as he did that evening. He chopped up some dung bricks, lighted a fire in the kitchen garden and boiled the millet for the bait. He made fresh knots for all the hooks, replacing any line that was rotten.

Mikhei watched his preparations eagerly. 'Take me with you, 'Mitry. You'll need help.'

'I'll manage.'

Mikhei sighed.

'We haven't been fishing together for a long time. I feel just like holding a carp on the line, a good sixteen-pounder.'

Mitka scowled into the steam from the boiled bait and

made no reply. When he was ready, he went to the front room.

Grandad Grishaka was sitting by the window, his nose saddled with a pair of metal-rimmed spectacles, reading the Gospel.

'Grandad!' Mitka called to him, leaning on the door-post.

The old man raised his eyes over his spectacles.

'Eh?'

'Wake me after first cock-crow.'

'Where would you be off to at that time in the morning?'

'Fishing.'

Old Grishaka was fond of fish, but for form's sake he started raising objections.

'Your father said the hemp would have to be scutched tomorrow. You can't go running off like that. Fishing!'

Mitka eased his shoulder away from the door-post and tried a trick.

'It don't matter to me one way or t'other. I wanted to treat Grandad to some fish but I can't go if the hemp has to be done.'

'Now steady there, where're you off to?' the old man pulled off his spectacles in panic. 'I'll talk to Miron. Perhaps I'll go right now. It wouldn't be a bad thing to have a bit of fish; tomorrow's Wednesday. Go along now, I'll wake you, you young jackanapes. Now what are you grinning at?'

At midnight the old man groped his way down the steps, holding up his linen pants with one hand and carrying a stick in the other. He floated across the yard to the barn like a trembling white ghost and poked the stick into Mitka, who was snoring quietly on a mat by one of the bins. The barn smelled of threshed grain, mice droppings, stale air and cobwebs. Mitka did not wake up at once. Grandad Grishaka poked him gently again and whispered, 'Mitka! Mitka, lad! Mitka, you rascal!'

Mitka pulled up his legs and went on snoring peacefully. In desperation the old man poked the blunt end of his stick into the lad's stomach and turned it like a drill. Mitka grabbed the stick with a gasp, and woke up.

'You sleep like a fool! It's terrible the way you sleep,' the old man scolded.

'All right, keep your shirt on,' Mitka whispered, groping for his boots.

He walked to the square. All over the village the

second cockcrow had begun. As he walked past Father Vissarion's house, he heard a flapping of wings in the chicken shed, then the cock bellowed in an archdeacon's bass and the hens broke into a frightened clucking.

The night watchman was dozing on the bottom step in front of the shop, his nose buried in the warmth of his sheepskin collar. Mitka reached the Mokhovs' fence, stacked his rods and bag of bait and, treading softly so as not to waken the dogs, mounted the steps. He turned the cold door-handle—the door was locked. He climbed over the rail of the veranda and went up to one of the windows. The sashes were half open. From the black slit came the sweet smell of a girl's body, warm with sleep, and the unfamiliar fragrance of perfume.

"Lizaveta Sergeyevna!"

His voice sounded very loud. He waited. Silence. 'What if I've picked the wrong window? Suppose it's the master himself sleeping here? Then I'll be for it! He'll shoot me down with a gun,' Mitka thought, gripping the sash handle.

"Lizaveta Sergeyevna, get up. Time to go fishing!'

It'll be some fishing if I'm at the wrong window, he thought.

'Get up now!' he said in exasperation, poking his head into the room.

'What? Who's that?' a frightened whisper came from the blackness.

'Are you coming fishing? It's me, Korshunov.'

'Oh! Just a moment.'

Something rustled in the room. The warm sleepy voice had a minty smell. Mitka saw something white and rustling move about the room.

'I'd rather get into bed with her than sit out there in the cold,' he thought vaguely, breathing in the scents of the bedroom.

A laughing face framed in a white kerchief appeared at the window.

'I'm coming out through the window. Give me your hand.'

'Come on then,' and Mitka helped her.

As she leaned on his arm she looked closely into his eyes.

'Wasn't I quick?'

'Quick enough.'

They walked towards the Don. She rubbed her slightly puffy eyes with a pink hand and said, 'I was sleeping

so sweetly. I could do with some more. It's early yet.'
'Now's the time.'

They went down to the Don by the first lane after the square. The water had risen during the night and the boat, which had been hitched to a stump on dry land the day before, was now afloat.

'We'll have to take our shoes off,' Liza sighed, trying to judge the distance.

'Let me carry you?' Mitka suggested.

'No ... I'd better take my shoes off.'

'It's easier to be carried.'

'No, really—' she hesitated in embarrassment.

Mitka hooked his left arm under her legs a little above the knee, lifted her easily and splashed through the water towards the boat. She involuntarily clutched his brown sturdy neck and broke into a soft, caressing laugh.

If Mitka had not stumbled on a boulder the village women used for beating out their washing, there would not have been a brief, accidental kiss. She gasped as her mouth pressed against Mitka's cracked lips, and Mitka came to a dead stop two paces from the grey side of the boat, water trickling into his boots and chilling his feet.

He unhitched the boat, pushed it hard and jumped in as it floated out. Standing in the stern, he paddled with a short oar. The water murmured and wept behind him. With its bows high out of the water the boat rode gently across the mainstream, heading for the other bank. The rods jumped and rattled.

'Where are you taking me?' she asked, glancing over her shoulder.

'T'other side.'

The boat ran up a sandy beach. Without asking, he took her in his arms and carried her into a clump of hawthorn. She bit and scratched, uttered one or two stifled screams and, as she felt her strength failing, began to sob angrily, without tears.

It was about nine o'clock when they returned. The sky was wrapped in a yellowish-red haze. The wind danced across the Don, whipping up white horses. The boat danced over the choppy waves and cold foaming splashes of water raised from the depths lashed Liza's pale drawn face and dripped from her eyelashes and the wet locks of hair that had slipped from under her kerchief.

She sat with her lids drooping over burnt-out eyes and twisted the stalk of a flower that had somehow fallen into the boat. Mitka rowed without looking at her. At his feet lay a small carp and a bream, its mouth set in the agony of death, an orange-rimmed eye bulging. A guilty look hovered on Mitka's face, mingling satisfaction with alarm.

'I'll take you to Semyonov's pier. It's nearer to your place,' he said, turning the boat downstream.

'All right,' she muttered.

The bank was deserted. The dusty wattle fences of the vegetable patches above the Don wilted in the hot wind and filled the air with the smell of scorched brushwood. The heavy sunflower tops, ravaged by sparrows, were bursting with ripeness and bowed to the earth, scattering their seeds. The meadow was emerald green with a new growth of grass. In the distance the foals were prancing and kicking, and the echoing laughter of the bells on their necks floated across the Don on the hot southern wind.

Mitka picked up the fish and offered it to Liza as she stepped out of the boat.

'Here! Take your catch!'

Her eyelashes fluttered in a startled look. She took it.

'Well, I'll be going.'

'All right.'

She walked off, holding the fish away from her on the willow twig threaded through its gills, pitiful and confused, all her recent confidence and gaiety left behind in the hawthorn.

"Lizaveta!'

She turned. There was irritation and surprise in the sudden jagged line of her brows.

'Come here a minute.'

And when she came nearer he said, resentfully, because of his own embarrassment, 'We was a bit careless... That skirt—at the back! There's a spot on it—only a little one though.'

She flushed to the collar-bones.

Mitka said nothing for a moment, then advised, 'Go by the back lanes.'

'I'll still have to cross the square. I meant to put on a black skirt,' she whispered, surveying Mitka's face with misery and a sudden hatred.

'Let me stain it green with a leaf,' he suggested simply, and was surprised to see tears welling in her eyes.

The word went round the village like a whispering wind. 'Mitka Korshunov had a night out with Sergei Platonovich's daughter!' It was the talk of the women as they drove their cows out at dawn, when they stood in the narrow dusty shade of the well-sweeps, with the water spilling from their pails, or knelt on the flat boulders by the Don, beating out their washing.

'That's what comes of having no mother of her own.'

'The master, he never has time, and that step-mother shuts her eyes to things.'

'Davydka the watchman was saying the other day, "I took a look round at midnight," he says, "and there was a man tapping at the far window. That must be a thief, I thought, trying to break in at Platonovich's. So I runs up and shouts 'Who's there? Police!' And it turns out to be Mitka!"'

'The way girls carry on nowadays, drat 'em...'

'Mitka was talking big to my Mikishka about it, "I'm going to marry her," he says.'

'Let him wipe the snot off his nose first.'

'He did it by force, they say, raped her...'

'We've heard that tale before...'

The talk trickled along the streets and side-lanes, and the girl's good name was soon tarred black as a harlot's gate.

It descended upon Sergei Platonovich's balding head and all but crushed him. For two days he made no appearance either in the shop or at the mill. The servants, who lived in one of the outbuildings, came in only to cook meals.

On the third day Sergei Platonovich had a dappled grey stallion harnessed to a light drozhky and drove off to the stanitsa, nodding haughtily to the Cossacks he passed on the road. In his wake a shining varnished carriage rolled out of the yard. Yemelyan, the coachman, sucking the curved pipe that had glued itself permanently to his short grizzled beard, shook out the silky blue reins and the fine pair of high-stepping raven-black horses clip-clopped away down the street. Behind him sat Liza, pale-faced, half-hidden by his craggy back. Holding a light suit-case on her lap and smiling wanly, she waved her glove to Vladimir and her step-mother, who were standing at the gate. Pantelei Prokofievich happened to be limping home from the shop at the time and inquired of Nikita the groom, 'Where is the heiress off to?'

Making allowance for the curiosity of common mortals, Nikita replied condescendingly, 'To Moscow, to study.'

The next day an event occurred that was for long afterwards to be told and retold down by the Don, under

125

the well-sweeps and on the cattle track... Just before dusk, when the herd had come in from the steppe, Mitka paid a visit to Sergei Platonovich (he had deliberately waited till late to avoid being seen). For he had come not to pay just a casual call, but to ask Liza's hand in marriage.

Before this he had seen her three or four times, not more. During their last encounter the following conversation had taken place between them.

'Wouldn't you like to marry me, 'Lizaveta, huh?'

'That's absurd!'

'I'll be good to you, I'll look after you well. We've got plenty of people to work for us. You'll be able to sit by the window and read your books.'

'You're a fool.'

Mitka had lapsed into offended silence. That evening he had gone home earlier than usual and in the morning made the announcement to his astonished father.

'Dad, I want to get married.'

'Mercy on you!'

'I mean it.'

'What's the great hurry?'

'Well, why not?'

'Who's smitten you this time—Marfa the Half-Wit?'

'Send the matchmakers to Sergei Platonovich.'

Miron laid out on the bench the tools he had been using to mend a harness and gave a short laugh.

'You're feeling merry today, my son.'

But Mitka stuck to his guns and his father flared up.

'You're a fool! Sergei Platonovich has capital of more than a hundred thousand. He's a merchant and what are you?.. Get out of here and stop your nonsense or I'll take this strap to the fine bridegroom!'

'But we've got fourteen pair of oxen, and what a farm! Besides, he's a peasant and we're Cossacks.'

'Go!' Miron ordered. He had no liking for long discussions.

Mitka found a sympathetic listener only in his grandfather. The old man hobbled off to speak to his son about it, his stick tapping on the floor.

'Miron!'

'What is it now?'

'Why're you agin it? If she's taken the lad's fancy—'

'Father, you're like a babe-in-arms, honestly you are! Mitka's a fool, but you beat everything!'

'Hold your tongue!' Grishaka thumped on the floor

with his stick. 'Or aren't we good enough for 'em? He ought to feel honoured to have a Cossack asking for his daughter. He'll be falling over himself to give her away. Our family is known all over the district. We're not rag-tag and bobtail. We've got a good farm. We have indeed! Go and see him about it, Miron! Don't hang back! And let him give us the mill for a dowry. Ask him for it!'

Miron snorted and went out into the yard, but Mitka decided to wait until evening and take matters into his own hands. He knew his father's obstinacy was like an elm. It could be bent, but it was no use trying to break it.

He walked up to the Mokhovs' house, whistling to himself, but at the front door his courage began to fail. He stood hesitating for a minute, then walked across the yard. At the steps of the veranda he asked a maid in a rustling starched apron, 'Is the master at home?'

'The master is having his tea. You'll have to wait.'

He sat down, smoked a cigarette, spat on his fingers to put it out, and then crushed the stub messily on the floor. Sergei Platonovich appeared, brushing the crumbs off his waistcoat; at the sight of Mitka his brows knitted.

'Come in.'

Mitka entered the cool study, which smelled of books and tobacco, feeling that the boldness he had started off with from home had been just enough to last him to the door of the study.

Sergei Platonovich went to his desk and swung round on heels that gave a loud squeak.

'Well?' His fingers were clawing the top of the desk behind him.

'What I came to find out was...' Mitka plunged into the cold slime of those drilling eyes and hunched his shoulders with a shiver. 'Would you give me 'Lizaveta in marriage?'

Desperation, resentment and fear bathed Mitka's confused face in perspiration as fine as dew during a drought.

Sergei Platonovich's left eyebrow twitched and his upper lip curled back, exposing the purple underside. He thrust his whole body forward.

'What?.. Wh-a-a-at?.. Scoundrel!.. Get out of here... I'll have you up before the ataman! You scum! You filthy cur!'

Emboldened by the other's shouting, Mitka watched the bluish blood pumping into Sergei Platonovich's cheeks.

'Don't take offence... I was only trying to put things right for her.'

Sergei Platonovich rolled his bloodshot, tear-filled eyes and flung a massive iron ash-tray down at Mitka's feet. It bounced and hit Mitka's knee-cap, but he bore the pain staunchly and swung the door open. Snarling now and made even more impudent by pain and resentment, he shouted:

'Well, it's up to you, Sergei Platonovich. I only wanted to do right... Who will want her now? So I thought I'd cover up her shame... Who wants a chewed bit? Even a dog wouldn't eat it.'

With a crumpled handkerchief pressed to his lips Sergei Platonovich lurched after Mitka, barring his way to the front door. Mitka ran out into the yard. A mere wink passed from Sergei Platonovich to Yemelyan the coachman, who was lounging near by. While Mitka was tugging at the tight bolt on the side gate, four dogs released from their chains rounded the corner of the shed and at the sight of a stranger galloped across the cleanly swept yard.

Sergei Platonovich had brought back two pups, a dog and a bitch, from a fair in Nizhny Novgorod in 1910. They were black, shaggy and heavy-jawed. In twelve months they grew as big as yearling calves. At first they tore the skirts of the women who passed the Mokhovs' yard, then they learned to pull the women down and bite their legs, and only when they had mauled to death a heifer belonging to Father Pankraty and a couple of Atyopin's pigs did Sergei Platonovich order them to be chained up. They were let off at night, and once a year, in spring, for mating.

Before Mitka could turn round, the leader, Bayan, pounced on him and sunk its teeth into the padding of his coat. The others tugged and tore, whirling round him in a black swarm. Mitka fought them off with his hands, trying not to fall. Out of the corner of his eye he saw Yemelyan, scattering sparks from his pipe, slip away into the kitchen and slam the painted door.

Sergei Platonovich stood at the corner of the porch, leaning against the drain-pipe and clenching those small white fists of his until the harsh shiny hair stood out on the backs. Staggering, Mitka managed to draw the bolt and drag himself out of the yard with the snarling, stinking knot of dogs clinging to his torn and bleeding legs. He strangled the life out of Bayan and eventually beat off the others with the help of some passing Cossacks.

III

Natalya fitted well into the Melekhov household. Miron had brought up his family strictly; despite his wealth and having other hands on the farm, he had trained his children in all kinds of farm work. The diligent Natalya soon won the hearts of her father- and mother-in-law. Ilyinichna, who, if the truth were known, had little liking for her elder daughter-in-law, the smart, clothes-loving Darya, took to Natalya from the first.

'Have a good sleep, my little one! What are you jumping out of bed for?' she would coo, padding heavily about the kitchen. 'Go and get your beauty sleep, we'll manage without you.'

And Natalya, who had risen with the dawn to help with the cooking, would go back to bed in the best room.

Strict though he was over household matters, even Pantelei would say to his wife, 'Don't wake Natalya. She tires herself out enough during the day. She and Grishka are going out to plough. You be after Darya. She's got an idle streak in her... Painting her cheeks and blackening her eyebrows, the bitch.'

'Yes, let her bask a bit for the first year anyway,' Ilyinichna sighed, remembering her own back-breaking life.

Grigory began to get used to his new, married state and lost some of his rough edges, but after the third week he realised with fear and a bitter anger that he had not finally broken with Aksinya, that something had stuck like a thorn in his heart. It was a pain that would not pass quickly. The wound which in the flush of courtship he had so light-heartedly dismissed, thinking it would soon heal and be forgotten, was still there. It showed no sign of healing, and memory made it bleed. Before the wedding Petro had asked him one day, when they were threshing, 'What about Aksinya, Grishka?'

'What about her?'

'You'll be sorry to drop her.'

'If I drop her, someone else will pick her up,' Grigory had said then, with a laugh.

'Well, watch your step.' Petro chewed his much chewed moustache. 'You can't go back on it, you know.'

'When the flesh is older, the flame is colder,' Grigory countered lightly.

But at night, as he dutifully caressed his wife and tried to stir her with his youthful zest, he encountered only coolness and embarrassed submission. Natalya had no taste for the joys of the flesh. She had inherited her mother's slow, unresponsive blood, and at the memory of Aksinya's frenzied love-making, Grigory would say with a sigh, 'Your father must have made you on an ice-floe, Natalya... You're too chilly by half.'

And Aksinya, for her part, would smile darkly when they met, and spin a clinging web of words.

'Hullo, Grisha dear! How's life? Does your young wife love you well?'

'All right,' he would answer vaguely, and try to escape as soon as possible from Aksinya's caressing gaze.

Stepan seemed to have made it up with his wife. He spent less time at the tavern and one evening in the threshing barn, when they were winnowing the wheat, he suggested for the first time in months, 'Come on, let's have a song.'

They sat down, leaning against a stack of dusty wheat straw. Stepan began to sing an army song and Aksinya put in the descant in her full-throated voice. They sang tunefully together, as they had in the first years of their married life. There had been times then when they were driving home from the fields in the crimson glow of the sunset and Stepan, as he sat swaying on the load, would strike up an old lament, as mournful as a deserted, weed-grown track across the steppes. Aksinya would sing with him, resting her head on the great mounds of her husband's chest. The horses would pull the big creaking wagon and the old men of the village would listen to the song from a distance.

'Stepan's got himself a wife with a fine voice.'

'What a lilt, eh!'

'Stepan's got a voice too, clear as a bell!'

And the old men sitting on the copings of their houses and watching the dusty purple sunset die away would call to one another across the street:

'It's a valley song they're singing.'

'Ay, mate, that one comes from Georgia.'

'No wonder Kiryushka was fond of it, rest his soul.'

Grigory would hear the Astakhovs singing of an evening. At threshing time (their barns were next door to each other) he would see Aksinya as sure of herself and as happy as she had ever been. Or at least so it seemed to him.

Stepan never so much as passed the time of day with the Melekhovs. He would go about the threshing floor with a fork, his big shoulders swinging, and sometimes making a joking remark to his wife. Aksinya would laugh, letting her dark eyes flash from under her kerchief. Her green skirt would surge before Grigory's eyes when he closed them, and some unknown force would twist his head in the direction of Stepan's barn. And he failed to notice how Natalya, who was helping Pantelei to spread the sheaves for threshing, caught her husband's every roving glance with her tortured, jealous eyes; nor did he see the faint grin that spread over Petro's face as he watched Grigory from where he was driving the horses.

Amid the dull rumble and clatter—the groan of the earth crucified under the stone rollers—Grigory wrestled with vague thoughts, trying to grasp slippery scraps of ideas that eluded his understanding.

The sounds of the threshing, the shouts of the drivers, the crack and whistle of the whips, the chatter of the winnowing drums from the near and distant threshing floors drifted away and melted over the meadow. The village, full and fat with the harvest, basked in the cool September sunshine and lay stretched out along the Don like a beaded snake across a road. In every yard, behind its wattle fences, under every roof a bitter-sweet life swirled separately from the others. Grandad Grishaka had caught a chill and was suffering from tooth-ache; Sergei Platonovich clutched his forked beard and in the privacy of his study wept and ground his teeth, crushed by his humiliation; Stepan nursed his hatred of Grigory and at night his iron fingers clawed the patchwork blanket in his sleep; Natalya would run away into the barn and throw herself on a heap of dried dung bricks, shaking and sobbing over her defiled happiness; Khristonya, who had sold a calf at a fair and drunk the proceeds, was conscience-striken; Grigory sighed with foreboding and renewed pain; Aksinya caressed her husband and drowned her hatred of him in tears.

Davydka, the mill-hand who had lost his job, sat for nights on end with Knave in the wattle-and-daub carter's shed, while the latter, his fierce eyes glittering, proclaimed, 'They won't get away with it! They'll soon have their throats cut! One revolution wasn't enough for them. There'll be another 1905, and then we'll get even! Yes, we'll get even all right!' He shook a scarred finger threateningly, then shrugged his jacket back onto his shoulders.

And over the village the days mingled into nights, the

weeks and months crept by, the wind blew, the hill moaned, warning of bad weather to come, and the Don, glazed with the transparent greenish azure of autumn, rolled on indifferently to the sea.

IV

One Sunday at the end of October Fedot Bodovskov made a journey to the stanitsa.

He took with him in a basket four brace of well-fattened ducks and sold them at the market; in a shop he bought his wife a length of pretty cotton print and was just about to leave (he was tightening the hame-strap) when a man, evidently a stranger to the locality, and not a Cossack either, came up to him.

'Good afternoon!' he said, touching the brim of his black felt hat with his brown fingers.

''Afternoon!' Fedot grunted guardedly, narrowing his Kalmyk eyes.

'Where are you from?'

'From a village, not from here.'

'What village?'

'Tatarsky.'

The stranger drew a silver cigarette case with a boat embossed on the lid from a side-pocket, offered Fedot a cigarette and went on with his questions.

'Is yours a large village?'

'No, thanks, I've just had one. Our village? Ay, it's pretty big. A good three hundred households.'

'Is there a church?'

'Of course.'

'And a forge?'

'A smithy? Ay, there's a smithy.'

'Does the mill have a workshop?'

Fedot slapped the restive horse with the reins, and shot a surly look at the black hat and the deep lines running down to the short black beard in the man's large white face.

'What do you want?'

'I intend to make my home in your village. I've just been to the local ataman. Are you going back empty?'

'Yes.'

'Will you give me a lift? But I'm not alone. I have my wife with me, and two trunks weighing about eight poods.'

132

'I can take 'em.'

Having agreed on a payment of two rubles, Fedot drove round to Froska the roll-maker, where his passenger had been lodging, helped a frail fair-haired little woman into the wagon, and placed the two iron-bound trunks in the back.

They drove out of the stanitsa. Fedot clicked his tongue, waved the horse-hair reins over his sturdy little horse, and kept turning his angular head; he was eaten up with curiosity. His passengers sat quietly behind him, saying nothing. To break the ice, Fedot asked for a cigarette, then he inquired, 'Where have you come from?'

'Rostov.'

'Hail from there?'

'What did you say?'

'I'm asking you: where were you born?'

'Oh, yes. That's where we're from. We're Rostov people.'

Fedot's brown cheeks creased as he peered at a distant clump of steppeland weed. The road led up a long incline and on the brow of the hill, in the brown withered grass, about half a verst from the road his sharp Kalmyk eyes had spotted the moving heads of a flock of bustards.

'Pity I've no gun or we could have a shot at the bustards. See 'em trotting along over there,' he said with a sigh and pointed.

'I can't say I do,' his passenger confessed, blinking short-sightedly.

Fedot watched the bustards make their way into the ravine and turned to face his passengers. The man was of medium height and thin, and his close-set eyes had a sly twinkle. He often smiled when speaking. His wife was dozing, wrapped up in a knitted shawl. Fedot could not see her face.

'What makes you want to live in our village?'

'I'm a mechanic, I want to start a workshop. I have some experience of cabinet-making too.'

Fedot eyed the man's big hands suspiciously. The man noticed his glance and added, 'I am also an agent for the Singer sewing-machine company.'

'What name do you go by?' Fedot inquired.

'My name is Stokman.'

'So you're not a Russian?'

'Yes, I am. But my grandfather was of Lettish origin.'

In next to no time Fedot learned that the mechanic Osip Stokman had formerly worked at the Aksai factory, then somewhere in the Kuban country, and after that in the South-East Railway workshops. And his inquisitive tongue gleaned a lot of other details about the stranger's life.

When they reached the State Forest the conversation flagged. Fedot watered his sweating horse at a roadside well-stream and, made drowsy by the constant jogging, began to doze. It was five versts to the village.

Fedot wound the reins round his wrist, put his feet up and made himself comfortable.

But he was not allowed to doze off.

'How's life in your village?' Stokman asked, swaying and bobbing with the motion of the wagon.

'We get along.'

'Are the Cossacks, in general, satisfied with life?'

'Some are, some aren't. You can't please everybody.'

'Yes, of course...' the mechanic agreed. And after a pause he went on asking his tricky, loaded questions. 'So you live well, you say?'

'Well enough.'

'Your army service must be a burden? Isn't it?'

'Serving in the army?... We're used to it. That's the only time you see life—on active service.'

'The bad side of it is that the Cossacks have to provide their whole outfit themselves.'

'Ay, that it is, damn their eyes!' Fedot burst out, and cast an apprehensive glance at the woman. She had turned away. 'Our authorities are a terrible lot... When I was due for service, I had to sell my oxen and buy myself a horse. And then they go and reject it.'

'Rejected it?' the mechanic sounded surprised.

'Yes, straight out. His legs are no good, they says. I tried to talk 'em round. "Put yourself in my place," I says. "He's got legs like a prize stallion, it's just his walk... He struts like a young cock."But no, they wouldn't have him. It's ruination!'

The conversation took a more lively turn. Fedot became so excited that he jumped off the wagon and chatted on willingly about the people of the village. He cursed the village ataman for his unfair division of the meadowland and praised the way things were run in Poland, where his regiment had been stationed. The mechanic's close-set eyes watched Fedot keenly as he strode along beside the wagon; he was smoking a mild cigarette in his bone cigarette-holder, and smiled frequently, but the slantwise furrow across his pale sloping

134

forehead moved slowly and ponderously, as though propelled from within by hidden thoughts.

They reached the village towards evening.

On Fedot's advice Stokman went to the widow Lukeshka Popova and rented two rooms in her house.

'Who did you bring back from the stanitsa?' the women from next door asked Fedot when he reached his gate.

'An agent.'

'What kind of agent?'

'Ah, you women, what a stupid lot you are! I've told you, he's an agent. Sells sewing-machines. He gives 'em away free to the pretty girls, but the ugly ones, like you Auntie Marya, have to pay for them.'

'That a fine thing for you to say, you bandy-legged devil. Just look at your Kalmyk mug! It'd frighten a horse!'

'The Kalmyk and the Tatar come first in the steppe, so mind your tongue, woman!' was Fedot's parting shot.

Before Stokman had passed a single night at the gossip-loving Lukeshka's, the women's tongue were wagging all over the village.

'Have you heard?'

'Heard what?'

'Fedot the Kalmyk has brought a German here.'

'Not really?'

'So help me God! He wears a felt hat and his name's Shtopol or Shtokal...'

'He must be a policeman?'

'No, he's an exciseman, my dear.'

'That's all gossip, girls. He's an accountant, they say, just like Father Pankraty's son.'

'Pashka, love, slip down to Lukeshka's and ask her on the quiet who she's got with her now.'

'Off you go, fast as your legs will carry you, my little one!'

The next day the newcomer reported to the village ataman.

Fyodor Manytskov, who had been carrying his staff of office for nearly three years, held the black oilcloth-covered passport for some time, turning it this way and that. Then it was fiddled with and examined by Yegor Zharkov, the clerk. They exchanged glances, and the ataman, true to his old sergeant-major's habit, swept his arm in a gesture of authority.

'You can stay.'

The newcomer bowed and took his leave. For a week he did not show his nose outside the house, kept himself to himself like a marmot in its burrow. All that could be heard was the tapping of his axe as he fitted out a workshop in the old tumbledown summer kitchen. The women's insatiable interest cooled and only the children hung about by the fence, watching the stranger with unabashed, animal curiosity.

V

Grigory and his wife went out to plough three days before Intercession. Pantelei was unwell; he came out to see them off, leaning on a stick and groaning because of the pain in his back.

'Plough the two strips on the other side of the common, near Red Ravine, Grishka.'

'All right. But what about the strip over Willow Ravine?' Grigory asked in a hoarse whisper. He had caught cold fishing and his throat was bandaged.

'After the holiday. You've got plenty to go on with. There's a good fifteen acres by Red Ravine. Don't be greedy.'

'Won't Petro be coming out to help?'

'He's going to the mill with Darya. We've got to get the corn ground before the rush starts.'

Ilyinichna slipped two freshly baked buns under Natalya's blouse and whispered, 'Why don't you take Dunyashka with you to drive the oxen?'

'We'll manage.'

'Well, it's up to you, little one. Christ be with you.'

Dunyashka walked across the yard, her slim figure bowed under the weight of an armful of wet washing that she was taking down to the Don to rinse.

'Natalya, love, there's heaps of sorrel in Red Ravine. Do pick us some!'

'I'll pick plenty.'

'You keep quiet, magpie!' Pantelei brandished his stick.

The three pairs of oxen pulled the upturned plough along the road, scratching a trail on the dry soil hardened by the dry autumn. Grigory tramped along the edge of the road, fiddling with the tight cloth round his throat, and coughing. Natalya walked beside him, the food bag bouncing on her back.

A cool crystal stillness had settled over the steppe. On

the hump of the hill beyond the common the ploughmen were combing the earth and the drivers whistling at the oxen, but here, by the road, there was only the stunted bluish-grey wormwood, the roadside broom that the sheep had nibbled, the knot-grass, bowed as if in prayer, and the ringing glassy coolness of the sky, streaked with flying threads of jewelled gossamer.

After seeing off Grigory and his wife, Petro and Darya got ready for the mill. Petro fitted up a sieve in the barn and winnowed the wheat. Darya filled the sacks and carried them out to the wagon.

Pantelei harnessed the horses, adjusting the straps with his usual care.

'How much longer are you going to be?'

'Just coming,' Petro responded from the barn.

* * *

It was crowded at the mill. The yard was cluttered with wagons and there was a crush round the weighing shed. Petro tossed the reins to Darya and jumped down from the wagon.

'Will you take my number soon?' he asked Knave, who was stationed at the scales.

'All in good time.'

'Whose are you grinding now?'

'Thirty-eight.'

Petro came out to unload his sacks. At that moment a row broke out in the weighing shed. A hoarse, angry voice barked, 'You missed your turn and now you want to push in? Keep away, Tufty, or I'll hurt you!'

Petro recognised the voice of Horseshoe Yakov and listened. The angry shouting swelled and burst out through the doors of the weighing shed.

A blow thudded home and an elderly, bearded Ukrainian with his black peaked cap awry reeled out of the shed backwards.

'What for?' he shouted, clutching his cheek.

'I'll scrag you!'

'Just wait!'

'Come on, Mikikhvor!'

A tough, pugnacious artilleryman known as Horseshoe Yakov (during his army service a horse he was shoeing had kicked him in the face; the hoof had broken his nose, cut his lips and left the oval scar with the bluish-black nail marks that gave him his nickname) ran out of the weighing shed, rolling up his sleeves. A tall Ukrainian in a pink shirt clouted him from behind. Horseshoe staggered but stayed on his feet.

'Help, lads! They're beating up Cossacks!'

Ukrainians (they had come in a group, all from the same district) and Cossacks poured out of the mill like grain through a funnel.

A fight broke out round the main entrance. The doors groaned and cracked under the weight of struggling bodies. Petro dropped his sack, gave a little grunt, and ran lightly on his toes towards the mill. Standing up on the load, Darya saw Petro punch his way into the middle, knocking men down right and left, then gasped in fright as he was battered to the wall and thrown down among the trampling feet. Mitka Korshunov came bounding round the corner of the engine shed, swinging a heavy metal bolt.

The Ukrainian who had clouted Horseshoe from behind, broke out of the scrimmage, a tattered pink sleeve trailing behind him like a broken wing. He ran crouching, scrabbling the ground with his hands, to the first wagon and with hardly an effort wrenched out the shaft. Hoarse cries and groans floated up over the yard, mingling with the thud of blows and the splintering of wood.

The three Shumilin brothers came running from home. One-armed Alexei tripped over a pair of reins someone had left lying near the gate, jumped to his feet and went leaping over the interlocked wagon-shafts, pressing his empty left sleeve to his belly. Martin, his brother, bent down to tuck a flapping trouser leg into his white sock, but a fresh burst of shouting came from the mill and a scream rose high above the sloping roof, like a wind-whirled thread of gossamer. Martin straightened up and rushed in pursuit of Alexei.

Darya watched from the top of the load, gasping and wringing her hands. Women all around were wailing and squealing. The horses laid their ears flat, the oxen lowed and backed up against the wagons... A pale-faced Sergei Platonovich limped past, lips flopping, belly rolling like a round egg under his waistcoat. Darya saw the Ukrainian in the torn pink shirt cut Mitka Korshunov's legs from under him with the wagon-shaft. But the next moment he dropped the shaft and fell himself with one-armed Alexei on top of him, hammering him with his leaden fist. Other scenes of the fray flashed before Darya's eyes like colourful scraps of patchwork. She saw, and was not surprised to see, Mitka Korshunov drag himself to his knees and fling the iron bolt at Sergei Platonovich's legs as he ran past; the merchant flapped his arms wildly, crashed to the ground and crawled crabwise towards the weighing shed; he was trampled on and thrown flat on his face. Darya broke into a fit of hysterical laughter that shattered the smooth curves of her pencilled eyebrows. The fit ended suddenly when she noticed Petro stagger out of the swaying, bellowing mass and lie down under a wagon, spitting blood. She darted over to him with a cry of alarm. Cossacks came running in from the village with fence stakes; one was swinging a crowbar. The fight was assuming monstrous proportions. It was quite different from the drunken brawls outside the taverns or the fisticuffs at Shrovetide. A young Ukrainian with a smashed skull lay by the door of the weighing shed, legs thrashing, head ducking in a dark, coagulating pool of blood; blood-soaked strands of hair were spread over his face. Evidently his days on this bright and merry earth were over.

The Ukrainians had huddled together like sheep and were being driven back towards the carters' shed. Things would have ended badly if one of them, an old man, had not hit upon an idea. He darted into the shed, pulled a flaming brand out of the stove and carried it into the yard. He ran to the barn where the milled wheat was kept—a thousand poods or more of wheat flour. A train of sparks, dulled by the daylight, fluttered over his shoulder.

'I'll burn it down!' he yelled, lifting the crackling brand to the reed-thatched roof.

The Cossacks hesitated and halted. A dry gusty wind was blowing from the east, carrying the smoke away from the roof of the carters' shed towards the huddled group of Ukrainians. One good spark in that dry thatch and the village would go up in flames.

The Cossack ranks broke into a subdued muttering. One or two backed away to the mill, but the Ukrainian went on waving the burning brand above his head, shaking blobs of fire from the bluish smoke.

'I'll burn the bloody place down! Get out of the yard!'

With many additional bruises on his disfigured face Horseshoe Yakov, the instigator of the fight, was the first to leave the mill yard. The other Cossacks followed him hastily.

The Ukrainians tossed their sacks on to the wagons and harnessed up. Waving the reins and lashing the horses, they charged out of the mill-yard and clattered away down the street.

The next moment one-armed Alexei was in the middle of the yard, his stump in its empty knotted sleeve jerking against his lean belly, his eyes and cheeks twitching violently.

'To horse, Cossacks!'

'After 'em!'

'They won't get further than the hilltop!'

Mitka Korshunov, despite a noticeable limp, made for the gate. A fresh ripple of fury stirred the Cossacks gathered round the mill, but at that moment a stranger in a black felt hat, whom no one had noticed before, emerged from the engine-shed and came striding towards them; scanning the crowd with sharp close-set eyes, he raised his hand.

'Wait!'

'Who are you?' Horseshoe Yakov knitted his twitching eyebrows in a frown.

'Where did he spring from?'

'Bash him!'

'Ga-a-a-rn!'

'Now let's wait just a minute, neighbours!'

'You're no neighbour of ours, you mongrel!'

'Muzhik!'

'Bumpkin!'

'Give him one, Yakov!'

'A good 'un—between his eyes!'

The man smiled awkwardly but with no sign of fear, took off his hat and with an astonishingly simple gesture wiped his forehead. The smile was totally disarming.

'What's all this about?' he waved his folded hat, indicating the dark, blood-soaked earth at the door of the weighing shed.

'We were beating up some Tufties,' one-armed Alexei replied peaceably and winked with both his eye and cheek.

'But what for?'

'For jumping the queue. Let 'em wait their turn,' Horseshoe explained, coming forward and wiping a clot of blood from under his nose with a sweep of the arm.

'We gave 'em something to remember us by!'

'We could still catch 'em!.. They couldn't set fire to anything in the steppe.'

'We gave up too easily. He'd never have done it.'

'A man'll do anything when he's desperate.'

'The Tufties are a terrible bad-tempered lot,' Afonka Ozerov said, grinning.

The man waved his hat at Afonka.

'Who are you?'

Afonka spat contemptuously through one of the many gaps between his teeth and stepped back to watch the flight of the spit.

'I'm a Cossack. What are you—a Gypsy?'

'No, you and I are both Russians.'

'That's a lie!' Afonka declared flatly.

'The Cossacks are descended from the Russians. Do you know that?'

'And I'm telling you that the Cossacks come from Cossacks!'

'In the old days there were serfs who ran away from their masters and settled on the Don. That's how they came to be called Cossacks.'

'All right then, chum, go your own way,' one-armed Alexei advised with suppressed anger, clenching his swollen fingers, and his face twitched more violently than ever.

'And that bastard's come to live here!.. Trying to make us into muzhiks!'

'Who is he? Eh, Afonka?'

'Someone who came here. He's lodging at cross-eyed Lukeshka's.'

The chance of pursuit was lost and the Cossacks dispersed, animatedly discussing the fight.

* * *

That night, in the steppe some eight versts away from the village Grigory said regretfully to Natalya as he wrapped himself in his coat of thick, prickly homespun, 'You're like a stranger to me... You're like that moon up there—not cold nor warm. I don't love you, Natalya. Don't be angry. I didn't want to say it, but we can't go on like this... I'm sorry for you because we're kind of together, but I've no feeling for you... My heart's as empty as this steppe.'

Natalya gazed up at the starry land above and the shadowy, phantomlike clouds floating across it, and said nothing. From that dark blue void the call of a few late migrating cranes echoed like silver bells as the birds winged their way south.

The withered grass smelled of sorrow and death. Somewhere on the hillside the red spot of a ploughman's campfire flared fitfully.

When Grigory awoke before dawn his coat was covered with more than three inches of snow. The steppe languished restlessly under the glittering virginal whiteness and quite close by the fresh snow was clearly marked by the blue tracks of a hare that had frisked about on the first snow of winter.

VI

It had long been the rule that if a Cossack riding alone on the road to Millerovo met Ukrainians (their settlements began from Nizhne-Yablonovsky and were dotted along the whole stretch of seventy-five versts to Millerovo) and did not give them the right of way, he would be beaten up. So whenever Cossacks travelled to the station, they would go together in a train of wagons and not be afraid to answer abuse with abuse during an encounter in the steppe.

'Heh, Tufty! Get out of the road! Think you can live on Cossack land, you bastard, and not make way for us?'

And it was no holiday either for the Ukrainians who brought their wheat to the Paramonov elevator on the Don. Fights broke out for no reason at all, simply because a man was a 'tufty' and 'tufties' had to be beaten up.

Many centuries ago a diligent hand had sown the seeds of caste enmity on Cossack soil. It had tended and fostered them and the seeds had yielded a rich crop. The soil was soaked with the blood shed in fights between Cossacks and newcomers, whether Russian or Ukrainian.

Two weeks after the fight at the mill a policeman and an inspector arrived in the village.

Stokman was the first person to be called in for interrogation. The inspector, a young official from a family of the Cossack nobility, rummaged in his brief-case and asked:

'Where were you living before you came here?'

'In Rostov.'

'What did you go to prison for in 1907?'

Stokman's eyes flashed like a polecat's at the brief-case and the bowed head of the inspector with its crooked scurf-flaked parting.

'For being involved in the disturbances.'

'Hem... Where were you working at the time?'

'In the railway workshops.'

'What trade?'

'Mechanic.'

'You're not a Jew, are you? Or a converted one?'

'No. I think—'

'I'm not interested in what you think. Were you ever in exile?'

'Yes.'

The inspector raised his head from his brief-case and munched his chapped clean-shaven lips.

'I advise you to leave here...' And to himself, 'In fact, I'll see to it that you do.'

'Why should I leave, inspector?'

The reply was another question.

'What did you talk about with the local Cossacks on the day of the fight at the mill?'

'Actually I—'

'All right, you may go.'

Stokman went out on to the veranda of Mokhov's house (officials always stayed at Sergei Platonovich's, preferring it to the inn) and looked back at the well painted double-doors with a shrug.

VII

Winter did not set in at once. The snow which fell at Intercession melted and the herds were again put out to graze. A south wind blew for a week, the weather grew warmer, the earth recovered and the late grass in the steppe was a mossy green.

The thaw lasted until St. Michael's Day, then there was a hard frost and snow fell; the days steadily grew colder, another seven inches of snow fell, and the winding tracks of hares appeared on the abandoned vegetable patches along the Don, where the drifts were already up to the tops of the fences. The village streets were deserted.

The smoke of dung fuel spread out over the village and the rooks, attracted by the human warmth, paraded round the scattered heaps of ash by the roadside. A smooth sledge road wound its way through the village like a faded blue ribbon.

One day the Cossacks assembled on the square to discuss the share-out of brushwood allotments. They crowded round the porch of the administration office in their sheepskins and topcoats, their felt boots squeaking on the crisp snow. Soon the cold drove them inside. The honoured members of the community with their silvery beards sat down at the table on either side of the ataman and the clerk; the younger ones with beards of different colours and some with no beards at all gathered in tight little groups, muttering to one another out of the warmth of their sheepskin collars. The clerk covered pages with his minute handwriting while the ataman watched over his shoulder, and a muffled hum of voices filled the cold room.

'The hay this year—'

'Ay, the meadow hay's good fodder, but there's nothing but broom in the steppe.'

'In the old days they used to graze in the steppes till Christmas.'

'That was all right for the Kalmyks.'

'Uh-huh—'

'The ataman's got a neck on him like a wolf's; he can't hardly turn his head.'

'He's been stuffing himself like a hog, the devil!'

'Hullo there, kinsman, are you trying to scare the winter away? That's a hell of a sheepskin you've got.'

'Ah, but the Gypsy's already sold his coat.'

'Here's a story for you then. During Holy Week there was some Gypsies out at night in the steppe and they didn't have nowt to cover 'emselves with, so one of 'em wrapped himself up in a fishing net. When the cold crept into his guts, the Gypsy, he woke up, poked his finger through one of the meshes and says to his mother, "Oh, Mummy," he says, "that's why it's so perishing cold!.."'

'Hope to God it don't get slippy.'

'We'll have to shoe the oxen if it does.'

'The other day I cut some white willow up Devil's Creek. Fine stuff.'

'Button your fly, Zakhar. Your old woman'll turn you out if you freeze it.'

'What's this I hear, Avdeich, about you taking in the village bull?'

'I decided not to. Paranka Mrykhina said she would. I'm a widow, she says, it'll be more cheerful with him around. All right, I says, you have him then, and if there'a an addition to the family—'

'Haw! Haw! Haw!'

'Ho! Ho!'

'Esteemed elders! Now what about the wood-cutting... Quiet there!'

'If, I says, there's an addition to the family ... I'll stand god-father to him...'

'Quiet, please!'

The meeting began. Fondling his rod of office, breathing steam, and flicking icicles out of his beard with his little finger, the ataman called out the names of the assigners of allotments. Steamy air poured into the room as more Cossacks squeezed through the door at the back, and there was a hearty blowing of noses.

'You can't start the wood-cutting on Thursday!' Ivan Tomilin tried to outshout the ataman. He cocked his head in its blue artilleryman's cap and rubbed his crimson ears furiously.

'Why not?'

'You'll rub your ears off, gunner!'

'We'll sew some bull's ears on him instead!'

'On Thursday half the village will be going out to bring in hay from the meadows. Couldn't you think of that!'

'You can bring in the hay on Sunday.'

'Esteemed elders!'

'What now?'

'Never mind the hay!'

Howls of disagreement rose from the assembled Cossacks.

Old Matvei Kashulin bent forward over the rickety table and croaked fiercely, poking his smooth ash stick at Tomilin.

'The hay can wait! Do as others do... You always have to stick your oar in. You're too young and stupid, my lad!.. Huh! Listen to him!'

'And you're old and still borrowing brains from your neighbours.' Popping his head up from the back rows, one-armed Alexei volleyed back with his eye winking and scarred cheek twitching.

For six years there had been a feud between him and old Kashulin over a scrap of ploughland. Alexei gave the old man a beating every spring, though the strip of land Kashulin had grabbed from him was so narrow you could spit across it with your eyes closed.

'Hold your tongue, twitcher!'

'Pity you're out of reach or I'd bloody your snout for you!'

145

'Why, you one-armed blinker!..'

'Quiet there, stop this bickering!'

'Go outside if you want a scrap.'

'Give over, Alexei, the old feller's so steamed up his busby will blow off in a minute.'

'Stick the rowdy ones in the cooler!'

'He started it...'

'Give him one on the ear tomorrow but now keep quiet.'

The ataman brought his fist down with a thump that made the table squeak.

'I'll call in the guard in a minute! Silence!'

The hubbub rolled to the back of the room and died away.

'On Thursday, at first light, you'll be going out for the felling.'

'What do you say, elders?'

'Good luck go with you!'

'Godspeed!'

'The old folk aren't listened to much these days.'

'They'll obey us all right. Or can't we bridle 'em? My Alexei, when I gave him his share, wanted to fight me over it, waved his fist in my face, he did. But I soon showed him. "I'll report you to the ataman and the elders and have you thrashed..." He knuckled under pretty quick, like grass in a spring flood.'

'And another thing, elders, we've had an order from the stanitsa ataman.' The ataman cleared his throat and twisted his head; the high collar of his uniform was cutting into his neck. 'This Saturday the young Cossacks are to take the oath. It's your duty to see they get to the stanitsa ataman's office in good time.'

Pantelei was standing with his lame leg tucked up under him like a crane by the window nearest the door. Miron was sitting on the windowsill with his long sheepskin unbuttoned, smiling into his chestnut beard. His short whitish eyelashes were fluffy with frost and his big brown freckles had turned grey from the cold. A group of younger Cossacks had gathered in a circle, winking and grinning as they listened to Avdeich, nicknamed the Braggart, who stood in the middle, his blue-topped and silver-crossed guardsman's busby perched on his balding pate, his unageing face as full and ruddy as a winter pippin.

The same age as Pantelei, Avdeich had once served in the Ataman's Life Guards. He had joined up as Ivan Avdeich Sinilin and come back as the Braggart. He was the first Cossack from the village to be recruited to the Ata-man's regiment. It had had a strange effect upon him. He had grown up like any other lad with a quirk or two. But when he came back from his army service the quirky element had snowballed. From the day he came home he began to tell the most fantastic tales about his service at the royal court and about his extraordinary adventures in St. Petersburg. His astonished audience at first listened open-mouthed, taking it all in good faith, but then they discovered that Avdeich was a liar such as the village had not seen since the day of its foundation; he was openly laughed at but he never blushed, even when caught out in monstrous fabrications (or perhaps he did blush but his face was always too ruddy to show it). Nor did he stop telling tall stories. When cornered, he would take offence and get fighting mad, but if people merely chuckled quietly, he would fly away into the realms of fantasy and not even notice his listeners' mocking remarks.

He was a working Cossack and a good farmer, managed his affairs sensibly, with a trick or two up his sleeve, but when it came to telling about his service with the Guards, he was incorrigible: people just held their sides for laughter.

Avdeich stood in the middle of the group, swaying to and fro in his worn-down felt boots and surveying the jostling throng around him. He spoke in a deep, imposing voice.

'Nowadays the Cossacks are nothing like they used to be. Only half-grown, they are. You could split any of 'em in half with a good sneeze. Well, to cut a long story short,' with a disdainful smile he put his boot down on a gobbet of spit, 'in the stanitsa of Vyoshenskaya I had the chance of seeing some dead men's bones. Ay, they were real Cossacks in those days!'

'Where did you dig 'em up, Avdeich?' a clean-shaven Cossack asked, nudging his neighbour.

'Why don't you stop lying for once, man, just for the sake of the coming Saint's Day?' Pantelei put in, wrinkling his hooked nose and tugging at his ear-ring. He had no liking for this windbag.

'I never tell a lie, chum,' Avdeich said impressively and stared wonderingly at Anikei, who was already shaking as if from fever. 'I saw the bones when we built a house for my brother-in-law. We found a grave when we were laying the foundation. So in the old days there must have been a graveyard here by the Don, next to the church.'

'What about bones then?' Pantelei asked gruffly, making for the door.

'There was an arm—like this,' Avdeich spread his rake-like arms, 'and a head—it's the honest truth, believe me—as big as an army cooking pot.'

'Come on, Avdeich, you'd do better to tell us the story of how you caught a brigand in St. Petersburg when you were young,' Miron suggested sliding off the windowsill and drawing his sheepskin round him.

'What is there to tell?' Avdeich became suddenly modest.

'Tell us!'

'Yes, go on!'

'Do us the honour, Avdeich!'

'Well, this is how it happened,' Avdeich cleared his throat and took a pouch out of his trousers pocket. He sprinkled some tobacco into his cupped palm, put back a couple of coins that had fallen out with the tobacco, and surveyed his listeners blissfully. 'A great villain had escaped from the fortress. The authorities were searching for him everywhere but couldn't find him. Run off their feet they were. He'd simply vanished and that was that! In the middle of the night I was summoned to the guard-room by the duty officer, and when I got there, what do you think he says? "Go at once to the royal chambers," he says. "His Imperial Majesty himself wants to see you." That scared me a bit, of course, but in I went. And there I was, standing at attention, but His Majesty graciously claps me on the shoulder and says, "Now, look here, Avdeich," he says, "the worst enemy of our empire has escaped and you've got to find him, even if you have to burrow underground. And if you don't find him, you'd better not show your face in here." "Very good, Your Imperial Majesty," I says. Well, that was a headache for me, lads, I can tell you. I took three of the finest horses from the tsar's stables and off I went.' Avdeich lighted a cigarette, surveyed the drooping heads of his listeners and with new inspiration boomed on out of the cloud of smoke that enveloped his face. 'I galloped all day, I galloped all night. And on the third day, near Moscow I caught him. So I pops him into the carriage and back we go. I arrives at midnight, up to the eyes in mud, and goes straight to the Emperor himself. Of course, there were all sorts of princes and counts trying not to let me in, but I took no notice of them. Well, I knocks at the door. "May I come in, Your Imperial Majesty." "Who is it?" he asked. "It's me, Ivan Avdeich Sinilin," I says. And then there was a fine old how-do-you-do! I could hear the

Emperor himself shouting, "Maria Fyodorovna, Maria Fyodorovna, get up quick and light the samovar. Avdeich is here!"'

An explosion of laughter rose from the back of the room. The clerk, who had been reading out notices about lost and found cattle, stumbled over the phrase, 'the left leg is stockinged down to the ankle.' The ataman craned his neck forward like a goose, peering at the guffawing Cossacks.

Avdeich jerked his hat forward. His face clouded and his eyes wandered uncertainly from one to another of his listeners.

'Just a minute!'

'Haw! haw! haw!'

'He'll be the death of us!'

'Ho! ho! ho!'

'Avdeich, you bald bastard, ho! ho!'

' "Light the samovar, Avdeich is here!" How d'you like that!'

The assembly broke up and a continuous creaking rose from the frozen wooden steps of the porch as the Cossacks jostled down them. In the trampled snow outside, Stepan Astakhov and a tall lean Cossack, the owner of the windmill, were wrestling to get warm.

'Throw the merry miller!' the onlookers round them urged. 'Shake the millings out of him, Stepan!'

'No scragging! You're too clever by half!' old Kashulin shouted excitedly, hopping around them like a sparrow and in his excitement failed to notice the large glistening drop dangling from the tip of his bluish-grey nose.

VIII

When he got back from the meeting, Pantelei went straight to the side-room that he and his wife occupied. Ilyinichna had not been well lately. There was pain in her tired puffy face. She was sitting up in bed on a high feather mattress with a pillow under her back. At the sound of familiar footsteps she turned her head and looked at her husband with the sternness that had long since taken possession of her face. Her gaze rested on the damp matted curls of his beard and moustache and her nostrils quivered, but the only smell that came from the old man was of frost and sour sheepskin. He's sober today, she thought, and laid down her knitting contentedly on the soft mound of her stomach.

'What have they decided about the wood-cutting?'

'It's to be on Thursday,' Pantelei smoothed down his moustache. 'Thursday, first thing in the morning,' he added, seating himself on the chest beside the bed. 'Well, how do you feel? Any better?'

A shadow of reticence fell upon his wife's face.

'About the same... Aches and pains in my joints.'

'I told you, you foolish woman, not to get into that water in autumn. Stay out of trouble when you know where it lies!' Pantelei burst out, scratching broad circles on the floor with his stick. 'Haven't we enough women in this house? Damn and blast your hemp! You had to do it and now... God almighty!'

'We can't afford to waste hemp. Who else was there? Grisha was out ploughing with Natalya. Petro and Darya had gone off somewhere.'

The old man leaned forward, breathing into his cupped palms.

'How's Natalya?'

Ilyinichna livened up and a note of anxiety came into her voice.

'I just don't know what to do. She was crying again the other day. When I went out into the yard I noticed someone had left the barn-door open. So I thought I'd go and close it. And there she was by the millet bin. "What is it, lovey?" I says. "I've got a head-ache, Mother," she says. It's no good expecting the truth, you know.'

'Mebbe she's ailing?'

'No, I've asked her... Either someone's put a spell on her or it's Grishka.'

'He's not carrying on with that other one again, is he?'

'Goodness, no! What a thing to say!' Ilyinichna threw up her hands in alarm. 'What do you take Stepan for—a fool? I haven't noticed anything like that.'

The old man stayed with her a while, then left the room.

Grigory was in his room, sharpening some fish hooks with a file. Natalya was smearing them with pork dripping and carefully wrapping each one in a piece of cloth. Pantelei gave her a keen look as he limped past. A faint flush lingered in her sallow cheeks, as in an autumn leaf. In a month she had grown noticeably thinner and there was something new and pitiful in the expression of her eyes. The old man stopped in the doorway. So that's the way he takes care of his wife, he thought, and glanced back at Natalya's smoothly combed head bowed over the bench.

Grigory was sitting by the window. The tousled black hair on his forehead jerked with each stroke of the file.

'Drop that, damn you!' Pantelei shouted, turning suddenly purple with rage, and gripped his stick to keep his hand in check.

Grigory gave a start and looked up at his father in surprise.

'I was trying to sharpen both points, Dad.'

'Drop it, I tell you! Get things ready for the wood-cutting!'

'I won't be a minute.'

'The sledges are all falling to bits and he sits there filing hooks,' the old man said more calmly. He lingered at the door for a moment, as if he had something else to say, then went out. He vented the rest of his anger on Petro.

As Grigory pulled on his coat, he heard his father shouting in the yard.

'The animals haven't been watered yet! What are you thinking about, you lazy bugger?.. And who's been at that rick by the fence? Didn't I tell you not to touch it? You'll use up all the best hay, you wasters. Then what will you have to feed up the oxen with for the spring ploughing?'

On Thursday Ilyinichna wakened Darya about two hours before daybreak.

'Get up, it's time to light the stove.'

Darya darted to the stove in nothing but her shift, found some matches in the cupboard and lighted the fire.

'Hurry up with the cooking,' Petro urged his wife, blinking sleepily through his tousled locks, and coughed as he lighted a cigarette.

'They don't wake Natalya. She sleeps as long as she likes, the shameless hussy. Do you expect me to break my back?' Darya grumbled sleepily.

'Go and wake her up,' Petro advised.

Natalya was up already. She pulled on a jacket and went to the shed for fuel.

'Bring some more kindling,' her sister-in-law commanded.

'Tell Dunya to go for the water. D'you hear, Darya?' Ilyinichna called, shuffling about the kitchen painfully.

The kitchen smelled of fresh yeast, leather harness and human warmth. Darya darted about in her floppy felt boots, clattering the iron pots and pans; she had rolled up her sleeves and her small taut breasts quivered under her pink shirt. Married life had not sallowed her; tall and slender, and supple as a willow branch, she still looked like a girl. She walked with a flick of the shoulders and a twist of the hips, laughed at her husband's bellowings, and a row of small close-set teeth showed under the thin curve of her shrewish lips.

'You'd better have put the dung-bricks in the stove yesterday evening. They'd have dried out overnight,' Ilyinichna grumbled testily.

'I forgot, Mother. More's the pity,' Darya answered for them all.

It was light by the time they had cooked breakfast. Old Pantelei ate in haste, burning his mouth on the thin gruel. Grigory chewed gloomily, the muscles working in his cheeks. When his father was not looking, Petro amused himself by teasing Dunya, whose cheek was bandaged because of tooth-ache.

From all over the village came the scrape of sledge runners. Ox-drawn sledges were making their way down to the Don in the grey murk of dawn. Grigory and Petro went out to harness up. Grigory muffled his throat in the soft scarf Natalya had given him before they married, and gulped in the dry, frosty air. A raven cawed lustily over the yard and the rustle of its slowly flapping wings sounded clearly in the frosty stillness. Petro watched it for a moment.

'It's making for the south, where it's warm,' he said.

Behind a small, pink cloud, as merry as a girl's smile, the thin edge of the young moon glimmered in the sky, and the rearing smoke from the chimney reached up with its one arm for that golden, inaccessibly distant pointed blade of light.

Near the Melekhov farm the Don was not yet frozen over. Greenish, snow-ridged ice was spreading from the bank and the water outside the grip of the main current was already bubbling and cleaving to it, while further out, beyond the middle, where the springs rose from below the Black Ravine on the left bank, a dangerous and enticing pool showed up darkly amid the white snowdrifts, its surface freckled with the busily diving wild duck that were wintering there.

The sledges began their journey from the square.

Pantelei drove off behind an older pair of oxen without waiting for his sons. Petro and Grigory followed soon after. At the slope down to the river they caught up with Anikei. He had driven his axe with its fine new handle into the side of the sledge and with a broad green sash wound around his waist was striding along beside his oxen. His wife, a puny ailing little woman, had taken the reins.

While still at a distance Petro shouted, 'Taking the wife with you, neighbour?'

Anikei, always ready for a laugh, skipped over to the brothers' sledge.

'Sure, I am. To keep me warm.'

'You won't get much warmth out of her.'

'I keep feeding her on oats, but she don't get any fatter.'

'Are we cutting in the same strip as you?' Grigory asked, jumping off the sledge.

'Yes, if you'll give me a smoke.'

'You're a one for cadging!'

'The sweetest things on earth are what you beg or steal,' Anikei chuckled, wrinkling his bare womanish face in a smile.

They drove on together. The forest stood white and stern in its lacework of frost. Anikei took the lead, flicking the overhanging branches with his whip and bringing bunches of crisp, prickly snow down on his muffled wife.

'Don't play about, you devil!' she cried, shaking herself.

'Push her nose in a snow-drift!' Petro shouted, trying to get his whip under the oxen's bellies to liven their pace.

At a turn in the road they met Stepan Astakhov. He was driving a pair of unharnessed oxen back to the village. His patched felt boots squeaked on the snow as he strode along with a curly frost-rimed lock of hair dangling from under his tall sheepskin cap.

'What's up, Stepan? Did you lose your way?' Anikei shouted as they passed.

'Like hell, I did! The sledge hit a stump and one of the runners has split right in half. Now I've got to go back—' Stepan swore violently and narrowed his fierce, light eyes at Petro as he walked past.

'What about your sledge?' Anikei shouted, turning round.

Stepan waved him aside and cracked his whip to bring the oxen back on to the track. He gave Grigory a long hard look as he passed. A little further on, Grigory saw the sledge that Stepan had abandoned in the middle of the road. Aksinya was standing beside it. She was watching the approaching sledges, her left hand holding the skirt of a fine fur-trimmed winter coat.

'Out of the way or I'll ride you down. Oho, what a wife, but she's not mine!' Anikei roared.

Aksinya stepped back smiling and sat down on the broken sledge.

'You've got yours with you.'

'Ay, she sticks to me like a burr in a pig's tail. Otherwise I'd give you a lift.'

'Thank you kindly.'

Petro glanced back at Grigory as they passed her. There was a rather wary smile on his face; alarm and expectation showed in every movement.

'Good morning to you, neighbour,' Petro greeted her, touching his cap with his glove.

'The Lord be praised.'

'So you've had an accident?'

'Yes, we have,' Aksinya answered slowly, turning away and rising as Grigory came up. 'Grigory Panteleyevich, I'd like to speak to you.'

Grigory turned towards her, shouting to Petro as he drove on, 'Keep an eye on my oxen.'

'Well, well!' Petro leered and tucked a bitter, tobacco-stained whisker into his mouth.

They stood facing each other in silence. Aksinya glanced round anxiously, then let her dark, liquid eyes rest on Grigory. Shame and joy were burning her cheeks, parching her lips. Her breath came in short, quick gasps.

The two sledges dropped out of sight behind a brown thicket of young oak-trees. Grigory looked straight into Aksinya's eyes and saw them flare wilfully, recklessly.

'Do what you like with me, Grisha, but I can't live without you,' she said firmly, and waited tight-lipped for his answer.

He said nothing. The forest stood fettered by the silence. His ears rang in the glassy void. The gleaming track polished by sledge runners, the grey rag of the sky, the mute forest in its deathly sleep... A sudden throaty call from a raven close by seemed to waken Grigory from a momentary drowsiness. He looked up. The burnished black-feathered bird had soared and its wings were waving farewell as it flew silently away. He was surprised when he heard himself say, 'It's going to be warm. It's flying to the warm lands.' He roused himself and laughed hoarsely... 'Well then?' Furtively, lowering his intoxicated eyes, he snatched Aksinya to him.

IX

It was a mixed bunch that gathered in Stokman's room at cross-eyed Lukeshka's in the evenings. Khristonya came, and from the mill there was Knave with his greasy jacket draped over his shoulders, the grinning Davydka, who had been at a loose end for three months, and the engine man, Ivan Alexeyevich Kotlyarov; Filka the cobbler turned up occasionally and Mishka Koshevoi, a young Cossack who had not yet done his active service, was a regular guest.

At first they played cards, then Stokman produced a slim volume of Nekrasov's verse. They started reading it aloud and it went down well. The next step was Nikitin and around Christmastime Stokman suggested that they should read a tattered notebook that had lost its cover. Koshevoi, who had been to a church school and did some of the reading, surveyed the greasy pages.

'You could make noodles out of it! It's greasy enough.'

Khristonya roared with laughter and Davydka grinned dazzlingly, but Stokman waited for the laughter to subside, and said, 'Read us some of it, Misha. It's interesting, about the Cossacks.'

Koshevoi bent his fair tousled head over the table and read out the title.

'A Short History of the Don Cossacks.' He surveyed his listeners, frowning expectantly.

'Go on,' said Ivan Alexeyevich.

They wrestled with it for three evenings. First they read about Pugachov, about Cossack freedom, about Stenka Razin and Kondraty Bulavin, and then they came to more recent times. The unknown author derided the poor life the Cossacks led now in clear and scathing terms. He poked fun at the administration, the tsarist authorities, and the Cossacks themselves, who had hired themselves out as the punitive troops of the monarchy. Tempers rose and they began to argue. Khristonya boomed his remarks, head touching the main beam of the ceiling. Stokman sat by the door, smoking a cigarette in his ringed bone cigarette-holder, only his eyes smiling.

'It's true! Fair said!' Khristonya pronounced.

'The Cossacks didn't bring this shame on themselves. It was forced on 'em,' Koshevoi spread his arms indignantly and a frown wrinkled his handsome dark-eyed face.

He was stockily built, as broad in the thighs as in the shoulders; the firm brick-coloured neck was mounted on a cast-iron foundation, and on such a neck it was strange to see a quite small, beautifully poised head with feminine lines in the softly coloured cheeks, a small obstinate mouth and dark eyes under a golden shock of curly hair. The engine man Ivan Alexeyevich, a tall big-boned Cossack, argued fiercely. Cossack traditions were ingrained in every fibre of his bony body. He defended the Cossacks and hammered Khristonya, his round prominent eyes flashing.

'You've grown just like a muzhik, Khristonya. And don't argue! There's only one measly drop of Cossack blood for every pail of muzhik blood in you. Your mother got you from a Voronezh egg-trader.'

'You're a fool! A real fool, man!' the big guardsman boomed. 'I'm sticking up for the truth!'

'I didn't serve in the Ataman's regiment,' Ivan Alexeyevich replied pointedly. 'That's where all the fools are.'

'There're plenty of thick-heads in other regiments.'

'Belt up, muzhik!'

'Muzhiks are human beings, aren't they?'

'Muzhiks are muzhiks, made of bast and stuffed with straw.'

'I saw all kinds, mate, while I was serving in Petersburg. A funny thing happened to me once,' Khristonya went on. 'We were on duty at the tsar's palace, standing guard over his chambers, inside and out. The outside guard used to ride along the wall, two this way and two that. When we met we'd ask if everything was quiet, no rebellions like. And when we got the answer, "All quiet", we'd ride on. But never any stopping and talking—not on your life! They chose us for our looks. When they picked a pair for the doors, they'd try to have 'em alike. Dark with dark, fair with fair. And not just the colour of their hair, but even their faces. I myself had to go to the barber's and have my beard dyed because of that bull-shit. It was my turn to be paired up with Nikifor Meshcheryakov—a Cossack from Tepikinskaya in our squadron—a bay he was. Damned if I know what made his hair like that at the temples; flaming red it was. But anyway they couldn't find another one like him in any of the squadrons. So our Lieutenant Barkin, he says to me, "Go to the barber's and have your beard and moustache dyed at once." Well, they did it for me, and when I looked in the glass, my heart sank into my boots. I thought I was on fire! When I touched that beard, it well-nigh burnt my fingers! Phew!'

'Grind away, organ-grinder! What are you talking about now?' Ivan Alexeyevich cut in.

'About the people, that's what.'

'Well, tell us about 'em then. Because right now you're stuck on your beard—and a fat lot of use that is to us!'

'That's what I'm telling you! Well, once we had to ride out on guard duty. Me and one of my mates. And round the corner comes a whole lot of students. Hordes of 'em! And at the sight of us they start caterwauling. Boo! Boo! And before we knew where we were, they'd surrounded us. "What are you riding around for, Cossacks?" "We're on guard duty," I says. "Now then, let go of my reins, keep your hands off!" And I reached for my sword. "Don't you worry, Cossack," he says, "I'm from Kamenskaya stanitsa myself. I'm only here to study at the uni— the university," or whatever it is. So we rode on and then one fellow with a long nose takes a tenner out of his wallet and says, "Here, have a drink, Cossacks, to the health of my late father." He gives us the tenner and takes a picture out of his bag. "Here's a portrait of my father," he says. "You can have it as a keepsake." Well, we took it, of course, it would have been a shame not to. The students moved off with more booing. And we rode away to the Nevsky Prospekt. And then a lieutenant rides out of the back gate of the palace with his troop and comes straight at us. "What's going on?" he says. So I says, "The students surrounded us and started talking. In accordance with regulations we were going to cut them down, but then they let us go, so we rode away." Well, when we were relieved, we says to the sergeant-major, "We've just earned ten rubles and we've got to spend it drinking to the memory of this old feller here." And we shows him the picture. So the sergeant-major brings in the vodka that evening and we have a binge for the next two days, and afterwards it all turned out to be a trick. That student, the scallawag, instead of giving us his father's picture had slipped us a picture of the biggest rebel that ever was, and a German at that! And for conscience's sake I'd gone and hung it up over my bed in his memory. He looked all right, with his grey beard, might have been a merchant or something, but the lieutenant, he spots it and asks me, "Where did you get that picture, you so-and-so?" Well, I told him. And he starts lamming into me, first across one cheek, then the other. 'Do you know,' he says, "that's their ataman Karl—"

Oh darn it, I've forgotten his other name. What was it now, if only I could remember...'

'Karl Marx?' Stokman suggested, barely suppressing a smile.

'That's it! Karl Marx!' Khristonya burst out joyfully. 'Let me in for it properly, he did... Sometimes, you know, the tsarevich Alexei came into that guardroom with his tutors. Suppose he'd seen it? What'd have happened then?'

'And you keep praising the muzhiks. They certainly led you up the garden path,' Ivan Alexeyevich chuckled.

'Still, we had a tenner's worth of booze out of him. Maybe we drank for the bearded Karl, but it was a good booze-up.'

'He deserves a toast,' Stokman said smiling, and fingered one of the rings of his nicotine-stained cigarette-holder.

'What's he done to deserve it?' Koshevoi asked.

'I'll tell you that another time. It's too late now.' Stokman knocked the butt of the cigarette out of the holder with his palm.

After much sifting and selection a group of ten Cossacks was formed and began to meet regularly in the tumbledown shack. Stokman was the leading spirit and he made straight for a goal that was known to him alone. Like a worm boring into wood, he undermined simple notions and habits, instilling dislike and hatred of the existing system. At first he encountered the cold steel of distrust, but instead of retreating he gnawed through it.

He had dropped the larva of discontent. Who was to know that in four years' time a strong and hardy embryo would emerge from its crumbling walls?

X

The stanitsa of Vyoshenskaya, the oldest of the upper Don stanitsas, stands on the sloping sandy left bank of the Don. Once the stanitsa of Chigonaki, sacked in the time of Peter I, it grew up again on a new site and was renamed Vyoshenskaya, which meant 'landmark', for it was then a landmark on the great waterway between Voronezh and the Azov Sea.

At Vyoshenskaya the Don bends like the stem of a Tatar bow. At first it seems about to swing away to the right, but a little further on, at the village of Bazki it straightens out again majestically and carries its greenish, blue-tinted waters past the chalky bluffs of the right-bank hills, past the villages that line the right bank, past the lonely stanitsas of the left bank, and on to the sea, the blue Sea of Azov.

At Ust-Khopyorskaya it joins the Khopyor, at Ust-Medveditskaya, the Medveditsa, and then flows on full-watered amid the riotous growth of populous villages and stanitsas of the lower reaches.

Vyoshenskaya was buried in yellow sand. A dreary, balding place with no orchards. The square was dominated by an ancient church, grey with age, and from here six streets followed the course of the Don. Where the Don swung away towards Bazki, a channel branching off into a poplar grove formed a lake that was as wide as the river itself in the dry season. The end of the lake was the end of the stanitsa. In a smaller square, overgrown with prickly golden thorn bushes, stood another church with green domes and a green roof matching the green of the poplars on the other side of the lake.

Beyond the stanitsa to the north lay a stunted pine grove, backwaters that were pink from the red clay of the soil, and a saffron flood of sands rolling away into the distance. Here and there a village, a grove of trees, a rusty scrub of willows stood out like an island amid the waves of sand.

One Sunday in December a dense crowd of some five hundred young Cossacks from all the villages of the district gathered in the square around the ancient church. The mass was nearly over and the bells were ringing for the anthem. A senior sergeant, a gallant old Cossack with long-service stripes, gave the order to fall in. The noisy crowd spread out and formed up in two long straggling lines. The sergeants ran to and fro, straightening out the wavy ranks.

'Ranks!' the senior sergeant drew out the word in a long shout and then, with a vague gesture, commanded, 'Form fours!'

The ataman in full dress, a new officer's greatcoat, and jingling spurs, marched into the churchyard, followed by the chief of military police.

Grigory Melekhov was standing in line next to Mitka Korshunov and they talked in whispers.

'My boot's pinching me something awful,' Mitka complained.

'Stick it out and they'll make you an ataman.'

'They'll be marching us inside soon.'

As if to confirm his words, the senior sergeant stepped back and swung round on his heels.

'Right turn!'

Five hundred pairs of booted feet responded with a sharp double thump.

'Right wheel, quick march!'

The column streamed through the open gate, hats were snatched off, and the church was filled to the dome with the tramp of marching feet.

Grigory did not listen to a word of the oath of allegiance that was being read out by the priest. He was watching Mitka's agonised face as he hopped about trying to relieve the pressure on his imprisoned foot. Grigory's raised hand began to go numb, thoughts swirled murkily through his head. As he approached the cross and kissed the silver, which was already moist from many mouths, he thought of Aksinya and his wife. Then, as if by a flash of forked lightning, his thoughts were slashed by a brief moment of recall: the forest, the brown tree-trunks in their splendid white raiments, and the hot, liquid glow of Aksinya's dark eyes under her fluffy shawl.

They came out into the square and formed up again. The senior sergeant blew his nose, wiped his fingers surreptitiously on the hem of his uniform, and began his speech.

'Now you're no longer boys, but Cossacks. You've taken the oath and so you ought to understand what's what. Now that you've grown up to be Cossacks, you must guard your honour, obey your parents, and all the rest of it. When you were boys, you used to fool about, played tip-cat in the street, I expect, but now that's all over and you've got to think about your future service in the army. In a year from now you'll be due for active service.' At this point the sergeant blew his nose again, shook his hand clean and, pulling on a fluffy rabbit-wool glove, concluded, 'And your father or mother, as the case may be, must give some thought to getting together your equipment. They must make sure you've got a proper army horse. And, in general... Well now, lads, off you go home and Godspeed!'

Grigory and Mitka waited by the bridge for the other lads from their village and they all set out for home together. They took the path along the bank. Smoke was melting into the sky over the chimneys of Bazki and a bell was ringing faintly. Mitka limped along behind, leaning on a knotty stake he had broken out of a fence.

'Take your boot off,' one of the lads suggested.

'And get frostbite?' Mitka said dubiously, lagging still further behind.

'You can keep your sock on.'

Mitka sat down in the snow, tugged his boot off, and walked on awkwardly in his sock, leaving the clear imprint of the thick crocheted wool in the crisp snow.

'What road shall we take?' asked short, stumpy Alexei Beshnyak.

'Along the Don,' Grigory answered for the others.

They walked on, chattering and pushing one another off the road.

By mute agreement each one, in turn, was pulled down and crushed into the snow, while the others piled on top of him. Between Bazki and the village of Gromkovsky, Mitka spotted a wolf picking its way across the Don.

'Look, lads—a wolf! There he goes!'

'Halloo!'

'Oho!'

The wolf loped on for a few yards and halted, standing sideways not far from the other bank.

'After him!'

'Boo!'

'Rotten devil!'

'Mitka, you're the one he's staring at because you're walking in your sock.'

'See the way he stands sideways on, he can't turn his head with that great scruff on him.'

'Ay, proper stiff-necked he is.'

'Look! Off he goes!'

The beast stood motionless and grey, as if carved out of rock, its tail sticking straight out. Then it sprang hurriedly aside and trotted towards the willows fringing the bank.

It was dusk by the time they reached the village. Grigory walked along the ice to his own lane and climbed up to the gate. A sledge lay abandoned in the yard; some sparrows were chirping in a heap of brushwood by the fence. The air smelled of habitation, charred wood, and the warm steamy stench of the cattle sheds.

As he climbed the steps of the porch Grigory glanced through the window. The lamp hanging from the ceiling cast a dim yellow light. Petro was standing with his back to the window. Grigory brushed the snow off his boots and stepped into the kitchen in a cloud of steam.

'Hullo! I'm back.'

'You've been quick. It's cold outside, eh?' Petro's answer was hasty and not quite natural.

Pantelei was sitting with his elbows on his knees and his head bowed. Darya had her foot on the treadle of a spinning wheel and was making it hum. Natalya was standing at the table with her back to Grigory and did not turn. Grigory's eyes scanned the kitchen and came to rest on Petro. From the anxious look on his face he realised that something had happened.

'Did you take the oath?'

'Uh-huh!'

Grigory removed his coat slowly, playing for time and running over in his mind all the possibilities that might have led to this chilly and silent reception.

Ilyinichna came in from the front room, a sad and worried look on her face.

'It's Natalya,' Grigory thought as he sat down on the bench beside his father.

'Get him his supper,' Ilyinichna said to Darya with a glance at Grigory.

Darya checked the song of the spinning wheel and went to the stove with a barely perceptible swing in her shoulders and slim girlish waist. The kitchen was choked with a silence broken only by the snuffing of a goat and its newborn, which had been brought in for the warmth.

Grigory glanced at Natalya as he ate, but could not see her face. She was sitting sideways to him with her head bowed over her knitting. Pantelei was the first to break under the strain of the general silence.

He cleared his throat in a deliberate, rasping way and said, 'Natalya is talking about going back to her parents.'

Grigory rolled some breadcrumbs into a ball and said nothing.

'Why is that?' his father asked, his lower lip quivering (the first sign of the frenzy that was about to break loose).

'I don't know why.' Grigory's eyes narrowed as he stood up, pushing the bowl aside and crossing himself.

'But I know!' his father said, raising his voice.

'Don't shout! Don't shout!' Ilyinichna broke in. 'I know why!'

'Now there's no need for all this fuss.' Petro stepped away from the window into the middle of the room. 'It's up to her. If she wants to live here she's welcome; if not, let her go and God be with her.'

'I'm not blaming her. Though it's a disgrace and a sin against God, I don't blame her; she's not the one that's to blame. It's him—that bastard!' And Pantelei pointed at Grigory, who had moved away and was leaning against the stove.

'But what have I done?'

'You mean to say you don't know... Don't you know, you devil?'

'No, I don't.'

Pantelei jumped up, knocking the bench over as he did so, and came close up to Grigory. Natalya dropped the stocking she had been knitting and the needle fell with a pinging clatter; in response to the sound a kitten sprang down from the ledge over the stove and with its head tilted to one side curved its paw and tapped the ball of wool towards the chest.

'Now this is what I have to say to you,' the old man began in a clear, restrained voice. 'If you don't want to live with Natalya, you can get out—go where your fancy takes you! That's all I have to say! Go where your fancy takes you!' he repeated in a calm ordinary voice and turned away, picking up the bench as he did so.

Dunyashka sat on the bed, her frightened eyes darting this way and that.

'And I say this to you, Father, but don't be angry,' Grigory's voice quivered huskily. 'I didn't marry Natalya; it was you who married me off. And I won't hold her. Let her go back to her father if she wants to.'

'And you get out too!'

'I will.'

'Go to the devil then!'

'I'm going. You needn't be in such a hurry!' Grigory reached out for the sleeve of the coat that he had dropped on the bed. His nostrils were flared and he was shaking with the same boiling anger as his father.

The same blood, laced with that of the Turk, flowed in their veins, and at that moment they were unbelievably alike.

'Where can you go?' Ilyinichna wailed, seizing Grigory's arm, but he pushed his mother roughly away and caught his cap with a quick snatch as it rolled off the bed.

'Let him go, the randy dog! Let him go, and be damned! Here you are, get out!' the old man thundered, throwing the door wide open.

Grigory strode onto the porch and the last he heard was the sound of Natalya's sobbing.

The night was frosty. Needle-sharp snow was falling from the black sky and from time to time the ice on the Don cracked and rumbled like gunfire. Grigory ran out of the gate, panting. Dogs were barking discordantly at the other end of the village. The darkness rose before him in a haze riddled with yellow pinpoints of light.

He walked aimlessly down the street. The windows of Stepan's house reflected the darkness like black diamonds.

'Grisha!' Natalya's sorrowful cry came from the gate.

'Go to hell, I'm sick of you!' Grigory muttered, gritting his teeth and walking on faster.

'Grisha, come back!'

Grigory turned his uncertain steps into the next lane and the bitter cry reached him for the last time, muffled by the distance, 'Grisha, darling!'

He crossed the square quickly and stopped at the fork, considering the names of the friends with whom he might be able to spend the night.

He decided on Mikhail Koshevoi. Mikhail lived on the outskirts, at the foot of the hill; the whole family consisted of him and his mother, a spinster sister, and two small brothers. Grigory entered the yard and tapped on the tiny window of the mud-walled cottage.

'Who is it?'

'Is Mikhail at home?'

'Yes. But who is it?'

'Me, Grigory Melekhov.'

A minute later Mikhail himself, roused from the sweet slumber of early night, opened the door.

'You, Grisha?'

'Yes.'

'What do you want at this time of night?'

'Let me in and we'll talk.'

In the porch Grigory gripped Mikhail's elbow and, furious with himself for not being able to find the right words, whispered, 'I want to stay the night with you... I've had a row with my people... I know you haven't got much room... Anywhere'll do.'

'We'll find room for you, don't worry. What was the trouble about?'

'Oh, that can wait... Where's your door? I can't see a thing.'

They made up a bed for Grigory on a bench. He pulled his coat over his head to keep out the whispering between Mikhail's mother and her daughter, who slept together in the same bed.

What was going on at home? Would Natalya really leave? Life was going to take a new turn for him. Where should he lay his head now? And the answer was not long in suggesting itself, 'I'll ask Aksinya tomorrow and we'll go away together to the Kuban, as far away from here as we can get.'

Steppeland hills, villages and stanitsas that he had never seen or loved rolled by before Grigory's eyes. And beyond those hills, at the end of that grey road, as in a fairy-tale, there rose a welcoming, sky-blue land and with it, for good measure, Aksinya's love, in all its late rebellious flower.

He fell asleep, troubled by a sense of the approaching unknown. As he dozed off he tried vainly to grasp the half-formed idea that was weighing on his mind. His thoughts flowed on smoothly in this half sleep, like a boat borne along by the current, but suddenly they would stop as if caught on a sandbank, and with a sick feeling of uneasiness he would struggle to guess what it was. 'What is it? What's in my way?'

And in the morning, as soon as he awoke, he remembered: 'My army service! How can I take Aksinya anywhere! In spring I'll be going to camp, and in autumn I'll start my active service... That's the snag!'

He ate his breakfast and called Mikhail out into the porch.

'Go to the Astakhovs for me, Misha. Tell Aksinya to come out to the windmill as soon it gets dusk.'

'What about Stepan?' Mikhail looked doubtful.

'Pretend you've come to see him about something.'

'All right, I'll go.'

'And remember to tell her she must come.'

'All right.'

That evening he sat by the windmill, smoking into his sleeve. Behind the mill the wind hissed and stumbled through the dead maize stalks. A torn strip of canvas was flapping on the moored sails. To Grigory it was like a big bird circling above him, flapping its wings and unable to fly away. Still Aksinya did not come. The west was bathed in the dim lilac gold of the sunset. From the east the wind blew faster and harder and the darkness swooped down, overtaking the moon trapped in the willows. The bruised, bluish-red sky grew deathly dark over the mill; the last murmurs of fretful day rose from the village.

Grigory smoked three cigarettes one after the other,

stubbed out the last in the trampled snow and looked round in angry misery. The half-thawed tracks from the mill to the village showed up like black tar. There was no one in sight. He stood up, stretched his shoulders until they cracked, and headed for the light that twinkled invitingly in the window of Mikhail's cottage. As he walked up to the yard, whistling through his teeth, he came face to face with Aksinya. She had been running or at least walking very fast. Her face was flushed and her fresh chilled mouth smelled of either the wind or a distant, barely recognisable scent of fresh steppeland hay.

'I waited so long. I thought you wouldn't come.'

'It was Stepan. I've only just managed to get him out of the house.'

'You've chilled me to the bone, you bitch.'

'I'm hot, I'll warm you.' She threw open the folds of her fur-trimmed coat and twined herself round him, like wild hops round an oak. 'What did you call me out for?'

'Wait a bit, let go... There may be people about.'

'You've fallen out with your family?'

'I've left home. I spent last night at Mishka's... I'm living like a stray dog.'

'What will you do now, then?' Aksinya released Grigory and pulled the coat round her with a shiver. 'Let's go by the fence. We can't stand in the middle of the road like this.'

They stepped off the road. Grigory kicked away the drifted snow and leaned back against the frozen, creaking fence.

'Do you know if Natalya has gone back home?'

'No, I don't... She should do. How can she go on living there?'

Grigory pushed Aksinya's chilled hand into his sleeve and, gripping her small wrist, asked, 'What shall we do?'

'I don't know, dearest. I'll do anything you say.'

'Will you leave Stepan?'

'Without a sigh. Now, if you like.'

'We'll get a job together, we'll find somewhere to live.'

'Oh, Grisha, I could live in a sty as long as it was with you.'

They stood for a while, keeping each other warm. Grigory didn't want to go. He stood with his face turned to the wind, nostrils quivering, eyes closed. Aksinya had tucked her face under his arm and was drinking in the sweet intoxicating smell of his sweat; hidden from

Grigory's eyes, her wanton, greedy lips quivered in a joyful smile of fulfilled happiness.

'Tomorrow I'll go and see Mokhov. Perhaps he'll take me on,' Grigory said, changing his grip on Aksinya's wrist, which had grown damp under his fingers.

Aksinya gave no answer. Nor did she raise her head. Her recent smile had vanished. Like a hunted animal, fear and misery lurked in her dilated eyes. 'Shall I tell him or not?' she wondered, thinking of her pregnancy. And just as she decided that she must tell, a spasm of fear drove the terrifying thought away. With a woman's instinct she sensed that this was not the time to speak of it, that she might lose Grigory forever. Not knowing for sure whose child it was that was beginning to stir under her heart, Grigory's or Stepan's, she allowed herself to dissemble and said nothing.

'Why did you start like that? Are you cold?' Grigory asked, opening his sheepskin and wrapping it round her.

'Yes, I am a bit... I must go, Grisha. Stepan will be after me if I'm out when he comes.'

'Where did he go?'

'He's playing cards at Anikei's. It was such a job to get him out of the house.'

They parted and that smell on her lips, of the winter wind or perhaps of steppeland hay sprinkled with May rain, stayed on Grigory's lips.

Aksinya turned off down a lane and, bending forward, almost ran. By a well, where the cattle had churned the autumn mud, she stumbled on a frozen rut and, feeling a sharp stab of pain in the belly, clutched at the posts of the fence. The pain subsided and she felt the living creature in her womb turn over and kick at her side with angry force several times in succession.

XI

The next day Grigory went to see Mokhov. The merchant had just come home from the shop for his morning tea. He was sitting with Atyopin in his dining room with its expensive imitation-oak wallpaper, sipping a strong, claret-coloured brew. Grigory left his cap in the hall and went in.

'I'd like a word with you, Sergei Platonovich.'

'Ah, you're Pantelei Melekhov's son, I believe?'

'Yes.'

167

'What can I do for you?'

'I came to ask you if you'd give me a job?'

Grigory turned as the door creaked behind him. A young officer in a green tunic with a lieutenant's insignia on the shoulder straps entered from the drawing room, carrying a folded newspaper. Grigory recognised him as the officer Mitka Korshunov had outgalloped in the race the year before.

'Why, is your father so hard-up that he sends his son out to work?'

'I'm not living with him any more.'

'You've left home?'

'Yes.'

'I would gladly take you on. I know your family, you're hard workers. But I have no vacancy.'

'What's all this about?' the lieutenant asked, sitting down at the table and eyeing Grigory.

'The lad wants a job.'

'Do you know how to look after horses? Can you drive a carriage team properly?' the lieutenant asked, stirring his tea.

'Yes, we kept six horses of our own.'

'I need a coachman. What are your terms?'

'I wouldn't ask much.'

'In that case come to my father's estate tomorrow. Do you know where the Listnitsky estate is?'

'Yes, I know it.'

'It's about twelve versts from here. Come first thing in the morning. We can settle matters there.'

Grigory hesitated for a moment and, with his hand on the door-handle, said, 'I'd like to speak to you for a minute in private, Your Honour.'

The lieutenant followed him out into the semi-dark corridor. A meagre rosy light filtered through the opaque glass of the veranda.

'What is it?'

'I'm not alone,' Grigory flushed heavily. 'I've got a woman with me. Maybe you could find a job for her too?'

'Your wife?' the lieutenant asked, raising his eyebrows, which looked pink in the dim light.

'Someone else's.'

'Ah, so that's it. Well, we can take her on as a kitchen maid. Where is her husband?'

'Here, in the village.'

'You mean you have stolen another man's wife?'

'She came of her own accord.'

'How romantic. Very well, then. Come over tomorrow. You may go now.'

Grigory arrived at Yagodnoye, the Listnitsky estate, at about eight in the morning. It lay in a dip. Behind a crumbling brick wall the outbuildings were scattered haphazardly over a large yard. There was a lodge with a tiled roof and a date, 1910, also tiled, as a centrepiece; there were servants' quarters, a bathhouse, stables, a poultry roost and cowshed, a long barn, and a coach-house. Separated from the yard by a low fence, the manor, old and rambling, stood back in an orchard. Behind it rose a grey wall of bare poplars and willows crowned with the brown caps of abandoned rooks' nests.

Grigory was greeted at the gate by a pack of black Crimean borzoi hounds. A half-lame bitch with watery, old-womanish eyes was the first to come up and sniff at Grigory, then she followed him, her lean head drooping. In the servants' quarters a cook was quarrelling with a young, freckled house-maid. By the door sat a loose-lipped old man muffled in a cloud of tobacco smoke. The maid conducted Grigory into the house. The hall stank of dogs and raw skins. A shotgun case and a game bag with a tattered fringe of green silk tassels were lying on a table.

'The young master wants to see you,' the maid said, looking out from a side-door.

Grigory glanced apprehensively at his boots and walked in.

The lieutenant was lying on a bed under the window with a box of tobacco and empty cigarette tubes in front of him on the coverlet. When he had filled a tube with tobacco, he buttoned the collar of his white shirt and said, 'You are too early. You will have to wait until my father comes down.'

Grigory stood by the door. After a minute or two the sound of shuffling footsteps came from the hall and a deep, resonant voice asked through the crack of the door.

'Are you asleep, Yevgeny?'

'Come in.'

An old man in black Caucasian felt boots entered the room. Grigory glanced sideways at him and the first thing he noticed was the fine slightly crooked nose and the broad half-moons of the white moustache beneath it, tawnied by tobacco. The old man was very tall, broad-shouldered and thin. His camel-hair morning coat hung loosely on his lean frame, and the collar was like a noose round his brown, wrinkled neck. The faded eyes were close-set.

'This is the coachman I recommended to you, Father. The lad is from a good family.'

'What family?' the old man boomed in his rumbling voice.

'Melekhov's.'

'Which Melekhov?'

'He's a son of Pantelei Melekhov.'

'I knew Prokofy. He was with me. And I know Pantelei too. He's lame, isn't he? And of Circassian origin?'

'Yes, he is lame.' Grigory drew himself stiffly to attention.

He recalled his father's stories about the retired General Listnitsky, a hero of the Russo-Turkish war.

'Why are you asking for work?' the voice boomed again from above.

'I am not living with my father, Your Excellency.'

'What kind of Cossack will you make if you hire yourself out like this? Did your father not give you anything when you left home?'

'No, Your Excellency, he didn't.'

'That's a different matter then. Do you want a job for your wife as well?'

The bed creaked suddenly. Grigory moved his eyes and noticed the lieutenant winking and shaking his head.

'Yes, Your Excellency.'

'None of that "Excellency" stuff. I don't like it! The wage is eight roubles a month. That's for both of you. Your wife will cook for the house servants and seasonal workers. Will you take it?'

'Yes.'

'You are to be here tomorrow. You will occupy the quarters where the previous coachman lived.'

'What sort of hunt did you have yesterday?' the lieutenant asked his father as he lowered his narrow feet on to a rug.

'We flushed a fine fox out of Gremyachy Ravine and chased it into the woods, but it must have been an old one. It fooled the dogs.'

'Is Kazbek still lame?'

'The leg is dislocated apparently. Hurry up, Yevgeny, breakfast is getting cold.'

The old man turned to Grigory and snapped his dry, bony fingers.

'Quick march! Mind you're here at eight o'clock to-morrow.'

Grigory walked out of the gate. By the back wall of the barn the borzois were basking on a patch of ground that had dried out after the thaw. The bitch with the old-womanish look in her eyes trotted up to Grigory, sniffed at him from behind and followed him as far as the first ravine, head drooping despondently, then turned and went back.

XII

Aksinya finished her cooking earlier than usual. She raked the embers, closed the damper in the chimney and glanced out of the small window that looked on to the yard. Stepan was examining some poles stacked near the fence between his and the Melekhovs' yard. A half-smoked cigarette hung from the corner of his firm lips; he was selecting a suitable pole from the stack. The left corner of the barn had collapsed and would have to be buttressed with two strong poles, then rethatched with any rushes that he had left.

Aksinya had woken that morning with a flush on her cheeks and a youthful brightness in her eyes. The change had not escaped Stepan's notice; at breakfast he had asked, 'What's come over you?'

'Me?' Aksinya's cheeks blazed.

'You look shiny, as if you'd been smeared with sun-flower oil.'

'The stove was so hot... It sent the blood to my face.' She turned away and her eyes darted furtively to the window to see if Mikhail Koshevoi's sister was coming.

The girl did not arrive until dusk. Worn out by the suspense, Aksinya started to her feet.

'Did you want to see me, Masha?'

'Come outside for a minute.'

Stepan was standing before a piece of looking-glass moulded into the clay breastwork of the stove. With a small comb fashioned from a bull's horn he was arrang-ing his forelock and smoothing down his chestnut moustache.

Aksinya glanced guardedly at her husband.

'Are you going out somewhere?'

Stepan did not answer at once. He put the comb away in his trousers' pocket and took a pack of cards and a pouch out of the little niche where he kept them.

'I'm going round to Anikei's for a while.'

'When'll you get tired of it? Playing cards till cockcrow every night!'

'That's enough. I've heard it all before.'

'Pontoon again?'

'Stop nagging, Aksinya. You're like a horse that's been fed on barley. There's someone wants to see you.'

Aksinya slipped out into the porch. Masha, pink and freckled, greeted her with a smile at the door.

'Grisha's at our place.'

'Well?'

'He said to tell you to come as soon as it's dark.'

Aksinya clasped the girl's hands and pushed her to the outer door.

'Not so loud, dear. What else did he say?'

'He says you're to bring all your things with you, all you can carry.'

Burning and shivering in agitation, Aksinya glanced round at the door.

'Oh God, how can I?' she stammered. 'So soon... Say I'll come... Where will he meet me?'

'Come to our house.'

'Oh, I couldn't!'

'All right then, I'll tell him and he'll come out.'

Stepan put on his uniform coat and reached up to the lamp to light a cigarette.

'What did she come about?' he asked between pulls.

'Who?'

'The Koshevois' girl.'

'Oh, she just wanted to see me ... about cutting out a skirt for her.'

Blowing the black flakes of ash off his cigarette, Stepan went to the door.

'Go to bed. Don't wait up for me.'

'All right.'

Aksinya darted to the window and, dropping on her knees, pressed her face to the frost-coated pane. She could hear the crunch of Stepan's footsteps in the snow as he walked away along the path to the gate. The wind flicked a spark from his cigarette and carried it towards the window. Through the melted spot on the pane Aksinya caught a glimpse of a gristly ear clamped under his lambskin hat and a white cheek lighted by the flaring cigarette.

She opened the chest and feverishly threw all that was

left of her dowry—skirts, jackets, kerchiefs—into a big shawl. Panting and wild-eyed, she took a last look round the kitchen, put out the light and ran on to the porch. Someone came out of the Melekhovs' house to attend to the animals. Aksinya waited until the footsteps had died away, fastened the chain on the door and ran down to the Don, clasping her bundle. Strands of hair fell loose from under her kerchief and tickled her cheeks. By the time she had reached the Koshevois' cottage by back lanes she was weak with exhaustion. Her feet felt like cast iron and she could scarcely drag them along. Grigory was waiting for her at the gate. He took the bundle and without a word led the way into the steppe.

After they had passed the threshing barn Aksinya slowed her steps and touched Grigory's sleeve.

'Wait a bit.'

'Why wait? We'd better hurry before the moon rises.'

'Wait, Grisha.' Aksinya stopped and leaned forward, shoulders sagging.

'What is it?' Grigory bent over her.

'It's... I've got a pain... I lifted something heavy the other day.' Licking her parched lips and wincing with a pain that made her see spurts of fire, Aksinya clasped her belly. She stood for a while in this pitiful posture and then, tucking her hair under her kerchief, walked on.

'It's over now. We can go.'

'You don't even ask where I'm taking you. Mebbe I'm looking for a cliff to push over?' Grigory smiled in the darkness.

'It's all the same to me now. I've got what I was asking for.' Aksinya's voice broke in a dreary little laugh.

Stepan returned home as usual at midnight. He went to the stable, forked up the hay the horse had scattered, took off the halter, and climbed the steps of the porch. She must have gone out for a gossip, he thought as he unfastened the door chain. He went into the kitchen, closed the door firmly and lighted a match. After winning at cards (they had been playing for matches), he was in a peaceful, sleepy mood. By the light of the match he stared without guessing the reason at the things scattered all over the kitchen. Rather surprised, he went to the front room. The dark mouth of the open chest gaped up at him. On the floor lay an old jacket that his wife had forgotten in her haste. Stepan tore off his coat and dashed to the kitchen for a lamp. A glance round the room told him what had happened. He flung down the lamp, and, hardly aware what he was doing, snatched his sabre off the wall and gripped the hilt until his fingers went black, then he lifted Aksinya's blue yellow-flowered jacket on the point of the sabre, tossed it in the air and with a quick stroke cut it in two.

Grey and savage in his wolfish misery, he went on tossing the sliced fragments to the ceiling and slashing them with whistling strokes of the well-honed steel. Then he tore off the sword-knot, threw the sabre into a corner, strode back to the kitchen and sat down at the table. Head lolling to one side, he sat stroking the unwashed table-top with trembling iron fingers.

XIII

Troubles never come singly. That morning, because of Hetko's carelessness Miron Grigorievich's thoroughbred bull gored the neck of his best brood-mare. Hetko ran into the house, white and shaking.

'A terrible thing, master! That bull, durn its hide...' he cried, breaking into Ukrainian.

'What's wrong with the bull? Out with it!' Miron exclaimed in alarm.

'He's ruined the mare ... gored her...'

Miron ran out into the yard without a coat. By the well Mitka was laying into a red five-year-old bull with a fence pole. The bull had lowered his head until its wrinkled dewlap brushed the snow and, as it pawed the ground and shook its head, clouds of silvery snow-dust were flung around its spiralling tail. Instead of retreating from the blows, it lowed huskily and gathered its hind legs as if to charge.

The lowing grew into a throaty bellow. Mitka hit it about the head and sides, swearing wildly. He took no notice of Mikhei, who was trying to hold him back by his belt.

'Come back, Dmitry! For the love of Christ! He'll rip your belly open, I tell you! Miron Grigorievich, why don't you stop him!'

Miron ran to the well. The mare was standing by the fence with her head hanging despondently. Her flanks were heaving and the deep black hollows under her loins were blotched with sweat. Blood was running from her neck on to the snow and over the round bulges of her chest muscles. Fine spasms raised the light bay hair on her back and sides and made the groin tremble.

Miron ran round to her front. The huge pink wound in the neck was steaming. The gash was deep enough to take a man's hand and the quivering windpipe was exposed. Miron gripped the mare's forelock and pulled her head up. Her glittering violet eye met his and seemed to ask 'What now?' Miron answered the mute question with a shout, 'Mitka! Tell 'em to scald some oak bark. Hurry!'

Hetko, his pointed Adam's apple wobbling in his dirty neck, ran to strip some bark off an oak. Mitka came up to his father, looking back at the red bull, which was now milling round and round in the melted snow of the yard pouring out an interminable bellow.

'Hold her forelock!' Miron ordered his son. 'Mikhei, run for some twine! And be quick or I'll clout you!'

They tied the mare's velvety, lightly haired upper lip with a tight twist of rope so that it would not feel the pain. Old Grishaka came out to them. An acorn-coloured brew was brought in a painted mug.

'Cool it, it'll be too hot like that! D'ye hear me, Miron?'

'Father, go away to the house in peace! You'll catch cold out here!'

'But I say it must be cooled. D'ye want to finish off the mare?'

They washed the wound. With chilled fingers Miron threaded the sailmaker's needle with coarse thread and put in the stitches himself. It was a fine seam. But before he could step away from the well, Lukinichna came running from the house, her pallid sagging cheeks crumpled with alarm. She called her husband aside.

'Natalya has come back!.. Oh, God-a-mercy!'

'What is it now?' Miron bristled up and even the freckles turned pale in his pale face.

'It's Grigory... Our son-in-law's left home!' Lukinichna flapped her arms like a rook about to take wing, and broke into a wail, 'It'll be the talk of the village! Oh, Father, what a misfortune! Oh! oh! oh!'

Natalya in a shawl and a short winter jacket was standing in the middle of the kitchen. Two tears were lodged near the bridge of her nose and would not fall. Her cheeks were flushed a blotchy red.

'What are you doing here?' her father stormed at her as he entered the kitchen. 'Had a beating from your husband? Quarrelled over something?'

'He's left me,' Natalya coughed out through dry sobs,

175

then swayed and fell on her knees before her father.

'Oh, Daddy dearest, there's nothing left for me in life! Take me back! Grisha's gone off with that woman of his!... I'm all alone! I feel like a cart had ridden over me!'

She babbled the words, gazing up imploringly at her father's ginger-red beard.

'Now hold on a minute!'

'I can't live there any more... Take me back!' Natalya crawled quickly to the big chest by the wall and buried her weeping head in her hands. Her kerchief slipped down her back and her black straight hair hung limply over her pale ears. At a tense moment tears are like rain in a May drought. Her mother clasped Natalya's head to her sunken belly, murmuring a woman's foolish words of comfort, while Miron, in a blazing temper, dashed out on to the porch.

'A two-horse sledge! And quick about it!'

Near the porch a cock that had just masterfully mounted a hen was scared off by the roaring voice and hobbled away bandy-legged towards the barns, squawking in indignation.

'Harness up!' Miron splintered the carved railings of the porch with his boots and only went indoors when Hetko had trotted a pair of black stallions out of the stable, throwing on their collars as he did so.

Mitka and Hetko drove off to fetch Natalya's belongings. In his confusion the Ukrainian ran over a pig that did not get out of the road in time. He had been thinking to himself, 'Mebbe the master will forget about the mare with a thing like this on his hands?' And was so overjoyed that he loosened his grip on the reins.

But the next moment another thought overtook the first, 'That mean old devil won't ever forget it!' And his lips twisted in a scowl.

'Get a move on, you bugger... I'll give it you!' And with a carefully aimed flick of the whip he lashed one of the stallions just under its throbbing spleen.

XIV

Lieutenant Yevgeny Listnitsky served in the Ataman's Life Guards. While racing against his fellow officers he had suffered a bad fall and broken his left arm. After a spell in hospital he had taken leave and gone off to Yagodnoye for six weeks.

The old general lived a lonely life on his estate. He had lost his wife in a suburb of Warsaw in the eighties of the last century. Shots fired at the Cossack general had hit his wife and coachman. The general had survived in a coach riddled with bullets. Yevgeny, the son his wife had left him, was two years old at the time. Soon after this event the general retired from the army, moved to Yagodnoye (his main estate of over ten thousand acres, granted to his great grandfather for participation in the war of 1812, was in the Saratov Province) and settled down to a stern, ascetic life.

As soon as Yevgeny was old enough, his father sent him to the cadet corps and devoted himself to the management of his estate. He raised thoroughbred cattle, bought racehorses from the imperial stud, crossed them with the finest mares from England and the Provalsk stables on the Don, and succeeded in developing a breed of his own. On the land apportioned to him as a Cossack and on other land that he had bought, he kept herds of horses, grew grain, or rather had other men grow it for him, rode to hounds autumn and winter, and once in a while locked himself up in the White Room and drank for weeks on end. He was troubled by an insidious stomach complaint and was strictly forbidden by his doctors to swallow any solid food; he chewed each morsel, sucked out the juices and spat the chewed remains on to a silver platter held out for him by the young servant Veniamin, a former peasant, who remained constantly in attendance at his side.

Veniamin was rather stupid. His dark face and round head were crowned with something that looked more like black plush than hair. He had been in service with Listnitsky for six years. At first, when he had to stand at the general's side, holding the silver platter, it made him feel sick to watch the old man spitting out the grey tooth-torn scraps of food, but he got used to it. One day about a year later, as he watched his master chewing cutlets made of white turkey meat and spitting them out, he thought, 'What a waste! He can't eat it and my tummy's rumbling. This is like the old dog in a manger. I'll try and finish up for him. What harm will it do me?' He tried and was not sick afterwards. So from then on he would carry the silver platter into the hall and hurriedly swallow what the doctors had forbidden his master to swallow. Whether from this or something else, he grew fat and sleek, and numerous folds appeared on his neck.

7–1106

Besides Veniamin, the house servants living on the estate were the cook Lukeria, a decrepit old stableman called Sashka, the herdsman Tikhon, and the newly engaged coachman Grigory with his Aksinya. The flabby, big-bottomed, pock-marked Lukeria, who looked like a yellow lump of unrisen dough, barred Aksinya from the stove from the start.

'You can do the cooking when the master hires the labourers for the summer. I'll manage quite well by myself for the time being.'

Aksinya's duties were to scrub the floors in the big house three times a week, feed the poultry and keep the poultry yard clean. She set about her work conscientiously, trying to please everyone, including Lukeria. Grigory spent most of his time in the large log-built stables with Sashka the stableman. The old man had lived till he was grey-haired without ever being called anything but Sashka. No one honoured him with a patronymic, and probably even old Listnitsky himself, with whom Sashka had been living for more than twenty years, did not know his surname. As a young man Sashka had driven the coaches, but as his sight and strength began to fail, he had turned to grooming. All covered with greenish grey hair (it was grey even on his hands) and with a nose that had been flattened by a blow with a rounders-bat when he was still a boy, the old fellow always had a gentle childish smile on his face and blinked at the world around him with simple red-lidded eyes. His apostolic face was spoiled by the humorously snub nose and by the scar that disfigured his lower lip. During a drinking bout in the Russian army (Sashka was Russian-born among the Ukrainians of Boguchar, hence a 'Moskal') he had by mistake taken a swig of *aqua regia* instead of vodka and the fiery liquid had folded his lower lip back on to his chin. As it trickled away, it had left a cheerful pink scar that would not grow hair. It was as though some unknown beast had licked Sashka's beard and left the mark of its thin rasp-like tongue on his chin. Sashka often indulged in vodka and would then strut about the yard as if he owned it. Swaying to and fro, he would stand under his master's bedroom windows and wag his finger slyly in front of his cheery little nose.

'Nikolai 'Lexeyich! Are you there, Nikolai 'Lexeyich?' he would shout in a loud stern voice.

The old general would come to the window, if he happened to be in the bedroom at the time.

'What, guzzling again, you old wretch?' he would thunder from the window.

Sashka would hitch up his trousers, wink and smile craftily. His smile danced right across his face, from the half-closed left eye to the pink scar running from the right corner of his mouth. It was a crooked smile, but a pleasant one.

'Nikolai 'Lexeyich, Your Grace, I know you!..' And doing a little caper, he would hold up his thin dirty finger and shake it threateningly.

'Go and sleep it off,' his master would say indulgently from the window, smiling and twirling his drooping moustache with all five of his nicotine-stained fingers.

'The devil can't fool Sashka!' Sashka would laugh, going up to the fence. 'Nikolai 'Lexeyich, you're like me. We're like a fish and water, you and me. Always together in any weather. You and me, we're rich, we are!..' Sashka held his arms wide apart. 'Everyone in the Don region knows us. You and me...' Sashka's voice became sorrowful and at the same time insinuating, 'we're a fine pair, Your Excellency, in every way, only our noses are all shitted up.'

'Why's that?' his master inquired, face blue with laughter, moustache and whiskers twitching.

'Because of vodka,' Sashka rapped out, blinking furiously and licking away the dribble that was creeping down the runnel formed by the pink scar. 'Don't drink, Nikolai 'Lexeyich. Or we'll both be done for! It'll all go down the drain!'

'Here, take a hair of the dog that bit you.'

The old general threw a twenty-kopeck piece out of the window. Sashka caught the coin in the air and tucked it into the lining of his cap.

'Well, good-bye, General,' he sighed, turning away.

'Have you watered the horses?' his master asked, smiling in anticipation.

'You dang rotten devil! You son-of-a-bitch!' Sashka turned purple, his voice cracked and he shook with anger. 'Sashka not water the horses?! Eh? Why, even if I was dying I'd crawl round and give 'em each a pailful of spring water! What does he take me for!'

Sashka walked off in a huff, swearing and shaking his fists. He got away with anything—his drinking, his familiarity to the master. And he got away with it because he was irreplaceable stableman. Winter and summer he slept in the stables, in an empty stall; no one could look after horses better than Sashka. He was both a groom and a farrier; in spring, in the full bloom of May he would go out into the steppe to pick herbs and dig up healing roots in the ravines and gulleys. Bunches of all kinds of dried herbs hung high up on the stable walls: yarrow to cure heaves, wild garlic as an antidote for snakebite, winter-green for hoof-rot, and a small white herb growing at the foot of willows on floodland to treat strains, and many other little-known herbs for curing horses' ills and injuries.

Summer and winter a sublte, throat-catching aroma hung like a fine gossamer curtain over the stall where Sashka slept. The hay on the wooden bunk was packed down hard as a rock under its horse-cloth cover and on top of this was Sashka's working coat, saturated in horse sweat. He had no other belongings except this coat and a short sheepskin.

Tikhon, a burly, thick-lipped, dull-witted Cossack, lived with Lukeria and for no reason at all was secretly jealous of Sashka. Once a month he would take Sashka by a button of his greasy shirt and haul him off behind the sheds.

'Now, granfer, you just stop making eyes at my woman!'

'That's as may be...' Sashka gave a meaningful wink.

'Keep off, granfer!' Tikhon begged.

'But I'm fond of the pock-marked ones, son. I can do without a tot as long as you find me a pock-marked woman. The more pock-marked she is, the more she loves the menfolk, the sly wench.'

'It's a shame and a sin at your age, granfer... You're a doctor, you cure horses, and you know the charms...'

'I'm a doctor in all things,' Sashka persisted.

'Keep off, granfer! It's wrong!'

'I'll have that Lukeria yet! You can say good-bye to her, the rogue, I'll have her off you. She's like a plum cake, she is. Only all the currants have been picked out. That's why she looks pock-marked. Just the kind I like!'

'Here you are then... And don't cross my path again or I'll kill you,' Tikhon would say with a sigh and produce some coins from his pouch.

And so it went on, month after month.

Life at Yagodnoye mouldered away in sleepy bemuse-ment. The estate lay in a dry valley, remote from any of the main routes across the steppe. Communication with the stanitsa and the villages petered out from autumn onwards. Whole families of wolves wintering in the Black Wood came out at night on to the sandy hill running down into the poplar grove behind the house, and frightened the horses with their howling. Tikhon would go out into the grove to scare them off with the master's double-barrelled shotgun and Lukeria would sit with a rough blanket round her huge, stovelike bottom, staring into the darkness from eyes half buried in the folds of her fat pock-marked cheeks, waiting in suspense for the sound of the shot. At such moments she imagined the ugly, balding Tikhon as a handsome and recklessly daring young man, and when the door of the servants' quarters opened to admit Tikhon and a cloud of cold steaming air, she would make room in bed and cooingly embrace her frozen mate.

In summer Yagodnoye hummed till late at night with the voices of the seasonal labourers. Listnitsky sowed about a hundred acres to various grain crops and hired labour for the harvest. Yevgeny would visit the estate occasionally in summer, stroll about the orchard and poplar grove, feeling bored. The mornings he spent with a rod and line by the pond. He was rather short and thickset, and wore his hair in Cossack fashion, with the forelock combed to the right. His officer's long tunic fitted well on his broad shoulders.

In his first days on the estate, when he and Aksinya had only just taken up their quarters, Grigory saw a lot of the young master. Veniamin would come to their room and incline his velvety head smilingly. 'The young master wants to see you, Grigory.'

When Grigory entered and stood by the door, the lieutenant would point to a chair, showing his large, widely spaced teeth in a smile.

'Take a seat.'

Grigory would sit down on the edge.

'How do you like our horses?'

'They're a fine lot. The Grey is real good.'

'Give him plenty of exercise. But don't gallop him flat out.'

'Grandad Sashka told me.'

'What about Sturdy?'

'The bay, you mean? No price would be too high for him. Right now he's chipped his hoof. We'll have to get him reshod.'

Listnitsky looked at him narrowly with his penetrating grey eyes and asked, "You should be going to camp in May, shouldn't you?'

'Yes.'

'I'll have a word with the ataman. You won't have to go.'

'Thank you kindly.'

Silence. The lieutenant unbuttoned his collar and stroked his womanishly white chest.

'Aren't you afraid that Aksinya's husband will try to get her back?'

'He's disowned her. He wouldn't take her.'

'Who told you that?'

'I had to go to the stanitsa for some shoeing nails and I met someone from our village. He says Stepan is drinking himself silly. Says he wouldn't give two pins for Aksinya now. "Let her do as she likes," he says, "I can find myself a tastier bit when I want."'

'Aksinya's a fine-looking woman,' the lieutenant said gazing thoughtfully a little above the level of Grigory's eyes and smiling vaguely.

'She's all right,' Grigory assented, and frowned.

Yevgeny's leave was nearly over. By now he could use his arm freely, without a sling, and lift it without bending it at the elbow.

During these last days he often came to sit in Grigory's half of the servants' quarters. Aksinya had cleaned and whitewashed the walls, washed the window frames and scrubbed the floor with crushed brick. The bare cheerful room had the cosiness that only a woman's presence can give. The small stove gave off a comforting heat. The lieutenant would drape his dark-blue worsted Romanov coat over his shoulders and head for the servants' quarters, choosing a time when Grigory was sure to be busy with the horses. He would first visit the kitchen and joke with the cook, then turn away to the other half. He would sit down on a stool by the stove, hunching his shoulders and looking at Aksinya with shamelessly smiling eyes. Aksinya was so embarrassed in his presence that she could scarcely hold her knitting needles.

'How are you getting on, Aksinya, my dear?' the lieutenant would ask, filling the room with blue smoke from his cigarette.

'Quite well, thank you.'

Aksinya flushed crimson as her eyes met the lieutenant's transparent gaze mutely telling of his desire. Those luminous naked eyes annoyed and repelled her. She would answer his trivial questions haphazardly and try to leave the room as soon as possible.

'I must go and feed the ducks.'

'Don't be in a hurry. You have plenty of time,' the

lieutenant smiled and his legs trembled in the close-fitting trousers.

He would go on and on, questioning Aksinya about her former life, playing on the deep notes of his voice, which was like his father's, and raping her with eyes that were as light and clear as spring water.

When Grigory came in after work, the lieutenant would moderate his glances, give Grigory a cigarette and leave.

'What was he sitting here for?' Grigory would ask thickly, not looking at Aksinya.

'How should I know?' she would force a laugh as she remembered the look in the lieutenant's eyes. 'He just came in and sat down. Like this.' And she imitated the lieutenant's hunched posture. 'He keeps on sitting here till it makes you sick. And that knee of his, it looks so sharp.'

'Have you been making eyes at him?' Grigory frowned fiercely.

'Not likely!'

'Well, watch out. Or I'll kick him down those steps like a shot.'

Aksinya looked smilingly at Grigory and could not decide whether he was serious or joking.

XV

Winter lost its grip in the fourth week of Lent. The ice of the Don frayed into long tassels, bulged porously and turned grey as its crust thawed. In the evenings the wind soughed over the hill, which according to tradition was a sign of frost, although in reality a thaw was on the way. The light morning frosts put an icy tinkle in the air, but by noon the earth softened and began to smell of March, of frozen cherry bark and rotted straw.

Miron Grigorievich was quietly preparing for the ploughing. As the days grew longer he busied himself under the overhang of the shed, mending the harrows, and with Hetko's help made two new wagon frames. In the fourth week of Lent old Grishaka began his fast. He would come home from church, almost black with cold, and complain to his daughter-in-law, 'That priest, he's frozen me stiff, the dozy fellow. He conducts the service like a carter with a load of eggs. It's terrible!'

'Why don't you fast in Easter week, Grandad? It would be warmer by then.'

'Ask Natalya to knit me some thicker socks. A grey wolf would freeze with his heels bare like mine.'

Natalya lived with her father like a bird of passage. She longed and hoped for Grigory's return, refusing to listen to the sober voice of reason; at night, crushed by the unexpected and undeserved wrong she had suffered, she burned with misery and anguish. But worse was to come and a cold fear brought Natalya to the limit of her endurance. In the room that had been hers before she married she fluttered exhaustedly like a wounded lapwing in a backwater. Ever since her return her brother Mitka had been giving her strange looks. One day he cornered her in the porch and asked straight out, 'Pining for Grishka, are you?'

'What's that to you?'

'I could help you forget him...'

Natalya looked into his eyes and was horrified by what she saw there. Those narrow slits of green gleamed oilily in the darkness of the porch. She darted into her grandfather's room at the side of the house, slammed the door, and stood listening to the anxious throbbing of her heart. The next day Mitka came up to her in the yard. He had been throwing hay to the cattle and green wisps were clinging to his straight hair and fur cap. Natalya was driving away the dogs that were trying to get at the pig's trough.

'Don't get uppish, Natalya.'

'I'll scream for Father!' Natalya cried, raising her hands as if to ward him off.

'You're crazy!'

'Go away, you wretch!'

'What are you squalling about?'

'Go away, Mitka! Or I'll go and tell Father!.. How can you look like this at your sister? Have you no shame? It's a wonder the earth don't open and swallow you up!'

'Well, it don't.' Mitka put his hands on his hips and stamped his foot to confirm the fact.

'Don't come near me, Mitka!'

'I won't right now, but I will at night. That's for sure!'

Natalya left the yard trembling. That evening she made up a bed on the big chest and took her younger sister to bed with her. She tossed and turned all night, driving her feverish eyes like wedges into the darkness, waiting for a rustle, a quiet footfall, ready to scream the house down, but the silence was broken only by the heavy breathing of Grandad Grishaka from the next room and the occasional snuffles of her sister, lying with arms and legs spread out at her side.

The skein of days unwound its thread, poisoned by a woman's inconsolable grief.

Mitka, who had still not recovered from the shame of his marriage proposal, was forever in a sullen spiteful mood. He went out in the evenings and seldom came home before dawn. He had taken up with some loose-living soldiers' wives and often went to Stepan's to play pontoon. Miron said nothing for the time being, but kept his eyes open. One day before Easter Natalya happened to meet Pantelei outside Mokhov's shop. His was the first greeting.

'Natalya, wait a minute.'

Natalya stopped and felt a fresh pang of misery as she looked at her father-in-law's face with its hooked nose that faintly reminded her of Grigory's.

'Why don't you ever come and see us old folk?' Pantelei began, avoiding her glance, as though he himself were to blame for what had happened. 'The wife's missing you, wants to know how you're getting on.'

Natalya recovered from her confusion. 'Quite well, thank you—' she hesitated a moment, for she had been going to say 'Father', and ended with, 'Pantelei Prokofievich.'

'Why don't you come and see us?'

'There's such a lot to do on the farm.'

'That Grishka...' The old man shook his head bitterly. 'He let us down properly, the stinker... Just when we were getting on so well together!'

'What's the use, Father...' Natalya's voice rang on a high, breaking note. 'Fate willed otherwise.'

Pantelei shifted his feet in embarrassment as he saw Natalya's eyes fill with tears. Her mouth twisted with the effort of checking them.

'Good-bye then, my dear!.. Don't you grieve over him, the rotten devil, he's not worth your little finger. He may come back. If I could see him, I'd make him smart!'

Natalya walked away with her head drawn into her shoulders, a beaten woman. Pantelei stood shifting his feet, as if he were about to break into a trot. When Natalya reached the corner, she glanced back. Her father-in-law was limping away across the square, leaning heavily on his stick.

XVI

The gatherings at Stokman's had become less frequent. Spring was on the way and preparations had to be made for work in the fields. Only the mill hands, Knave and Davydka, and Ivan Alexeyevich Kotlyarov, the engine-man, still attended. Towards evening on the Thursday before Easter they met in the workshop. Stokman was sitting on the bench, filing a ring he had made from a silver half-rouble piece. A sheaf of rays from the setting sun streamed through the window, casting a dusty yellowish-pink square of light on the floor. Ivan was toying with a pair of pliers.

'I saw the boss the other day about the piston. It'll have to be taken to Millerovo. They'll fix it. What can we do here? There's a crack in it about this big.' For the benefit of no one in particular Ivan held up his little finger to show the size of the crack.

'There's a factory in Millerovo, isn't there?' Stokman asked, powdering his finger with fine silver dust as he used the file.

'Yes, they've got an open-hearth furnace. I was there last year.'

'Many workers?'

'Hell of a lot. About four hundred.'

'What kind of ... mood are they in?' Stokman shook his head as he worked, and the words came out between pauses.

'Oh, they live fine. They're no proletarians... They're just—shit.'

'Why?' Knave, who was sitting beside Stokman with his stumpy fingers locked under his knees, asked the engine-man.

Davydka, still grey-headed from the flour dust that had worked its way into his hair, was clumping about the workshop, kicking aside the foamy shavings and listening with a smile to their dry fragrant rustling. It was like walking through a wooded ravine strewn with purple gently yielding leaves and feeling the youthful springiness of the damp soil beneath.

'Because they're all comfortably off. Every one of them has his own house, his wife, and all they could wish for. And besides, half of 'em are Baptists. The owner himself is a preacher, so they all look after each other, but the dirt on 'em is so thick you couldn't scrape it off with a hoe.'

'Baptists? What are they, Ivan Alexeyevich?' Davydka halted at the sound of the unfamiliar word.

'The Baptists? They believe in God in their own way. Something like the Old Believers.'

'Every fool goes mad in his own way,' Knave added.

'Well, I went to see Mokhov,' Ivan went on with his story, 'and he had Lispy Atyopin sitting with him. He told me to wait in the hall. So I sat down and waited. And through the door I could hear what they were saying. The boss, he tells Atyopin all about it. Very soon, he says, there's going to be a war with the Germans. He'd read it in some book or other. And old Lispy, you know what he says? "I don't agree with you, of courth, about the pothibility of war."'

Ivan imitated Atyopin so well that Davydka gave a brief laugh but, noticing Knave's sarcastic glance, fell silent.

' "Germany can't go to war with Russia because they feed themselves on our grain",' Ivan continued his account of the conversation he had overheard. 'And then another voice chimes in. I didn't recognise it, but afterwards it turned out to be General Listnitsky's son, the officer. "There will be a war between Germany and France over the vineyards," he says, "but it has nothing to do with us."'

'What do you think, Osip Davydovich?' Ivan asked Stokman.

'I'm no prophet,' Stokman answered evasively, examining the finished ring at arm's length.

'If they start scrapping, we'll be in it as well. They'll drag us in by the hair, whether we like it or not,' Knave reasoned.

'The thing is this, lads...' Stokman began, gently relieving Ivan of the pliers.

He spoke seriously, evidently intending to go into the problem thoroughly. Knave settled himself more comfortably, pulling up his legs that had begun to slip off the bench. Davydka's lips fell open, revealing his glistening close-set teeth. In his concise, vivid way Stokman described the struggle between the capitalist countries for markets and colonies. Before he could finish, Ivan interrupted indignantly, 'But what has this got to do with us?'

'Your heads and a lot of others will ache from the wine that other people drank,' Stokman replied with a smile.

'Don't talk like a kid,' Knave sneered at Ivan. 'You

know the old saying, "When masters fall out their men get the clout".'

'Hm-m-m.' Ivan frowned as he grappled with a massive, unyielding chunk of thought.

'Why is that Listnitsky hanging about round the Mokhovs? Is he after their daughter?' Davydka asked.

'The Korshunov brat has been after her already,' Knave said maliciously.

'Hear that, Ivan Alexeyevich? What's the officer nosing around for there?'

Ivan started, as if he had been lashed behind the knees.

'Eh? What did you say?'

'Been having a doze, have you? We're talking about Listnitsky.'

'He was on his way to the station. Yes, and here's another bit of news. When I came out, who do you think I met on the porch? Grishka Melekhov, standing there with a whip in his hand. "What are you doing here, Grigory?" I asks. "Taking Lieutenant Listnitsky to Millerovo," he says.'

'He's working for them as a coachman,' Davydka put in.

'Picking up crumbs from the rich man's table.'

'You're like a dog on chain, Knave. You've got a snarl for everyone.'

The talk broke off for a minute. Ivan rose to go.

'Hurrying off to service?' Knave got in a final dig.

'I do enough serving every day.'

Stokman saw his guests off, locked up the workshop and went into the house.

On Easter Eve the sky was banked with heavy black-breasted clouds and the first drops of rain began to fall. The dank darkness hung oppressively over the village. At dusk the ice on the Don cracked with a long reverberating roar and the first floe was forced out of the water. The ice broke up all at once over a distance of about four versts, as far as the first bend below the village, and then began to move. To the steady tolling of the church-bell the ice-packs crushed and battered one another, making the banks shudder. At the bend, where the Don turns left, a jam began to form. The grinding roar of the colliding floes reached the village. A flock of village lads had gathered in the churchyard, amid the shining pools of thaw water. The resonant sound of chanting rolled out through the open doors into the porch and from the porch into the churchyard. The latticed windows glowed with a festive brightness, and in the darkness of the yard the boys tickled and kissed the giggling girls and whispered dirty stories to each other.

The churchwarden's lodge was crowded with Cossacks who had come for the Easter service from near and distant villages. Tired out by the journey and the stuffiness of the room, some of them had fallen asleep on the benches and windowsills, and even on the floor.

A group had gathered on the crumbling steps. They were smoking and chatting about the weather and the winter crops.

'When will your people be going out into the fields?'

'Come St. Thomas's, I reckon.'

'That's where you've been lucky. Yours is sandy steppe out there, an't it?'

'Sandy loam, but this side of the ravine it's salt marshes.'

'Well, the earth'll have a good drink now.'

'At ploughing time last year, it was like gristle, baked hard all over.'

'Dunya, where are you?' a thin, high-pitched voice piped from the bottom of the lodge steps.

And by the gate of the churchyard a rough, husky voice grumbled, 'You've found a fine place for necking. Why, you... Get out of here, you young brats. Isn't there anywhere else!'

'Feel left out of it, do you? Go and kiss the bitch in our yard,' a wobbly young voice answered cheekily from the darkness.

'Bitch! Just you wait, I'll—'

A squelch of running feet, a quick rustle of skirts.

Moisture was dripping off the roof with a glassy tinkle; and again a slow, drawling voice, like the black-earth mud, 'The other day I was trying to buy a plough off Prokhor. Offered him twelve rubles, but he wouldn't take it. He won't sell anything cheap, that one won't.'

From the Don came a steady swishing, rustling and crunching, as though a fine, buxom woman, dressed up and tall as a poplar, were striding past the village, her huge skirt rustling.

At midnight, when the slushy darkness had thickened, Mitka Korshunov rode up to the church on an unsaddled horse. He dismounted, tied the reins to the mane and gave the excited horse a hard slap. He stood for a moment, listening to its hooves churning the ground, then straightened his belt and walked into the yard. In the porch he took off his cap, bowed his unevenly trimmed head and, pushing the women aside, made his way to the altar. The men were gathered in a black drove on the left and there was a colourful array of women's finery on the right. Mitka sought out his father in the front row and went up to him, took him by the elbow just as he was about to make the sign of the cross, and whispered in his ear, 'Come outside for a minute, Father.'

Mitka's nostrils twitched as he pushed his way out of the church through a solid curtain of smells. He was almost overpowered by the reek of hot wax, the odour of women's sweating bodies, the funereal smell of clothes that came out of the family chests only at Christmastime and Easter, and the stench of wet boot leather, moth balls, and bad breath from hungry, fasting stomachs.

In the porch Mitka pressed his chest against his father's shoulder and said, 'Natalya's dying!'

XVII

After taking Yevgeny to the station at Millerovo, Grigory did not get back to the estate until Palm Sunday. The thaw had swallowed up the snow and in a mere two days the road had gone to pieces.

In Olkhovy Rog, a Ukrainian settlement about twenty-five versts from the railway, he nearly drowned his horses while crossing a small river. He had reached the settlement towards evening. The ice had broken up and floated away downstream and the river, swollen by brown freshets of thaw water, was already threatening the streets of the settlement.

The inn where travellers stopped to feed their horses on the way to the station was on the other side. The water might rise even higher during the night and Grigory decided to cross.

He drove to the spot where only the day before he had crossed solid ice; now the river had burst its banks and the muddy waters swept along, spinning part of a fence and half a cartwheel in midstream. The sand where the snow had melted was freshly marked by sledge runners. Grigory reined in the sweating foam-flecked horses and jumped down to examine the narrow tracks cut by the runners. At the water's edge they swerved to the left and disappeared. Grigory judged the distance across by eye— not more than fifty paces. He went back to the horses and checked their harness. At that moment an elderly Ukrainian in a foxskin cap came out of the house nearest the bank.

'Is there a crossing here?' Grigory asked, waving his reins at the surging brown flood.

'Ay, they got across this morning.'

'Is it deep?'

'No, but it might swamp your sledge.'

Grigory gathered up the reins and with his whip at the ready sent the horses off with a sharp, 'Giddyup!' The horses started unwillingly, snorting and sniffing at the water.

'Giddyup!' Grigory cracked his whip and stood up on the box.

The sturdy bay on the left tossed its head valiantly and tugged hard at the traces. Out of the corner of his eye Grigory saw the water foaming round the side of the sledge. It rose first to the horses' knees, and then, suddenly to their chests. Grigory tried to turn them back, but they had lost their footing and with frightened snorts had begun to swim. The sledge swung round, forcing the horses to face the current. Water rolled over their withers and the sledge heaved and dragged them back.

'Hi!.. Hi!.. Drive 'em!' the Ukrainian shouted running along the bank and for some reason waving his fur cap.

Grigory whooped and urged on the horses in a frenzy. The water swirled behind the sinking sledge. Suddenly the sledge struck a pile sticking out of the water (all that was left of the bridge) and turned over. Grigory gasped and went under, but kept hold of the reins. He could feel the stream tugging at the skirts of his sheepskin, at his legs, dragging him with gentle persistence and turning him over beside the tossing sledge. He managed to grab a runner, let go of the reins and began to pull himself along hand over hand, trying to reach the swingle-tree. His fingers had just touched the metal tip, when the bay in its efforts to fight the current kicked him hard on the knee. Choking, Grigory changed hands and managed to grab one of the traces. He felt himself being dragged away from the horses and the strain on his fingers was doubled. Pierced by fiery needles of cold, he reached out for the bay's head and found himself staring into the animal's bloodshot eye just as it fixed its maddened, mortally frightened gaze on him.

Again and again Grigory lost his hold on the slippery leather reins, struck out and recovered his grip, then lost it again; as he snatched once more, his foot unexpectedly scraped on firm ground.

'Giddy-y-up!!' he strained forward with all his strength

and fell flat in the foaming shallows, knocked off his feet by the horse behind him.

The horses trampled over him, dragged the sledge out of the water in a mad rush, and halted a few paces further on, shuddering with exhaustion, their wet backs steaming.

Oblivious of pain, Grigory jumped to his feet; the cold wrapped itself round him like an unbearably hot dough. He was trembling more than the horses and felt as weak on his feet as a baby. Recovering his wits, he turned the sledge over on to its runners and sent the horses off at a gallop to warm them up. He drove down the street as if in a cavalry charge and swung in at the first open gate without slowing down.

He was lucky enough to strike upon a hospitable host, who put his son in charge of the horses, himself helped Grigory to undress, and in a tone that brooked no argument ordered his wife to heat the stove. Grigory lay on the stove-bed in his host's trousers until his own clothes were dry, then, after a supper of meatless cabbage soup, went to bed.

He set off in the morning well before dawn. He had a distance of one hundred and thirty-five versts to cover and every minute was precious. There were turbulent streams in every ravine and gully and any day now the steppe would be made impassable by the spring floods.

The bare black road was killing the horses. While the ground was still hard with the morning frost, he got as far as the fork in the road leading to a Ukrainian settlement, four versts away, and halted there. Steam was rising from his sweating horses and a long gleaming trail lay behind him. Grigory abandoned the sledge at the fork, tied up the horses' tails and mounted one of them bareback, leading the other by its halter. On the morning of Palm Sunday he reached Yagodnoye.

The old general listened to his detailed account of the journey and went to look at the horses. Sashka was walking them in the yard, squinting crossly at their sunken flanks.

'How are the horses?'

'What d'ye expect?' Sashka grunted and walked on, shaking his round greenish-grey beard.

'Are they ruined?'

'No. The bay got his chest chafed a bit. That's nothing.'

'Go and get some sleep,' Listnitsky said, motioning the waiting Grigory away.

Grigory went to his quarters, but he was allowed only

a night's rest. The next morning Veniamin appeared in a new blue sateen blouse and with his habitual fat smile on his lips.

'Grigory, the master wants you. At once!'

The general was shuffling up and down the drawing room in felt slippers. Grigory stood hesitantly at the door and coughed once, then again. The master raised his head.

'What do you want?'

'Veniamin told me to come.'

'Ah, yes. Go and saddle the stallion and Sturdy. Tell Lukeria not to feed the hounds. We'll be hunting!'

When Grigory turned to go, the general brought him back with a shout. 'D'you hear? And you'll be going with me.'

Aksinya slipped an unleavened bun into Grigory's pocket and hissed, 'He doesn't even give you time to eat, the old devil!.. They're working you to death. At least put a scarf on, Grisha.'

Grigory led the saddled horses to the fence and whistled up the hounds. The general came out in a dark-blue waisted coat with a richly decorated belt. A nickel-plated flask with a cork protector was slung over his shoulder; a riding whip dangled from his wrist, trailing like a snake behind him.

While he held the reins, Grigory watched the old man and was amazed at the ease with which he swung his bony frame into the saddle.

'Follow me,' Listnitsky commanded briefly, gathering the reins lovingly in a gloved hand.

The four-year-old stallion that Grigory was riding pranced and sidestepped, cocking its head. Its hind hooves were not shod and slithered on the patches of ice, making the horse use all four feet at once. The old general sat comfortably on Sturdy's broad back in a slightly stooped but firm posture.

'Where are we going?' Grigory asked, drawing level.

'To Olshansky Ravine,' the general's deep voice responded.

The horses kept up a lively pace. The stallion wanted its head. It arched its short neck like a swan, squinted with a protruding eye at its rider and snapped at his knee. They rode up a gentle slope and the general put Sturdy into a swinging canter.

The hounds had fanned out a little behind Grigory. The old black bitch loped along with her humped muzzle touching the tip of the horse's tail. The stallion squatted excitedly and tried to kick its persistent follower, but the bitch dropped behind and her mournful old-womanish eyes tried to catch Grigory's eye as he looked back.

They reached their destination in half an hour. The general guided his horse along the shaggy weed-grown ridge, while Grigory rode down into the ravine, peering cautiously at the pitted water-worn bottom. Now and then he glanced up at his master. Through the steely blue of the bare and sparse alder scrub the figure of the old man was silhouetted clearly against the sky. When he rose in the stirrups and leaned over the saddle-bow, his belted blue coat rumpled at the back. The hounds tracked over the undulating slope, keeping together in a bunch. Grigory lurched in his saddle as he crossed a steep water-course.

If only I could have a smoke, he thought, taking off his glove and rummaging in his pocket for paper. I'll let go of the reins when I get across and find my pouch.

'After him!' the shout from the ridge cracked like a rifle shot.

Grigory looked up sharply and saw the general ride up on to the sharp crest of the ridge and, waving his whip high, throw his horse into a gallop.

'After him!'

A moulting dirty-brown wolf, still shaggy about the loins, was running quickly across the soggy reed-grown bottom of the ravine. It leapt across a dip, stopped and, turning quickly, caught sight of the hounds. The pack had spread out like a horseshoe to head it off from the wood that began at the end of the ravine.

The wolf leaped springily on to a mound over a marmot's burrow and made a dash for the wood. The old bitch was cutting across its front with long bounds. A tall grey dog known as Hawk, one of the best and fiercest in the pack, was coming up from behind.

The wolf seemed to hesitate for a moment. Grigory wheeled to get out of the ravine and lost sight of it for a moment. By the time he rode on to the ridge the wolf was a faint blur in the distance and the black hounds were bounding through the steppe. Further to the left Listnitsky was galloping along the edge of a steep bank, belabouring Sturdy with the butt of his whip. The wolf was making for the next ravine, but the dogs were closing in, and Hawk—from where Grigory was, a mere whitish streak—was snapping at the wolf's shaggy groin.

'After him!' the shout reached Grigory again.

He gave the stallion its head, trying vainly to make out what was going on in front. His eyes were bleared, his ears blocked by the roar of the wind. Seized by the spirit of the chase, he crouched over the stallion's neck and whirled into a mad gallop. When he reached the ravine there was no sign of either wolf or dogs. A minute later Listnitsky came up. Reining in his horse at full gallop, he shouted, 'Where did he go?'

'Into the ravine, I reckon.'

'Take the left side!.. Off you go!..'

Listnitsky drove his heels into the flanks of the rearing horse and rode off to the right. Grigory reined in as he went down the slope, then whooped and dashed up the other side. For about a verst and a half he urged on the sweating horse with his voice and whip. The soft, still moist earth clung to its hooves and spattered his face. The long ravine winding across the side of the hill, turned to the right and branched out into three gullies. Grigory crossed the first of these and was pounding down a gentle slope when he spotted the black chain of hounds chasing the wolf across the steppe. They must have headed it off from the heart of the ravine, which was thick with oak and alder. Where the dark-blue gullies sloped away, the wolf had taken to the open and, having gained a couple of hundred yards, was making a fresh dash, this time for a dry valley covered with tall withered scrub and thistle.

Wiping the tears from his eyes, Grigory rose in his stirrups and watched the wolf, but a glance to the left told him that these were his home acres. The strip that he and Natalya had ploughed in autumn spread out before him in a rough greasy-looking square. He deliberately rode over the ploughed land and in the few minutes it took the horse to stumble across the furrows all the zest died out of him. He urged on the panting stallion indifferently and, keeping an eye on the general in case he looked round, reduced his speed to a leisurely canter.

In the distance, near Red Ravine, the deserted ploughmen's shelter came into view. A team of six oxen was pulling a plough, leaving fresh velvety furrows behind it.

They must be from our village. Whose land is that? Anikei's? Grigory screwed up his eyes, trying to recognise the oxen and the man behind the plough.

'Take him!'

Grigory saw two Cossacks leave their plough and run to cut off the wolf as it headed for the ravine. One of them, a big man with the strap of his red-banded Cossack cap lowered under his chin, was waving a short iron bar he had taken from the oxen's yoke. And then, quite unexpectedly, the wolf stopped and sat down in a deep furrow. The leading hound flew straight over him and fell on its forepaws; the old bitch slithered on its hindquarters over the loose soil, trying to stop, but cannoned straight into the wolf. It jerked its head fiercely and the bitch was flung aside on the rebound. With dogs all over it the wolf staggered on for a few more paces, then began to roll like a great black ball. Grigory galloped up a few moments before the general, sprang out of the saddle and crouched by the tangle of bodies, his hunting knife drawn back to strike.

'That's the spot!.. Underneath!.. Get him in the throat!' the Cossack with the iron bar shouted in a panting voice that sounded strangely familiar. He knelt down beside Grigory, seized the big hound tearing at the wolf's belly by the scruff of the neck and pulled it off, then gripped the wolf's feet in his huge hand. Grigory groped for the windpipe under the bristling fur and drew the knife across it.

'The dogs! Keep the dogs off!' Listnitsky croaked, going blue in the face as he dropped out of his saddle on to the soft ground.

With some difficulty Grigory drove off the dogs and looked round at the general.

Stepan Astakhov, still wearing his cap with the shiny chin-strap lowered, stood at a distance, toying with the iron bar. His lower jaw and eyebrows were working strangely.

'Where are you from, young fellow?' Listnitsky asked him. 'What village?'

'Tatarsky,' Stepan answered after a pause, and took a step towards Grigory.

'What name?'

'Astakhov.'

'Listen to me then. When are you going home?'

'Tonight.'

'Bring us this carcass.' Listnitsky pointed his foot at the wolf that lay in its death agony, teeth gnashing slowly, one hind leg with a brownish matted tuft of hair on the ankle rigidly erect. 'I'll pay anything it costs,' the general promised and, mopping his purple face with his scarf, walked away and leaned over to slip the flask off his shoulder.

Grigory went back to his horse. As he put his foot in

the stirrup he glanced round. Shaking uncontrollably, Stepan was walking towards him, neck working, heavy fists bunched against his chest.

XVIII

On Good Friday night there was a gathering of women at Pelageya Maidannikova's, a neighbour of the Korshunovs. Her husband, Gavrila, had written to her from Lodz, promising that he would be home for Easter. Pelageya had whitewashed the walls and tidied up the little cottage on Monday, and had been waiting and watching for her husband since Thursday. She would stand by the fence bareheaded and gaunt, her face covered with the blotches of pregnancy, shading her eyes and looking to see if he was coming. She was expecting a baby, but with a good conscience. The previous summer Gavrila had come home on leave from his regiment, bringing his wife a length of Polish cotton. His visit had been a short one. He had slept with her only four nights, and on the fifth day had got drunk, started swearing in Polish and German, and with tears rolling down his cheeks, struck up an old Cossack song about Poland, dating from 1831. His friends and brothers who had come to see him off were at the table. They had all had plenty of vodka before dinner and joined in the song.

> They said of Poland, it's a very rich land,
> But we found out it's as poor as the damned.
> And in this said Poland there stands an inn,
> A Polish inn, belongs to the Polish king.
> Three lads in the inn were knocking it back,
> A Prussian, a Pole and a young Don Cossack.
> The Prussian, he drinks vodka, and pays his score.
> The Pole, he drinks vodka, and pays some more.
> The Cossack, he drinks—and the inn's as poor as before.
> Then he walks around with clinking spur
> And the barmaid sees his eye is on her.
> 'Oh, mistress dear, come live with me,
> Come live with me, on the quiet Don,
> The folk of the Don, they don't live your way,
> Don't weave, don't spin, don't sow, don't mow,
> Don't sow, don't mow, but they dress very gay.'

After dinner Gavrila said good-bye to his family and left, and ever since that visit Pelageya had been keeping an eye on the hem of her skirt.

She gave Natalya Korshunova the following explanation of her pregnancy:

'Afore Gavrila came home I had a dream, dear. It was as if I was walking across the meadow and in front of me was the old cow we sold last summer. There it was walking along and milk was dripping from its udder and leaving a trail behind it. Goodness gracious, I thinks to myself, how could I have milked her like that? And after that Granny Drozdikha came to ask for some hops. So I told her about my dream and she says to take a lump of wax to the cowshed. "Break it off a candle," she says, "roll it in a ball and bury it in some fresh cow dung, because there's trouble watching at your window." Well, I started looking right away but couldn't find a candle. We did have one but the children must have taken it—to tempt the tarantulas out of their holes, I expect. Then Gavrila comes home and with him comes trouble. Before that my petticoat hadn't been tight for three years, but now look...' And Pelageya pointed woefully at her rounded belly.

Pelageya grew lonesome waiting for her husband, so on Friday she asked her women neighbours round to keep her company. Natalya came with a stocking she had not yet finished knitting (with spring coming on old Grishaka felt the cold even more). She was lively and laughed rather too readily at the other women's jokes because she did not want them to see how she was pining for her husband. Pelageya sat on the stove-bed, dangling her bare violet-veined legs and made fun of Frosya, a shrewish young woman.

'How could you give your Cossack such a beating, Frosya?'

'Don't you know how? On the back, the head, wherever I could get at him.'

'I don't mean that. I mean, how did it all start?'

'It just started,' was the reluctant reply.

'What would ye do if ye caught your man with another woman? Keep quiet about it?' Kashulin's sister-in-law, a tall, bony woman, asked slowly and deliberately.

'Tell us all about it, Frosya.'

'Why should I! Can't you think of anything better to talk about?'

'Come on, don't be shy. We're all friends here.'

Frosya spat out the husks of the sunflower seed she had been chewing and smiled.

'I'd had my eye on him for some time, and then I got word that he was out by the mill, carrying on with a grass-widow from across the Don. So off I went and there they were by the millet mill.'

'Well, Natalya, and what's the latest about your husband?' Kashulin's sister-in-law changed the subject.

'He's at Yagodnoye,' Natalya answered quietly.

'D'ye expect to live with him any more?'

'She may be expecting to, but he's not having any,' Pelageya interrupted.

Natalya felt the hot blood surge into her cheeks. She bowed her head over the stocking, then glanced up at the women. Seeing that they were all looking at her and it was no use trying to hide her blushes, she deliberately but awkwardly, so that they all noticed it, let the ball of wool roll from her lap, and then bent down, groping for it over the cold floor.

'Say good riddance to him, woman. As long as you've got a neck you'll always find someone to put a yoke on it,' one of the guests advised with unconcealed pity in her voice.

Natalya's feigned liveliness had died like a spark in the wind. The women began discussing the latest gossip and rumours. Natalya knitted in silence and could barely sit through the evening. She left with a half-formed decision in her mind. The shame of not knowing where she stood (she still hoped that Grigory had not left her for ever, and was waiting and ready to forgive him) hardened her resolve. She decided to get in touch with Grigory secretly and find out whether he had gone for good or perhaps had changed his mind. It was late when she came back from Pelageya's. Her grandfather was sitting in his room, reading an old leather-bound copy of the Gospel, whose dog-eared pages were stained with candle wax. Her father was in the kitchen, tying another ring to his fish-trap and listening to Mikhei, who was telling him about a murder that had happened long ago. Her mother had put the children to bed and was herself asleep on the stove-bed, the black soles of her feet pointing towards the door. Natalya took off her coat and walked aimlessly through the rooms. From the big front room came the sound of mice squeaking and scuffling behind a board in the corner, where a pile of hempseed had been stored for sowing.

She lingered for a minute in her grandfather's room, standing by the corner table staring dully at the stack of religious books piled under the ikon.

'Grandad, have you any paper?'

'What kind of paper?' the old man gathered a sheaf of wrinkles above his glasses.

'For writing on.'

Old Grishaka thumbed through a book of psalms and produced a sheet that smelled strongly of Saint's Day honey and incense.

'And a pencil?'

'Ask your father for that. Go along, my dear. Don't bother me now.'

Natalya got a stump of pencil from her father, sat down at the table and once again struggled with the thoughts that she had struggled with for so long already, and that had left a dull ache in her heart.

Next morning she promised Hetko some vodka and sent him off to Yagodnoye with a letter.

'Grigory Panteleyevich!

'Write and tell me how I am to live and whether or not my life is ruined for ever. You left home without a single word to me. I did never offend you and I expected you to untie my hands and say whether you had gone forever, but you have cut yourself off from the village and are silent as the grave.

'I thought you left because you got angry and would come back, but I don't want to put myself between the two of you. It is better for me alone to be trampled on than that two should suffer. Do me this last kindness and write. When I know for sure, I shall have only one thing to think about, but now I stand at a crossroads.

'Don't be angry with me, Grisha, for love of Christ.

Natalya.'

Gloomily anticipating the long spell of drinking that he was about to embark on, Hetko led a horse out on to the threshing floor and, keeping out of sight of his master, threw on the bridle and rode away bareback. He had none of the Cossack horsemanship. His ragged elbows stuck out and the children playing in the street shouted after him as he rode away at a rapid trot.

'Tufty!.. Tufty Ukrainian!'

'Tufty tar-barrel!'

'You'll fall off!'

'Look at that dog on a fence!'

It was nearly evening when he returned bringing with him a scrap of blue sugar wrapping paper. He produced it from his shirt-front with a wink at Natalya, 'It's a terrible road, little mistress! It nearly shook the guts out of poor Hetko!'

Natalya turned grey in the face as she read the message. Something sharp and jagged entered her heart in four short jabs.

The four words scrawled across the scrap of paper were: 'Live alone. *Grigory Melekhov.*'

Hurrying as though her strength were about to fail, she almost ran indoors and lay down on her bed. Her mother had lighted the stove so that she could finish her cooking and have time to bake her Easter cakes.

'Come on, Natalya, give me a hand!' she called to her daughter.

'I've got a head-ache, mother. I'll just lie down for a bit.'

Lukinichna poked her head round the door. 'Why don't you take some pickle juice? It'll put you right in no time.'

Natalya licked her cold lips without answering.

She lay till evening with a warm woollen shawl over her head, hunched up and shivering. Miron and her grandfather were about to go to church when she got up and came out into the kitchen. Beads of perspiration gleamed under the smoothly combed black hair at her temples and her eyes were glazed.

Her father shot a reproachful glance at his daughter as he fastened the long row of buttons on his baggy trousers.

'This is a fine time to get ill, girl. Come with us to the morning service.'

'I'll come along later.'

'When it's all over?'

'No, I must get dressed first. I'll dress up properly, then I'll come.'

The men went off, leaving only the two women in the house. Natalya wandered aimlessly from the chest to the bed, staring with hatred at the rumpled heap of finery, struggling with a half-formed idea and muttering to herself. Her mother thought she was hesitating over what to wear and tried to be helpful.

'Put on my blue skirt, dear. It'll be just right for you now.'

No new Easter clothes had been made for Natalya, and

her mother, remembering the close-fitting blue skirt of hers that her daughter had loved to put on before she married, offered it to her in the belief that Natalya was upset because she had so little to choose from.

'Will you wear it? I'll get it out.'

'No, I'll go in this one.' Natalya carefully took out her green skirt and suddenly remembered that this was the skirt she had been wearing when Grigory had come to see her during their engagement and in the cool of the shed made her blush with that first fleeting kiss. She began to shake and fell forward on to the open lid of the chest in a fit of sobbing.

'Natalya! What is it, dear?' Lukinichna exclaimed.

Natalya stifled the cry that rose to her throat and forced herself to laugh. It was a creaking, wooden laughter.

'Oh, something's come over me today.'

'Yes, dear, I've noticed—'

'What have you noticed, Mother?' Natalya cried with unexpected malice, crumpling the green skirt in her fingers.

'You can't go on like this... You must get married.'

'Once was enough!'

Natalya went to her own little room to dress and soon appeared in the kitchen again attired for church, a slim girlish figure, her wan face tinged with the transparent bluish flush of unhappiness.

'Go by yourself, I'm not ready yet,' said her mother. Natalya tucked a handkerchief into her sleeve and went out on to the porch. The wind carried the rustle of floating ice from the Don and the bland refreshing smell of the thaw. Holding up the hem of her skirt with her left hand and stepping round the pinkish-blue puddles, she walked to church. On the way she tried to recover her former balanced state of mind. She thought of the festival, of many things, intermittently and vaguely, but her mind stubbornly returned to the scrap of wrapping paper tucked away in her bosom, to Grigory and that lucky woman, who was now laughing at her condescendingly and perhaps even—pitying her.

She entered the churchyard. There were some boys standing in her path and, as she walked round them, she heard them talking.

'Did'ye see who that was?'

'Yes, it's Natalya Korshunova.'

'They say she's got rupture. That's why her husband left her.'

'Don't give me that! She was carrying on with her father-in-law, old Pantelei with the gammy leg.'

'So that's why Grigory ran away from home?'

'Sure it is. And this time she's—'

Natalya stumbled on over the uneven paving stones and reached the steps of the church. A whispered obscenity was thrown after her like a stone. To the sound of giggles from the girls standing on the steps, she made her way to the other gate and, swaying like a drunkard, ran back home. She paused for breath at the gate, then went in, tripping over her skirt and biting her already bleeding and swollen lips. The half open door of the shed loomed in the shifting lilac darkness of the yard. With a fierce effort she gathered her remaining strength, ran to the door and stepped hurriedly inside. The shed was dry and cool and smelled of leather harness and stale straw. With no thought or feeling, only black misery clawing at her shame-filled, desperate heart, Natalya groped her way to a corner. She found a scythe, removed the handle (her movements were now deliberately slow and precise) and, throwing back her head, drew the blade sharply and with a rush of joyous resolution across her throat. The searing pain flung her to the ground and, with a vague sense of not having completed what she had set out to do, she dragged herself on to her hands and knees, then hurrying (the blood streaming over her breast frightened her) and tearing at the fasteners with trembling fingers, she for some reason undid her jacket. With one hand she pushed aside the firm unyielding breast, and with the other pointed the scythe at her heart. She crawled to the wall, wedged the blunt end of the blade, where the handle should have been, into a chink, forced her hands back behind her head and thrust her chest forward. Forward, forward... She clearly heard and felt the cabbage-like crunch as the blade cut into the flesh; a mounting wave of pain rose like fire from her chest to her throat and drove ringing needles into her ears...

The house door creaked. Lukinichna felt with her foot for the first step and walked down from the porch. A church bell was ringing out steadily. From the Don came the ceaseless rumble of rearing massive ice-floes as the liberated river, joyous and full-watered, carried its icy captivity away, down to the Azov Sea.

Stepan came up to Grigory, seized his stirrup and pressed hard against the horse's sweating flank.

'Well, how are you, Grigory!'

'Praise the Lord.'

'What are you thinking now? Huh?'

'Why should I think?'

'You ran off with another man's wife and now you're—having a good time with her?'

'Let go of the stirrup.'

'Don't be scared... I won't hit you.'

'I'm not scared. You'd better drop that!' Grigory snapped, reddening at the cheekbones.

'I won't fight you today, I don't feel like it... But mark my words, Grishka: sooner or later I'll kill you!'

'Wait and see, the blind man said.'

'Yes, just you remember that, and remember it well. You've done me a great wrong!.. Taken all the sap out of my life, gelded me like a hog. Look!' Stepan held out his hands with their grimy palms upward. 'I'm ploughing, but I don't know what I'm doing it for. Do I need much for myself? I could get through the winter without taking all this trouble. But it's the loneliness of it that kills me... Ay, you did me a great wrong, Grigory!'

'Don't come crying to me. The well-fed don't understand the hungry.'

'There's something in that,' Stepan assented, looking up into Grigory's face, and suddenly he gave a simple boyish smile that split the corners of his eyes into a multitude of fine wrinkles. 'There's one thing I regret, lad... Remember the year before last, the fights we had at Shrovetide?'

'When?'

'The year the felter got killed. The bachelors were fighting the married men, remember? Remember how I chased you? You were a lightweight compared to me, just a green bulrush. I took pity on you. But if I'd hit you when you was running, I'd have split you in two! Running that quick you was, and all tense; if I'd given you a real one in the ribs—that would have been the end of you!'

'Don't grieve too much, we'll bump into each other again one day.'

Stepan rubbed his forehead, trying to remember something.

Listnitsky, who was leading his horse by the bridle, shouted to Grigory to get moving.

Still holding the stirrup, Stepan kept up with the stallion. Grigory watched him guardedly. From above he could see Stepan's drooping chestnut moustache and the thick scrub on his long unshaven cheeks. The cracked patent-leather strap of his cap hung down under his chin. His face, grey with dirt and streaked with the sweat that had run down it, was almost that of a stranger. Grigory felt as if he were looking down from a hill at a distant steppe wrapped in a haze of drizzle. Stepan's face was grey with lassitude and boredom. He dropped behind without saying good-bye and Grigory rode on at a walk.

'Wait a bit! How... How's Aksinya?'

Grigory knocked a lump of mud off his boot.

'All right.'

He checked the horse and looked round. Stepan was standing with his legs wide apart, teeth bared and biting at a stalk. Grigory suddenly felt unaccountably sorry for him, but jealousy drove out pity. He turned round on the creaking saddle and shouted, 'She's not pining for you, don't worry!'

'Is that so?'

Grigory lashed the stallion between the ears and rode away without replying.

XX

Aksinya told Grigory of her pregnancy only in her sixth month, when it could no longer be concealed. She had kept it from him for fear that he would not believe it was his child she was carrying under her heart. Her face had grown sallow from the fits of fright and misery that overcame her, from waiting and putting things off.

Even in the first months the sight of meat had made her sick, but Grigory had not noticed it, or, not guessing the cause, had given it little thought.

The conversation took place one evening. When she had told him, Aksinya scanned his face anxiously for any signs of change, but he only turned away to the window and coughed irritably.

'Why didn't you tell me before?'

'I was afraid, Grisha... I thought you'd leave me.'

Grigory's fingers drummed on the back of the bed.

'How soon will it be?'

'In August, I think.'

'Is it Stepan's?'

'It's yours.'

'Is it?'

'Work it out yourself... From the time of the wood-cutting it'd be—'

'Don't make things up, love! Even if it is Stepan's, you can't help it now. I want a straight answer.'

Aksinya sat on the bench with angry tears in her eyes, speaking in a choking whisper.

'I lived with him so many years and nothing happened! Can't you see? I wasn't ailing in any way... So it must be you who gave it to me.'

Grigory said no more on the subject. A new thread of wary aloofness and slightly mocking pity wove itself into his feeling for Aksinya. She withdrew into herself and made no attempt to beg affection. Her looks had faded during the summer but her shapely figure was hardly spoiled by pregnancy; its fullness hid the roundness of her belly and her thin face was softened by the warmer light in her eyes. She coped easily with her work. There were fewer hired hands that year and less cooking to be done.

With an old man's capricious affection Sashka had become attached to Aksinya. Perhaps it was because she looked after him like a daughter, washing his clothes, patching his shirts and giving him the softest morsels at table. When he had finished with the horses, Sashka would bring water to the kitchen, mash the potatoes that had been boiled for the pigs, and do all kinds of small services, each with a little caper, spreading his arms and showing his bare gums.

'You've been good to me, lass, and I'm going to pay you back! I'd find a noggin for you, Aksinya, love, if I had to draw it from my own heart. In a right bad way I was without a woman's care! The lice were eating me up! So you just say if there's anything you need.'

Grigory, who had been excused training camp at the request of the younger Listnitsky, helped with the mowing, occasionally drove the old general to the stanitsa, and spent the rest of the time with him shooting or riding down bustards. The easy, well-fed life had spoiled him. He had grown lazy, put on weight and looked older than his years. Only one thing worried him—the prospect of serving in the army. He had neither a horse nor equipment and it would be no use counting on his father to provide them. He spent as little as he could of the wage he received for himself and Aksinya, and even denied himself tobacco in the hope of saving enough to buy a horse without begging from his father. The general had also promised to help. Grigory's conjecture about his father was soon confirmed. At the end of June he had a visit from Petro. In the course of the conversation he mentioned that their father was still angry and had actually said he would not provide a cavalry mount, so Grigory had better join the local infantry unit.

'Well, he can drop that nonsense. I'm going to ride my own horse.' And Grigory stressed the 'own'.

'How'll you get one? Dance for it?' Petro grinned, munching his moustache.

'I'll steal one, if I can't get it any other way.'

'Good for you!'

'I'll buy it out of my wages,' Grigory explained more seriously.

Petro sat on the porch, asked about the work, the food and the money, nodding his assent to everything and munching the well-chewed tip of his moustache and, having found out all he wanted to know, finished up by saying, 'Why don't you come home? It's no use riding the high horse. Think you're going to make your fortune?'

'I'm not doing it for that.'

'D'you reckon to live with her now?' Petro changed the subject.

'Who do you mean by "her"?'

'This one here.'

'Yes, I reckon so. Why?'

'I was just asking, out of interest.'

When he was seeing his brother off, Grigory asked, 'How are things at home?'

Petro gave a mocking little laugh as he untethered his horse.

'You've got as many homes as a hare has holes. We're not doing too badly. Mother misses you. And what a hay crop we raked in this year! Three stacks of it.'

With a wistful feeling Grigory examined the old stubby-eared mare Petro was riding.

'Hasn't she foaled?'

'No, brother, she turned out to be barren. The Bay, the one we got off Khristonya—she had a foal.'

'What was it?'

'A colt, brother. And what a colt—worth his weight in gold! Long legs, good pasterns and a fine chest on him.

He'll make a grand horse.'

Grigory sighed.

'I'm missing the village, Petro. And the Don. You never see flowing water out here. It's a sickening place!'

'Come and see us,' Petro grunted, heaving himself on to the horse's knobbly back and swinging his leg over the crupper.

'I will one day.'

'Well, good-bye!'

'Safe journey!'

Petro had ridden out of the yard when he suddenly remembered something, and shouted to Grigory, who was still standing on the porch.

'Ay, and about Natalya... I forgot... A terrible thing...'

The wind that had been hovering over the yard like a kite snatched the last phrase. Petro and his horse were swaddled in the silken dust and Grigory turned away with a shrug to go to the stables.

It was a witheringly dry summer. There was hardly a dribble of rain and the corn ripened early. They had only just got the rye in when the barley was ready, showing up in yellow patches of drooping bristled ears. Four extra labourers had been hired for the reaping season and Grigory went out to work with them.

Aksinya finished her cooking early and persuaded Grigory to take her too.

'What for? Why not stay at home?' he had argued, but Aksinya insisted and, quickly wrapping a kerchief round her head, ran out of the gate to catch up with the wagon carrying the hired men.

The thing that Aksinya had awaited with such anxiety and yet with a joyous impatience, and which Grigory had vaguely feared, happened during the reaping. Aksinya was raking when certain signs made her drop the rake and lie down under a rick. Soon she was in labour. She lay on her back, biting her blackened tongue. The labourers on the reaper drove past, shouting at the horses as they went round the field. A young fellow with a syphilitic nose and deep lines in his yellow board-like face jeered at Aksinya as he rode by, 'What's up? Got stuck in an awkward place? Get up or you'll melt!'

Grigory changed places on the reaper and came over to her.

'What's the matter?'

Aksinya gasped out through her writhing lips, 'It's started.'

'I told you not to come, you stupid bitch! Now what are we going to do?'

'Don't be angry, Grisha... Oh!.. Oh!.. Grisha, harness up. I'd rather it was at home... How can I have it here? With men all round...' Aksinya moaned as the iron hoop of pain tightened.

Grigory ran for the wagon horse, which was grazing in a hollow. By the time he had harnessed it and driven up, Aksinya had crawled away and thrust her head into a pile of dusty barley and was spitting out the prickly ears that she had gnawed in her agony. She stared with swollen uncomprehending eyes at Grigory and sank her teeth into her crumpled apron so that the labourers would not hear her ugly animal-like scream.

Grigory lifted her into the wagon and drove hard for the estate.

'Oh, not so fast!.. Oh, death!.. You're ... shaking me!..' Aksinya screamed, rolling her dishevelled head back and forth on the bottom of the wagon.

Grigory silently plied his whip and swung the reins above his head without looking back at the source of those harsh, rending cries.

With her hands pressed to her cheeks and her half-crazed eyes rolling wildly Aksinya was flung about as the wagon danced from side to side over the bumpy, little used track. The horse was going at full gallop; Grigory kept his eyes fixed on the shaft-bow rising and falling smoothly against a dazzling white cloud that hung in the sky like polished crystal. Aksinya's screams broke off for a minute. The wheels rattled and her helpless head knocked against the back of the wagon. At first Grigory remained unaware of the sudden hush, then it hit him and he glanced round. Her face contorted, Aksinya was lying with her cheek pressed against the side of the wagon, gasping like a fish out of water. Sweat was rolling down her forehead into the sunken eyesockets. Grigory lifted her head and put his crumpled cap under it. She squinted up at him and said firmly, 'I'm dying, Grisha. It's ... it's all over!'

He shuddered, suddenly chilled to the toes of his sweating feet. Shakenly he sought words of comfort and affection, but found none; his lips curved harshly and he blurted out, 'You stupid fool!' He shook his head and, bending almost double, reached down and pressed Aksinya's awkwardly twisted leg. 'Aksinya, love!..'

The pain that had abated for a minute returned with

redoubled force. Feeling something tear in her belly, Aksinya arched her back and shook Grigory with a terrible mounting scream. Grigory lashed the horse frantically.

Amid the rumble of the wheels he scarcely heard her call his name 'Grisha!'

He reined in and turned his head. Aksinya was lying in her own blood, her arms outstretched; under her skirt something living stirred and squealed...

Grigory jumped dazedly to the ground and staggered like a hobbled horse to the back of the wagon. As he leaned over Aksinya and felt the hot breath from her mouth he guessed rather than heard the words, 'Bite through the cord ... and ... tie it up ... with thread ... from your shirt...'

With shaking fingers Grigory ripped a bunch of threads from his calico shirt and, screwing up his eyes till they hurt, bit through the umbilical cord and tied the bleeding stump firmly with thread.

XXI

The Listnitsky estate clung to the broad dry valley like a growth on a tree-trunk. The wind changed, blowing from the south or north; the sun floated in the bluish whiteness of the sky like the yolk of an egg; autumn rustled in, treading on the skirts of summer, winter descended with its frosts and snow, but Yagodnoye remained wrapped in its wooden torpor. The days with their routine that cut the estate off from the rest of the world were as alike as peas in a pod.

The black whistling ducks with their red-ringed eyes still waddled about the yard, the guinea-fowl were scattered here and there like sprinklings of coloured beads, and the gawdy plumed peacocks strutted about the roof of the stables, uttering their hollow cat-like cries. The old general liked all kinds of birds. He even kept a wounded crane, and in November it would tug at the strings of human hearts with its mournful response to the faint call of its migrating brothers. But its broken wing hung limply at its side and it could not fly. The general would watch from his window as it bucked and jumped about trying to leave the ground; his big mouth would open wide under the grey overhang of his moustache and his deep laughter would resound through the empty white-walled drawing room.

Veniamin held his velvety head as high as ever, his big thighs shook like jellied meat, and he still spent days on end playing rummy with himself on the big chest in the hall. Tikhon still cherished his pock-marked mistress and was jealous of Sashka, the labourers, Grigory, his master, and even of the crane, on which Lukeria lavished the overflow of her widowly tenderness. And from time to time Sashka would get drunk and go to the window to wheedle kopecks out of his master.

Only two events occurred to disturb this mouldering, somnolent life: the birth of Aksinya's child and the disappearance of a thoroughbred gander. Everyone soon got used to the baby girl that Aksinya had brought into the world, and when the feathers of the gander were found at the bottom of the bank below the poplar grove (evidently the work of a fox), calm once again descended on the estate.

As soon as he awoke in the morning the general would call for Veniamin. 'Did you have any dreams?'

'Oh yes, such a wonderful dream.'

'Tell me about it,' his master would command briefly, making himself a cigarette.

And Veniamin would tell his dream. If it was boring or frightening, the old man would take him to task.

'What a fool! An oaf! You must be a fool to have such foolish dreams!'

So Veniamin took to inventing cheerful, interesting dreams. The trouble was that he had to use his imagination. He would start thinking them up several days in advance, while he sat on the chest, plastering the rug with playing cards as thick and greasy as the cheeks of the player. He would stare so long at one spot and think so hard that eventually he stopped having any dreams at all. He would wake up and try to remember them, but his mind was a blank. He could not recall even a face, let alone a dream.

As Veniamin came to the end of his meagre stock of invention, his master grew even more demanding and would catch the narrator repeating himself.

'You, stupid dolt, you told me that dream about a horse last Thursday. What's the matter with you?'

'I had it again last night, Nikolai Alexeyevich! It came back, honestly it did, may God be my witness!' Veniamin would lie readily enough.

In December Grigory was summoned by courier to the stanitsa administration in Vyoshenskaya. He was given one hundred rubles to buy a horse, and also notice that on the second day of Christmas he was to report at the recruiting centre in the town of Mankovo.

Grigory returned from the stanitsa in a state of dismay. Christmas was approaching and he had nothing ready. With the money he had received from the administration and his own savings he bought himself a horse in the village of Obryvsky for one hundred and forty rubles. Old Sashka went with him and they struck a reasonable bargain for a six-year-old bay with drooping haunches; it had one barely visible defect. Old Sashka tugged at his beard and said, 'You won't find anything cheaper, and the officers won't spot it. They an't got the gumption.'

Grigory rode the horse home, trying it at the walk and the canter. And a week before Christmas Pantelei himself arrived at Yagodnoye in a sledge. He tethered the mare to the fence and limped to the servants' quarters, stripping icicles off his beard, which lay across the collar of his sheepskin like a block of black wood. Grigory was taken aback when he saw his father through the window.

'Look at that!.. It's Father!'

For some reason Aksinya darted to the cradle and wrapped up the child.

Pantelei stumped into the room in a cloud of cold air, took off his fur cap, crossed himself before the ikon, and let his eyes roam slowly round the room.

'Good health to you!'

'Hullo, Father,' Grigory responded, and rose from the bench. He took a step forward and halted in the middle of the room.

Pantelei offered Grigory his chilled hand, sat down on the edge of the bench and drew his sheepskin round him, ignoring Aksinya, who was standing stiffly by the cradle.

'Getting ready for the army?'

'Of course.'

Pantelei said nothing and gave his son a long, testing look.

'Take your coat off, Father. You must be frozen?'

'Never mind that.'

'We'll heat the samovar.'

'Thank ye.' Scratching an old speck of dirt off his coat, he said, 'I've brought you your equipment: two greatcoats, a saddle, trousers. Go and take it... It's all out there.'

Grigory went out bareheaded and carried the two sacks in from the sledge.

'When do you muster?' his father inquired, rising.

'The second day of Christmas. Are you going already, Father?'

'Ay, I'm in a hurry. I want to get back early.'

He said good-bye to Grigory and, still ignoring Aksinya, went to the door. With his hand on the latch he shot a glance at the cradle and said, 'Your mother asked to be remembered to you. She's having trouble with her legs.' And after a pause, with an effort, as though lifting something heavy, 'I'll come to see you off as far as Mankovo. Get yourself ready.'

He went out, plunging his hands into the warmth of a pair of knitted mittens. Pale from the humiliation she had suffered, Aksinya said nothing. Grigory walked about the room, glancing at her sideways and always treading on the same creaking floorboard.

On the first day of Christmas Grigory drove Listnitsky to Vyoshenskaya.

The general attended mass, had lunch with his cousin, the mistress of a large estate near by, and ordered Grigory to harness up.

Grigory had not finished his bowl of thick pork and cabbage soup, but he rose at once and went to the stable.

The light city sledge was drawn by a dappled grey trotter from the Orlov stud. Grigory led it out of the stable, using all his weight to hold the bridle, and harnessed it hastily to the sledge.

The wind was winnowing the crisp prickly snow and low silvery gusts were hissing across the yard. The trees in the garden were draped with soft tassels of hoarfrost. As the wind shook them off, they rainbowed in the sunshine. On the roof of the house, near a sooty smoking chimney some shivering jackdaws were jabbering at each other. They flew up at the sound of footsteps, circled over the house like grey snowflakes and flew westwards towards the church, darkening to a deep blue against the violet morning sky.

'Say the sledge is ready!' Grigory shouted to a housemaid who had run out on to the porch.

Listnitsky came out, dipping his moustache into the collar of his raccoon coat. Grigory wrapped up his master's feet and fastened the velvet-covered wolfskin rug.

'Warm him up,' Listnitsky commanded with a glance at the horse.

As he leaned back, gripping the quivering reins with

213

tense hands, Grigory glanced apprehensively at the polished ruts, remembering how when the sledge swerved awkwardly during their first winter ride the general had jabbed the back of his head with a by no means feeble fist. They drove down to the bridge and only when crossing the Don did Grigory slacken the reins and rub his wind-seared cheeks with his glove.

They reached Yagodnoye in two hours. Listnitsky was silent all the way, only occasionally tapping Grigory's back with a crooked finger to halt the sledge while he turned away from the wind and lit a cigarette.

As they were driving down the slope towards the estate, he asked, 'Do you start early tomorrow?'

Grigory turned sideways and only just managed to force a 'Yes' from his frozen lips. It was as though his tongue had swollen from the cold and stuck to his teeth.

'Did you get all your money?'

'Yes.'

'Don't worry about your wife, she can live here. Serve well. Your grandfather was a fine Cossack. You too must...' the old general's voice became muffled as he sheltered his face in his coat collar, 'you too must be worthy of your grandfather and your father. Your father won first prize for trick riding at the Imperial Review in 1883, didn't he?'

'Yes, he did.'

'There you are then,' the general ended severely, almost threateningly, and buried his face completely in his overcoat.

Grigory handed the horse over to Sashka and went to the servants' quarters.

'Your father's here!' Sashka shouted after him, throwing a cloth over the horse's back.

Pantelei was sitting at the table, finishing a plate of jellied meat. He's had a drink or two, Grigory decided, noticing the softened lines of his father's face.

'So you're back, soldier?'

'Yes, and frozen stiff,' Grigory replied, clapping his hands; and to Aksinya, 'Untie my hood, I'm all fingers and thumbs.'

'You were unlucky, the wind was right in your face,' his father grunted, ears and beard twitching as he chewed.

On this visit he was far more gentle. With a brief but friendly command he told Aksinya to cut him some more bread. 'Don't be stingy now.'

As he rose from the table and went to the door for

a smoke, he rocked the cradle once or twice as if by accident, pushed his beard under the canopy and asked, 'A Cossack?'

'It's a girl,' Aksinya answered for Grigory and, noticing the disappointment that passed over the old man's face and lodged in his beard, added hastily, 'She's the living image of Grisha.'

Pantelei briskly surveyed the dark little head poking out of the covers and affirmed with some pride, 'Yes, that's our blood all right... Humph!.. Well, I'll be...'

'How did you come, Father?' Grigory asked.

'Two horses—the filly and Petro's.'

'One would have been enough. We could have put mine in harness.'

'No need for that. Let him go light. That's not a bad horse you've got there.'

'So you've seen it?'

'Just a look.'

They talked of various unimportant matters with only one thing at heart. Aksinya took no part in the conversation and sat forlornly on the bed, her full, firm breasts all but bursting her blouse. She had filled out since giving birth and acquired a new assurance in her posture.

They went to bed late. Aksinya clung to Grigory, soaking his shirt with salty tears and the milk that oozed overabundantly from her breasts.

'I'll die of loneliness here... How can I stay here all alone?'

'You'll manage,' Grigory whispered back.

'Think of the long nights ... when the baby won't sleep... I'll miss you so much, I'll just wither!.. Think of it, Grisha—four years!'

'They used to serve twenty-five years in the old days, so I've heard.'

'What do I care about the old days.'

'Enough of that!'

'Oh, curse your rotten service that parts us like this.'

'I'll be coming home on leave.'

'On leave,' Aksinya echoed with a moan, sobbing and wiping her nose on his shirt. 'A lot of water will go down the Don before that.'

'Don't whimper... You're like an autumn drizzle, you go on and on.'

'What would you be like in my shoes!'

It was nearly daybreak before Grigory fell asleep. Aksinya nursed the baby and, leaning on her elbow, gazed unblinkingly into the hazy lines of Grigory's face, saying good-bye to him. She remembered the night when she had tried to persuade him to go off with her to the Kuban; there had been a moon then and the yard outside had been flooded with its pale light.

The moon was the same, but Grigory now was the same and yet not the same. A long path, well trodden by the days, lay behind them.

Grigory turned over and said clearly in his sleep, 'At Olshansky village...' His voice broke off without finishing the sentence.

Aksinya tried to fall asleep, but her thoughts scattered sleep as the wind scatters a haycock. Until daybreak she pondered this unconnected phrase, trying to guess its meaning.

Pantelei awoke as soon as daylight foamed through the frost-coated windows. 'Get up, Grigory, it's getting light.'

Kneeling on the bed, Aksinya pulled on her skirt and with a sigh began searching for matches.

By the time they had breakfasted and packed up, the day dawned. The morning light was tinged with a liquid blue. The fence rose toothily out of the snow and the roof of the stables loomed dark against the tender lilac haze of the sky.

Pantelei went out to harness the horses. Grigory broke away from Aksinya's frenzied kisses and went to say good-bye to Old Sashka and the others.

Aksinya wrapped up the baby and came out to see him off.

Grigory let his lips rest for an instant on his daughter's small damp forehead and went to his horse.

'Get into the sledge!' his father shouted, starting the horses.

'No, I'll ride.'

Taking his time, Grigory tightened the saddle-girths, then mounted and shook out the reins. Aksinya kept tapping his leg with her fingers and repeating, 'Grisha, wait... There was something I wanted to say...' Trembling and confused, she frowned as she tried to remember.

'Well, good-bye! Look after the little one... I must be off. Look where Dad is now!'

'Wait, darling!..' With her left hand Aksinya seized the cold stirrup and, clasping the swaddled baby in her right, gazed up at him insatiably with no free hand to wipe the tears falling from her wide unblinking eyes.

Veniamin came out on to the porch.

'Grigory, the master wants to see you.'

Grigory swore, swung his whip and galloped out of the yard. Aksinya ran after him, stumbling through the snow-drifts in her felt boots.

Grigory overtook his father on the brow of the hill. Bracing his will, he glanced back. Aksinya stood at the gate, clasping the swaddled baby to her breast, the ends of her red shawl fluttering and twisting in the wind.

Grigory rode up beside the sledge and they slowed to a walk. His father turned his back on the horses and asked, 'So you're not thinking of living with your wife?'

'That's an old story... It's all over and done with.'

'So you won't?'

'So I won't.'

'Hadn't you heard that she tried to take her own life?'

'I heard about it.'

'Who from?'

'I had to drive the master to the stanitsa and saw some of our people there.'

'And what about God?'

'Oh, Father, after all... What's the use of crying over spilt milk.'

'Don't come that on me! I'm saying this for your own good,' Pantelei rapped out, beginning to lose his temper.

'What is there to talk about? You've seen, I've got a child. I can't change anything now.'

'Are you sure you're not rearing another man's child?'

Grigory's face paled. His father had touched an open wound. Ever since the birth of the child Grigory had been wrestling with a suspicion that he would not confess to Aksinya or even himself. At night, while Aksinya slept, he would often go up to the cradle and stare at the baby's pinkish brown face, trying to detect features of his own, and would turn away as uncertain as before. Stepan's hair was also a dark brown, almost black. How could you tell whose blood flowed in those delicate blue veins that showed up through the baby's skin? At times he thought his daughter was like himself, but at others she reminded him painfully of Stepan. Grigory had no feeling for her, except perhaps hostility at the thought of what he had been through when driving back from the fields with Aksinya writhing in labour behind him. Only once, when Aksinya was busy in the kitchen, had he taken his daughter out of the cradle and, as he changed the wet nappy, felt a sharp tickling of excitement. He had bent over her furtively and pressed his teeth into one of the baby's little red toes that was sticking up.

Now his father had jabbed the wound ruthlessly. He folded his hands on the saddle-bow and replied huskily, 'I won't leave the child, no matter whose it is.'

Pantelei swung his whip at the horses without looking round.

'Natalya's spoiled her looks... She holds her head crooked now, like she'd been struck with the paralysis. She cut a main sinew and her neck is all to one side.'

He was silent for a time. The sledge runners scraped over the snow, Grigory's horse was knocking its hooves as it walked.

'How is she now?' Grigory asked, carefully picking a half-rotten burr out of the horse's mane.

'She's got over it, I think. She was in bed for seven months. At Whitsun we thought it was all up with her. Father Pankraty came to anoint her... But she pulled through. She's been getting better since then. Now she's up and about. She aimed that scythe at her heart, but her hand shook and she missed. It would have been the end of her otherwise.'

'Faster down the hill!' Grigory plied his whip and, rising in the stirrups, rode on ahead of his father. The horse broke into a canter, kicking lumps of snow from its hoofs into the sledge.

'We'll have Natalya to live with us!' Pantelei shouted, overtaking him. 'She don't want to live with her own folk. I saw her a while ago and invited her.'

Grigory made no reply. They rode on to the next village in silence and his father did not raise the subject again.

In one day they covered about seventy versts. At the end of the next, when the lights were on in the houses, they arrived in Mankovo.

'Where're the Vyoshenskaya men?' Pantelei asked the first person they met.

'Straight on down the main street.'

In the lodging they found five other recruits with fathers who had come to see them off.

'What villages are ye from?' Pantelei asked, as he sheltered the horses.

Several voices answered from the darkness that they were from the River Chir.

'What village?'

'Some are from Kargin, some from Napolov, from Likhovidov. Where would you be from?'

'From the cuckoo's nest,' Grigory said with a laugh, unsaddling the horse and feeling its sweating back.

The next morning Ataman Dudarev of Vyoshenskaya stanitsa took his recruits before the medical commission. Grigory saw the lads of his age from his own village; Mitka Korshunov, mounted on a tall light-bay horse with a flashy new saddle and a richly decorated bridle and breast-band, had galloped past on his way to the well in the morning. He had noticed Grigory at the gate of his lodgings, but had ridden past without so much as a greeting, his left hand steadying his jauntily tilted cap.

In the unheated waiting room of the *volost**　administration the recruits undressed in turn. Army clerks and an assistant police officer hurried to and fro. The A. D. C. to the *okrug* ataman, wearing short patent-leather boots, scurried past from time to time; his agate signet ring and dark handsome eyes with their prominent pinkish whites brought out the whiteness of his skin and shoulder cords. The conversation of the doctors and occasional remarks filtered through from the inner room.

'Sixty-nine.'

'Pavel Ivanovich, give me an indelible pencil,' a morning-after voice requested huskily from near the door.

'Chest measurement...'

'Oh yes, obviously hereditary.'

'Syphilis, make a note of that.'

'Why are you covering yourself with your hand? You're not a girl.'

'What a physique!..'

'...in the village, it's a hot-bed of this disease. Special measures ought to be taken. I have already reported the matter once to His Excellency.'

'Pavel Ivanovich, just look at this specimen. What a physique!'

'Yes, indeed...'

Grigory undressed beside a tall ginger-haired lad from the village of Chukarinsky. A clerk appeared and, straightening his shoulders till his tunic creased at the back, rapped out, 'Panfilov Sevastyan, and Melekhov Grigory.'

'Hurry up!' Grigory's neighbour whispered, flushing and rolling down his socks.

Grigory went in with goose-flesh all over his back. His

---

* *Volost, okrug*—administrative sub-divisions of Cossack territory, *okrug* being the largest.—*Tr.*

body was the colour of stained oak and he suddenly felt confused at the sight of his own legs covered with thick dark hair. A gawky lad was standing naked on the scales in the corner. Someone, evidently an assistant doctor, moved the balance and shouted, 'Four, ten. Get down.'

The humiliating process of examination upset Grigory. A grey-haired doctor in a white coat tested his chest with a stethoscope, another, somewhat younger, rolled back his eyelids and looked at his tongue, a third—in horn-rimmed spectacles—hovered in the background, with his sleeves rolled up to the elbows, rubbing his hands.

'Get on the scales.'

Grigory stepped on to the cold ribbed platform.

'Five, six and a half,' the assistant announced, when he had flicked the metal balance to and fro.

'What the devil! The fellow's not very tall...' the grey-haired doctor purred, taking Grigory's arm and spinning him around.

'Amazing!' the younger one stuttered.

'How much?' one of the doctors sitting at the table asked in astonishment.

'Five poods, six and a half pounds,' the grey-haired doctor replied, his eyebrows still raised.

'Shall we put him in the Guards?' the regional military police chief asked, inclining his black smoothly brushed head to his neighbour at the table.

'He has the face of a bandit—quite savage.'

'Here, turn round! What's that on your back?' an officer with colonel's insignia on his shoulder straps exclaimed, tapping the table impatiently.

The grey-haired doctor mumbled something. Grigory turned his back towards the table, scarcely able to control the shivers rippling through his body, and answered, 'I had a chill in spring. They're boils.'

By the time all his measurements had been taken, the officers discussing the case at the table had decided that he would have to go into an ordinary regiment of the line.

'You will be drafted into the Twelfth Regiment, Mele-khov. D'you hear?'

He was allowed to go. As he went to the door he heard the supercilious whispers behind him.

'Oh, quite impossible! Just imagine if His Majesty were confronted with a face like that? Those eyes...'

'Some sort of cross-breed! From the East, I suppose.'

'And his body's not clean either. Boils...'

The lads of his village waiting their turn surrounded him as he came out.

'Well, what's it to be, Grishka?'

'Where've they put you?'

'The Ataman's Regiment, I expect?'

'How much did you knock up on the scales?'

Hopping about on one leg, Grigory pulled on his trousers and answered through clenched teeth, 'Leave me alone! What the hell is all the fuss about? Where did they put me? The Twelfth Regiment.'

'Korshunov Dmitry and Kargin Ivan.' The clerk called out.

Grigory ran down the steps, buttoning his sheepskin.

A warm wind had brought a sudden thaw and the bare patches on the road were steaming. Clucking chickens ran across the street and some geese were wading a puddle streaked with ripples. In the water their pink webbed feet had the orange-red flush of frost-seared autumn leaves.

The inspection of the horses began a day later. Officers bustled about the square; a veterinary surgeon and his assistant with a measuring-stick walked past with the skirts of their long greatcoats flapping. The horses, a motley bunch, were strung out along the wall in a long line. Ataman Dudarev ran slipping and stumbling from the scales to the table that had been set up in the middle of the square. The military police chief walked past, explaining something to a young lieutenant, legs jerking as if he were angry.

Grigory, who was number 108 in the line, led his horse to the scales. They measured every section of the horse's body, weighed the animal, and before it could leave the platform the veterinary surgeon again, with an habitual air of authority, seized its upper lip and examined its mouth, squeezed and pressed the chest muscles, then ran his strong fingers, like a spider, down the legs.

He squeezed the knee joints, tapped the ligaments of the tendons, and pressed the bone above the fetlocks. He poked, pinched and listened until the horse itself became suspicious, then he walked away, flapping the skirts of his white coat and spreading a strong odour of carbolic acid all around him.

The horse was rejected. Old Sashka's hopes had proved unfounded. The hawk-eyed surgeon had all the 'gumption' that was required to find the hidden defect Sashka had spoken of.

Grigory conferred anxiously with his father and half an hour later, in between turns, Petro's horse was put on the scales. The surgeon let it through with hardly a look.

Grigory chose a fairly dry spot, spread out his horse cloth and arranged all his equipment on it; Pantelei stood behind him, holding the horse and chatting to another old man who was also seeing off his son.

A tall grizzled general in a pale-grey greatcoat and a silvery Astrakhan hat walked past them. Swinging a white-gloved hand, he took longer strides with his left leg than with his right.

'That's the *okrug* ataman,' Pantelei whispered, jabbing Grigory in the back.

'He's a general, isn't he?'

'Major-General Makeyev. He's mad strict!'

The ataman was followed by a crowd of officers who had come in from the regiments and batteries. A captain, broad in the shoulders and thighs and wearing artillery uniform, was talking loudly to a tall handsome officer of the Ataman's Life Guards.

'What the devil! Here was an Estonian village, where nearly everyone is fair, and this girl such a sharp contrast! And she was not the only one! We made various conjectures and it turned out that twenty years before...' The officers walked on and as the wind carried their words away Grigory only just managed to hear the concluding phrase mingled with the officers' laughter, '...your Life Guards had been stationed in that village.'

Buttoning his tunic with trembling ink-stained fingers, a clerk ran past pursued by an angry shout from the assistant chief of military police, 'In triplicate, I told you! I'll have you put under arrest!'

Grigory stared curiously at the unfamiliar faces of the officers and officials. A passing A. D. C. fixed a pair of bored watery eyes on him and turned away on encountering his attentive gaze; a worried-looking elderly lieutenant chased after the A. D. C., biting his upper lip with yellowed teeth. Grigory noticed the twitch just above his ginger eyebrow.

The equipment at Grigory's feet was laid out according to regulations on a fresh, unused horse-cloth. It consisted of a saddle with a metal-trimmed frame painted green, front and rear saddle-bags, two greatcoats, two pairs of trousers, a tunic, two pairs of top-boots, underclothes, a pound and a half of rusks, a tin of corned beef, cereals and all the other food supplies a mounted soldier was supposed to carry. The open saddle-bags revealed a set of horse-shoes for all four feet, nails wrapped in an oily rag, a soldier's hussif containing two needles and thread, and a towel.

Grigory checked his belongings for the last time and bent down to give the stained buckles of his saddle-bags a rub with his sleeve. The inspecting commission approached slowly along the line of Cossacks standing behind their equipment. The officers and the ataman were meticulous in their inspection, holding up the skirts of their light-grey greatcoats as they squatted down to rummage in saddle-bags, turn out hussifs, and test the weight of the food bags on their hands.

'Look at that tall one, lads,' a young Cossack next in line to Grigory exclaimed, pointing to the *okrug* chief of military police, 'he's digging like a dog in a polecat's burrow.'

'The devil!.. He's turning out the bag!'

'Must be something wrong or he wouldn't pull it to bits like that.'

'He's not counting the nails, is he?'

'Nosey dog!'

The remarks died away as the commission came nearer. It would soon be Grigory's turn. The *okrug* ataman was carrying his glove in his left hand and swinging his right arm stiffly. Grigory drew himself to attention; behind him his father cleared his throat. The wind wafted the smell of horse's urine and melted snow across the square. A dismal sun looked down blearily on the scene.

The officers took their time with Grigory's neighbour and came on to him one by one.

'Surname? Christian name?'

'Melekhov, Grigory.'

The police chief lifted one of the greatcoats by its back-strap, sniffed at the lining and quickly counted the fastenings; another officer with a cornet's insignia fingered the good woollen cloth of the trousers; a third, bending over so far that the tails of his coat flapped up on to his back, rummaged in the saddle-bags. The police chief felt the rag containing the nails with his thumb and little finger, as though it were something hot, and his lips moved as he counted.

'Why only twenty-three nails? What does this mean?' he exclaimed, tugging the corner of the rag in annoyance.

'No, Your Honour, there are twenty-four.'

'D'you think I'm blind?'

Grigory hastily turned back the corner of the rag covering the twenty-fourth nail and, as he did so, his rough dark fingers touched the police chief's sugar-white hand. The police officer snatched his hand away as though it had been pricked, wiped it on the side of his grey greatcoat and, frowning with disgust, pulled on his glove.

Grigory noticed this and smiled maliciously as he straightened up. Their eyes met and a flush appeared on the police officer's cheeks. He raised his voice.

'Is that the way to look, Cossack! How dare you look at me like that?' His cheek, which bore the dried-up scar of a razor cut, reddened from the top down. 'Why are the buckles of your saddle-bags dirty? What's all this? Are you a Cossack or a peasant lout?.. Where is your father?'

Pantelei Prokofievich pulled the horse's bridle and took a step forward, bringing his lame leg up with a click of the heels.

'Don't you know the regulations?' the police chief, who had woken up in a bad temper after losing at cards the night before, pounced on the old man.

The *okrug* ataman came up and the police officer subsided. The ataman touched the saddle seat with the toe of his boot, hiccoughed and walked on to the next Cossack. The movements officer of the regiment Grigory had been drafted to politely went through everything, down to the thread in the hussif, and was the last to leave, walking away backwards as he lighted a cigarette in the wind.

The next day a train of red railway vans loaded with Cossacks, horses and fodder left the station of Chertkovo for Liski and Voronezh.

In one of the vans, leaning against a wooden manger, stood Grigory. The sliding doors were open and the unfamiliar flat countryside floated past with a gentle blue braid of forest forever encircling it in the distance.

The horses champed the hay and shifted their feet, uncertain of the foothold on the swaying floor.

The van smelled of steppe wormwood, horse sweat, and the spring thaw, and the distant braid of forest glimmered on the horizon, blue, pensive and unattainable as the faintly shining evening star.

PART THREE

I

On a melting, merry day in March 1914, Natalya returned to her father-in-law's house. Pantelei was weaving fuzzy blue willow twigs into a fence the bull had broken. The roof was dripping, the icicles dangling from it gleamed like silver, and the eaves were streaked with tarry black stains from the water that had trickled down them.

A redder, warmer sun nuzzled the thawing brow of the hill like an affectionate calf, the earth was swelling with moisture, and an early crop of grass shone like malachite on the bald chalky headlands running down to the Don.

Natalya, changed and thin, came up to her father-in-law from behind and inclined her scarred, misshapen neck.

'Hullo, Father.'

'Natalya, lass! Hullo, m'dear, hullo!' In his excitement Pantelei dropped the twig he had been bending. It twisted and straightened as it fell. 'Where have you been all this time? Come into the house, dear. Mother'll be right glad to see ye.'

'Father, I've come...' Natalya made a vague gesture and turned away. 'I've come to stay, if you'll have me.'

'What a question, lass! You're no stranger here. Grigory has been asking about you in his letters. Yes, my girl, he wanted to know how you're getting on.'

She walked into the house with Pantelei stumping along agitatedly and joyfully beside her.

A little chain of tears trickled down Ilyinichna's cheek as she embraced Natalya, then, blowing her nose on her apron, she whispered, 'If only you'd got a baby. That'd make him stick to you... Sit yourself down now. I'll get you some pancakes, shall I?'

'God bless you, Mother. You see, I've come—'

Dunyashka, glowing like a sunrise, burst into the kitchen from the back yard, and in one bound flung her arms round Natalya's knees.

'Oh, you shameless creature! You've forgotten all about us!'

'You crazy young filly!' her father reprimanded her with mock severity.

'What a big girl you've grown!' Natalya exclaimed, freeing herself from Dunyashka's arms and gazing into her face.

They all spoke at once, interrupting one another, then suddenly falling silent. Ilyinichna put her hand to her cheek and looked sadly at her daughter-in-law, so unlike the former Natalya.

'Have you come to stay?' Dunyashka wanted to know, plucking at Natalya's fingers.

'It's not for me to say.'

'Of course, she is. She's his wife, isn't she! Where else should she live! Stay with us!' Ilyinichna declared, sliding an earthenware bowl full of pancakes along the table towards her daughter-in-law.

Natalya had returned to her husband's family after long hesitation. Her father, reluctant to let her go, had scolded and reproached her, but after her recovery she found it hard to live with her own family and feel herself almost a stranger among those who had once been dear to her. Her attempted suicide had set her apart from them. But Pantelei, ever since seeing Grigory off into the army, had been trying to win her over. He had firmly resolved to take her back into his own family and reunite her with his son.

So from that day on Natalya was once again a member of the Melekhov household. Darya did nothing to show her displeasure; Petro treated her as one of the family, and his wife's occasional hostile glances were redeemed by Dunyashka's ardent affection and the old couple's parental warmth.

The very next day after Natalya's arrival, Pantelei made Dunyashka write Grigory a letter that he dictated.

Greetings, our dear son Grigory Panteleyevich!

Your mother Vasilissa Ilyinichna and I send you our deepest regards and parental blessing from the bottom of our hearts. Your brother Pyotr Panteleyevich and his wife Darya Matveyevna send their regards and wish you good health and providence; your sister Yevdokiya and the rest of the family also send you their regards. We have received the letter that you sent on February 5th and heartily thank you for it.

If the horse, as you write, is hitching, you must smear the fetlocks with lard, as you know, and don't shoe his hind feet unless it's slippery. Your wife Natalya Mironovna is living with us and is in good health and comfortable.

Your mother sends you some dried cherries and a pair of woollen socks, some fat-back and other good things. We are all well, but Darya's baby has died, as we hereby inform you. The other day Petro helped me to put a new thatch on the barn and he says you must look after the horse and take good care of it. The cows have calved; the old mare is in foal, her udder's tight and you can see the young one kicking in her belly. She was mated with a stallion from the stanitsa stud called Donets and we are expecting her to foal in the fifth week of Lent. We are glad to hear you are doing well in the army and that your officers approve of you. Do your duties well. Service for the Tsar will never be wasted. Natalya will be living with us now and you must think about that. And we've had trouble too. At Shrovetide a wolf killed three of our sheep. Well, keep well and God bless you. Don't forget your wife—that's an order from me. She's an affectionate woman and lawfully wedded to you. So don't kick across the traces and listen to your father.

Your parent, Senior Sergeant,

Pantelei Melekhov.

Grigory's regiment was stationed four versts from the Russo-Austrian border, in the small town of Radzivilovo. Grigory wrote only occasional letters home. He was restrained in his response to the news that Natalya was living at his father's house and asked only to give her his regards; the substance of his letters was usually evasive and vague. Pantelei would make Dunyashka or Petro read them to him time and time again, while he tried to fathom the thoughts hidden between the lines. In a letter before Easter he asked Grigory straight out whether he intended to live with his wife on his return from the army, or stay with Aksinya.

Grigory was slow in answering. After Whitsuntide they

227

received a short letter from him. Dunyashka read it quickly, swallowing the ends of words and Pantelei had difficulty in catching the meaning behind all the countless greetings and questions. Grigory ended his letter with a reference to Natalya:

...You ask me to write whether I will be living with Natalya or not, but all I can say to you, Father, is that a cut loaf can't be stuck together. What can I offer Natalya now, when, as you know, I have a child myself? I can't promise her anything and I am sick of talking about it. The other day a smuggler was caught on the border and we talked to him. He told us we'll soon be at war with the Austrians, and that their tsar came to the border to see where he could start the war from and what lands he could grab. If war breaks out, I may not live to see the end of it, so it's no good trying to decide things beforehand.

* * *

Natalya worked for her father-in-law, unconsciously cherishing the hope of her husband's return and relying on it to keep up her broken spirit. She wrote nothing to Grigory, but no one else in the family awaited his letters with such pain and yearning.

The life of the village followed its usual inviolable course. The Cossacks who had served their time in the army came home; the week-days were swallowed up by humdrum tasks, on Sundays whole families went in droves to church; the men wore their tunics and best trousers and the women rustled by in long different-coloured skirts that swept the dust, and bright-patterned blouses, puffed at the shoulders, gathered at the wrists, and rotting and faded under the armpits from acid-sweet women's sweat that tickled the nostrils like mustard.

On the square the parked carts stood with their shafts pointing skywards, horses whinnied, and a mixed crowd milled to and fro. By the fire-shed the Bulgarian market gardeners offered their vegetables for sale on long mats, while gangs of children stood gaping at the unharnessed camels behind them, which in their turn haughtily surveyed the market-place and the crowd seething with red-banded caps and a motley sprinkling of women's kerchiefs. Resting from their ceaseless toil on the water-wheel, the camels chewed their weedy cud with dribbling mouths, and their eyes gradually became set in a somnolent greenish solder.

In the evenings the streets groaned with the beat of dancing feet; here and there a gathering would burst into song or jig to the accordion, and not until late at night did the last melodies die away on the warm dry air.

Natalya never went out in the evenings but she listened gladly to Dunyashka's artless tales. All of a sudden the youngest Melekhov had grown up into a slim-waisted girl with a beauty of her own. She had matured quickly, like an early-ripening apple. This was the year when her older girl-friends forgot her past adolescence and took her into their circle. Dunyashka was her father's girl, dark and stocky.

Her fifteenth spring came and went without rounding out her slim, gawky figure. She remained an innocent, pitiful mixture of childhood and blossoming youth; her small breasts, no bigger than a fist, were firming up under her blouse, her shoulders were broadening out, but in the long slanting slits of her eyes the black pupils still sparkled shyly and mischievously amid the bluish whites. After the evening's outing she would confide her simple secrets only to Natalya.

'Natalya, darling, I want to tell you something.'

'I'm listening.'

'Mishka Koshevoi sat with me all yesterday evening on the oak stumps by the stores.'

'What are you blushing for?'

'I'm not blushing one little bit.'

'Look in the glass—you're all aflame.'

'Wait a bit. It was you who made me blush.'

'Go on then, I won't make any more remarks.'

Dunyashka rubbed her flaming cheeks with her dark hands, pressed her fingers to her temples and let out a tinkle of young, causeless laughter.

' "You're like the gentle tulip of the steppes," he says!'

'Yes, and then what?' Natalya encouraged her, rejoicing in the other's joy and forgetting her own that had been trampled on.

'And I says to him, "None of your fibbing, Mishka!" So then he swears it by Almighty God.' Dunyashka's laughter rang through the room like harness bells. She shook her head, and her black, tightly plaited braids darted like lizards over her shoulders and back.

'And what else did he tell you?'

'Give me a handkerchief as a keepsake, he says.'

'Did you give him one?'

'No, I didn't. "No," I says, "you can ask your lady-

love for that." You see, he's going with the Yerofeyevs'
daughter-in-law... She's a grass-widow now, having a good
time.'

'Then you'd better keep away from him.'

'Oh, I'm far enough away as it is.' Dunyashka mastered
the smile that was hovering on her lips, and went on,
'There were three of us girls going home together, and
then Grandad Mikhei caught up with us and he was ever
so drunk. "Kiss me, girls," he cries. "I'll give you a kopek
apiece, my lovelies." And he just jumped on us, but
Nyurka whacked his forehead with a switch. We only just
got away from him!'

It was a dry, smouldering summer. The Don grew
shallow by the village, and where the current had once
been fast and dangerous a crossing formed that the oxen
could ford without wetting their backs. At night a clinging sultriness slid down the hill into the village and the
breeze filled the air with the cloying scent of scorched
grass. During the night storm clouds would build up
beyond the Don and thunder would crash and rumble,
but no rain fell on the fevered earth and the lightning
blazed for nothing, chopping the sky into jagged blue
slices.

Every night an owl hooted from the bell-tower. Its
weird wavering cries lingered over the village, and then it
would fly from the bell-tower to the cemetery, which had
recently been trampled by stray calves, and moan over
the brown disturbed graves.

'It's a bad sign,' the old men predicted when they
heard the owl hooting over the graveyard.

'There's a war coming.'

'It used to hoot like that before the Turkish campaign.'

'Mebbe there's cholera about again?'

'No good will come of it. It's flying from the church
to the dead.'

'Oh, merciful Saviour, blessed Saint Nicholas...'

Martin Shumilin, the brother of one-armed Alexei,
stalked the bird of ill omen for two nights by the cemetery wall, but it flew silently over his head, invisible
and mysterious, alighted on a cross in the other corner of
the cemetery and continued to send its ominous cries
over the sleepy village. Martin swore and let fly at the
black hanging belly of a cloud that was passing overhead.
He lived near the cemetery. His wife, a nervous woman,
ailing but as fertile as a rabbit—she had a baby every
year—greeted her husband with reproaches.

'Oh, what a fool you are! A proper fool! Is the bird interfering with you, you brute? And what if God punishes us? Here I am in my last month and suppose I can't give birth because of you, you devil?'

'Be quiet, woman! You'll have it all right! What are you stamping about for, like a cooper's horse! Why should the darn creature give us all the willies? It's calling down trouble on us. If there's a war, they'll want me in the army, and look at the litter you've given me.' Martin waved his hand towards the corner, where the squeaking of the mice mingled with the snuffling of a heap of youngsters all sleeping together on a mat.

When discussing the matter with the old men in the market-place, Pantelei would offer his own weighty argument.

'Our Grigory writes that the Austrian tsar came to the border and gave orders for all his troops to be mustered in one place and march on Moscow and Petersburg.'

The old men recalled past wars and shared their conjectures.

'There's not going to be any war. You can see that from the harvest.'

'The harvest has nothing to do with it.'

'It's them students causing trouble, I reckon.'

'We'll be the last to hear about that.'

'Like in the war against Japan.'

'Have you got your son a horse?'

'No need to rush things...'

'It's all a lot of talk!'

'Who would we go to war with?'

'With the Turks, because of the sea. They can't share out the sea properly.'

'What's so hard about that? Just cut it up into strips like we do with the meadow, and there you are!'

The talk usually ended in a joke and the old men went their ways.

There were urgent matters to be attended to. The meadow grass on the other side of the Don was ripening fast and had to be mowed. Feeble and without fragrance, it was not a patch on the grasses of the steppe. The soil was the same, but the grass sucked different juices from it. Out in the steppe beyond the hill the hard-baked black earth was like gristle; a drove of horses could gallop over it without leaving a hoofmark. The soil was hard, but the grass on it grew strong and fragrant, tall enough to tickle a horse's belly; but down by the Don, and on the other side, the soft, oozing soil sent up a flabby, joyless crop that in some years even the cattle would not touch.

Scythes were being sharpened and rakes repaired all over the village; the women were brewing kvass to comfort the mowers, and just at this moment an event occurred that shook the village from end to end. The district chief-of-police, a police inspector, and a black-toothed puny little officer in a uniform that no one had ever seen before arrived in the village. They demanded to see the ataman, assembled witnesses, and marched straight to cross-eyed Lukeshka's.

The police inspector had taken off his badged, canvas-topped cap and was carrying it in his hand. The party proceeded down the left side of the street; the path by the fence was dappled with patches of sunlight and as the inspector tramped across them in his dusty boots he questioned the ataman, who was strutting along in front like a cockerel.

'Is the newcomer Stokman still here?'

'Yes, Your Honour.'

'How is he employed?'

'We know he's a craftsman. Always sawing and planing.'

'Have you noticed anything untoward him?'

'No, Your Honour.'

As he walked, the chief-of-police pressed a pimple that had come up between his eyebrows; he was puffing and sweating in his thick woollen uniform. The black-toothed little officer was picking his teeth with a straw and wrinkling the limp reddish folds round his eyes.

'Who comes to see him?' the inspector went on with his questions, hauling back the hurrying ataman with his hand.

'Some people do, indeed. Sometimes they play cards.'

'But who?'

'Mostly from the mill. The workers there.'

'Who precisely?'

'The engine-man, the scalesman, the rollerman Davyd-ka, and one or two of our Cossacks go there sometimes.'

The inspector halted and waited for the black-toothed officer to catch up, wiping the sweat from the bridge of his nose with his cap. He said something to the officer, twisting a button on his uniform, and beckoned the ataman. The latter ran up on tip-toe, holding his breath; a tangle of veins stood out quivering on his neck.

'Get two of your men and go and arrest the lot. Bring them to the office and we'll be along there in a moment. Do you understand?'

The ataman drew himself up and held the upper part of his body so far forward that the biggest vein in his neck bulged over the high collar of his uniform like blue whip-cord, then with a little grunt he marched off in the direction from which he had come.

Stokman was sitting with his back to the door, cutting a pattern out of plywood with a fret-saw. He was wearing only an undervest with the collar unbuttoned.

'Stand up. You are under arrest.'

'What is this all about?'

'Do you occupy two rooms?'

'Yes.'

'We're going to make a search.' Stumbling as his spur caught on the door-mat, the officer walked to the table, narrowed his eyes and picked up the first book he saw.

'I shall want the keys of that trunk.'

'To what do I owe the honour of this visit, Inspector?'

'There will be time to discuss that with you later. Witness! This way!'

Stokman's wife looked out from the next room and left the door ajar. The inspector went in, followed by a clerk.

'What's this?' the officer asked softly, holding a book in a yellow binding at arm's length.

Stokman shrugged. 'A book.'

'Keep your witticisms for a more suitable occasion. I shall expect a different kind of answer to my questions!'

Stokman leaned back against the stove, suppressing a wry smile. The police chief glanced over the officer's shoulder and fixed his eyes on Stokman.

'Are you studying this?'

'I'm interested in the subject,' Stokman answered drily, dividing his black beard into two equal portions with a small comb.

'I see.'

The officer turned over a few pages and threw the book down on the table; he glanced through another, put it aside, read the cover of a third, and turned to Stokman.

'Where do you keep this kind of literature?'

Stokman closed his left eye, as though taking aim. 'All that I have is here.'

'You're lying!' the officer said crisply, waving the book.

'I demand—'

'Search!'

The police chief steadied his sword and went over to

the trunk, where a Cossack guard with small-pox scars on his face and evidently frightened by what was happening, was rummaging among the clothes and underwear.

'I demand polite treatment,' Stokman completed the phrase, and with one eye still closed took aim at the bridge of the officer's nose.

'Be quiet, fellow.'

They rummaged through everything that could be rummaged through in the half of the house occupied by Stokman and his wife. The workshop was also searched. The zealous police chief even tapped the walls with a crooked finger.

Stokman was marched off to the administration building. He walked down the middle of the street with the Cossack guard behind him, one hand tucked into the lapel of his shabby grey jacket, the other swinging as if to shake dirt off his fingers; the rest kept to the sun-dappled path by the fence. Once again the inspector stamped on sunny patches with boots now stained green by the goosefoot but, instead of carrying his cap in his hand, he had clamped it down firmly over his white gristly ears.

Stokman was the last to be interrogated. Ivan Alexeyevich, who had not even had time to wash the engine grease off his hands, Davydka with an awkward smile on his face, Knave with his jacket draped over his shoulders, and Mikhail Koshevoi, had already been interrogated and were sitting together in the waiting room, guarded by a Cossack.

The inspector leafed through a pink folder while Stokman stood facing him on the other side of the desk.

'When I questioned you about the murder at the mill, why did you conceal the fact that you are a member of the Russian Social Democratic Labour Party?'

Stokman stared over the inspector's head without answering.

'That has been proved. You will pay the penalty for your work,' the inspector snapped, irritated by this stubborn silence.

'Please begin your interrogation,' Stokman said in a bored tone, and with a glance at a vacant stool asked permission to sit down.

The inspector rustled his papers instead of replying, but looked up resentfully when Stokman calmly seated himself.

'When did you take up residence here?'

'Last year.'

'On the instructions of your organisation?'

'Without any instructions.'

'How long have you been a member of your party?'

'What are you talking about?'

'I am asking you,' the inspector stressed the 'I', 'how long you have been a member of the RSDLP.'

'I think that—'

'I am not in the least interested in what you think. Answer the question. Concealment is useless and could only harm you.' The inspector detached one of the papers and pinned it to the desk with his forefinger. 'This is a report from Rostov confirming your membership of the party in question.'

Stokman scanned the white slip of paper with narrowed eyes, let them rest on it for a moment, and then, rubbing his knee, replied firmly, 'Since 1907.'

'Very well. And you deny that you were sent here by your party?'

'Yes.'

'In that case, why did you come here?'

'There seemed to be a demand for people with mechanical skills.'

'Why did you choose this district?'

'For the same reason.'

'Are you, or were you at any time during this period, in contact with your organisation?'

'No.'

'Do they know that you are here?'

'Probably.'

The inspector sharpened a pencil with a small mother-of-pearl penknife and pursed his lips. He did not look at Stokman.

'Are you in correspondence with any of your members?'

'No.'

'For what purpose did the workers from the mill assemble at your lodgings?'

Stokman shrugged, as if in astonishment at the absurdity of the question.

'We merely gathered on winter evenings... Simply to pass the time. We played cards...'

'And read books forbidden by law,' the inspector added.

'No. They are all uneducated.'

'But the engine-man from the mill and the other mill-hands do not deny the fact.'

'That is not true.'

'It seems to me you haven't the least idea...' At this point Stokman smiled and the inspector lost the thread of what he had been going to say. He ended with suppressed anger. 'You simply have no common sense! You are only harming yourself by your denials. It is quite obvious that you were sent here by your party to spread disaffection among the Cossacks, to subvert their loyalty to the government. I don't understand why you are playing this shifty game. It won't alleviate your guilt.'

'These are mere conjectures on your part. May I smoke? Thank you. And your conjectures have no foundation.'

'Excuse me, did you read this book to the workers who visited you?' The inspector laid his hand on a small volume, covering the title. Above it a name showed up clearly in black and white: 'Plekhanov.'

'We read poetry,' Stokman sighed, and drew at his cigarette held firmly between his fingers.

The next morning, under a sickly overcast sky, a postal tarantass drawn by two horses drove out of the village. Stokman was sitting in the back, muffling his beard in the thin greasy collar of his overcoat and dozing. Two Cossack guards armed with sabres sat squeezed in on either side of him. One of them, a curly-headed pock-marked fellow, was gripping Stokman's elbow with gnarled grimy fingers and squinting at him with frightened whitish eyes while keeping his left hand on the battered sheath of his sabre.

The tarantass went down the street at a smart pace, raising the dust. Outside the Melekhovs' yard, with her back to the fence of the threshing floor a small woman wrapped in a shawl stood waiting. Her face was obliterated by tears, like a defaced coin, and looked pitifully yellow and pasty with its vacant tear-filled eyes.

As the tarantass swung past, the woman clasped her hands to her breast and ran after it.

'Osip! Osip! Oh, what shall I do!'

Stokman was about to wave, but the pock-marked guard jumped up, dug his dirty fingers like pincers into his arm, and shouted in a savagely hoarse voice, 'Sit down! Or I'll cut you down!..'

It was the first time in all his simple life that he had set eyes on a man who had dared to go against the tsar.

II

Somewhere behind him, in the slimy grey mist lay the long road from Mankovo to the small township of Radzivilovo. Grigory tried to recall the journey but nothing connected came to mind; only the red station buildings, the clicking of the wheels under the swaying floor, the smell of hay and horses' excrement, the endless threads of steel unreeling behind the engines, the smoke that sometimes billowed in through the doors of the vans, the moustached bloated face of a gendarme on the platform at Voronezh or Kiev.

At the wayside station where they detrained they were met by a crowd of officers and people with their hair cut very short and wearing long grey coats, who spoke in a strange incomprehensible tongue. It took some time to unload the horses, which had to be led down ramps from the vans. The assistant movements officer gave the order to saddle up and led the three hundred or more Cossacks to the veterinary station. The lengthy process of examining the horses was followed by allocation to squadrons. The N. C. O.s were kept running to and fro. Light-bay horses were assigned to the first squadron; grey and dun to the second, dark bays to the third; Grigory's mount was assigned to the fourth, with the plain and golden bays; the sorrels went to the fifth, and the blacks to the sixth. The sergeants-major then formed the Cossacks up into troops and led them off to their squadrons, which were spread out among the various estates and townships of the locality.

Sergeant-Major Kargin, pop-eyed and debonair, with long-service stripes, asked Grigory as he rode past, 'What stanitsa are you from?'

'Vyoshenskaya.'

'Bob-tailed, are you?'*

The Cossacks from other stanitsas chuckled as Grigory swallowed the insult in silence.

The road led out on to a highway. The horses from the Don, which had never seen a made-up road before, snorted and flattened their ears, as if they were setting foot on a river covered with thin ice. They soon got used to it, however, and trotted along with their fresh, unworn shoes clicking crisply. All around lay the strange land of Poland,

---

* All the stanitsas had nicknames. Vyoshenskaya's was Dogs.— *Author.*

sliced by blades of stunted forest. The dull warm day was humid. Even the sun, hidden behind a cheesecloth curtain of cloud, seemed different from that of the Don.

The Radzivilovo estate was four versts from the station. Half way there the Cossacks were overtaken by the movements officer and his orderly, who went by at a fast canter. The troop reached the estate half an hour later.

'What *khutor** is that?' a young Cossack from Mitya-kinskaya stanitsa asked, pointing to a cluster of bare tree-tops in an orchard.

'*Khutor*? You forget your *khutors* here, young shaver! This isn't the Don Army Region.'

'What is it then, uncle?'

'And I'm not your uncle! A fine nephew you'd make! That, my lad, is the estate of the Princess Urusova. That's where our fourth squadron is stationed.'

Despondently stroking his horse's neck, Grigory rose in the stirrups and gazed at the neat two-storeyed house, the wooden fence and the unfamiliar outbuildings. As they rode past the orchards, the bare branches whispered to the wind in the same language as those in the faraway Don homeland he had left behind.

A tedious and stultifying life began. Deprived of their usual occupations, the young Cossacks could at first find nothing to do but relieve their feelings in desultory talk. The squadron was quartered in big, tiled outbuildings; they slept on wooden bunks under the windows. Over Grigory's bunk the paper sealing that had come unstuck from the frame hummed all night like a distant shepherd's horn, and as Grigory lay listening to it amid the chorus of snores he felt a stony misery eating into him. That fine vibrating hum seemed to put pincers on his heart, and at such times he longed to get up, go to the stables, saddle his horse and ride all the way home at a wild gallop, leaving flecks of foam on this deaf, unresponsive earth.

At five in the morning they were wakened to groom the horses and clean up. In the half an hour while they were feeding their tethered mounts with oats they would toss brief remarks to one another.

'Rotten place this is, lads!'

'Can't stand it!'

'And the sergeant-major—he's a swine! He makes you wash the horses' hooves.'

---

* The Cossack word for village.—*Tr.*

'Back home now they'll be stuffing themselves with pancakes. It's Shrovetide...'

'I'd like to get my hands on a girl, eh?'

'Last night, lads, I dreamed I was out mowing with my Dad and there was a ring of people all round, like daisies round a threshing floor,' docile Prokhor Zykov recounted, his gentle calf-like eyes shining. 'We were mowing and the grass was falling under our scythes... It was grand!'

'The wife will be saying, "I wonder what my Mikola is doing now?"'

'Oho! She'll be belly-rubbing with your father most likely!'

'Go on with you...'

'There isn't a woman living who won't have a bit on the side while her husband's away.'

'What are you moaning about? A woman's big enough jug o'milk. There'll still be some left for us when we come back from the army.'

Yegor Zharkov, who had the liveliest and lewdest tongue in the squadron, and impudence enough for two, broke into the conversation, winking and grinning suggestively.

'You can bank on that. Your dad won't miss any chances with his daughter-in-law. He's a he-dog all right. It's happened before...' He rolled his eyes, surveying his listeners. 'One old buck was making a real nuisance of himself round his daughter-in-law, wouldn't give her a minute's peace, but her husband was in the way. And you know what he thought of? One night he went out and opened the shed on purpose, so that all the cattle would come into the yard. Then he says to his son, "You so-and-so," he says, "why'd you leave the gate open? Look, the animals are all over the yard. Go and get 'em in!" You see, he thought he'd jump into bed with his daughter-in-law while his son was out. But his son was lazy and whispers to his wife, "You go and get 'em in." So out she went and he stayed in bed, listening. Then his father climbs down from the stove-bed and crawls over to their bed on his hands and knees. The son's no fool, picks up a rolling pin from the bench and waits. And as soon as his father gets to the bed and starts groping around, the son bonks him one on his bald patch. "Shoo, you damned animal!" he says. "What's this habit you've got of chewing the blanket!" You see, they were keeping the calf indoors at night and it had a habit of chewing their bed-clothes. So the son gives his dad a bonk and pretends to be talking to the calf. After that he keeps quiet for a bit and the old fellow crawls back to bed and lies there feeling the bump that's as big as a goose's egg. Well, after a bit, he says, "Ivan, d'you hear me, Ivan?" "What's the matter, Dad?" "Who was that you hit just now?" "The calf, of course." And then the old man says with tears in his voice, "What kind of a farmer will you make, darn you," he says, "if you knock the animals about like that?"'

'You're a great one for making things up!'

'Like a dog barks. Ought to be put on a chain.'

'What's this—the market-place? Break it up!' the sergeant-major bawled as he came up, and the Cossacks went back to their horses, chuckling and firing jokes at each other. After breakfast the sergeants set about knocking their home-bred ways out of them on the parade ground.

'Pull that belly in, pig's trash!'

'Right dress! Quick march...'

'Troop, halt!'

'March!'

'Left marker, is that the way to stand, blast you?'

The officers remained at a distance, watching the Cossacks being marched about the big yard, smoking and sometimes intervening.

As he glanced at the smart, well-groomed officers in their trim pale-grey greatcoats and well cut uniforms, Grigory felt separated from them by an invisible, insurmountable wall; the life on the other side of that wall was very different from that of the Cossacks, smart and clean, without lice, without fear of the sergeants-major, who often brought their fists into play.

An episode that occurred on the third day after their arrival at the estate made a painful impression on Grigory and all the other young Cossacks. They were engaged in mounted exercises when the lively, mettlesome horse ridden by Prokhor Zykov—the lad with the gentle calf-like eyes who often dreamed of home—happened to kick the sergeant-major's mount as it went past. The glancing blow only opened the skin on the upper part of the other horse's left leg, but the sergeant-major lashed Prokhor hard across the face with his whip and rode into him shouting, 'Why the hell don't you look where you're going? You, little bastard! I'll have you on guard duty for the next three days.'

The squadron commander, who was giving the troop officer some instructions, witnessed this scene and turned away, toying with the hilt of his sword and yawning. Prokhor wiped the blood from the weal that had come up on his cheek and his lips trembled.

As he brought his horse into line, Grigory watched the officers, but they went on chatting as if nothing had happened. About five days later, while watering his horse, Grigory dropped a pail into the well. The sergeant-major swooped on him like a hawk and lifted his fist.

'Hands off!' Grigory snapped huskily, looking down at the rippling water.

'What? Climb down there and get it, you bastard! I'll smash your face!..'

'I'll get it, but keep your hands off me!' Grigory said slowly, without raising his head.

If there had been other Cossacks by the well, the incident would have taken a different turn. The sergeant-major would have thrashed Grigory on the spot, but the others were attending to their horses by the fence and were out of earshot. The sergeant-major stepped closer to Grigory, looked back at them, rolled his eyes in insensate anger, and croaked, 'Who do you think you are? Is that the way you talk to your superiors?'

'Don't look for trouble, Semyon Yegorov!'

'Are you threatening me? I'll beat you into a pulp!'

'Now get this straight,' Grigory lifted his head from the well, 'If ever you hit me, I'll kill you! Understand?'

The sergeant-major opened his square, carp-like mouth in astonishment, but could think of nothing to say. The moment for punishment was lost. Grigory's pale, drawn face looked dangerous and the sergeant-major was at a loss. He walked away from the well, slipping in the mud churned up round the gutter that they used for pouring water into the wooden troughs. When at a distance he turned round and heaved his fist into the air like a sledge-hammer.

'I'll report you to the squadron commander! I'll report you!'

For some reason he did not carry out his threat, but for the next fortnight he hounded Grigory ruthlessly, picking on every little thing and putting him on extra sentry duty, though he was careful not to look him in the eye.

The dreary routine crushed the life out of everything. The whole day, until last post sounded in the evening, was spent in foot and mounted exercises, in grooming, cleaning and feeding the horses, and learning nonsensical 'regulations' by heart. At ten o'clock, after inspection and assignment to sentry duty, they would form up for prayers and the sergeant-major, running his round, pellet-like eyes, over the assembled ranks, would begin in that born-gruff voice, 'Our Father, who art...'

The same rigmarole began the next morning and the days followed one another, different but alike as twins.

Besides the elderly wife of the manager there was only one other woman on the whole estate—the Polish girl Frania, the manager's young and pretty maid. The target of all eyes, including the officers', she often ran to and fro from the house to the kitchen, where the old browless cook was in charge.

Sighing and winking, the drilling troops watched Frania's grey skirt as she rustled past. Constantly watched by Cossacks and officers, Frania bathed in the streams of lust that flowed from three hundred eyes and swayed her hips provocatively as she ran to and fro between the kitchen and the house, smiling at each troop in turn, and at the officers in particular. Her favours were courted by everyone, but rumour had it that only a certain lieutenant with curls all over his head and hair all over his body had won them.

It was an early spring day when it happened. Grigory was on duty in the stables. Most of the time he was at one end of the building, where the officers' stallions were falling out over a mare that was with them. It was the dinner-break. Grigory had just been calming down a major's white-stockinged stallion with his whip and had glanced into the stall where his own horse was munching the hay. The horse looked round at its master, showing a pinkish eyeball and lifted its hind leg, which had been bruised during the sabre exercises. As he adjusted the halter, Grigory heard sounds of a scuffle and a muffled scream coming from a dark corner of the stable. He walked along past the stalls, slightly surprised by the unusual sounds. A clammy darkness suddenly descended on him as the door of the stable was slammed shut and a voice called in a restrained whisper, 'Come on, lads! Quick!'

Grigory walked faster.

'Who's there?'

He bumped into Sergeant Popov, who was groping his way to the door.

'Is that you, Grigory?' he whispered, feeling Grigory's shoulders.

'Wait. What's happening?'

The sergeant let out a guilty titter and grabbed Grigory's sleeve.

'Here... Stop. Where're you off to?'

Grigory tore his arm afree and threw open the door. A gawdy-feathered hen with a docked tail, all unaware that tomorrow the cook intended making her into a soup for his master, was scratching casually in the dung and clucking thoughtfully over where to lay her egg.

Momentarily blinded by the flood of light, Grigory shaded his eyes with his hand and turned towards the noise from the corner of the stable, which had grown louder. He groped along the wall; a reflected sunbeam danced on the wall and the mangers near the door. He walked forward, half closing his dazzled eyes. Soon he bumped into Zharkov the jester, who was coming towards him buttoning up his trousers and shaking his head.

'What are you doing here?'

'Hurry up!' Zharkov whispered, panting stale breath into Grigory's face. 'It's marvellous!.. The lads have got Frania in there... Laid her out...' His snigger broke off and his back thudded against the log wall of the stable as Grigory pushed him aside. Grigory ran towards the sound of the scuffling. His dilated eyes that had now grown accustomed to the darkness were white with fear. A crowd of Cossacks, the whole of the First Troop, were jostling in the corner where the horse-cloths were usually piled. Grigory silently elbowed his way through, and there was Frania lying on the floor, quite still, her head bound up in horse blankets, her skirt torn and dragged up above her breasts, her legs, white in the darkness, shamelessly and terrifyingly flung apart. One of the Cossacks had just risen from her, holding up his trousers, and with a wry grin, not looking at his friends, was stepping aside to make way for the next. Grigory recoiled and dashed for the door.

'Sergeant-major!..'

They caught him just before he reached it and dragged him back, clamping their hands over his mouth. He ripped someone's uniform from collar to hem and kicked another in the stomach, but he was thrown down, his head muffled like Frania's in a horse-blanket and his hands tied. They tossed him into an empty manger keeping silent so that he should not recognize their voices. Choking in the stinking woollen blanket, he tried to shout and kicked wildly at the wooden partition. He heard the whispers from the corner and the creak of the door as Cossacks entered and left. After about twenty minutes he was untied. The sergeant-major and two Cossacks from another troop were standing at the door.

'You keep quiet!' the sergeant-major said, blinking and looking away.

'You'd better not blab or we'll chop your ears off,' Dubok, a Cossack from another troop, advised with a grin.

Grigory saw Cossacks pick up the grey bundle that was Frania (her legs hung motionless, jutting out under her skirt), climb on to a manger and push her out through a gap in the wall where there were some loose boards. The stable overlooked an orchard, and above every stall there was a small grimy window. With a clatter of boots the Cossacks climbed up on the partitions to see what Frania would do; some of them hurried outside. Grigory, too, was moved by the same bestial curiosity. Gripping a beam, he pulled himself up to one of the windows, found a foothold and looked down. Scores of eyes stared through the grimy windows at the figure lying by the wall. Frania lay on her back, her legs working like scissors, her fingers scrabbling at the half melted snow. Grigory could not see her face, but he heard the suppressed gasps of the other Cossacks gathered at the windows and the soft pleasant crunch of the hay under their feet.

Frania lay for a long time, then dragged herself to her knees. Her arms trembled and seemed about to give way. Grigory saw that clearly. She struggled to her feet, a strange, unrecognizably dishevelled figure, and looked up at the windows in a long, lingering stare.

Then she staggered away, one hand clutching at the honeysuckle bushes, the other reaching out along the wall.

Grigory jumped down from the partition and rubbed his throat; he was choking.

At the door someone—afterwards he could never remember who—said to him in a matter-of-fact way, 'If you breathe a word to anyone, by Christ, we'll kill you! Get me?'

During the drill period the troop officer noticed a button missing from Grigory's greatcoat.

'Who's been pulling you about? What's this new fashion?'

Grigory glanced down at the small round mark left by the button on the cloth; memory seared through him and for the first time in years he felt like crying.

III

The steppe was wrapped in sultry yellow sunshine. Yellow dust rose from the unreaped waves of ripened wheat. The metal of the reaping machines was too hot to touch, the bluish-yellow canopy of the sky too hot to look at. And where the wheat ended, the broom spread its saffron blossom.

The whole village had migrated into the steppe to cut the rye. They were wearing out their horses on the reapers, and they themselves were nearly choking in the pungent dust and heat. The occasional ripples of air from the river lifted the dust and a thick haze muffled the stinging sun like a veil of horsehair.

Petro, who was throwing the swathes off the reaper, had drunk half a cask of water since morning. He gulped down the tepid, tasteless liquid, and the next moment his mouth was dry again, his shirt and trousers even wetter, and more sweat streamed down his face. There was a constant ringing and crackling in his ears and words stuck in his throat like burrs. Darya with her face completely covered and her blouse unbuttoned was tying the sheaves and shooking them. Grey grains of sweat rolled into the hollow between her brownish breasts. Natalya was urging on the horses harnessed to the reaper. Her scorched cheeks were beetroot red, her eyes watering. Pantelei plodded along the rows, looking as if he had just had a ducking. His soaked shirt was scalding his back and his bedraggled beard dripped from his chin like melting black cart grease.

'Got yourself in a lather, eh?' Khristonya shouted from a wagon as he rode past.

'Wet through!' Pantelei waved him aside and tramped on, mopping his belly with the hem of his shirt.

'Petro,' Darya shouted, 'I've had enough!'

'Hold on, let's finish the row.'

'Let's wait for the heat to go down. I give up!'

Natalya stopped the horses, panting as if she had been hauling the reaper herself. Darya walked slowly towards them over the stubble, her feet sore and black from the rub of her boots.

'Petro, there's a pond not far away from here.'

'Not far! About three versts!'

'I'd like a swim.'

'While you'd be walking back from there...' Natalya sighed.

'Why the devil should we walk? We'll unhitch the horses and ride!'

Petro glanced apprehensively at his father, who was stacking a shook, then made a sweeping gesture.

'Take 'em out, girls!'

Darya unhitched the traces and sprang agilely on to the mare's back. Natalya pursed her cracked lips in a smile and led the horse to the reaper, so that she could use the seat as a step.

'I'll give you a leg up,' Petro said, helping her.

They rode off, Darya galloped ahead with her skirt rucked up over her knees and her kerchief slipping off the back of her head. She sat the horse in Cossack style and Petro couldn't resist shouting after her, 'Mind you don't make it sore!'

'Who cares!' Darya threw back with a wave of her hand.

As they crossed the summer track, Petro glanced to the left. Far away along the grey hump of the highway a whirling speck of dust was rapidly approaching from the direction of the village.

'Someone's in a hurry,' he said, screwing up his eyes.

'Yes, he must be! Look at the dust he's making!' Natalya exclaimed.

'What for? Darya!' Petro shouted, overtaking his wife. 'Wait a bit! Let's have a look at that rider over there!'

The speck dropped into a hollow and came out enlarged to the size of an ant.

The figure of the horseman began to emerge through the dust. In another five minutes it was quite distinct. Petro put a grimy hand to the brim of the straw hat he used for work and stared.

'His horse won't last long at that rate. He's going flat out.'

He frowned and lowered his hand. A confusion had come upon his face and settled in the fork between the raised eyebrows.

Now the rider was clearly visible. He was still going at a hard gallop, holding his cap on with his left hand and gripping a dusty red pennant in his right.

He galloped by so close that Petro, who had just ridden

246

off the road, heard the hollow gasping of the horse, as it gulped the scorching air into its lungs. The rider's mouth looked like a square of grey stone as he shouted, 'Alarm!'

A fleck of yellowish foam fell on a hoofmark left in the dust. Petro followed the rider with his eyes, and all that he could ever remember afterwards was the laboured breathing of the exhausted horse and the steely gleam of its wet crupper.

Still not fully aware of the calamity that had occurred, Petro gazed stupidly at the foam quivering in the dust and the steppe sloping away in long waves to the village. Cossacks were galloping in from all sides across the yellow patches of stubble. All over the steppe, as far as the hill that was barely visible in the yellow haze, little tufts of dust were springing up and, where the horseman had reached the highway, a long grey tail stretched all the way to the village. Every Cossack eligible for military service had downed tools, unhitched a horse from a reaper and was riding hard for the village. Petro saw Khristonya unharness his guards stallion from his wagon and fling it into a gallop, bunching up his long legs and glancing back from time to time.

'What's it all about?' Natalya gasped, looking at Petro in fright and it was that look—the look of a startled hare—that shook him out of his stupor.

He galloped back to the camp, jumped off his horse before it stopped, pulled on the trousers he had thrown off in the heat of the work and, with a wave to his father, melted away in a cloud of dust that was like any of the others flickering like grey freckles of ash on the smouldering steppe.

IV

A dense grey crowd was gathering on the square. Horses, Cossack kit and equipment, the shoulder-straps bearing the various numbers of regiments, were drawn up in long rows. The Life Guards of the Ataman's regiment, a head taller than the Cossacks of the ordinary regiments, strutted about in their light-blue caps, like Dutch ganders among the lesser breeds of farmyard fowl.

The tavern was closed. The military police chief looked gloomy and worried. Women in their Sunday best lined the fences along the street. There was only one word on the lips of this motley crowd: 'mobilisation'. Flushed, tipsy faces. The sense of alarm spread to the horses, and an angry neighing broke out as they fought and snapped at one another. Dust hung low over the square, which was strewn with empty vodka bottles and the wrappers of cheap sweets.

Petro walked up, leading his saddled horse by the bridle. By one of the fences a burly, black-haired guardsman was buttoning up his baggy dark-blue trousers, his lips parted in a wide white-toothed grin. Beside him, a stocky Cossack woman—his wife or mistress—was piping away like a little grey quail.

'I'll give it you for that bitch you've been going with!' she was promising him.

She was drunk, there were sunflower husks in her lank dishevelled locks, and the ends of her colourful shawl were dangling loose. As he tightened his belt, the grinning guardsman planted his feet apart, making an arch wide enough for a year-old calf to pass through under his billowing breeches.

'Lay off, Mashka!'

'You randy dog, you skirt-chaser!'

'Well, what of it?'

'You and your brazen eyes!'

Near by a sergeant-major, his face framed in a red beard, was arguing with an artilleryman.

'Nothing's going to happen! We'll stand by for a day or so, then they'll send us home again.'

'But supposing there's a war?'

'God bless you, friend! What country in the world could stand up to us?'

Next to them a rambling discussion was taking place; a handsome elderly Cossack was beginning to lose his temper.

'It's nothing to do with us. Let 'em fight if they want to, but we haven't got our grain in yet!'

'Terrible this is! Look at all the men they've got together here. And every day counts at this time o'year!'

'The cattle'll be pulling our shooks to bits.'

'We'd just made a start on the barley.'

'So they've knocked off the Austrian tsar, have they?'

'His heir.'

'What regiment are you in, Cossack?'

'What's up with you, mate? Got rich all of a sudden?'

'Why, if it isn't Steshka! Where'd you spring from?'

'The Ataman says they've got us here just in case anything blows up.'

248

'Watch out, then, Cossacks!'

'If only they'd wait another year I'd be out of the third reserve.'

'What you here for, Grandad? Or haven't you done your time yet?'

'Once they start mowing us down, they'll get to the grandads soon enough.'

'They've shut the booze-shop.'

'Shut yourself! Marfutka here can sell you a barrel if you want it.'

The commission started its inspection. Three Cossacks were marching a drunk with blood on his face to the administration office. He hung back, tearing at his shirt, rolling his Kalmyk eyes, and bawling, 'I'll have the blood of those muzhiks! I'll show 'em what a Don Cossack's like!'

People stood back to let them pass with approving chuckles and sympathetic remarks.

'That's right, pitch into 'em!'

'What did he get knocked about for?'

'He beat up one of the muzhiks.'

'That's what they need!'

'We'll give 'em some more.'

'In 1905, boy, I was with the troops that was sent to put some of 'em in order. That was a laugh!'

'If there's a war, they'll have us on that job again.'

'Well, they can stuff it! Let 'em use volunteers. Or the police. It's not the thing for Cossacks.'

There was a crush round the counter in Mokhov's shop. The tipsy Ivan Tomilin was having a row with the owners. Sergei Platonovich, arms outspread, was remonstrating with him; his partner Lispy Atyopin was backing away towards the door.

'Really thith ith outrageouth!' he complained. 'Run and geth the athaman ath once, boy!'

Wiping his sweating hands on his trousers, Tomilin advanced on the frowning Sergei Platonovich.

'You dirty bastard, squeeze me dry, would you? And now you're scared? I'll smash your face in and you won't get a thing out of me! Robbing us of our Cossack rights! You dirty dog! You creep!'

The village ataman was painting a rosy picture for the benefit of the Cossacks gathered round him.

'War? No, there won't be any war. His Honour the Superintendent of Military Police says it's just for show. You can rest assured on that score.'

'Well, that's a good thing! As soon as I get home I'll be out in the fields.'

'The work's at a standstill now.'

'What are the authorities thinking about, if you please? I've got more than 250 acres under corn.'

'Timoshka! Tell our folk we'll be back tomorrow.'

'That must be a notice they're reading? Let's hear what it's all about!'

The square buzzed till late at night.

* * *

Four days later the red-painted goods-vans carried the Cossack regiments and batteries away to the Russo-Austrian border.

War...

From the stalls came the snorting of horses and the rich smell of dung. From the bunks where the men lay, the same kind of talk and songs, mostly this one:

> *The Don's awake and stirring,*
> *The truly Christian Don,*
> *Obedient to the monarch's call,*
> *It marches on, it marches on.*

At the stations they were met with curious and reverent glances that roved over the Cossack stripes on their trousers, over the Cossack faces that had not yet lost the deep tan from their work in the fields.

War!..

Frantic howls in the newspapers...

At the stations the women waved their kerchiefs smilingly at the Cossack troop trains and threw the men cigarettes and sweets. It was only at Voronezh that a tipsy old fellow, a railwayman, happened to put his head into the van where Petro and thirty other Cossacks were sweltering, and asked with a twitch of his thin little nose, 'Going off to war, eh?'

'Jump in and come with us, Grandad,' one of the Cossacks answered for all of them.

'What fine young ... bullocks for slaughter!' And he stood there, shaking his head reproachfully.

V

In the last days of June Grigory's regiment began manoeuvres. On orders from Divisional H. Q. it marched to the town of Rovno, where two infantry divisions and a number of cavalry units were deploying. The Fourth Squadron was stationed in the village of Vladislavka.

Some two weeks later, when the squadron, exhausted by the prolonged manoeuvring, took up its quarters in the township of Zaboron, the squadron commander, Captain Polkovnikov, rode in from Regimental H. Q. at a gallop. Grigory, who was resting in his tent with other Cossacks of his troop, saw the squadron commander charging down the narrow street on a foam-flecked horse.

The Cossacks in the yard stirred into life.

'Does that mean we're off again?' Prokhor Zykov suggested, and listened expectantly.

The troop sergeant pushed a needle into the lining of his cap (he had been sewing up his trousers).

'Looks like it.'

'They don't give you a bit of rest, the devils.'

'The sergeant-major said the brigade commander would be arriving soon.'

At that moment the bugler sounded the alert.

The Cossacks jumped up.

'What's become of my pouch?' Prokhor exclaimed, searching frantically.

'Boot and saddle!'

'To hell with your pouch!' Grigory shouted as he ran out.

The sergeant-major pounded into the yard and, steadying his sword, ran to the tethering posts. The horses were saddled in the regulation time. As Grigory tore up the tent pegs, the troop sergeant whispered to him, 'It's war, lad!'

'You're kidding?'

'God's own truth, the sergeant-major told me himself!'

They struck their tents and formed up in the street.

The squadron commander wheeled on his excited horse before the assembled ranks.

'In troop columns!..' his nasal voice hung over the ranks.

There was a great clatter of hooves as the squadron rode out of the town at a brisk trot. From the village of Kusten the First and Fifth Squadrons were also proceeding to the station at a trot.

One day later the regiment detrained at the station of Verba, thirty-five versts from the Austrian border. The dawn was coming up behind the station birch-trees and it promised to be a fine morning. A locomotive rumbled by. A shunting-engine was puffing up and down in a siding. The dew on the rails shone like varnish. The horses clattered down the ramps from the vans, snorting. Shouts and deep-voiced commands could be heard from beyond the water-tower.

The Cossacks of the Fourth Squadron led their horses out over the level crossing. Their voices clung stickily to the crumbling lilac darkness. Faces showed up bluishly, the shapes of the horses dissolved in the gloom.

'What squadron?'

'Where did you spring from?'

'I'll spring you, you lout! Is that the way to talk to an officer?'

'Sorry, Your Honour!.. Didn't recognise you.'

'Keep moving!'

'What are you lolling about for? There's an engine coming. Get moving.'

'Sergeant-Major, where is your third troop?'

'Squa-a-adron! Bring up the rear!'

And in the column, mutterings, half-whispers:

'Bring up the bloody rear, when you've missed two nights' sleep.'

'Syomka, give me a drag, I haven't had a smoke since yesterday evening.'

'Hold that stallion.'

'He's chewed through the halter, the devil.'

'Mine's lost a shoe on his foreleg.'

The Fourth Squadron found its path barred by another squadron that was turning off the road.

The shapes of the riders stood out clearly against the bluish whiteness of the sky, as though drawn in Indian ink. They were riding four abreast. Their lances swayed like bare sunflower stalks. Now and then a stirrup-iron clanked or a saddle creaked.

'Hey, lads, where are you heading for?'

'To our cousin's christening party.'

'Ha! ha! ha!'

'Silence! What's all the talk about!'

Prokhor Zykov clasped his metal-clad saddle bow and peered into Grigory's face, speaking in a whisper.

'Aren't you scared, Melekhov?'

'What is there to be scared of?'

'Well, we might be going into battle right now.'

'If we do, we do.'

'I'm scared,' Prokhor confessed, and his fingers played nervously with the reins, which were wet and slippery from the dew. 'Couldn't sleep a wink on the train last night. Darned if I could.'

The head of the column jerked and crawled forward, bringing the Third Troop into motion. The horses loped on steadily. The lances hitched to the riders' legs, swayed and floated forward.

Grigory let the reins hang loose and dozed. No, it was not his horse, with its springy step, that was carrying him lightly in the saddle, but he himself, walking alone along a warm black road, and the going was somehow unusually light and easy.

Prokhor kept muttering something in his ear. His voice mingled with the creaking of the saddle and the clip-clop of hooves without disturbing the thoughtless drowsiness that had overcome him.

They were riding along a cart-track. The stillness rang soothingly in his ears. The ripened oats gave off dewy vapours. The horses reached down for the low-hanging panicles, jerking the reins out of the riders' hands. Gradually a gentle glow crept under Grigory's tired, swollen lids; he lifted his head and again became aware of Prokhor's voice, monotonous as the creak of a wagon.

He was awakened by a deep, rumbling roar from far away across the oatfields.

'Gunfire!' Prokhor almost shouted.

Terror flooded murkily into his calf-like eyes. Grigory looked up. The troop sergeant's grey greatcoat was rising and falling in time with the horse's back. A field with unreaped strips of rye and a lark fluttering over it at about the height of a telegraph pole lay basking obliviously beside the track. The squadron came to life, electrified by the intense rumble of gunfire. Captain Polkovnikov, spurred on by the firing, led the squadron at a trot. They came to a crossroads where several tracks met at a deserted tavern, and from then on began to encounter wagons carrying refugees. A squadron of splendidly equipped dragoons swung past the Cossack unit. The dragoon captain with light-brown sideburns mounted on a chestnut thoroughbred, surveyed the Cossacks ironically and spurred his horse. A little further on a howitzer battery was stuck in a marshy hollow. The drivers were belabouring the horses while the gun-crews tried to manhandle the guns. A burly pock-marked gunner was coming from the tavern with an armful of boards that he must have torn out of the fence.

The squadron passed a regiment of infantry. The soldiers were marching fast with their greatcoats rolled on their backs and the sunlight glancing off their polished mess-tins and flowing down the sting-like blades of their bayonets. A corporal bringing up the rear of his company, small but cocky, threw a lump of dried mud at Grigory, 'Catch! You can throw it at the Austrians!'

'Don't play about, smarty.' Grigory cut the lump in two with his whip as it flew towards him.

'Take 'em our kind regards, Cossacks!'

'You'll be meeting them yourselves soon!'

The leading column was bawling out a lewd ditty; a fat-bottomed soldier of womanish appearance was walking backwards beside the column, slapping his hands on his short-topped boots. The officers were laughing. The sharp whiff of approaching danger had brought them closer to the men and made them more tolerant.

From the tavern to the village of Horovischuk the road was alive with infantry units, baggage trains, batteries and field hospitals, crawling along like caterpillars. The air was charged with the deadly breath of imminent battle.

At the village of Berestechko the Fourth Squadron was overtaken by the regimental commander Colonel Kaledin. He was accompanied by a lieutenant-colonel of the Cossacks. As Grigory watched the colonel's splendid figure riding away, he heard the lieutenant-colonel saying worriedly to him, 'This village is not marked on the three-verst map, Vassily Maximovich.'

Grigory did not catch the colonel's reply. An A. D. C. galloped past after them, his horse stepping heavily on its left hind leg. Grigory mechanically judged the animal's reliability.

A tiny hamlet appeared below the gently sloping fields in the distance. The regiment was going at a canter, and the horses began to sweat. Grigory ran his hand over his horse's darkened neck and looked around. Beyond the hamlet a ridge of forest lunged its green spears into the deepening blue of the sky. The rumble of artillery fire had swollen to a roar; now it was thundering in the ears of the riders and alarming the horses. The lulls were filled with the crackle of rifle fire. Distant puffs of smoke from bursting shrapnel shells melted away behind the forest, and the volleys of rifle-fire moved to the right, dying away, then flaring up again.

Grigory listened intently to every sound and his nerves became more and more strained. Prokhor Zykov fidgeted in his saddle and talked incessantly.

'Listen to that shooting, Grigory. It's like kids banging the fences with a stick, isn't it?'

'Keep quiet, you talker!'

The squadron rode into the hamlet. The yards were swarming with troops; dismayed villagers were running to and fro, packing up to leave. As he rode past one of the yards, Grigory noticed that some soldiers had lighted a fire under the overhang of a shed. The owner—a tall grey-haired Byelorussian—was so crushed by his sudden misfortune that he paid no attention. While his family threw pillows in red pillow-cases and other odds and ends on to a wagon, the man carefully carried out a perfectly useless wheel rim that had probably been lying in the yard for the past ten years.

Grigory marvelled at the stupidity of the women, who were bringing out flower-pots and ikons and leaving essential and valuable things behind. Feathers from a ripped eiderdown whirled about the street like snowflakes in a storm. The air smelled of burned soot and musty cellars. On the road out of the village a Jew came running towards them. The narrow slit of his mouth looked as if it had been cut open by a sword. 'Mr. Cossack! Mr. Cossack! Oh, my God!' he cried.

A small round-headed Cossack was trotting away from him, waving his whip and paying no attention to the shouts.

'Halt!' a captain from the Second Troop shouted at him.

The Cossack crouched over his saddle-bow and turned down a by-lane.

'Stop, damn you! What regiment are you from?'

The Cossack's round head ducked down over the horse's neck and he went into a mad gallop. At a high fence he brought the horse up on its hind legs, cleared it neatly, and disappeared.

'The 9th Regiment is stationed here, Your Honour. He must be with them,' the sergeant-major reported.

'To hell with him,' the captain frowned, and looked down at the Jew, who was clinging to his stirrup. 'What did he take from you?'

'Oh, sir, ... my watch, sir!' The Jew turned his handsome face towards the other officers who had ridden up and blinked rapidly.

The captain kicked his stirrup free and rode on. 'You'd lose it anyway if the Germans get here,' he remarked, smiling into his moustache.

The Jew stood in the middle of the street, staring confusedly. His face was twitching.

'Make way, Mr. Jew!' the squadron commander shouted sternly, and raised his whip.

The Fourth Squadron rode past amid a clatter of hooves and a creaking of saddles. The Cossacks glanced mockingly at the disconcerted Jew and passed remarks.

'Our lot can't live without nicking something.'

'A Cossack's light-fingered by nature.'

'Shouldn't leave their stuff lying about.'

'That was a smart one, that was...'

'The way he went over that fence, like a borzoi!'

Sergeant-Major Kargin dropped behind and, to the accompaniment of laughter from the Cossack ranks, lowered his lance.

'Run or I'll spear yer!'

The Jew gasped in fright and took to his heels. The sergeant-major gave chase and lashed him from behind with his whip. Grigory saw the Jew stumble and turn towards the sergeant-major, covering his face with his hands. Blood was seeping between his thin fingers.

'What was that for?' he sobbed.

The sergeant-major's rapacious bird-like eyes gleamed derisively, and as he rode away he shouted over his shoulder, 'Don't stick your neck out, you fool!'

Outside the village, in a dip overgrown with yellow waterlilies and sedge, some engineers were completing the construction of a wide bridge. A motor-car stood near by, humming and vibrating. The chauffeur was fussing round it. A stout grey-haired general with a pointed beard and baggy cheeks was reclining on the back seat. Colonel Kaledin, the commander of the Twelfth Regiment, and the commander of an engineer battalion, were standing at attention beside him, their hands raised in salute. Tugging at the strap of a map-case, the general was shouting angrily at the engineer.

'Your orders were to have this work finished yesterday. Silence! You should have brought up the materials beforehand. Silence!' he thundered again, though the officer was keeping his mouth tightly shut and only his lips were twitching. 'How do you expect me to cross over to the other side now?.. Well, Captain, I'm asking you—how?'

A young black-moustached general sitting on his left struck a match to light his cigar and smiled. The commander of the engineers bent forward and pointed to something that was happening beside the bridge. The squadron rode down into the hollow. Brownish-black mud came up over the horses' knees and white shavings from the bridge sprinkled on them like feathers.

They crossed the border at noon. The horses jumped over the striped border post that had been knocked down. A rumble of gunfire was now coming from the right. The red-tiled roof of an Austrian farmstead could be seen in the distance. The sun's rays were beating down almost vertically. Bitter, greasy dust was settling everywhere. The regimental commander ordered out an advance guard, and it was the Fourth Squadron's Third Troop under Lieutenant Semyonov that rode ahead. The remaining squadrons of the regiment were left behind in the swirling grey dust. A detachment of some twenty Cossacks rode along a rutted track past the farmstead.

The lieutenant led his patrol on for some three versts and stopped to check his position on the map. The Cossacks got together for a smoke. Grigory was about to dismount and loosen his saddle-girths, but the sergeant-major glared at him.

'What the bloody hell!.. Get back on your horse!'

The lieutenant lit a cigarette and carefully polished the field-glasses he had taken out of their case. Ahead lay a flat stretch of country bathed in the noonday sun. To the right a jagged wall of forest was pierced by the long pointed sting of the road. About a verst and a half further on, another hamlet could be seen with a steep clayey cliff and a cool glassy stream below it. The lieutenant scanned the dead, deserted streets through his field-glasses, but the place was as empty as a graveyard. The blue thread of water beckoned temptingly.

'That must be Korolevka?' the lieutenant indicated the village with his eyes.

The sergeant-major rode up to him without replying. His expression said without words, 'You know best. Our job is to obey.'

'We'll take that direction,' the lieutenant said undecidedly, putting away his glasses and wincing as if from tooth-ache.

'Mightn't we run straight into 'em, Your Honour?'

'We'll be careful. Get moving.'

Prokhor Zykov edged up closer to Grigory. Their horses were trotting side by side. They rode into the deserted street apprehensively. Every window threatened vengeance, every open door evoked a sense of loneliness and sent a shiver down the spine. Fences and ditches attracted the eye with the force of a magnet. They had come like beasts of prey, just as wolves approach a house on a winter night. But the streets were deserted. The silence was stupefying. The innocent chimes of a wall clock coming from the window of one of the houses exploded in their ears like gun-shots, and Grigory noticed the lieutenant snatch frantically at the holster of his revolver.

There was not a living soul in the village. The patrol forded the stream. The water came up to the horses' bellies and they entered it gladly, drinking as they did so despite the urgings of their riders. Grigory gazed longingly at the muddied water; so near and yet beyond his reach it beckoned irresistibly. If only it had been possible, he would have sprung out of his saddle, sprawled in it without taking off his clothes and let the stream whisper drowsily over him until his back and sweating chest were chilled and shivering.

From the hill beyond the village they sighted a town: square upon square of brick buildings, gardens, church spires.

The lieutenant rode up on to the sunken crest of the hill and put his field-glasses to his eyes.

'There they are!' he cried, moving the fingers of his left hand.

The sergeant-major and then the Cossacks, one by one, rode up on to the sun-scorched hilltop to look. People were scurrying about the tiny streets; some sidestreets were blocked by wagons; horsemen were galloping to and fro. When he shaded his eyes, Grigory could make out the alien grey of the uniforms. The brown, freshly dug trenches round the city yawned like the lairs of wild beasts; men were swarming over them.

'What a lot of 'em...' Prokhor exclaimed in astonishment.

The others, all gripped by the same feeling, were silent. Grigory listened to the quickened beat of his heart (it was as if someone very small but heavy had got into the left side of his chest and was running on the spot) and realised that this was quite a different feeling from what he had experienced at the sight of the 'enemy' during manoeuvres.

The lieutenant was making notes. The sergeant-major brought the Cossacks down from the summit, ordered them to dismount, and rode up to the lieutenant. After a moment the lieutenant beckoned Grigory.

'Melekhov!'

'Here.'

Grigory walked up the hill, easing his numb legs. The lieutenant handed him a folded sheet of paper.

'Your horse is better than the others. Take this to the regimental commander at the gallop.'

Grigory slipped the message into his breast pocket and went back to his horse, lowering the strap of his cap under his chin.

The lieutenant watched him, waited until he had mounted, then glanced at his wrist-watch.

The regiment was approaching Korolevka when Grigory rode in with his despatch.

Colonel Kaledin gave some instructions to his aide, who rode off in a cloud of dust to the First Squadron.

The Fourth Squadron streamed through Korolevka and deployed smartly on the outskirts, as if at exercises. Lieutenant Semyonov rode in from the hill with the other Cossacks of the Third Troop.

The squadron wheeled into line, horses shaking their heads, flies biting, bridles jangling. Hooves thudded dully in the noonday hush as the First Squadron rode out of the village to join them.

Captain Polkovnikov pranced out in front of the formation on his tall caracoling horse, held it on a tight rein, and slipped his hand through the knot of his sword. Grigory held his breath, waiting for the command. A muffled rumble came from the left flank as the First Squadron rode into position.

The captain tore the sword from its sheath and the blade flashed a faint blue.

'Squa-a-a-dron!' The sword swung left, then right, and fell forward until it was suspended just above the horse's rigidly erect ears. 'Charge!' Grigory rehearsed the as yet unuttered command in his mind. 'Lances at the ready, sabres out, into the attack—forward!' the captain ended the order abruptly and gave his horse full rein.

The earth groaned as it was crucified by a thousand hooves. Grigory had barely managed to lower his lance

(he was in the first rank) when his horse, caught up in
the already moving flood, plunged forward, straining for
its head. Captain Polkovnikov showed up in front against
the grey background of the field. A black stretch of
ploughland came racing towards them. The First Squadron
let out a ragged, wavering cheer that was taken up by the
Fourth. The horses bunched their legs and flung themselves forward in great bounds. Through the roar of the
wind in his ears Grigory heard the popping of as yet
distant shots. The first bullet pinged high overhead,
furrowing the glassy haze of the sky with its long whine.
Grigory pressed the hot shaft of his lance to his side till
it hurt. His hand was clammy with sweat. The whistle
of flying bullets forced his head down to the horse's
moist neck, and the pungent smell of the animal' sweat
stung his nostrils. He saw the brown ridge of trenches
and the grey figures running back to the town as if
through misted binoculars. A machine-gun hammered
ceaselessly, spreading a shrieking fan of bullets over the
Cossacks' heads, more bullets tore up cotton-wool puffs
of dust before and under the horses' feet.

The thing in Grigory's chest that before the charge had
been pumping so hard seemed to have turned into wood.
He could feel nothing but the ringing in his ears and a
pain in the toes of his left foot. Fear reduced his thoughts
to a heavy congealing tangle.

The first to fall from his horse was Cornet Lyakhovsky.
Prokhor rode over him.

A fragment of what he saw as he looked back engraved
itself on Grigory's mind. Prokhor's horse, having leapt
over the prostrate officer, bared its teeth and fell, twisting its neck. Prokhor was flung out of the saddle by the
impact. Like a diamond cutting glass, Grigory's memory
carved and retained the picture of the pink gums and
bared teeth of Prokhor's horse and Prokhor himself lying
flat and trampled by the horse coming up from behind. The
scream was inaudible, but Prokhor's face with its contorted
mouth and calf-like eyes starting out of their sockets told
him that the cry must be inhuman. More Cossacks fell.
With and without their horses. Through the tears whipped
into his eyes by the wind Grigory stared ahead at the grey
froth of Austrians running from their trenches.

The squadron, which had begun its charge in close
formation, was now raggedly scattered. The front-rankers,
including Grigory, were already approaching the trenches;
the rest were strung out behind them.

A tall fair-browed Austrian with his peaked cap tilted forward over his eyes took aim and fired almost point-blank at Grigory from a kneeling position. The heat of the molten lead scorched Grigory's cheek. He aimed his lance and reined in with all his strength. The blow landed as the Austrian jumped to his feet and was so powerful that the lance went right through him, burying half its length in his body. Grigory was unable to withdraw. He felt the convulsions of the falling body coming up the shaft and saw the Austrian, bent backwards (only the tip of his unshaven chin visible) clawing and clutching at the shaft with hooked fingers. Grigory released his grip on the lance and reached for the hilt of his sabre with a numbed hand.

The Austrians were running into the streets of the suburbs. Cossack horses reared over the clump of grey uniforms.

In the first minute after he had dropped the lance Grigory wheeled his horse without knowing why. He had a glimpse of the sergeant-major galloping past him with his teeth bared in a snarl. Grigory struck his horse with the flat of his sword and, arching its neck, it carried him off down a street.

An Austrian was running along beside a high iron railing swaying from side to side, crazed with fear. He had no rifle and was clutching his cap in his hand. Grigory's eyes focussed on the back of his head, jutting over the damp hem of his collar. He overtook him, and inflamed by the madness that was going on all around him, lifted his sabre. The Austrian was keeping close to the railing and Grigory was out of position for a slash. Leaning out of his saddle he held the sabre at an angle and let it fall on the Austrian's temple. Without a cry the man pressed his hand to the wound and swung round with his back to the railing. Grigory, unable to rein in his horse, galloped on, then turned and rode back at a trot. The Austrian's rectangular face, lengthened by fear, grew black as iron. He held his arms stiffly to his sides and his ashen lips moved rapidly. The glancing blow of the sabre had taken off a sliver of skin and it was hanging down his cheek, like a red rag. Blood was trickling in a crooked stream on to his uniform.

Their eyes met. The Austrian's were flooded with the horror of death. He began to sag at the knees and a gurgling cry rose from his throat. With half closed eyes Grigory swung his sabre. The long, swinging stroke split the skull. The Austrian fell with his arms outstretched, as though he had tripped; the shattered cranium thudded dully on the stone pavement. Grigory's horse jumped away with a snort and carried him out into the middle of the street.

Scattered shots still sounded in the streets. A foaming horse dragged a dead Cossack past Grigory. The man's foot was caught in the stirrup and his battered, half-naked body bumped and swung over the paving stones.

Grigory noticed only the red stripe of the trousers and the torn green tunic rucked up in a bundle round the head.

Confusion flooded his brain like molten lead. He got off his horse and shook his head. Cossacks of the Third Squadron that had come up in support galloped past him. A wounded man was carried by on a greatcoat. A crowd of Austrian prisoners were driven past at the double. They ran in a grey huddled herd with an eerie clattering of their iron-tipped boots. Their faces merged into a jellied, clay-coloured blob. Grigory dropped the reins and, without knowing why, walked over to the Austrian soldier he had cut down. The man was lying there, by the fanciful ironwork of the railings, holding out a dirty brown palm, as if for alms. Grigory looked into his face. It seemed to him small, almost child-like, despite the drooping moustache and the stern twisted mouth, tortured by recent suffering or perhaps by the joyless life it had known before.

'Heh, you!' an unknown Cossack officer riding down the middle of the street called to him.

Grigory looked up at the dusty white cockade on the officer's cap and stumbled back to his horse. His steps were fettered and heavy, as if an insupportable load had been placed on his shoulders; disgust and bewilderment were crushing his spirit. He grasped a stirrup, but for a long time could not lift his leaden foot into it.

VI

The second-line reservists from Tatarsky and the neighbouring villages spent their second night after leaving home in the village of Eya. The Cossacks from the lower end of Tatarsky kept aloof from those of the upper half. So Petro Melekhov, Anikei, Khristonya, Stepan Astakhov, Ivan Tomilin and a few others were all billeted together. Their host, a tall gangling old man, who had taken part in the Turkish campaign, engaged them in conversation when they had bedded down on their blankets in the kitchen and the front room and were having a last smoke before going to sleep.

'So you're off to the war, soldiers?'

'That's it, grandad.'

'It'll be a different war, I reckon, from the one against the Turks? Look at the weapons they've got now.'

'No difference! They killed off plenty in the Turkish war and it'll be just the bloody same in this,' Tomilin grunted angrily, though it was not clear who he was angry with.

'That's foolish talk, my boy. It'll be a different kind of war.'

''Course, it will,' Khristonya affirmed lazily, with a yawn, stubbing out his cigarette on a fingernail.

'We'll do our bit of fighting,' Petro Melekhov yawned and, making the sign of the cross over his mouth, pulled his greatcoat over his head.

'Now, my sons, there's something I want to ask of you. Something real important and one day you'll remember what I told you,' the old man said.

Petro turned back his greatcoat and listened.

'Remember one thing: if you want to stay alive, and come out of mortal battle unharmed, you must abide by human righteousness.'

'Righteousness?' asked Stepan Astakhov, who was lying at the end of the row. He smiled distrustfully. He had started smiling again ever since he had heard about the war. It attracted him, and the general consternation, the pain that other people were suffering were a balm to his own.

'Well, I'll tell you. In war you must never take anything that doesn't belong to you—that's one thing. And never touch women, heaven forbid. And besides that, you've got to know a prayer.'

The Cossacks stirred and all began talking at once.

'It's more a matter of hanging on to what's your own than taking someone else's.'

'How d'ye mean—never touch the women? Don't force 'em—that I understand. But what if you can talk her into it?'

'How'd anyone stick it that long?'

'Ay, that's the thing!'

'What's this prayer you're talking about?'

The old man fixed his eyes on them severely and answered all their questions at once.

'No women! That's flat! If you can't stick it out, you'll lose your head or get wounded. Then you'll remember, but it'll be too late. I'll tell you the prayer. I went all through the Turkish war and had death on my shoulders like a knapsack, but I came out of it alive thanks to that prayer.'

He went into the front room, rummaged about under the ikon and brought in a tattered, yellow sheet of paper.

'Here you are. Up you get and copy it. Tomorrow you'll be off before cock-crow, won't you?'

The old man smoothed the crackling sheet on the table and went out. Anikei was the first to get up. Unsteady shadows from the lamp flame, stirred by the draught from the window, flickered across his bare, womanish face. All of them sat down and copied the prayer except Stepan. Anikei finished before the others, folded the scrap of paper he had torn from an exercise book and tied it above the cross that he wore round his neck. Stepan sat swinging his leg and making fun of him.

'Nice place you've made for lice. They wouldn't find it cosy enough on the cord, so you've built 'em a paper house. Just the thing!'

'Young man, if you don't believe, you should keep quiet!' their host interrupted him. 'Don't stand in the way of others and don't mock the faith. It's a shame and a sin!'

Stepan lapsed into a grinning silence; to overcome the awkwardness of the moment, Anikei asked the old man, 'In one of these prayers there's something about a bear spear and arrows. What's all that for?'

'The Prayer in Attack was not written in our day. It was handed down to my grandfather from his grandfather. And mebbe it goes back further than that. In the old days they fought with spears and bows and arrows.'

There were three prayers and the Cossacks could take their choice.

THE PRAYER AGAINST ARMS

God bless us. On the mountain there lies a white stone like a horse. As water enters not the stone, so may no bullet or arrow enter into me, a slave of God, or my comrades, or my horse. As the hammer rebounds from the anvil, so may the bullet rebound from me; as millstones turn, so may the arrow turn and not touch me.

As the sun and moon are bright, so may I, a slave of God, be strong. Beyond the mountain stands a gate. This gate is locked and I shall throw the keys into the sea, under the burning white rock of Altor that cannot be seen by witch or wizard, by monk or nun. Even as the waters flee not from the ocean and the yellow sands cannot be counted, so may I, a slave of God, remain unvanquished. In the name of the Father, the Son, and the Holy Ghost. Amen.

THE PRAYER AGAINST ASSAULT

There is a great ocean, and in this great ocean there is the white rock of Altor. And on that rock there is a man of stone three times nine cubits high. May I, a slave of God, and my comrades, be clad in stone from east to west, from earth to sky, against sharp sabre and sword, against lance, damask blade, and bear spear; against dagger tempered and untempered, against knife, axe and cannon ball; against lead bullets and all missiles; against all arrows, trimmed with the feathers of eagles, swans, geese, cranes or ravens; and against all assault from Turks, Crimeans, Austrians, against invading foes, against Tatars, Lithuanians, Germans, Siberians and Kalmyks. Holy Fathers and Heavenly Powers, protect me, a slave of God. Amen.

THE PRAYER IN ATTACK

Immaculate Virgin, Holy Mother of God and our Lord Jesus Christ. Bless, Lord, thy servant entering battle, and my comrades that are with me. Wrap them in cloud, protect them with thy heavenly hail of stone. Saint Dmitry of Salonica, defend me, a slave of God, and my comrades on all four sides; suffer not evil men to shoot, nor with spear to pierce, nor with battle-axe to strike, nor with club to smite, nor with axe to hew down, nor with sabre to slash or pierce, nor with knife to stab or cut; neither old nor young, neither brown nor black; neither heretic, nor sorcerer, nor any wizard. All lieth before me, a slave of God, naked and alone before my judgment. In the sea, in the ocean on the Island of Buyan there stands an iron post. On that post there is a man of iron resting on an iron staff, and he charmeth all iron, steel, blue tin, lead, and all who shoot them: 'Go thou, iron, into your mother-earth away from the slave of God and past my comrades and my horse. The arrow that is made of wood, go thou into the forest, and the feather, into its mother-bird, and the glue, into the fish.' Defend me, a slave of God, with a golden shield from blade and bullet, from cannon-balls, from spear and knife. May my body be stronger than armour. Amen.

The Cossacks carried away with them under their shirts the prayers they had copied. They tied them to their crosses, to their mother's blessings, and to the little bundles of their native soil that they carried, but death claimed even those that carried these prayers.

Their bodies rotted on the fields of Galicia and East Prussia, the Carpathians and Romania, wherever the flames of war lit the sky and the earth was marked by the hooves of Cossack horses.

VII

The usual practice was to put the Cossacks from the upper stanitsas of the Donets Region—Yelanskaya, Vyoshenskaya, Migulinskaya and Kazanskaya—into the 11th and 12th Cossack regiments of the line and the Ataman's Life Guards.

In 1914, however, some of the Vyoshenskaya Cossacks who had been called to the colours were for some reason drafted into the 3rd Don Cossack Regiment named after Yermak Timofeyevich, which was manned mainly by Ust-Medveditsa Cossacks. Among those so drafted was Mitka Korshunov.

The regiment was stationed in Vilno along with some units of the 3rd Cavalry Division. In June the squadrons rode out of town to the grazing grounds.

It was a warm overcast summer's day. Hazy clouds flocked across the sky, hiding the sun. The regiment was in marching order. The band was blaring. The officers in their white-topped summer caps and light tunics rode along together with blue puffs of cigarette smoke floating above them.

The peasants and their gaily dressed womenfolk mowing the meadows along the country road shaded their eyes and stared at the Cossack columns.

The horses were beginning to sweat. Yellowish flecks of foam gathered round their groins. The gentle breeze from the south-east did not dry the sweat and only made the air more sultry.

Half way to their destination, not far from a small hamlet, a yearling colt strayed in among the Fifth Squadron. It dashed out from behind a fence, spotted the solid mass of horses and with a joyful whinny galloped towards them. Its youthfully fluffy tail streamed sideways, grey bubbles of dust curled up from under its shell-like hooves and settled on the trampled green. It galloped up to the leading troop and foolishly plunged its head into the groin of the sergeant-major's horse. The horse bucked but did not kick, evidently out of pity.

'Out of the way, stupid!' the sergeant-major shouted, raising his whip.

But the colt looked so homely and friendly that the Cossacks could only laugh. And then, to everyone's surprise, it pushed its way impudently among the ranks and the troop was thrown out of formation. Despite the Cossacks' urgings, the horses hesitated and backed away. Pushed out of their ranks, the colt ran alongside and tried to bite the horse nearest to it.

The squadron commander came charging up.

'What's going on here?'

At the spot where the unruly colt had made its absurd intrusion, the horses were jibbing and snorting and the smiling Cossacks were laying on with their whips. While the troop milled about, other troops bore down on it from behind. An enraged troop officer galloped up from the end of the column.

'What's going on?' the squadron commander boomed, steering his horse into the milling throng.

'It's this colt...'

'It's got in here amongst us...'

'We can't get rid of the young devil!'

'Use your whip! What are you being so gentle for?'

The Cossacks grinned sheepishly, trying to rein in their excited mounts.

'Sergeant-major! What the devil are you doing, Lieutenant! Put your troop in order! This is the limit...'

As the squadron commander rode away, his horse stumbled and its hind legs slid down into the roadside ditch. He dug in his spurs and the horse leapt out on to a bank overgrown with goosefoot and yellow-white daisies. A group of officers had halted at a distance. A lieutenant-colonel had thrown back his head and was drinking from a flask, while his other hand fondled the splendidly fashioned pommel of his saddle.

The sergeant-major broke up the troop and with much swearing drove the colt off the road. The troop formed up again and a hundred and fifty pairs of eyes watched the sergeant-major cantering after the colt. Every now and then it would stop and rub its dung-encrusted flank against the sergeant-major's mighty steed, then prance

267

away with its tail erect before the sergeant-major could reach its back with his whip. The lash landed on the colt's fluffy tail, which sank for a moment, when sprang up again and waved valiantly in the wind.

The whole squadron was laughing, including the officers. Even the major's gloomy face twisted into a semblance of a smile.

Mitka Korshunov was riding in the third rank of the leading troop with Mikhail Ivankov, a Cossack from the village of Kargin, near Vyoshenskaya, and Kozma Kryuchkov, nicknamed the Camel, a pock-marked, roundshouldered Cossack, constantly found fault with Mitka. Kryuchkov was an 'old Cossack', that is, he was in his last year of active service and according to an unwritten law he had the right, like any other 'old Cossack', to chase up the youngsters, drill them, and hand out 'buckles' for every trifling offence. The established penalties were thirteen strokes of the belt buckle for the 1913 draft and fourteen for the 1914. The sergeant-majors and officers encouraged this practice as a means of instilling respect for age as well as rank.

Kryuchkov, who had just received his corporal's stripes, sat in his saddle, hunched up like a bird. He frowned at a grey, full-breasted cloud and, imitating the voice of the burly squadron commander, Major Popov, asked Mitka, 'Now ... tell me, Korshunov, what's the name of our squadron commander?'

Mitka, who had felt the sting of a good many buckles for his obstinacy and unruliness, forced a respectful expression on his face.

'Major Popov, Corporal!'

'What?'

'Major Popov, Corporal!'

'That's not what I'm asking. You tell me what he's called among us, Cossacks.'

Ivankov winked warningly at Mitka and parted his hare-lip in a grin. Mitka glanced round and saw Major Popov riding up from behind.

'Come on, answer up!'

'Major Popov is the correct form of address, Corporal.'

'Fourteen buckles! Now tell me, scum!'

'I don't know, Corporal!'

'Well, when we get to the grazing grounds,' Kryuchkov said in his real voice, 'I'll give you a proper belting. Answer my question!'

'I don't know.'

'You, bastard, don't you know the name we've got for him?'

Mitka heard the soft, furtive tread of the major's horse behind him and said nothing.

'Well?' Kryuchkov frowned angrily.

A guarded chuckle rose from the ranks behind. Not realising what the laughter was about and thinking it was at him, Kryuchkov flared up, 'All right, Korshunov. When we get there, I'll give you fifty of the best!'

Mitka shrugged resignedly.

'Black Nose!'

'Ah, that's better.'

'Kryu-u-uchkov!' a voice bellowed from behind.

The 'old Cossack' jumped in the saddle and drew himself up to attention.

'What's this name, you're playing, you scoundrel?' Major Popov said as he drew level. 'Is that what you teach a young Cossack?'

Kryuchkov blinked with half-closed eyes. His cheeks were a deep purple. Restrained chuckles came from behind.

'Who was it I taught a lesson last year? Whose face did I break this fingernail on?' The major held up the long sharp nail of his little finger under Kryuchkov's nose. 'So mind I don't hear any more of it! D'you understand, my friend?'

'Yes, I understand perfectly, Your Honour!'

The major waited a minute, then rode aside and reined in his horse to watch the squadron go past. The Fourth and Fifth squadrons went by at a trot.

'Squadron, keep up the pace!'

Kryuchkov straightened his shoulder strap, glanced back at the receding figure of the major and shook his head bemusedly as he adjusted his lance.

'That's Black Nose for you! Where did he spring from?'

Perspiring with laughter, Ivankov told him, 'He'd been riding behind us for a long time. He heard everything. Must have guessed it was about him.'

'You should have given me a wink, you fool.'

'Why should I?'

'I'll show you why. Fourteen of the best on your bare buttocks!'

The squadrons were spread out over the surrounding estates. During the day they mowed the clover and meadow grass for the owners and at night grazed their hobbled horses on the plots assigned to them, playing cards round their smoking campfires, telling yarns and fooling about.

The Sixth Squadron was working for the big Polish landowner Schneider. The officers lived in the lodge, gambling and drinking, and courting the estate manager's daughter en masse. The Cossacks pitched their tents three versts from the manor. Every morning the manager would drive out to them in a light racing drozhky. The stout Polish worthy would get out of his carriage, easing his stiff fleshy legs, and invariably greet the Cossacks with a wave of his tall white cap with a patent-leather peak.

'Come and do a bit of mowing with us, master!'

'Get your fat down!'

'Take a scythe or you'll get the staggers!' voices responded from the white-shirted ranks of Cossacks. The manager would smile back imperturbably, wiping the sundown pink of his bald spot with a bright-bordered handkerchief, then go off with the sergeant-major to mark out new strips of grass to be mown.

At noon the kitchen would arrive. The Cossacks would wash and come in for their meal.

They ate in silence, but in the half-hour rest period after dinner they would make up for any lack of conversation before.

'The grass here is rotten stuff. Not a patch on our steppe grass.'

'There's hardly any quitch.'

'Our folk down on the Don will have finished mowing by now.'

'We'll soon be finished here. There was a new moon born yesterday. It's got to be washed by the rain yet.'

'He's a miserly Pole. He might stand us a bottle apiece for our pains.'

'Haw! Haw! He'd piss on the altar for a bottle.'

'So what's that mean, lads? The richer they are, the meaner they get, eh?'

'Better ask the tsar that one.'

'Anyone seen the landowner's daughter?'

'What about her?'

'That girl's got some meat on her!'

'Nice juicy bit of lamb?'

'That's it!'

'She'd go down well with some of the hard stuff.'

'Is it true she was courted by a prince of the blood?'

'A tasty bit like her wouldn't come an ordinary man's way!'

'Other day, lads, I heard a rumour we're going to be reviewed by one of the royals.'

'The fat cat's got nothing to do, so he...'

'Come off it, Taras!'

'Give us a puff, eh?'

'You're a cadger, you devil, with your long arm. Go and beg at the church door!'

'Look, mates, Fedotka's a good puffer, but he's got nothing to puff at.'

'There's only ash left.'

'Open your eyes, mate. Plenty of fire left there, like in a good woman!'

They lay on their bellies, smoking and burning their bare backs red in the sun. To one side five 'old Cossacks' were questioning a young recruit.

'What stanitsa are you from?'

'Yelanskaya.'

'From the goats, eh?'

'Yes, Corporal.'

'What animal do they use for carting salt round your way?'

Kozma Kryuchkov was lying on a horse-cloth not far away, winding his scanty whiskers on his fingers and looking bored.

'Horses.'

'And what else?'

'Oxen.'

'And what do they use to bring the roach from the Crimea? You know 'em. They're a kind of bullock with bumps on their backs and they eat prickles. What are they called?'

'Camels.'

'Aha! Haw! Haw! Haw!'

Kryuchkov got up lazily and came over to the culprit, hunching his shoulders like a camel, stretching his sallow neck with its large Adam's apple, and unbuckling his belt.

'Bend over!'

In the iridescent dusk of the June evenings the Cossacks would sing round their camp-fires.

> To a distant land a Cossack rode
> On a sturdy steed of burnished black,
> For ever he'd left his native abode

A silvery tenor voice sobbed mournfully, and then the basses came in, spreading a deep velvet sorrow:

271

And never would he come back.

The tenor rose to a higher pitch, touching the very quick:

> *In vain did his youthful Cossack bride*
> *Gaze northward at morn and eve.*
> *Waiting in hope for her Cossack to ride*
> *From a land he ne'er will leave.*

Many voices tended the song and it grew rich and heady, like the beer of Polesye:

> *For beyond the hills where in wintertime*
> *The frosts bite deep and the blizzards blow,*
> *Where grimly nod the fir and pine,*
> *The Cossack's bones lie beneath the snow.*

The voices told their simple tale of Cossack life while the tenor descant quivered like a skylark over the thawing earth of April:

> *As the Cossack lay dying he begged and prayed*
> *That a mound be piled at the head of his grave.*

And again the basses came in to share its sorrow:

> *Where a guelder-rose from his native land*
> *Its blossoms bright should forever wave.*

At another camp-fire the group was smaller and the song was in a different strain:

> *From the stormy Azov Sea*
> *The ships are sailing up the Don,*
> *For back to his own country*
> *A young ataman has come.*

At yet another, the squadron story-teller, coughing in the smoke, was spinning a fanciful tale. He was listened to with unflagging attention. Only occasionally when the hero of the tale cleverly escaped from the traps laid for him by the Muscovites or the Evil Spirit, would someone's hand gleam in the firelight as it slapped the top of a boot, and a voice, hoarse from the smoke, gasp its approval.

'Well, I'll be damned! That's great, that is!'

Then the smooth tones of the story-teller would flow on once again.

...A week after the regiment had arrived at the grazing grounds, Major Popov called in the squadron blacksmith and the sergeant-major.

To the sergeant-major, 'How are the horses?'

'Not so bad, Your Honour. Pretty good, in fact. Their backs have filled out. They're putting on a bit of flesh.'

The major made an arrow out of his black moustache (hence the nickname Black Nose) and said, 'We have orders from the regimental commander that all stirrups and bridles are to be tinned. The regiment is to be present at an imperial review. So everything has got to be shining bright—saddles and all the rest. The Cossacks must be a sight for sore eyes. When will you be ready, my friend?'

The sergeant-major looked at the smith. The smith looked at the sergeant-major. They both looked at the major.

'How about Sunday, Your Honour?' the sergeant-major suggested, and respectfully touched his own greenish tobacco-stained moustache.

'Mind it is Sunday!' the major warned grimly, and that was that.

The preparations for the imperial review began at once. Mikhail Ivankov, the son of a Karginskaya blacksmith, and a competent smith himself, helped to tin stirrup-irons and bits, while the others gave the horses extra grooming, cleaned the bridles, and polished the snaffle-rings and other metal parts of the harness with broken brick.

A week later the regiment was shining like a new twenty-kopeck piece. Everything from the horses' hooves to the Cossack's faces wore a glossy sheen. On Saturday the regimental commander Colonel Grekov inspected the regiment and thanked the officers and men for their zealous preparations and fine turn-out.

The azure thread of July days unwound loop by loop. The Cossack horses flourished on the good fodder and only the Cossacks fretted. With not a sign of the review in the offing they were harassed by their own conjectures. A week passed in rambling discussion, spit and polish and other preparations. Then like a bolt from the blue came the order to march to Vilno.

By evening they were there and a second order went round the squadrons: the Cossacks were to stow their baggage in the warehouse and prepare to take the field.

273

'What's it all about, Your Honour?' the Cossacks asked plaintively, trying to get the truth out of the troop commanders.

But the officers only shrugged. They themselves would have crossed anyone's palm with silver to know the truth.

'I don't know.'

'Mebbe it's manoeuvres in the presence of His Majesty?'

'We have not yet been informed.'

That was all the consolation to be had from the officers. Towards evening on July 19th the regimental commander's messenger managed to pass the word on to a friend of his, Cossack Mrykhin of the Sixth Squadron, who was on duty in the stables.

'It's war, boy!'

'You're lying!'

'God's truth. But keep it under your hat!'

The next morning the regiment was drawn up in squadrons in front of the dustily glinting barrack windows. The formations were mounted and waiting for the regimental commander.

Major Popov positioned himself in front of the Sixth Squadron on a fine horse, holding the reins tight in his white-gloved left hand. The horse was arching its great wheel-like neck and scratching its face on its rippling chest muscles.

The colonel of the regiment rode round the corner of the barracks and reined in his horse so that it stood sideways on to the formation. His aide took out a handkerchief and held it with his little finger elegantly extended, but did not have time to blow his nose. In the tense silence the colonel shouted, 'Cossacks!..' and with that one word took command of everyone's attention.

'Here it comes!' was the thought in each man's mind. The excitement had the tension of a compressed spring. Mitka Korshunov dug his heels into the sides of his restless horse. Next to him Ivankov sat squarely in his saddle, listening with his harelipped mouth open and showing an array of blackened uneven teeth. Next in line was Kryuchkov, hunched and frowning, beyond him, Lapin, his ears twitching like a horse's, and next to him, Shchegolkov with his big razor-scarred Adam's apple.

'...Germany has declared war on us.'

A rustle like a wave of wind passing over a field of ripe barley ran through the well aligned ranks. A horse's neigh cut the air like a scream. Round eyes and the oblong blackness of open mouths turned in the direction of the

First Squadron, on the left flank, where the horse had neighed.

The colonel went on speaking. Using words in the required order, he tried to arouse a sense of national pride, but what the thousands of Cossacks saw in their minds' eye was not the rustling silk of foreign banners lowered at their feet, but their wives, children and sweethearts, the ungarnered grain, the unmanned villages. Everything that was a part of their everyday lives, that flowed like blood in their veins, howled and raved in protest.

'Entrainment in two hours' was the only phrase that stamped itself on everyone's memory.

The officers' wives who had gathered near the parade ground were weeping into their handkerchiefs. The Cossacks rode away in bunches to their barracks. Lieutenant Khoprov almost had to carry his blonde Polish wife, who was expecting a baby.

The regiment rode to the station singing. Their voices drowned the bank and half way there it faded into a confused silence. The officers' wives rode with them in carriages, a colourful crowd seethed on the pavements, hooves kicked up the gritty dust and, jeering at his own and others' grief, jerking his left shoulder so that the blue shoulder-strap tossed deliriously, the regiment's song-leader roared out the words of a bawdy Cossack song.

Oh, lovely lass, I caught a pike...

The squadron wrapped its grief in the song and carried it to the station, to the red-painted vans that were to be its home. Deliberately slurring the words and shifting the stress, they bawled to the beat of the horses' newly shod hooves:

O-ff-á-corn, o-ff-á-corn mash...
Oh, lovely lass, I made a soup
O-f-á-cup, o-f-á-cup o 'lentils...

The regimental A. D. C. rode up from the end of the squadron, purple with laughter and embarrassment. The song-leader flung his reins aside and winked cynically at the dense crowds seeing off the Cossacks. And it was not sweat but a bitter brew of wormwood that flowed down the scorched bronze of his cheeks into his black moustache.

275

> *Oh, lovely lass, I fed a man*
> *O-f-á-Cossack, o-f-á-Cossack squadron...*

A locomotive getting up steam at the station gave a warningly sober roar.

* * *

Troop trains... Troop trains... Troop trains without number!

Seething, distracted Russia was pumping its grey-coated blood along the country's arteries, along the rail routes to its western border.

VIII

In the small town of Torzhok the regiment was split up into squadrons. On the instructions of divisional headquarters the Sixth Squadron was put at the disposal of the Third Army Infantry Corps. It marched to the township of Pelikalie and set up its outposts.

The frontier was still guarded by border units. Infantry and artillery were being brought up from the rear. By the evening of July 24th a battalion of the 108th Glebov Regiment and a battery arrived in the town. At the nearby manor there was an outpost manned by nine Cossacks under the command of a troop sergeant.

On the night of the 26th Major Popov summoned the sergeant-major and a Cossack named Astakhov.

It was dark by the time Astakhov returned to the troop. Mitka Korshunov had just come back from watering his horse.

'Is that you, Astakhov?' he called out.

'Yes, it's me. Where's Kryuchkov and the lads?'

'Over there, in the house.'

Astakhov, a big, ponderous black-haired Cossack, entered the house, blinking. At the table, by the light of an oil-lamp Shchegolkov was mending a broken rein. Kryuchkov was standing by the stove with his hands behind his back, winking at Ivankov and pointing to the master of the house, a Pole suffering from dropsy, who was lying on the bed. They had just shared a joke and Ivankov's pink cheeks were still twitching with laughter.

'Tomorrow, lads, we'll be on the road at first light.'

'Where to?' Shchegolkov asked, and dropped the needle he had been trying to thread.

'A place called Lubow.'

'Who'll be going?' Mitka Korshunov asked as he came in and put the empty pail down by the door.

'Shchegolkov, Kryuchkov, Rvachov, Popov and you, Ivankov.'

'What about me?'

'You'll stay behind, Mitka.'

'To hell with you then!'

Kryuchkov eased his back away from the stove, stretched himself until his bones cracked, and asked their host, 'How many versts is it to this Lubow place?'

'Four miles.'

'It's not far from here,' Astakhov said, and sat down on a bench to take off his boots. 'Where can you dry your footcloths here?'

They rode out at dawn. At a roadside well a bare-footed peasant-girl was lowering a pail for water. Kryuch-kov reined in his horse.

'Give us a drink, sweetheart!'

Holding down her homespun skirt, the girl splashed pink-legged through a puddle and, smiling with eyes fringed in long, soft lashes, offered him the pail. Kryuch-kov took it and held it in one hand, though his arm trembled with the strain and water splashed and dripped down the red stripe of his trousers as he drank.

'Christ save you, Grey Eyes!'

'By the Lord Jesus.'

She took the pail and walked away, looking round and smiling.

'What're you grinning at, come for a ride with me!' Kryuchkov shifted on his saddle as if to make room for her.

'Get moving!' Astakhov shouted, riding off.

Rvachov glanced mockingly at Kryuchkov.

'Can't take your eyes off her, eh?'

'Her legs are as red as a turkey's,' Kryuchkov said with a laugh and they all looked round as if at a word of command.

The girl was bending over the well, her pink legs parted and her skirt drawn tight over her buttocks.

'I'd like to get married...' Popov sighed.

'Suppose I marry you with my whip,' Astakhov proposed.

'A whip's not what you marry with...'

'Feeling skittish?'

'We'll have to have him bending over!'

'Geld him, like a bullock.'

The Cossacks cantered away laughing. The little town of Lubow came into view, spread out in the dip below the next hill. The sun rose over the hill behind them. A lark was singing its heart out over the cup-shaped insulator of a telegraph pole.

Astakhov, who had just finished a training course, had been put in command of the new outpost. He chose the last house on the frontier side of the town to quarter his men. The owner, a bandy-legged Pole with a shaven head on which he wore a white felt hat, took the Cossacks out to the shed and showed them where to put their horses. Behind the shed there was a thin wattle fence and beyond that, a green strip of clover. The land rose to a promontory of woodland close by, and farther on there was a whitish sweep of cornfields cut by a road, then more glossy green strips of clover. From the ditch behind the fence the Cossacks kept watch in turn with a pair of field-glasses, while the others rested in the cold shed, which smelled of stale straw, dusty chaff, mice droppings and the musty sweetness of mouldering earth.

Ivankov made a bed for himself in a dark corner by a plough and slept till evening. He was wakened at sunset. Kryuchkov took a pinch of the skin on his neck and pulled it.

'What a scruff he's got from guzzling the government's grub! Get up, sonny, and go and watch out for the Germans!'

'Don't muck about, Kozma!'

'Get up!'

'Ouch, let go! Don't muck about... I'm getting up.'

Ivankov got up, red-faced and puffy, worked his boiler-like head, which was firmly attached to his broad shoulders by a short neck, and snuffling (he had caught a chill from sleeping on the damp ground), adjusted the straps on his bandolier and walked out of the shed, trailing his rifle behind him. He relieved Shchegolkov, adjusted the binoculars and stood scanning the north-west and the forest.

The whitish sweep of the cornfields billowed in the wind and the green promontory of the alder woods caught the deep-red rays of the setting sun. Shouting children were bathing in a stream that lay beyond the town in a gentle blue curve. A women's contralto voice was calling her child in Polish. Shchegolkov rolled a cigarette and said as he was leaving, 'What a red sunset, eh! It's going to be windy.'

'That it will,' Ivankov agreed.

That night the horses were left unsaddled. The lights went out and a hush fell on the little town. The next morning Kryuchkov called Ivankov from the shed.

'Let's go into town.'

'What for?'

'Get something to eat, have a drink.'

'Not much chance,' Ivankov demurred.

'Yes, there is. I asked. See that little house over there, near the tiled shed?' Kryuchkov pointed a swarthy long-nailed finger. 'A Jew lives there and he's got some beer. Shall we go?'

As they were leaving, Astakhov called to them from the door of the shed.

'Where're you off to?'

Kryuchkov, who was Astakhov's superior in rank, waved him aside.

'We'll be back soon.'

'Come back!'

'Don't bark!'

The old Jew with long temple curls and a loose eyelid bowed to the Cossacks as they entered.

'Got any beer?'

'No, there's none left, Cossack sir.'

'We'll pay for it.'

'Jesus-Maria, would I think of... Believe me, an honest Jew, I have no beer!'

'You're lying, yid!'

'But, Cossack sir, I have told you there is none.'

'Now, you look here...' Kryuchkov interrupted crossly, and groped in his pocket for his shabby purse. 'You give it to us or I'll get angry.'

The Jew pressed the coin to his palm with his little finger, lowered his twisted eyelid and went out into the porch.

After a minute or two he reappeared with a bottle of vodka, damp on the outside and coated with barley chaff.

'And you said you hadn't got any. That's not the way, Dad!'

'I said I had no beer.'

'Give us something to eat with it.'

Kryuchkov slapped the bottom of the bottle to eject the cork and filled a cup to its chipped brim.

They left the tavern half drunk. Kryuchkov cut a caper and shook his fist at the dark, hollow-eyed windows.

Astakhov was sitting in the shed, yawning. Behind a partition the horses were champing the hay.

In the evening Popov rode off with a report. The day had passed in complete idleness.

Evening darkened into night. A young yellow moon that looked as if it had been slashed by a sabre hung high over the township.

Now and then a ripe apple would fall with a damp thud in the orchard behind the house. It was near midnight when Ivankov heard the sound of approaching hoof-beats. He crawled out of the ditch, but there was a cloud over the moon and he could see nothing in the grey darkness.

He shook Kryuchkov, who was sleeping by the door of the shed.

'Kozma, there's some horsemen coming! Get up!'

'Where from?'

'From town.'

The two men went outside. The mutter of hooves from the road about a hundred paces away was now quite distinct.

'Let's go into the orchard. We can hear better from there.'

They darted past the house into the orchard and flattened themselves by the fence. Muffled talk. The thwack of stirrups. Creaking saddles. The sounds came nearer. Soon the dim outlines of the horsemen appeared.

They were riding four abreast.

'Who goes there?'

'What's that to you?' a tenor voice responded from the leading rank.

'Who goes there? I'll fire!' Kryuchkov rattled the bolt of his rifle.

'Whoa!' someone reined in, then rode up to the fence. 'What's this, a border post?'

'Yes, it is.'

'What regiment?'

'Third Cossack.'

'Who're you talking to there, Trishin?' someone asked from the darkness.

The rider who had approached answered, 'It's a Cossack outpost, Your Honour.'

Another rider approached.

'Hullo, Cossacks!'

'Hullo,' Ivankov responded after a pause.

'Have you been here long?'

'Since yesterday.'

The second rider lit a cigarette and by the light of the match Kryuchkov saw an officer in border guard's uniform.

'Our border regiment has been withdrawn from the frontier,' the officer said, puffing at his cigarette, 'So remember—you're in the front line. The enemy will probably advance in this direction tomorrow.'

'Where're you heading for, Your Honour?' Kryuchkov asked, keeping his finger on the trigger.

'Two versts from here we are to join up with our squadron. Come on, lads, get moving. Good luck, Cossacks!'

'Good journey.'

The wind tore the cloud bandage ruthlessly off the moon and a deathly yellow light flowed like pus over the town, the clumps of orchard, the knobbly top of the shed, and the detachment riding up the hill.

In the morning Rvachov rode off to the squadron with a report. Astakhov had a word with the master of the house and for a small payment he allowed them to mow some clover for the horses. That night they kept the horses saddled. The Cossacks were alarmed by the news that they had been left face to face with the enemy. Before, when they had known the border guards were in front, there had not been this feeling of isolation and loneliness; the news that the frontier was now unguarded had all the greater impact.

Their host's field was not far from the shed. Astakhov set Ivankov and Shchegolkov to do the mowing. The Pole with his felt hat flopping over him like a white burdock leaf led them to their strip. Shchegolkov mowed while Ivankov raked the damp, heavy grass and pushed it into forage sacks. Meanwhile Astakhov, who had been watching the road to the frontier through the field-glasses, noticed a boy running across the fields from the south-west. He came bounding down the slope like a brown half-moulted hare, shouting while still at a distance and waving the long arms of his jacket. He ran up panting and round-eyed.

'Cossack, Cossack, *przyszedl* German! The German is here!

He pointed with his long floppy sleeve and Astakhov with his eyes to the glasses saw a distant cluster of horsemen.

'Kryuchkov!' he snapped, keeping the glasses to his eyes.

Kryuchkov ran out of the wide doors of the shed, looking round.

'Run and call the lads! The Germans are here! A German patrol!'

He heard Kryuchkov clumping away, and through the glasses his eyes focussed clearly on the group of horsemen floating along behind a reddish bank of grass.

He could even make out the reddish brown of their horses and the dark-blue of their uniforms. There were more than twenty of them. They were riding in a tight bunch, in no set formation; they had come from the south-west, when they were expected from the north-west. They crossed the road and trotted on up the ridge above the town.

With the tip of his tongue poking out between pursed lips, panting with exertion, Ivankov was stuffing an armful of grass into a forage sack. The bandy-legged Polish farmer was standing beside him, sucking a pipe. He had tucked his hands into his belt and was glowering from under the brim of his hat at Shchegolkov, who was mowing.

'Call this a scythe?' Shchegolkov was grumbling, brandishing the toy-like mowing hook. 'Do you mow with this?'

'I mow,' the Pole replied, curling his tongue round the chewed mouthpiece of the pipe and freeing one hand from under his belt.

'You know what your scythe is good for—mowing a woman on her special spot!'

'Uh-huh,' the Pole assented.

Ivankov tittered and was about to say something, but as he looked round he noticed Kryuchkov running towards them over the field, holding the hilt of his sabre as he stumbled over the lumpy furrows.

'Stop work!'

'What's up now?' Ivankov asked, jabbing the point of the scythe into the ground.

'Germans!'

Ivankov dropped his sack. Their host ran for home, bending so low that his hands almost touched the ground, as if bullets were already whistling over his head.

They had only just reached the shed and jumped on their horses when they saw a company of Russian soldiers entering the town from the direction of Pelikalie. They rode to meet them and Astakhov reported to the company commander that a German patrol was riding along the ridge above the town. The major glared severely at the dust-rimmed toes of his boots and asked, 'How many of them?'

'More than twenty.'

'Ride out and cut them off. And we'll keep them under fire from here.' He turned to his company, formed them up and led them on at a quick march.

By the time the Cossacks rode up on to the hill, the Germans were ahead of them and trotting across the road to Pelikalie. They were led by an officer on a short-tailed sorrel horse.

'After 'em! We'll drive 'em towards the second outpost!' Astakhov commanded.

The mounted border guard who had joined them in the town dropped behind.

'What's up? Had enough already, mate?' Astakhov shouted, turning round.

The border guard waved and turned away at a walk towards the town. The Cossacks went on at a swift trot. The blue uniforms of the German dragoons were now visible even to the naked eye. They were trotting in the direction of the second outpost, which was at the manor, some three versts from the town. From time to time they looked back at the Cossacks. The distance between them had noticeably decreased.

'Let's have a shot at 'em!' Astakhov shouted huskily, and dismounted.

From a standing position, with the reins wound round their wrists they fired a volley. Ivankov's horse reared and pushed him over. As he fell he saw one of the Germans drop from his horse. At first he leaned lazily sideways, then suddenly threw out his arms and fell. The Germans neither stopped nor drew their carbines; instead they quickened their pace to a gallop and spread out. The wind fluttered the pennants on their lances. Astakhov was the first to remount. They plied their whips hard. The German patrol swung sharply to the left and the pursuing Cossacks galloped past the body of the fallen German at a distance of about a hundred paces. The terrain became hilly, with numerous dips and jagged ridges. As soon as the Germans came up on the other side of a dip, the Cossacks would dismount and fire a volley after them. Near the second outpost they brought down another dragoon.

'Got him!' Kryuchkov shouted, pushing his foot into the stirrup.

'Our lads'll be here from the manor in a minute!.. That's where the second outpost is...' Astakhov muttered, pushing a new cartridge clip into the magazine with a yellow, nicotine-stained thumb.

The Germans changed to a steady trot. They stared at the manor as they rode past, but the yard with the sun licking insatiably at the tiled roofs was deserted. Astakhov fired from the saddle. A German who had fallen behind the others shook his head and spurred on his horse.

Later it turned out that the Cossacks had withdrawn from the second outpost the night before, on learning that the telegraph wires half a verst from the manor had been cut.

'We'll drive 'em to the first outpost!' Astakhov shouted, turning to the others.

At that moment Ivankov noticed that Astakhov's nose was peeling and a thin sliver of skin was hanging from one nostril.

'Why don't they make a stand?' he asked plaintively, adjusting his rifle on his back.

'Mebbe they will...' Shchegolkov shouted, panting like a broken-winded horse.

The Germans rode down into the next dip without looking back. On the other side there was a dark stretch of ploughland; the near side bristled with tall weeds and scattered bushes. Astakhov reined in his horse, pushed back his cap and wiped the big beads of sweat with the back of his hand. He looked at the others, spat hard and said, 'Ivankov, go down into the dip and see where they are.'

Ivankov, his face brick-red, his back wet with sweat, licked his parched lips thirstily, and rode off.

'Oh, for a smoke,' Kryuchkov muttered, flicking away the gadflies with his whip.

Ivankov rode at walking pace, standing up in his stirrups and looking down into the dip. First he spotted the waving tips of the lances, then the Germans suddenly appeared. They had turned their horses and were coming up the slope in a charge. At their head was an officer, his sword raised picturesquely. In the brief moment while he was wheeling his horse Ivankov had an impression of the officer's frowning, beardless face and his fine riding posture, but the thunder of German hooves rained like hailstones on his heart and the stinging chill of death seared his back. He swung his horse round and galloped away without even a shout.

Astakhov had no time to fold his pouch, and dropped it as he tried to stuff it into his pocket.

Kryuchkov saw the Germans coming up behind Ivankov and was the first to gallop forward. The Germans on the right flank were riding across to cut Ivankov off and were overtaking him at fantastic speed. He was lashing his horse and looking back. His face was grey and contorted, his eyes bulging out of their sockets. Astakhov, flat over his saddle pommel, took the lead. A whirl-wind of brown dust rose behind Kryuchkov and Shchegolkov.

'They'll catch me!' the thought froze in Ivankov's mind and it never occurred to him to defend himself; he hunched his big, fleshy body into a ball and crouched forward till his head touched the horse's mane.

He was overtaken by a burly ginger-haired German, who jabbed him in the back with his lance. The point pierced his belt at an angle and went almost an inch into his body.

'Turn back, lads,' he shouted madly, and drew his sabre. He parried a second blow aimed at his side and, rising in his stirrups, slashed at the back of a German who had ridden up on his left. He was surrounded. A tall German horse charged into his horse's flank and nearly knocked it off its feet and right in front of him was the frightening blur of a foreign face.

Astakhov was the first to reach them. He was pounced on and forced aside. He fought back with his sabre, twisting and turning in the saddle, his face contorted and grinning like a death's head. A German sword slashed Ivankov's neck. A dragoon loomed up on his left and raised sword flashed pallidly in his eyes. Ivankov parried with his sabre and steel met steel with a shriek. A lance had been poked under his shoulder strap from behind and was persistently tugging it off his shoulder. Behind the rearing muzzle of a horse he glimpsed the sweating flushed face of a freckled elderly German. Lower jaw trembling, the German was lunging wildly at Ivankov's chest with his sword, but could not reach him. The German dropped it and wrenched at a carbine in a yellow sheath attached to his saddle, keeping his frightened, blinking brown eyes on Ivankov. Before he could draw the carbine, Kryuchkov reached him across the horse with his lance. The German, tearing at the front of his dark-blue tunic as he fell backwards, gave a frightened and astonished gasp.

'*Mein Gott!*'

About eight dragoons surrounded Kryuchkov, trying to capture him alive. But he reared his horse and, swinging his body from the waist, fought them off with his sabre. When it was knocked out of his hand, he snatched a lance from the nearest German and wielded it as if at exercises.

The Germans backed away and hacked at the lance with their swords. By that small strip of loamy sombre ploughland they charged and grappled with one another, swaying to and fro in the struggle, as if driven by the wind. Brutalised by fear, Cossacks and Germans stabbed and hacked at anything they saw: backs, arms, horses, weapons. The fear-crazed horses cannoned into each other at random. Recovering some of his self-control, Ivankov struck several times at the head of the blond long-faced dragoon who was attacking him, but the sabre hit the steel sidepieces of his helmet and glanced off.

Astakhov broke out of the ring, bleeding profusely. The German officer came after him and was killed by a shot at pointblank range from Astakhov's rifle, which he had managed to rip off his shoulder. This was the turning-point in the fight. The Germans, all wounded by clumsy random blows and now deprived of their officer, scattered and withdrew. No one gave chase or fired a shot in pursuit. The Cossacks rode straight back to Pelikalie and their own squadron; the Germans picked up the wounded comrade who had fallen from his horse and retired to the border.

After galloping about half a verst, Ivankov swayed in his saddle.

'Can't go on... I'm falling!' He reined in his horse, but Astakhov jerked the reins forward.

'Keep going!'

Kryuchkov smeared the blood on his face and felt his chest. Wet spots of red showed on his tunic.

At the manor where the second outpost had been stationed they split up.

'Now we go right!' Astakhov said, pointing to the bright green of a boggy patch in the alders beyond the yard.

'No, it's to the left!' Kryuchkov insisted.

They parted and Astakhov and Ivankov arrived in the

town later. A party of Cossacks from their squadron was waiting for them on the outskirts.

Ivankov dropped his reins, sprang off his horse, swayed and fell. They had difficulty in removing the sabre from his convulsed fingers.

One hour later almost the whole squadron rode out to the place where the German officer had been killed. The Cossacks took his boots, clothes and weapons and crowded round, staring at his young, frowning and already yellowish face. Tarasov, an Ust-Khopyorskaya man, who had been quick enough to take possession of the dead man's watch with a silver guard, sold it on the spot to a troop sergeant. In the man's wallet they found a little money, a letter, a lock of fair hair in an envelope, and a photograph of a girl with a haughty smiling mouth.

IX

The incident was later blown up into a feat of arms. Kryuchkov, the squadron commander's favourite, received the St. George Cross on his recommendation. His comrades were left in the shade. The hero was transferred to Divisional Headquarters, where he loafed till the end of the war, and was awarded three more crosses for having influential ladies and officers from Petrograd and Moscow come to look at him. The ladies sighed in admiration and regaled the Don Cossack with expensive cigarettes and delicacies. At first he lambasted them with all the names under the sun, but later, under the salutary influence of the headquarters bootlickers in officers' uniform, he made a lucrative profession out of it; he described his 'exploit', laying on the colours with a trowel and lying without a qualm of conscience, and the ladies enthused and gazed in adoration at the Cossack hero's pock-marked brigandish face. Everyone was pleased, everyone was happy.

When the tsar visited G. H. Q., Kryuchkov was taken there as an exhibit. The somnolent ginger-haired emperor looked Kryuchkov over like a horse, blinked his liverish, baggy eyelids, and patted him on the shoulder.

'Good fellow, Cossack!' he said, and turned to his retinue, 'Bring me some Seltzer.'

Kryuchkov's face with its long forelock won a permanent place in the newspapers and magazines. There was a brand of cigarettes with Kryuchkov's picture on it.

The merchants of Nizhny Novgorod presented him with a golden sword.

The uniform of the German officer killed by Astakhov was pinned to a sheet of plywood and the Russian General von Rennenkampf put Ivankov and his A. D. C. in his car with this exhibit and drove out in front of the troops leaving for the fighting line and made the usual fire-eating speeches.

But what had really happened was that a few men, not yet practised in the art of destroying their fellow creatures, had met each other on the field of death and, overcome by animal fear, had charged and battered one another, striking blindly and maiming themselves and their horses. At the sound of a shot that had killed one of their number they had scattered in panic and ridden away morally crippled.

And this was called a feat of arms.

X

The front had not yet grown into the long unyielding viper that it was later to become. Cavalry skirmishes and battles flared up on the border. In the first days after the declaration of war the German command put out feelers in the shape of strong cavalry patrols that alarmed the Russian units by slipping past the outposts and spying out the positions and strength of their forces. The front of Brusilov's Eighth Army was covered by the 12th Cavalry Division under the command of General Kaledin. To the left, the 11th Cavalry Division had crossed the Austrian border and was advancing. It captured Lesznjów and Brody and came to a standstill when the Austrians were reinforced and the Hungarian cavalry clashed head on with the Russian horse, harassing it and driving it back towards Brody.

Since the action at the town of Lesznjów, Grigory Melekhov had been wrestling with a nagging inward pain. He had grown noticeably thinner and lost weight. Often on the march and while resting, asleep or dozing, he dreamed of the Austrian he had cut down by the iron railing. Time and again he relived that first encounter, and even in his sleep, pursued by memories, he felt the convulsion that the lance had transmitted to his right hand; when he awoke, he would try to banish the dream by pressing his eyes until they hurt.

The cavalry trampled the ripe grain and the fields were pitted with the marks of sharp-studded hoofs, as though the whole of Galicia had been swept by hailstorms. Heavy soldiers' boots hardened the cart-tracks, chipped the highways and churned the August mud.

Where battles had been fought the earth's sombre face was pock-marked with shell-holes, and splinters of iron and steel rusted in it, yearning for human blood. At night scarlet dawns stretched their long arms to the sky as villages and towns flared like summer lightning. In August, the time of mellowing fruit and ripening corn, the sky remained an unsmiling grey and the few fine days were oppressively hot and humid.

August was drawing to a close. The leaves in the orchards turned a greasy yellow, a deathly purple seeped from their stems, and at a distance the trees looked as if they were covered with ragged wounds and streaming with their crimson blood.

Grigory observed with curiosity the changes that came over the other Cossacks in the squadron. Prokhor Zykov, who had only just returned from the field hospital with the ridged scar of a horse's hoof on his cheek, still had that look of pain and astonishment in the corners of his lips, and his gentle calf-like eyes blinked frequently; Yegor Zharkov used the foulest possible oaths on any occasion, told even more filthy stories than usual, and cursed everything under the sun; a fellow villager of Grigory's, Yemelyan Groshev, a serious and practical-minded Cossack, had a charred, burnt-out look and would suddenly, for no apparent reason, break into absurd and sullen laughter. A change had occurred in every face; each man in his own way was nursing, germinating the seeds sown by war and all of them together, young Cossacks uprooted from their villages, in the atmosphere of death and destruction that surrounded them, were already wilting and changing shape like stalks of mown grass.

The regiment had been withdrawn from the line and was given three days' rest to receive the reinforcements that had arrived from the Don. Grigory's squadron was just about to go and bathe in the landowner's pond when a large detachment of cavalry set out from the station three versts away.

While the Cossacks of the Fourth Squadron were walking to the dam, the detachment rode down the slope from the station and were soon recognised as Cossacks.

Prokhor Zykov leaned forward to pull off his tunic and, as he freed his head, peered into the distance.

'They're ours, from the Don.'

Grigory stared frowningly at the column as it trooped into the grounds of the estate.

'They're reserves.'

'It must be a reinforcement for us.'

'They're calling up the second-line men.'

'Look, lads! Isn't that Stepan Astakhov? In the third rank!' Groshev exclaimed, and gave a little grating laugh.

'Yes, they're taking that lot now.'

'And there's Anikei!'

'Grishka! Melekhov! There's your brother! See him?'

'I see him.'

'That's a drink you owe me, slow-coach. I saw him first!'

The skin on Grigory's high cheekbones puckered as he tried to recognise the horse Petro was riding. They must have bought him a new one, he thought, and transferred his glance to his brother's face, strangely altered since their last meeting—sun-burnt, the wheaten-coloured moustache clipped short and the brows scorched silver by the sun. Grigory went to meet him, taking off his cap and waving mechanically as if on parade. The other Cossacks, half-naked, streamed after him from the dam, breaking through a brittle scrub of hollow-stemmed chervil and withered burdock.

The reserve squadron rode round the orchard into the grounds of the estate where the regiment was stationed. It was led by an elderly thick-set major with a freshly shaven head and hard, wooden lines round his clean-shaven mouth.

That one's a growler, Grigory thought, smiling at his brother and casting a quick glance at the major's erect figure and the hook-nosed horse under him, probably of a Kalmyk breed.

'Squadron!' the major shouted in a clear, well-trained voice, 'In troop columns, by the left, march!'

'Hullo, brother!' Grigory shouted, smiling at Petro and feeling a sudden thrill of joy.

'Praise the Lord! Here we are, come to back you up. How are things?'

'Not so bad.'

'Still alive?'

'So far.'

'Greetings from the family.'

'How are they?'

'All well.'

Petro turned round resting his hand on the crupper of the sturdy sorrel horse he was riding, scanned Grigory with smiling eyes and rode on, dropping out of sight behind the dusty backs of the other Cossacks, friends and strangers.

'Hullo there, Melekhov! Greetings from the village.'

'You here too?' Grigory smiled as he recognised Mikhail Koshevoi by his thick golden forelock.

'Yes, here I am. We're like chickens after corn.'

'A fat lot you'll find here! You're more likely to get pecked yourself.'

'Come off it!'

Yegor Zharkov came hopping along on one leg in only his shirt, struggling with his trousers as he tried to get the other leg into them.

'Hi there, Cossacks!'

'Well! If it isn't Yegor Zharkov!'

'What's up, stud-horse, have they hobbled you?'

'How's my mother back there?'

'Still alive.'

'She sent you her love, but I didn't take the present she had for you. I had enough to carry as it was.'

Yegor listened to the reply with an unusually serious face, then sat down on his bare bottom on the grass, trying to hide his disappointment and still unable to get his shivering leg into his trousers.

The half-naked Cossacks lined up along a blue-painted fence, while the squadron of reinforcements from the Don trooped down an avenue of chestnut trees into the yard.

'Hi there, Cossack!'

'Is that you, cousin Alexander?'

'The very same.'

'Andreyan! You lop-eared devil, don't you recognise me?'

'Greetings from your wife, soldier!'

'Christ save you.'

'Where's Boris Belov?'

'What squadron was he in?'

'The Fourth, I reckon.'

'Where's he from?'

'Zaton, Vyoshenskaya stanitsa.'

'What d'you want him for?' another joined in the fleeting exchange.

'I've got a letter for him.'

'Well, chum, he was killed at Raibrody the other day.'

'You don't say?'

'God's truth! I saw it with my own eyes. The bullet hit him just under the left nipple.'

'Anyone here from Chornaya Rechka?'

'Nobody, keep moving.'

The squadron halted and formed up in the middle of the yard. The dam again became crowded with Cossacks who had returned to their bathing.

A little later those who had just arrived with the reserve squadron started coming over. Grigory sat down with his brother. The clay of the dam smelled unpleasantly of damp. The sluggish water was green at the edges. Grigory killed the lice in the seams and folds of his shirt while he talked.

'I'm real heartsick, Petro. I feel like a man who's been not quite killed... Like I'd been between a couple of millstones—they've ground me to pulp and spat me out.' His voice was plaintive and cracked, and a dark furrow (Petro noticed it with twinge of fear) ran diagonally across his forehead, suggesting a strange and frightening alienation.

'What's it like?' Petro asked, pulling off his shirt and revealing a white body with a clear deep line of sunburn on the neck.

'Well, it's like this,' Grigory hurried on, and his voice strengthened with anger. 'People have been set against one another and you'd better not get caught! People are worse than wolves. There's hatred everywhere. I reckon if I bit someone he'd get the rabies.'

'Have you had to—kill anyone?'

'Yes, I have!' Grigory almost shouted, crumpling the shirt and throwing it down at his feet. Eyes averted, he clutched his throat and rubbed it, as though trying to push down a word that had stuck there.

'Tell me about it,' Petro commanded, afraid to meet his brother's glance.

'My conscience is killing me. At Lesznjów I stuck my lance right through a man... That was in battle... It was the only thing to do... But why did I cut down that other one?'

'What other one?'

'The one I killed for nothing, and now I'm sick, I can't get him out of my mind, damn his guts. I dream about the bastard at night. But was it my fault?'

'You aren't broken in yet. You'll get into the way of it.'

'Is your squadron from the reserve?' Grigory asked.

'Why should it be? No, we're part of the 27th Regiment.'

'I thought you'd come to give us a hand.'

'Our squadron is to be attached to some infantry division or other. We're catching up with it now. But there was a reserve squadron with us. They're giving you the youngsters.'

'So that's it. All right, let's have a swim.'

Grigory hurriedly slipped off his trousers and went out on to the ridge of the dam, brown, well-knit, slightly stooped and, so it seemed to Petro, somewhat aged since their last meeting. He threw out his arms and dived; a heavy green wave folded over him and spread out in ripples. He swam out to a bunch of shouting Cossacks in the middle, slapping the water affectionately and moving his shoulders with indolent ease.

Petro was a long time taking off the cross he wore round his neck and his mother's blessing sewn together with the prayer he had copied. He slipped the little bundle under his shirt and entered the water gingerly, wetting his chest and shoulders, then gave a gasp, dived and swam out to catch Grigory; they broke away from the others and swam together to the opposite shore.

Soothed by the cool motion through the water, Grigory spoke more calmly, with none of the passion he had just shown.

'The lice have got me, I'm so homesick. I'd love to be home again. I'd fly there if only I had wings. Just for one little look. What's it like there now?'

'Natalya's with us.'

'Eh?'

'She's living with us.'

'How about Mum and Dad?'

'They're all right. And Natalya's still waiting for you. She's got the idea into her head that you'll come back to her.'

Grigory snorted and spat water without answering. Petro turned his head and tried to catch his eye.

'You might at least send her greetings in your letters. You're everything to her.'

'Does she think she can mend a broken pot?'

'Well, how shall I put it... It's hope that keeps her alive. She's a fine girl. And strict too. Keeps a tight rein on herself. No playing around for her. She wouldn't have any of that.'

'Why doesn't she get married?'

'That's a daft thing to say.'

'No, it's not. That's how it should be.'

'Well, it's your business. I'm not interfering.'

'How about Dunyashka?'

'She's the marrying age, brother! She's shot up this past year, you wouldn't recognise her.'

'Has she?' Grigory looked surprised and more cheerful.

'Sure as God. She'll be married off and we won't be there to dip our whiskers in the vodka. They may even kill us, the bastards.'

'Only too likely!'

They scrambled out on to the sand and lay down together arm in arm, warming themselves in the late summer sun. Mishka Koshevoi swam past, thrusting his body half out of the water.

'Come in, Grisha!'

'I will soon.'

Burying a beetle in the sand, Grigory asked, 'What's the news of Aksinya?'

'I saw her in the village before war was declared.'

'What did she come there for?'

'To collect her belongings from her husband.'

Grigory coughed and swept a heap of sand over the beetle.

'Didn't you speak to her?'

'Only passed the time of day. She's filled out and looks quite happy. Seems to be living well enough on his lordship's grub.'

'What about Stepan?'

'He gave her the things. Treated her decently. But you be careful of him. Be on your guard. The Cossacks told me that when he was drunk he threatened he'd put a bullet through you in the first battle.'

'Uh-huh.'

'He won't forgive you.'

'I know.'

'I've got myself a horse,' Petro changed the subject. 'Did you sell the oxen?'

'Ay, the baldies. For a hundred and eighty. And the horse cost a hundred and fifty. It's great! I bought it at Tsutskan.'

'How's the grain?'

'Fine. Didn't have time to harvest it though, before they roped us in.'

Their talk turned to farming matters and lost its tension. Grigory listened eagerly to the news of home and for a few minutes he was the same straightforward, high-spirited lad he had been before.

'Well, let's take another dip, then get dressed,' Petro suggested, brushing the sand off his stomach and shivering. The skin on his back and arms was all gooseflesh.

They returned from the pond in a crowd. By the fence that separated the orchard from the yard of the manor they were overtaken by Stepan Astakhov. He was combing his matted forelock into place under the peak of his cap as he drew level with Grigory.

'Hullo, friend!'

'Hullo,' Grigory dropped behind a little, meeting his glance with embarrassment and a touch of guilt.

'You haven't forgotten me?'

'I had—almost.'

'But I still remember you,' Stepan smiled mockingly and strode on, putting his arm round the shoulder of a Cossack with sergeant's stripes, who was walking in front.

After dark that evening a telephone message came through from Divisional Headquarters, ordering the regiment to take the field. Within a quarter of an hour the reinforced squadrons were mustered and rode off singing—to fill a breech made in the line by the Hungarian cavalry.

As they said good-bye, Petro gave his brother a folded slip of paper.

'What is it?' Grigory asked.

'I copied out a prayer for you. Here take it.'

'Does it do any good?'

'Don't laugh, Grigory.'

'I'm not laughing.'

'Well, good-bye, brother. Look after yourself. Don't go charging ahead of the others. Death's on the lookout for hotheads! Take care!' Petro shouted.

'What's the prayer for then?'

Petro waved the remark aside.

Until eleven they rode without taking any precautions. After that the sergeants-major went round the squadrons, ordering the utmost silence and no smoking.

Flares tinged with lilac-coloured smoke blazed over a distant ridge of forest.

A small brown morocco notebook. The corners frayed and broken; it must have spent a long time in its owner's pocket. The pages are covered with rather elaborate sloping handwriting.

* * *

...For some time I have felt this need to put pen to paper. I want to keep a sort of 'diary of the heart'. First of all, about her. In February (I don't remember the date), I was introduced to her by a person from her part of the country, a student called Boyaryshkin. I ran into them outside a cinema. When Boyaryshkin introduced her he said, 'This is Liza, she's a Cossack girl, from Vyoshenskaya stanitsa. Be nice to her, Timofei. She's a great girl.' I remember uttering some incoherent remark and taking her soft sweaty hand in mine. That was how I met Yelizaveta Mokhova. I realised at once that she was no longer a virgin. Such women have eyes that tell you too much. The first impression of her, I admit, was unfavourable; it must have been that warm, damp hand. I have never met anyone whose hands perspired so much; and then those eyes, very beautiful eyes actually, with a glorious hazel tint in them, but unpleasant.

Vasya, old friend, I find myself consciously touching up my style, even resorting to imagery, so that when in the course of time this 'diary' reaches you in Semipalatinsk (I am thinking of sending it to you after this affair I have started with Yelizaveta Mokhova is over; it should amuse you considerably), you will have a clear idea of what happened. I shall describe things in chronological order. Well, as I have said, we were introduced and the three of us went to see some sentimental cinema rubbish. Boyaryshkin kept quiet (he had toothache, 'tusk-ache', as he called it) and I found it difficult to make conversation. We turned out to be from the same neighbourhood, that is, from neighbouring stanitsas, but after we had shared a few reminiscences about the beauties of steppe scenery and so on, we had nothing more to say. I maintained an unconstrained silence, so to speak, and she suffered the lack of conversation without the slightest discomfort. I learned from her that she was a second-year medical student, that she came from a merchant family, and that she was fond of strong tea and Asmolov's snuff. Extremely scanty information, as you can imagine, for getting to know a girl with hazel eyes. When we said good-bye (we saw her off to the tram-stop), she invited me to call on her. I made a note of her address. I think I shall drop in on April 28th.

April 29th

Called on her today, she gave me tea and halvah. As a matter of fact, there is something in her. Sharp tongue, moderately clever, but she's got hold of that Artsibashev do-as-you-please theory, you can smell it even at a distance. I got home late, made myself cigarettes and thought of things completely unconnected with her, mainly money. My suit is in an appalling state, but I have no 'capital'. On the whole, things are bloody.

May 1st

Today was marked by an event of some importance. While passing the time quite harmlessly in Sokolniki Park we got involved in an incident. The police and a detachment of Cossacks, about twenty of them, were dispersing a workers' May Day meeting. A drunk hit one of the Cossacks' horses with a stick and the Cossack brought his whip into play (I don't know why, but some people persist in calling a whip a riding crop. It has its own glorious title—why not use it?). I decided to intervene. I was impelled by the most noble feelings, I assure you. I told the Cossack he was a 'chapura'* and one or two other things besides. He was going to take a swing at me with his whip, but then I said pretty firmly that I was a Cossack of Kamenskaya stanitsa myself and could knock hell out of him any day of the week. The Cossack happened to be a good-natured young fellow who hadn't been in the army long enough to get sour. He replied that he was from the stanitsa of Ust-Khopyorskaya and a useful man with his fists. We parted peaceably. If he had started anything against me there would have been a fight; and something else, rather worse for me personally. My intervention may be attributed to Liza's presence, which induces in me a purely childish desire to perform some 'exploit'. I can actually see myself turning into a young cockerel and feel an invisible red comb sprouting under my cap... What am I coming to!

---

* Don dialect for 'heron', i. e. in this context 'clumsy oaf.'—*Tr.*

The only thing to do in my present mood is to get drunk. On top of everything I have no money. My trousers are hopelessly split just where it matters most (in the crotch, to put it bluntly), like an overripe water-melon down on the Don. The chances of my darn holding out are remote indeed. Might as well try to sew up a water-melon. Volodka Strezhnev has been round. Tomorrow I shall attend lectures.

Money from Father. Rather a grumpy letter, but I don't feel a scrap of shame. If only Dad knew his son's moral supports have rotted like this... I have bought a suit. My new neck-tie attracts the attention even of cab-men. After a shave at the best barber's in town, in Tver-skaya Street, I came out as fresh as a daisy. The police-man at the corner of the Sadovo-Triumfalnaya Boulevard grinned at me. The old scoundrel! Still, in my present get-up he and I have something in common! But three months ago? Oh well, it's better not to rummage in the linen of past history... I saw Liza quite by chance through the window of a tramcar. She waved her glove and smiled. What a man, eh?

'To love all ages are submissive...' I can still see the mouth of Tatyana's husband gaping up at me like the barrel of a cannon. From my seat in the gallery I had an irresistible desire to spit into it. Whenever I think of that phrase, particularly the 'sub-miss-ive' at the end, my jaws ache to yawn. Probably a nervous tick.

But the thing is that I, at my age, am in love. Though it makes my hair stand on end to write it... I called on Liza. Began with a very long and high-flown introduction. She pretended not to understand and tried to change the subject. Is it too early yet? Devil take it, this new suit put me up to it. When I look in the glass, I feel I am irresistible. Now is the time, I think. Actually my main consideration is common sense. If I don't propose now, in two months' time it will be too late; my trousers will be worn out and begin to rot in a place that will make a proposal out of the question. As I write this, I overflow with self-admiration. What a brilliant combination I am of all the best qualities of the best people of our time. Here you have gentle yet fiery passion as well as the 'voice of reason firm'. A Russian salad of all the virtues, not to mention a host of other admirable qualities.

Well, I got no further with her than my preliminary speech. We were interrupted by her landlady, who called her out into the corridor and, as I heard, asked her for a loan. She refused, although she had the money. I knew that for a fact and I pictured her face as she said she just couldn't manage it in that truthful voice of hers and with such sincerity in those hazel eyes. I didn't want to talk about love after that.

May 13th

I am well and truly in love. There can be no doubt about it. Everything tells me so. Tomorrow I shall propose. I have not yet decided what role to play.

May 14th

The thing came about in a most unexpected fashion. It was raining, a nice warm drizzle. We were walking along Mokhovaya, the wind was sweeping rain across the pavement. I talked and she was quiet, with her head down as if she were thinking. Rain was trickling off the brim of her hat on to her cheek and she was beautiful. I quote our conversation:

'Yelizaveta Sergeyevna, I have told you what I feel. Now it is up to you.'

'I doubt the sincerity of your feelings.'

I shrugged my shoulders in an idiotic fashion and blurted out that I was ready to take an oath, or some such silliness.

She said, 'Look here, you're talking like a character out of Turgenev. Can't you make it simpler?'

'Nothing could be simpler. I love you.'

'And now what?'

'Now it's up to you.'

'You want me to say I love you, too?'

'I want you to say something.'

'You see, Timofei Ivanovich... How shall I put it? I like you just a little bit... You're very tall.'

'I'll get taller,' I promised.

'But we know so little of each other, we...'

'We'll know each other a lot better when we've lived together for a while.'

She rubbed her wet cheeks with a pink hand and said, 'Well, all right then, let's live together. Time will show.

But you must let me break off my former attachment first.'

'Who is he?' I inquired.

'You don't know him. He's a doctor, a venerologist.'

'When will you be free?'

'By Friday, I hope.'

'Shall we be living together? In the same flat, I mean?'

'Yes, I think that will be more convenient. You will move in with me.'

'Why?'

'My room's very comfortable. It's clean and the landlady is a nice person.'

I raised no objection. At the corner of Tverskaya we parted. To the great astonishment of a lady who happened to be passing we kissed.

What does the future hold in store?

May 22nd

This is our honeymoon. Today my 'honeymoon' mood was spoiled by Liza's telling me I must change my underwear. Of course, my underwear is in a disgusting state. But the money, the money... We are spending mine and there's not much left... I shall have to find work.

May 24th

Today I decided to buy some new underwear but Liza put me to an unexpected expense. She suddenly had an irresistible desire to dine at a good restaurant and buy herself a pair of silk stockings. We have dined and bought, but I am in despair. No underwear for me!

May 27th

She's sucking me dry. I am physically no more than a bare sunflower stalk. Not a woman but a smouldering fire.

June 2nd

We woke up today at nine. My idiotic habit of wriggling my toes led to the following results. She pulled back the bedclothes and subjected my foot to a prolonged examination. Then she summed up her observations thus:

'You have a foot like a horse's hoof! Worse! And those hairs on your toes—ugh!' She jerked her shoulders in a kind of feverish disgust, buried her head under the bedclothes and turned away to the wall.

I was abashed. I tucked my feet out of sight and touched her on the shoulder.

'Liza!'

'Leave me alone!'

'Liza, this won't do at all. I can't change the shape of my feet, they weren't made to order, you know. And as for the vegetation, you can never tell where hair will grow next. It grows everywhere. You're a medical student, you ought to know the laws of nature.'

She turned over. There was a nasty glint in her hazel eyes.

'For goodness sake buy some deodorant powder. Your feet stink like a corpse!'

I remarked reasonably enough that her hands were always clammy. She remained silent and, to put it in lofty terms, a murky cloud descended on my soul... It has nothing to do with feet or hair...

June 4th

Today we took a boat out on the River Moskva. We recalled the Don countryside. Liza's conduct is deplorable. She keeps making cutting remarks at my expense, and sometimes they are very rude. To pay her back in her own coin would mean breaking off our relations and I don't want that. In spite of everything, I am getting more and more attached to her. She is simply spoiled. But I fear my influence will not be strong enough to produce any radical change in her character. A lovable, spoiled little girl. A little girl, moreover, who has seen things that I know of only by hearsay. On the way home she dragged me into a chemist's and, with a smile on her face, bought some talcum powder and some other rubbish.

'This'll stop you perspiring so much.'

I made a gallant bow and thanked her.

Absurd, but there it is.

June 7th

She has very little intellect, but she knows all the other things.

Every night before going to bed I wash my feet in hot water, pour Eau-de-Cologne over them and powder them with some disgusting stuff.

June 16th

Every day she becomes more and more intolerant. Yesterday she had hysterics. It is very hard to live with such a woman.

301

We have absolutely nothing in common! We are not even talking the same language. The element of unity is the bed. Life has lost its sap.

This morning she looked in my pocket for money before going to the baker's and came across this little book. She looked at it.

'What's this you're carrying about?'

I felt hot all over. Suppose she glanced through it? I was surprised to hear myself answer in such a natural voice. 'Just a notebook for calculations.'

She pushed it back into my pocket quite indifferently and went out. I must be more careful. Witty observations are only worthwhile when the other person knows nothing about them.

They shall be a source of entertainment to my friend Vasya.

June 21st

I am astounded at Liza. She is twenty-one. When did she have time to become so depraved. What kind of family has she got, how was she brought up, who had a hand in her development? These are questions that interest me intensely. She is devilishly beautiful. She takes pride in the perfection of her figure. The worship of self—nothing else exists for her. I have tried several times to talk to her seriously... It would be easier to convince an Old Believer that God doesn't exist than to re-educate Liza.

Life together has become impossible and absurd. Yet I hesitate to break things off. I must confess that I like her in spite of everything. She has grown upon me.

June 24th

The answer to the puzzle was quite simple after all. We had a heart-to-heart talk today and she told me I don't satisfy her physically. The break is not yet official, in a few days probably.

June 26th

What she needs is a stallion from the stanitsa stud. A stud-horse!

June 28th

It is very difficult to give her up. She drags me down like mud. Today we took a ride out to the Vorobyovy

Hills. She sat by the hotel window and the sun filtered under the carved eaves on to her curls. Her hair is the colour of pure gold. There's a piece of poetry for you!

July 4th

I have left my work. Liza has left me. Today I drank beer with Strezhnev. Yesterday we drank vodka. Liza and I parted as educated people should, politely. No nonsense. Today I saw her in Dmitrovka Street with a young man in jockey boots. She acknowledged my greeting with a mere nod. It is time to stop writing these notes—the source has run dry.

I am quite unexpectedly impelled to take up the pen again. War. An explosion of bestial enthusiasm. Every top-hat stinks of patriotism, the smell's as bad as a worm-ridden dog. The other fellows are indignant, but I am glad. I am eaten up with longing for my 'paradise lost'. Last night I had a lustful dream about Liza. She has left a deep mark of yearning... I should be glad of some diversion.

August 1st

I'm fed up with all the brouhaha. The old longing has returned. I suck it like a baby sucking its dummy.

August 3rd

A way out! I shall go to the war. Foolish? Very. Shameful?

But what does it matter? There is nowhere else for me to go. At least, I shall have a taste of something different. Yet there was no such blasé feeling two years ago. Am I getting old?

August 7th

I am writing in the train. We have just left Voronezh. Tomorrow I get off at Kamenskaya. I have made up my mind to fight 'for the Faith, the Tsar, and the Fatherland'.

August 12th

What a send-off they gave me. The ataman had a drink too many and came out with a fire-eating speech. Afterwards I told him in a whisper he was a fool. He was flabbergasted and so offended his cheeks turned green. Then he hissed spitefully, 'Call yourself educated, do you? You wouldn't be one of those we flogged in 1905, would you?' I replied that, to my regret, I was not 'one

303

of those' and advised him to join the Social Democrats. My father wept and tried to kiss me with a dewdrop hanging from the tip of his nose. Poor dear father! He ought to be in my shoes. I suggested jokingly that he should come with me and he exclaimed in alarm, 'But what about the farm?' Tomorrow I leave for the station.

August 13th

Unharvested fields. Sleek marmots on the hillocks. They bear a striking resemblance to the Germans we see impaled on Kozma Kryuchkov's lance in the cheap lithograph. Once upon a time I was a student of mathematics and other exact sciences. Little did I think I should live to become such a 'jingoist'. When I get into the regiment, I'll have a proper talk with the Cossacks.

August 22nd

At one of the stations along the line I saw the first party of prisoners. A fine-looking Austrian officer with the bearing of an athlete was being taken under guard to the station building. Two young ladies strolling along the platform smiled at him. He managed a very neat bow without stopping and blew them a kiss.

Even as a prisoner he was clean-shaven, gallant, his brown boots glistened. I watched him as he walked away. A young handsome fellow, a pleasant, friendly face. If you met him in battle, your arm wouldn't lift to strike.

August 24th

Refugees, refugees, refugees... Every line is crowded with trains packed full of refugees and troops.

The first hospital train has just passed. When it stopped, a young soldier jumped out. His face was bandaged. We got talking. He had been wounded by grapeshot. Awfully glad he probably won't have to do any more fighting; an eye was damaged. He was actually laughing.

August 27th

I am with my regiment. The regimental commander is a very fine old man. A Cossack from the lower Don. One can smell blood around here. There are rumours that we shall be in the front line the day after tomorrow. Mine is the Third Troop of the Third Squadron—Cossacks from Konstantinovskaya. A dull lot. Only one wag and songster.

We are going up. It's very noisy out there today. Sounds like thunder rumbling in the distance. I actually sniffed the air for rain. But the sky is like blue satin.

Yesterday my horse went lame, grazed its leg on the wheel of a field-kitchen. Everything is new and strange. I don't know what to start on, what to write about.

Yesterday there was no time to write. Now I am writing in the saddle. The jolting makes my pencil perform some monstrous antics. There are three of us riding with forage sacks for grass.

The lads are filling the sacks and I am lying on my stomach making a belated record of what happened yesterday. Yesterday Sergeant-Major Tolokonnikov (he addresses me contemptuously as 'student'. 'Hi there, student, can't you see your horse has got a shoe coming off?') sent six of us out on reconnaissance. We rode through a little town that had been partly burnt down. It was very hot. The horses were sweating, and so were we. Cossacks should not have to wear serge trousers in summer. Outside the town I saw my first corpse. A German. Lying on his back with his legs in a ditch. One hand twisted under him, a cartridge clip in the other. No rifle anywhere near. A ghastly sight. A cold shiver runs down my spine as I think of it... He looked as if he had been sitting with his feet in the ditch and had then lain back to rest. Grey uniform and helmet. I noticed the leather lining patterned like the protective sheet of tissue paper in a cigarette box. I was so dazed by this first experience that I don't remember his face. Only the big yellow ants crawling over the yellow forehead and the glassy, half-closed eyes. The Cossacks crossed themselves as they rode past. I looked at the small spot of blood on the right side of the uniform. The bullet had hit him in the right side and gone straight through. As I rode by I noticed that where the bullet had come out, the stain on the uniform and the clot of blood on the ground was much bigger, and the tear in the uniform was ragged.

I rode past shuddering. So that's how it happens...

A senior sergeant, nicknamed Teaser, tried to raise our fallen spirits by telling us a dirty joke, but his own lips were trembling.

About half a verst from the town we came to a gutted factory: just brick walls blackened with smoke at the top.

We were afraid to ride straight along the road because it lay past this burnt-out hulk, so we decided to go round it. As soon as we struck off the road, somebody opened fire on us from the factory. The sound of that first shot, ashamed though I am to admit it, nearly toppled me out of the saddle. I clutched at the pommel and instinctively ducked down, tugging at the reins. We galloped back into the town past the ditch where the dead German lay and didn't recover our wits till the town was behind us. Then we turned round and dismounted. We left two men with the horses, while the other four of us made our way back to that ditch. We crouched down to go along it. From a distance I saw the legs of the dead German in short fawn boots dangling over the edge. I held my breath when I passed him, as if he were asleep and I were afraid of waking him. The grass under him was moist and green.

We lay down in the ditch and a few minutes later nine German uhlans rode out from behind the ruins of the factory. I could tell they were uhlans by their uniforms. One of them, evidently an officer, shouted something in a guttural voice and the whole troop rode in our direction... The lads are calling for me to come and help them load the grass. I must go.

August 30th

I want to finish describing how I fired my first shot at a man. The German uhlans rode down on us and I can still see those lizard-green uniforms, the glistening bell-shapes of their helmets, their lances with the pennants fluttering at the tips.

They were mounted on dark bay horses. For some reason I let my glance wander to the bank of the ditch and noticed a small emerald-green beetle. It grew larger and larger before my eyes until it seemed enormous. Brushing aside the blades of grass like a giant, it lumbered towards my elbow, which rested on the dry crumbling clay of the ditch; it climbed the sleeve of my tunic and crawled quickly on to the rifle, then from the rifle, on to the sling. I was still watching it on its journey when I heard the Teaser's voice bawling, 'Fire! What's the matter with you?!'

I settled my elbow more firmly, screwed up my left eye and felt my heart swelling till it was as huge as that emerald beetle. My sights trembled against a background of grey-green uniform. Next to me there was a shot from Teaser. I pressed the trigger and heard the moaning flight of the bullet. I must have had my sights too low because the bullet ricochetted off a tussock and kicked up a spurt of dust. That was the first shot I had ever fired at a man. I emptied the magazine without aiming. I had another look at the Germans only when I pulled the trigger and got no response. They were galloping back in the same good order as before, with the officer bringing up the rear. There were nine of them and I could see the dark bay croup of the officer's horse and the metal plate on the top of his uhlan's helmet.

September 2nd

In *War and Peace* Tolstoy has a passage in which he speaks of the line between opposing armies, the line of the unknown that seems to divide the living from the dead. The squadron in which Nikolai Rostov is serving goes into an attack and Rostov sees that line in his mind's eye. I remembered that passage particularly vividly when today, at dawn, we attacked a unit of German hussars. Since early morning their troops, with excellent artillery support, had been harassing our infantry. I saw our men—the 241st and 273rd infantry regiments, I think—fleeing in panic. They were literally demoralised after being thrown into an attack with no artillery support. Enemy fire had accounted for nearly a third of them and the rest were being pursued by German hussars. Then our regiment, which had been standing in reserve in a forest clearing, was thrown into action. This is how I remember the affair. We left the village of Tyszwici between two and three in the morning. The darkness was very intense just before dawn. The air was heavy with the smell of oats and pine needles. The regiment proceeded in squadrons. We turned off the road and struck across the fields. The horses snorted as their hoofs sprinkled the heavy dew off the oats.

It was chilly even in a greatcoat. They kept the regiment tracking across the fields for a long time and an hour passed before an officer rode up and handed an order to the regimental commander. Our old man passed on the order in a dissatisfied tone and the regiment wheeled into the woods. The columns were bunched up very close on the narrow path. Fighting was going on somewhere to the left. Judging by the noise, a large number of German batteries were in action. The sound of the shots came in waves and it felt as if all this scented pinewood was on fire about us. Until sunrise we could only listen. A cheer went up, a limp, ragged sort of cheer—and then stillness, punctuated by the sharp, clear hammering of machine-guns. At that moment my mind was in a turmoil and the only thing I could imagine with any clarity—but that picture was utterly and painfully distinct—was the lines of our infantry as they advanced.

I could see those baggy grey figures in their flat field caps and clumsy soldier's boots pounding over the autumn earth and I could hear the sharp hoarse chuckle of the German machine-guns as they set to work transforming those living sweating human bodies into corpses. The two regiments were mown down and fled, abandoning their arms. They were pursued by a regiment of German hussars. We were on their flank at a distance of seven hundred paces or less. An order was given. We formed up instantly. I heard a single cold command. 'Forward!' It seemed to hold us back for an instant, like a bit in the mouth, then we were flying ahead. My horse's ears were pressed so flat against its head, you couldn't have prised them up with your fingers. I glanced round—behind me were the regimental commander and two officers. Yes, this was the line dividing the living from the dead. Here it was, the great moment of insanity!

The hussars wavered and turned back. Before my eyes Lieutenant Chernetsov cut down a German hussar. I saw a Cossack of the Sixth Squadron overtake a German and hack madly at his horse's croup. Ribbons of skin streamed from the sabre as it rose and fell. It was inconceivable! There was no name for it! On the way back I saw Chernetsov's face, intent and controlledly cheerful—he might have been sitting at the card table instead of in the saddle, having just murdered a man. Lieutenant Chernetsov will go far. A capable fellow!

September 4th

We are resting. The Fourth Division of the Second Army Corps is being brought up to the front. We are stationed at the small town of Kobylino. This morning, units of the 11th Cavalry Division and the Urals Cossacks passed through the town on a forced march. Fighting continues in the west. A constant rumble. After dinner I went to the field hospital. A train of wounded had just arrived. Stretcher-bearers were unloading a big wagon and laughing. I went up to them. A tall ginger-haired soldier had just climbed down with the help of an orderly. 'What do you think of that, Cossack?' he said, addressing me.

'They've given me a load of peas in the backside. I've got four lumps of grapeshot in it!' The orderly asked if the shell had burst behind him. 'Behind me be damned, I was advancing arse-first myself.' A nurse came out of the cottages. I glanced at her and suddenly felt so weak I had to lean against the wagon. The resemblance to Liza was extraordinary. The same eyes, the same oval face, same nose, hair. Even her voice was similar. Or was I imagining things? Now, I suppose, I shall see a resemblance in every woman I meet.

September 5th
The horses have had a day's feeding in the stalls and we are off to the front again. Physically I am a wreck. The bugler is sounding the order to mount. There's a man I'd love to put a bullet through!

* * *

The squadron commander had sent Grigory Melekhov with a message to regimental headquarters. As he rode through the district where recent fighting had taken place Grigory noticed a dead Cossack lying at the side of the highway. He lay with his fair head resting on the hoof-pitted road. Grigory dismounted and, holding his nose (the dead man already reeked of decay), searched the body. In his trouser pocket he found this notebook, a stub of indelible pencil and a purse. He removed the cartridge belt and glanced at the pale, damp face that was already beginning to decompose. The temples and the bridge of the nose were turning a moist black; on the forehead a slantwise furrow fixed in mortal concentration was grimed with dust.

Grigory covered the face with a cambric handkerchief that he had found in the dead man's pocket and rode on to headquarters, glancing back occasionally. He handed in the notebook to the headquarters clerks, who gathered round to read it and laugh over this other man's brief life and its earthly passions.

XII

After the capture of Lesznjów the 11th Cavalry Division had stormed Stanislawszyk, Radzivilovo and Brody and on August 15th deployed outside the town of Kamionka-Strumiłowa. In its wake came the army, concentrating infantry on the important strategic sectors and crowding the junctions with staffs and supplies. The front stretched southward from the Baltic like a death-dealing lash. Headquarters worked out plans for a broad offensive, generals pored over maps, messengers galloped to and fro with orders, and hundreds of thousands of soldiers went to their deaths. Reconnaissance reported that powerful enemy cavalry forces were being brought up to the town. Cossack patrols skirmished with enemy reconnaissance in the woods along the roads.

All through the campaign, ever since his brother had left, Grigory Melekhov had been trying vainly to get a grip on himself, check his morbid thoughts and recover his former equable state of mind. The latest reinforcements to arrive in the regiment had included some men of the third-line reserve. One of them, Alexei Uryupin, a Cossack of Kazanskaya stanitsa, was assigned to the same troop as Grigory. Uryupin was tall, slightly stooped, with a prominent lower jaw and a long thin Kalmyk moustache; his merry, fearless eyes always had a gleam of laughter in them; though he was still young, his head was bald and shining and scanty tufts of light-brown hair grew only at the sides of the knobbly, bulging skull. The Cossacks at once nicknamed him 'Curly'.

After the battle at Brody the regiment was allowed a day's rest. Grigory was billeted in the same house as Curly and they got talking.

'You look washed out, Melekhov.'

'Washed out?' Grigory frowned.

'Seedy, like a sick man,' Curly explained.

They fed their tethered horses and leaned back on the rickety moss-grown fence for a smoke. Hussars were riding down the street four abreast. Corpses were still lying about by the fences (there had been fighting in the streets when the Austrians were driven out) and acrid smoke was rising from the ruins of a burnt-out synagogue. The town presented a picture of destruction and eerie desolation amid the rich colours of evening.

'I'm fit enough,' Grigory looked away and spat.

'Come off it! I can see.'

'What can you see?'

'Scared, are you, snuffer? Afraid of death?'

'You're a fool,' Grigory said contemptuously, and frowned at his fingernails.

'Now tell me this, have you killed a man?' Uryupin

rapped out, scanning Grigory's face intently.

'Yes. What about it?'

'Is your soul snivelling?'

'Snivelling?' Grigory gave a dry little laugh.

Curly drew his sabre.

'Want me to cut off your head?'

'And what then?'

'It won't worry me. I have no pity!' Uryupin's eyes were laughing, but Grigory realised from his voice and the rapacious quiver of his nostrils that he meant what he said.

'You're a crazy fellow,' he said, looking closely at Uryupin's face.

'And you're a chicken-hearted one. Do you know the Baklanov stroke? Look!'

Uryupin chose an old birch-tree growing near by and walked straight towards it, shoulders hunched, measuring the distance with his eye. His long, sinewy arms with their enormously thick wrists, hung motionless at his sides.

'Look!'

He raised his sabre slowly, crouched a little and suddenly brought it down in a slanting stroke of terrible force. The tree, severed at a height of less than five feet from the root, toppled over, clutching at the bare window frames and scratching the walls of the house with its branches.

'Did you see that? Learn it. Baklanov was an ataman. Heard of him? His sabre was loaded with quicksilver. It was heavy to lift, but one stroke would split a horse in two. Like that!'

It took Grigory a long time to master the complexities of the stroke.

'You're strong, but you're a fool with a sabre. This is how it's done,' Curly taught him, and a slanting blow of his sabre would slice through the target with tremendous force.

'Cut a man down boldly. He's soft as dough, a man is,' Curly instructed, eyes laughing. 'Don't think about what it's all for. You're a Cossack. It's your duty to cut people down without question. It's sacred work to kill a man in battle. God pardons one of your sins for every man you kill, just the same as for a snake. You mustn't harm animals without need, a calf, say, or something like that. But destroy man. Man is poisonous. He's unclean, he fouls the earth like a toadstool.'

In reply to Grigory's objections he merely frowned and maintained a stubborn silence.

Grigory noticed with surprise that for no apparent reason all horses feared Uryupin. When he approached the tethering posts, they would flatten their ears and huddle together as if a wild animal and not a man were approaching them. When the squadron was advancing over marshy wooded country near Stanisławszyk it was forced to dismount. The horse-minders led the horses away to cover in a hollow. Uryupin was detailed for the task but he refused outright.

'Uryupin, you arse-hole, what the hell are you playing at? Why don't you take the horses?' the troop sergeant bawled at him.

'They're scared of me. Honestly, they are!' Curly insisted, with that constant gleam of laughter in his eyes.

He had never been a groom. He was gentle with his own horse and looked after it well, but Grigory always noticed that as soon as its master approached, arms hanging motionless at his sides as usual, the horse's back would twitch nervously.

'Well, my saintly man, tell me why the horses jib like that when you come near,' Grigory asked one day.

'Who knows?' Uryupin shrugged. 'I'm kind to them.'

'They can tell a drunk by the smell and that scares them, but you're dead sober.'

'I've got a firm heart and they sense it.'

'You've got a wolf's heart. Or mebbe you haven't got one at all, just a stone instead.'

'Mebbe,' Uryupin agreed readily.

At Kamionka-Strumilowa the whole of the Third Troop went out on reconnaissance with the troop officer. The day before, a Czech deserter had informed the command of the positions of the Austrian units and the likelihood of a counter-attack on the Goroshi-Stawintski line. The road along which the enemy units were expected to advance had to be kept under constant observation. The troop officer left four Cossacks with the troop sergeant on the fringe of the woods and rode with the rest towards the tiled roofs of a farm that were just visible over the next hill.

Grigory, the troop sergeant and some of the younger Cossacks—Silantyev, Uryupin and Mikhail Koshevoi—formed the group that stayed behind on the edge of the wood beside an old shrine with a sharp pointed roof and a rusty crucifix on top.

The sergeant told them to dismount.

'Off you get, lads,' the sergeant told them. 'Koshevoi, take the horses behind the pines over there. Ay, where they're thicker.'

The Cossacks stretched themselves out by a fallen pine-tree and smoked, while the sergeant kept constant watch through field-glasses. About ten paces away, a field of unreaped rye was waving in the breeze. The empty ears bowed and murmured sorrowfully. For about half an hour the Cossacks lay exchanging idle remarks. Artillery fire rumbled incessantly somewhere to the right of the town. Grigory crawled out to the rye, found a few full ears, crushed them in his hand and munched the hard, overripe grain.

'Austrians!' the sergeant called in a low voice.

'Where?' Silantyev sat up startled.

'Coming out of the woods. Over to the right there!'

A bunch of horsemen rode out from behind a distant coppice. They stopped, scanned the field with its jutting headlands of forest, then moved on in the direction of the Cossacks.

'Melekhov!' the sergeant called.

Grigory crawled back to the pine.

'We'll let 'em get a bit nearer, then give 'em a volley. Have your rifles ready, lads!' the sergeant whispered feverishly.

The approaching horsemen veered to the right and came on at a walk. The four Cossacks lay behind the pine-tree, holding their breath.

'...*aucht, Kapral!*' a young resonant voice reached them on the wind.

Grigory raised his head. Six Hungarian hussars in handsome braided tunics were riding up in a bunch. The leader, mounted on a big black stallion, was holding a carbine and laughing quietly, in a deep voice.

'Let 'em have it!' the sergeant whispered.

The volley crashed out and was followed by a long echo.

'What's up?' Koshevoi shouted in alarm from behind the trees, and, to the horses, 'Whoa there! Damn you! Mad lot! Down, you devil!' His voice was soberingly loud.

The hussars broke up and galloped away through the rye in a straggling line. One of them, the one who had been riding in front on the sleek black stallion, fired into the air. The last man, lagging behind, flattened himself over his horse's neck and looked back, holding on his cap with his left hand.

Uryupin was the first to jump up and run forward. He ran with his rifle at the ready, stumbling through the corn. About a hundred paces away a horse that had fallen was kicking and trying vainly to rise. Its rider was standing beside it, rubbing his knee. He shouted something while the Cossacks were still at a distance and raised his hands, looking round at his comrades galloping away into the distance.

It all happened so quickly that Grigory realised what had happened only when Uryupin brought in the prisoner.

'Take that off, soldier-boy!' he shouted, tugging roughly at the hussar's sword.

The prisoner smiled sheepishly and fumbled with the buckles. He was quite ready to take off the belt, but his fingers would not obey him. Grigory helped him cautiously, and the hussar, a tall plump-cheeked young fellow with a small wart on the corner of his clean-shaven upper lip, smiled gratefully and nodded. He seemed glad to be relieved of his weapons and, looking at the Cossacks, fumbled in his pockets, took out a leather pouch and, speaking quickly, offered it round.

'He's offering us a smoke,' the sergeant said with a grin, and felt in his pocket for cigarette paper.

'Try some free 'baccy,' Silantyev said with a chuckle.

The Cossacks rolled themselves cigarettes and lighted up. The strong black pipe tobacco went to their heads.

'Where's his rifle?' the sergeant asked, pulling greedily at his cigarette.

'Here,' Uryupin pointed to the stitched fawn-leather sling of a rifle that he had hitched over his shoulder.

'He'll have to be taken to the squadron. Headquarters will want a "tongue". Who'll take him, lads?' the sergeant asked, coughing and looking squiffily at the Cossacks.

'I will,' Uryupin volunteered.

'Go on, then.'

The prisoner seemed to understand what was in store for him and a wry, miserable smile spread over his face, but he mastered his feelings, turned out his pockets hurriedly and offered the Cossacks a soft shapeless bar of chocolate.

'*Ich russin ... russin ... nicht austritz!*'* he mispronounced the words, making absurd gestures and pressing the Cossacks to take his squashed tasty-smelling chocolate.

---

* I am a Galician ... not Austrian.—*Tr.*

314

'Any other weapons?' the sergeant asked. 'You needn't babble like that, we won't understand anyway. Got a revolver? Got a bang-bang?' he pressed an imaginary trigger.

The prisoner shook his head frantically.

'No! No!'

He willingly allowed himself to be searched. His plump cheeks were trembling.

Blood was trickling from the torn knee of his breeches, and the scratched pink flesh was showing. He pressed his handkerchief to it, frowned and smacked his lips, talking incessantly. His cap was still lying by his dead horse and he was asking to be allowed to go and fetch his blanket, cap and a notebook where he kept a photograph of his family. The sergeant tried vainly to understand what he was saying and eventually gave up with a wave of his hand.

'Take him away.'

Uryupin took his horse from Koshevoi, mounted, adjusted the sling of his rifle and pointed ahead.

'Get moving, soldier-boy, you poor sod!'

Encouraged by his smile, the prisoner smiled too, and as he stepped off beside the horse even gave Uryupin's bony knee an ingratiatingly familiar pat. Uryupin thrust his hand away sternly, reined in his horse and let him walk on ahead.

'Get moving, you devil! What are you playing at?'

The prisoner hurried on guiltily and his face was serious as he turned to look back at the other Cossacks. His fair, almost white curls rose cheerfully from the top of his head. This was how Grigory would later remember him, with his braided hussar tunic draped over his shoulders, his blond unruly curls and confident, debonair walk.

'Melekhov, go and get the saddle off his horse,' the sergeant ordered and spat regretfully on the stub of his cigarette, which he had smoked till it was burning his fingers.

Grigory took the saddle off the dead horse and for some reason picked up the cap and smelled the lining, which reeked of cheap soap and sweat. He carried the saddle back, still holding the hussar-cap gingerly in his left hand. The Cossacks squatted down by the pine-tree, rummaged through the saddle bags and examined the strangely shaped saddle.

'That was good 'baccy, we should've asked him for another smoke,' Silantyev said regretfully.

'Ay, it was right good stuff.'

'Went down your throat like butter.' The sergeant sighed at the memory, and swallowed as his mouth began to water.

A few minutes later a horse's head appeared from among the pines and Uryupin rode up.

'What happened?' the sergeant asked worriedly. 'Did he give you the slip?'

Uryupin rode up flicking his whip, dismounted and stretched his shoulders.

'What've you done with the Austrian?' the sergeant persisted, coming up to him.

'Lay off!' Uryupin snarled. 'He ran ... he tried to run away.'

'And you let him?'

'He tried when we got out on the road... I cut him down.'

'You're lying!' Grigory shouted. 'You killed him for nothing!'

'What's all the noise about? What business is it of yours?' Uryupin fixed his eyes on Grigory in an icy stare.

'Wha-a-t?' Grigory rose slowly to his feet, groping around him with unsteady hands.

'Don't butt in where you're not needed! Get me? Don't butt in!' Uryupin repeated harshly.

Grigory seized his rifle by the sling and flung it to his shoulder.

But his trembling finger could not find the trigger. His face was blotchy and strangely twisted.

'Now then!' the sergeant shouted as he ran up.

His push forestalled the shot and the bullet sang away through the tree-tops knocking off pine-needles.

'Good Lord!' Koshevoi gasped.

Silantyev sat where he was, gaping.

The sergeant pushed Grigory back, trying to wrench the rifle out of his hands. Only Uryupin made no attempt to move; he stood with his feet apart and his left hand tucked into his belt.

'Have another shot.'

'I'll kill you!' Grigory shouted, struggling to reach him.

'What are you doing! Want to get yourself court-martialled? Shot? Drop that gun!' the sergeant bawled and thrusting Grigory aside, stood between them, arms spread out as if crucified.

'Bullshit! You won't kill me!' Uryupin sneered, shifting his foot slightly.

It was dusk when they rode back and Grigory was the first to notice the hacked body by the roadside. He rode on ahead of the others and reined in his snorting horse to look at it. The dead man lay with his face buried in the curly roadside moss, one arm twisted and flung out. His hand glowed yellowishly, like an autumn leaf, on the grass. The savage blow, probably delivered from behind, had cleft the prisoner from the shoulder to the waist.

'He chopped him down all right,' the sergeant said huskily as he rode by, glancing apprehensively at the dead man's twisted head with its already drooping curls.

The Cossacks rode back to the squadron in silence. The twilight deepened. A breeze sprang up, driving a black feathery cloud from the west. A smell of marsh grass, damp and decay rose from a bog somewhere nearby; a bittern boomed. The drowsy silence was broken only by the jingle of harness, the thwack of sabre on stirrup, and the crunch of pine-needles under hooves. The ruddy glow of the vanished sun faded from the trunks of the pine-trees over the path. Uryupin smoked one cigarette after another. The glowing tip showed up his thick fingers and bulging black finger nails clamped over the butt.

The cloud drifted over the forest, intensifying the faded, inexpressibly sad colours of evening that had fallen upon the earth.

XIII

The assault on the town was launched early in the morning. The infantry, supported by cavalry on their flanks and in the reserve, were to attack from the forest at dawn, but a muddle occurred. Two infantry regiments failed to reach their starting positions in time. One of them, the 211th, had been ordered to move over to the left flank and the other was fired on by its own battery while attempting an encircling movement. Havoc ensued, plans went awry and the attack threatened to end in failure, if not a rout. While the infantry was being sorted out and the artillery were extricating the guns and ammunition trains that during the night had on someone's orders been sent into a bog, the 11th Cavalry Division launched its offensive. The marshy, thickly wooded terrain precluded a broad frontal attack and on some sectors the assault had to be made by individual troops.

The Fourth and Fifth Squadrons of the 12th Regiment were held in reserve; the rest had already been drawn into the wave of the offensive. After a quarter of an hour the reserve squadrons heard a long rumble and scattered cheering. Now and then a Cossack spoke.

'They've started!'

'Hear that machine-gun going!'

'Mowing down our lot, I bet...'

'They're quiet now, aren't they?'

'They must have got there.'

'It'll be our turn next.'

The squadrons were stationed in a forest clearing, their view blocked by towering pines. A company of infantry went by almost at the double, their brisk, smart-looking sergeant-major bringing up the rear and shouting hoarsely, 'Don't straggle!'

The company thudded past, their metal water-bottles clanking, and disappeared into a grove of alders.

From far away across the forest another weaker and more ragged cheer went up, then broke off suddenly. The silence became oppressive.

'Now they're at it!'

'Hacking away at each other!'

They all listened intently, but the silence was impenetrable. On the right flank the Austrian artillery began to pound the attacking forces and machine-guns stitched the air with staccato sound.

Grigory Melekhov looked round at the men of his troop. They were nervous and the horses stirred restlessly as if gadflies were stinging them. Uryupin had hung his cap on his saddle pommel and was wiping the sweat off his bald bluish pate. Next to Grigory, Mikhail Koshevoi was pulling furiously at a cigarette. All objects were intensely and exaggeratedly real, as one sees them after a sleepless night.

The squadrons waited for about three hours. The firing died away, then swelled up again. An aeroplane roared overhead, made a few circles at a great height and flew off eastwards, gaining altitude; milky puffs of smoke from shrapnel shells burst in the blue expanse beneath it as the anti-aircraft guns opened up.

The reserve was sent in at noon. All stocks of tobacco had been exhausted and the men were worn out by the suspense when a hussar messenger galloped up. The commander of the Fourth Squadron immediately led his troops out on to the forest path and rode away with them. (Grigory had the impression they were going back). For about twenty minutes they rode through thickets, abandoning formation. The sounds of battle came nearer; somewhere, not far behind them a battery was firing rapidly; shells shrieked and whined over their heads. After its ragged advance through the forest the squadron straggled out into open fields. On the fringe of a wood half a verst away Hungarian hussars were cutting down the gun crews of a Russian battery.

'Squadron, formation!'

And before they could spread out in line, 'Squadron, sabres out, into the attack—forward!'

A blue cloudburst of blades. The squadron quickened its pace from a trot to a gallop.

About six Hungarian hussars were busy round the battery's nearest gun. One of them was dragging the rearing horses by their bridles; another was beating them with the flat of his sword, while the others, dismounted, were heaving at the spokes of the gun-carriage wheels. An officer on a dock-tailed chocolate-coloured horse was bellowing orders at them from the side. At the sight of the Cossacks, the Hungarians abandoned the gun and galloped away.

'Like that, and that, and that!' Grigory counted the horse's galloping strides. His foot lost its stirrup for a second and fear surged through him as he felt his unsteadiness in the saddle and tried to regain his foothold; he leaned over, caught the stirrup and pushed his toe into it and, on raising his eyes, saw the gun crew's team of six horses. The driver was flat on the first horse's back with his arms round its neck, his shirt covered in blood and brains from his shattered skull. The next moment Grigory felt and heard the crunch of his horse's hooves trampling the body of one of the crew. Two more were lying beside an overturned ammunition crate and a third was lying face downwards on the gun-carriage. At that moment Silantyev overtook and galloped ahead of Grigory. The officer on the dock-tailed mare fired at him almost point-blank. Silantyev jerked in the saddle and fell backwards, his arms thrown out as if to embrace the blue distance. Grigory wheeled to the left to attack from the side where he could best use his sabre; the officer noticed his manoeuvre and fired at Grigory from under his arm. He emptied his revolver and drew his sword. Evidently a skilled fencer, he parried three smashing blows with ease. Grigory, mouth twisted, rose in his stirrups and attacked for the fourth time. Their horses were now running almost abreast and he could see the Hungarian's ash-grey shaven cheek and the number sewn on the collar of his tunic. At the last moment he changed the direction of the blow and lunged with the point of the sabre between the shoulder blades. His next blow landed on the neck, at the tip of the spinal column. The Hungarian's sword-arm went limp, he dropped the reins, straightened up for a moment as if he had been stung, then fell forward on the pommel of his saddle. With a monstrous feeling of relief Grigory hacked at his head. He saw the sabre bite into the bone just above the ear.

The next moment he himself was stunned by a terrible blow from behind. He felt hot salt in his mouth and realised that he was falling—the stubble-clad earth came spinning up to meet him from the side.

The impact as he hit the ground brought him back to reality for an instant. He opened his eyes, only to have them washed with blood. A drumming of hooves and the laboured breathing of a horse. For the last time he opened his eyes and saw the pink nostrils of a horse and a boot in stirrup iron. 'It's all over!' the soothing thought slithered through his mind. Then came a roar and a black void.

XIV

At the beginning of August, Yevgeny Listnitsky decided to get himself transferred from the Ataman's Life Guards to a Cossack regiment of the line. He sent in his application and within three weeks obtained a transfer to one of the regiments of the active army. When the formalities were complete, before leaving Petrograd he wrote his father a brief letter informing him of his decision.

Dear Father,

I have managed to get myself transferred from the Ataman's Regiment to the army. Today I received my appointment and am leaving to take up a post under the commander of the Second Army Corps. You will probably be surprised by my decision but the explanation is this. The atmosphere I had to endure here set my teeth on edge. I am sick and tired of the whole business of service at court with its parades, receptions, changing of the guard and so on. I want real-life action or, if you prefer it, I want to do something heroic. I suppose it is my blood that is beginning to tell, the glorious blood of the Listnitskys, who ever since the Patriotic War of 1812 have woven laurels into the crown of Russian arms. I am going to the front. I ask your blessing. Last week I saw the Emperor before his departure for General Headquarters. I worship the man. I was with the household guard in the palace. He came in with Rodzyanko and as he passed he looked at me and said in English, 'These are my gallant guardsmen. In due course I'll use them to trump Wilhelm's card.' I adore him like a college girl. I am not ashamed to confess this to you, even though I am now over twenty-eight. I am deeply disturbed by the palace rumours that are being spread around the monarch's glorious name like a spider's web. I will not and cannot believe them. The other day I nearly shot Major Gromov for referring disrespectfully to his Imperial Majesty in my presence. It is disgusting and I told him that only a churl could stoop to spreading such vile slander. The incident occurred in the presence of several officers. I was seized by a paroxysm of rage. I drew my revolver and was about to spend a bullet on this lout, but I was disarmed by my fellow officers. Every day it became more and more difficult for me to remain in this cesspit. In the guards regiments, particularly among the officers, there is no real patriotism and—frightening though it may be to say so—there is not even any love of the dynasty. These people are not aristocrats but rabble. Essentially this is the reason for my breaking with the regiment. I cannot endure the company of people for whom I have no respect. Well, that seems to be all. Forgive the incoherence, I am in a hurry. I must strap up my suitcase and go to see the commandant. Keep well, Father. I will write in more detail from the army.

Your Yevgeny

The Warsaw train left at eight o'clock in the evening. Listnitsky took a cab to the station. Petrograd spread out behind him in a murky blue glitter of lights. The station was crowded and noisy. Most of the passengers were military. The porter put Listnitsky's suitcase on the rack and, on receiving a few coins, wished the gentleman a good journey. Listnitsky took off his sword belt and greatcoat, unfastened the straps of his equipment and spread a coloured silk Caucasian quilt on his berth. Below him, by the window an ascetically thin-faced priest was partaking of the home-cooked provisions he had spread on the table. Shaking crumbs out of his scanty beard, he offered some of the dainties to a dark skinny girl in high-school uniform sitting opposite him.

'Won't you have a bite?'

'No, thank you.'

'Now don't be shy. A girl as thin as you ought to be eating more.'

'Thank you.'

'Here, try some of the curd cake. Perhaps you will have some, Lieutenant?'

Listnitsky looked down from his bunk.

'Are you speaking to me?'

'Yes, I am.' The priest's morose eyes bored into him and only the thin lips smiled under the drooping patchy moustache.

'Thank you, but I'm not hungry.'

'That's a pity. What the Lord gives cannot defile. Are you bound for the army?'

'Yes.'

'May the Lord help you.'

Through a haze of drowsiness Listnitsky heard the priest's muffled voice as if from a great distance, and soon it seemed to be not the priest's complaining bass but that of Major Gromov.

'...I have a family, you know, and it's a poor parish. So I have to go as a regimental priest. The Russian people can't live without faith. And year by year, you know, the faith is growing. There are some, of course, who fall by the wayside, but they are from the intelligentsia. The ordinary folk cleave unto God. Indeed they do...' the deep voice sighed, then launched into another stream of words that no longer entered his consciousness.

Listnitsky dozed off. His last sensation was of the smell of fresh paint from the narrow boarding of the carriage ceiling and a shout outside the window.

'The luggage office accepted it. It's no business of mine!'

What did the luggage office accept? The question hovered in his mind for a moment, then the thread broke again. After two restless nights he plunged into a deep refreshing sleep and did not awake until the train had covered a distance of some forty versts from Petrograd. The wheels were clicking steadily and the carriage swayed as the engine tugged it up a gradient. In the next compartment several voices were singing quietly. A lantern cast slanting lilac shadows.

The regiment to which Listnitsky had been assigned had suffered heavy losses in the recent fighting. It had now been withdrawn from the battlefield and was being replenished with men and horses.

Regimental headquarters was in the big trading village of Bereznyagi. Listnitsky left the train at a tiny wayside station, where a field hospital was also being unloaded. He had learned from the doctor in charge that the hospital was being transferred from the South-Western Front to this sector and would soon be proceeding on a route through the villages of Bereznyagi, Ivanovka and Krysho-vinskoye. The big purple-faced doctor gave an unflattering account of his immediate superiors, berated the staff officers of the division and, tugging at his beard and glinting anger from under his gold pince-nez, poured out bitterness and disillusion to his chance acquaintance.

'Will you take me to Bereznyagi?' Listnitsky interrupted him.

'Get into the cart, Lieutenant. Come with us,' the doctor assented. At once becoming familiar, he twisted a button on Listnitsky's greatcoat and rumbled on in an appeal for sympathy, 'Just think of it, Lieutenant. Travelling two hundred versts in those cattle trucks to hang about here with nothing to do while on the sector my hospital was transferred from there had been two days of the bloodiest fighting possible and hundreds of wounded still in need of our help.' With angry relish the doctor repeated the phrase, 'Yes, the bloodiest fighting possible.'

'What is your explanation of this absurd muddle?' Listnitsky inquired out of politeness.

'Explanation?' the doctor raised his eyebrows ironically above his pince-nez and boomed, 'The slackness, muddle-headedness and stupidity of the people in charge, that's what! Those scoundrels sit there on their behinds and make a muddle of things. There is no efficiency, not even common sense. Remember Veresayev's *A Surgeon's Notes*? Well, there you have it, sir! Quadrupled!'

Listnitsky saluted and walked away to the carts with the angry doctor croaking behind him.

'We'll lose the war, Lieutenant! We lost to the Japanese and learned nothing from that. It's going to be a walkover, we say, so what else do you expect...' And he strode away along the tracks, stepping over the oily-hued puddles and shaking his head in despair.

It was dusk when the hospital arrived at Bereznyagi. A wind was stirring the yellow stubble. Storm-clouds were writhing and rearing in the west. In the heights they glowed a violet black, but lower down their menacing hues faded into gentle lilac, its pastel reflections flowing across the dull homespun of the sky; in the middle this shapeless mass was breaking up like a jumble of ice-floes on a river, and a stream of orange-coloured sunset rays was pouring through the gap. The fan of refracted blazing light plunged precipitously, generating an indescribable bacchanalian spectrum of colours.

A light-bay horse that had been shot was lying in a roadside ditch. One of its hind legs was sticking up weirdly and the worn shoe was glittering. As Listnitsky jolted past in the cart he stared curiously at the dead horse. A medical orderly who was riding with him spat at the animal's swollen belly and explained, 'It bust itself—ate too much grain,' he added more correctly, with a glance at the lieutenant, and was about to spit again but swallowed it out of politeness and wiped his lips on his sleeve. 'Now it's dead and no one bothers to clear it away... The Germans don't live the way we do.'

'How do you know?' Listnitsky asked in unreasoning anger, and at that moment felt a similarly unreasoning hatred of the orderly's face, in which indifference was mingled with a faint air of superiority and contempt. The face was grey and dreary, like the September stubble; it had nothing to distinguish it from the thousands of other peasant-soldier faces that Listnitsky had encountered on his way from Petrograd to the front. They all seemed faded, drained of colour, there was nothing but stupidity in the eyes, grey, blue, green or whatever colour; they reminded him of old copper coins worn smooth by use.

'I lived in Germany for three years before the war,' the orderly replied unhurriedly. This voice had the same shade of superiority and contempt that the lieutenant had noticed in his face. 'I worked at a cigar factory in Königsberg,' he went on drearily, lashing the little cart-horse with the knotted leather reins.

'Oh, be quiet!' Listnitsky said severely, and turned away to stare at the dead horse's head with its long fore-lock falling over its eyes and bare teeth, weathered by wind and sun. The leg that was sticking up was bent at the knee. The hoof was slightly split by the shoe nails but the hollow beneath was firm and glowed with a bluish freshness, and by the leg and the delicate pastern the lieutenant could tell that the horse had been young and of a good breed.

The cart jolted on over the rutty country road. The colours died out of the western sky and the wind sucked away the clouds. The leg of the dead horse stood out blackly behind like a broken cross. As Listnitsky sat staring at it, the horse was suddenly caught in a bunch of sunrays and the leg with its smooth reddish fur blossomed like some magical leafless branch in inexpressible orange splendour.

As they drove into Bereznyagi, the hospital met a wagon train of wounded.

The elderly shaven-headed Byelorussian in charge of the first wagon was walking beside his horse with the rope reins wound round his hand. A Cossack with a bandaged head and no cap was lying on the wagon, propping himself up on his elbow. Eyes wearily closed, he was munching a piece of bread and spitting out the black chewed mush. A soldier was lying flat on his face beside him. His trousers were horribly torn and stiff with congealed blood at the buttocks. He was swearing obscenely without raising his head and Listnitsky was horrified to recognise in his voice the intonations of the truly religious at prayer. On the second wagon there were about six soldiers, lying together. One of them, feverishly elated, his inflamed, bloodshot eyes half closed, was speaking excitedly.

'...he says as how an ambassador came from their emperor and offered to make peace. And the main thing is he's a reliable man. I hope he's right in what he says.'

'Not very likely,' another said, shaking a round head that bore the scars of a long past attack of scrofula.

'But why not, Filipp? Mebbe he did come to make an offer,' said a third, sitting with his back to the others.

The red bands of Cossack caps showed up on the fifth wagon. Three Cossacks who had made themselves comfortable on the roomy wagon eyed Listnitsky in silence and in their dusty faces he found none of the respect that he was accustomed to see in the ranks.

'Hullo, Cossacks!' the lieutenant greeted them.

'Good health,' the nearest to the driver, a handsome Cossack with a silvery moustache and heavy eyebrows, answered indifferently.

'What regiment are you from?' Listnitsky asked, trying to spot the number on the Cossack's blue shoulder strap.

'The twelfth.'

'Where is it at present?'

'We don't know.'

'Where were you wounded then?'

'At one of the villages round here... Not far away.'

The Cossacks whispered among themselves and one of

them, holding his wounded arm wrapped in a strip of linen, jumped down from the wagon.

'Your Honour, wait a tick!' He padded along the road, on bare feet, nursing his bullet-torn arm that showed signs of festering, and smiled at Listnitsky.

'You're not from Vyoshenskaya stanitsa, are you? Are you Listnitsky?'

'I am.'

'Ah, we thought so. Have you got any baccy with you, Your Honour? For Christ's sake, give us a bit. We're dying for a smoke!'

He held on to the side of the cart, walking beside it. Listnitsky took out his cigarette case.

'Could you manage a dozen? There's three of us here,' the Cossack looked up with a beseeching smile.

Listnitsky turned out his whole supply of cigarettes on to the Cossack's brown hand.

'Are there many of your wounded here?'

'Couple of dozen.'

'Have you had heavy losses?'

'A lot killed. Give me a light, Your Honour. Thank you kindly.' As he got his cigarette going and dropped behind, the Cossack shouted, 'Three men from Tatarsky, near your estate, were killed today. They've knocked off a lot of us Cossacks.'

And with a wave of his sound arm he turned to catch up his wagon. The wind ruffled his unbelted field tunic.

The commanding officer of the regiment to which Listnitsky had been appointed had taken up his quarters in Bereznyagi at the house of a local priest. On the square Listnitsky said goodbye to the doctor who had hospitably given him a seat in his cart and went off in search of regimental headquarters, brushing the dust off his uniform and making inquiries of passers-by. A red-bearded sergeant-major came towards him, marching a soldier to the guard-house. He saluted the lieutenant without getting out of step, answered his question, and pointed out the house. The headquarters was placidly quiet, like any such establishment well behind the lines. The clerks were dozing over a big desk, an elderly major was engaged in a joking conversation with some invisible person at the other end of the field telephone line. Flies were buzzing against the windows of the large cottage and a nagging mosquito-like buzz of telephones came from other parts of the house. An orderly escorted the lieutenant to the quarters of the regimental commander.

In the hall he was greeted in an unfriendly manner by a tall colonel with a triangular scar on his chin, who seemed disgruntled about something.

'Yes, I am the commander of the regiment,' he replied in answer to Listnitsky's question. Listnitsky reported that he had the honour to present himself for duty, and was motioned silently to the colonel's room. Closing the door behind him, the colonel ran his fingers through his hair with a gesture of extreme weariness and said in a soft, monotonous voice, 'I was told about you yesterday by brigade headquarters. Do sit down.'

He asked Listnitsky about his previous service, about the news from the capital, and about his journey. Throughout the brief conversation he never once raised his weary, heavy-lidded eyes to the lieutenant's face.

He must have had a bad time at the front. He looks mortally tired, Listnitsky thought sympathetically, eyeing the colonel's lofty forehead. But as if to disillusion him, the colonel scratched the bridge of his nose with his sword hilt and said, 'Go and make the acquaintance of your fellow officers, Lieutenant. You see, I haven't slept for three nights. There's absolutely nothing to do in this hole except drink and play cards.'

Listnitsky saluted, smiling wryly to conceal his scorn. He went out in disgust, recalling ironically the respect evoked by the colonel's tired appearance and the scar on his broad chin.

XV

The division was given the task of forcing the River Styr and breaking through to the enemy's rear in the vicinity of Lowiszczy.

It took Listnitsky only a few days to get used to the officers of the regiment and the atmosphere of action quickly drove out the sense of ease and placid drowsiness that had taken possession of him.

The division performed its task brilliantly. It struck at the left flank of a massive enemy force and broke through into its rear. At Lowiszczy the Austrians, supported by Hungarian cavalry, tried to counter-attack, but were mown down by shrapnel from the Cossack batteries. The Hungarian squadrons fell back in disorder under deadly fire from machine-guns on their flank and were pursued by Cossacks.

Listnitsky rode with his regiment in the counter-attack and his battalion was sent to harass the retreating enemy. The troop under his command lost one Cossack killed and four wounded. With outward calm he rode past one of the wounded, a young, hook-nosed Cossack from Krasnokutskaya stanitsa, trying not to hear his faint, husky cries. The man's name was Loshchenov, and he was pinned under his dead horse. He was wounded in the forearm, but lay quietly, only begging the passing Cossacks to release him. 'Don't leave me, brothers! Help me out of this!'

His low, tortured voice was beginning to fade, but there was no compassion in the surging hearts of the Cossacks that passed him or, if there had been, it was suppressed by the will that drove them on relentlessly. The troop rode for five minutes at a walk to rest their horses, which were still panting from the furious gallop. The broken squadrons of Hungarian cavalry were falling back only about half a verst away from them. The blue-grey uniforms of infantry could be seen among their splendid fur-trimmed tunics. An Austrian baggage train was creeping along a ridge of hills with white puffs of shrapnel smoke waving it farewell. Somewhere to the left a battery was pumping shells at it. The sound of the shots rolled across the fields and echoed back from the nearest wood in a variety of voices.

Lieutenant-Colonel Safronov, who was leading the cavalry battalion, gave an order and the three squadrons broke into a straggling trot. The horses swayed under their riders, scattering yellowish-pink flecks of foam.

They passed the night in a small hamlet.

Twelve officers were billeted together in one hut. They turned in, utterly exhausted and hungry. At about midnight the field kitchens arrived. Cornet Chubov came in with a mess-tin of cabbage soup and its greasy aroma woke the sleepers.

A quarter of an hour later the puffy-faced officers were eating hungrily and in silence, trying to make up for the two days spent in battle. The late meal banished sleep. Heavy with food, the officers lay back on their astrakhan cloaks and on the straw and smoked.

Captain Kalmykov, a small tubby officer, whose face as well as his name bore witness to Mongolian descent, began to speak in a sharp, gesticulating manner.

'This is no war for me! I was born about four centuries too late. I won't live to see the end of this war.'

'Drop the fortune-telling,' Lieutenant Tersintsev grunted from under his cloak.

'It's not fortune-telling. It's my predestined end. I'm
atavistic, there's no place for me in this world, honestly
there isn't. When we were advancing under fire today,
I was trembling with fury. It's a disgusting sensation,
similar to fear. They shoot at you from a distance of
several versts. You ride your horse like a bustard under
the aim of a sportsman's gun.'

'In Kupalka I had a look at an Austrian howitzer.
Did any of you see it, gentlemen?' Major Atamanchukov
asked, licking the traces of bully beef off his clipped
English-style moustache.

'Splendid piece of work! The sight and the whole
mechanism are sheer perfection,' exclaimed Cornet
Chubov, who had by now emptied a second mess-tin of
soup.

'I saw it but I wouldn't say too much about my
impressions. I'm an ignoramus when it comes to artillery. To my mind it was just a cannon, with a big mouth.'

'I envy the men who used to fight in the old primitive
way,' Kalmykov continued, now addressing Listnitsky.
'Charging the enemy in honourable battle, slicing a man
in two with your sword—that I understand! But this is
the devil knows what!'

'The role of the cavalry will be reduced to nothing in
future wars.'

'To be more precise, it simply won't exist.'

'Well, that's only a supposition.'

'No doubt about it.'

'Look here, Tersintsev, you can't replace men entirely
by machines. That's going too far.'

'I'm talking about the horses, not the men. They will
be replaced by a motor-cycle or a car.'

'I can just imagine a motor-car squadron.'

'Nonsense,' Kalmykov burst out hotly. 'The horse
will still be of use in the army. That's an absurd fantasy!
We don't know what will happen in a hundred or two
hundred years, but today, at any rate, the cavalry...'

'What will you do, Dmitry Donskoi, when the front is
one long line of trenches? Now then? Answer that one!'

'Break through, raid deep into enemy territory behind
the lines—that's the cavalry's job.'

'Rubbish.'

'Well, we shall see, gentlemen.'

'Let's go to sleep.'

'Enough argument, you fellows. There's a limit to everything. Other people want some sleep.'

The argument died down. Someone was already snoring and whistling under his cloak. Listnitsky, who had taken no part in the conversation, lay on his back, breathing in the heady smell of the rye straw that had been spread for bedding. Kalmykov crossed himself and lay down beside him.

'Have a talk with volunteer Bunchuk, Lieutenant. He's in your troop. He's an interesting fellow!'

'In what way?' Listnitsky asked, turning his back on Kalmykov.

'He's a Russified Cossack. Lived in Moscow. He's just an ordinary working man but he has a fine grasp of this kind of problem. He's a fearless fellow and a first-class machine-gunner.'

'Let's go to sleep,' Listnitsky replied.

'Yes, I suppose we should,' Kalmykov agreed, thinking of something else. He twiddled his toes and frowned apologetically. 'You must excuse me, Lieutenant, the smell is from my feet... I haven't had my boots off for over two weeks. My socks are rotten with sweat... It's revolting, you know. I must get some footcloths off the Cossacks.'

'Never mind,' Listnitsky murmured as sleep surged over him.

Listnitsky forgot the conversation with Kalmykov, but the next day he chanced to meet Bunchuk. At dawn the squadron commander ordered him to carry out a reconnaissance and, if possible, make contact with the infantry regiment that was continuing the offensive on the left flank. Listnitsky came out into the morning dusk of the yard and began searching for the troop sergeant among the sleeping Cossacks.

'Detail five Cossacks for a patrol with me and tell them to get my horse ready. And be quick about it.'

Five minutes later a shortish, thick-set Cossack appeared on the threshold of the hut.

'Your Honour,' he began, addressing Listnitsky, who was filling his cigarette-case, 'the sergeant won't send me on patrol because it's not my turn. Won't you allow me to go?'

'Are you trying to make up for something? What have you done wrong?' the lieutenant asked, scanning the Cossack's face in the gloom.

'I have done nothing wrong.'

'Well, you may come with us then,' Listnitsky said rising.

'Wait a minute!' he called to the Cossack as he walked away. 'Come back.'

The Cossack turned.

'Tell the sergeant...'

'My name is Bunchuk,' the Cossack interrupted.

'A volunteer?'

'Yes.'

'Will you tell the sergeant,' recovering from a momentary confusion, Listnitsky continued, 'tell him to... All right, you may go, I'll tell him myself.'

The darkness thinned. The patrol rode out of the hamlet past the guard posts and sentries and headed for the village marked on the map.

When they had covered about half a verst, the lieutenant slowed his pace to a walk.

'Volunteer Bunchuk!'

'Yes, sir.'

'Kindly come a little closer.'

Bunchuk rode his unimpressive mount up beside Listnitsky's thoroughbred Don stallion.

'What stanitsa are you from?' Listnitsky asked, examining the volunteer's profile.

'Novocherkasskaya.'

'May I learn the reason that prompted you to join up as a volunteer?'

'By all means,' Bunchuk drew out the phrase with a touch of mockery in his voice, and looked at the lieutenant with hard greenish eyes. His unblinking gaze was firm, not easily broken. 'I'm interested in the art of war. I want to learn it.'

'There are military schools for that purpose.'

'I know there are.'

'Then why have you chosen this way?'

'I want to see what it's like in practice first. The theory will come later.'

'What was your occupation before the war?'

'Worker.'

'Where did you work?'

'In Petersburg, Rostov-on-Don, and Tula, at the arsenal there... I'm going to ask to be transferred to a machine-gun platoon.'

'Do you know anything about the machine-gun?'

'I know the Chauchat, Berthier, Madsen, Maxim, Hotchkiss, Bergmann, Vickers, Lewis and Schwarzlose guns.'

'Oho! I will speak to the commander of the regiment about you.'

'Please do.'

The lieutenant glanced again at the stocky, thickset figure beside him. Bunchuk reminded him of a Don-side cork-elm. There was nothing striking about him. Everything was ordinary; only the firmly set jaws and challenging eyes distinguished him from the mass of other faces.

He seldom smiled, and only with the corners of his lips. The eyes did not soften and the faint gleam in them remained as unassailable as ever. He grudged colour and was coldly restrained—a cork-elm, that rugged tree of iron strength that grows in the grey loam of the uninviting land beyond the Don.

For a time they rode on in silence. Bunchuk's big hands rested on the pealing green pommel of his saddle. Listnitsky took out a cigarette, lighted it from a match that Bunchuk offered him, and noticed the sweet tarry smell of horse sweat on his hand. The brown hair on the back of it was as thick as horse fur. Listnitsky involuntarily felt like stroking it. Inhaling the pungent smoke, he said, 'From this wood you and one more Cossack will take the path to the left. Do you see it?'

'Yes.'

'If you don't meet our infantry within half a verst, you will turn back.'

'Yes, sir.'

They broke into a trot. The wood was fringed with a cluster of young birches, but behind them stood clumps of yellow stunted pines, scrub and bushes mangled by the rapid retreat of the Austrian supply trains. Over on the right the earth was shaking with the thunder of artillery, but here, by the birches it was unbelievably quiet. The ground was drinking in the rich dew, the grass was turning pink, every stalk brightly coloured and heavy with the blossom of late summer, which cries out that death is near. Listnitsky halted by the birches to study the ridge beyond the wood through his field-glasses. A bee settled on the brass hilt of his sword and spread its wings.

'Stupid,' Bunchuk said with a quiet pity in his voice, as if disapproving of the bee's foolhardiness.

'What?' Listnitsky jerked his eyes away from the glasses.

Bunchuk glanced at the bee and Listnitsky smiled.

'Its honey will be bitter, don't you think?'

But it was not Bunchuk who answered him. From a distant clump of pines a machine-gun tore the silence to shreds with its piercing magpie chatter and a spray of howling bullets cut through the birches. A severed twig spiralled down on to the mane of the lieutenant's horse.

They galloped back to the hamlet, urging on their horses with whip and voice. The Austrian machine-gun fired off the rest of its ammunition in their wake.

Listnitsky met Bunchuk on several occasions after that and was always surprised by the indomitable strength of will that gleamed in those hard eyes. He could not fathom what was behind the elusive secretiveness that hung like a cloud shadow on the face of this apparently ordinary man. Even when he spoke, Bunchuk seemed to leave something unsaid, keeping a smile tucked away in the corners of his lips, as though he were following a devious path around a truth that he alone knew. He was transferred to a machine-gun platoon. About ten days later, when the regiment had a day's rest, Listnitsky happened to overtake Bunchuk on his way to the squadron commander. Bunchuk was walking past a fire-gutted shed, playfully flicking his wrist.

'Ah, the volunteer!'

Bunchuk turned his head and stepped aside, saluting.

'Where are you going?' Listnitsky asked.

'To the platoon commander.'

'Then we are probably going the same way?'

'Probably we are.'

They walked down the street of the ruined village in silence. People were hurrying about round the few sheds that were still standing. Horsemen rode by. In the middle of the street a field kitchen stood smoking with a long queue of Cossacks waiting beside it. There was a fine chilling drizzle in the air.

'Well, have you been studying war?' Listnitsky asked with a glance at Bunchuk, who was lagging slightly behind him.

'Yes ... I suppose I have.'

'What do you expect to do after the war?' Listnitsky asked for some reason, looking at the volunteer's hairy hands.

'Someone will reap what has been sown, and I... Well, I'll see.' Bunchuk narrowed his eyes.

'What do you mean by that?'

'You know the saying, Lieutenant,' Bunchuk's eyes

narrowed into mere slits: "He who sows the wind shall reap the whirlwind"? So there it is.'

'Leave out the allegories and make yourself clear.'

'It's clear enough as it is. Goodbye, Lieutenant, I turn left here.'

Bunchuk put his hairy fingers to the peak of his Cossack cap and turned off to the left.

The lieutenant shrugged and stood staring after him.

'Is the fellow trying to be original or is he just a crank,' he thought irritably as he turned away and walked into the squadron commander's clean, well-kept dug-out.

XVI

The third-line reserves had left with the second, and the stanitsas and villages of the Don were as deserted as at hay-making or harvest time.

But on the frontiers it was a bitter harvest that the men toiled for that year; death laid its hand on the reapers and many a bareheaded Cossack woman wept and keened for the slain. The cry went up over the villages. 'Oh, love... Who will care for me now?'

The loved ones fell on all sides, the red Cossack blood flowed, and eyeless in sleep from which there was no awakening, they rotted while the guns thundered their funeral dirge in Austria, in Poland, in Prussia... Even the east wind could not carry the mourning voices of their wives and mothers to their ears.

The flower of Cossack manhood left its homeland and perished out there amid the slaughter, the lice, and the horror.

One fine September day a milky rainbow-coloured gossamer was floating over the village of Tatarsky. The bloodless sun wore the pinched smile of a widow and the stern virginal blue of the sky was repellently pure and proud. The yellow-tinged forest on the far side of the Don stood in bleak sadness, the poplars shone pallidly, the oaks were dropping their intricately carved leaves, and only the alders kept their gawdy green and gladdened the quick eye of the magpie with their vitality.

On that day Pantelei Melekhov received a letter from the army in the field. Dunyashka brought the letter from the post office. On handing it to her, the postmaster bowed, shook his balding head and spread his arms in abject apology.

'For mercy's sake, forgive me, but I unsealed the letter. Tell your father it was Firs Sidorovich who opened it. He was so anxious to find out about the war... You must forgive me and tell Pantelei Prokofievich so with my respects.'

He was unusually embarrassed and came out to see Dunyashka off, oblivious of the smudge of ink on his nose.

'Don't be offended with me, God forbid... It was only because we have known each other so long...' He was so profuse in his apologies that Dunyashka felt instinctively alarmed.

By the time she got home she was trembling and could barely retrieve the letter from her bosom.

'Hurry up!' Pantelei shouted, stroking his quivering beard.

'The postmaster said he read the letter because he was so interested like and you mustn't be offended with him, Father.'

'To hell with him! Is it from Grigory?' the old man questioned, panting excitedly in Dunyashka's face. 'It must be from Grigory? Or from Petro?'

'No, Dad ... the handwriting's someone else's on the envelope.'

'Read it then, don't keep us on edge!' Ilyinichna burst out, hobbling to a bench (her legs were swollen and she rolled rather than walked).

Natalya came running in from the yard and stood by the stove, pressing her hands to her breast and holding her scarred neck to one side. A smile trembled like a sunbeam on her lips. She was expecting a greeting from Grigory, just a word in passing in reward for her dog-like devotion.

'Where's Darya?' Ilyinichna whispered.

'Be quiet!' Pantelei snapped with a glint of fury in his eyes and, turning to Dunyashka, 'Read, girl!'

' "I have to inform you..." ' Dunyashka began, then slid off the bench, howling with grief. 'Oh, Father! Father!.. Oh, Mother! Our Grisha... Oh! oh! oh! ... he's been killed!'

A striped wasp, trapped among the yellowed geranium leaves, buzzed furiously against the windowpane. A hen clucked peacefully in the yard, and the distant tinkle of children's laughter could be heard from the open door.

A convulsion seized Natalya's face before her lips could abandon their recent trembling smile.

Pantelei rose jerking his head paralytically and stared in frenzied astonishment at his daughter writhing on the floor.

I have to inform you that your son, Grigory Panteleyevich Melekhov, a Cossack of the 12th Don Cossack Regiment, was killed in action on the night of September 16th near the town of Kamionka-Strumiłowa. Your son died the death of the brave. May this be some comfort to you in your irreparable loss. All that is left of his belongings will be passed on to his brother Pyotr Melekhov. The horse remains in the regiment.

Captain Polkovnikov,
Commander of the Fourth Squadron,
Field Army, September 18th, 1914

After the news of Grigory's death Pantelei went to pieces all at once. The family saw him growing older before their very eyes. Nothing, it seemed, would avert his decline. His memory began to fail, his mind became clouded. He walked about the house, back bent and face as dark as cast-iron; the feverish oily gleam in his eyes betrayed his inner distress.

He put the letter from the squadron commander under the ikon and several times a day would come out into the porch and beckon Dunyashka.

'Come here, my girl.'

She would go up to him.

'Bring me the letter about Grigory. Read it!' he would command her, glancing furtively at the door of the front room, where Ilyinichna was lying in inconsolable grief. 'Read it quietly, to yourself like.' And he would wink cunningly, hunching his whole body and indicating the door with his eyes. 'Read quietly, or else mother there ... she's in a bad way...'

Choking back her tears, Dunyashka would read the first sentence and Pantelei, who at this point usually squatted down on his haunches, would raise his swarthy hand that was as broad as a horse's hoof.

'That's enough! I know the rest... Take it and put it under the ikon... Don't make a noise, though, or else mother...' And again he would wink repulsively and writhe, like bark in a fire.

He went grey in circles and soon his head was spotted with dazzling white patches and white threads spread through his beard. He became gluttonous, eating hugely and carelessly.

On the ninth day after the funeral service they invited the priest Vissarion and their relatives to a feast for the dead warrior Grigory.

Pantelei ate quickly and greedily, his beard festooned with noodles. Ilyinichna, who had been keeping a worried eye on him over the past few days, burst into tears.

'Father! What has come over you!'

'What's the matter?' the old man blurted out, looking up from his bowl with bleary eyes.

Ilyinichna dropped her hand and turned away, crushing an embroidered cloth to her eyes.

'You're gobbling as if you hadn't had anything to eat for three days, Father!' Darya said angrily, and gave him a sharp look.

'Eating a lot am I?.. Well ... well ... I won't then any more,' Pantelei ended up disconcertedly. He stared bewilderedly at the others seated at the table, munched his lips and fell silent, frowning and answering no questions.

'Be brave, Prokofievich. Aren't you taking it a little too hard?' the priest tried to cheer him after the wake was over. 'He died a holy death. Don't anger God, old man. Your son wore a crown of thorns for the tsar and the fatherland, and you... It's a sin, Pantelei Prokofievich, a sin! The Lord will not forgive you!'

'I know, Father, I'm doing my best... His commanding officer wrote that he died the death of the brave, didn't he?'

The old man kissed the priest's hand, leaned against the doorpost, and for the first time since receiving the news of his son's death, broke into a violent flood of tears.

That day he overcame himself and recovered his spirit.

Each member of the family licked his wounds in his own way.

When Natalya heard the news of Grigory's death from Dunyashka, she ran out into the yard with only one thought—to put an end to herself. 'It's all up with me now. I'll kill myself!' She struggled furiously in Darya's arms and accepted oblivion with a sense of joyful relief, for it would at least postpone the moment when consciousness would return and remind her inescapably of what had happened. She spent a week in a dull delirium and returned to the world of reality changed and quiet, gnawed by a wasting sickness. An invisible corpse haunted the Melekhov house and the living breathed the cornflower-sweet smell of its decay.

12–1106

XVII

On the twelfth day after the news of Grigory's death the Melekhovs received two letters at once from Petro. Dunyashka read them at the post office and set off for home at a mad run, now flying like a straw in a whirlwind, now leaning helplessly against a fence. She caused a good deal of confusion in the village and indescribable excitement at home.

'Grisha's alive!.. He's alive, our dearest!' she yelled in a sobbing voice while still at a distance. 'Petro says so in his letter!.. Grisha's wounded, not killed!.. He's alive, alive!'

'Greetings, dear parents,' Petro wrote in his letter dated September 20th. 'I have to inform you that our Grisha nearly gave up the ghost, but that now, thank the Lord, he's alive and well, which is what we wish for you too, God willing, and good health and happiness. At the town of Kamionka-Strumiłowa their regiment was in action and the Cossacks of his troop saw a Hungarian hussar cut him down with his sword and Grigory fell off his horse, and that was all we knew. I questioned them, but that was as much as they could tell me. It was only afterwards that I heard from Mikhail Koshevoi—he came to our regiment on messenger duty—that Grigory lay there on the ground till nightfall, and in the night he came to and started crawling. He found his way by the stars and happened on one of our officers that was wounded. This wounded officer was a lieutenant-colonel of the dragoons and he had been wounded in the belly and legs by a shell. Grigory got him on his shoulders and carried him for six versts. And for that he's been decorated with the St. George Cross, and he's also been promoted to Junior Sergeant. Just think of that! Grigory's wound is a mere scratch, it was a glancing blow, just took a bit of the skin off his head; he was knocked out when he fell off his horse. Now he's back in action, Mikhail told me. Excuse me for writing like this. I'm writing in the saddle and it's mighty shaky.'

In his next letter Petro wanted some dried cherries to be sent to him 'from the dear orchards of the Don' and asked the family not to forget him and write more often; he also scolded Grigory for, so the Cossacks had told him, not taking good care of his horse. This was too bad of him because the Bay was Petro's own property. So he wanted his father to write to Grigory himself about it.

'Through the Cossacks I let him know that if he didn't look after that horse as if it was his own, I'd bloody his nose for him even if he had won the George Cross,' wrote Petro, after which came an endless list of greetings. Despite their bravado the crumpled rain-blurred lines of the letter were tinged with a bitter sadness. Evidently Petro was not having an easy time either.

The joy-struck Pantelei was a pitiful sight to watch. He grabbed both letters and went about the village, buttonholing the literate and making them read them aloud. Not that he really wanted to listen to them over and over. It was his belated joy that he wanted to share and boast about.

'Aha! See what my Grishka is like?' He would raise his hooflike hand when the stumbling reader reached the place where Petro described Grigory's feat in carrying the wounded lieutenant-colonel six versts on his back.

'His is the first cross in the whole village,' the old man would declare proudly and, jealously retrieving the letters, he would tuck them away in the lining of his crumpled cap, and go on to look for another person who could read.

Sergei Platonovich Mokhov himself spotted the old man from the window of his shop and came out to greet him, taking off his cap.

'Come in, Prokofievich.'

He took the old man's hand in his fleshy white palm.

'Congratulations, congratulations... That's a son to be proud of—and you were holding a wake for him! I've just read about his exploit in the papers.'

'Is it in the papers?' Pantelei almost choked as his throat suddenly went dry.

'Yes, there's a report about it. I've read it.'

Sergei Platonovich himself took down three quarter-pound packets of the best Turkish tobacco and filled a bag with expensive sweets without weighing them. He handed it all to Pantelei and said, 'When you write to Grigory Panteleyevich, send him my regards and this too.'

'Goodness me! Lord be praised! What an honour for Grisha!.. The whole village is talking about him... That I should live to see the day...' the old man whispered as he hobbled down the steps of Mokhov's shop. He blew his nose, smeared away a tear that was tickling his cheek with the sleeve of his coat, and thought to himself, 'I must be getting old. The tears come too easily... Ah, Pantelei, Pantelei, you're not the man you were! You used to be hard as flint, you could hump two-hundred-weight sacks off the barges. But now? Grishka's knocked the stuffing out of me, that he has.'

He limped down the street, clasping the bag of sweets to his chest and his thoughts hovered over Grigory, like a lapwing over a bog, as he recalled the words of Petro's letter. And at that moment he met his in-law Miron Korshunov. Miron was the first to hail him.

'Hi there, kinsman! Wait a minute!'

They had not seen each other since the day of the declaration of war. After Grigory had left home, the relations between them had been, if not hostile, rather strained and cold. Miron was furious with Natalya for humiliating herself before Grigory and waiting for what crumbs he might throw her. And for making him, Miron, endure a similar humiliation.

'That stray bitch!' was what he called Natalya in the family circle. 'Why can't she live at home with her father. Going off to her in-laws like that, as if their bread tasted better than ours. She's put her own father to shame! He can't look people in the face now because of her, the fool.'

Miron marched up to Pantelei and shoved out his freckled hand.

'Good health to you!'

'The Lord be praised.'

'Been shopping?'

Pantelei raised his free right hand and shook his head.

'These are gifts for our hero. Sergei Platonovich, our benefactor, read about his valour in the newspapers and has given him these sweets and some special mild tobacco. Send your hero my regards, he says, and these gifts, and may he go on distinguishing himself in future. He even shed a tear, would you believe it, kinsman?' Pantelei boasted unrestrainedly and peered into Miron's face, trying to assess the impression he had made.

Light and shade mingled under Miron's whitish eyelids, giving a mocking glint to his lowered eyes.

'Oh, so that's it,' Miron grunted, and walked away to the fence on the other side of the street.

Pantelei hurried after him, opening the bag of sweets angrily with trembling fingers.

'Here, have a chocolate!' he offered maliciously. 'Do take one, please, I offer it to you on behalf of your son-

340

in-law... You don't have a very sweet life, so mebbe this will make up for it. Who knows if your son will ever win such an honour?'

'You leave my life out of it. I don't need you to tell me about that.'

'Try one, do me the honour!' Pantelei bowed with exaggerated courtesy, hobbling ahead of his kinsman. His gnarled fingers skinned the sweet of its fine silver-paper wrapping.

'We aren't used to sweet things,' Miron pushed his hand aside. 'We aren't used to them and our teeth don't take kindly to other people's sweets. And you shouldn't be going about begging on behalf of your son. If you're in need, you should come to me. I'd always help my son-in-law. Natalya's eating your bread, after all. I could help you out in your poverty.'

'No one in our family has ever begged, and don't lie with that wooden tongue of yours, kinsman! There's a lot of hoity-toity in you—far too much! Mebbe it's because you've got such a rich home that your daughter left you to live with us?'

'Now wait!' Miron cut in peremptorily. 'There's no reason for us to quarrel. I didn't come to quarrel; so calm down, man. Let's go and have a chat. I've business to discuss with you.'

'There's nothing for us to discuss.'

'Yes, there is. Come on.'

Miron seized Pantelei's sleeve and turned down a by-lane. They walked past the houses and out into the steppe.

'What's this all about?' Pantelei asked, calm now that his fit of anger had passed.

He glanced sideways at Korshunov's freckled face. Miron tucked up the long skirts of his coat, sat down on the edge of a ditch and pulled out an old tobacco pouch with a tasseled fringe.

'Well, Prokofievich, you jumped at me for nothing, like a fighting cock, but that won't do among kinsmen. Will it now? What I want to know,' his voice changed to a firm, brusque tone, 'is how much longer is your son going to make a fool of my daughter? Tell me that!'

'Ask him yourself.'

'It's not for me to ask him. You're the master in your own house, so it's you I'm talking to.'

Pantelei squeezed the sweet in his fist and the sticky chocolate oozed between his fingers. He wiped his hand on the brown crumbling clay of the bank and silently set about making himself a cigarette. He folded a slip of paper, sprinkled a pinch of the Turkish tobacco into it and handed the packet to Miron. His kinsman took it unhesitatingly and also made himself a cigarette out of Mokhov's generous gift. They lighted up. A full-breasted foam-white cloud hung overhead and, stirred by the wind, the tenderest wisp of gossamer, reached up from the earth toward those unthinkable heights.

The day was on the wane. The autumn stillness was peaceful, ineffably sweet, like a lullaby. The sky had lost the deep radiance of summer and shone a faded blue. Apple leaves brought from God knows where scattered their rich purple over the ditch. The forked highway disappeared over the wavy crest of the hill. In vain it pointed towards the dream-like emerald thread of the horizon and the unknown lands beyond. Bound fast to their homes, their daily cares, people toiled beyond their strength on the threshing floor, while the road—a deserted, dreary track—flowed away across the horizon into the unseen. Only the wind came that way, stirring the dust.

'This tobacco's weak as grass,' Miron said, and let out a little unmelting puff of smoke.

'Ay, it's rather mild ... but pleasant,' Pantelei assented.

'Answer me now, kinsman,' Miron said in a more relaxed voice, and stubbed out his cigarette.

'Grigory don't write anything about that. At the moment he's wounded.'

'So I've heard.'

'What's going to happen later, I don't know. Mebbe they will kill him properly next time. How about that?'

'But how can it go on like this!' Miron protested, blinking in pitiful confusion. 'The way she lives now—not a girl, not a woman, nor even an honest widow. It's a shame and a disgrace. If I'd known such a thing would happen, I'd never have let you or your matchmakers into the house. That I wouldn't! Ah, kinsman... Every man's sorry for his own child... It's the call of the blood in us.'

'But what can I do?' Pantelei launched into the attack with restrained fury. 'Tell me that! D'you think I'm glad my son's left home? Has that done me any good? What people you are!'

'You must write to him,' Miron dictated huskily, and the clay trickling from under his hand into the ditch rustled in time with his words. 'Let him say once and for all.'

'He's got a child from that one...'

'And he'll have a child from this one!' Miron shouted, turning purple. 'How can he treat a living creature so? How can he? She tried to take her life once and now she's a cripple... Is she to be trampled into the grave? Has he no heart at all?' Miron's voice dropped to a choking whisper; one hand clawed his chest, the other tugged at the skirt of his kinsman's coat. 'Or is it the heart of a wolf?'

Pantelei breathed heavily and turned his head away.

'...the woman's pining for him, there's no life for her without him. She's just a maid of all work in your house!'

'She means more to us than any of our own! Hold your tongue, man!' Pantelei shouted, and stood up.

They walked away in different directions without saying goodbye.

XVIII

When life bursts its banks, it spreads into many streams and there's no telling what treacherous and cunning move it will make next. Where today it looks as shallow as a sandbanked stream, so shallow that you can see its wretched pebbly bottom, tomorrow it will flow rich and well-watered.

The decision to go to Aksinya at Yagodnoye and beg her to give Grigory back ripened suddenly in Natalya's mind. For some reason it seemed to her that everything depended on Aksinya, and that if only she pleaded hard enough, Grigory would come back and with him, her former happiness. She gave no thought to whether this was feasible or how Aksinya would react to her strange request. Driven by an unconscious urge, she set about putting her sudden decision into effect at once. At the end of the month the Melekhovs had received a letter from Grigory. After his greetings to his father and mother, he sent greetings and deepest respects to Natalya Mironovna. Whatever the reason that prompted him to do so, it gave Natalya the push that she needed and the following Sunday she made ready to go to Yagodnoye.

'Where are you off to, Natalya?' Dunyashka asked, watching Natalya as she studied her face severely in a bit of looking-glass.

'To see my folk,' Natalya lied, and the blood rushed

to her cheeks as she realised what humiliation and moral torture she was inviting.

'Why don't you come out for an evening with me, just for once, Natalya,' Darya suggested, dolling herself up. 'What about tonight?'

'I don't know, I don't think so.'

'Oh you, little nun! This is just the time for us, while our husbands are away,' Darya said, winking playfully, and bent her supple body almost double to examine the embroidered hem of a new pale-blue skirt in front of the mirror.

A noticeable change had come over Darya since Petro's departure; her husband's absence was beginning to tell. There was restlessness in her eyes, movements, even her walk. She dressed with special care on Sundays and came home late from the evening gatherings. Bad-tempered and dark under the eyes, she would complain to Natalya, 'It's awful, really it is!.. They've taken all the good Cossacks, there's no one left in the village but boys and old men.'

'What does it matter to you?'

'Of course, it matters!' Darya exclaimed. 'There's no one to lark about with in the evenings. If only they'd send me to the mill alone. There's not much fun going with my father-in-law watching over me.'

And she was brazen enough to ask Natalya. 'How do you stand it, my dear, being so long without a man?'

'Stoppit—you shameless creature!' Natalya blushed violently.

'And you don't even want it?'

'It seems that you do?'

'Yes, girl, I do and all!' Darya laughed till she was quite pink and the steep arches of her eyebrows quivered. 'Why should I hide it... I'd even tumble on old man, honestly I would! Just think, it's two months since Petro left.'

'You'll get yourself into trouble, Darya.'

'Go on with you, you honoured old maid! We know these quiet ones. You're just not letting on!'

'I haven't anything to let on about.'

Darya glanced at her scornfully and, biting her lips with her small, spiteful teeth, related, 'The other night Timoshka Manytskov, the ataman's son, came and sat down beside me. All sweaty he was. I could see he was afraid to start anything... Then he got his hand into my armpit, and it was trembling! I put up with it for a bit, but then my temper got the better of me. If only he'd been a bit more of a man—not this young snot! He's not more than sixteen; that's the kind we get now... Well, I sat quiet and he kept pawing me, and then he whispers, "Let's go off to our barn!" And then I let him have it!..'

Darya laughed gaily, her brows fluttered, and merriment spurted from her half-closed eyes.

'A proper scolding I gave him! "You young so-and-so," I said, jumping up. "You slobbering puppy! How can you say such a thing? How long is it since you stopped wetting the bed?" Told him good and proper, I did!'

Her relationship with Natalya was simple and friendly. The dislike Darya had felt at first had worn off, and the two women, so different in character and in every other way, got on well together.

Natalya put on her coat and went out.

Darya overtook her in the porch.

'Will you open the door for me tonight?'

'I expect I'll stay the night with my folk.'

Darya scratched the bridge of her nose thoughtfully with her comb, then shook her head.

'All right, off you go. I didn't want to ask Dunyashka, but I suppose I'll have to.'

Natalya told Ilyinichna that she was going to see her family and set out. Wagons from the market were driving across the square. People were coming out of church. Natalya walked past two side-lanes and turned off into the third. She climbed the hill hurriedly, looking back only once, from the top. The village lay in a flood of sunlight, the whitewashed cottages gleamed, sunbeams danced on the sloping roof of the mill, and the sheet iron glistened like molten ore.

XIX

The war had also plucked Yagodnoye of its menfolk. Veniamin and Tikhon had gone and the estate was even duller, drearier and more isolated than before. Veniamin's place as valet to the old general had been taken by Aksinya; the broad-bottomed Lukeria, who showed no signs of getting any thinner, took over the work in the scullery and the poultry yard. Grandad Sashka combined the duties of stableman with guarding the orchard, and the only new face was that of the coachman—the aged and dignified Cossack Nikitich.

That year the general reduced his sowing area and supplied nearly a score of horses as remounts to the army, keeping only the thoroughbred racers, and three Don work-horses for the needs of the estate. The general passed the time hunting, using Nikitich to beat the bustards for him, and occasionally rousing the district with his borzois in a wolf-hunt.

From Grigory Aksinya occasionally received brief letters to tell her that so far he was safe and well and getting through his service. Either out of reticence or reluctance to display weakness in a letter, he never wrote a word about his having a hard time or missing her. There was a note of coolness in his letters, as if he were forced to write them. The phrase that slipped out in one of his last letters was exceptional, '...I'm in action all the time and I'm getting a bit tired of fighting and carrying death with me in my saddle-bags.' In every letter he asked about his daughter. '...Write to me how my little Tanya is getting on and what she looks like now. The other night I dreamt of her quite grown up and wearing a red dress.'

Outwardly Aksinya seemed to be bearing up well. All her love of Grigory overflowed on to her daughter, particularly after she became sure that it was his child. The evidence that life provided was irrefutable. The little girl's chestnut fluff fell out and was replaced by a black curly head of hair; her eyes also changed colour, growing darker and more slanting. Every day the resemblance to her father became more and more striking and even her smile was Grigory's; it had that wild Melekhov gleam. Now Aksinya had no doubt at all as to who was the father of her child and became fervently attached to it. There was none of the old feeling of revulsion that she had experienced on going up to the cradle and finding in the girl's small sleeping face some remote resemblance to Stepan's hated face.

The days seeped away, leaving a bitter sediment in Aksinya's heart. Fear for the life of her beloved bored into her brain and lodged there in her waking hours. It came at night too, and then all that will power had held in check broke its bonds. Aksinya would writhe the whole night through in tears and silent screams of grief. She would gnaw her fists so as not to wake the child, stifling her cries and killing the moral pain with the physical. The rest of her tears she would weep out into the baby's napkins, thinking in her childlike innocence, 'It's

Grigory's child, he ought to feel in his heart how much I miss him.'

After such nights she would rise in the morning, feeling as if she had been beaten. Her body ached, little silver hammers drummed ceaselessly at her temples, and a mature grief settled in the corners of what had once been her girlishly full lips. How those nights of grieving aged Aksinya!

One Sunday she served the master his breakfast and went out on to the porch. A woman had come to the gate. There was something frighteningly familiar in those burning eyes that gazed from under the white kerchief... The woman lifted the latch and entered. Aksinya turned pale as she recognised Natalya, and slowly walked towards her. They met in the middle of the yard. Natalya's boots were coated with dust. She halted and let her big toil-worn hands fall lifelessly to her sides, breathing heavily and trying vainly to straighten her deformed neck, with the result that she seemed to be looking in another direction.

'I've come to see you, Aksinya,' she said, licking her parched lips with a dry tongue.

Aksinya cast a quick glance at the windows of the house and without a word walked to her room in the servants' quarters. Natalya followed her. The rustle of Aksinya's dress rasped painfully on her ears, and among a jumble of thoughts her mind seized on one, 'It must be the heat that's made my ears hurt like this.'

Aksinya let Natalya in and closed the door. When she had done so, she planted herself in the centre of the room and pushed her hands under her apron. The game was under her control.

'What brings you here?' she asked softly, almost in a whisper.

'Could I have a drink...' Natalya asked, and her eyes roamed heavily round the room.

Aksinya waited. Natalya began to speak, raising her voice with difficulty.

'You took my husband away from me... Give me back Grigory! You ... you've ruined my life... Look what I've become...'

'Give you back your husband?' Aksinya gritted her teeth and the words, like raindrops on stone, worked slowly, corrosively. 'Your husband? Who are you asking? Why did you come here? It's too late... It's too late to come cadging now!'

Aksinya thrust forward, swinging her whole body and laughing harshly.

She peered into her enemy's face mockingly. Here she was—the lawful deserted wife—standing before her, humiliated and crushed by grief; here was the woman who had made her suffer all the grief and pain of parting with Grigory, who had thrust a jagged rock into her heart. While Aksinya had endured such agony, this woman had been fondling him and probably laughing over the hapless mistress that he had left.

'So you've come to ask me to give him up!' Aksinya panted. 'You creeping snake! It was you who stole Grigory from me! Yes, you! Not me! You knew he was living with me, so why did you marry him? I got back what was mine and he is mine. I have a child by him, and you...'

She stared into Natalya's eyes with a storm of hatred and poured out the words that had been seething in her mind for so long.

'Grishka's mine and I won't give him up to anyone!.. He's mine! He's mine! D'you hear? Mine!.. Get out, you shameless bitch! You're no wife of his. You want to take the father away from his child? Oho! Why didn't you come before? Why didn't you, eh?'

Natalya stepped sideways to a bench and sat down, dropping her head on her hands and covering her face.

'You left your own husband... Don't shout like this.'

'I've no husband except Grishka. I've no one in the world!'

Feeling the pent-up anger rise again within her, Aksinya stared at the strands of straight black hair that had slipped from under Natalya's kerchief.

'You think he needs you? Look at your crooked neck! You think he'll fancy you now? He gave you up when you were all right. Will he want a cripple? You'll never get Grishka back! That's all I have to say! So get out!'

Aksinya was fighting ferociously to protect her nest and getting her own back for everything she had suffered in the past. She could see that Natalya, despite her slightly crooked neck, was still as lovely as before. Her cheeks and mouth were fresh and uncrumpled by time, while she, Aksinya, had a fine web of wrinkles under her eyes, wrinkles for which Natalya herself was to blame.

'Do you think I had any hope you would do as I ask?' Natalya raised her tortured eyes.

'Then why did you come?' Aksinya asked in one breath.

348

'Heartache made me.'

Aksinya's daughter, wakened by the sound of voices, began to cry and sat up in her crib. The mother took the child in her arms, sat down and turned away to the window. Shaking all over, Natalya stared at the child and a dry spasm seized her throat. It was Grigory's eyes that were looking at her with intelligent curiosity from the child's face.

She went out into the porch, sobbing and swaying. Aksinya made no attempt to see her off.

A minute or two later Sashka came in.

'Who was that woman?' he asked, evidently guessing the truth.

'Oh, just a woman from the village.'

Natalya walked about three versts from the estate and lay down under a thorn bush. She lay thinking of nothing, crushed by an inexpressible misery. Those dark, rather gloomy eyes of Grigory's that she had seen in the child's face were constantly before her.

XX

Grigory recalled that night with a vivid, blinding intensity. He had come to his senses in the early hours and groped about the prickly stubble, groaning from the throbbing pain that filled his head. With an effort he raised his hand and felt his matted forelock, stiff with congealed blood. The touch of his finger on the raw wound burned like a red-hot ember. He gritted his teeth and lay back. Leaves nipped by an early frost rustled glassily on a tree overhead. The black shapes of branches stood out clearly against the deep-blue sky and stars shone between them. Grigory stared unblinkingly, wide-eyed; to him they were not stars but strange bluish-yellow fruits dangling on their stalks.

Realising what had happened and gripped by a dawning sense of horror, he began to crawl on all fours, gritting his teeth. Pain romped over him and threw him flat on his face. When he seemed to have been crawling for an infinitely long time, he forced himself to look round. The tree where he had lain unconscious loomed only fifty paces away. Once he crawled over a dead man, his elbows digging into the hard sunken belly. Sick from loss of blood, he wept like a child and chewed the dew-fresh grass to stop himself from fainting. Beside an overturned ammunition crate, he dragged himself to his feet, stood swaying for a while, and then walked on. His strength gradually returned, his step grew firmer, and soon he was able to find his way east, using the Great Bear as a guide.

On the edge of a wood he was halted by a gruff warning.

'Don't come any nearer or I'll shoot!'

A revolver drum clicked. Grigory peered in the direction of the sound; dimly he made out a pine-tree and beside it, a man propping himself on one elbow.

'Who are you?' Grigory asked, hearing his own voice as if it were a stranger's.

'You're Russian? My God!.. Come here!' the man by the pine slumped to the ground.

Grigory went up to him.

'Bend down.'

'I can't.'

'Why not?'

'I'll fall and won't be able to get up again. I've been wounded in the head.'

'What unit are you from?'

'Twelfth Don Regiment.'

'Help me, Cossack.'

'I'll fall, Your Honour.' (Grigory had recognised an officer's insignia on his greatcoat.)

'At least, give me a hand up.'

Grigory helped the officer to his feet and they walked on together. But with every step the wounded officer leaned more heavily on Grigory's arm. As they climbed out of a hollow he seized Grigory's sleeve and said through chattering teeth, 'Leave me here, Cossack... I'm wounded in the stomach. The bullet went right through.'

The eyes behind the pince-nez grew dull and the open unshaven mouth gasped for air. The officer fainted. Grigory carried him, falling, pulling himself up, and falling again. Twice he abandoned his burden, only to go back and pick it up, and then struggle on, as if in a waking dream. At eleven in the morning they were spotted by a signals detachment and taken to a dressing station.

A day later Grigory slipped away without permission, ripped the dressing off his head and strode along, waving the bloodstained bandage with a feeling of relief.

'Where did you spring from?' the squadron commander asked in wonder.

'I've come back to the regiment, Your Honour.'

The next person Grigory saw was the troop sergeant.

'Where's my horse—the Bay?'

'He's safe and sound, lad. We caught him right away after we'd seen off the Austrians. How are you? We've been praying for your soul in heaven.'

'You were in too much of a hurry.'' Grigory gave a wry grin.

EXCERPT FROM ORDERS

For saving the life of Colonel Gustav Grosberg, Commander of the 9th Dragoon Regiment, Grigory Melekhov, 12th Don Cossack Regiment, is promoted to the rank of Corporal and recommended for the St. George Cross, 4th class.

The squadron rested for two days in the town of Ka-mionka-Strumiłowa and was to be on the march the following night. Grigory found the house where his troop was billeted and went to inspect his horse.

A set of underwear and a towel were missing from the saddle-bags.

'They pinched it under my very eyes, Grigory,' Mikhail Koshevoi confessed guiltily. He had been in charge of the horse. 'They herded a whole lot of infantry into this yard. Thick as flies, they were. It was the infantry that took 'em.'

'To hell with it. All I need is something for my head, this bandage is soaked.'

'Take my towel.'

Uryupin came into the shed where they were talking. He held out his hand to Grigory as if nothing had happened between them.

'Ah, Melekhov! Alive and kicking, eh?'

'Just about.'

'There's blood on your forehead, wipe it off.'

'All in good time.'

'Let me see how they marked you.'

Uryupin pulled Grigory's head down and gave a sniff.

'Why did you let 'em shave your head? What a sight you are!.. Those doctors, they'll make a proper hash of it. Let me treat you.'

Without waiting for Grigory's consent he took a cartridge out of his ammunition pouch, removed the bullet and tipped the gunpowder on to his swarthy hand.

'Get me a cobweb, Mikhail!'

Koshevoi reached up with his sabre, flicked a cobweb off one of the rafters and gave it to him. With the same

351

sabre Uryupin dug a lump of earth out of the floor, mixed it with the cobweb and the gunpowder, and chewed it for some time. He plastered the thick paste over the bleeding wound and grinned.

'In three days it'll be gone. See how I'm looking after you, and you wanted to shoot me.'

'Thanks for your attention, but if I'd killed you it would have been one sin less to my account.'

'You're a straightforward lad.'

'I'm just as God made me. What's the place like on my head?'

'There's a cut seven inches long. That's a keepsake for you.'

'I won't forget it.'

'You couldn't, if you wanted to; the Austrians don't sharpen their sabres. You were slashed with a blunt one. Now you'll have a scar for the rest of your life.'

'Lucky for you it was a glancing blow, Grigory, or we'd have buried you in foreign soil,' Koshevoi said with a smile.

'What shall I do with my cap?'

Grigory looked perplexedly at the cap in his hands with its torn and blood-stained top.

'Throw it away, the dogs will eat it.'

'Grub's up, lads, come and get it!' someone shouted from the door of the house.

The Cossacks left the shed. The Bay whinnied after Grigory and rolled its eyes.

'He was pining for you, Grigory,' Koshevoi said with a nod towards the horse. 'I was real surprised. He wouldn't eat his food, and kept whinnying.'

'When I was finding my way out of there, I kept calling him,' Grigory said huskily, turning away. 'I thought he wouldn't have left me and he's hard to catch, won't let a stranger take him.'

'Yes, we only just managed it. We had to rope him.'

'He's a good horse—my brother Petro's.' And Grigory turned his head to hide his feelings.

They entered the house. In the front room Yegor Zharkov lay snoring on a mattress taken from the bed and spread on the floor. The indescribable disorder indicated that the owners had left in haste. Broken crockery, scraps of paper, books, bits of cloth stained with honey, children's toys, old shoes, the flour sprinkled all over the floor were evidence of a hurried retreat.

Yemelyan Groshev and Prokhor Zykov had cleared

a space on the table and were eating their dinner. Prokhor's calf-like eyes bulged at the sight of Grigory.

'Gri-i-sha! Where are you from?'

'The other world.'

'Run and get his soup. What are you goggling at?' Uryupin snapped at him.

'The kitchen's right here, in the lane. I won't be a minute.'

Prokhor darted out into the yard, chewing as he went.

Grigory sat down wearily in his place.

'I don't remember when I last ate,' he said, smiling apologetically.

Units of the 3rd Corps were passing through the town. The narrow streets were choked with infantry, baggage trains and cavalry units. The crossroads were jammed and the rumble of traffic penetrated the closed doors of the house. Prokhor soon reappeared with a mess-tin of soup and a large paper cone of boiled buckwheat.

'Where can I put the buckwheat?'

'Here's a saucepan with a handle.' Groshev took a chamber-pot off the windowsill, not knowing its true function.

Prokhor frowned. 'Your saucepan stinks.'

'Never mind. Tip it out, we'll bother about that later.'

Prokhor unfolded the paper and the soft wholesome mash with an amber fringe of melted butter round the edges spilled out steaming. They ate and talked at the same time. Wetting a grease-spot on his faded trouser stripe with spit, Prokhor related, 'There's a battery of mountain artillery next door, feeding up their horses. Their warrant officer says he read in the paper that the allies have given the Germans a real pasting.'

'You missed something this morning, Melekhov,' Uryupin purred through a mouthful of buckwheat. 'We received a message of thanks.'

'Who from?'

'Lieutenant-General von Divid, the divisional O. C., inspected us and thanked us for beating off the Hungarian hussars and saving the battery. They nearly got away with the guns, see. "Well done, Cossacks," he says. "The Tsar and the Fatherland will not forget you."'

Grigory gave a non-committal grunt.

Shots rang out in the street and were followed by a long burst of machine-gun fire.

'Outside!' a voice bawled from the gate.

The Cossacks dropped their spoons and rushed into

the yard. An aeroplane was circling low overhead, its engine roaring menacingly.

'Down by the fence! He'll start dropping his bombs in a minute; there's a battery right by!' Uryupin shouted.

'Wake Yegor! He'll get killed on his soft mattress!'

'Get the rifles!'

Uryupin aimed carefully and fired from the porch.

Soldiers ran down the street, half crouching for some reason. From the neighbouring yard came the neigh of a horse and a harsh command. Grigory emptied his magazine and glanced over the fence. The gunners were running to and fro, wheeling the guns into a shed. Screwing up his eyes against the abrasive blue of the sky, he watched the great roaring bird as it went into a dive; at that moment something broke away from it and glinted in the sunlight. A shattering explosion shook the little house and the Cossacks crouching round the porch; in the neighbouring yard a horse screamed in mortal agony. Pungent sulphurous fumes drifted over the fence.

'Down!' Uryupin shouted, darting off the porch.

Grigory sprang after him and fell by the fence. An aluminium section of the plane's wing flashed as it banked away smoothly. Volleys and single shots echoed from the street in a chaos of ragged firing. Grigory had just reloaded when an even more violent explosion threw him a couple of paces from the fence. A great chunk of earth landed heavily on his head, sprinkling dirt in his eyes.

He was lifted to his feet by Uryupin. A sharp pain in his left eye temporarily blinded him; with difficulty he forced open the right. Half the house had been demolished; the bricks lay in an ugly red pile of rubble with pink dust swirling over it. Yegor Zharkov was crawling out of the wrecked porch on his hands and knees. His whole face was screaming and bloody tears were flowing from his empty eye sockets. He kept his head between his shoulders and cried out, apparently without opening his deathly dark lips.

One leg, severed at the hip, was dragging behind him on a thin rag of skin and a scorched trouser leg. The other leg was missing. He moved his hands slowly and the whimpering, almost childlike, cry drilled its way out of his mouth. Then the cry broke off and he fell sideways, pressing his face into the damp, unfriendly earth fouled with horse dung and rubble. No one went to help him.

'Pick him up!' Grigory shouted, his hand still pressed to his left eye.

354

Some infantrymen ran into the yard. A signallers' cart stopped by the gate.

'Keep moving! What are you stopping for?' an officer shouted as he galloped past. 'You gaping brutes!'

An old man in a long black coat and two women walked up from somewhere. A crowd gathered round Zharkov. Grigory pushed his way through and saw that he was still breathing, in sobbing, shuddering gasps. Great beads of sweat had broken out on his deathly yellow forehead.

'Pick him up! What are you—men or devils!'

'No need to bite our heads off!' a tall infantryman snapped back. ' "Pick him up!" Where d'you expect us to take him? Can't you see he's done for?'

'Both legs gone.'

'Look at all the blood!'

'Where are the stretcher bearers?'

'What good would they be?'

'He's still conscious.'

Grigory looked round as Uryupin touched him on the shoulder.

'Don't move him,' Uryupin whispered. 'Go round the other side and look.'

Keeping a grip on Grigory's sleeve, he walked round the crowd and pushed his way through. Grigory looked once and walked away to the gate, shoulders hunched. Zharkov's intestines lay steaming in a tender pink and blue heap under his belly. The end of the tangled mess, smeared with sand and dung, was writhing and swelling. The dying man's hand seemed to be groping sideways.

'Cover his face,' someone suggested.

Zharkov suddenly pulled himself up, threw his head back till it knocked between his hunched shoulder blades, and screamed in a hoarse, inhuman voice:

'Brothers, put an end to me! Brothers!.. Brothers!.. What's the use of staring?.. Ah-a-a-ah!.. Brothers! Put an end to me!'

XXI

The carriage swayed gently, the rhythm of the wheels kept up a drowsy lullaby, half the seat was wrapped in yellow patterns of light from the lantern. It was good to stretch out at full length and have your boots off for the first time in a fortnight, to feel free of all duties, to know that life held no dangers and that death was far, far away. The best thing of all was to listen to the varying tones of the wheels, when you knew that every turn and every tug of the engine was taking you farther from the front. And Grigory lay listening, twiddling the toes of his bare feet, and basking in the ease of the fresh underwear he had only just put on. It was as if he had cast off a dirty outer skin and was entering another life spotlessly clean.

His serenity was disturbed only by the nagging pain in his left eye. It would die away for a while, then suddenly return, searing the eye with fire and squeezing out involuntary tears under the bandage. At the hospital in Kamionka-Strumiłowa a young Jewish doctor had examined Grigory's eye and written something on a scrap of paper.

'We'll have to send you to the rear. That eye is in serious trouble.'

'Will I be one-eyed?'

'Certainly not,' the doctor smiled reassuringly, noticing the unconcealed alarm in Grigory's question. 'But you need treatment, perhaps an operation. We'll send you right back into the rear, to Petrograd, for example, or Moscow.'

'Thank you kindly.'

'Don't be afraid, your eye will be all right.' The doctor patted him on the shoulder, slipped the paper into his hand, and pushed him gently into the corridor, rolling up his sleaves in readiness for an operation.

After a lot of bother Grigory got on a hospital train and lay back for a day and a night, enjoying the rest while the old and undersized locomotive pulled the heavy train laboriously towards Moscow.

They arrived at night. The badly wounded were carried out on stretchers; those who could walk without help had their names taken and stepped out on to the platform. The doctor in charge of the train called out Grigory's name from the list and, pointing him out to a nurse, said, 'Doctor Snegiryov's hospital. Kolpachny Lane.'

'Have you got your belongings?' the nurse asked.

'What belongings has a Cossack! A saddle-bag and a greatcoat, that's all.'

'Come along then.'

She rustled away, patting her hair into place under her cap. Grigory followed her unsteadily. They took a cab. The hum of the big city, the clang of the tramcars, the blue shimmering light of electricity overwhelmed Grigory. He sat leaning back in the seat of the cab, gazing eagerly at the streets, which were still crowded despite the lateness of the hour; the exciting warmth of a woman's body beside him added to the strangeness. In Moscow it was already autumn. The trees on the boulevards gleamed yellowishly in the light of the street lamps, the night was dank and chilly, the pavements glistened damply and the stars on the clear horizon were bright and autumnally cold. From the centre they drove into a deserted side-street. The horse's hooves clattered on the cobble-stones. The driver, wearing a long dark-blue coat, like a priest's, swayed on his high box, and flicked his lop-eared nag with the ends of the reins. Somewhere on the outskirts locomotives were whistling. May be one of them is heading for the Don right now, Grigory thought wistfully, and was overcome by pangs of homesickness.

'Are you dozing?' the nurse asked.

'No.'

'We'll soon be there.'

'What did you say, miss?' the cabman said turning his head.

'Hurry up.'

The waters of a pond gleamed oilily behind a wrought-iron grill, a railed landing-stage with a boat tied to it flashed by. Damp air drifted into the cab.

They even keep their water behind bars here. It's not like the Don, Grigory thought vaguely. Leaves rustled under the rubber tyres.

The driver drew up outside a three-storey building. Grigory straightened his greatcoat and jumped out.

'Give me your hand,' the nurse said, bending forward.

Grigory took the small soft hand in his and helped her down.

'You do smell of soldier's sweat,' the carefully toileted nurse exclaimed, laughing softly, and rang the door bell.

'You ought to be there yourself, nurse. Mebbe you'd stink of something else besides,' Grigory said with quiet fury.

The door was opened by a liveried porter. They mounted a fine staircase with gilded bannisters to the first floor. There the nurse rang again. They were admitted by a woman in a white coat. Grigory sat down at a small circular table. The nurse spoke quietly to the woman in white, who took notes.

Heads wearing spectacles of different colours peered out of the doors on each side of a long narrow corridor.

'Take off your greatcoat,' the woman in white told him.

An attendant, also in white, took the greatcoat from Grigory and led him to the bathroom.

'Take everything off.'

'What for?'

'You're going to have a bath.'

While Grigory was undressing and looking round in astonishment at the room and the frosted glass of the windows, the attendant filled the bath, read the temperature, and told him to get in.

'This tub's not for me,' Grigory muttered in embarrassment as he lifted a dark hairy leg over the side.

The attendant helped him to wash thoroughly and gave him a towel, underwear, slippers, and a grey dressing gown with a belt.

'What about my clothes?' Grigory asked in surprise.

'In hospital you'll wear this. Your clothes will be returned when you leave.'

Grigory scarcely recognised himself as he passed a large wall mirror in the hall. The tall swarthy-faced individual with sharp cheekbones and blotches of high colour in his cheeks, wrapped in a dressing-gown and with a bandage biting into his black hair, bore only a remote resemblance to the former Grigory. His moustache had bushed out and he had a short curly beard.

'Life has made me look a lot younger,' he muttered to himself with a wry smile.

'Ward Six, third door on the right,' the attendant told him.

As Grigory entered the large white room a priest in dark-blue spectacles rose to meet him.

'Ah, a new neighbour? Glad to see you; it won't be so lonely. I'm from Zaraisk,' he said companionably and offered Grigory a chair.

After a few minutes a stout assistant doctor with a big ugly face entered the room.

'Come with me, Melekhov, we must have a look at your eye,' she said in a deep-throated voice, and stepped back to let Grigory into the corridor.

XXII

On the south-western front in the region of Shevel the army command had decided to pierce the enemy's front with a grandiose cavalry onslaught. A large cavalry force would follow this up with a raid along the front, destroying lines of communication and spreading confusion among enemy units with sudden attacks from the rear. The command placed great hopes on the success of this plan and cavalry in unprecedented numbers was assembled in the area. The regiments thus transferred included the Cossack regiment in which Lieutenant Listnitsky was serving. The attack was planned for August 28th but had been postponed until the 29th because of rain.

That morning the whole division was assembled in readiness for the attack.

Some eight versts away on the right flank the infantry staged a diversionary attack to draw the enemy's fire; two squadrons of cavalry were also sent in another direction to deceive the enemy.

Ahead, for as far as the eye could see there was no sign of the opposing forces. A verst away from his squadron Listnitsky spotted a line of dark deserted trenches. Beyond them a field of rye loomed out of the bluish early morning mist that was swirling about it in the light breeze.

The enemy command had either received word of the intended attack or had foreseen it, and on the night of the 28th their troops had been withdrawn from their trenches and moved back some six versts, leaving concealed machine-gun nests that harassed the Russian infantry along the whole sector, wherever they came into contact.

Somewhere behind the billowing clouds the sun was shining, but the low ground lay in a creamy yellow fog. The order to attack was given and the regiments swung into motion. Thousands of hooves set up a hollow, seemingly subterranean rumble. Listnitsky held back his thoroughbred to prevent it breaking into a gallop. When they had gone about a verst and a half the orderly ranks of the attackers were confronted by the rye. More than waist high and well plaited with grass and bindweed, it made the going extremely heavy for the horses. Ahead of them the reddish-brown rye rose wave upon wave; behind them it lay crushed and trampled by their hooves. By the fourth verst the horses began to stumble and sweat, but still there was no sign of the enemy. Listnitsky glanced round at the squadron commander; the major's face was full of dumb dismay.

Six versts of this impossible riding ripped all the strength out of the horses. Some of them fell under their riders. Even the sturdiest were on their last legs. And just at that moment the Austrian machine-guns opened up and the big guns began a steady pounding... The murderous fire mowed down the foremost ranks. The uhlans were the first to waver and turn back, then the Cossack regiment crumpled; in their panic flight they were sprayed by machine-guns and shelled by the artillery. Owing to the criminal negligence of the high command a cavalry attack of unprecedented dimensions ended in an utter rout. Some regiments lost half their men and horses; in Listnitsky's regiment the casualties amounted to about four hundred men and sixteen officers.

Listnitsky's horse was shot from under him and he himself received two wounds, in the head and leg. He was saved by Sergeant-Major Chebotaryov, who leapt off his horse, heaved Listnitsky across his saddle and galloped clear.

The divisional chief of staff Golovachov, a colonel of the General Staff, took several snapshots of the attack and later showed them to the officers. Lieutenant Chervyakov, who had been wounded, was the first to strike him in the face, then broke down in tears. Some passing Cossacks ran up and tore Golovachov to pieces, desecrated the body and flung it into the filth of a roadside ditch. Thus ended a brilliantly inglorious attack.

From a Warsaw hospital Listnitsky informed his father that as soon as he recovered he would come to Yagodnoye to spend his convalescent leave. On receiving the letter, the old man locked himself up in his study and came out only on the next day, as black as a thundercloud. He ordered Nikitich to harness a racehorse to the droshky, ate his breakfast and drove off to Vyoshenskaya, where he sent his son four hundred roubles by telegraph and dispatched a brief letter.

I can only be glad that you, my dear boy, have received your baptism of fire. It is your noble fate to be there, and not at the palace. You are too honest and intelligent to be able to kowtow with an untroubled conscience. No member of our family ever had that proclivity. For that your grandfather fell into disgrace and lived the rest of his days in Yagodnoye without hope or expectation of pardon from the monarch. Good health to you, Zhenya, and get well. Remember you are the only one I have in this world. Your aunt asks to be remembered to you. She is quite well. As for myself, there is nothing to write. You know how I live. What is going on at the front? Are there no people left with the power of reason? I don't believe the reports in the newspapers. They are mendacious from beginning to end, as I know from past experience. Surely, Yevgeny, we are not going to lose the campaign?

I await your arrival home with the greatest impatience!

It was true enough that the old Listnitsky had nothing to write about his life. It dragged along in its old rut, as monotonous and unchanging as ever. Perhaps the only difference was that the cost of labour had risen and there seemed to be a shortage of liquor. The general drank more often and had become more irritable and fault-finding. One day he summoned Aksinya at an unearthly hour and said, 'You are serving badly. Why was the breakfast brought to table cold yesterday? Why was the coffee glass not properly washed? If this continues, I shall dismiss you—d'you hear?—dismiss you! I have no patience with slovens!' He slashed the air with his hand. 'D'you hear? I can't stand them!'

Aksinya, who had been standing tight-lipped, suddenly burst into tears.

'Nikolai Alekseyevich! My little girl is ill. Couldn't you let me off work for a bit... I can't leave her for a minute.'

'What's wrong with her?'

'She's got strawberry tongue... It's choking her...'

'Scarlet fever? Why didn't you say so, you fool? The devil take you, you stupid hussy! Run and tell Nikitich to harness up and drive to the stanitsa for the doctor. Look lively!'

Aksinya ran out under a bombardment of thunderous shouts from the old man.

'You stupid woman! Stupid fool!'

The next morning Nikitich arrived with an assistant doctor. He examined the little girl, who was unconscious and in a high fever, and without answering any of Aksinya's questions, went straight to the house to see the general. Listnitsky received him in the hall, standing and without offering his hand.

'What's wrong with the child?' he asked, answering the greeting with a casual nod.

'Scarlet fever, Your Excellency.'

'Will she get better? Is there hope?'

'Very little. She'll probably die... Remember her age.'

'Fool!' the general turned purple in the face. 'What were you taught at medical school? Cure her!'

He slammed the door in the face of the frightened doctor and paced about the room.

Aksinya knocked at the door and came in.

'The doctor wants horses to take him to the stanitsa.'

The old man swung round on his heels.

'Tell him he's a blockhead! Tell him he won't leave here until he cures the girl for me! Give him a room in the lodge and feed him!' the old man shouted, brandishing his bony fist. 'Give him all he can eat and drink, feed him up like a prize bull, but he's not leaving here!' He broke off and went to the window, drummed his fingers on the sill, then turned to an enlarged photograph of his son, taken in his nursemaid's arms. He stepped back a couple of paces and stood peering at it, as if unable to recognise the child.

The day her daughter fell ill, Aksinya had remembered Natalya's bitter phrase, 'My tears will be your tears...' So this, she decided, was God's punishment for mocking her rival.

In her fear for the life of the child she had lost her head and rushed about senselessly, unable to cope with her work.

'Surely He won't take her from me?' the feverish thought throbbed in her brain and, while not believing and refusing to believe it, she prayed frenziedly and begged God in his mercy to save the life of the child.

'Oh God, forgive me!.. Don't take her away! Have pity, Lord, be merciful!'

But disease was strangling the life out of the small body. The little girl lay on her back with the breath coming from her swollen throat in short wheezing gasps. The doctor, now lodged in the servants' quarters, visited her three or four times a day. In the evenings he stood on the porch, smoking and gazing at the autumn stars sprinkled across the sky.

Aksinya spent the nights on her knees by the bed. And night after night, the little girl's wheezing gurgle cut her heart like a whip.

'Mu-u-mmy!' the small parched lips made the merest rustle.

'Little one, my little daughter!' the mother called mutedly. 'My little flower, don't go away, Tanya! Look at me, my pretty one, open your eyes. Wake up now! My little dove, my dark eyes... Oh God, why do you punish me so?'

Now and then the child raised her inflamed lids, all swollen with bad blood and gave a wandering, elusive look. Her mother tried desperately to catch that glance, but it seemed to withdraw inwardly, sad and resigned.

She died in her mother's arms. The small blue mouth sobbed and gaped for the last time, the small body shuddered; the little sweating head, eyes half closed over the dead pupils, fell back over Aksinya's arm, and one gloomy Melekhov eye looked up in surprise.

Sashka dug a tiny grave near the pond, beside an old branching poplar, carried the small coffin out under his arm and buried it with a haste that was not a bit like him, then waited long and patiently for Aksinya to rise from the loamy mound. But it was no use waiting. He blew his nose with a sound like the crack of a whip and went off to the stables... From the hay loft he fetched a bottle of Eau-de-Cologne and a small, only partly full bottle of methylated spirits, mixed the two in a bottle and, as he shook it and admired the colour, said, 'God rest her innocent soul!'

He drank, shook his head frantically, helped it down with a squashed tomato and, staring sorrowfully at the bottle, said, 'Don't forget me, dear, and I won't forget you!..' and wept.

Three weeks later Yevgeny Listnitsky sent a telegram saying that he had been given leave and was on his way home. A team of three horses was sent to the station to meet him, all the servants were roused; turkeys and geese were killed, Sashka was busy, dressing a slaughtered sheep. There were enough preparations for a grand gathering of guests.

On the eve of his arrival an escort was sent out to the settlement of Kamenka. The young master arrived at night. An icy drizzle was falling and the lanterns cast rippling streams of light on the puddles. The horses drew up at the porch with their bells tinkling. An excited, smiling Yevgeny stepped out of the carriage, threw off his warm cloak on to Sashka's arm, and mounted the steps of the porch with a noticeable limp. Knocking over furniture in his haste, the old general shuffled forward to meet him.

Aksinya put supper on the table in the dining room and went to say that the meal was ready. Looking through the keyhole, she saw the old man clasping his son and kissing him on the shoulder; his flabby, wrinkled neck was quivering. When Aksinya looked again a few minutes later, Yevgeny, his field-service tunic unbuttoned, was kneeling beside a large map spread on the floor.

The old general, puffing ragged smoke rings from his pipe, was rapping the arm of his chair with his knuckles and booming indignantly.

'Alexeyev? Impossible! I can't believe it.'

Yevgeny argued quietly and at some length, tracing lines on the map with his finger while the old man rumbled restrainedly in reply.

'In this particular case the Commander-in-Chief is mistaken. This is sheer narrowness of vision! Now, if you'll forgive me, Yevgeny, here's a similar example from the Russo-Japanese campaign. With respect!'

Aksinya knocked.

'What, supper ready? Just a minute.'

The old man came out jovial and animated, with a youthful gleam in his eye. He and his son drank a bottle of wine that had been dug out of the ground only the day before. The faded date—1879—was still visible on the musty green label.

The sight of their merry faces while she served at table only made Aksinya the more aware of her loneliness. She was tormented by a grief that would not be relieved by tears. In the first days after the death of her little girl she had longed to cry. The sobs rose in her throat, but no tears would come and the load on her heart was twice as heavy. She slept a great deal, seeking relief in a drowsy oblivion, but even in her dreams she was troubled by the ghostly crying of her child. Sometimes she would imagine that the child was asleep beside her and would reach out across the bed; at others she would hear the barely audible whisper, 'Mummy ... thirsty.'

'Dearest heart...' Aksinya would whisper with chilled lips.

Even in her sombre waking hours she sometimes felt a child clinging to her knees and would suddenly find herself reaching down to fondle the curly head.

On the third day after his arrival, Yevgeny sat with old Sashka in the stable until late evening, listening to his guileless tales about the free life that the Cossacks used to live on the Don in the old days. It was past eight o'clock when he left the stable; the wind was swirling round the yard and the ground squelched muddily underfoot. A young yellow-whiskered moon was riding high among the clouds. By its light Yevgeny glanced at his watch and made for the servants' quarters. At the steps he lit a cigarette, stood thinking for a moment, then, with a sudden shrug, walked resolutely on to the porch. He lifted the latch cautiously and the door opened with a creak. As he entered Aksinya's room, he struck a match.

'Who's there?' Aksinya asked, pulling up the bed-clothes.

'It's me.'

'I'll get dressed.'

'Never mind that. I won't be more than a minute.'

He threw off his greatcoat and sat down on the edge of the bed.

'Your little girl has died.'

'Yes,' Aksinya murmured.

'You have changed a great deal. And no wonder. I can imagine what it's like to lose a child. But surely you shouldn't torment yourself like this. You can't bring her back and you're still young enough to have children. Really you shouldn't! Take a grip on yourself... You haven't lost everything with the death of the child. Just think, you have your whole life before you.'

Yevgeny pressed Aksinya's hand and fondled it with affectionate authority. His voice played softly on the lower notes, then dropped to a whisper and, as he heard Aksinya begin to shake with suppressed grief, and then break into wild sobs, he began to kiss her tear-wet cheeks and eyes.

A woman's heart is easily won by sympathy and affection. In her blind despair Aksinya yielded to him with all her violent, long forgotten passion. And when the over-whelming, blinding wave of shameless ecstasy had passed, she opened her eyes, let out a sudden cry, and ran madly out on to the porch in only her shift. Yevgeny hurried out after her, leaving the door open. He pulled on his greatcoat as he went and strode away to the house. By the time he reached it he was panting. As he mounted the steps to the veranda he laughed joyfully and with satisfaction. He was elated. When he lay in bed rubbing his soft fleshy chest, he thought, 'From the point of view of honour it's underhand and immoral. Grigory... I have robbed my neighbour, but out there at the front I risked my life. If the bullet had been just a little to the right, it would have gone through my head. I would be rotting in the ground by now and my body would be feeding the worms... One must live and lust after every moment of life. For me everything is permitted!' For a moment he was horrified by his own thoughts, but imagination again conjured up the fearful picture of the attack and the moment when he rose from his fallen horse only to be cut down by bullets. And as he dropped off to sleep, he told himself contentedly, 'I'll think about that tomorrow. Now it's time to sleep, to sleep...'

The next morning, when he was left alone in the dining room with Aksinya, he came up to her, smiling guiltily; she shrank back against the wall and seared him with a frenzied whisper, 'Don't come near me, you devil!'

But life dictates its unwritten laws. Three days later Yevgeny came to Aksinya's room again at night and was not refused.

XXIII

There was a small garden adjoining Doctor Snegiryov's eye hospital.

It was one of the many uninviting well-clipped gardens in Moscow's backstreets, where the eye obtained no relief from the stone-bound boredom of the city and one was reminded all the more painfully of the wild freedom of the forest. Autumn had taken over the hospital garden; it had strewn the paths with orange and bronze leaves, crushed the flowers with the morning frosts, and flooded the lawns with a watery green. On fine days the patients paced the paths, listening to the pealing churchbells of the devout city. In bad weather (and that year it was mostly bad) they drifted about from ward to ward, lay on their beds in silence, as tired of other people's company as they were of themselves.

Most of the patients were civilians; the war wounded were kept together in one ward. There were five of them: Jan Vareikis, a tall brown-haired Lett with a neat clipped beard and light-blue eyes; Ivan Vrublevsky, a handsome dragoon, aged twenty-eight, born in Vladimir Province; a Siberian marksman Kosykh; a fidgety sallow-faced soldier named Burdin, and Grigory Melekhov. At the end of September a new patient was brought in. During evening tea the doorbell gave a long urgent peal. Grigory looked out into the corridor. Three people had entered the hall: a nurse, a man in a Circassian tunic, and a third person, supported by the other two. He had evidently only just arrived from the station, judging by his filthy soldier's tunic with brownish bloodstains down the chest. He was operated on the same evening. After only a few brief preparations (the sound of the instruments being sterilized could be heard in the wards), the new patient was taken to the operating theatre. A few minutes later muffled singing was heard.

Under the influence of chloroform the newcomer sang and uttered incomprehensible curses while all that a shell-splinter had left of his eye was removed. When it was over he was put in with the other wounded. A day later, after the effects of the chloroform had worn off, he related that he had been wounded near Wehrberg on the German front, that his name was Garanzha, that he had been a machine-gunner and was a native of Chernigov Province. It took him only a few days to become especially attached to Grigory; their beds were next to each other and after the doctor's evening round they would have long whispered conversations.

'Well, Cossack, how are things?'

'As bright as mud.'

'How's your eye?'

'I'm having injections.'

'How many have you had so far?'

'Eighteen.'

'Does it hurt?'

'No, it's a treat.'

'Ask 'em to cut it out for you then.'

'We don't all have to be one-eyed.'

'That's so.'

Grigory's bitter, sarcastic neighbour was dissatisfied with everything. He cursed the government, the war, his own fate, the hospital food, the cook, the doctors, everything that came within range of his sharp tongue.

'What have you and me been fighting for, boy?'

'The same thing as everyone else.'

'That's no good, give me a proper answer.'

'Lay off!'

'Bah! You're a fool. You've got to understand these things. We've been fighting for the bourgeois, don't you see? And what's a bourgeois? It's the kind of bird that lives in a hemp field.'

He explained the strange words to Grigory, sprinkling his speech with peppery invective.

'Don't jabber! I don't understand your Ukrainian lingo,' Grigory would interrupt him.

'There now! What is it you don't understand, you Russian clod?'

'Speak slower.'

'I'm speaking pretty slow as it is, m'deary. You say you're for the tsar, but what is he, this tsar? The tsar's a drunkard, the tsaritsa's a whore, and the bosses are doing well out of the war, but for us it's a rope round our necks. Get me? That's how it is! The factory-owner drinks his vodka, the soldier swats his lice, they both have a tough time. The factory-owner gets his money-bags, the worker gets his rags, that's the way things are. Serve well, Cossack! Serve well! You'll soon earn another cross—a fine big one, made of oak...' Usually he spoke Ukrainian, but at times, when he grew excited, he would break into Russian and, loading it with curses, express himself quite correctly.

Day after day he fed Grigory's mind with truths that he had never heard before, showed him the actual causes of the war and fiercely derided the autocracy. Grigory tried to argue, but Garanzha cornered him with simple, murderously simple questions and Grigory would be forced to agree.

The worst of it was that in his heart he felt Garanzha was right and was powerless to offer any counter-arguments; he had none and could find none. Grigory realised in horror that this clever and aggressive Ukrainian was slowly but surely destroying all his previous notions of the tsar, the fatherland, and his Cossack's military duty.

In the month since Garanzha's arrival all the pillars on which his view of life had rested had crumbled to dust. They had already been undermined and corroded by the monstrous absurdity of the war, and only a push was needed. The push was given and thought awakened, nagging and oppressing Grigory's simple, straightforward mind. He thrashed about looking for a solution to a problem that was beyond his comprehension and was glad to find it in the answers provided by Garanzha.

Late one night Grigory rose from his bed, wakened Garanzha, and sat down on the edge of his bed. The greenish light of the September moon was filtering through the lowered window blind. Dark, earthy ruts showed up in Garanzha's face and the black sunken hollow of his eye gleamed moistly. He yawned and wrapped the blanket round his feet with a shiver.

'Why aren't you asleep?'

'I can't. Sleep won't come. Explain this to me. The

war's doing some people a lot of good, and for others it's ruin...'

'Well? A-a-ah...' Garanzha yawned.

'Wait a minute!' Grigory whispered, burning with anger. 'You say they're sending us to our deaths for the sake of the rich, but what about the people? Or don't they understand? Couldn't anyone tell 'em about it? Someone who'd come forward and say, "Brothers, look what you're dying for, giving your blood for."'

'Someone who'd come forward? Are you crazy? I'd just like to see you come forward. Here we are, whispering together like geese in the reeds, but just try and speak out and you'll get a bullet. The people are stone deaf. The war will wake them up. After the thunder comes the storm.'

'What shall we do? Tell me, you snake! You've roused my heart.'

'What does your heart tell you?'

'I can't understand it,' Grigory confessed.

'If someone tries to push me off a cliff, I'll push him off instead. We've got to turn the rifles round. We've got to shoot the men who're sending people into this hellfire. Let me tell you this,' Garanzha sat up, gritting his teeth and stretching out his arms, 'a great wave will rise up and sweep everything away!'

'So, the way you look at it ... everything's got to be turned upside down?'

'Yes! We've got to throw out the government like a dirty old pair of pants. We've got to flay the hide off the gentlefolk because they've made life such a hell for the people.'

'And when you've got a new government, what will you do about the war? Men will still want to fight. If we don't want to, our children will. How can you put a stop to war? How can you destroy it, when men have fought all through the ages?'

'Ay, it's true there've been wars since time began, and they'll go on as long as there are blood-sucking governments in the world. That's how it is! But if each country had a workers' government, they wouldn't go to war with each other. That's what you've got to bring about. And that's what will happen, and to hell with 'em! It will be! The Germans and the French, they'll all have governments of workers and peasants. Why should we fight each other then? Down with frontiers! Down with hatred! Life all over the world will be beautiful. Ah!' Garanzha sighed,

369

bit the tip of his moustache, and with a gleam in his one eye smiled dreamily. 'Ah, Grisha, I'd give my blood drop by drop to see that day... My heart's burning to see it...'

They talked until daybreak. In the grey light of dawn Grigory fell into a restless sleep.

In the morning he was awakened by voices and the sound of weeping. Ivan Vrublevsky was lying face down on his bed, sobbing and snuffling; a nurse, Jan Vareikis and Kosykh were standing round him.

'What's he snivelling about?' Burdin grunted, poking his head out from under the covers.

'He's broken his eye. He was taking it out of the glass and dropped it on the floor,' Kosykh replied with more malicious satisfaction than sympathy.

A russified German, who ran a business in artificial eyes, had been moved by patriotic sentiments to supply the war wounded free of charge. Only the day before, a splendidly fashioned glass eye, as blue and handsome as any real one, had been selected for Vrublevsky. When it was put in, he had laughed and jumped for joy like a child.

'When I get home,' he said in his broad Vladimir accent, 'I'll catch the prettiest girl going. I'll marry her first, then confess I've got a glass eye!'

'He will and all, darn him!' laughed Burdin, who was always singing a ditty about a girl whose sarafan had been nibbled by a cockroach.

And now because of an unlucky accident the handsome young man would go back to his native village a one-eyed freak.

'They'll give you a new one, stop bawling,' Grigory comforted him.

'No, they won't. You know how much an eye costs—three hundred rubles. They won't give another.'

'And that one was a real beauty! It had every little vein drawn on it,' Kosykh kept on gloatingly.

After morning tea Vrublevsky drove with the assistant doctor to the German's shop and the German found another eye for him.

'The Germans are better than the Russians!' Vrublevsky enthused wildly. 'You'd get damn all out of a Russian merchant, but this one didn't say a word.'

September passed. Time counted the days with parsimonious care. They dragged out their endless length, filled with deathly boredom. At nine in the morning the tea came round and every patient was given two wafer-thin slices of French bread and a small finger of butter on a plate. After dinner they were still hungry. In the evening they drank more tea, taking sips of cold water in between for variety's sake. Patients came and went. The first to leave the 'military ward', as the ward for the wounded was called by the patients, was the Siberian Kosykh. He was followed by the Lett Vareikis. Grigory's turn came at the end of October.

Doctor Snegiryov, the handsome, neatly bearded owner of the hospital, tested Grigory's eyesight in a dark room with illuminated letters and figures and passed it as satisfactory. He was released from the eye hospital and sent to another in Tverskaya Street, because the wound on his head had unexpectedly opened and was slightly festered.

'Will we see each other again,' Grigory asked as he said goodbye to Garanzha.

'Mountains never meet, but we're men.'

'Well, Ukrainian, thanks for opening my eyes for me. I can see now and I've got a score to settle!'

'When you get back to your regiment, have a word or two with your Cossacks.'

'All right, I will.'

'And if you're ever down Chernigov way, near the village of Gorokhovka, ask for blacksmith Andrii Garanzha. I'll be glad to see you. Goodbye, lad!'

They hugged each other. And for a long time Grigory would remember the Ukrainian with that one stern eye and the friendly lines round his mouth and in his earthy cheeks.

Grigory spent about ten days in the other hospital. The corrosive venom of Garanzha's teaching was at work in his brain and he was wrestling with half-formed decisions. He hardly spoke to the other men in the ward and his troubled state of mind showed in every movement. 'Disturbed' was the conclusion reached by the head doctor who received him, as he ran a casual glance over Grigory's un-Russian face.

For the first few days Grigory was feverish and lay on his bed listening to the incessant ringing in his ears.

And it was at this time that the following incident occurred.

On his way home from Voronezh a distinguished member of the imperial family graciously condescended to visit the hospital. On being notified that morning, the hospital staff scuttled about like mice in a burning

371

barn. The wounded were dressed up as well as possible; those confined to bed were lifted and had their bed linen changed before it was due. A junior doctor went round trying to teach them how to answer His Highness and how to behave in his presence. The general alarm spread to the wounded, and some even dropped their voices to a whisper beforehand. At noon a motor-horn sounded at the entrance and, accompanied by the requisite number of persons in attendance, His Highness entered the doors of the hospital that had been flung open to greet him. (One of the wounded, a wag and practical joker, after-wards assured his mates that at the moment of the titled visitors' arrival the hospital's red-cross flag suddenly began to flap wildly, though the weather that day was exceptionally fine and windless, and that the elegantly coiffured gentleman on the sign of the barber's shop across the street bent over in a bow, or something like it.) The inspection began. The royal personage asked the kind of futile questions befitting his rank and the circum-stances; the wounded, on the advice of the junior doctor, made their eyes bulge even wider than they had been taught on the parade ground, and answered, 'Yes, Your Imperial Highness' and 'No, Your Imperial Highness'. Comments to their answers were supplied by the head of the hospital, who wriggled like a snake under a pitch-fork and looked a pitiful sight even from a distance. The royal personage went from bed to bed, giving out miniature ikons. The retinue of resplendent uniforms rolled towards Grigory in a wave of expensive perfume. He stood by his bed, unshaven, gaunt, his eyes bloodshot and inflamed, the tightly drawn skin on his prominent brown cheekbones quivering with an inner tension.

'Here they are, the ones for whose sakes we're driven from our homes and thrown to the slaughter. The rotten bastards! Bloodsuckers! Scum! These are the worst lice we've got on our backs!.. And this one! Was it to please him we rode over other folk's grain and killed people who'd done us no wrong? And I crawled through the stubble crying out in pain? And the fear? They took us from our families, starved us in their stinking barracks...' The thoughts whirled through his brain. Foaming anger convulsed his lips. 'How fat and sleek you all are! You ought to be sent out there, you bloody bastards! On horseback, with a rifle on your back, swarming with lice and fed on rotten bread and maggoty meat!'

Grigory scanned the sleek officers of the royal retinue

and fixed his fevered glance on the baggy cheeks of the royal personage.

'A Don Cossack, decorated with the St. George Cross,' the head of the hospital bent forward in an elaborate bow and imparted the information as if it were he himself who had earned the decoration.

'What stanitsa are you from?' the royal personage asked, holding an ikon ready.

'Vyoshenskaya, Your Imperial Highness.'

'How did you win your cross?'

Tedium and satiety lingered in the bright vacant eyes. The gingerish left eyebrow was raised in a movement designed to make the royal face more expressive. For a moment Grigory was aware of a sudden coolness and prickling in his chest; it was the feeling he always had in the first moment of a charge. His lips trembled and twitched uncontrollably.

'I... I think I want to... A call of nature, Your Imperial... Just a number one...' Grigory bent over like a broken stem and made a sweeping gesture under the bed.

The royal personage's left eyebrow reared vertically and the hand holding the ikon stopped half way. His pouting lip sagged in astonishment. He turned to the grey-haired general accompanying him and said something in English. A barely perceptible ripple of confusion passed over the suite. A tall officer with epaulettes touched his eye with a hand clad in a snow-white glove; another lowered his head, a third looked round questioningly at a fourth. Smiling respectfully, the grey-haired general reported something to His Highness in English and the personage graciously consented to place the ikon in Grigory's hands and even conferred upon him the highest favour of allowing his hands to touch his shoulder.

After the departure of the distinguished guests Grigory dropped on to his bed, buried his face in the pillow and lay with his shoulders shaking for several minutes. It was impossible to tell whether he was crying or laughing, but he rose with dry and much brighter eyes. He was immediately summoned to the head doctor's office.

'You scum!' the doctor began, crumpling his beard that was the colour of a moulting hare.

'Don't you call me scum, you bastard!' Grigory said, his lower jaw shaking as he strode up to the doctor. 'There's none of your lot at the front!' Mastering himself, he added with more restraint, 'Send me home!'

The doctor backed away behind his desk and said in

a controlled voice, 'We certainly shall. Go to the devil!'

Grigory went out with a trembling smile on his face and frenzy in his eyes.

For his monstrous and unforgivable antics in the royal presence the hospital administration deprived him of food for three days. He was fed by his fellow patients in the ward and by the soft-hearted cook, who suffered from a rupture.

XXIV

On the night of November 3rd, Grigory Melekhov arrived at Nizhnye-Yablonovsky, the first Cossack village on the road from the station. From there it was only a few dozen versts to the Yagodnoye estate. Grigory tramped past the scattered houses, rousing the dogs; among the riverside willows young, boyish voices were singing.

> *Through the trees, swords glinting, goes*
> *A squadron all with fine moustachios.*
> *An officer young rides at their head,*
> *By him an hundred Cossacks led.*

A powerful tenor began with resounding clarity:

> *Fear not, brothers, follow me!*

Then the well-attuned voices took up the refrain fiercely:

> *Up the ramparts rapidly!*
> *On him who first shall reach the foe*
> *Honours and glory we'll bestow!*

The familiar words of the old Cossack song that he himself had often sung wafted an inexplicable warmth and fondness into Grigory's heart. His eyes began to prick, his chest tightened. Eagerly drinking in the pungent dung smoke from the chimneys of the Cossack dwellings, Grigory walked through the village and the song followed him:

> *On the ramparts we stood our ground*
> *While bullets buzzed like bees all round.*

Than Cossacks of the Don none braver
When they charge with bayonet or sabre!

'It's a long time since I sang like that. Not since I was
a lad. Now my voice has dried up and life has cut short
my song. Here I am, going on leave to another man's
wife, without a home of my own, like a wolf in a ravine.'
Such were Grigory's thoughts as he tramped on with a
weary steadiness, mocking himself bitterly for the strange
course his life had taken. He climbed the sloping hill out
of the village and looked back. The yellow light of a lamp
showed in the window of the last house, where an elderly
Cossack woman was sitting at her spinning wheel.

Grigory stepped off the road and walked on over the
moistly brittle, frosted grass. He decided to spend the
night at the first village along the Chir, so as to reach
Yagodnoye before nightfall on the following day. It was
past midnight when he reached the village of Grachov.
He stopped at a house on the outskirts and left as soon
as the lilac morning dusk began to clear.

It was dark when he reached Yagodnoye. He jumped
silently over the fence and, as he walked past the stables,
heard Grandad Sashka coughing.

'Grandad Sashka, are you asleep?'

'Wait, who's that? I know that voice... Who be it?'

Old Sashka threw a coat over his shoulders and came
out into the yard.

'By all the saints! Grigory! Where the devil did you
spring from? That's a guest for you!'

They embraced. Sashka looked up into Grigory's eyes
and said, 'Come in and have a smoke.'

'No, tomorrow. I'd better go now.'

'Come in, I tell ye.'

Grigory reluctantly obeyed. He sat down on the plank
bed and waited for the old man to clear his throat.

'Well, Granfer, how're you getting on? Still alive and
kicking?'

'Jogging along. I'm like an old flintlock, I'll never wear
out.'

'How's Aksinya?'

'Aksinya... She's all right, thank the Lord.'

The old man broke in to a fit of coughing. Grigory
realised it was an attempt to hide his confusion.

'Where did you bury little Tanya?'

'In the orchard, under the poplar.'

'Well, and what else have you got to tell me?'

'I've got such a cough, Grigory. It's doing me in...'

'Come on now!'

'Everyone's well. The master, he's drinking... The stupid feller, he drinks beyond all reason.'

'How about Aksinya?'

'Aksinya? She's a maid now.'

'I know.'

'Why don't you make yourself a smoke? Eh? Have a smoke, I've got some first-rate 'baccy.'

'I don't want to. Come on, out with it, or I'll go. I feel...' Grigory turned heavily and the plank bed creaked under him, 'I feel you've got something to tell me and you're keeping it hidden, like a stone up your sleeve. Come on, strike!'

'And I will!'

'Strike!'

'I will strike. I can't hold it back, Grigory. It'd grieve me more to keep it from you.'

'Tell me then,' Grigory said, letting his hand fall fondly but with a rock-like heaviness on the old man's shoulder. He sat hunched and waiting.

'You've warmed a snake in your bosom!' Old Sashka burst out suddenly in a sharp falsetto, splaying his fingers in a strange gesture. A viper! She's been lying with Yevgeny! What d'you say to that?'

A sticky drop of spit crept down the pink groove on the old man's chin. He brushed it away and wiped his hand on his rough homespun underpants.

'Are you sure?'

'I saw it myself. He comes to her every night. Go and see, he'll be with her now, like as not.'

'So that's how it is...' Grigory clenched his fingers till the knuckles cracked, and sat for a long time with hunched shoulders trying to relax the convulsed muscles of his cheeks. A sound like harness bells was jangling in his ears.

'A woman's like a cat; she cuddles up to anyone who pets her. Don't trust 'em, don't put no faith in 'em!' Sashka told him.

He made a cigarette for Grigory, lighted it and pushed it into his hand.

'Have a smoke.'

Grigory drew twice at the cigarette, then stubbed it out between his fingers and left without another word. By the window of the servants' quarters he halted, breathing deep and fast. Several times he raised his hand to knock, then dropped it again as though his arm had broken. His first knock was restrained, with a bent finger, then he lost control and leaned against the wall, hammering furiously on the window frame. The frame shook and moaned with the sound of vibrating glass and the blue of the night trembled in the pane.

Grigory caught a glimpse of Aksinya's face, lengthened by fear. She opened the door and gave a cry. Grigory took her in his arms at once and gazed into her eyes.

'Oh, how you knocked! I was asleep... I never expected you... My dearest!'

'I'm cold.'

Aksinya felt the shivers running through Grigory's massive frame, and yet his hands were burning hot. She fussed about, lighting the lamp and hurrying about the room, a soft woollen shawl thrown over her plump glowing shoulders as she kindled a fire in the grate.

'I wasn't expecting you... It's such a long time since you wrote... I thought you wouldn't be coming... Did you get my last letter? I was going to send you some goodies, but then I thought I'd better wait. I might get a letter from him, I thought.'

She glanced up occasionally at Grigory. The stiff smile seemed to have congealed on her red lips.

Grigory sat on the bench without taking off his great-coat. His unshaven cheeks were flaming, his eyes hidden in the deep shadow of his hood. He was about to untie the hood, but instead, in a sudden fit of indecision he took out his pouch and rummaged in his pocket for paper. In utter misery he scanned Aksinya's face.

She had grown so much more beautiful during his absence.

Something new and imperious had appeared in the poise of that handsome head. Only the thick fluffy curls and the eyes were the same... But this irresistible, flaming beauty was not his. How could it be when she was the mistress of a gentleman's son.

'You ... you don't look like a maid. You're more like a housekeeper.'

She shot a frightened glance at him and forced a laugh.

Dragging his pack behind him, Grigory went to the door.

'Where are you going?'

'Outside, for a smoke.'

'The eggs are nearly ready, won't you wait?'

'I won't be a minute.'

On the porch Grigory opened his soldier's pack and took out an embroidered shawl carefully wrapped in a clean army shirt. He had bought it in Zhitomir from a Jewish street-trader for two rubles and had been guarding it like the apple of his eye. He would take it out while they were on the march, admire its flowing rainbow of colours and think of Aksinya's delight when he came home and showed her its glorious pattern. What a pitiful gift! How could Grigory rival the bounty of the son of the richest landowner on the upper Don? Stifling the dry sobs that rose to his throat, Grigory tore the shawl to shreds and stuffed them away under the steps, then threw the pack down on a bench and entered the room.

'Sit down and let me take your boots off, Grisha.'

With soft white hands that had grown unaccustomed to rough work Aksinya drew off Grigory's heavy soldier's boots and, clasping his knees, broke into long silent weeping. Grigory waited for her to finish, then asked, 'Why are you crying? Aren't you glad to see me?'

He was soon asleep.

Aksinya went out on to the porch without a coat and in the biting cold, with the funereal wail of the north wind in her ears stood clinging to a wet post and did not move until dawn.

In the morning Grigory put on his greatcoat and went to the house. The old general was standing on the porch, dressed in a fur jacket and a yellowed Astrakhan hat.

'Here he is, the knight of St. George. Well, you have grown into a real man, my good fellow!'

He saluted Grigory and held out his hand.

'Is it to be a long stay?'

'Two weeks, Your Excellency.'

'We have buried your daughter. A great pity.'

Grigory said nothing. Yevgeny had come out on the porch, pulling on his gloves.

'Grigory? Where have you sprung from?'

Everything went dark before Grigory's eyes, but he smiled.

'From Moscow. On leave.'

'So that's it. You were wounded in the eye, weren't you?'

'Yes.'

'I heard about that. What a fine fellow he's become—hasn't he, Father?' The lieutenant nodded to Grigory and turned away towards the stables. 'Nikitich, bring the horses!'

The dignified Nikitich finished adjusting the harness and, squinting with hostility at Grigory, led an old grey race-horse up to the porch. The ice-coated earth crunched under the wheels of the light droshky.

'Your Honour, allow me to drive you, for old time's sake?' Grigory made the request with an ingratiating smile.

'He suspects nothing, the poor fellow,' Yevgeny thought with a smile of satisfaction and his eyes gleamed through his pince-nez.

'Very well then, we'll go for a drive.'

'What's this? Are you abandoning your young wife when you've only just come home? Didn't you miss her?' the old general asked with a gracious twinkle.

Grigory laughed.

'A wife isn't a bear, she won't run away into the woods.'

He climbed on to the box, tucked the whip away under the seat and shook out the reins.

'Ah, I'll give you a fine ride, Yevgeny Nikolayevich!'

'You'll be well rewarded.'

'We have enough to thank you for as it is. For keeping my Aksinya like this and—feeding her.'

Grigory's voice broke suddenly and an unpleasant suspicion stirred in the lieutenant's mind. Surely he doesn't know? Nonsense! How could he! Impossible! He leaned back in his seat and lit a cigarette.

'Don't be long!' the old general shouted after them.

Frosty, needle-sharp dust spurted from under the wheels.

Grigory tore the horse's lips with the reins and lashed it to a gallop. In a quarter of an hour they were on the other side of the hill. In the first dip Grigory leapt down from the box and pulled the whip out from under the seat.

'What's this?' the lieutenant frowned.

'I'll show you what!'

Grigory gave a short swing of the whip and hit the lieutenant across the face with sickening force. Then, changing his grip, he used the handle on his face and arms, giving him no chance to recover. A splinter from the broken pince-nez cut Yevgeny above the eyebrow. Blood streamed down over his eyes. At first the lieutenant tried to protect his face with his hands, but the blows came faster and harder. He sprang up with his face disfigured by blood and anger and tried to defend himself, but Grigory stepped back and paralysed his right arm with a blow on the wrist.

'That's for Aksinya! That's for me! For Aksinya! And another for Aksinya! For me!'

The whip whistled and struck home with a soft slap. Then Grigory knocked the lieutenant down on the hard rutted road and dragged him about, kicking him brutally with the iron-tipped heels of his soldier's boots. When he had no more strength left, he jumped into the droshky and with a whoop lashed the horse into an exhausting gallop. At the gate he abandoned the carriage, bent the whip double and, stumbling over the skirts of his unbuttoned coat, ran to the servants' quarters.

Aksinya looked round as the door crashed open. 'Slut!.. Bitch!..'

The whip squealed and wrapped itself round her face.

Grigory ran out panting into the yard and, ignoring Sashka's questions, strode away from the estate. He had gone more than a mile before Aksinya caught up with him.

Panting violently, she walked at his side, trying to touch his hand.

At a fork in the road, beside a weathered steppeland shrine, she said in a strange, distant voice, 'Grisha, forgive me!'

Grigory showed his teeth in a snarl, hunched his shoulders, and turned up the collar of his greatcoat.

Aksinya was left standing by the shrine. Grigory walked on without a backward glance and did not see her hands stretched out imploringly after him.

As he walked down the hill into the village of Tatarsky he noticed in surprise that he was still carrying the whip. He flung it away and walked with long strides up the lane. Astonished faces were pressed to windows, the women he passed bowed low on recognising him.

At the gate of his own yard a dark-eyed young beauty flung herself headlong on to his neck and clung there. Gripping her cheeks between his hands, Grigory lifted her face and saw that it was Dunyashka.

Pantelei limped down from the porch, and in the house his mother broke into loud weeping. Grigory hugged his father with his left arm while Dunyashka kissed his right.

The steps gave a painfully familiar creak and Grigory was on the porch. His aged mother ran out like a girl, wept into his buttonholes and, holding her son as if she would never let go, babbled something that could not be expressed in words, while in the inner porch, clinging to the door post to stop herself falling, Natalya stood with a tortured smile on her pale face until she was cut down by Grigory's brief confused glance.

* * *

That night Pantelei nudged his wife and whispered, 'Take a quiet look. Have they gone to bed together or not?'

'I made the bed up for the two of them.'

'Go and have a look!'

Ilyinichna peeped through a crack in the door into the front room and came back.

'They're together.'

'Well, thank God! Thank God!' the old man raised himself on his elbow and made the sign of the cross, whimpering quietly.

BOOK TWO

BOOK TWO

PART FOUR

I

The year 1916. October. Night. Rain and wind. The
Pripet Marshes. Trenches above a bog overgrown with
alders. Barbed wire entanglements in front. Cold slush
in the trenches. The wet glimmering shield of an observation platform. Here and there a gleam of light
from the shelters. At the entrance to one of the officers' dug-outs a stockily built individual paused for a
minute, felt with wet fingers for the fastenings of his
greatcoat, hurriedly unbuttoned them, shook the water
off the collar, wiped his boots on a bunch of straw
stamped into the mud, and only then pushed open the
door, lowering his head as he entered.

A yellow pennant of light from a small kerosene lamp
cast an oily gleam on the face of the newcomer. An
officer in an unbuttoned leather jacket rose from a plank
bed, passed his hand over his tousled greying hair and
yawned.

'Is it raining?'

'It is,' his visitor replied, and hung up his greatcoat
and sodden cap on a nail by the door. 'It's warm in here.
You've worked up quite a fug.'

'We had the stove going. The worst thing is this sub-
soil water—it seeps in. The rain's making life a bloody
misery, damn it. Don't you think so, Bunchuk?'

Rubbing his hairy hands, Bunchuk hunched his shoulders and squatted by the stove.

'Put some boards down. Our dug-out's in splendid

shape. You could walk about barefoot. Where's Listnitsky?'

'Asleep.'

'Since when?'

'He turned in after making his rounds.'

'Isn't it time to wake him?'

'Go ahead. We'll have a game of chess.'

Bunchuk flicked the wet off his broad, thick eyebrows with his forefinger and called softly, without raising his head.

'Yevgeny Nikolayevich!'

'Still asleep,' the greyish-haired officer sighed.

'Yevgeny Nikolayevich!'

'Well, what is it?' Listnitsky raised himself on his elbow.

'Want a game of chess?'

Listnitsky swung his legs off the bed and sat rubbing his plump chest with the soft pink cushion of his palm.

As they were finishing the first game, two more officers came in—Major Kalmykov and Lieutenant Chubov of the Fifth Squadron.

'News!' Kalmykov exclaimed from the threshold. 'The regiment will in all probability be taken out of the line!'

'Where did that come from?' Captain Merkulov, the officer with greying hair, smiled incredulously.

'Don't you believe me, Uncle Petya?'

'To be quite frank, no.'

'The battery commander told me over the phone. How does he know? Of course, he does. He came back from divisional headquarters only yesterday.'

'I could do with a good steaming in a bath-house.'

Chubov smiled blissfully and went through the motions of whacking his buttocks with a bunch of birch-twigs. Merkulov laughed.

'All you need in this dug-out is a boiler—there's plenty of water.'

'Yes, you're very wet in here, gentlemen,' Kalmykov grumbled, surveying the log walls and the oozing earthen floor.

'There's a bog just outside.'

'Thank the Almighty that you're tucked away safely behind a bog,' Bunchuk broke into the conversation. 'If the ground was firm, we'd be attacking, but here we use about one clip of cartridges a week.'

'Attacking would be better than rotting alive in this hole.'

'That's not what they're keeping the Cossacks for,

Uncle Petya. They don't want them wiped out in attacks. Don't pretend you don't know that.'

'What do you think they're keeping them for then?'

'At the required moment the government will try, as usual, to solve its troubles with Cossack help.'

'That's nonsense,' Kalmykov waved the suggestion aside.

'Why so?'

'Because it is.'

'Oh, come now, Kalmykov. There's no point in denying the truth.'

'What truth?'

'It's public knowledge. Why pretend you don't know it?'

'Attention, please, gentlemen!' Chubov exclaimed and with a theatrical bow pointed to Bunchuk. 'Cornet Bunchuk will now recite to us from the Social-Democratic book of dreams.'

'Are you trying to be funny?' Bunchuk laughed drily, and his direct gaze forced the other to look away. 'Well, keep it up—every man has his calling. I say that we haven't seen anything of the war since the middle of last year. Ever since this positional warfare started, the Cossacks have been tucked away in safe corners and are being kept under wraps until such time as they are needed.'

'And what then?' Listnitsky asked, clearing away the chessmen.

'Then, when the discontent breaks out at the front—and that's inevitable, the men are getting tired of the war, as can be seen from the increasing number of deserters—then they'll bring in the Cossacks to put down the mutinies. The government is keeping the Cossack forces like a stone in a sling. When the time comes, it'll try to use that stone to crack the skull of the revolution.'

'You're going too far, my dear fellow!' Listnitsky retorted. 'Your assumptions are somewhat shaky. For a start, no one can predetermine the course of events. How do you know about these future outbreaks and so on? Suppose we make a different assumption -- that the Allies smash the Germans and the war is brought to a brilliant conclusion, then what role do you assign to the Cossacks?'

Bunchuk smiled thinly.

'It doesn't look very much like the end, and certainly not a brilliant one.'

'The campaign's hanging fire...'

'There'll be plenty of hanging,' Bunchuk promised.

'When did you come back from leave?' Kalmykov asked.

'The day before yesterday.'

Bunchuk rounded his lips, released a puff of smoke with his tongue, and threw away the butt of his cigarette.

'Where were you?'

'In Petrograd.'

'Well, how's the capital? Bursting with life? By God, what wouldn't I give to spend a week there?!'

'Not very encouraging,' Bunchuk replied, weighing his words carefully. 'Bread's in short supply. The working class districts are hungry, discontented; protest is brewing.'

'Something's going to happen before we get out of this war. What do you think, gentlemen?' Merkulov looked round inquiringly at the other officers.

'The Russo-Japanese war sparked off the revolution of 1905; this war will end in a new revolution. And not only revolution, but civil war.'

Listnitsky listened to Bunchuk and made a vague gesture, as if trying to interrupt the cornet, then rose and paced about the dug-out, frowning. When he spoke there was suppressed anger in his voice.

'What surprises me is that among our officers there are such'—a gesture at Bunchuk's hunched figure—'individuals. I find it surprising because it is still not clear to me what his attitude is to the Motherland, to the war... In conversation he once expressed himself very vaguely, but plainly enough for one to understand that he is in favour of our defeat in this war. Did I understand you rightly, Bunchuk?'

'I am in favour of defeat.'

'But why? As I see it, no matter what one's political views, to desire the defeat of one's country is ... treason. For any decent person it's complete dishonour!'

'Remember the Bolshevik group in the Duma was agitating against the government and thus contributing to defeat!' Merkulov intervened.

'Do you share their point of view, Bunchuk?' Listnitsky questioned.

'Of course, I share it if I advocate defeat, and it would be absurd for me, a member of the RSDLP, a Bolshevik, not to share the view of the party's parliamentary group. What I find far more surprising, Yevgeny Nikolayevich, is that an educated man like you should be politically ignorant.'

'Above all, I'm a soldier devoted to the monarch. The mere sight of the "socialist comrades" sets my teeth on edge.'

Bunchuk checked the smile that was hovering on his lips. Above all, you're an ass, and on top of that, a self-satisfied blimp, he thought to himself.

'There is no other god but Allah...'

'Army life's rather exceptional,' Merkulov put in almost apologetically. 'We have all tended to keep away from politics and treat it as none of our business.'

Major Kalmykov sat fingering his long, drooping moustache, a sharp glint in his fiery Mongolian eyes. Chubov lay on his bed listening to the conversation and examining a smoke-stained drawing by Merkulov that was pinned to the wall. A half-naked woman with the face of a Magdalene was looking down at her bare breast, smiling languidly and wantonly. With two fingers of the left hand she had lifted the brown nipple, little finger carefully crooked, her eyes glowing in the shadow of the lowered lashes. One shoulder was slightly raised to keep the strap of her slip from falling and the hollows formed by the collar-bones nursed soft pools of light. There was so much unaffected grace and truth in the woman's posture, the pastel shades were so expressive that Chubov's face broke into a smile of admiration and, though he heard what was being said, it no longer penetrated his consciousness.

'How very good!' he exclaimed, turning away at last from the drawing, and at a most unfortunate moment because Bunchuk had only just uttered the phrase, '...tsarism will be destroyed, you can be sure of that!'

Smiling caustically as he rolled his cigarette, Listnitsky looked now at Bunchuk, now at Chubov.

'Merkulov, you're a real artist!' Chubov blinked, as though dazzled.

'Oh, it's just a hobby...'

'We may lose a few hundred thousand soldiers but surely it's the duty of everyone who was nurtured by this soil to defend the Fatherland from subjugation.' Listnitsky lit a cigarette and, as he polished the lenses of his pince-nez with a handkerchief, looked expectantly at Bunchuk with short-sighted, unprotected eyes.

'The workers have no Fatherland,' Bunchuk punched

389

the phrase home. 'Those words of Marx contain a profound truth. We have no Fatherland and never have had! Patriotism is the breath of life for you! You were fed and nurtured by this cursed soil, but we ... grew like weeds, like wormwood on wasteland... You and we can't flourish together.'

He pulled a wad of papers out of his side pocket and rummaged through them, standing with his back to Listnitsky, then went up to the table and smoothed out a yellowed page from a newspaper with his big thick-veined hand.

'Will you listen?' he asked, turning to Listnitsky.

'What is it?'

'An article about war. I'll read part of it. I'm not very educated myself, I won't get it right. But it's all here, in a nutshell.'

' "...the socialist movement cannot win in the old framework of the Fatherland. It creates new, higher forms of human community, in which the legitimate needs and progressive aspirations of the working masses of every nationality will be satisfied for the first time in international unity, provided that the present national barriers are destroyed. To the attempts of today's bourgeoisie to divide and disunite the workers by means of hypocritical appeals for 'defence of the Fatherland' the politically conscious workers will reply with new and constantly repeated efforts to unite the workers of different nations in the struggle to overthrow the bourgeoisie of all nations.

' "The bourgeoisie is deluding the masses by disguising imperialist plunder with the old ideology of 'national war'. The proletariat exposes this trickery by proclaiming that the imperialist war should be turned into civil war. This was the slogan outlined by the Stuttgart and Basle resolutions, which had in mind not war in general but specifically this present war, and which spoke not of 'defence of the Fatherland' but of 'accelerating the collapse of capitalism', of using the crisis created by the war for this purpose, and of the example provided by the Paris Commune. The latter was an instance of a war between nations being transformed into a civil war. Of course, such a transformation is not easy and cannot be accomplished 'at the whim' of one party or another. But such a transformation is inherent in the objective conditions of capitalism in general, and the period of the end of capitalism in particular. It is in that direction and that direction alone that socialists must conduct their activities. It is not their business to vote for war credits or to encourage chauvinism in their 'own' country (and allied countries), but primarily to strive against the chauvinism of their 'own' bourgeoisie without confining themselves to legal forms of struggle when the crisis has matured and the bourgeoisie has itself repealed the legality it has created. Such is the line that leads to civil war and will bring about civil war at some point or other in the general European conflagration. War is not an accident, not a 'sin', as the Christian parsons think (who preach patriotism, humanity and peace no worse than the opportunists) but an inevitable stage of capitalism, just as legitimate a form of capitalist life as peace. Present-day war is a people's war. What follows from this truth is not that we must swim with the 'popular' current of chauvinism, but that the class contradictions dividing the nations continue to exist in wartime and manifest themselves in conditions of war. Refusal to serve with the forces, anti-war strikes, etc., are sheer nonsense, the miserable and cowardly dream of an unarmed struggle against the armed bourgeoisie, the vain yearning for the destruction of capitalism without a desperate civil war or series of wars. It is the duty of every socialist to conduct propaganda of the class struggle during wartime as well; work for the transformation of a war between nations into a civil war is the only socialist activity in the era of an imperialist armed conflict between the bourgeoisie of all nations. Down with the sanctimonious, sentimental and stupid sighs for 'peace at any price'! Let us raise the banner of civil war! Imperialism is gambling with the fate of European culture: this war will soon be followed by others unless there are a series of successful revolutions; the legend that this is the 'last war' is an empty and dangerous legend, a piece of petty-bourgeois mythology..." '

Bunchuk, who had been reading slowly and quietly, raised his deep cast-iron voice as he came to the last sentences and ended amid general strained attention, ' "If not today, then tomorrow, if not during the present war, then after it, if not in this war, then in the next, the proletarian banner of civil war will gather round it not only hundreds of thousands of class-conscious workers, but also the millions of semi-proletarians and petty-bourgeois now deluded by chauvinism, whom the horrors of war will not only frighten and depress, but also enlighten, teach, awaken, organise, harden and prepare for the war against the bourgeoisie of their 'own' and 'foreign' countries..." '

After a long silence Merkulov asked, 'That wasn't printed in Russia, was it?'

'No.'

'Where then?'

'In Geneva. It's from No 33 of *The Social Democrat* for 1914.'

'Who wrote it?'

'Lenin.'

'He's ... the leader of the Bolsheviks, isn't he?'

Bunchuk left the question unanswered; his fingers were trembling slightly as he folded the newspaper. Merkulov ruffled his greying hair and, without looking at the others, said, 'He has great power of persuasion... Damn it, but there's a lot there that makes you stop and think...'

Listnitsky spoke up heatedly. In his agitation he buttoned the collar of his shirt and, pacing rapidly from one corner of the dug-out to the other, poured out words like peas out of a sack.

'That article is a pitiful attempt by a man the Fatherland has expelled from its borders to influence the course of history. In our realistic times prophecy does not command success, especially prophecy of that kind! Any true Russian would ignore these hysterical ravings with contempt. Empty chatter! Turn a war between nations into a civil war. God, how despicable it all is!'

Listnitsky glanced at Bunchuk with a grimace of disgust. Bunchuk was rummaging in his sheaf of papers, head lowered, brows knitted; a swollen vein in his thick brown neck was pulsing rapidly. Listnitsky blurted out his phrases fiercely, but his low soft voice made no impression.

'Bunchuk!' Kalmykov exclaimed. 'Wait a minute, Listnitsky!... Bunchuk, d'you hear?... All right, let's suppose that this war turns into a civil war. What then? All right, you overthrow the monarchy. What kind of government do you want then? What kind of power?'

'The power of the proletariat.'

'Parliament, you mean?'

'You're not going far enough,' Bunchuk smiled.

'What precisely then?'

'There must be a workers' dictatorship.'

'So that's it!.. And what about the intellectuals, the peasants? What role will they play?'

'The peasantry will follow us. So will some of the thinking intellectuals. As for the rest... This is what we'll do with them!' With a flick of the wrist Bunchuk crumpled a piece of paper that he happened to be holding and shook it, then ground out through his teeth, 'That's what we'll do!'

'You're flying high,' Listnitsky said sarcastically.

'And we'll land high,' Bunchuk countered.

'You'd better spread some straw beforehand.'

'Why the devil did you volunteer for the front and even take the trouble to earn yourself a commission? How does that fit in with your views? How very strange! The man is against war, against the destruction of his—what do you call them?—his class brothers, and suddenly he becomes an officer!'

Kalmykov slapped his boots and laughed heartily.

'How many German workers have you and your machine-gunners disposed of?' Listnitsky asked.

Bunchuk rummaged through his bundle of papers and, still leaning over the table, said, 'How many German workers have I gunned down, that's ... a question. I volunteered because I'd have been called up anyway. I think the knowledge I've gained here in the trenches will come in useful in the future... Yes, in the future. Listen to what it says here. "Take the army of today. It is a good example of organisation. This organisation is good only because it is *flexible* and is able at the same time to give millions of people *a single will*. Today these millions are living in their homes in various parts of the country; tomorrow mobilisation is ordered, and they report for duty. Today they live in the trenches, and this may go on for months; tomorrow they are led to the attack in another order. Today they perform miracles in sheltering from bullets and shrapnel; tomorrow they perform miracles in hand-to-hand combat. Today their advance detachments lay minefields; tomorrow they advance scores of miles guided by airmen flying overhead. When, in the pursuit of a single aim and animated by a single will, millions alter the forms of their communication and their behaviour, change the place and the mode of their activities, change their tools and weapons in accordance with the changing conditions and the requirements of the struggle — all this is genuine organisation.

' "The same holds true for the working-class struggle against the bourgeoisie. Today there is no revolutionary situation..." '

'What do you mean by "situation"?' Chubov interrupted.

Bunchuk started as if he had just been wakened from a dream, and rubbed his big bulging forehead with the knuckle of his thumb, trying to understand the question.

'I asked you what you mean by the word "situation"?'

'You see, I understand what it means, but I can't explain it properly...' Bunchuk's face broke into an innocent, boyish smile that looked strange on that big gloomy face, like a young light-grey hare frolicking across a dreary, rainswept autumn field. 'A situation means what is happening at the moment, the way things are. Isn't that it?'

Listnitsky shook his head vaguely.

'Read on.'

' "Today there is no revolutionary situation, the conditions that cause unrest among the masses or heighten their activities do not exist; today you are given a ballot paper—take it, learn to organise so as to use it as a weapon against your enemies, not as a means of getting cushy legislative jobs for men who cling to their parliamentary seats for fear of having to go to prison. Tomorrow your ballot paper is taken from you and you are given a rifle or a splendid and most up-to-date quick-firing gun—take this weapon of death and destruction, pay no heed to the mawkish snivellers who are afraid of war; too much still remains in the world that must be destroyed with fire and sword for the emancipation of the working class; if anger and desperation grow among the masses, if a revolutionary situation arises, prepare to create new organisations and *use* these useful weapons of death and destruction *against* your *own* government and your *own* bourgeoisie..." '

Bunchuk was interrupted by a knock and the entry of the sergeant-major of the Fifth Squadron.

'Your Honour,' he said to Kalmykov, 'there's an orderly here from regimental headquarters.'

Kalmykov and Chubov put on their greatcoats and left. Merkulov, whistling softly to himself, sat down to draw. Listnitsky continued to pace about the dug-out, plucking at his moustache and pondering over something. Presently Bunchuk also took his leave. He made his way along the mud-choked communication trench, holding his collar with his left hand and the skirts of his great-coat with his right. The wind hosed the narrow passage, splashing over the steps, whistling and whirling. Bunchuk smiled vaguely to himself as he walked along in the darkness. By the time he reached his dug-out he was again saturated with damp and the smell of rotting alder leaves. The commander of the machine-gun platoon was asleep. His dark black-moustached face was haggard (he had been gambling at cards for three nights running). Bunchuk rummaged in the soldier's pack that he had kept since his days in the ranks, went to the door with a bunch of papers and burnt them, slipped two tins of meat and several handfuls of revolver cartridges into his trousers' pockets, and went out. The wind burst in as he opened the door, scattering the grey ash from the papers he had burnt on the threshold and extinguishing the smoking lamp.

After Bunchuk had left, Listnitsky paced his dug-out for another five minutes in silence, then went up to the table. Merkulov was drawing, his head tilted to one side. His fine-pointed pencil moved across the sheet, shading in smoky shadows, and Bunchuk's face, creased by its habitual withdrawn, almost forced smile, looked up from the white square of paper.

'It's a strong face,' Merkulov said, holding the drawing away from him and turning to Listnitsky.

'Well, what do you think?' asked the other.

'Damned if I know!' Merkulov replied, guessing what the question was about. 'He's a strange fellow. Things are much clearer now that he's explained himself, but I didn't know what to make of him before. He's enormously popular with the Cossacks, you know, specially the machine-gunners. Haven't you noticed that?'

'Yes,' Listnitsky replied non-committally.

'The machine-gunners are Bolsheviks to a man. That's his work. I was surprised that he put his cards on the table. Why? Just to spite us, I suppose! He knows that none of us can possibly share these views, but for some reason he opened up. Though he's by no means a hothead. He's a dangerous man.'

While discussing Bunchuk's strange behaviour, Merkulov put the drawing aside and began to undress. He hung his damp socks on the stove, wound up his watch, finished his cigarette, and turned in. Soon he was asleep. Listnitsky sat down on the stool where Merkulov had been sitting a quarter of an hour before, and on the other side of the drawing, breaking the sharp tip of the pencil, scrawled the following message.

Your Excellency,

The suppositions which I previously conveyed to you have now been fully confirmed. Cornet Bunchuk in a conversation that took place today with the officers of our regiment (Major Kalmykov and Lieutenant Chubov of the Fifth Squadron and Captain Merkulov of the Third, were also present besides myself), and for reasons that I must confess are still not altogether clear to me, explained the tasks that he is performing in accordance with his political beliefs and probably on the instructions of his party leadership. He was carrying on his person a bundle of papers of a forbidden character. For instance, he read out excerpts from his party newspaper *The Social Democrat*, published in Geneva. Cornet Bunchuk is undoubtedly engaged in underground activities in our regiment (it has been suggested that this was his reason for volunteering in the first place), and the machine-gunners have been the direct target of his agitation. They are thoroughly disaffected. His pernicious influence has affected the morale of the regiment as a whole. There have been cases of refusal to carry out orders, of which I have already informed the divisional special department.

Cornet Bunchuk recently returned from leave (in Petrograd) amply supplied with subversive literature; he will now try to step up his activities.

In view of the foregoing I have reached the following conclusions: (a) Cornet Bunchuk's guilt is fully established (the officers present during the conversation will confirm my information under oath); (b) to stop his revolutionary activities he must be arrested and brought before a field court-martial; (c) the machine-gun platoon must be screened at once; the most dangerous men among them should be taken in charge and the rest taken out of the line or dispersed among other regiments.

I beg you not to overlook my sincere desire to serve my country and the Monarch. A copy of this letter has been forwarded to S.T. Korp.

Major *Yevg. Listnitsky*.

No 7 Sector,
20 October 1916

The following morning Listnitsky sent his report to divisional headquarters by special messenger, ate his breakfast and left the dug-out. Beyond the slimy wall of the parapet a mist was hovering over the marsh; tattered fragments clung to the wire as if caught on the barbs. The liquid mud at the bottom of the trench was a good inch deep; brown rivulets were flowing from the gun ports. Cossacks in wet muddy greatcoats were boiling up tea on the iron shields from the parapets; some were squatting on their haunches, smoking, their rifles propped against the trench wall.

'How many times have you been told not to light fires on the shields! Don't you understand anything, you swine?' Listnitsky shouted angrily as he reached the first group of Cossacks sitting round their smoky fire.

Two men rose reluctantly; the others stayed as they were, holding up the skirts of their greatcoats. A dark, bearded Cossack with a silver ear-ring dangling from one wrinkled lobe replied as he pushed a handful of twigs under the pot.

'We'd be only too glad to do without 'em, Your Honour, but how can ye light a fire? Look at the water all round!'

'Remove that shield at once!'

'Are we to go hungry then?! Is that it?' a Cossack with smallpox scars on his broad face said frowning and looking away.

'None of your insolence! Remove that shield!' Listnitsky flicked the burning twigs from under the pot with the toe of his boot.

The bearded Cossack with the ear-ring gave a smile that was half a scowl as he tipped the hot water away.

'You've had your tea, boys,' he muttered.

The Cossacks watched the major walk away down the line. Fiery glow-worms trembled in the bearded one's moist glance.

'He spat on us, the bastard!'

Another gave a long sigh as he slung his rifle on to his shoulder.

In the Forth Troop's sector Listnitsky was overtaken by Merkulov. He came up panting, his new leather jacket creaking slightly, his breath staled by heavy smoking. He took Listnitsky aside and breathed hurriedly in his ear.

'Heard the news? Bunchuk deserted last night.'

'Bunchuk? Wha-a-at?'

'He deserted... Ignatich, the commander of the machine-gun platoon — he's in the same dug-out as Bunchuk —says he didn't come in last night. So he must have cleared out as soon as he left us.'

Listnitsky stood polishing his pince-nez and frowning.

'You seem upset?' Merkulov eyed him closely.

'I? Upset? Are you quite sane? Why should I be? I'm simply surprised.'

II

The next morning an embarrassed sergeant-major came to Listnitsky's dug-out, coughed nervously, and made his report.

'This morning some of the Cossacks, Your Honour, found these papers in the trenches. It's a bit awkward like. So I thought I'd better report it to you. Otherwise we might find ourselves in trouble.'

'What papers?' Listnitsky asked, rising from his bunk.

The sergeant-major held out a fistful of crumpled pamphlets.

The typewritten text stood out clearly on the sheets of cheap paper. Listnitsky's eyes raced through it.

Workers of all countries, unite!

COMRADE SOLDIERS!

This cursed war has been going on for two years! For two years you have been rotting in the trenches, defending interests that are alien to you. Hundreds of thousands of men killed and disabled, hundreds of thousands of orphans and widows—such are the results of this slaughter. What are you fighting for? Whose interests are you defending? The tsarist government has put millions of soldiers under fire in order to seize new lands and oppress the populations of these lands, as it oppresses enslaved Poland and other nationalities. The industrialists of the world cannot come to terms over the available markets for the goods produced by their factories and mills; they cannot agree about the profits—the carve-up is being carried out by armed force—and you, ignorant souls, are going to your deaths in the struggle for their interests, and killing other toilers like yourselves.

Enough of your brothers' blood has been shed! Working people, come to your senses! Your enemy is not the Austrian and German soldier, who is just as deluded as you, but your own tsar, your own industrialist and landowner. Turn your rifles against them. Fraternise with the German and Austrian soldiers. Reach out through the wire fences with which they have caged you off from one another like wild beasts. You are brothers in toil, your hands still bear the bloody callouses of your toil, you have nothing to go to war about. Down with the autocracy! Down with the imperialist war! Long live the unbreakable unity of the working people of the whole world!

Listnitsky was panting by the time he read the final lines. Now it's started, he thought, overcome by hatred and foreboding. He telephoned the regimental commander and informed him of what had happened.

'What are your orders, Your Excellency?' he asked in conclusion.

Through a mosquito-like hum and distant buzzing the general's words came over the line in clipped phrases.

'Take the sergeant-major and the troop officers. Make an immediate search. Of the whole regiment, including the officers. I'll ask divisional headquarters today when they intend relieving the regiment. I'll tell them to hurry. Inform me at once if you find anything.'

'I think it's the work of the machine-gunners.'

'Do you? Then I'll order Ignatich at once to search his Cossacks. Good-day, Major.'

Listnitsky assembled the troop officers in his dug-out and told them the regimental commander's orders.

'But this is preposterous!' Merkulov burst out indignantly. 'Are we expected to search each other?'

'Your turn first, Listnitsky!' young, beardless Lieutenant Razdortsev called out.

'Let's draw lots.'

'Take us in alphabetical order.'

'Joking aside, gentlemen,' Listnitsky interrupted sternly. 'The Old Man is going too far, of course. The officers in our regiment are above suspicion. There was only Cornet Bunchuk and he has deserted; but the Cossacks will have to be searched. Call the sergeant-major.'

The sergeant-major, an elderly Cossack with three St. George crosses, came in, gave a cough, and looked round at the officers.

'Who are the suspicious characters in your squadron? Who do you think might have been distributing these proclamations?' Listnitsky asked him.

'None in our squadron, Your Honour,' the sergeant-major replied confidently.

'But the proclamation was found in your squadron's sector. What strangers have been visiting your trenches?'

'There ain't been anyone from the other squadrons.'

'We'd better go and comb through the lot,' Merkulov declared with a wave of dismissal, and made for the door.

The search began. The Cossacks' faces expressed various feelings. Some frowned sullenly, others sent scared looks at the officers rummaging in their scanty Cossack kit, others chuckled quietly to themselves. A jaunty young sergeant, a patrol leader, asked, 'Why don't you tell us what you're looking for? If something's been stolen, maybe someone's seen it.'

The search yielded no results, except for the crumpled sheet that one Cossack of the First Troop was found to be carrying in his pocket.

'Did you read this?' Merkulov asked, dropping the sheet in a comic display of fright.

'I picked it up to make a fag with,' the Cossack smiled without raising his eyes.

'What are you grinning at?' Listnitsky shouted hotly, turning purple as he bore down on the Cossack; his short golden eyelashes were twitching nervously under his pince-nez.

The smile vanished from the Cossack's face, as if swept away by the wind.

'Beg pardon, Your Honour! I can hardly read. I only picked it up because there's no paper to make a fag with. I had the baccy but no paper. That's why I picked it up.'

The Cossack's voice was loud with resentment and under the resentment there was bitterness.

Listnitsky spat and walked away. The officers trailed after him.

A day later the regiment was withdrawn from its positions and sent back some ten versts into the rear. Two men of the machine-gun platoon were arrested and court-martialled and the rest were transferred either to the reserve or to regiments of the Second Cossack Division. During its few days' rest the regiment recovered some of its smartness. The Cossacks steamed the dirt off themselves and shaved properly, and not as they had done in the trenches, where a simple but painful method of removing the hair from their cheeks, known as 'pig-singeing', was commonly in use. The beard was lighted with a match and a wetted towel applied as soon as the flames reached the skin.

'Want a pig-singe or how?' the troop barber would ask his client.

During this period of rest the Cossacks looked outwardly smarter and more cheerful, but Listnitsky, and the other officers as well, knew that this cheerfulness was like fine weather in autumn—here today and gone tomorrow. At the mere mention of a return to the trenches their expressions changed and discontent and sullen animosity oozed from under their lowered eyelids. They seemed tired to death, strained beyond breaking-point, and this weariness broke their morale. Listnitsky knew only too well how terrible a man in such a state could be when possessed of an aim.

In 1915 he himself had seen a company go into the attack five times, suffering appalling losses, only to receive the order that the attack was to be renewed. The remnants of the company left their sector of their own accord and made for the rear. Listnitsky and his squadron were ordered to stop them, and when he lined up his troops to do so, they were fired upon. There were not more than sixty men left out of the whole company and he saw the crazed desperation and daring with which they defended themselves from the Cossacks, dying under their sabres but flinging themselves to their destruction in the knowledge that they must die anyway.

The incident had stayed with him as a grim reminder and, as he studied the Cossack's faces anxiously and with fresh eyes, he asked himself, 'Will these turn on us too one day, so that nothing but death will stop them?' And at the sight of those weary, embittered glances, he knew that the honest answer was yes.

A fundamental change had come over the Cossacks. Even their songs were new, born of the war and tinged with a black despair. In the evenings, as he passed the big factory shed where the squadron was quartered, the song Listnitsky heard most frequently was an inexpressibly sad lament. It was always sung by three or four voices. The pure tenor of the second part would soar up vibrantly over the richly flowing basses:

> *Oh, dearest land where I was born,*
> *Oh, land where I belong,*
> *Never more I'll see you, never hear at dawn*
> *The nightingale's awakening song.*
> *And you, dear Mother mine,*
> *Don't grieve so sore,*
> *My dearest, never pine,*
> *We can't all be killed in t'war.*

Listnitsky would stop and listen, feeling that he too was moved by the song's simple grief. A string tautened in his heart and the low tones of the descant plucked at this string, making it throb painfully. Listnitsky stood at a distance from the shed, staring into the autumnal gloom of evening and felt the sweet sting of tears on his eyelids.

> I ride and I ride o'er the open field
> And my heart, it tells me for sure,
> It tells of the fate, a fate that is sealed—
> Of a brave lad who'll come back no more.

While the basses were still holding the final words, the descant soared over them and the sounds, fluttering like a white-breasted bustard in flight, hastily told this story:

> Fast the leaden bullet sped,
> It pierced my breast right through.
> Forward I fell on my horse's head
> And bloodied his black mane red.

Only once while the regiment was resting did Listnitsky hear the stirring words of an old Cossack song. As he walked past the shed on his usual evening stroll, he heard the sounds of half-tipsy voices and laughter and guessed that the quartermaster had been on a trip to the township of Nesviska, brought back some moonshine and treated the Cossacks. With plenty of rye vodka inside them the Cossacks were arguing and laughing about something or other. On his way back, while still at a distance, Listnitsky heard the thunder of the song and the wild, piercing but rhythmical whistles:

> The man who's never been to war
> Hasn't seen what horrors are.
> Soaked by day, at night we shiver,
> All night long no sleep whatever.

The whistles spiralled up in a steady vibrating flow and were drowned in the blare of at least thirty voices:

> There's fear and grief at every turn,
> Every day and every hour.

One lively fellow, evidently a youngster, was giving short deafening whistles as he thumped his heels on the wooden floor. Their beat sounded clearly through the blare of the song:

> *Amid the roaring Black Sea waves*
> *Our fleet's ablaze, ablaze, ablaze.*
> *Fires we damp out,*
> *Turks we stamp out,*
> *Glory to our Cossack braves!*

A smile came involuntarily to Listnitsky's lips and he tried to fall into step with the beat of the song. Was the yearning for home as strong among the infantry, he asked himself. But reason objected coldly. Why should they be any different? Certainly the Cossacks reacted more painfully to enforced idleness in the trenches—the very nature of their service had accustomed them to being constantly on the move. But for two years now they had been forced to lie low or waste their strength in fruitless efforts to advance. The army was weaker than it had ever been before. It needed a strong hand, success, a great drive forward—that would shake it out of its lethargy. History could provide examples of long wars when even the most steadfast and disciplined troops had become demoralised. Even Suvorov had experienced that. But the Cossacks would hold out. If they did leave the front, they would be the last to do so. After all, they were a small, isolated nation, warlike by tradition, not just a mob of peasants or factory hands. As if deliberately to disillusion him, a strained uncertain voice from the shed began to sing *Snowball-Tree*. Other voices joined in and as he walked away Listnitsky again heard the same Cossack yearning, translated into song:

> *The young officer prays to God,*
> *The young Cossack begs to go home:*
> *'Oh, young officer,*
> *'Let me go home,*
> *'Let me go home*
> *'To my father.*
> *'To my father and mother,*
> *'To my father and mother,*
> *'And to my young wife.'*

In the evening, three days after he had deserted, Bunchuk reached a large merchant town in the frontline zone. Lights were on in the houses. Frost had spread a thin crust of ice over the puddles and the footsteps of the few people who were still about could be heard from afar. Bunchuk listened intently as he walked into the town, avoiding the lighted streets and making his way along the deserted back-lanes. On the outskirts he had nearly run into a patrol and now he moved with wolf-like haste, hugging the fences and keeping his right hand in the pocket of his filthy greatcoat; he had spent the day hiding in a barn, buried in a heap of chaff.

An army corps had its supply base in the town and various units were stationed there. There was always a risk of running into a patrol, so Bunchuk's hairy fingers were constantly pressed to the ribbed butt of the revolver in his greatcoat pocket.

On the other side of the town Bunchuk walked several times up and down a deserted side-street, glancing in at the gates and studying the shape of each poverty-stricken little dwelling. After about twenty minutes he approached a shabby house on the corner, peeped through a crack in the shutters, smiled, and resolutely entered the gate. His knock was answered by an elderly woman in a shawl.

'Does Boris Ivanovich lodge with you?' Bunchuk asked.

'Yes. Come in, please.'

Bunchuk squeezed past the woman and heard behind him the cold clank of the door-latch. In the low-ceilinged room lighted by a tiny lamp an elderly man in military uniform was seated at a table. He peered frowningly for a moment, then rose and with restrained joy held out his hands to Bunchuk.

'Where are you from?'

'The frontline.'

'Well!'

'And now I'm here...' Bunchuk smiled and, touching the other man's uniform belt with his finger-tip, said quietly, 'Have you a room?'

'Yes, certainly. Come this way.'

He led Bunchuk into an even smaller room; without lighting the lamp, he gave him a chair, closed the door behind him, pulled the curtain and said, 'Are you through now?'

'Yes.'

'How're things out there?'
'Everything's ready.'
'Lads you can trust?'
'Definitely.'

'I think you'd better take those clothes off, then we'll have a talk. Give me your greatcoat. I'll bring you something to wash with.'

While Bunchuk was washing his hands and face over a mildewed-green copper basin, the man in uniform stroked his cropped hair and spoke in a quiet, tired voice:

'At present they're far stronger than we are. What we have to do is grow, extend our influence, work tirelessly to explain the true causes of the war. And we are growing—you can be sure of that. All who leave them inevitably come to us. Any grown man is stronger than a boy, but when that man grows feeble with age, the boy will do away with him. And what we see in this case is not just senility, but a progressive paralysis of the whole organism.'

Bunchuk finished washing and, as he rubbed his face with the rough towel, said, 'Before I left I told those officer fellows my views. It was rather funny. Now I've gone, they're bound to give the machine-gunners a shaking up. Some of the lads may be court-martialled, but what can they do if there's no evidence? I hope they'll scatter them. That'll play into our hands; let the seed fall on fresh soil... There're some fine lads there! Hard as nails!'

'I've had a note from Stepan. He wants me to send him someone who knows about warfare. You're the man for him. But how about identification papers? Can we manage it?'

'What's the job?' Bunchuk asked, reaching up to hang the towel on a nail.

'Training the youngsters. You still haven't grown any taller, eh?' his host smiled.

'No reason to,' Bunchuk retorted. 'Specially in my present position. I'd better stay short and not be noticed.'

They talked until the grey dawn. A day later Bunchuk, disguised and made up so that he was quite unrecognisable, and carrying papers in the name of one Nikolai Ukhvatov, a soldier of the 441st Orsha Regiment, invalided out of the army on account of a chest wound, walked out of town and headed for the station.

III

On the Vladimir-Volynsk and Kovel sectors, in the area of operations of the Special Army (it was the thirteenth of the Russian armies, but since 'thirteen' was an unlucky number and even generals are superstitious, a different designation was deemed appropriate), preparations for an offensive were launched towards the end of September. A convenient springboard for the attack was chosen near the village of Svinukha and the artillery softening-up began.

By this time the front was so jam-packed with death-dealing weapons of war that enormous effort and monstrous sacrifices of human life were needed to make the slightest impression on its outline. An unprecedented quantity of artillery had been assembled. For nine days hundreds of thousands of shells of various calibre pounded an area occupied by two lines of German trenches. On the very first day, as soon as the barrage began, the Germans withdrew from the first line, leaving only observers in the trenches. A few days later they abandoned the second line and withdrew to the third.

On the tenth day, infantry units of the Turkestan Corps attacked. The attack was launched by the French method—in waves. Sixteen waves splashed out of the Russian trenches. Heaving, thinning, surging up round the ugly bunches of blasted wire entanglements, the grey billows of this human tide rolled forward. And from the German side, from behind the charred stumps of a blue-grey alder scrub and the battered sandy earthworks a crackling, roaring inferno of rifle and gun fire shook the air and ground.

Occasionally a salvo from one particular battery would interrupt the general uproar, then the firing would flare up again over the whole area.

Ratt-a-tat-a-tat-tat the German machine-guns chattered in mad haste.

The whirling pillars of explosions rose from the torn sandy earth over an area nearly a mile across and the attacking waves broke up and fell back from the shell-holes like foaming surf, then surged forward again.

More and more often the earth was churned up by black shell-bursts, the attacking troops were blasted ever more intensely by whining shrapnel, and machine-gun fire swept even lower and more fiercely across the battlefield. Most of the attackers were mown down even before they reached the wire. Out of sixteen waves only the last three got as far as the charred uprooted posts and heaps of tangled wire, broke against them, recoiled and flowed back in mere trickles and droplets... More than nine thousand lives were splashed out that day on to the desolate sandy soil round the village of Svinukha.

Two hours later the offensive was renewed. Units of the 2nd and 3rd divisions of the Turkestan Rifle Corps were thrown into action. Units of the 53rd Infantry Division and the 307th Siberian Rifle Brigade were brought up along communication trenches to the left, while battalions of the 3rd Grenadier Division advanced on the Turkestan right flank.

At this point Lieutenant-General Gavrilov, commander of the 30th Army Corps of the Special Army, received from Army H. Q. an order to transfer two divisions to the Svinukha area. That night the 320th Chembarsky, the 319th Bugulminsky and the 318th Chernoyarsky regiments of the 80th Division were withdrawn from their positions and replaced by Latvian rifles and newly arrived volunteer units. The manoeuvre was to take place at night, but only that evening one of the regiments had been demonstratively moved in another direction, and not until it had marched twelve versts along the frontline did it receive the order to turn back. The regiments of the 80th Division were all moved in the same direction but along different roads. On their left the 283rd Pavlograd and the 284th Węgrów regiments of the 71st Division were also on the march, closely followed by a regiment of Urals Cossacks and the 44th dismounted Cossack Regiment.

Before being transferred, the 318th Chernoarsky Regiment had been stationed on the River Stok od, in the neighbourhood of the small town of Sokal and not far from the Rudka-Merinskoye estate. After marching all night the regiment was quartered in some abandoned shelters in a forest. For four days it was trained in the French method of attacking in half-companies instead of battalions. The Grenadiers were taught the quickest way of cutting wire entanglements and given a fresh course in grenade-throwing. Then the regiment was again moved on. For three days they marched through forests and clearings, and along remote overgrown cart-tracks rutted by artillery. Thin, cotton-like mist floated with the wind, catching on the tops of the pine-trees, drifting across the clearings, and hovering over the bluish green of the warm marshes, as a kite hovers over a dead carcass. A rainy murk seeped out of the sky. The men marched on and on, soaked to the skin and in a bitter mood. After three days they halted not far from the zone of the offensive, in the villages of Big and Little Porek. There they rested for a day, preparing for the road of death.

Meanwhile a special Cossack squadron escorting the staff of the 80th Division was also approaching the scene of action. The squadron was made up partially of third-line reserves from the village of Tatarsky. The Second Troop consisted entirely of Tatarsky men: Martin and Prokhor Shamil, the two brothers of one-armed Alexei, Ivan Alexeyevich Kotlyarov, the former engineman at Mokhov's mill, gap-toothed Afonka Ozerov, the former village ataman Manytskov, the Shamils' bow-legged neighbour Yevlanty Kalinin, the tall and gawky Borshchev, the short-necked, bear-like Zakhar Korolyov, and the merriest man in the whole squadron Gavrila Likhovidov, an unusually brutal-looking Cossack, who unprotestingly endured constant beatings from his seventy-year-old mother and his plain-faced but spirited wife; many more Tatarsky men were to be found in this and other troops of the squadron. Some of the Cossacks were serving as orderlies for the divisional staff, but on October 2nd they were replaced by Uhlans and on the instructions of General Kitchenko, the divisional commander, the squadron was dismounted and sent into the line.

Early in the morning on October 3rd the squadron marched into the village of Little Porek, just when the First Battalion of the 318th Chernoyarsky Regiment was leaving it. The infantrymen were running out of the abandoned half-ruined houses and forming up in the street. A swarthy young ensign was hanging about beside the leading platoon. He took a bar of chocolate out of his map-case (his moist, bright-pink lips were already rimmed with chocolate), unwrapped it and paced along the column, his long threadbare greatcoat with its mud-caked skirts flapping between his legs, like a sheep's tail. The Cossacks were marching along the left-hand side of the street, and Kotlyarov was in the right-hand file. He was looking down carefully at his feet and trying to step over the puddles. A voice called to him from the infantry and he turned his head to glance at their ranks.

'Ivan Alexeyevich! Old pal!'

A little soldier broke away from his platoon and came trotting towards him, flat-footed as a duck. He kept hoisting his rifle over his shoulder as he ran, but the sling slipped and the butt thumped dully on his drinking mug.

'Don't you recognise me? Have you forgotten?'

In the little soldier whose face was covered right up to the cheekbones with a prickly smoky-grey stubble Ivan managed with some difficulty to identify Knave.

'Where did you spring from, laddie?'

'Can't you see? I'm in the army.'

'What regiment?'

'The 318th Chernoyarsky. I never thought ... never had a hope of meeting any of our lot.'

Ivan clasped Knave's small grimy hand in his big rough palm and held it, smiling joyfully. Knave again broke into a trot to keep up with his long strides. He gazed up into Ivan's face and the look in his spiteful, close-set eyes was unusually soft and moist.

'We're going up for the offensive.'

'So are we.'

'How are you, Ivan Alexeyevich?'

'What's the good of talking!'

'That's how I feel too. Haven't been out of the trenches since 'fourteen. I never had a home or family myself, but here I am busting my guts out for somebody's sake. The foal just follows the mare's tail.'

'D'you remember Stokman? Our dear Osip Davydovich! He'd tell us what it's all about. What a man he was, eh? What a man, eh?'

'Yes, he'd have sorted it out!' Knave exclaimed enthusiastically, shaking his small fist and wrinkling his narrow hedgehog face in a smile. 'I remember him better than my own father. Never thought much of my father... You never heard what happened to him, did you?'

'He's in Siberia,' Ivan sighed. 'Doing time.'

'What?' Knave questioned, hopping along like a tom-tit beside his big companion and cupping his hand under a gristly pointed ear.

'He's in prison. He may be dead by now.'

Knave walked for a while in silence, glancing now back to where his company had formed up, now at Ivan's jutting chin and the deep round dimple just below the lower lip.

'Goodbye!' he said, freeing his hand. 'I reckon we won't see each other again.'

Ivan took off his cap with his left hand and bent down to hug Knave's thin shoulders. They kissed as if saying goodbye for ever, and Knave fell behind. He suddenly tucked his head between his shoulders so that only the sharp brownish-pink tips of his ears showed above the grey collar of his greatcoat and walked away, hunched and stumbling.

Ivan stepped out of the ranks and with a quiver in his voice called out, 'Heh, old chum! You used to be fierce—remember? You were tough once, weren't you?'

Knave turned his tear-aged face and shouted, beating his fist on his dark bony chest that showed under his unbuttoned greatcoat and the torn collar of his shirt, 'Yes, I was! I was tough, but now I've had a real bashing! The hills were too steep for the old horse!'

He shouted something else, but the squadron turned down the next street and Ivan lost sight of him.

'That was Knave, wasn't it?' Prokhor Shamil asked from behind him.

'That was a man,' Ivan replied huskily, his lips trembling as he clapped his rifle on to his shoulder.

On the way out of the village they began to encounter the wounded. At first they came in ones and twos, then in groups, and later, in crowds. Some of the wagons were so overloaded that they could barely crawl along. The nags that were pulling them were horribly thin. Their sharp backbones had been flayed by constant blows of the whip and the pinkish red-spotted bones stood out with only a few tufts of fur to cover them. Their foam-flecked muzzles nearly touched the mud as they strained at the traces. Sometimes a panting mare would stagger to a halt with its sunken, sharp-ribbed flanks heaving helplessly. A blow of the whip would force it into motion again and, swaying from side to side, it would stumble on, and the wounded men, clinging to the wagon on all sides, would stumble on with it.

'What unit?' the squadron commander asked, choosing one of the better natured faces.

'Turkestan Corps. Third Division.'

'Were you wounded today?'

The soldier turned away without replying. The squadron left the road and headed for a forest that was visible about half a verst away. By now the companies of the 318th Chernoyarsky Regiment had also left the village and squelched along behind them, churning up the mud with their heavy infantry boots. In the distance a German observation balloon hung like a yellow-grey blob in the washed-out hazy sky.

'Look up there, Cossacks, there's a wonder for you!'

'What a sausage!'

'He's watching us from there, the bugger, to see how our troops are moving.'

'Did you think he'd climb that high for nothing?'

'He's a long way off!'

'Even a shell wouldn't go that far, I reckon.'

In the forest the Cossacks were overtaken by the First Company of the Chernoyarsky Regiment. Until evening they huddled under the wet pines with the water trickling down their necks and sending shivers down their backs; they were not allowed to light fires, and it would have been difficult to do so in the rain. Just before dusk they were marched into a communication trench. With walls barely high enough to cover a man, it was several inches deep in water. It smelled of river mud, rotting pine needles, and the fresh, velvety-soft scent of the rain. The Cossacks gathered up their greatcoats and squatted on their haunches, smoking and unravelling a brittle grey thread of conversation. The Second Troop, having shared out the ration of tobacco it had received before setting off, crowded round the troop sergeant. He was seated on an abandoned drum of wire, telling them about General Kopylovsky, who had been killed on the previous Monday, and in whose brigade he had served in peace-time. His story was cut short by the troop officer's call 'To arms!' The Cossacks jumped up, burning their fingers as they greedily finished their cigarettes. From the communication trenches the squadron again emerged into the darkening pine forest. They pushed on, encouraging each other with jokes. One tried to whistle.

In a small clearing they came across a row of corpses. The dead were lying shoulder to shoulder, in various postures, most of them obscene and frightening. A soldier with a rifle and a gasmask hanging from his belt was standing guard. The damp earth round the corpses was churned up; there were many footmarks and the grass was deeply scarred by wagon wheels. The squadron passed at a distance of only a few paces. Already the air was heavy with the sickly-sweet scent of decaying flesh. The squadron commander halted his men and, accompanied by the troop officers, went up to the soldier on guard. Meanwhile the Cossacks broke ranks and edged closer to the dead, removing their caps and surveying the bodies with that tremulous, hidden fear and animal curiosity that every living person feels towards the mystery that surrounds a dead man. All the dead were officers. The Cossacks counted forty-seven. Most of them were young, between twenty and twenty-five by the look of them, and only the one on the far right, with a Captain's shoulder-straps, could be called elderly. His thick black moustache drooped mournfully over the gaping mouth that still held the mute echoes of its last cry, and the broad boldly flared eyebrows frowned over the death-bleached face. Some of the dead men were wearing mud-caked leather jackets, the rest were in greatcoats. Two or three had no caps. The Cossacks' attention was captured by the figure of a lieutenant, who still looked handsome even in death. He lay on his back with his left hand pressed firmly to his chest while the outstretched right hand held the butt of a revolver in a grip that would never be broken. Evidently someone had tried to recover the revolver, for the broad yellow wrist bore white scratches, but flesh and steel were firmly joined and not to be parted. The fair curly head from which the cap had fallen lay with one cheek pressed lovingly to the earth and the orange blue-tinged lips were twisted in sorrowful bewilderment. The man to the right of him lay face downwards, his greatcoat had lost its back-strap and was rucked up, revealing the tensed muscular legs in khaki breeches and short chrome-leather boots with misshapen heels. His cap was missing and so was the top of his skull, which had been shorn clean away by a shell splinter; the empty cranium, framed with a few damp strands of hair, was filled with light pink water, left there by the rain. Next to him lay a stocky thick-set figure with his jacket open and shirt torn. There was no face; the lower jaw lay askew on the bared chest, and just beneath the hair line there was a narrow white band of forehead, the skin of which was scorched and curled up at the edges; between the jaw and the top of the forehead there was nothing but shattered bones and a thin blackish-red pulp. Further on lay a carelessly assembled heap of limbs and the tattered remains of a greatcoat with a torn mangled leg where the head should have been; and further on still, lay a mere boy with full lips and an adolescently oval face; a stream of machine-gun bullets had slashed his chest, his greatcoat was pierced in four places and scorched flakes of cloth protruded from the holes.

'That one... Who did that one cry for before he died? His mother?' Ivan stammered through chattering teeth and, turning away abruptly, walked off like a blind man.

The Cossacks retreated hurriedly, crossing themselves

and not looking back. And for some time afterwards no one spoke as they made their way through the narrow clearings, hurrying as if to escape the memory of what they had seen. The squadron halted near a line of empty, abandoned dug-outs. The officers and an orderly who had ridden over from the headquarters of the Chernoyarsky Regiment entered one of them; and it was only then that gap-toothed Afonka Ozerov gripped Ivan's hand and whispered, 'That lad ... the last one ... I reckon he'd never kissed a woman in his life. And now he's dead, eh?'

'Where did they get chopped up like that?' Zakhar Korolyov interrupted.

'In an attack. That's what the guard said,' Borshchev replied after a pause.

The Cossacks were ordered to stand easy. Darkness gathered over the forest. The wind hurried on the clouds, now and then ripping them apart to reveal the lilac pin-points of distant stars.

Meanwhile in the dug-out where the officers of the squadron had assembled, the squadron commander dismissed the orderly and opened the letter he had brought. He scanned the contents by the light of a short stub of candle and read aloud:

At dawn on October 3rd the Germans used poison gas against three battalions of the 256th Regiment and captured the first line of our trenches. I order you to advance to the second line, make contact with the First Battalion of the 318th Chernoyarsky Regiment and occupy the second line with the aim of knocking the enemy out of the first line on the same night. On your right flank you will have two companies of the Second Battalion and a battalion of the Fanagoriysky Regiment of the 3rd Grenadier Division.

The officers discussed the situation, smoked their cigarettes and left the dug-out. The squadron continued its march.

While the Cossacks had been waiting, the First Battalion of the Chernoyarsky Regiment had marched on ahead and reached the bridge over the River Stokhod. The bridge was guarded by a strong machine-gun post of one of the Grenadier regiments. The sergeant-major explained the situation to the battalion commander and, having crossed the bridge, the battalion split up. Two companies turned to the right, one to the left, and the last, with the battalion commander, stayed in reserve. The companies advanced in dispersed lines. The scanty woodland was deeply rutted. The men groped their way forward, tripping and swearing under their breath. In the company on the extreme right the sixth man from the end of the line was Knave. After the order to be at the ready, he had cocked his rifle and walked forward holding it out in front of him, scratching the bushes and trunks of the pines with the bayonet. Two officers passed him on their way along the line. They were talking in subdued tones. He heard the company commander's fruity baritone complaining.

'An old wound of mine has opened again. Damn that treestump! This is terribly unfortunate, Ivan Ivanovich, I caught my foot on a stump in the darkness. The wound has opened and I can't walk, I shall have to go back.' The voice broke off for a minute, then came again, fading into the distance. 'Take over command of the first half-company. Bogdanov will take over the second, and I'll ... honestly, I can't go on. I have no choice.'

Ensign Belikov's light tenor voice yelped hoarsely in reply.

'How surprising! As soon as we're in action your old wounds start troubling you.'

'Kindly be silent, Ensign!' the company commander raised his voice.

'Oh, drop that, please! Go on back!'

As he listened to the sound of his own and the other men's footsteps, Knave heard a hurried crunching behind him and realised that the company commander was making off. A minute or two later Belikov passed him with the sergeant-major on his way to the company's left flank.

'They've got a nose for trouble, those dodgers! As soon as things get serious, they either fall ill or their old wounds start troubling them. And you, the newcomer, have to take over a half-company... What scoundrels! I'd have those ... to the ranks...'

The voices broke off suddenly and Knave could hear only the damp squelching of his own footsteps and high-pitched ringing in his ears.

'Heh, chum!' someone called in a husky whisper from the left.

'What?'

'Keeping up?'

'Just about,' Knave replied as he fell over and slid on his bottom into a water-filled shell-hole.

'Dark, isn't it!' came the voice from the left.

They went on for a minute, invisible to each other, and

414

then, unexpectedly, right by Knave's ear the same husky voice said, 'Let's keep together! It's not so creepy.'

Again they fell silent, clumping along in their wet boots. A waning mottled moon suddenly dived out from behind a ridge of cloud, showed its scaly yellow face for a few seconds, dived back again, like a carp, into the flowing cloud billows, then emerged into a patch of clear sky and poured down its dusky light; the wet needles of the pine-trees gleamed phosphorescently, and in this light their scent seemed to grow stronger and the breath of the wet earth, colder. Knave glanced at his neighbour. The man halted suddenly, jerked his head back as if he had been struck, and parted his lips.

'Look!' he breathed.

Three paces away from them, by a pine-tree, stood the figure of a man, his feet planted wide apart.

'It's a man,' Knave either said or thought to himself.

'Who's there?' the soldier with him shouted, throwing his rifle to his shoulder. 'Who is it? I'll fire!'

The figure under the pine-tree made no response. The head was hanging to one side, like the top of a sunflower.

'He's asleep!' Knave gave a grating chuckle and stepped forward, trembling and trying to cheer himself with forced laughter.

They approached the standing figure. Knave craned forward and stared. His comrade touched the motionless grey figure with the butt of his gun.

'Hi, you! You asleep? Hi, chum!' he said derisively. 'What are you—a dummy?' his voice broke off. 'It's a corpse!' he shouted, recoiling.

His teeth chattering, Knave jumped back and on the very spot where his feet had been a second before the standing man fell like a sawn tree. They turned him over and only then did they realise that the pine-tree had been the last refuge of a gassed soldier fleeing from the death that he already carried in his lungs, a soldier of one of the three battalions of the 256th Infantry Regiment. A tall, broad-shouldered fellow, he lay with his head thrown back, his face smeared with the sticky mud into which he had fallen, his eyes eaten away and liquefied by the gas; the swollen fleshy tongue stuck out between the teeth like a piece of shiny black wood.

'Come on. Come on, for God's sake! Let him lie,' Knave's companion muttered, tugging at his arm.

They started off and at once encountered another corpse. As they walked on, they found more and more.

Some lay in little stacks, others had frozen in a squatting position, others, on all fours, like grazing cattle, and one, at the entrance to the communication trench leading to the second line of trenches, lay curled up in a ball with one hand, bitten in agony, thrust into his mouth.

Knave and the soldier who had joined him ran to catch up with the line and, having got ahead of it, again walked on together. Together they jumped into a dark maze of trenches zigzagging away into the darkness.

'Let's have a look in the dug-outs. Maybe there's some grub going,' the other man suggested.

'All right.'

'You go right, I'll go left. While our lot's coming, we'll check.'

Knave struck a match, stepped through the open door of the first dug-out—and flew out again as if propelled by a spring; in the dug-out there were two corpses lying across one another. In the course of his fruitless search he groped through three dug-outs, kicked open the door of a fourth, and was almost knocked off his feet when a foreign voice rasped metallically, '*Wer ist das*?'*

Feeling as if he had been sprinkled with hot ash, Knave recoiled without answering.

'*Das bist du, Otto? Weshalb bist du so spät gekommen*?** the German asked, stepping out of the dug-out and swinging his shoulders lazily to adjust the greatcoat draped over them.

'Hands up! Put 'em up! Surrender!' Knave shouted hoarsely and crouched as if he had orders to shoot.

Dumbfounded, the German slowly raised his hands and turned round, gazing spellbound at the sharp glinting point of the bayonet. The greatcoat fell from his shoulders, his single-breasted grey-green tunic crinkled under the armpits, his big, working man's hands shook, and his fingers moved as though playing on invisible keys. Knave remained crouching and stared up at the tall burly figure, the metal buttons of his uniform, the short boots with seams at the sides, and the peakless cap tilted slightly sideways. Then he changed his position all at once, as though he had been shaken out of his ill-fitting greatcoat, and, uttering a strange throaty sound, something between a cough and a sob, he stepped towards the German.

'Run!' he said in an empty brittle voice. 'Run, Ger-

---

*'Who's that?'

**'Is that you, Otto? Why are you so late?'

416

man! I've got no grudge against you. I won't shoot.'

He leaned his rifle against the wall of the trench and reached up for the German's right hand. His confident movements overcame the prisoner's fears and he lowered his hand, listening intently to the strange intonations of the foreign voice.

Without hesitation Knave held out his rough hand with all the scars of twenty years' hard work, squeezed the German's cold limp fingers, and then turned his hand upwards; lilac petals of light from the waning moon fell on the small yellow palm, dotted with the brown mounds of old callouses.

'I'm a worker,' said Knave, shaking as if from fever. 'Why should I kill you? Run!' And he gave the German a gentle push on the shoulder, pointing to the black tangle of the forest. 'Run, you nut! Our lot will be here soon.'

The German stood staring intently at Knave's outstretched hand, leaning slightly forward, straining to grasp the hidden meaning in these incomprehensible sounds. This lasted for perhaps a second or two; his eyes met Knave's and his glance suddenly quivered into a joyful smile. He stepped back, threw out both hands in a sweeping gesture, grasped Knave's hands tightly and shook them, smiling radiantly and leaning forward to look into Knave's eyes.

'*Du entlässt mich?.. O, jetzt hab ich verstanden! Du bist ein russischer Arbeiter? Sozial-Demokrat, wie ich? So? O! O! Das ist wie im Traum... Mein Bruder, wie kann ich vergessen? Ich finde keine Worte. Nur du bist ein wunderbarer wagender Junge... Ich...*'*

In the boiling flood of foreign words Knave caught only one that was familiar, the interrogative 'Social-Democrat'?

'Yes, I'm a Social-Democrat. And you'd better run... Goodbye, old chum. Give us your hand!'

Understanding had come intuitively and they stood staring into each other's eyes—the tall well-built Bavarian and the little Russian soldier.

The Bavarian whispered, '*In den Zukünftigen Klassenkämpfen werden wir in denselben Schützengräben sein,*

---

*'You're letting me go? Oh, now I understand! You are a Russian worker? A Social-Democrat like me? Yes? Oh! Oh, this is like a dream. My brother, how can I ever forget this?.. Words fail me... But you're a wonderful, brave man... I...'

nicht wahr, Genosse?'* and he sprang over the parapet like a big grey animal.

From the woods came the squelching footsteps of the approaching skirmish line. It was preceded by a platoon of Czech reconnaissance scouts with its own officer. They nearly shot down Knave's companion as he emerged from a dug-out where he had been looking for something to eat.

'I'm one of yours! Can't you see... Drat your eyes!' the man shouted at the sight of the dark muzzle of a rifle pointing at him.

'It's your own men here,' he repeated, clasping a loaf of black bread to his chest, like a baby.

Recognising Knave, an N. C. O. jumped across the trench and brought the butt of his gun down hard on Knave's back.

'I'll smash you! I'll bloody your nose for you! Where've you been?'

Knave was so limp and exhausted that even the blow did not have the desired effect on him. He swayed forward, and astounded the N. C. O. with a good-natured reply that was not at all like them.

'I was pushing on ahead. You needn't knock me about.'

'Then don't dangle like the cow's tail! Now he's lagging behind, now he's in front. Don't you know the regulations? Is this your first year in the army?' He paused for a minute, then asked, 'Got any baccy?'

'It's a bit crushed.'

'Out with it.'

The N. C. O. lighted up and went off to the end of the platoon.

Just before dawn the Czech scouts ran smack into a German observation post. The Germans shattered the silence with a volley. It was followed by two more, at regular intervals. A red flare soared up over the trenches, voices were heard, and before the scarlet sparks of the flare had died out of the sky, the Germans launched an artillery attack.

The first resounding shots were quickly followed by two more.

The shells drilled through the air with a clucking sound that rose to a grinding roar as they flew over the heads of

*'In the coming class battles we shall be in the same trenches. Won't we, comrade?'

the men of the first half-company; there was a moment's silence, then from far away, near the crossing over the Stokhod, came the relaxing crash of explosions.

The line that had been advancing at a distance of fifty paces behind the Czech scouts dropped to the ground after the first volley. As the flare burst in a scarlet glow, Knave saw the men crawling like ants between the bushes and trees, no longer shunning the muddy earth but clinging to it for protection. They swarmed round every rut, pressed themselves into every fold of the ground, pushed their heads into every hole. And even so, when the chattering streams of machine-gun fire splashed and pattered through the forest like a May downpour, they faltered and began to crawl back, pulling their heads down into their shoulders, flattening themselves to the ground like caterpillars, slithering like snakes without bending legs or arms, and leaving snake-like trails behind them in the mud. Some jumped up and ran. Explosive bullets tore and smacked their way through the forest, slashing pine-needles, splintering the trees, and burying themselves in the ground with a viper-like hiss.

The first half-company had lost seventeen men by the time it regained the second line of trenches. Not far away the Cossacks of the special squadron were re-forming their ranks. They had been advancing to the right of the half-company and, having quietly disposed of the sentries, they might have taken the Germans by surprise, but the volley fired at the Czech scouts had alerted the whole sector. Shooting at random, the Germans had killed two Cossacks and wounded one. The Cossacks had brought their dead and wounded back with them and as they formed up they talked among themselves.

'We ought to bury our lads.'

'Somebody'll do that.'

'Better think about the living—the dead don't care.'

Half an hour later an order was received from regimental headquarters: 'After an artillery softening-up I order the battalion together with the Special Cossack Squadron to attack the enemy and knock them out of the first line of trenches.'

The feeble artillery barrage lasted until noon. The Cossacks and infantry posted sentries and rested in the dug-outs. At noon they attacked. To the left, on the main sector, the gun-fire was heavy—the attack had been renewed there too.

On the extreme edge of the right flank there were

Baikal Cossacks. On their left they had the Chernoyarsky Regiment and the Special Cossack Squadron. Next to them was the Fanagoriysky Grenadier Regiment, then the Chembarsky, Bugulminsky, the 208th and 211th Infantry, the Pavlograd and Węgrów regiments; in the centre regiments of the 53rd Division were developing the offensive; and the whole left flank was occupied by the 2nd Turkestan Infantry Division. The Russians were attacking everywhere and the whole sector shook with the rumble of gunfire.

The squadron advanced in open formation, its left flank linked with the Chernoyarsky Regiment's right. As soon as the Cossacks got within sight of the German breastworks they came under heavy fire. They advanced silently in short dashes, falling flat, emptying their rifles and running on. At about fifty paces from the trenches they dropped down and stayed down, firing without lifting their heads. The Germans had rigged up wire netting on posts all along the line. Two grenades thrown by Afonka Ozerov rebounded from the netting before they exploded. He lifted his arm to throw a third, but a bullet hit him just below the left shoulder and came out of his backside. Ivan, who was lying near by, saw Afonka kick feebly and lie still. Prokhor Shamil, the brother of one-armed Alexei, was killed outright; Manytskov, the former village ataman, was the third victim, and the next moment a bullet picked off the Shamils' bow-legged neighbour Yevlanty Kalinin.

In the space of half an hour the Second Troop lost eight men. When the major in command of the squadron and two troop officers were killed, the squadron began to fall back without waiting for orders. When they were out of range, the Cossacks got together and found that half their number were missing. The Chernoyarsky men also retreated. In the First Battalion the losses were even heavier, but another order soon arrived from regimental headquarters: 'The attack must be renewed at once and the enemy driven out of the first line of trenches at all costs. The ultimate success of the operation along the whole front depends on success in restoring the initial situation.'

The squadron spread out in a thin line and advanced again. Under devastating fire they hit the ground at a distance of about one hundred paces from the German trenches.

Again the units began to melt away and the men clung

madly to the ground, without raising their heads, without moving, intoxicated with the horror of death.

Just before evening the second half-company of the Chernoyarsky Regiment broke up and began to run. The shout 'we're surrounded!' reached the Cossacks, who also scrambled to their feet and ran back, tearing their way through bushes, tripping over roots and dropping their weapons. When he reached safer ground, Ivan collapsed under a pine-tree that had been cut down by a shell. Soon he saw Gavrila Likhovidov coming towards him. Likhovidov was staggering along drunkenly, his eyes on the ground, snatching at the air with one hand and groping over his face with the other, as if to wipe away a cobweb. He had neither rifle nor sword, his straight dark-brown sweat-sodden hair was hanging down over his eyes. After wandering round the clearing, he came up to Ivan, halted and rammed his wavering glance into the ground. His knees were half bent and trembling, and to Ivan he looked as if he were about to leap into the air.

'Well, that's the way it is...' Ivan began, trying to say something, but a shudder convulsed Likhovidov's face.

'Halt!' he shouted and crouched on his haunches, splaying his fingers and glancing fearfully over his shoulder. 'Listen! I'm going to sing you a song. A little bird flew up to an owl and said:

> 'Tell me, tell me, mistress owl,
> Who's the bigger, senior fowl?
> Here's the eagle, he's the tsar,
> Here's the kite, he's a major,
> Harrier's a captain,
> Ring-doves are Urals men,
> Turtle-doves are guardsmen,
> Stock-doves are linesmen,
> Starlings are Kalmyks,
> Jackdaws are Gypsies,
> Magpies are ladies,
> Grey ducks are infantry
> And goosies are lassies...'

'Hold on there!' Ivan turned pale. 'Likhovidov, what's up, man? Are you ill?'

'Don't interrupt!' Likhovidov went purple in the face and, again twisting his bluish lips into an inane smile, resumed his weird chant:

> *Goosies are lassies,*
> *Bustards are asses,*
> *Bitterns are bullies,*
> *Rooks are shooties,*
> *Crows are diddlers,*
> *Didappers are fiddlers...*

Ivan jumped to his feet.

'Come on, let's get back to the squadron. Or the Germans'll grab us! D'you hear?'

Snatching his hand away and hurrying along, Likhovidov went on shouting, warm spit dripping from his lips:

> *Nightingales be songsters,*
> *Swallows be rompsters,*
> *Blackbird's a bare-belly,*
> *Tom-tit's a taxman,*
> *Sparrow's a foreman...*

Suddenly he broke off and began to sing in a hoarse, croaking voice. It was not a song but a rising wolf-like howl that burst from his snarling mouth. Pearly spit glowed on the sharp, fanglike teeth. Ivan stared in horror at the madly squinting eyes of the man who had but recently been his friend, at his head with its plastered hair and waxen ears. In bitter desperation Likhovidov howled:

> *Loud the glorious bugles blow,*
> *Across the Danube Cossacks go.*
> *The Sultan's Turks we put to flight*
> *And freed the Christians from his might.*
>
> *We flew across those little hills*
> *Like locusts in a swarm,*
> *Shooting surely with our rifles,*
> *All Cossacks of the Don.*
>
> *Soon we'll pluck your turkeys*
> *Like chickens to the bone,*
> *Then catch your wives and children*
> *And march them captive home.*

'Martin! Martin, come over here!' Ivan shouted as he spotted Martin Shamil hobbling across the clearing.

Martin came up, using his rifle as a crutch.

422

'Help me to take him back. See what he's like?' Ivan indicated the madman with his eyes. 'It was too much for him. The blood's gone to his head.'

Shamil bandaged his wounded leg with a sleeve torn from his vest and, without looking at Likhovidov, took him by the arm. Ivan took the other arm and they led him away.

> *We flew across those little hills*
> *Like locusts in a swarm...*

Likhovidov shouted, but quieter now. Frowning painfully, Shamil tried to soothe him.

'Don't make all that noise now! Stuff it, lad, for Christ's sake. You've done your flying, I reckon! Stuff it!'

> *Soon we'll pluck your turkeys,*
> *Like chickens to the bone...*

But the madman tried to break away from them and went on singing, only occasionally stopping to press his hands to his temples, gnash his teeth and with shaking lower jaw jerked his head sideways under the scorching breath of madness.

IV

Heavy fighting was going on about forty versts away down the Stokhod. For two weeks the howl and rumble of gunfire had been continuous. At night the distant violet sky was sliced by the reflections of searchlight beams, and their irridescent flashes, winking across to one another, aroused inexplicable fears in those who were watching the glow and flare of war from afar.

The 12th Cossack Regiment was deployed on a wild, marshy sector. During the day the Cossacks took occasional shots at the Austrians scurrying along the shallow trenches; at night, protected by the marshes, they slept or played cards; and only the sentries observed the ominous orange splashes of light from the battle zone.

One frosty night, when the distant reflections were tracing particularly bright patterns in the sky, Grigory Melekhov left his dug-out, made his way along a communication passage into the grey stubble of trees that bristled on the black skull of the hill behind the trenches, and lay down in the open amid the scents of earth. The air in the dug-out had been foul and choked with the brown tobacco smoke that hung like a heavy fringed cloth over the table, where eight Cossacks were playing cards. But here, among the trees on the crest of the hill, there was a gentle breeze, which seemed to come from the wings of a bird flying invisibly overhead, and an indescribably sad smell arose from the grass that had perished in the frost. The disfigured, shell-shorn trees were wrapped in darkness, the smoky fires of the Pleiades were dying to ashes, the Great Bear lay beside the Milky Way like an overturned wagon with its shaft askew, and only the North Star still poured down its steady shimmering light.

Grigory looked up at it through half-closed lashes and the star's gentle but frigid rays stung equally cold tears from his eyes.

As he lay there on the hill he for some reason recalled the night he had walked from the village of Lower Yablonovskoye on his way home to Aksinya, in Yagodnoye; and with a sharp stab of pain he recalled her, too. Memory moulded the time-faded features of a face that was infinitely dear and yet alien to him. With a sudden quickening of the pulse he tried to picture instead the face he had seen last, contorted with pain, with the purple weal left by the whip on its cheek, but memory stubbornly offered another, tilted a little to one side and smiling triumphantly. There she was, turning her head playfully and fondly, and thrusting at him from below with those dark fiery eyes, her wantonly greedy red lips whispering something inexpressibly tender and passionate. Then she slowly averted her glance and turned away, revealing the two big fluffy curls on her neck that he had once loved to kiss.

Grigory gave a start. For a second it seemed to him that he had smelt the faint intoxicating aroma of Aksinya's hair; he sat up, arching his back, nostrils wide and twitching—but no, it was only the poignant smell of fallen leaves. The oval of Aksinya's face blurred and faded. Grigory closed his eyes and laid his hand on the rough earth, then stared up at the far edge of the sky, where beyond a broken pine the North Star still quivered like a beautiful blue butterfly in motionless flight.

Unconnected bits of memory eclipsed the image of Aksinya. He recalled the weeks he had spent with his family in Tatarsky after the break with her; at night, the avid, ravaging caresses of Natalya, who seemed to be trying to make up for her previous virginal frigidity; during the day, the almost ingratiating attention of his family and the honour that the village people accorded to their first winner of the St. George Cross. Everywhere, even in his own family, Grigory noticed the sidelong glances of astonished admiration. People studied him as if unable to believe that this was the same headstrong, high-spirited lad they had known before. In the village square the old men would chat with him as with an equal, hats were raised in response to his bow, and the women gazed with unconcealed admiration at the gallant, slightly stooped figure with the cross and striped ribbon on his greatcoat. He noticed the obvious pride that his father took in walking beside him to church or the parade ground. And gradually this subtle poison of flattery, respect and admiration destroyed and swept from his mind the seeds of truth that Garanzha had planted. Grigory was one man when he came home from the front and another when he left. The Cossack traditions that he had drunk in with his mother's milk and cherished all his life conquered the greater human truth.

'I knew it, Grisha,' his father said after a farewell drink and passed his hand agitatedly over his silver and black hair, 'I've known for a long time that you'd make a fine Cossack. On your very first birthday, according to the old Cossack custom, I carried you out into the yard—remember, mother?—and put you astride a horse. And you, you son-of-a-bitch—grabbed hold of its mane with your little hands! Even then I guessed you'd turn out well. And you did.'

When Grigory left for the front, he was a good Cossack again. Though inwardly unreconciled to the senselessness of war, he valiantly defended Cossack glory.

May 1915. Near the village of Olkhovchik the 13th German Iron Regiment was attacking across a bright green sward of meadowland. The machine-guns were chirping like cicadas. The heavy machine-gun of a Russian company entrenched above the river was pounding ponderously. The 12th Cossack Regiment went into action. Grigory was running forward from cover to cover with the Cossacks of his squadron and, as he glanced back over his shoulder, he saw the molten disk of the sun in the noonday sky and another, exactly the same, in a backwater trimmed with a fuzzy yellow fringe of catkins.

The horse-minders were behind the poplars on the other side of the river. Ahead was the line of Germans, the brass eagles gleaming yellow on their helmets. Grey wormwood-coloured puffs of smoke from the shots stirred in the breeze.

Grigory emptied his gun unhurriedly, taking careful aim, and, as he listened between shots for the troop officer's target orders, he gently brushed away a mottled ladybird that had settled on the sleeve of his tunic. Then they charged. Grigory felled a tall German lieutenant with the metal-trimmed butt of his rifle, took three prisoners and, firing over their heads, forced them to run down to the river.

At Rava-Russkaya, in July 1915, he and a troop of Cossacks recaptured a Cossack battery that had fallen to the Austrians. During the fighting in the same sector he slipped through the enemy lines, opened fire with a light machine-gun and turned the Austrians' attack into a rout.

In an encounter near Bayanets he captured a stout Austrian officer, slung him across his saddle like a sheep and galloped clear. All through the ride he was aware of the nauseating smell of human excrement coming from the officer and the trembling of his fat, fear-drenched body.

And with special clarity, as he lay on the black bare crest of the hill, Grigory remembered the incident that had brought him face to face with his sworn enemy Stepan Astakhov. It had occurred when the 12th Regiment was withdrawn from the front and transferred to East Prussia. The Cossack horses trampled the neat German fields and the Cossacks burned the German homes and farmsteads, leaving a trail of reddish smoke, charred smouldering walls and cracked tile roofs. Near the town of Stallupönen the regiment attacked together with the 27th Don Cossack Regiment. Grigory caught a glimpse of his brother, looking much thinner, the clean-shaven Stepan, and other Cossacks from his village. During the battle both regiments were worsted. The Germans surrounded them and, when the twelve squadrons, one after the other, charged the German lines to break out of the encirclement, Grigory saw Stepan throw himself clear of the black horse that had been shot from under him and roll head over heels. Seized by a sudden joyful resolution, Grigory managed with difficulty to rein in his horse and, when the last squadron had thundered past, nearly trampling on Stepan, he galloped up to him and shouted, 'Grab my stirrup!'

Stepan clutched the stirrup leather and ran for about half a verst beside Grigory's horse.

'Don't ride so fast! For Christ's sake, not so fast!' he begged, panting.

They passed safely through the breach and had no more than a hundred paces to go to the wood where the squadrons were dismounting, when a bullet hit Stepan in the leg; he lost his grip on the stirrup and fell flat on his back. The wind snatched Grigory's cap off his head and flung his hair in his eyes. He tossed it back and looked round. He saw Stepan run limping to a bush, throw his Cossack cap into it and sit down, hurriedly pulling off his trousers with their bright scarlet stripes. A squad of German infantry was advancing over the hill and Grigory realised that Stepan was tearing off his Cossack trousers so that he could pass for an ordinary soldier. At that time the Germans took no Cossack prisoners... Obeying an impulse of the heart, Grigory turned and galloped over to the bush, jumping off as he came to it.

'Get into the saddle!'

Grigory would never forget the quick upthrust of Stepan's eyes. He helped him to mount and himself ran beside the sweat-bathed horse, holding the stirrup.

The hot whine of a bullet broke off with a ping as it flew past out of hearing. But this drilling, downward-curving whine of bullets continued—over Grigory's head, over Stepan's chalk-white face, and from both sides, while from behind came the crack of rifle shots, like the popping of locust-tree pods.

In the wood Stepan slid out of the saddle, grimacing with pain, dropped the reins and limped away. Blood was oozing over the top of his left boot and at every step a thin cherry-red stream spurted from the loose sole. He leaned against the trunk of a branching oak and beckoned Grigory.

'The boot's full of blood,' he said as Grigory came up.

Grigory looked aside without replying.

'Grisha... When we were attacking today... D'you hear, Grigory?' Stepan's sunken eyes sought Grigory's. 'When we were attacking, I took three shots at you, from behind... It wasn't God's will for me to kill you.'

Their eyes clashed. Stepan's pain-sharpened glance shone unbearably bright from the sunken sockets. He scarcely parted his clenched teeth as he spoke.

'You saved me from death... For that I thank you... But I can't forgive you for Aksinya. I can't bring myself to... So don't force me, Grigory.'

'I'm not forcing you,' Grigory replied.

They parted still unreconciled.

And another memory. In May Grigory's regiment with other units of Brusilov's army, had broken through the front at Lutsk and raided far behind the enemy lines, striking some hard blows and taking some itself. Near Lvov, Grigory on his own initiative had led the squadron in a charge and captured an Austrian howitzer battery with all its crew. A month later he had swum the River Bug at night for an information prisoner. He had surprised a sentry and knocked him down, but the tough, stocky German had fought furiously with his half-naked attacker and tried to yell for help before he was tied up.

Grigory smiled as he remembered the incident.

And there had been many such days that time had scattered across the recent and not so recent battlefields. Loyally Grigory had defended his Cossack honour and seized every chance of showing the wildest daring. He had risked his life in madcap adventures, slipped through the Austrian lines in disguise, and brought back sentries alive. He had done all that a Cossack rough-rider could do and at last the pain of human compassion that had tortured him in the first days of war seemed to have gone for ever. His heart had hardened like a salt-marsh in a drought, and just as the salt-marsh absorbs no water, so Grigory's heart had become impervious to pity. With cold contempt he staked his own life and the lives of others; this was how he had won his reputation for bravery—along with four crosses of St. George and four medals. During the rare parades he stood by the regimental banner with its aura of the battle smoke of many wars; but he knew that he would never again laugh as he used to; knew that his eyes had sunk deep into their sockets and his cheekbones were sharper than ever before; knew that when he kissed a child it was hard for him to look into those clear eyes. Yes, Grigory was well aware of the price he had paid for his row of crosses and his promotion.

He lay on the hill with his greatcoat tucked under him, leaning on his left elbow. Memory obligingly revived the past and into the meagre patchwork of his wartime memories there sometimes crept the fine blue thread of some distant happening in childhood. Grigory would linger over it wistfully for a moment, then return again to the recent past. In the Austrian trenches someone was skilfully playing a mandolin. The thin sounds, modulated by the wind, came across the Stokhod and tripped lightly over the blood-soaked earth. The stars overhead were burning even more fiercely, the darkness was more intense, and already the midnight mist was crouching over the marsh. Grigory smoked two cigarettes one after the other, stroked the sling of his rifle with a rough fondness and, heaving himself up with the fingers of his left hand, rose from the hospitable ground and walked back to the trenches.

In the dug-out they were still playing cards. Grigory dropped on to his bunk with the intention of continuing his wanderings along the overgrown paths of memory that he had so often visited before, but sleep drugged him and he dozed off in the awkward posture that he had taken on lying down. In his dreams he saw a boundless wind-scorched steppe, tufts of pinkish mauve everlastings, and among the shaggy lilac thyme the marks of unshod horses' hoofs... The steppe was deserted and terrifyingly quiet. He was walking on firm sandy ground but could not hear his footsteps and this made him afraid. He awoke and lifted his head, cheeks deeply creased from the awkward posture in which he had been sleeping. For a time he munched his lips, like a horse that had momentarily caught and lost the scent of some wonderful grass. After that he slept without waking and without dreams.

He got up in the morning, feeling wretched and inexplicably depressed.

'What are you looking so glum about today? Been dreaming of home?' Uryupin asked him.

'You've guessed it. I dreamed of the steppe. I feel all boxed up... If only I could have a spell at home. I'm fed up with serving the tsar.'

Curly chuckled condescendingly. All this time he had lived in the same dug-out as Grigory and treated him with the respect that one strong beast feels for another; since their first quarrel, in 1914, there had been no further outbreaks and Curly's influence was clearly having its effect on Grigory's mind and character. The war had worked a deep change in Uryupin's view of the world. He was unwillingly but steadily moving towards rejection of the war. He would talk at length about traitor generals and the Germans who had firmly installed themselves at the tsarist court. A phrase he once let slip was, 'What can you expect when the tsaritsa herself has German blood in her. When the time comes, she'll sell us for the flick of a horse's tail.'

One day Grigory told him the gist of Garanzha's teaching, but Curly would have none of it.

'The song's a good one, but the voice croaks,' he said with a scornful grin, slapping his bald bluish pate. 'Mishka Koshevoi is always crowing about that, like a cock on a fence. There's no sense in these revolutions, they're just tomfoolery. What you've got to understand is that we Cossacks must have our own government, and not someone else's. We need a strong tsar, someone like Nikolai Nikolayevich.* Our road's not with the peasants—you can't pair a goose with a pig. The peasants are out for more land, the workers want more wages, and what will they give us! We've got plenty of land as it is! So what else do we need? The nose-bag's empty—that's the trouble. The tsar's no bloody good—there's no denying that. His father was a bit tougher, but this one will end up with a revolution on his hands like in 1905, then the whole bloody lot will come crashing down. That won't do us any good. If, God forbid, they kick out the tsar, they'll be after us too. And then, with the grudge they've got against us, they'll start carving up our land amongst the peasants. So you'd better keep your ear to the ground.'

'You always see only one side of the question,' Grigory replied frowning.

'That's a daft thing to say. You're still a youngster, you haven't been broken in. You wait! When they've knocked some of the stuffing out of you, then you'll know what side the truth is on.'

Usually their discussion went no further. Grigory would fall silent and Uryupin would try to talk of other things.

That day Grigory got involved in an unpleasant incident. The field kitchen arrived as usual, stopping on the other side of the hill, and the Cossacks hurried along the communication trenches to get there first. Mishka Koshevoi went to fetch the food for the Third Troop. He came back with the steaming mess-tins on a long stick and, on entering the dug-out, shouted, 'This won't do, lads! What do they think we are—dogs?'

'What are you on about?' Uryupin asked.

'They're feeding us on rotten meat!' Koshevoi exclaimed indignantly.

---

*The Grand Duke Nikolai Nikolayevich (1856-1929), Commander-in-Chief of the Russian Army in World War One. During the Civil War that followed he fled abroad, where he was supported by Wrangel and most of the monarchists in his claim to the Russian throne.

He tossed back a golden forelock that was like a tangled bunch of wild hops, dumped the mess-tins down on a wooden bunk, and shot a sidelong glance at Uryupin.

'The soup stinks. Smell it!'

Curly bent over his mess-tin, twitched his nostrils and made a face. Unconsciously imitating him, Koshevoi did the same.

'It's the meat that stinks,' Curly decided.

He put the mess-tin down in disgust and glanced at Grigory. Grigory bounded forward off the bunk and made his long nose even longer over the soup, then stepped back and with a lazy flick of the foot tipped it out on the floor.

'Now why do that?' Curly said doubtfully.

'Can't you see why? Look. Or are you blind? What's that?' Grigory pointed at the murky liquid spreading towards his feet.

'Ah!.. Maggots! By my old mother... And I never spotted 'em! That's a dinner for you. It's not cabbage soup, it's noodles—with maggots instead of tripe.'

The boiled puffy white maggots lay limply beside a blood-red lump of meat amid the greasy blobs of fat on the floor.

'One, two, three, four...' Koshevoi counted, for some reason in a whisper.

For a minute none of them spoke. Grigory spat through clenched teeth. Koshevoi drew his sword and said, 'We're going to arrest this soup and march it to the squadron commander.'

'That's a good idea!' Curly approved.

He hurriedly unscrewed his bayonet.

'We'll bring the soup along and you, Grishka, must come with us and report to the squadron commander.'

Uryupin and Koshevoi, their swords drawn, carried a full mess-tin of soup on the bayonet. Grigory followed behind them and a grey-green wave of Cossacks rolled after them along the zigzags of the trenches.

'What's up?'

'Did they sound the alarm?'

'Mebbe it's something about peace?'

'Want peace, do you? Anything else you want?'

'They've arrested some maggoty soup!'

Uryupin and Koshevoi halted at the officer's dug-out. Bending forward and holding his cap on with his left hand, Grigory stepped inside.

'Stand back!' Curly snarled bad-temperedly, looking

round at a Cossack who had shoved him from behind.

The squadron commander came out, buttoning up his greatcoat and glancing in surprise and some alarm at Grigory, who had come out behind him.

'What's the matter, lads?' The commander's eyes roved over the Cossacks' heads.

Grigory came forward and answered amid the general silence.

'We've brought in a prisoner.'

'What prisoner?'

'Here he is.' Grigory pointed to the mess-tin of soup at Curly's feet. 'That's the prisoner... Smell what your Cossacks are being fed on.'

His eyebrow jagged up into a triangle and straightened out again. The squadron commander studied the expression on Grigory's face, then looked at the soup.

'They've started feeding us on carrion!' Mishka Koshevoi shouted fiercely.

'Change the quartermaster!'

'He's a creep!'

'The greedy hog!'

'He guzzles ox-kidney soup.'

'And we get it with maggots instead!'

The squadron commander waited until the uproar had died down, then said sharply, 'Quiet there! Silence! That's enough. The quartermaster will be changed today. I shall appoint a commission to investigate his activities. If the meat doesn't come up to standard...'

'Court-martial him!' several voices boomed from the back.

The officer's voice was swept away in a fresh uproar.

The quartermaster had to be replaced on the march. A few hours after the rebellious Cossacks had arrested and marched their soup to the squadron commander, the headquarters of the 12th Regiment received orders to withdraw from the trenches and march to the Romanian border by a specified route. That night the Cossacks were relieved by Siberian infantry. In the township of Rynvichi the regiment collected its horses and the next morning set out by forced marches for Romania.

Massive reinforcements were being sent to help the Romanians, who had been suffering one defeat after another. This was clear from the mere fact that on the first evening the billeting officers sent ahead to find accommodation for the squadron returned empty-handed; the village shown in the itinerary was already packed with infantry and artillery that was also moving in the direction of the Romanian border. The regiment was obliged to march an extra eight versts before it found somewhere to stay the night.

They rode on for seventeen days. The horses were half starved. There was no fodder in the war-ravaged frontline zone; the local people had either fled into the Russian hinterland or were hiding in the forests; the abandoned houses gaped with the blackness of bare walls; only occasionally the Cossacks would meet a sullen, frightened local inhabitant, who at the sight of armed men would make off hurriedly. The Cossacks, exhausted by the endless march, chilled to the bone and angered by the treatment they and their horses were receiving, ripped the straw thatch off the roofs, and in villages that had survived the passage of war unhesitatingly pillaged the meagre food stocks. No threats from the officers could restrain them from marauding.

In a prosperous little village not far from the Romanian border Curly managed to steal a peck of barley from a barn. The owner caught him in the act, but Curly beat up the elderly mild-mannered Bessarabian and got away with the barley for his horse. The troop officer found him at the tethering post. Curly had hung the nose-bag on his horse's muzzle and with trembling hands was stroking the animal's sunken flanks, gazing into its eyes as if it were a human being.

'Uryupin! Give back that barley, you son-of-a-bitch! You'll get yourself shot for this, you scoundrel!'

Curly flicked a glazed, squinting look at the officer, flung his cap down and for the first time since he had joined the regiment burst into frantic yelling.

'Court-martial me! Shoot me! Kill me on the spot! But I won't give you the barley! Why should my horse starve to death? I won't give it back. Not one grain of it!'

He clutched now at the head, now at the mane of the greedily munching horse, now at his sword.

The officer stood staring silently at the animal's horribly jutting ribs, then nodded and said, 'Why are you feeding a hot horse?'

There was a note of embarrassment in his voice.

'Nay, he's cooled off by now,' Uryupin replied almost in a whisper, gathering up the grains that had scattered out of the nose-bag and tipping them back.

15–1106

* * *

By the beginning of November the regiment reached its new positions. High winds swirled over the mountains of Transylvania, freezing mists billowed in the gorges, the frost-seared pinewoods gave off a powerful fragrance, and on the first, virginal snow the men often came across the tracks of wild animals—wolves, elk, wild goats frightened out of their fastnesses by the war and fleeing into the hinterland.

On November 7th the 12th Regiment stormed Hill 320. The day before, the enemy trenches had been manned by Austrians, but the next morning they were relieved by Saxon troops, who had just been transferred from the French front. In infantry formation the Cossacks made their way up the stony, snow-powdered slopes. Frozen gravel slid away from under their feet and fine snow-flakes drifted round them. Grigory was marching beside Uryupin and there was a guilty and strangely embarrassed smile on his face.

'I'm feeling a bit scared today. As if this was my first attack.'

'You don't say?' Curly responded wonderingly.

He still had his battered rifle slung over his shoulder and was sucking at the icicles dangling from his moustache.

The Cossacks advanced in ragged lines, holding their fire. The ridges of the enemy trenches remained menacingly silent. Behind the German earthworks a Saxon lieutenant, his face red from the wind, his nose peeling, was leaning back with a broad smile on his face and shouting encouragement to his men.

'*Kameraden! Wir haben die Blaumäntel oft genug gedroschen! Da wollen wir's auch diesen einpfeffern, was es heisst mit uns'n Hühnchen zu rupfen! Ausharren! Schiesst noch nicht.*'*

The Cossack squadrons advanced for the assault. Loose rock and stones scattered away from under their feet. Grigory tucked in the ends of his weather-stained hood and smiled nervously. His hooked nose and the gaunt cheeks covered with the black stubble of a long-unshaven beard were a yellowish blue, and his eyes glittered like chips of anthracite from under his frost-rimmed brows.

*'Friends! We've beaten the bluecoats often enough! Let's show them once again what it's like to take us on. Steady now! Hold your fire!'

His habitual calm had deserted him. Fighting this un-expected return of fear, he talked to Uryupin as he nervously scanned the grey snow-sprinkled ridge of trenches.

'They're keeping quiet, letting us get nearer. I'm scared and not ashamed to say so... What about turning back, eh?'

'What's the matter with you today?' Uryupin snapped back irritably. 'This is like a card game, chum. If you don't have faith in yourself, you'll get clobbered. You've gone all yellow in the face, Grishka... Either you're sick or you're going to catch a packet. Heh, look at that! Did you see that?'

A German in a short greatcoat and spiked helmet had risen to his full height above the trenches and then disappeared.

To Grigory's left a handsome Yelanskaya Cossack with light-brown hair kept peeling the glove off his right hand and pulling it on again as he walked. He seemed to have difficulty in bending his knees and affected an exaggeratedly loud cough. He's like someone walking in the dark and coughing to keep his spirits up, Grigory thought. Beyond this Cossack he caught a glimpse of Sergeant Maksayev's freckled cheek, and beyond him was Yemelyan Groshev, firmly gripping his rifle with its fixed bayonet. Grigory remembered that a few days ago Yemelyan had stolen a sack of maize from a Romanian after forcing the lock of his cupboard with that bayonet. Mishka Koshevoi was only a short distance from Maksayev. He was smoking greedily and often blew his nose, wiping his fingers on the skirt of his greatcoat.

'I'm thirsty,' Maksayev said.

'My boots are pinching me, Yemelyan,' Mishka Koshe-voi complained. 'I can hardly walk.'

Groshev interrupted him fiercely, 'Don't worry about your boots. The Germans'll start ripping us with their machine-guns in a minute.'

At the first volley Grigory fell with a gasp as a bullet flung him to the ground. He reached for his field bag, where he had a bandage, but the feeling of blood gushing into his sleeve from his wounded arm robbed him of his strength. He lay face downwards, pushed his heavy head behind the cover of a rock, and licked greedily at a small curl of snow. With quivering lips he mouthed the fine light snow and listened with unusual fear and trembling to the dry whine and snicking of bullets and the general

435

crash of firing. When he raised his head again, he saw the Cossacks of his squadron running down the slope, sliding, falling, and firing back at random. An unreasoning fear brought him to his feet and forced him to run down the slope towards the jagged seam of pine forest from which the regiment had launched its attack. He overtook Yemelyan Groshev, who was dragging the wounded troop officer down the steep slope at a run; the lieutenant's legs were sagging drunkenly under him and once or twice he fell forward on to Groshev's shoulder, spitting up black clots of blood. The squadrons rolled down towards the forest like an avalanche, leaving the grey lumps of their dead on the grey slopes; the wounded that no one had managed to pick up crawled back themselves with machine-guns cutting them down from behind.

A ceaseless flood of firing tore the air to shreds and sent long echoes across the mountainside.

Grigory reached the forest, leaning on Mishka Koshevoi's arm. A German machine-gun was thudding heavily on the left flank and bullets were ricochetting off the surrounding slope like stones skated by a strong arm across the first fragile ice of autumn.

'They've given us a pasting this time!' Uryupin shouted, almost as if he were glad. Leaning against the reddish trunk of a pine-tree, he was shooting lazily at the Germans as they darted across from one trench to another.

'Fools need a lesson! A damn good lesson!' Koshevoi shouted breathlessly, tearing his arm away from Grigory. 'The people are just a mob! Worse! They'll bleed to death before they understand what they're being clobbered for!'

'What are you getting at?' Curly frowned.

'Anyone with any sense would understand, but what's the use of talking to a fool? You can't knock sense into him!'

'What about your oath? You took the oath of allegiance, didn't you?' Curly persisted.

Giving no answer, Koshevoi dropped on his knees, scooped up some snow with shaking hands and gulped it down greedily, shivering and coughing.

V

Away to one side of the village of Tatarsky the autumn sun was riding across a sky wrinkled with rippling grey clouds. Up there, in the heights, a light breeze was nudging the clouds along gently, helping them to float westwards, but over the village, over the green plain of the Don, over the bare forests, the wind flowed in powerful streams, bending the crowns of the willows and poplars, furrowing the Don and driving droves of russet leaves along the streets. On Khristonya's threshing floor a carelessly topped rick of wheat straw was shaking its shaggy locks. The wind pounced on it, chewed away the top, knocked the pole down, then suddenly forked up the whole golden load, carried it across the yard, whirled it about the street and, having generously spread the bare road with straw, dumped the bristling bundle on the roof of Stepan Astakhov's house. Khristonya's wife rushed bareheaded into the yard and, holding her skirt between her knees, watched the wind making free on the threshing floor, then went back indoors.

The third year of the war was beginning to tell on the affairs of the village. Deprived of their menfolk, the farmsteads with their crumbling sheds and dilapidated fences had a toothless look; all of them bore the unsightly marks of gradual decay. Khristonya's wife was keeping the farm going with her nine-year-old son; Anikei's had stopped bothering and took care only of herself, as her grass-widow's status seemed to warrant; she painted her cheeks and dressed herself up and for lack of any full-grown Cossacks accepted the attentions of lads of fourteen and upwards, as could be seen from the condition of her gate, which had been amply smeared with tar and still bore the brownish tell-tale marks. Stepan Astakhov's house stood empty. Before his departure the owner had boarded up the windows; parts of the roof had caved in and burdock was sprouting all over it, the lock on the door was rusty, the gates hung open and the overgrown yard could be invaded at any time by stray cattle seeking shelter from the heat or bad weather. The wall of Ivan Tomilin's house was toppling into the street and was held up only by a forked branch; evidently fate was taking its revenge on the valiant artilleryman for all the German and Russian homes he had destroyed as a gun-layer.

And so it was in every street and side-lane of the village. At the lower end only Pantelei's farm looked trim and in proper working order. But even here all was not well. Age had toppled the tin cocks on the roof of the barn; the barn itself had sunk sideways and an experienced eye could have observed signs of bad husbandry. The old man could not cope with everything; he had even reduced

his sowings, not to mention other things. Only the Melekhov family had not grown less; to make up for the
absence of Petro and Grigory, who were still away at the
war, Natalya had in the previous autumn given birth to
twins. She had managed to please both her mother- and
father-in-law by having a baby boy and a baby girl. Her
pregnancy had been a hard one; some days she had been
scarcely able to walk because of the agonising pains in her
legs. She would drag herself about, wincing with the pain
but not giving in to it, and it left no mark on her brown,
thin but happy face. Tiny beads of perspiration would
break out on her forehead at moments when the ache in
her legs was particularly bad and this was the only sign
by which Ilyinichna could tell what she was suffering.
'Go and lie down, you mad creature!' she would chide,
shaking her head. 'What are you torturing yourself for?'

One bright September day Natalya felt the first signs
and walked out of the house.

'Where are you off to?' her mother-in-law asked.

'To the meadow. I must have a look at the cows.'

Natalya hurried away from the village, glancing over
her shoulder, moaning and holding her belly, then she
crept in among some thorn bushes and lay down. It was
dark when she made her way home by the back-lanes.
In her homespun apron she was carrying twins.

'Oh, you poor dear thing! You wretch! How could
you? Where have you been?' Ilyinichna wailed.

'I was too ashamed... I couldn't let Father... I'm clean,
Mother, and I've washed them too... Take them,' Natalya
replied, pale and apologetic.

Dunyashka dashed off for the midwife. Darya fussed
about spreading a blanket over a sieve and Ilyinichna,
laughing and crying at the same time, exclaimed, 'Darya!
Put that sieve away. D'you think they're kittens? Lord
above, there're two of them! Oh, goodness, and one's
a boy! Natalya, love!.. Well, make up her bed for her!'

Pantelei, who was in the yard when he was told that
his daughter-in-law had given birth to twins, at first
spread his arms in astonishment, then tugged joyfully
at his beard and wept, and then for no good reason burst
into a tirade against the midwife who had just hurried
up to the house.

'You're lying, old woman!' He shook a long-nailed
finger in front of the woman's nose. 'You're lying!
The Melekhov breed won't die out for a long time yet!
A Cossack and a lass—that's what my daughter's given

438

me! There's a daughter-in-law for you! Good Lord in heaven! How can I ever thank her, the darling, for such a favour!'

And what a fruitful year it was. The cow also had twins, and on St. Michael's day there were twins among the sheep and goats. Marvelling over the situation, Pantelei reasoned to himself, 'This must be a lucky year, a year of plenty! Everything's having twins. Ho! Ho! How we are multiplying!'

Natalya gave her babies the breast until they were a year old. In September she weaned them, but it was late autumn before she recovered her looks; her teeth gleamed a milky white in her thin face and there was a fresh warm glow in her eyes, which seemed too big on account of her thinness. She neglected herself and devoted her whole life to the children, giving them every minute free of housework. She washed and scrubbed, darned and knitted and would often perch herself on the bed, take the twins out of the cradle and, freeing her big melon-like breasts from her loose blouse with a movement of the shoulders, nurse the two of them together.

'They've sucked you dry as it is. You feed them too often!' Ilyinichna would say, slapping her grandchildren's plump creased little legs.

'Feed 'em up! Don't grudge your milk! You haven't got to save it for cream,' Pantelei would intervene with a jealous roughness.

In these years life was on the ebb, like the Don after a flood. The dull days dragged by one after another amid the constant humdrum of work and want, small joys and a great unsleeping anxiety for those who were away at the war. Occasional letters came from Petro and Grigory with the army in the field; they arrived in thumbed, greasy envelopes covered with postmarks. Grigory's last letter had been in strange hands; half of it was neatly blotted out with violet ink and there was a strange ink mark in the margin of the grey paper. Petro wrote more often, and his letters to Darya were full of threats and entreaties that she should stop her nonsense; evidently rumours of his wife's dalliance had reached him. With his letters Grigory also sent money—his army pay and the extra for his crosses. He promised to be coming home on leave, but for some reason did not come. The brothers were taking different roads; the war was weighing on Grigory, sucking the ruddiness from his cheeks and painting them with bile, and he longed for it to end;

but Petro was rising quickly and smoothly up the ladder of promotion; in the autumn of 1916 he had received the rank of sergeant-major and earned himself two crosses by sucking up to the squadron commander, and now he spoke in his letters of trying to get himself sent to an officers' training school. With Anikei, who had been home on leave that summer, he sent a German helmet and greatcoat, and a photograph of himself. His somewhat aged face stared complacently from the grey square of cardboard, the tips of his waxed blonde moustache stood erect, and under his snub nose the firm teeth showed in the smile his family knew so well. Life itself was smiling on Petro, and he was enjoying the war because it opened up such wonderful prospects. Could he, an ordinary Cossack lad who had followed the plough since he was a boy, ever have dreamed of becoming an officer and enjoying the sweet things of life? But war had flared up and in its ruddy glow he clearly glimpsed the life of ease that the future promised him... Only one corner of Petro's life displayed an unsightly flaw. Dark rumours about his wife were going round the village. Stepan Astakhov had been on leave that autumn and on his return to the regiment had boasted to the whole squadron of having had a fine time with Petro's grass-widow. Petro refused to believe the tales he heard from his friends; his face darkened, but he smiled and said, 'Stepan's making it all up! He's trying to get his own back on me for what Grigory did to him.'

But one day, whether deliberately or by chance, Stepan dropped an embroidered handkerchief as he left the dug-out; Petro, who was behind him, picked up the delicately woven piece of lace and recognised his wife's needlework. And once again a tight Kalmyk knot of enmity was tied between Petro and Stepan. Petro was only waiting for his chance, and it looked as if Stepan would soon be lying on the bank of the Western Dvina with Petro's mark on his skull. But it so happened that Stepan went out to raid a German outpost and failed to return. The Cossacks who were with him came back with the story that the German sentry must have heard them cutting the wire entanglements and thrown a grenade, but they had managed to rush the outpost; Stepan had bowled the sentry over with his fist, but another had got a shot in and Stepan had fallen. The Cossacks had stabbed the second sentry and dragged away the German who had been knocked senseless by Stepan's leaden fist.

Yet when it came to lifting Stepan he had proved too heavy and they had been forced to leave him. The wounded man had begged, 'Brothers! Don't leave me to my death! How can you, brothers!' But a burst of machine-gun fire had splashed over the wire and the Cossacks made off. Stepan's imploring cry had followed them, but men value their own skins more than that of others.

When he heard the news, Petro felt a little better, as if the smarting sore had been smeared with marmot fat. All the same, he told himself, when I go home on leave, I'll have Darya's blood! I'm not Stepan, I won't leave it like that. He thought of killing her, and at once rejected the idea. 'I'll kill a snake and it'll spoil my whole life for me. I'll rot in gaol and all my work'll be wasted, I'll lose everything.' So he decided to give her a beating, and one that would rid the woman for life of all desire for any more philandering. 'I'll bash her eye out, the snake. Then only the devil will want her.' Such was the conclusion reached by Petro while he sat it out in the trenches above the steep, clay-strewn bank of the Western Dvina.

Autumn crushed the trees and grass, the morning frosts seared them, the earth grew colder, the autumn nights blacker and longer. The Cossacks went about their duties in the trenches, fired off a few rounds at the enemy, wrangled with the sergeants-major over warm clothing, ate what they could get and often went hungry, but none of them ever stopped thinking about the Don homeland that was so far away from this unfriendly Polish soil.

That autumn Darya Melekhova was making up for all the time she had spent without her husband. On the first day of Intercession, Pantelei woke up as usual before anyone else in the house, stepped out into the yard and clutched his head in dismay. Somebody's mischievous hand had lifted the gate off its hinges and laid it across the road. This was a disgrace. The old man put the gate back at once and after breakfast called Darya into the summer kitchen. What was said there no one ever knew, but a few minutes later Dunyashka saw Darya dash out of the kitchen with her kerchief falling about her shoulders, her hair all over the place and tears streaming down her cheeks. As she passed Dunyashka, she jerked her shoulders and the dark arches of her eyebrows quivered on her angry tear-stained face.

'Just you wait, you old bastard! I'll give you something

441

to remember me by!' she hissed through her swollen lips.

Darya's blouse was torn at the back and a crimson-blue weal showed on the white skin. She flounced up the steps of the house and disappeared into the porch, and Pantelei limped out of the kitchen as furious as the devil, gathering a new pair of leather reins in his fist as he came.

Dunyashka heard her father's husky voice, 'You deserved a lot more than that, you bitch! Slut!'

Order was restored in the house. For a few days Darya remained on her best behaviour, went to bed earlier than anyone else, and smiled coldly in response to Natalya's sympathetic glances, merely shrugging a shoulder and raising an eyebrow as much as to say, 'Never mind, we'll see what happens next.' And on the forth day an incident occurred that never became known to anyone but Darya and her father-in-law. For a whole week afterwards Darya kept a triumphant smirk on her face and the old man went about embarrassed and confused, like a cat that had misbehaved; he said nothing to his wife about the incident and even at confession kept the whole affair and his sinful thoughts afterwads a secret from Father Vissarion.

It happened like this. Soon after Intercession, Pantelei, having convinced himself of Darya's reformed character, said to Ilyinichna, 'Don't be soft with Darya! Put as much work as you can on her shoulders. While she's busy, she won't have time to go a-roaming. She's a sleek young filly... All she can think about is gallivanting around.'

With this in mind he made Darya clean out the threshing barn, tidy up the old firewood in the back yard, and himself helped her to clear out the chaff shed. Towards evening he decided to carry the winnower from the barn to the chaff shed and called out his daughter-in-law.

'Darya!'

'What is it, Father?' she responded from the shed.

'Come and help me to carry the winnower.'

Darya came out of the shed, shaking out the chaff that had sprinkled down the collar of her blouse and adjusting her kerchief, and made for the barn through the gate of the threshing floor. Pantelei, wearing a loose padded jacket and torn trousers, limped on ahead of her. The yard was deserted. Dunyashka and her mother were spinning the autumn crop of wool, Natalya was kneading dough. The sunset was burning out in a crimson glow and the churchbells were ringing for evensong. A small raspberry-coloured cloud hung high up in the transparent sky and across the Don the rooks clung to the grizzled poplar branches like black charred rags. In the brittle hollow stillness of evening every sound had its own perfect clarity and pitch. A persistent smell of fresh dung and hay drifted over from the cattle pen. Grunting and straining, Pantelei with Darya's help carried the pealing rusty-red winnower into the shed, set it down in a corner, raked up a heap of chaff and turned to leave the shed.

'Father!' Darya called him in a low voice, almost a whisper.

He stepped behind the winnower and, suspecting nothing, asked, 'What's the matter?'

Darya was standing facing him with her blouse open and her hands behind her head, doing up her hair. A blood-red sunset ray coming through a chink in the wall had caught her in its glow.

'Here, Father, there's something... Come and have a look,' she said, bending sideways and glancing furtively over her father-in-law's shoulder at the wide-open door of the shed.

The old man came closer and Darya suddenly flung her arms round his neck, locked her fingers and dragged him after her, whispering, 'Here, Father, here... It's nice and soft here.'

'What are you at?' Pantelei gasped in fright.

He struggled to free his neck from Darya's grasp but she pulled his head toward her face with even greater force and her hot mouth breathed into his beard, laughing and whispering.

'Let go, you slut!' As the old man struggled to free himself he felt the pressure of his daughter-in-law's taut belly.

She clung to him and fell over on her back, pulling him with her.

'What the devil! You're mad!.. Let me go!'

'Don't you want it?' Darya asked panting, then unlocked her arms and pushed her father-in-law in the chest. 'Don't you want it? Or can't you do it any more?.. Well, don't judge me then! So there!'

Jumping to her feet, she hurriedly pulled down her skirt, brushed the wheat chaff off her back and shouted in the face of the dazed Pantelei.

'What did you beat me for the other day? D'you think I'm an old woman? You weren't like this when you were young, were you? My husband's been away for a year now! Am I supposed to have it with a dog? Nothing doing, cripple! And put that in your pipe and smoke it!'

Darya made a rude gesture and flounced away to the door, eyebrows dancing. At the door she took another careful look at herself, brushed the dust off her blouse and kerchief and said without looking at her father-in-law, 'I can't live without it. I've got to have a man. If you don't want it, I'll find someone else, and you'd better keep quiet!'

She flounced away to the gate of the threshing floor and disappeared without looking back. Pantelei stood by the rusty side of the winnower, munching his beard, and staring sheepishly at the shed and the toes of his patched working shoes. 'Could be she's right, after all? Mebbe I ought to have sinned with her?' he was thinking at that moment, stunned by what had happened.

VI

In November the frosts gained a firm hold. Snow fell early. At the bend near the upper end of the village the Don froze over and people would sometimes venture across the thin blue sheath to the other side, but lower down the river only the edges were coated with porous ice and the midstream rip was high and swollen with swirling grey-green waves. Eleven fathoms down amid the sunken wood in the pool by Black Ravine the sheat-fish had long since bedded down for the winter; alongside them lay the slimy carp, and only the small fish still coursed about the Don with sometimes a pike darting across the narrows in pursuit. The sterlet were lying on the shingle, and the village fishermen were waiting for keener, harder frosts, so that they could get out on the first firm ice and nab the valuable fish.

In November the Melekhovs received a letter from Grigory. He wrote from Cuvinski in Romania to say that he had been wounded in the first engagement of the campaign; the bullet had smashed a bone in his left arm and he was being sent home for treatment in his own district, at Kamenskaya. In the wake of this letter another misfortune descended on the Melekhov household. About a year and a half ago Pantelei, finding himself in need of money, had borrowed a hundred rubles in silver from Sergei Platonovich Mokhov and given him a promissory note. In summer the old man had been summoned to the shop and Atyopin, peering over his gold-rimmed pince-nez at Melekhov's beard, had asked, 'Well, Panthelei Prokofievich, are you going to pay uth back or not?'

Pantelei's glance roamed over the empty shelves and the counter that had grown shiny with age, and he shifted his feet uncomfortably.

'Wait a bit, Yemelyan Konstantinich, give me time to get things straightened out and I'll pay.'

They had left it at that. There had been no opportunity for Pantelei to straighten things out—it had not been that kind of harvest; nor were there any well fattened animals that he could sell. And then, all of a sudden, like snow in June, the bailiff arrived in the village, sent for the defaulter, and demanded the money on the nail.

Without allowing himself to be interrupted the bailiff read from a long sheet of paper spread on the table in front of him.

COURT ORDER

By order of His Imperial Majesty of the 27th day of October of the year 1916, I, Justice of the Peace of the Seventh Department of the Donetsk District, have heard the claim of merchant Sergei Mokhov against Sergeant Pantelei Melekhov in respect of 100 rubles owing by promissory note. On the basis of articles 81, 100, 129, 133 and 145 of the Civil Code, I hereby decree:

Sergeant Pantelei Prokofievich Melekhov shall pay the claimant merchant Sergei Platonovich Mokhov the sum of one hundred rubles owing by the promissory note of 21 June 1915, and also three rubles costs. The court's decision is not final and shall be announced as passed by default.

The said decision has legal force, on the basis of Article 156 of the Civil Code, Clause 3, and shall be put into effect forthwith. By order of His Imperial Majesty the Justice of the Peace of the Seventh Department of the Donetsk District hereby orders:

The above decision shall be executed in exact accordance with the law by all persons and institutions concerned. The officer charged with the execution of the court's decision shall be accorded due support in the performance of his duty by all local, police and military authorities.

When the order had been read out to him, Pantelei asked permission to go home, promising to bring the money that very day. But instead of going home he went straight to his son's father-in-law Miron Korshunov. On his way across the square he happened to meet one-armed Alexei Shamil.

'Limping along all right, Prokofievich?' Shamil greeted him.

'Just about.'

'Going far on God's errand?'

'To my kinsman. We've a little matter to discuss.'

'Oh! Well, it's a day of rejoicing for them. Haven't you heard? Miron's son Mitka is back from the war.'

'Is he really?'

'That's the story I heard,' Shamil said, winking with his eye and cheek at the same time and pulling out his pouch as he came up to Pantelei, 'Let's have a smoke! My paper, your baccy.'

As he lighted up, Pantelei wondered whether he ought to go to the Korshunovs or not. In the end he decided he should, and, taking leave of Alexei, limped on his way.

'Mitka's got a cross now too! He wants to catch up with your lads. There're as many crosses in the village now as sparrows in a woodpile!' Alexei boomed after him.

Pantelei took his time getting to the end of the village and approached the gate of the Korshunovs' house, glancing up at the windows. The master himself came to the door. Old Korshunov's freckled face looked as though it had been washed with joy; it seemed both cleaner and less freckled.

'Have you heard our good news?' Miron asked, shaking Pantelei's hand.

'I heard it from Alexei Shamil on the way here. There's something else I wanted to see you about, kinsman.'

'Let it wait! Come in now and greet our soldier. I must admit we've had a drink already to celebrate. My old woman had been keeping a bottle of royal for the occasion.'

'No need to tell me that,' Pantelei said with a smile, nostrils twitching. 'I smelt it a long way off.'

Miron threw open the door and stepped back to admit his guest. Pantelei crossed the threshold and found himself looking straight at Mitka, who was seated at the table in the place of honour.

'Here he is, our soldier!' Old Grishaka exclaimed, weeping and leaning his head on Mitka's shoulder as he rose from the table.

'What are you looking at, kinsman?' Mitka said in a deep rather husky voice, smiling.

'Well, it's like a miracle. When we saw you and Grigory off to the army, you were mere boys. But now look at

446

you—a real Cossack, good enough for the Ataman's Guards!'

Gazing at Mitka with tearful eyes, his mother poured a glass of vodka and let it overflow.

'You, clumsy cow! Spilling good stuff like that!' Miron shouted at her.

'Congratulations all, and here's to your happy arrival, 'Mitry Mironovich!'

Pantelei rolled the bluish whites of his eyes and in one breath, eyelashes quivering, drained the bulbous glass. Slowly wiping his lips and moustache with his hand, he shot a glance at the bottom of the glass and, throwing back his head again, tossed a last orphaned drop into his gaping black-toothed mouth, then took a deep breath as he bit into a cucumber and screwed up his eyes blissfully. Lukinichna brought him another glass, and the old man at once became absurdly drunk. Mitka watched him, smiling. His catlike pupils would first narrow to green rush-like slits, then grow big and dark. He had changed beyond recognition in the past few years. In this burly black-moustached Cossack there was almost nothing left of the former slim, agile Mitka they had seen off to the army three years before. He had grown much taller, his shoulders had broadened and acquired a stoop, and he had filled out. He probably weighed a good fourteen stone at least. His face and voice had coarsened and he looked old for his age. Only the eyes were the same, disturbing and restless; his mother wallowed in them, laughing and crying, and sometimes passing her wrinkled faded hand over her son's short straight hair and narrow white forehead.

'So you've come home with a cross on your chest?' Pantelei asked, smiling tipsily.

'What Cossack hasn't got one these days?' Mitka said with a frown. 'They've given Kryuchkov three crosses just for hanging around at headquarters.'

'He's proud, our lad is,' Old Grishaka put in hastily. 'He takes after me, the scoundrel, after his grandfather. He won't bow to no man.'

'That's not what they give 'em crosses for, I'd say.' Pantelei looked sulky, but Miron steered him away into the front room, sat him down on the family chest and asked, 'How's Natalya and the grandchildren? Doing well? Thank the Lord! Didn't you say you had come on business, kinsman? What is it then? Out with it or we'll have another drink and you'll be tipsy.'

447

'Give me some money. For God's sake! Help me out, or I'll be in a right mess over this—this money business.'

Pantelei made his request with a sweeping drunken self-abasement. Miron interrupted him.

'How much?'

'A hundred.'

'A hundred what?'

'A hundred rubles.'

'Well, say so then.'

Miron rummaged in the chest, pulled out a packet wrapped in a greasy handkerchief and untied it; rustling the crisp banknotes, he counted out ten tens.

'Thanks, kinsman, you've got me out of a hole.'

'What's a little thing like that among kinsmen. We'll settle up one day.'

Mitka was home for five days; he spent the nights with Anikei's wife, taking pity on the dire need of a woman, and this one in particular, a simple, ever willing soul. During the day he roamed around the village, visiting relatives and friends. Tall and wearing only a light trench jacket, he strolled jauntily along the streets with his cap tilted at a rakish angle, showing off his hardiness. One evening he dropped in at the Melekhovs', bringing with him into the well-heated kitchen the fragrance of frost and the unforgettable pungent smell of soldiery. He sat for a while, discussing the war and the village news, narrowed his green, rush-like eyes at Darya, and got up to go. Darya, who hadn't taken her eyes off him since he entered the house, swayed like a candle flame when Mitka banged the door behind him and, setting her lips, was about to slip on her shawl, but Ilyinichna intervened.

'Where're you off to, Darya?'

'I've got to go outside.'

'I'll come with you.'

Pantelei was sitting with his head sunk on his chest, as though he had heard nothing. Darya brushed past him on the way to the door, with a vixenish gleam from under her lowered lashes; her mother-in-law followed her, dragging her feet ponderously and sighing. Mitka lingered at the gate, boots creaking, a cigarette glowing in his cupped hand. At the click of the latch he took a step towards the porch.

'Is that you, Mitka? Did you get lost in our yard?' Ilyinichna called to him slyly. 'Bolt the gate when you go out, or it'll be banging all night. How windy it is, eh!'

'No, I didn't get lost. I'll bolt it,' Mitka said irritably

after a pause, then cleared his throat and went straight across the street to Anikei's place.

Mitka lived a thoughtless, bird-like life. Today he was alive and tomorrow could take care of itself. He served without any overexertion and, though fearless blood flowed in his veins, made little attempt to distinguish himself. On the other hand, Mitka's army record was somewhat stained. He had been convicted twice, for the raping of a Polish woman who was a Russian subject, and for robbery; in three years of war he had received countless punishments and reprimands, and on one occasion a court-martial had been on the point of sentencing him to be shot. But Mitka had a way of wriggling out of trouble and, although he had the worst reputation in regiment, he was liked by the Cossacks for his cheerful, smiling disposition, his bawdy songs (Mitka's merits in this respect were by no means undistinguished), his comradeship and down-to-earth simplicity, and by the officers, for his brigandish daring. Mitka smiled and trod the earth with a light wolfish step and there was much of the wolf breed in him: in his loping gait, in his way of looking from under lowered brows with those green glittering eyes, and even in the way he turned his head—Mitka never twisted his shell-shocked neck to look round, but turned his whole body. Closely knit out of hard muscle and broad bone, he was light and sparing in his movements; his body had that astringent smell of health and strength, like black earth raised by the plough. For Mitka life was straight and uncomplicated; it ran like a ploughed furrow and he followed it as though it were his by right. And his thoughts were equally primitive and straightforward: if he was hungry, he could and should steal, even from a friend, and when he was hungry he stole; if his boots were worn out, the simplest thing on earth was to take a pair off a German prisoner; if he had been caught in some wrongdoing, he would have to make up for it, and Mitka did so by going out on patrol and bringing back half-suffocated German sentries he had overpowered at their posts, and volunteering for other dangerous expeditions. When taken prisoner in 1915, he had been beaten and hacked with swords, but during the night he had torn a hole in the roof, leaving most of his fingernails in the thatch, and escaped, taking a cart harness with him as a keepsake. For this kind of reason Mitka got away with a lot of things.

On the sixth day Miron drove his son to Millerovo,

put him on the train, listened to the chain of green boxes rattling away into the distance, and stood for a long time, digging his whip handle into the slag of the embankment and not raising his lowered, misty eyes. Lukinichna wept for her son, Old Grishaka grunted in his room, and kept blowing his nose into his hand and wiping it on the greasy hem of his long uniform coat. And Anikei's wife wept, too, as she remembered Mitka's big, passionate body and suffered from the clap her soldier boy had left her with.

Time plaited the days as the wind plaits a horse's mane. Before Christmas there was a sudden thaw; for a whole day it rained and the water gushed madly down the Donside hills; last season's grass and mossy slabs of chalk grew green again on the headlands where the snow had melted; the edges of the Don foamed where the ice had been eaten away and the ice swelled up and turned a deathly blue. The bared black earth gave off an inexpressibly sweet smell. The water bubbled in the old ruts along the Hetman's highway. Fresh landslides left yawning gaps in the clayey ravines outside the village. The south wind wafted from the Chir the stewed smell of rotting grass and by noon the tenderest of blue shadows glowed on the skyline as in spring. Dappled puddles appeared by the piles of ash tipped out along the village fences. The earth round the ricks on the threshing floors thawed out and passers-by felt their noses tingling from the sweetness of rotten straw. Tarry water ran down the eaves from the ice-fringed thatch, the magpies cawed with all their might on the fences and, overcome by the premature languors of spring, the village bull that was spending the winter in Miron's yard bellowed incessantly, mauled the fences with his horns, rubbed up against an old worm-eaten oak ploughshare, shook out his silky dewlap, and pawed the mushy, thawing snow in the yard.

On the second day of Christmas the Don began to break up. A jam of ice got moving in midstream with a great crunching and grinding. Floes heaved themselves out onto the bank like sleepy monster fish. On the other side of the Don the poplars, goaded by the exciting southern wind, strained forward as though in a bounding gallop. And their muffled hissing murmur floated across the river.

But towards nightfall the hill began to howl, the crows flocked together on the square, Khristonya's pig bolted past the Melekhov's house with a wisp of hay in its mouth, and Pantelei decided that spring had been nipped in the bud and tomorrow the frosts would strike again. That night the wind swung round to the east and a light frost patched the thaw-ravaged puddles with crystal shards of ice. By morning a Moscow wind was blowing and the frost had clamped down hard. Winter was restored to its rights. Out in the middle of the Don what was left of the ice floated by like big white leaves in memory of the thaw and the bare earth steamed frostily on the hill.

Soon after Christmas at a meeting in the stanitsa Pantelei heard from the local clerk that he had seen Grigory in Kamenskaya, and had been asked to tell the family that he would soon be home.

VII

Sergei Platonovich Mokhov was in the habit of feeling life from all sides with his small brown hands, the backs of which were sparsely coated with shiny hairs. Sometimes life responded playfully to his touch, sometimes it hung like a millstone round the neck of a drowning man. Sergei Platonovich had seen a great deal in his time and been in various tight corners. Long ago, when he had been in the grain storage business, he had bought grain from the Cossacks for next to nothing only to be faced with the task of carting four thousand poods of burnt wheat out of the village and dumping it in Bad Luck Ravine. He also remembered 1905, when someone in the village one dark autumn night had let fly at him with a shot-gun. But Mokhov had survived and grown rich. Eventually he had saved sixty thousand and stashed it away in the Volga-Kama Bank, but now some sixth sense told him that a time of great upheaval was imminent. He lived in expectation of bad times ahead, and was not mistaken. In January of the year 1917 the schoolmaster Balanda, who was slowly dying of consumption, complained to him,

'The revolution's just round the corner and here am I, dying of the silliest and most sentimental disease imaginable. It's such a shame, Sergei Platonovich!.. Such a shame that I shan't live to see your capital done away with and you flushed out of your cosy little nest.'

'Why is it a shame?'

'Of course, it is! After all, you know, it would be nice to see everything go up in smoke.'

'No, thank you, my friend! You'd better die now and I'll wait till tomorrow!' Sergei Platonovich replied, fuming inwardly.

In January, echoes of the St. Petersburg gossip about Rasputin and the royal family were still floating around the villages and stanitsas, and at the beginning of March Sergei Platonovich was caught like a bustard under a net by the news of the overthrow of the autocracy. The Cossacks received the news with restrained alarm and waited. That day the old men and some of the younger ones hung about in a crowd round Mokhov's closed shop until evening. The village ataman Kiryushka Soldatov (Manytskov's successor), a big, ginger-moustached and slightly cross-eyed Cossack, was depressed. He took hardly any part in the discussions that had flared up round the shop, and let his squinting eyes rove over the Cossacks, occasionally offering some confused remark such as 'They've made a fine mess of it!' or 'What a thing to happen!' or 'How shall we carry on now?'

At the sight of the crowd round his shop Sergei Platonovich decided to go and talk to the old men. He put on his racoon coat and, leaning on a brown cane embossed with a modest silver monogram, walked out on to his front porch. The murmur of voices reached him from the shop.

'Well, Platonich, you're a learned man, tell us, ignorant folk, what's going to happen now?' Matvei Kashulin asked, smiling nervously and gathering a bunch of crooked wrinkles round his chilled nose.

In response to Sergei Platonovich's bow the old men respectfully raised their hats and stepped back to admit him to their circle.

'We'll have to live without a tsar,' Sergei Platonovich began hesitantly.

The old men all spoke at once.

'Without a tsar! How can we?'

'Our fathers and their fathers before them lived under the tsars—how come we don't need one now?'

'Cut the head off and the legs won't live, I reckon.'

'What kind of government will there be?'

'Speak up, Platonich! Tell us the truth... What are you afraid of?'

'Mebbe he don't know himself,' Avdeich the Braggart said with a grin that made the dimples in his cheeks even deeper.

Sergei Platonovich stared dully at his old rubber over-boots and said, spitting the words out painfully, 'The State Duma will rule the country. We'll have a republic.'

'So that's what we've come to, in the devil's name!'

'When we were serving under the late Alexander the Second,' Avdeich began, but a sombre old Cossack named Bogatiryov interrupted him sternly, 'We've heard that before! That's got nothing to do with it.'

'So it looks like the end of the Cossacks?'

'While we're busy with these strikes, the Germans will be at the gates of Saint Petersburg.'

'If it's equality they're out for, they'll be wanting to make us equal with the peasants.'

'They'll soon be after our land, if we don't look out.'

Forcing himself to smile, Sergei Platonovich surveyed the old men's worried faces and a feeling of disgust and depression gripped his mind. He parted his sandy beard with a habitual gesture and began to speak, raging against no one knew whom.

'Yes, this is what they've brought Russia to, elders... They want to cut you down to the level of common peasants, rob you of your privileges, and soon they'll start paying off old scores. There are grim times ahead... It all depends on what hands take the reins of power, but it may well mean the end of everything.'

'We'll see about that, if we're still alive!' Bogatiryov shook his head and eyed Sergei Platonovich mistrustfully from under his shaggy brows. 'You've got your own axe to grind, Platonich, but mebbe things will work out a bit easier for us?'

'Easier for you—how?' Sergei Platonovich retorted sarcastically.

'Mebbe the new government will end the war... Such a thing could happen, couldn't it now?'

Sergei Platonovich dismissed the idea with a wave of his hand and with all his years on his shoulders stumped away to his smart blue-painted porch. As he walked, he thought distractedly of money, of the mill and the fall-off in trade, remembered that Liza was now in Moscow, and that Vladimir was soon to arrive from Novocherkassk. The dull prick of anxiety for his children did not interrupt the riotous flow of his thoughts. He reached the porch, feeling that in this one day all the brightness had gone out of life and that even he himself had somehow faded inwardly. A sour taste of rust filled his mouth with saliva. Glancing round at the old men by the shop, he spat over the carved rail of the porch and shuffled across the veranda into the house. Anna Ivanovna met her husband in the dining room, scanned his face with the usual indifferent glance of her colourless eyes, and asked, 'Will you have a drink before tea?'

'A drink? Of course, not!' Sergei Platonovich brushed the suggestion aside disdainfully.

He took off his coat with the same taste of rust in his mouth and a dull void in the head.

'There's a letter from Liza.'

Anna Ivanovna plodded fussily into the bedroom (the large household was such a burden to her, she had walked like this ever since her marriage) and brought out a letter with the seal broken.

Sergei Platonovich wrinkled his nose at the smell of perfume from the thick envelope. 'The girl's quite empty-headed, and stupid too,' he told himself. It was the first time he had thought of his daughter in this way. He read the letter unattentively and for some reason paused at the word 'mood', pondering over it as if it might have some strange and incomprehensible meaning. Liza ended her letter with a request for money. Sergei Platonovich was still aware of the aching void in his head as he read the closing lines. He suddenly wanted to hide himself in a corner and weep. At that moment life had reared up before him and revealed its utter emptiness.

'She's a stranger to me,' he thought about his daughter. 'And I'm a stranger to her. The only family feelings she ever has are when she needs money. The girl's a slut, she has lovers. But when she was small, she was my own fair-headed little darling. God, how everything changes! And I was fool enough in my old age to believe in the good life I was going to have in the future, but the fact is I'm as lonely as a wayside cross. My money wasn't made cleanly—but you can't make it otherwise!—I thieved and squeezed, and now there's been a revolution and to-morrow my servants may be turning me out of my own home. Everything will go to blazes! As for the children... Vladimir's a fool... Oh, what does it matter anyway?'

By some absurd twist of memory he recalled an incident that had occurred years before at the mill. A Cossack who had brought his corn to be milled made a row about there being a big shortfall in the flour and refused to pay. Sergei Platonovich who had been in the engine-room at the time, came out and, on hearing what all the noise was about, told the scalesman and the millers not to give the Cossack his flour. The little runt of a Cossack had tugged the sack one way and Zakhar, the burly, broad-chested miller, had pulled it the other. When the Cossack tried to push him away, the miller turned round and hit him on the temple with his big fist. The Cossack went down, then jumped to his feet and stood swaying, with blood seeping from the cut on his left temple. Suddenly he stepped up to Sergei Platonovich and breathed in a whining whisper, 'Take the flour then! Stuff yourself with it!' and walked out with his shoulders trembling.

Without any apparent connection Sergei Platonovich remembered this incident and its consequences. The Cossack's wife had come to ask for the flour to be given back. Forcing tears from her eyes and trying to win the other customers' sympathy, she had wailed, 'What do they think they're doing, good folk! What right have they? Give us back our flour!'

'Get out, woman, while the going's good, or I'll tear your hair out!' Zakhar retorted chuckling.

Sergei Platonovich had been shocked and annoyed to see Knave the scalesman, as small and puny as that Cossack, go for Zakhar with his fists. He was given a cruel thrashing, and then came asking to be paid off. All this passed swiftly through Mokhov's mind while he folded the letter he had just read and stared unseeingly at nothing in particular.

The day left him with an ugly throbbing pain. He slept badly, tossing and turning in the grip of absurd thoughts and half-conscious desires. He fell asleep after midnight and, on hearing in the morning that Yevgeny Listnitsky was back from the front and staying with his father in Yagodnoye, decided to pay them a visit, find out the true state of affairs and relieve the bitter ferment of foreboding that had gathered in his mind. Yemelyan, sucking his pipe as usual, harnessed a cob to the town sledge and drove his master off to Yagodnoye.

The sun ripened over the village like an orange apricot; beneath it the clouds smoked and smouldered. The keen frosty air was charged with a rich, fruity smell. The thin shards of ice on the road crackled under the horse's hoofs, the steam from its nostrils drifted back on the wind and coated its mane with hoarfrost. Soothed by the rapid drive and the cold, Sergei Platonovich dozed and swayed from side to side, rubbing his shoulders on the carpeted back of the sledge. Behind him a crowd of Cossacks in their black sheepskins loomed darkly on the village square and the women in their fur-trimmed winter coats stood about in sheep-like clusters.

The schoolmaster Balanda with a handkerchief pressed to his green-tinged mouth and a red ribbon in his button-hole was addressing the crowd, his eyes shining feverishly.

'...The rule of the accursed autocracy has ended! From now on your sons will no longer be sent to whip the workers into submission. Your shameful service to the blood-sucker tsar is over. The Constituent Assembly will be the master of the new, free Russia. It will succeed in building a different, a brighter, so to speak—life!'

Behind him his mistress stood tugging at the folds of his short, waisted overcoat and whispering imploringly, 'No more, Mitya! Stop now! It's bad for you! You'll be coughing up blood again... Mitya!'

The Cossacks listened to Balanda with eyes on the ground, giving occasional grunts and hiding their smiles. He didn't manage to finish his speech. A sympathetic voice boomed from one of the front rows, 'Life's going to be bright enough, by the looks of it, but you won't last that long, old chum. You'd better go home. It's pretty fresh outdoors today.'

Balanda mumbled a half-finished phrase and stumbled away out of the crowd, looking exhausted.

Sergei Platonovich arrived at Yagodnoye at noon. Yemelyan led the cob to the wicker mangers by the stables and while his master was climbing out of the sledge and fishing for his handkerchief under the skirts of his sheepskin, found time to unbridle the animal and cover its back with a horse-blanket. At the porch Sergei Platonovich was met by a tall borzoi hound with ruddy patches on its grizzled coat. It rose to meet the stranger, stretching its long, sinewy legs and yawning; the other dogs that had been lying like black bundles round the porch followed its example.

'What a crowd of them, damn it!' Sergei Platonovich mounted the steps backwards, eyeing them apprehensively.

The dry well-lighted hall stank of dogs and vinegar. Over a chest, on a branching pair of antlers hung an officer's astrakhan busby, a hood with a silver tassle and a sheepskin cloak. Sergei Platonovich glanced up at them and for a moment it seemed to him as if a black, shaggy figure was standing on the chest, shoulders hunched in astonishment. A plump dark-eyed woman appeared from a side room. She studied the newcomer attentively and asked, without changing the serious expression on her darkly handsome face, if he wished to see the master.

'I'll go and tell him.'

She disappeared into the drawing room without knocking and closed the door firmly behind her. With some difficulty Sergei Platonovich had recognised this plump dark-eyed beauty as Aksinya Astakhova. She, too, had recognised him and, compressing her cherry-red lips, walked away holding herself unnaturally erect and displaying her smooth bare elbows. A minute later she reappeared followed by old Listnitsky himself. With a measured smile of welcome he boomed condescendingly, 'Ah, my worthy merchant! What brings you here? Please...' And he stepped aside, motioning his guest into the drawing room.

Sergei Platonovich bowed with the esteem for social dignitaries that had long since become part of his nature, and entered the room. Yevgeny Listnitsky rose to meet him, looking at him narrowly from under his pince-nez.

'This is splendid, my dear Sergei Platonovich! Very glad to see you! What's this? Not getting older, are you?'

'Not at all, Yevgeny Nikolayevich! I still hope to outlive you. How are you? Safe and well?'

Showing his gold-capped teeth in a smile, Yevgeny escorted the guest to a chair. They sat down together at a small table, exchanging trivial remarks and searching each other's faces for the changes that had occurred there since their last meeting. Having ordered tea, the general joined them. He was smoking a big curved pipe. He halted beside Sergei Platonovich's chair, laid his long bony hand on the table, and asked, 'How are things in your village? Have you heard—the good news?'

Sergei Platonovich looked up at the clean-shaven sagging folds on the general's chin and neck and sighed.

'Indeed I have!'

'What a fatal predetermination was at work there...' The general's throat quivered as he swallowed smoke. 'It was bound to happen. I foresaw it from the day war broke out. But, of course ... the dynasty was doomed. Just now I recalled Merezhkovsky—do you remember, Yevgeny? His *Peter and Alexei*? After he has been tortured, Tsarevich Alexei says to his father, "My blood will fall on your descendants."'

'We have nothing definite to go on, you see,' Sergei Platonovich began anxiously; he fidgeted in his chair for a moment, lit a cigarette and went on, 'We haven't seen a newspaper for a week. Only these incredible rumours, utter confusion. It's terrible, really it is! When I heard that Yevgeny Nikolayevich had come home on leave, I decided to drive out here and ask what's going on, what we can expect.'

There was not a trace of a smile on Yevgeny's pale, carefully shaven face as he gave his account of the situation.

'Menacing events... The men are literally all demoralised. They don't want to fight, they're tired. What it amounts to is that since the beginning of this year we haven't had any soldiers in the generally accepted sense of the word. The soldiers we once had have turned into gangs of criminals run wild. Father here, for example—he simply can't imagine it. He can't imagine to what extent our army has disintegrated... They leave their positions in defiance of orders, rob and kill civilians, murder their own officers, go about marauding... Refusal to obey orders is the usual thing nowadays.'

'A fish rots from the head,' old Listnitsky puffed out the phrase with his smoke.

'I wouldn't say so,' Yevgeny frowned, and a veined eyelid ticked nervously. 'No, I wouldn't say so... The army is rotting from below, demoralised by the Bolsheviks. Even the Cossack units, and especially those which are in close contact with the infantry, are morally unstable. There is tremendous war weariness and yearning for home... And on top of that you have the Bolsheviks.'

'What is it they want?' Sergei Platonovich could not refrain from asking.

'Oh!..' Listnitsky gave a dry laugh. 'What they want... It's worse than cholera germs! Worse in the sense that it more easily infects a man and spreads among the mass of the rank-and-file. I'm talking about an idea. No quarantine is of any use against it. Among the Bolsheviks there are undoubtedly gifted people—I have met some of them— and there are just plain fanatics, but the overwhelming majority are irresponsible thugs. They are not interested in the substance of the Bolshevik doctrine, but only in the possibility of plunder and getting out of the fighting. Their chief desire is to seize power, put an end to what they call the "imperialist" war, even by means of a separate peace, then give the land to the peasants and the factories to the workers. The whole thing, of course, is as utopian as it is foolish, but the soldiers' sympathies are won by such primitive means.'

Yevgeny spoke with suppressed anger. The ivory cigarette-holder danced in his fingers. Sergei Platonovich listened leaning forward as though he were about to jump to his feet. The elder Listnitsky shuffled about the room in his shaggy black astrakhan boots, nibbling the greenish-grey tip of his moustache.

Yevgeny told them how even before the February events he had been forced to flee the regiment in fear of Cossack revenge, and about what he had seen later in Petrograd.

The conversation faltered for a minute. Old Listnitsky stared at the bridge of Sergei Platonovich's nose and asked, 'Well, will you buy the grey, the one you had a look at in autumn—Boyarinya's son?'

'Is this the time for such things, Nikolai Alexeyevich?' Sergei Platonovich wrinkled his forehead pitifully and made a hopeless gesture.

Meanwhile in the servants' quarters Yemelyan had warmed himself and was drinking tea, mopping the perspiration from his ruddy-brown cheeks and talking about the village and its news. Aksinya stood by the bed, her bosom resting on the carved headboard, a fluffy woollen shawl drawn round her shoulders.

'Our house must've tumbled down by now?' she said.

'No, why should it? It's still standing! What could happen to it?' Yemelyan replied, keeping her in suspense over every word.

'How are our neighbours, the Melekhovs, getting on?'

'Getting on all right.'

'Has Petro been home on leave?'

'Don't think he has.'

'And Grigory?.. Their Grisha?'

'Grigory was home after Christmas. His woman's given him twins. Ay, o'course, Grigory was home, he's been wounded.'

'Wounded?'

'O'course, he was. Wounded in the arm. He's got marks all over him now, like a dog after a fight. You can't tell what he's got more of—crosses or scars.'

'What's he like now?' Aksinya asked with a dry spasm rising in her throat, and coughed to steady her faltering voice.

'Just the same—hook-nosed and dark. A Turk all over, as he's supposed to be.'

'I didn't mean that... Has he aged?'

'How the devil should I know? Mebbe he has a bit. His wife had twins, so he can't have aged all that much.'

'There's a draught in this room,' Aksinya said with a shiver, and went out.

Yemelyan watched her go, poured himself his eighth cup of tea and, placing his words slowly, as a blind man places his feet, muttered, 'The stinking, dirty bag! Rotten as they come she is! Used to be running about the village in farm boots and now she's a fine lady. She can't even talk straight. I can't stick women like her, the bitches. I'd have 'em all... The creeping, slimy snake! I'd... "There's a draught in this room..." Mare's snot, that's what she is!'

He was so offended that he left his eighth cup unfinished. Rising from the table, he crossed himself and walked out with his nose in the air, deliberately dirtying the well polished floor with his boots.

All the way home he was as sullen as his master. He vented his spite on the horse, flicking the tongue of the whip round the animal's genitals and calling it all the names he could think of. Contrary to his habit, he did not exchange a single word with his master throughout the journey. Sergei Platonovich also maintained a frightened silence.

VIII

Just before the February revolution the First Brigade of one of the infantry divisions in the reserve of the South Western Front and the 27th Don Cossack Regiment that was attached to it had been withdrawn from the front line with the idea of bringing them up to the capital and using them to subdue the disorders that had broken out there. The brigade was moved back behind the lines, fitted out with new winter clothing, fed well for a day, and on the next day loaded into trains and sent off towards Minsk. But events forestalled them; even on the day of their departure there had been persistent rumours that the Emperor had signed the act of abdication at the headquarters of the Commander-in-Chief.

The brigade was turned back before completing half its journey. At the station of Razgon the Cossacks were ordered to detrain. The tracks were choked with vans and wagons. Soldiers with red ribbons on their greatcoats and new well-made rifles of Russian pattern but English manufacture were milling about the platform. Many of them seemed excited and glanced apprehensively at the Cossacks as they formed up in squadrons.

It had been a wet, dreary day. Water was trickling off

the roofs of the station buildings; the oily puddles between the tracks reflected the grey soggy sheepskin of the sky. The whistle blasts of the shunting engines sounded muffled and flabby. Behind a warehouse the Cossack regiment formed up in mounted order to meet the brigade commander. The horses' legs, wet to the fetlocks, were steaming and crows alighted fearlessly behind the assembled ranks, scratching and pecking at the orange apples of their droppings.

The brigade commander, mounted on a tall raven-black horse, rode up to the Cossacks accompanied by the commander of the regiment. He drew rein and surveyed the squadrons, then began speaking with nervous motions of his bare hand, as though pushing away the uncertain, muffled words he was uttering.

'Cossacks! By the will of the people the hitherto reigning Emperor Nicholas the Second has—er—been deposed. Power has passed to the Provisional Committee of the State Duma. The army, yourselves included, must take this—er—news calmly... The duty of the Cossacks is to defend their Motherland from the attacks of external and—er—so to speak, external enemies. We shall stand aside from the disturbances that have begun and allow the civilian population to choose ways of organising a new government. We must stand aside! As far as the army is concerned, war and politics are incompatible... At a time of such upheaval of—er—all the foundations, we must be firm as...' the brigade commander, a stolid old general, not used to making speeches, cast around hesitantly for comparisons, his eyebrows twitching and a look of dumb agony on his flaccid face; the squadrons waited patiently: '...er—as steel. It is your duty as Cossacks to obey your commanders. We shall fight the enemy as valiantly as we have always done, and back there...' a vague sweep of the hand behind him, '...back there, let the State Duma decide the fate of the country. First we'll finish the war, then we, too, will take part in the internal life, but as things are now—er--it wouldn't do. We cannot sacrifice the army... There must be no politics in the army!'

At the same station a few days later the Cossacks took the oath of allegiance to the Provisional Government; they began attending meetings, keeping together in small groups made up of men from their own districts, aloof from the army rank-and-file that had flooded into the station. They discussed at great length the speeches they had heard, recalling and probing mistrustfully every doubtful word. All of them for some reason had formed the opinion that if there was to be freedom, it must mean the end of the war, and this firmly entrenched notion presented a grave challenge to the officers, who maintained that it was Russia's duty to fight on to the end.

The dismay that had seized the high command since the overthrow of the tsar was reflected at lower levels; divisional headquarters seemed to have forgotten the existence of the marooned brigade. By now the men had eaten what was left of the eight days' rations that had been issued to them and went off in droves to forage in the surrounding villages; illicitly distilled spirits appeared on sale at the markets and it was by no means an uncommon sight to see drunken officers and N. C. O.s in the streets.

Knocked out of their routine by the transfer, the Cossacks hung about in the vans, waited impatiently to be sent home to the Don (a rumour that the second-line reserves were to be demobilised had gained a firm hold), paid scant attention to their horses and spent days on end in the market square, trading saleable articles that they had kept since their days in the front line: German blankets, bayonets, saws, greatcoats, leather field bags, and tobacco.

The order to return to the front was received with open grumbling. The Second Squadron refused to leave and would not allow the locomotive to be coupled to the train, but the regimental commander threatened to disarm them and gradually the tumult died down. The trains got under way and headed for the front. In the vans the talk went on:

'What d'ye make o' this, lads? They call it freedom, but there's no let-up from the war—more bloodshed, eh?'

'They've got the screw on us again!'

'What was the idea of kicking out the tsar then?'

'We'll be as well off without him as with him.'

'It's the same old pair of pants, only back to front.'

'Ay, that's it!'

'How much longer will this go on?'

'Three years with a rifle on your back!'

At the next junction the Cossacks tumbled out of the vans as if the word had gone round secretly among them and, defying the threats and warnings of the regimental commander, held a meeting. In vain the commandant and aged station-master flapped about among the grey mass of Cossack greatcoats, urging the men to clear the tracks and go back to their vans. The Cossacks listened intently to a speech by a sergeant of the Third Squadron. The next to speak was a small well-knit Cossack named Manzhulov. Angry words spurted from his white-lipped, twisted mouth.

'Cossacks! This can't go on! We're being led up a tree again! They want to trick us! Now there's been a revolution and all the people have been given freedom, they ought to stop the war, because the people don't want war and nor do we! Aren't I right?'

'That you are!'

'Up the mare's arse with it!'

'We're sick and tired of it, all of us are!'

'We can't hardly keep our trousers up, let alone fight a war!'

'We—don't—want—war!'

'Let's go home!'

'Unhitch that engine! Come on, Fedot!'

'Cossacks! Wait a minute! Cossacks! Brothers! Can't you listen, you devils, blast you!.. Brothers!' Manzhulov's voice rose to a yell as he tried to make his voice heard above the roar of a thousand throats. 'Wait! Don't touch the engine! We don't need it. The thing here is this trickery... Let His Honour the regimental commander show us the document! Are we really being ordered back to the front or is it just one of their fine ideas?'

The regiment went back to the vans only when the commander, lips trembling, unable to control himself, had read aloud the telegram he had received from divisional headquarters, recalling the regiment to the front.

In one of the vans there were six men from Tatarsky, all of them serving in the 27th Regiment: Petro Melekhov, Mikhail Koshevoi's uncle, Nikolai Koshevoi, Anikei, Fedot Bodovskov, Merkulov, who with his curly black beard and wild light-brown eyes looked like a Gypsy, and Maxim Gryaznov, the Korshunovs' neighbour, a happy-go-lucky fellow, who before the war had earned a bad reputation throughout the district as a fearless horse-thief. The Cossacks were always laughing at him, 'It's Merkulov who ought to be stealing horses—he looks like a Gypsy, but never steals any. But you, Maxim, get all worked up as soon as you see a horse's tail!' Maxim would flush, screw up his flax-blue eyes, and hit back maliciously, 'A Gypsy spent the night with Merkulov's mother and mine must have got jealous.

I wouldn't be this way otherwise—not to save my life!'

'The wind blew gustily right through the van; the horses stood at the makeshift mangers with blankets on their backs; on the floor, on a heap of frozen earth, some damp sticks were burning smokily and the acrid smoke was floating away through a chink in the door. The Cossacks sat around on their saddles, drying their foot-cloths, which stank of sweat and damp. Fedot Bodovs-kov was warming his bare bandy legs by the fire. His angular, Kalmyk face wore a smile of content. Gryaznov was sewing on the sole of his boot as best as he could with hempen thread, and muttering to no one in particular in his husky smoker's voice.

'When I was a kid, I'd get up on the stove-bed some-times and my Granny (she was over a hundred years old by then!) would feel my head for lice and say, "Ah, Maximushka, my little berry! In the old days the people didn't like this—they lived a proper, orderly life and no troubles ever came upon them. But you, my little one, will live to see a time when the earth will be all tied up with wire and there'll be birds with iron beaks flying about in the blue sky, and they'll peck people like a rook pecks a watermelon. And death and dearth will come upon the land, and brother will rise against brother, and son against father... And there will be no more people left than there is grass after a fire."' Maxim made a pause, then went on, 'That's just what's happened. They've invented the telegraph—there's your wire for you! And the iron birds are the aeroplanes. Haven't they pecked plenty of our lads? And there'll be famine all right. Compared with other years, my folk are sowing only half of what they used to, and every farmer's the same. There's no one left in the villages but the old folk and the youngsters. If the harvest fails, you'll know what "dearth" is.'

'What about brother rising against brother—that's not happened yet, has it?' asked Petro Melekhov, poking the fire.

'It'll come to that too.'

'They won't agree about a government, and they'll start scrapping amongst themselves,' Fedot Bodovskov put in.

'Then we'll have to pacify 'em.'

'You'd better pacify the Germans first,' Koshevoi said laughing.

'Well, why not? We're good for some more fighting yet.'

Anikei wrinkled his hairless womanish face in feigned alarm and exclaimed, 'By our hairy-legged tsaritsa, how much longer will we be good for fighting?'

'Till you grow some hair on your face, you gelding,' Koshevoi jeered.

A laugh went up. Petro got some smoke down his throat and stared at Anikei with tears in his eyes, pointing at him.

'Hair's stupid stuff,' Anikei mumbled lamely. 'It sometimes grows where it shouldn't. I wouldn't swing my legs like that if I was you, Koshevoi.'

'No, we've had enough! A lot more than enough!' Gryaznov burst out unexpectedly. 'Here we are going through hell, getting eaten up by lice while our families are hungry. You know how bad it is? They wouldn't bleed, even if you cut 'em!'

'What're you blowing your top for?' Petro asked derisively, chewing the tip of his wheaten moustache.

'Everyone knows what for,' Merkulov replied for Gryaznov, and buried his smile firmly in his curly Gypsy beard. 'Everyone knows the Cossack's fed up, homesick... It's like when a herdsman's grazing his herd. While the sun's still drying the dew, the animals don't mind, they go on feeding. But when the sun climbs the oak and the gadflies get a-buzzing, and tearing into the cattle, that's when it happens...' Merkulov shot a cunning look at his companions and went on, turning to Petro. 'That's when the cattle get their rag out, Sergeant-Major! You know that yourself! You're not one of the pen-pusher types, are you! You've twisted the oxen's tails yourself, I reckon. What mostwise happens is that one of the heifers flicks her tail up and starts a-mooing, then off she goes! And the whole herd after her! The herdsman chases 'em, "Hi there, where're you off to?" But what's the use?! That herd's charging at full gallop, no worse than we did at the Germans at Nezviska. So how can you hold 'em?'

'What are you driving at?'

Merkulov did not answer at once. He wound a lock of his tar-black beard round his finger, tugged at it fiercely, then spoke coolly and without a trace of a smile.

'We've been fighting for well over two years, haven't we? This is our third year in the trenches. Why or what for, no one knows... So what I say is, it won't be long before some Gryaznov or some Melekhov will get his rag out and make for home, and the regiment will follow him, and then the army... We've had enough!'

465

'So that's it...'

'Sure it is! I'm not blind. I can see everything's hanging by a thread. You've only got to shout "Scat!" and the whole lot will fall to bits, like an old coat off your shoulders. In this third year of war the sun has climbed the oak for us too.'

'Take it easy!' Bodovskov advised. 'Petro's a sergeant-major, you know.'

'I've never harmed my own mates,' Petro flared up.

'Keep your shirt on! I was only joking,' Bodovskov looked confused, twiddled the gnarled toes of his bare feet, then stood up and padded over to a manger.

In a corner by some bales of pressed hay another group of Cossacks was talking quietly. Two of them—Fadeyev and Kargin—were from the village of Karginsky, and the other eight were from various villages and stanitsas.

After a while they began to sing. They were led by Alimov, a Cossack from the River Chir. He struck up a dancing song, but someone thumped him on the back and bawled hoarsely, 'Not that!'

'Hi there, you orphans, come over to the fire!' Koshevoi invited them. They fed the fire with some chips of wood (all that was left of a station fence) and with a blaze going the songs grew merrier:

> By the churchyard gates
> A snorting warhorse awaits.
> An old woman wails with her grandson
> The young wife weeps for her husband.
> Then from the holy shrine's door
> Comes a Cossack girded for war.
> His wife holds his stirrup,
> His nephew the lance...

In the next van an accordion was wheezily attacking a Cossack dance. The heels of government-issue boots were thumping the floorboards ruthlessly and someone was squawking out in a cracked voice:

> Oh, what a life of trouble and care,
> Tsardom's yokes are hard to bear.
> The Cossacks' necks are chafed and sore,
> They can't breathe freely any more.
> Pugachov roams the Don country,
> Sends his call out to the poor,
> 'Atamans, Cossacks, come, follow me...'

Then a second voice, drowning the first, broke into a mad high-pitched gabble:

> *The tsar in faith and truth we serve*
> *And for our wives we sorely yearn.*
> *With a wench we'll yearn no more*
> *And on tsar's ... hot tin we'll pour.*
> *Whip it up! Heh! Hot it up!*
> *Ho! Ho! Ho! Haw! Haw! Haw!*

The Tatarsky men had long since given up their song and listened grinning and winking to the wild commotion in the next van. Petro Melekhov burst out laughing.

'They've got devils inside 'em!'

Merkulov's brown and yellow spotted eyes suddenly glowed with merriment; he jumped to his feet and after waiting a moment for the measure, got a beat going with the toe of his boot that sounded like fine corn being poured into a bin, then suddenly he stamped his foot and, squatting down, went round and round in a circle with springy ease. They all danced in turn, warming themselves up with the exercise. By this time the accordion had stopped playing in the next van and husky voices were cursing heavily. Meanwhile the Tatarsky men tried so hard to outdance one another that the horses grew excited and it did not end until Anikei in the midst of one of his wildest capers fell backwards on to the fire. Amid much laughter they picked him up and by the light of a candle-stump examined his new trousers, now fatally burned at the seat, and the hem of his scorched jacket.

'Take your pants off!' Merkulov advised sympathetically.

'Are you mad, you Gypsy? What'll I wear then?'

Merkulov rummaged in his saddle-bags and pulled out a woman's coarse linen petticoat. They got the fire going again. Merkulov held up the petticoat by its narrow shoulder-straps, leaning back and moaning with laughter.

'Here you are! Haw! Haw! I pinched it off a station fence. I was keeping it for footcloths... Haw! Haw! But I won't rip it up now... You can have it!'

While they forced Anikei to put on the petticoat the laughter reached such a pitch that curious heads peered out of the doors of adjoining vans and envious voices called out in the darkness:

'What're you at there?'

'Blasted stallions!'

'What'ye bellowing about?'

'Found 'emselves a toy, the daft devils!'

At the next stop they got the accordion-player in from the front van and Cossacks from other vans jostled in with him, breaking the mangers and pushing the horses to the walls. In the tiny circle that was left Anikei did his act. The white petticoat, evidently from a huge woman, was far too long for him and wrapped itself round his legs but, spurred on by the cheers and chuckles, he danced till he dropped.

The stars looked down sadly on blood-soaked Byelorussia. The night sky yawned black overhead and floated away amid the smoke. The wind clung close to the earth, which was steeped in the bitter smells of rotted leaves, sodden, rusty clay, and the snows of March.

IX

Within twenty-four hours the regiment was once again approaching the front. The troop trains pulled into a junction and the sergeant-major went round with the order to detrain. Hurriedly the Cossacks led their horses down the ramps and scurried about, saddling up, running back for things they had left behind in the vans, and throwing ragged bales of hay out on to the wet sand between the tracks.

Petro Melekhov was summoned by the regimental commander's orderly.

'Go to the station, the commander wants to see you.'

Petro straightened the belt he was wearing over his greatcoat and headed unhurriedly for the platform, telling Anikei to keep an eye on his horse.

Anikei said nothing. His face, which now wore its usual gloomy expression, was a mixture of anxiety and boredom. Petro walked on, looking down at his boots that were already ochred with mud and wondering what the regimental commander wanted him for. His attention was diverted by a small crowd that had gathered at the end of the platform, by an urn of boiling water. He walked up and listened to the talk. About twenty men had gathered round a burly red-haired Cossack, who was standing with his back to the urn in an awkward, hunted attitude. Petro leaned forward to peer at the vaguely familiar bearded face of the red-haired Cossack guardsman, and at the figure 52 sewn on to his sergeant's blue shoulder strap; he decided that he had seen this man somewhere before.

'What was the fine idea? And with sergeant's pips on your shoulders!' a volunteer with a freckled intelligent face was questioning the Cossack gloatingly.

'What's it all about?' Petro inquired, touching the shoulder of a man who was standing near by. The man turned his head. 'They've caught a deserter. One of your Cossacks,' he replied reluctantly.

Petro racked his brains, trying to think where he had seen the guardsman's broad face with its ruddy moustache and eyebrows. Ignoring the volunteer's pesterings, the guardsman sipped hot water from a mug made of a copper shell-case and nibbled the lump of dry black bread he had dipped in the water. His widely spaced eyes were half closed and looked only down or sideways; his eyebrows moved as he munched and swallowed. Beside him stood his escort, an elderly stocky soldier gripping his rifle by its fixed bayonet. The deserter drained the mug and, as his weary gaze roamed the faces of the staring soldiers, a sudden spark of bitterness leaped into his blue, childlike eyes. He swallowed hurriedly, licked his lips and shouted in a rough unrepentant voice:

'What're you gaping at? Can't you let a man eat, you bastards! Haven't you ever seen a human being before?'

The infantrymen laughed and Petro, as often happens, the moment he heard the deserter's voice, recalled with astonishing clarity that this guardsman was from the village of Rubezhin, Yelanskaya stanitsa, that his name was Fomin, and that long ago, before the war, he and his father had haggled with him over a three-year-old bullock at the Yelanskaya annual cattle fair.

'Fomin! Yakov!' he sang out, pushing his way through the crowd.

The guardsman put the mug back on the urn with an awkward self-conscious gesture and, still chewing, looked at Petro in confusion.

'I don't recognise you, chum.'

'You're from Rubezhin, aren't you?'

'That's right. Are you from those parts?'

'I'm from Vyoshenskaya, I remember you. Five years ago my Dad and me, we bought a bullock off you.'

With the same embarrassed boyish smile on his face Fomin made an effort to remember.

'No, it's gone.. I can't recall you,' he said with obvious regret.

'Were you in the 52nd?'

'I was.'

'So you ran away? What made you do it, chum?'

Fomin pulled off his tall lambswool hat and took out a battered pouch. Hunching his shoulders, he slowly tucked the hat under his arm and tore a strip of paper, and only then clamped a stern, moistly glittering eye on Petro.

'Couldn't stand any more, brother,' he said quietly.

That look stung Petro. He grunted and gathered his tawny moustache into his mouth.

'Come on, you two, finish talking, or you'll get me into trouble,' the stocky guard said with a sigh, lifting his rifle. 'Get moving, Dad!'

Fomin hurriedly tucked the mug into his field-bag, said goodbye to Petro without looking at him again, and set off for the commandant's office with a lumbering, bear-like gait. At the station, in what had once been the first-class buffet, the regimental commander and two squadron commanders were bending over a small table.

'You have kept us waiting, Melekhov.' The colonel gave him an irate look and blinked wearily.

Petro heard the news that his squadron was to be placed at the disposal of divisional headquarters, and that he must keep a close watch on the Cossacks and report any change in their mood to the squadron commander. He looked the colonel in the eye unblinkingly and listened with attention, but he could not forget Fomin's moistly glittering glance and his quiet, 'Couldn't stand any more, brother.'

He left the hot fug of the station building and walked back to the squadron. The regiment's baggage train was in a siding near the station. As he approached his own van, Petro noticed the support-unit Cossacks and the squadron blacksmith. The sight of the smith cleared Petro's head instantly of all thoughts of Fomin and what he had said, and he quickened his pace, hoping to come to some agreement about having his horse reshoed. His mind turned to everyday cares and anxieties, but suddenly a woman appeared from round the corner of a red van. She was wearing a beautiful fluffy white scarf and her dress distinguished her from the women of these parts. The unexpectedly familiar lines of her figure made Petro look at her more closely. Suddenly she turned and hurried towards him, walking with a slight, almost imperceptible swing of her shoulders and slender hips. And even before he recognised the face, Petro knew from that light swinging walk that it was his wife. · A pleasant tingling shiver reached his heart. The unexpectedness of the joy made it all the stronger. Deliberately shortening his stride so that the support-unit men should not think he was out-of-the-way glad, Petro went to meet her. He embraced his wife with dignity, kissed her three times, and was going to ask her something, but a deep inner wave of emotion broke through to the surface, his lips quivered and he seemed to lose his tongue.

'I—I wasn't expecting you,' he managed to say at last.

'Oh, sweetheart! How changed you are!' Darya exclaimed. 'You're like a stranger to me. Look, I've come to see you! Our folk wouldn't let me. "How can you go all that way?" they said. But no, I thought to myself, I'll go and see my darling...' She chattered away, clinging to her husband and looking up at him with dewy eyes.

There was a crowd of Cossacks by the vans; at the sight of Petro and his wife, they coughed and winked and bemoaned their own fate.

'Petro's in luck!'

'My she-wolf wouldn't come to see me, she's queening it somewhere else now, I reckon.'

'While one's away, she'll have ten to stay.'

'Melekhov could at least let the troop have his for a night. Take pity on our need, eh!'

'Come on, lads, let's go. It's killing me the way she cuddles up to him!'

At that moment Petro completely forgot that he had intended to give his wife the hiding of her life. He fondled her in public, smoothed the pencilled arches of her brows with his big tobacco-stained thumb, and his heart sang. Darya also forgot that only two nights ago she had slept with a veterinary surgeon of the Dragoons who was on his way from Kharkov to join his regiment. The Dragoon had sported such a wonderful fluffy black moustache... But that had been two nights ago, and now she was hugging her husband and looking at him with tears of sincere joy in her clear truthful eyes.

X

After his leave Major Yevgeny Listnitsky was appointed to the 14th Don Cossack Regiment. Instead of returning to the regiment from which he had been so shamefully forced to flee even before the February revolution, he had reported straight to Divisional Headquarters, and the chief of staff, a young general from a famous family of the Don Cossack nobility, had readily arranged the transfer.

'I know you would find it difficult to work in your old surroundings, Major,' he said, taking him into a private room. 'The Cossacks' feelings have been roused against you, your name is anathema to them. Of course, it will be wiser for you to go to the Fourteenth. The officers there are an exceptionally fine lot and the Cossacks are steadier, more stolid—from the southern stanitsas of the Ust-Medveditsa district, most of them. You'll be better off there. You are the son of Nikolai Alexeyevich List-nitsky, are you not?' He paused and, on receiving an affirmative answer, went on, 'For my part I can assure you that we value officers like you. Even among the officers the majority nowadays are playing a double game. Nothing is easier than to change one's faith or worship two gods at once,' the chief of staff concluded bitterly.

Listnitsky gladly accepted the transfer. On the same day he left for Dvinsk, where the 14th Regiment was stationed. Within twenty-four hours he reported to Colonel Bykadorov, and was happy to find that the chief of staff had told him the truth. Most of the officers were monarchists; the Cossacks, a third of whom were Old Believers of the Ust-Khopyorskaya, Kumylzhenskaya, Glazunovskaya and other stanitsas, were in no mood for revolution, had only reluctantly sworn their allegiance to the Provisional Government, and neither understood nor wanted to understand the events seething around them. Those who had been elected to the regimental and squadron committees were of the time-serving, obedient type. In his new surroundings Listnitsky breathed a sigh of happy relief.

Among the officers he met two who had been with him in the Ataman Regiment and were stand-offish; the others were unusually friendly and united, and openly talked of restoring the dynasty. After two months in Dvinsk, the regiment was as solid as a clenched fist, well rested and braced for action. Before this its squadrons, attached to various infantry divisions, had roamed the frontline from Riga to Dvinsk, but in April they had been brought together by someone's considerate hand and the regiment was now in readiness. Under the strict surveillance of the officers, the Cossacks did their training, fed up their horses and lived a moderate vegetable existence, safely removed from any outside influence.

The Cossacks had only a vague notion about the purpose for which the regiment was being prepared, but among themselves the officers openly maintained that before long the regiment would be taken over by some firm hand and used to turn the wheel of history.

Close by, the front was in ferment. Short of ammunition, short of food, the armies were panting in a mortal fever; millions of hands in them were groping for the ephemeral word 'peace'. The armies' attitude to the country's temporary ruler Kerensky was mixed but, goaded on by his hysterical appeals, they stumbled forward in the June offensive. As their anger matured, it seethed and spurted like well waters forced up by hot subterranean springs.

But in Dvinsk the Cossacks lived a quiet, peaceful life; the horses' stomachs digested their oats and cattle cake; the Cossacks began to forget the hardships they had endured at the front; the officers attended the officers' club regularly, dined reasonably well, and argued heatedly about Russia's destiny.

And so it went on till the early days of July. On the 3rd of the month the order arrived: 'March at once, without delay.' And the troop trains rolled towards Petrograd. On July 7th the horses' hoofs clattered over the capital's cobbled streets.

The regiment was quartered on the Nevsky Avenue. Listnitsky's squadron was given an empty commercial building. The Cossacks' arrival had been eagerly awaited, as could be seen from the care and consideration the city authorities had lavished in preparing their accommodation. The walls had been freshly white-washed, the floors scrubbed and polished, the newly built wooden bunks smelled of fresh pinewood, and the clean, tidy semi-basement was almost cosy. Frowning over his pince-nez, Listnitsky inspected the premises thoroughly, walked along by the dazzlingly white walls, and decided that nothing better in the way of comfort could be expected. Satisfied by his inspection, he walked towards the exit into the yard, accompanied by the dapper little official from the City Council who had been charged with the task of meeting the Cossacks; but then an unpleasant incident occurred. As he grasped the door-handle he noticed an emblem skilfully scratched on the wall with some sort of sharp instrument. It consisted of a dog's head with its teeth bared in a snarl, and a broom. Evidently one of the workers employed to decorate the room had known who it was intended for.

'What's this?' eyebrows quivering, Listnitsky asked the official who had been showing him round.

The official ran his busy, mouse-like eyes over the drawing and breathed hard. The blood flooded so plentifully into his face that even his starched shirt-collar seemed to turn pink.

'Forgive me, Major. Some criminal hand—'

'I hope I am right in assuming that the Oprichnik* emblem was drawn without your knowledge?'

'But of course! God forbid! It's a Bolshevik trick. Some ruffian had the impudence to do such a thing! I shall have the wall redone at once. Quite appalling. Do forgive me! Such a ridiculous incident! I assure you I am ashamed of this vile action.'

Listnitsky began to feel genuinely sorry for this humiliated and embarrassed civilian. He relaxed his implacably cold glance and said with some restraint, 'A slight miscalculation on the part of the artist—Cossacks don't know Russian history. But that does not mean we can encourage such attitudes towards us.' The official obliterated the drawing with a hard well manicured finger-nail, and smudged his expensive English overcoat with fine white dust as he stood on tiptoe by the wall. Listnitsky stood polishing his pince-nez and smiling, but could not shake off a bitter, resentful sense of regret.

'So this is how they welcome us, this is the other side of all the flummery! Surely we are not seen as Oprichniks by the whole of Russia,' he thought as he paced across the yard to the stables, listening half-heartedly to the remarks of the official hurrying after him.

The sun's rays fell steeply into the deep spacious well of the courtyard. People leaned out of the windows of the surrounding houses to watch the Cossacks as they put their horses in the stables and gathered in the yard, standing or squatting on their haunches in the shade of the walls.

'Why don't you go inside?' Listnitsky asked.

---

*A dog's head and a broom were attached to the saddles of the *Oprichniki*, the notoriously brutal bodyguard of Ivan the Terrible, as a sign that they would sink their fangs into the tsar's enemies and then sweep them away. —*Tr*.

'Plenty of time, Major.'

'Too much mebbe.'

'Let's get the horses stabled first.'

Listnitsky made a strict inspection of the warehouse that had been turned into a stable, trying to recover his former dislike of the official representing the city authorities.

'Contact whoever you need to and see to it that another door is made. We can't keep one hundred and twenty horses in a place with only three doors. If there were an alarm, it would take us half an hour to get them out. Extraordinary that this factor was not taken into account beforehand. I shall be obliged to report the matter to the regimental commander.'

Having received an assurance that not one but two doorways would be made that very day, Listnitsky took his leave of his escort, thanking him curtly for his services. He then approved the duty roster and went upstairs to the quarters temporarily assigned to officers of the squadron. As he mounted the back stairs he unbuttoned his tunic and wiped the sweat from under his cap, enjoying the damp coolness of the building. There was no one else but Captain Atarshchikov in the room.

'Where are all the others?' Listnitsky asked, dropping on to his campbed and heaving up his feet in their dusty boots.

'In town. Seeing the sights of Petrograd.'

'Why aren't you?'

'Oh, I don't see much sense in it. Rushing off to town as soon as you arrive. I thought it would be better to read about what happened here a few days ago. Fascinating!'

Listnitsky lay in silence, the damp shirt pleasantly cool on his back. He felt too lazy to get up and wash. The effects of the journey were beginning to tell. Making an effort, he rose and called his batman. He changed his underclothes and washed thoroughly, snorting contentedly and rubbing his plump tanned neck with a rough towel.

'Have a wash, Vanya,' he advised Atarshchikov. 'It'll make you feel much better. Well, what's in the papers?'

'Perhaps I will. Make me feel better, you say?... What's in the newspapers? Reports of what the Bolsheviks are doing, government measures... Read about it.'

In better spirits after his wash, Listnitsky was about to settle down with the newspaper, but was summoned to see the regimental commander. Rising reluctantly, he put on a new tunic that smelled of soap and was still creased from the journey, buckled on his sword and went out onto the Nevsky. He crossed the street and turned to look back at the building where the squadron was quartered. Outwardly, it was indistinguishable from the others beside it; five stories with a façade of porous smoke-coloured stone, just one in a row of similar buildings. Listnitsky lit a cigarette and strolled along the pavement. The crowd flowed past him, foaming with boaters, bowlers and cloth caps and the elegantly simple and smart hats of the women. The democratic green blob of an army cap occasionally floated up out of the general stream only to disappear again in the riot of colour.

A bracingly fresh breeze blew from the sea but was soon broken up by the massive bulwarks of the buildings and flowed through the city in feeble uneven trickles. Billowing clouds were drifting southwards across the steely, lilac-tinged sky. Their milky white crests stood out in sharp relief. The city was wrapped in the humid sultriness that heralds a rainstorm. The air smelled of hot asphalt, exhaust fumes, the nearby sea, the faint exciting aroma of perfume, and something else, indefinable, that characterises any large city.

As Listnitsky strolled along smoking and keeping to the right-hand side of the pavement, he noticed the respectful sidelong glances of those he passed. At first he was embarrassedly aware of his creased tunic and dusty cap, but soon he decided there was no reason for a frontline man to feel ashamed of his appearance, especially one who had only just got off the train.

Indolent olive-yellow shadows from the awnings over the entrances to shops and cafes sprawled across the pavements. As the breeze flapped the faded canvas, the pools of shade stirred and writhed under the feet of the passing crowds. Though it was the after-dinner hour, the avenue was swarming with people. Listnitsky, who in the years of war had grown unaccustomed to city life, experienced a joyous satisfaction as he drank in the hum of voices interlaced with laughter, the tooting of motor horns, and the cries of the news vendors. Though he felt at home among this well-dressed, well-fed crowd, he could not help thinking, 'How smug, contented, and happy you all are, merchants and stockbrokers, officials of one rank or another, landowners, blueblooded aristocrats! But how did you feel three or four days ago? How did you look when the mob and the soldiery came flowing down this avenue, these streets, like molten ore? To be honest, I'm both glad and sorry to see you. And I don't know whether to rejoice over your present well-being.'

He tried to analyse his ambivalent feelings and find their source, and without much difficulty decided that he thought and felt like this because there was a war on and what he had experienced out there had set him apart from this smug, well-fed crowd.

'That fat young fellow over there,' he thought as his eyes met those of a stout, red-cheeked, beardless young man, 'why isn't he at the front? He's probably the son of some factory owner or business tycoon and has dodged the army. The scoundrel doesn't give a damn for his country. He's supposed to be "on defence work", while he gets fat and indulges in comfortable love affairs.'

'But whose side are you on if it comes to that?' he asked himself, and decided smilingly, 'With these people, of course! They're a part of me and I'm a part of them. Everything good and bad in them exists to some degree in me. Perhaps I have a slightly thinner skin than that fat hog over there, and that's why I react more painfully to everything, and certainly that's why I'm honestly at the war and not "on defence work" and precisely for that reason last winter in Mogilyov, when I saw the deposed emperor leaving GHQ in his car, saw his sorrowful lips and the indescribably moving way his hand lay help-lessly on his knee, I threw myself down in the snow and wept like a child... Yes, I am honest in not accepting the revolution, I can't accept it! My heart and mind are both against it. I'll give my life for the old world, I'll give it unhesitatingly, without posturing, like a soldier. But are there many who will do that?'

Emotion drove the blood from his face as he resurrect-ed in his memory that February day dying in a blaze of colour, the governor's house in Mogilyov, the iron railings damp with condensation from the frosty air, and the snow beyond, mottled by the scarlet rays from the low-hanging sun in its smoky aura of frost. On the other side of the Dnieper the sky above the sloping far bank was painted with azure, vermilion and tarnished gold and every brush-stroke on the horizon was so fine, so intan-gibly ethereal that it was almost painful to the eye. A small crowd of General Staff officers, soldiers and civilians had gathered in the drive. The limousine moved off. Yes, there was Frederiks* behind the windscreen, and the tsar, leaning back in his seat. A drawn face with a faint violet tinge. Black semi-circle of a tall lambskin hat across a pale forehead, uniforms of the Cossack escort.

Listnitsky almost ran past the astonished, head-turning strollers on the avenue. He could still see the tsar's hand that had been raised in salute falling from the edge of the black hat, and his ears still rang with the soundless motion of the car and the humiliating passivity of the crowd as it saw off Russia's last emperor in silence...

Listnitsky slowly mounted the steps of the building taken over by regimental headquarters. His cheeks were still quivering, his eyes bloodshot and swollen with tears. On the first-floor landing he smoked two cigarettes in quick succession, wiped his pince-nez and ran up the stairs two at a time to the floor above.

The regimental commander marked out on a map the district of Petrograd where Listnitsky's squadron was to guard government offices, listed them and informed him in minute detail how many sentries should be posted and at what times.

In conclusion he said, 'For Kerensky, in the Winter Palace...'

'Don't speak to me about Kerensky!' Listnitsky whispered loudly and his face went deathly pale.

'Yevgeny Nikolayevich, get a grip on yourself.'

'Colonel, please!'

'But, my dear fellow...'

'I beg you!'

'Your nerves...'

'Do you want me to send patrols to the Putilov Works now?' Listnitsky asked, breathing heavily.

The colonel bit his lip, smiled and shrugged his shoulders. 'Yes, at once! And there must be a troop officer with them.'

Listnitsky left the headquarters demoralised and crushed by memories of the past and his conversation with the regimental commander. He had nearly reached his quarters when he saw a Cossack patrol of the 4th Don Regiment that was also stationed in Petrograd. A bunch of flowers hung drooping from the bridle of the troop officer's light-bay horse. The officer's face wore a slight smile under the fair moustache.

'Hurrah for the saviours of the Motherland!' an excit-

---

*Count Frederiks, a minister of the royal court. —Tr.

able elderly gentleman shouted, stepping off the pavement and waving his hat.

The officer saluted politely and the patrol went off at a trot. Listnitsky looked at the excited wet-lipped face of the gentleman who had welcomed the Cossacks, at his flashy carefully knotted neck-tie, and with a grimace of disgust hunched his shoulders and slipped into the doorway of his house.

XI

General Kornilov's appointment as Commander-in-Chief of the South-Western Front was wholeheartedly approved by the officers of the 14th Regiment. Kornilov was spoken of with love and respect as a man of iron character who would undoubtedly be able to lead the country out of the impasse to which the Provisional Government had brought it.

Listnitsky was particularly enthusiastic about the appointment. Through the junior officers of the squadrons and the Cossacks of his acquaintance he tried to find out how the Cossacks felt about it, but the information he received was not encouraging. The Cossacks were either silent or gave apathetic answers:

'It's all the same to us.'

'Who knows what he's like!..'

'If he tried to do something about peace, then, o'course...'

'His being promoted won't make things any easier for us.'

A few days later persistent rumours began circulating among the officers with wider contacts in civilian and military circles that Kornilov was pressing the Provisional Government to restore the death penalty at the front and take many decisive measures on which the fate of the army and the outcome of the war depended. It was said that Kerensky feared Kornilov and would probably make every effort to replace him with a more flexible commander-in-chief. The names of several generals well known in the military sphere were being bandied about.

On July 19th everyone was astounded by the government announcement of Kornilov's appointment as Supreme Commander-in-Chief. Soon afterwards Captain Atarshchikov, who had a wide circle of acquaintances in the Main Committee of the Officers' Association, cited thoroughly reliable sources to the effect that Kornilov in a memorandum prepared for the Provisional Government had insisted on the necessity of the following crucial measures: extension of martial law to cover all military units in the rear and the civilian population throughout the country, including the right to administer the death penalty; restoration of the disciplinary powers of military commanders; drastic restriction of the activities of the soldiers' and sailors' committees, and so on. That evening Listnitsky discussed the situation with the officers of his and other squadrons and put the question to them squarely. Whose side were they on?

'Gentlemen!' he said with suppressed emotion. 'We are a united family. We know each other well but there are certain difficult questions that need clearing up. Today, when there is a distinct possibility of divergence between the Supreme Commander and the Government, we must get this thing straight. Who are we with? Who do we support? So let's talk it over in a spirit of comradeship without holding anything back.'

Captain Atarshchikov was the first to answer.

'For General Kornilov I would give my own blood and anyone else's, drop by drop! He is a man of perfect integrity and he and he alone is capable of putting Russia on her feet again. Look what he's doing in the army! Only thanks to him have the hands of the army commanders been partially freed. Up to now we've had nothing but bullying from the committees, fraternisation and desertion. What question can there be? Every decent person is bound to support Kornilov.'

Slim-legged and disproportionately broad in the chest and shoulders, Atarshchikov spoke with blazing conviction. Obviously he had deep feelings on the matter. When he had finished, he surveyed the officers gathered round the table, expectantly tapping his cigarette-case with the butt of his cigarette. He had a brown mole the size of a pea on the lower lid of his right eye. It prevented the upper lid from closing properly and at first sight people were apt to think that he was looking at them with a perpetually watchful and condescending sneer.

'If it's a choice between the Bolsheviks, Kerensky and Kornilov, we naturally support Kornilov.'

'It's hard for us to judge what Kornilov wants. Is it only the restoration of public order in Russia or perhaps the restoration of something else besides?'

'That's no answer on a question of principle!'

'Yes, it is!'

'Well it's not a very clever one, if it is an answer.'

'What are you afraid of, Lieutenant? Restoration of the monarchy?'

'I'm not afraid of it. On the contrary, that's what I want.'

'Then where's the difficulty?'

'Gentlemen!' Dolgov, a former sergeant-major, who had been promoted to cornet for bravery in action, spoke up in a firm, weathered voice. 'What's all the argument about? Why don't you say outright that we Cossacks had better hang on to General Kornilov like a child to its mother's skirts. I'm putting it to you straight, without any double talk! If we break away from him, we'll be done for! Russia will shovel us out like horse-shit. It's as plain as a pikestaff: where he goes, we must follow.'

'That's the way to talk!'

Atarshchikov slapped Dolgov admiringly on the shoulder and fixed a pair of laughing eyes on Listnitsky. The latter smiled agitatedly, smoothing down the trouser creases over his knees.

'Well, gentlemen?' Atarshchikov exclaimed on a rising note. 'Are we for Kornilov?'

'Of course!'

'Dolgov cut the Gordian knot at a stroke.'

'All the officers are for him.'

'We don't want to be the exception.'

'For dear Lavr Georgievich Kornilov, a Cossack and a hero—hip, hip, hurrah!'

The officers drank their tea, laughing and clinking glasses. Relieved of its previous tension, the conversation turned to the events of recent days.

'Yes, we're all for the Supreme Commander, but the Cossacks now, they're hanging back,' Dolgov said hesitantly.

'Hanging back?' Listnitsky repeated.

'Ay, there's no getting away from it. They want to get back to their homes and their women, the buggers. They're fed up with roughing it.'

'It's our duty to give the Cossacks a lead!' Lieutenant Chernokutov thumped on the table with his fist. 'Yes, a lead! That's what we're officers for!'

'The Cossacks need to have it patiently explained to them whose road they should follow.'

Listnitsky tapped his glass with his spoon and, having secured attention, said in clearly enunciated phrases, 'I would ask you to remember, gentlemen, that we should concentrate, as Atarshchikov says, on explaining the true

481

state of affairs to the Cossacks. We must get them out of the clutches of the committees. This will call for as drastic a change of character as most of us experienced after the February coup—if not deeper. In the old days—in 1916, say—I could punch a Cossack's face and risk his shooting me in the back during battle, but since February we have had to draw in our horns because now, if I were to strike some fool or other, I'd be murdered on the spot, in the trenches, without any waiting for a convenient moment. The situation today is quite different from what it used to be. We *must*,' Listnitsky stressed the word, 'we must bind ourselves closer to the Cossacks! Everything depends on it! Do you know what is happening at this moment in the 1st and 4th regiments?'

'Appalling!'

'Yes, it is appalling!' Listnitsky continued. 'The officers isolated themselves from the Cossacks as they always had done, and the result is that the Cossacks, every man jack of them, have fallen under Bolshevik influence and ninety per cent have become Bolsheviks themselves. After all, it's quite obvious that momentous events are in the offing... The 3rd and 5th of July were only an ominous warning to all who are complacent about the future. Either we shall have to fight for Kornilov against the troops of revolutionary democracy, or else the Bolsheviks, when they have built up their strength and expanded their influence, will stage another revolution. They have been given a breathing space, time to concentrate their forces, and we are just letting things slide. But how can we allow it?! In the coming upheaval a reliable Cossack will be very useful.'

'Without the Cossacks, of course, we're a useless bunch,' Dolgov said with a sigh.

'Quite true, Listnitsky!'

'Very true indeed.'

'Russia has one foot in the grave.'

'D'you think we don't know it? We know it all right, but sometimes we are powerless to do anything. Order No. 1* and *Okopnaya Pravda*** are sowing their seeds.'

---

*Passed by the Executive Committee of the Petrograd Soviet under pressure from the revolutionary masses, Order No. 1 (1 March 1917) introduced elected organizations in military units and control by these organizations over the activities of the old tsarist command.—*Ed.*

**Okopnaya Pravda* (Trench Truth)—militant Bolshevik newspaper.—*Ed.*

'And we stand admiring the young shoots instead of rooting them out and burning them!' Atarshchikov cried.

'We don't admire them! We're helpless!'

'No, Cornet! We're simply slack!'

'That's not true!'

'Prove it!'

'Quiet, gentlemen!'

'They've smashed up the *Pravda* office. Kerensky's very good at acting too late.'

'What is this—the market-place? You can't all shout at once!'

The uproar slowly subsided. The commander of one of the squadrons, who had listened to Listnitsky's remarks with intense interest, asked for attention.

'I suggest that we allow Major Listnitsky to finish what he was saying.'

'Hear! Hear!'

Rubbing his angular knees with his fists, Listnitsky went on, 'I say that in the battles to come, in the civil war—and I have only just realised that it's inevitable—loyal Cossacks will be badly needed. We've got to try and win them away from the committees that are leaning towards the Bolsheviks. This is an absolute necessity! If there're any fresh upheavals, the Cossacks of the 1st and 4th regiments will shoot their officers to a man.'

'That's quite clear!'

'They won't stand on ceremony!'

'And we must learn from their experience, a very bitter one. In the future one out of every two Cossacks of these regiments—although what kind of Cossacks are they now?—will have to be hanged. Or we may have to do away with the whole lot of them... The field must be cleared of weeds! So let's save our own Cossacks from mistakes for which they will later have to pay a heavy price.'

The next to speak after Listnitsky was the squadron commander, who had listened to him with such interest. An old regular officer, who had served nine years in his regiment and been wounded four times during the war, he spoke of the hardships and disappointments of the old days. The Cossack officers were regarded as the lowest of the low, treated shabbily, promotion was slow and the rank of lieutenant-colonel was the highest most regular officers could aspire to. Hence the inertia of the Cossack upper crust at the moment of the overthrow of the autocracy. But despite all this, he said, Kornilov must be given every support and there should be closer contact with him through the Council of the Union of Cossack Armies and the Main Committee of the Officers' Alliance.

'Let Kornilov become a dictator. That will be salvation for the Cossack armies. Under him we might have a better life than we did under the tsar.'

The time was long past midnight. A simple flaxen-haired night had spread straggling locks of cloud over the city. The dark spire of the Admiralty tower and a yellow flood of lights could be seen from the window.

The officers talked till dawn. It was decided that discussions with the Cossacks on current affairs should be held three times a week, and troop officers were instructed to keep their men busy with physical training and the study of regulations in order to divert their thoughts from the demoralising influence of politics.

Before retiring, they sang *The Don's Awake and Stirring, the Quiet and Christian Don*, drank their tenth samovar of tea, and proposed humorous toasts as they clinked glasses. And just before the end Atarshchikov, after a whispered consultation with Dolgov, proclaimed, 'Now, as a dessert, we shall treat you to an ancient Cossack song. Quiet, please! And it wouldn't be a bad thing to open the window—it's rather smoky in here.'

The two voices—Dolgov's weathered bass and Atarshchikov's mellow, unusually pleasant tenor—struck up falteringly at first, for each had its own pace, but then they mingled in a song of overwhelming beauty:

How proud our Don, our quiet Don, our father,
That never to the Tatar bowed its head, nor Moscow's
custom borrowed,
And ever met the Turk with sabre sharp and smote him
hip and thigh...
So through the ages the Don country, our mother,
For the Virgin Pure, for its Christian faith,
And for the free Don with surging wave 'gainst heathen
raised its battle cry.

Atarshchikov sat clasping his knees and led the song in the higher register, never losing the tune, although his variations ranged far ahead of Dolgov's stubborn bass; the young officer's face was unusually stern and only towards the end of the song did Listnitsky notice the cold glint of a tear slipping over the brown mound of the mole on his lower lid.

When the officers of the other squadrons had left, and their own had turned in, Atarshchikov sat down on the edge of Listnitsky's bed, tugging at the faded blue braces that spanned the broad arch of his massive chest. 'Well, you see, Yevgeny...' he began in a whisper, 'I'm devilishly in love with the Don, with all this old Cossack way of life that has taken centuries to grow. I love my Cossacks—and the Cossack women! The smell of steppe wormwood brings tears to my eyes... And when the sunflowers are in bloom and you get that smell of rainwashed vineyards over the Don, I love it so deeply, so desperately... I'm sure you'll understand. But now I'm wondering if we aren't going to bring these Cossacks to ruin. Is the road we want them to take the right one?'

'What exactly do you mean?' Listnitsky asked guardedly.

Atarshchikov's neck showed up youthfully and innocently brown against the white collar of his shirt. The blue edge of his upper lid hung heavily on the brown mole, and in profile only the moist light of one half-closed eye was visible.

'I'm wondering if this is what the Cossacks need?'

'In that case, what do they need?'

'I don't know... But why are they leaving us so spontaneously? It's as though the revolution had divided us into the sheep and the goats, as though we now have different interests.'

'You see, it's like this,' Listnitsky began cautiously. 'It's the difference in the way we perceive events. We're better educated, we're able to judge facts critically, but with them everything is much more primitive and simple. The Bolsheviks keep drumming it into their heads that the war must be brought to an end, or rather, turned into a civil war. They're setting the Cossacks against us, and because the Cossacks are tired, brutalised, and lack the strong moral sense of duty and responsibility to the motherland that we have, it's quite understandable that all this falls on fertile soil. After all, what does the word "motherland" mean to them? It's just an abstract concept. The Don Army Region is miles away from the front and the Germans will never get there—that's their reasoning. And that's the whole trouble. We've got to explain to them what the consequences will be of turning the war into a civil war.'

Even as he spoke, Listnitsky was subconsciously aware that his words were not reaching their target, and that

Atarshchikov was about to withdraw into his shell.

And this was what happened. Atarshchikov muttered something inaudible and sat for a time in silence, and, try as he would, Listnitsky could not guess the dark ramblings in the mind of his silent fellow officer.

I ought to have let him finish what he was saying, he thought regretfully.

Atarshchikov wished him good-night and rose without another word. For a minute he had yearned for a candid exchange of views, raised the black curtain of the unknown with which every man protects himself, then lowered it again.

Irritated by the unsolved mystery of what was in the other man's mind, Listnitsky lay on his bed smoking and staring into the grey woolly darkness. Suddenly he remembered Aksinya and the days of his leave that had been so full of her. He fell asleep, calmed by his thoughts and occasional memories of the women whose paths had at some time crossed his own.

XII

In Listnitsky's squadron there was a Cossack named Ivan Lagutin, from the stanitsa of Bukanovskaya. In the first elections he had been voted a member of the regiment's Military-Revolutionary Committee. Up to the time of the regiment's arrival in Petrograd he had done nothing to draw attention to himself, but in the last days of July his troop officer informed Listnitsky that Lagutin was attending the military section of the Petrograd Soviet of Workers' and Soldiers' Deputies and probably had close connections with its members. It had been noticed that he held frequent discussions with the Cossacks of his troop and was having a bad influence on them. In the squadron there had been two instances of refusal to go on sentry duty and patrol. The troop officer attributed these cases to Lagutin's influence upon the Cossacks.

Listnitsky decided that he should get to know Lagutin better and sound him out, but since it would have been foolish and indiscreet to tackle the Cossack directly, he waited. The chance soon presented itself. At the end of July it was the Third Troop's turn to patrol the streets in the vicinity of the Putilov Works.

'I will ride with the Cossacks,' Listnitsky told the

troop officer beforehand. 'Tell them to saddle up the Black for me.'

Listnitsky kept two horses—'in case of emergencies', as he put it. He dressed with his batman's assistance and went down into the yard. The troop was already mounted. In the murky lamplit darkness they rode through several streets. Listnitsky deliberately fell behind and called Lagutin to his side. The Cossack rode up, turned his shabby little horse and glanced warily at the major.

'What's the news in your committee?' Listnitsky asked.

'Nothing new.'

'What stanitsa are you from, Lagutin?'

'Bukanovskaya.'

'What village?'

'Mityakin.'

Their horses were now riding abreast. By the light of the street-lamps Listnitsky observed the Cossack's bearded face. The hair showing under his cap was combed back, the short curly beard grew unevenly over his plump cheeks, and the shrewd eyes were set deeply under the overhanging arches of the brows.

'He looks a simple enough fellow, but what's going on in his mind? Probably he hates me, like everything else connected with the old regime and the "corporal's cane",' Listnitsky told himself, and for some reason felt a desire to learn about Lagutin's background.

'Have you any family?'

'A wife and two kiddies.'

'And what kind of farm?'

'Call it a farm?' Lagutin said derisively, with a note of regret in his voice. 'We make ends meet just about. The ox works for the Cossack and the Cossack for the ox. We've been struggling all our lives... Our soil is mostly sand,' he added grimly after a moment's thought.

Listnitsky had once driven to the stanitsa of Sebryakovo through Bukanovskaya and he had a vivid recall of the remote stanitsa that lay well off the main highway, bordered by grassland and the capricious meanderings of the River Khopyor. From the crest of the hill above Yelanskaya, some twelve versts away he had seen the green haze of orchards in a hollow and the tall bell-tower standing among them like a gnawed white bone.

'Yes, our soil is sandy loam,' Lagutin added with a sigh.

'I expect you want to go home, eh?'

'That I do, Major! Of course, I'd like to get back.

487

We've had a pretty hard time during this war.'

'I doubt if you'll be going back soon.'

'Yes, I will.'

'The war isn't over yet, is it?'

'It soon will be. It won't be long now before we go home,' Lagutin insisted stubbornly.

'There's still some fighting to be done among ourselves, don't you think?'

Keeping his eyes on the pommel of his saddle, Lagutin paused for a while, then asked, 'Who have we got to fight?'

'Plenty of people... The Bolsheviks, for instance.'

And again Lagutin lapsed into a long silence, as though he had dozed off to the tapping of the horses' hoofs. They rode on for about three minutes. Slowly, choosing his words, Lagutin said, 'We've got no quarrel with them.'

'What about the land?'

'There's enough land for everyone.'

'Do you know what the Bolsheviks wish to achieve?'

'I've heard a bit here and there.'

'Well, what do you think we should do if the Bolsheviks attack us in order to seize our lands, to enslave the Cossacks? After all, you fought the Germans, you defended Russia, didn't you?'

'With the Germans it was different.'

'And the Bolsheviks?'

'Well, Major,' Lagutin said as if he had reached a decision, and raised his eyes to catch Listnitsky's glance. 'The Bolsheviks won't take my last scrap of land away from me. All I've got is my own share, just the one allotment, they won't need my land... But what about, for example—only don't be offended now!—your father's twenty-five thousand acres?'

'Not twenty-five, but ten.'

'Makes no difference, let's call it ten. Not so little, eh? Well, is that right? And if you take Russia as a whole, you'll find quite a lot of people like your father. So judge for yourself, Major, every mouth wants to be fed. You want to eat, and everyone else wants to eat. It was only the Gypsy who taught his old mare not to eat because he thought she'd get used to going without. But the old dear kept on trying and on the tenth day she kicked the bucket... The system was all lop-sided under the tsar, and for the poor people it was real rough... They gave your father a fine big slice of the pie—ten thousand—but he don't eat all that much, does he? He eats the same as other folk. So, of course, you can't help feeling people have been hard done by! The Bolsheviks are on the right track, and you talk about fighting them.'

Listnitsky listened with an inward sense of alarm. By the time the Cossack reached his conclusion he realised that he was powerless to offer any worthwhile argument against it, that with his straightforward, deadly simple reasoning the Cossack had driven him into a corner, and because a deeply suppressed awareness of his own misjudgement had stirred within him, Listnitsky became confused and angry.

'What are you then—a Bolshevik?'

'The name makes no difference,' Lagutin drawled derisively. 'It's not the name that matters, but the truth. The people want the truth, but it's always kept hidden away out of sight. Some say it's been dead and buried long ago.'

'So that's the stuff the Bolsheviks from the Soviet have been filling you up with. You haven't wasted your time in their company, have you?'

'No, Major, it's life that's filled us up, us patient ones, and the Bolsheviks have only got to light the fuse.'

'You'd better drop that kind of talk! This is no time for tomfoolery!' Listnitsky burst out angrily. 'Answer me this: you spoke of my father's land, of the landed estates in general, but that's private property. If you have two shirts and I have one, should I take yours? Is that what you think?' Listnitsky could not see Lagutin's face, but he heard the smile in his voice.

'I'd give away a shirt I didn't need of my own accord. I've done it before now, at the front, and not one I didn't need, but my one and only, and wore my greatcoat on my bare body. But when it comes to land, somehow no one wants to share.'

'Why, haven't you got enough land? Is that what you want?' Listnitsky raised his voice.

Lagutin turned pale and with a catch in his voice almost shouted in reply, 'D'ye think I only care about myself? We were in Poland. How do people live there? Didn't you see? And how do the peasants all around us live? Well, I've seen it! And it makes my blood boil! D'you think I've no pity for them? Mebbe I've been real sorry for the Poles, thinking about the rotten scraps of land they have to make do with.' Listnitsky was about to make a sarcastic reply, but a piercing shout came from the massive grey buildings of the Putilov Works—'Hold him!' Then a thunderous clatter of hoofs and a shot rang out. Listnitsky swung his whip and threw his horse into a gallop.

He and Lagutin rode up to the troop almost at the same time. The Cossacks had gathered at a crossroads, some were dismounting with a clatter of sabres, and a man they had seized was struggling in their midst.

'What's all this?' Listnitsky thundered, riding his horse into the crowd.

'Some bastard threw a stone...'

'And tried to run away.'

'Give him one, Arzhanov!'

'You swine! Have a shy at us, would you?'

Troop sergeant Arzhanov was leaning out of his saddle, gripping the collar of a shortish man in an unbelted black blouse. Three Cossacks who had dismounted were tying his hands.

'Who are you?' Listnitsky shouted, beside himself.

The prisoner looked up, silent lips twisted in the white half-visible face.

'Who are you?' Listnitsky repeated the question. 'Throwing stones, were you, you scoundrel! Well? So you won't speak? Arzhanov!'

Arzhanov let go of the prisoner's collar, jumped down and hit him full in the face.

'Give it to him!' Listnitsky ordered, wheeling his horse sharply.

Three or four of the dismounted Cossacks threw the bound man to the ground and laid on with their whips. Lagutin sprang down from his saddle and ran up to Listnitsky.

'Major!.. How can you? Major!' He gripped Listnitsky's knee with trembling tenacious fingers. 'You can't do that to a human being! What are you doing?'

Listnitsky said nothing and flicked his horse into motion with the reins. Lagutin rushed over to the Cossacks, flung his arms round Arzhanov and, stumbling over his own sword, tried to pull him away. The other resisted, muttering:

'Don't get so worked up! Does he think he can chuck stones at us and get away with it? Let go! Lemme go, before I give you one too!'

One of the Cossacks slung the rifle off his back and started battering the prostrate body with blows that made a soft crunching sound. After about a minute a low animal-like cry rose above the cobbles.

There followed a few seconds of silence, then the same voice, but with a youthful break in it and choking, half crushed with pain, gasped out between the blows, 'Swine!.. Counter-revolutionaries!.. Beat me then! O-o-oh!'

And *thud, thud, thud* came the blows.

Lagutin ran up to Listnitsky, clung to his knee, scratching the saddle flap with his nails, and gave a sobbing shout.

'Have mercy!'

'Get away!'

'Major!.. Listnitsky!.. D'you hear? You'll answer for this!'

'I despise you!' Listnitsky hissed and rode his horse at Lagutin.

'Brothers!' Lagutin shouted, running to the Cossacks who were standing aside. 'I'm a member of the regimental revolutionary committee. I order you to save this man from death! You'll have to answer... Yes, it's not the old days!'

Insane, blinding hatred took possession of Listnitsky. He lashed his horse between the ears and charged at Lagutin. Thrusting the barrel of his black oily-smelling revolver into his face, he screamed, 'Silence, you traitor! You Bolshevik! I'll shoot you!'

With an enormous effort of will he tore his finger off the trigger, reared his horse and galloped away.

A few minutes later three Cossacks rode off in his wake. A man in a soaked shirt that clung stickily to his body hung limply between the horses of two of them— Arzhanov and Lapin. He swayed gently in the Cossack's grip, his feet trailing over the cobbles. His shattered, blood-stained head with the chin sticking up whitely hung back between the jutting shoulder-blades. The third Cossack kept at a distance. At a lighted crossroads he spotted a cab and, rising in his stirrups, trotted over to it. He made some brief remark, slapped his boot expressively with his whip and the cabman drove hastily over to the other two, who had halted in the middle of the road.

The next day Listnitsky awoke with a feeling of having committed a great and irretrievable blunder. Biting his lips, he recalled the beating of the man who had thrown a stone at the Cossacks and what had happened between him and Lagutin. A frown crossed his face and he coughed thoughtfully. As he dressed, he reflected that he had better not do anything about Lagutin just yet, to avoid trouble with the regimental committee. Better wait until the other Cossacks who had been present had forgotten the incident, and then quietly get rid of him.

So that's how I set about 'binding ourselves closer to the Cossacks', he reflected ironically on his own words, and for some days afterward could not shake off the hateful impression of what had occurred.

On a fine sunny day at the beginning of August Listnitsky was out walking in the city with Atarshchikov. Nothing had happened to dispel the reticence that had come between them since the day of the officers' meeting. Atarshchikov remained wrapped up in thoughts that he did not care to express, and reacted to Listnitsky's repeated attempts to draw him out by dropping the curtain that most people use to screen their true self from others' eyes. To Listnitsky it always seemed that under the outward appearance that a person presented to the world there was another personality that often remained undiscovered. He firmly believed that if the outer shell was removed, the naked kernel, unadorned by any pretence, would reveal itself. So he always felt an urge to discover what lay beneath the coarse, stern, fearless, arrogant, complacent or cheerful appearance in the various people he met. In this case, he could only surmise that the young officer was desperately seeking a way out of the knot of contradictions and trying to find a link between the Cossack and the Bolshevik. This supposition forced him to abandon his attempts at intimacy and to maintain a certain aloofness.

They walked down the Nevsky, exchanging an occasional insignificant remark.

'Shall we go in for a bite?' Listnitsky suggested, indicating the door of a restaurant with his eyes.

'Perhaps we should,' the other agreed.

They went in and found themselves standing rather helplessly in a room where all the tables were taken. Atarshchikov had already turned to leave when a paunchy, well-dressed gentleman who had been studying them from a table by the window, where he was sitting in the company of two ladies, rose and came up to them, hat in hand.

'Won't you take our table? We are leaving now.' He smiled, exposing a row of widely spaced, nicotine-stained teeth, and motioned the officers forward. 'It's a pleasure to oblige an officer. We are very proud of you.'

The ladies had also risen. One, a tall brunette, was

adjusting her hair and the other, somewhat younger, toyed with her umbrella while she waited.

The officers thanked the man and made their way to the window. Shredded rays of light pierced the lowered blind and stuck themselves into the tablecloth like yellow needles. The disturbingly subtle aroma of the flowers on the tables was overlaid by the smells of food.

Listnitsky ordered a cold beet soup with ice and, while he waited, thoughtfully plucked the petals from a reddish-yellow nasturtium that he had taken from its vase. Atarshchikov mopped his perspiring forehead and his wearily lowered eyes blinked as they watched the reflections of light from a knife on the next table.

They had not finished their *hors d'oeuvres* when two officers came in talking loudly.

As he looked for a free table, the one in front turned his smoothly tanned face towards Listnitsky and joy blazed in his slanting black eyes.

'Listnitsky! Is it you?!' the officer cried, walking confidently towards him.

His white teeth gleamed from under a black moustache. Listnitsky recognised Major Kalmykov. The officer behind him was Chubov. They shook hands warmly. After introducing his former regimental comrades to Atarshchikov, Listnitsky asked, 'How do you come to be here?'

Kalmykov twirled his moustache and sent a quick glance round the room.

'We're on a mission. I'll tell you later. Let's hear about yourself. How're you getting on in the 14th Regiment?'

...They left the restaurant together. Kalmykov and Listnitsky dropped behind, turned down a side-street and half an hour later, having left the crowded quarter of the city, were walking alone, talking in low tones and with an occasional cautious glance over their shoulders.

'Our Third Corps is in the reserve of the Romanian Front,' Kalmykov recounted excitedly. 'About ten days ago I had orders from the regimental commander to hand over command of my squadron and proceed with Lieutenant Chubov to divisional headquarters. Splendid! I handed over the squadron and we arrived at headquarters. There Colonel M. of the operations department—you know him—informs me confidentially that I must go at once to General Krymov. So off we go to corps headquarters. Krymov receives me and, since he knows what kind of officers are being sent to him, he comes straight out with the following statement: "The government is in the hands of men who are deliberately leading the country to destruction. The ruling clique, and possibly the Provisional Government itself, must be replaced by a military dictatorship." He named Kornilov as the probable candidate, then asked me to go to Petrograd and put myself at the disposal of the Main Committee of the Officers' Alliance. We now have several hundred reliable officers grouped in the city. You realise what our role is to be? The Main Committee is in close contact with our Council of the Union of Cossack Armies. It's organising shock battalions at rail junctions and in the divisions. Everything that will prove very useful in the near future—'

'What d'you think will come of it all?'

'Well, you surprise me! Haven't you been able to size up the situation while you've been living here? There will certainly be a *coup d'état* and Kornilov will take over. The army is backing him up to the hilt. The way our people see it is that there are two equal quantities—Kornilov and the Bolsheviks. Kerensky is between two fires—if one doesn't get him, the other will. Let him sleep in Alice's bed while he can. He's only king for a day.' Kalmykov paused and toyed thoughtfully with the hilt of his sword, then said, 'The fact is that we're pawns on a chessboard, and pawns don't know where the player's hand will move them... I, for example, can't imagine what's going on just now at G.H.Q. I know there is some sort of secret connection or understanding among the generals Kornilov, Lukomsky, Romanovsky, Krymov, Denikin, Kaledin, Erdeli, and a good many others.'

'But the army? Will the whole army follow Kornilov?' Listnitsky asked, quickening his pace.

'The rank-and-file won't, of course. We shall lead them.'

'You know that Kerensky, under pressure from the Left, wants to replace the Supreme Commander?'

'He won't dare! He'd be brought to his knees the very next day! The Main Committee of the Officers' Alliance has let him know its view on that question pretty firmly.'

'Yesterday a delegation from the Union of Cossack Armies went to see him,' Listnitsky said smiling. 'They declared that the Cossacks wouldn't hear of Kornilov's replacement. And you know what his answer was? "This is an insinuation. The Provisional Government is not contemplating anything of the kind." He tries to reassure the public and at the same time winks like a whore at the Executive Committee of the Soviet.'

Kalmykov pulled an officer's field notebook from his pocket and read aloud as he walked along.

'"The Conference of Public Men welcomes you, the supreme leader of the Russian Army. The conference declares that it regards as criminal any attempt to undermine your authority in the army or Russia as a whole and joins its voice to that of the officers, the holders of the St. George Cross, and all Cossacks. At this time of grave trial all thinking Russia looks to you with hope and faith. May God help you in your great undertaking to rebuild a powerful army and save Russia! Rodzyanko." Well, that's clear enough, isn't it? Any replacement of Kornilov is out of the question. And by the way, did you see his arrival yesterday?'

'I didn't get back from Tsarskoye Selo till last night.'

Kalmykov's face broke into a smile that revealed an even row of teeth and healthy pink gums. His slanting eyes narrowed, radiating innumerable weblike wrinkles from the corners.

'It was classic! A squadron of Tekins as his bodyguard. Armoured cars with machine-guns. And the whole lot driving up to the Winter Palace. A pretty unambiguous warning, eh!' He laughed gutturally. 'You should have seen those faces under their great shaggy hats. That was a sight to see! They make a unique impression.'

After walking a little further round the Moscow-Narva district, the two officers parted.

'We mustn't lose touch with each other, Yevgeny,' Kalmykov said in farewell. 'There are grim times ahead. Keep your feet firmly on the ground or you'll fall!'

As Listnitsky walked away, he turned and shouted after him.

'Oh, I forgot to tell you. Remember our Merkulov? The artist?'

'What about him?'

'He was killed in May.'

'Not really!'

'And it was a pure accident. You couldn't imagine a more foolish death. A grenade exploded in the hands of a scout, blew his arms off at the elbow, and there was nothing left of Merkulov but a few guts and a smashed pair of field-glasses. After death had spared him for three years...'

Kalmykov shouted something else but a gust of wind

stirred the dust and carried only the voiceless ends of his words. Listnitsky waved and walked on, occasionally looking over his shoulder.

XIII

On August 6th General Lukomsky, the Supreme Commander's chief of staff, received an order brought to him by General Romanovsky, First Quartermaster General of General Headquarters, to concentrate the 3rd Cavalry Corps and the Native Division in the Nevel—Lower Sokolniki—Velikiye Luki area.

'Why send them to this particular area? These units are part of the reserve of the Romanian front,' Lukomsky asked in some perplexity.

'I don't know. I have given you the Supreme Commander's order exactly as it was conveyed to me.'

'When did you receive it?'

'Yesterday. The Supreme Commander called me in at 11 o'clock last night and ordered me to give you the message this morning.'

Romanovsky paced back and forth by the window, then halted in front of the strategic map of Central Europe that covered half of one wall in Lukomsky's office, and with his back to Lukomsky as he studied the map with exaggerated attention, said, 'Go and have it out with him... He's in his office at the moment.'

Lukomsky gathered the papers on his desk, pushed back his chair and walked across the room with the deliberately firm tread affected by all elderly military men that are putting on weight. As he stepped back to make way for Romanovsky at the door, he said as if in answer to his own thoughts, 'Yes. Quite right.'

A tall lean colonel unknown to Lukomsky had just left Kornilov's room. He stepped aside respectfully and walked away down the corridor, limping noticeably and jerking a shell-shocked shoulder in an absurd and frightening manner.

Kornilov was leaning forward slightly with his hands resting crosswise on his desk, speaking to the elderly officer in front of him.

'...that was to be expected. Have I made myself clear? Kindly inform me as soon as you arrive in Pskov. You may go.'

Kornilov waited for the door to close behind the

officer and sat down with a youthful lightness in his chair; as he pulled up another for Lukomsky, he asked, 'Did you get my instructions from Romanovsky on the transfer of the Third Corps?'

'Yes. That's what I came to talk to you about. Why did you choose that particular area for concentrating the corps?'

Lukomsky studied Kornilov's brown face attentively. It was impenetrable, Asiatically impassive; the familiar curving lines descended from the nose to a haughty mouth fringed by a sparse drooping moustache. The harsh, austere expression of the face was alleviated only by the lock of hair that fell forward boyishly over the forehead.

With one elbow on the desk and his chin resting in a small lean hand, Kornilov narrowed his glittering Mongolian eyes and placed his other hand on Romanovsky's knee.

'I want to concentrate the cavalry not especially behind the Northern front, but in an area from which it would be easy, if the need arose, to switch it to either the Northern or Western fronts. In my view the area I have chosen is the best answer. You have a different view? What is it?'

Lukomsky gave a vague shrug.

'There's no reason to worry about the Western front. It would be better to concentrate the cavalry in the area of Pskov.'

'Pskov?' Kornilov leaned forward with a frown that curled his thin faded upper lip, and shook his head. 'No! The Pskov area is not suitable.'

Lukomsky placed his hands on the arms of his chair with a tired, elderly gesture and, choosing his words carefully, said, 'Lavr Georgievich, I'll give the necessary instructions at once, but I have the impression that you're leaving something unsaid... The area you have chosen for concentrating the cavalry would be a very good one, should it prove necessary to send it to Petrograd or Moscow, but it won't secure the Northern front, if only because of the transport problem. If I'm not mistaken and you really have left something unsaid, then I must ask you either to send me away to the front line, or to make all your plans known to me. A chief of staff can remain at his post only if he enjoys the complete confidence of his commander.'

Kornilov listened intently with his head bowed, but

his quick eye had caught the faint flush of emotion on Lukomsky's outwardly cold face. He thought for a few seconds before replying.

'Yes, you're right. There are certain considerations which I have not yet mentioned to you... Please, give instructions for the transfer of the cavalry and summon, at once, General Krymov, the commander of the 3rd Cavalry Corps. You and I will talk the whole thing over on my return from Petrograd. Believe me, Alexander Sergeyevich, I have no desire to hide anything from you.' Kornilov stressed his final phrase and turned quickly at the sound of a knock on the door, 'Come in.'

The newcomers were von Wiezin, Assistant Commissar at G. H. Q. and a stocky tow-headed general. Lukomsky rose and, as he went out, heard Kornilov reply sharply in answer to von Wiezin's question.

'I have no time at present to reconsider the case of General Miller. What?.. Yes, I am leaving.'

Lukomsky returned to his office and stood looking out of the window. Stroking his greying wedge-shaped beard, he thoughtfully watched the wind smoothing the rebellious curls of the chestnut-trees and rippling the bowed sunlit grass.

An hour later the 3rd Cavalry Corps received the order from the Supreme Commander's chief of staff to prepare to move. The same day its commander General Krymov, who had at one time, on Kornilov's request, refused an appointment to the command of the 11th Army, was summoned urgently to G. H. Q. by coded telegram.

On August 9th Kornilov left by special train for Petrograd, guarded by a squadron of Tekins.

The next day the word went round headquarters that the Supreme Commander had been replaced and perhaps even arrested, but on the morning of the 11th Kornilov was back in Mogilyov.

He called in Lukomsky immediately. Having read the telegrams and communiqués, he carefully adjusted the immaculate white cuffs framing his slim olive-brown wrists and fingered his collar. The fussiness of his movements suggested an unwonted agitation.

'Now we can finish the discussion that was interrupted before,' he said quietly. 'I want to go back to the considerations that have compelled me to move the 3rd Corps in the direction of Petrograd and that I have not yet discussed with you. You know that on August 3rd, when I was at a cabinet meeting in Petrograd, Kerensky and

Savinkov warned me not to raise any particularly important questions of defence because some of the ministers,
they said, were not to be trusted. I, the Supreme Commander-in-Chief, am unable when reporting to the government to speak of operational plans because there is no
guarantee that what I say will not within a few days
become known to the German high command! Do you
call that a government? How can I believe after this that
it will save the country?' Kornilov walked with quick
firm steps to the door, locked it and paced about agitatedly in front of his desk. 'It is a bitter shame that the
country should be ruled by such worms. Lack of will,
lack of character, of ability, of resolution, and even
downright treachery—these are the qualities that deter-
mine the actions of this "government", if such it may be
called. With the connivance of individuals like Chernov,
the Bolsheviks will sweep Kerensky aside... Yes, Alexander
Sergeyevich, that is the situation in which Russia now
finds itself. Guided by principles that are known to you,
I wish to protect the country from fresh upheavals. The
main reason why I am moving the 3rd Cavalry Corps is to
get it deployed near Petrograd by the end of August, and
then, if the Bolsheviks act, it will be able to mete out the
proper treatment to all traitors to the Motherland. I am
putting General Krymov in direct charge of the operation. I am convinced that, if need be, he will not hesitate
to hang the whole Soviet of Workers' and Soldiers' Deputies. As for the Provisional Government... Well, we
shall see... I seek nothing for myself. We must save
Russia—at all costs, no matter what the sacrifice!'

Kornilov halted in front of Lukomsky, and asked bluntly, 'Do you share my conviction that the future of the
country and the army can be safeguarded only by such an
operation? Will you go with me in this to the end?'

Lukomsky half rose from his chair, gripping Kornilov's
dry hot hand emotionally.

'I share your view entirely! I will go with you, to the
end! The whole thing must be properly thought out, and
then we must strike. Entrust me with the task, Lavr
Georgievich.'

'I have the plan worked out already. The details are
being elaborated by Colonel Lebedev and Major Rozhen-
ko. You have plenty of work as it is, Alexander Sergeyevich. Put your trust in me. We shall have time to discuss
everything and make any adjustments that may prove
necessary.'

17*

For the next few days G. H. Q. lived in a fever of excitement. Every day the governor's residence in Mogilyov was visited by volunteers offering their services: sunburnt, weather-beaten officers in dusty field tunics from frontline units, smart-looking representatives from the Officers' Alliance and the Council of the Union of Cossack Armies, and messengers from the Don, from Kaledin, the first Cossack Vice-Ataman of the Don Army Region. Occasional civilians appeared. Among the visitors there were some who sincerely wished to put back on its feet the old Russia that had fallen in February, but there were also vultures, who had scented great bloodshed from afar and, guessing whose masterful hand would open the country's veins, had flocked to Mogilyov in the hope of snatching a share of the spoils. Dobrynsky, Zavoiko and Aladin were named at headquarters as men closely associated with the Supreme Commander. At G. H. Q. and the headquarters of the Campaign Ataman of the Don Army it was whispered that Kornilov was too trusting and had fallen into the hands of adventurers. At the same time the prevailing belief among the broad mass of officers was that Kornilov was the banner of the revival of Russia. And fervent supporters of restoration thronged to this banner from all sides.

On August 13th Kornilov left to attend the state conference in Moscow.

It was a warm, slightly overcast day. The sky looked as though it had been moulded out of bluish aluminium. A lambskin cloud with a lilac edging hung in the zenith. It burst iridescently and the slanting abundant rain fell on the fields, on the train clattering along the line, on the woods already fantastically trimmed by frosts, on the pure water-colour tracings of a distant birchgrove, on the earth dressed in the widow's weeds of early autumn.

The train rolled back one expanse after another, leaving behind a reddish trail of smoke. At the window stood a slightly built general in a field tunic with crosses of St. George on his chest. Narrowing his slanting coal-black eyes, he put his head out of the window and the fresh warm raindrops splashed generously on his deeply tanned face and black drooping moustache; the wind ruffled and combed back the lock of hair falling boyishly over his forehead.

The day before Kornilov's arrival in Moscow Major Listnitsky reported there with a message of special importance from the Council of the Union of Cossack Armies. When he handed in the packet at the headquarters of the Cossack regiment stationed in Moscow, he learned that Kornilov was expected on the following day.

By noon Listnitsky was at Alexandrovsky Station. The waiting room and the first- and second-class buffets were choked with waiting crowds, most of them military. A guard of honour from the Alexandrovsky War College had formed up on the platform and the Moscow Women's Death Battalion was on guard at the viaduct. At about three in the afternoon the train steamed in. All talk ceased at once. A fierce fanfare from the band, then the crunch and shuffle of a multitude of feet. Listnitsky was picked up by the surging crowd and thrown on to the platform. When he had struggled clear, he saw two ranks of Tekins forming up in front of the Supreme Commander's carriage. Its gleaming varnished side shimmered with the reflections of their long scarlet coats. Kornilov appeared with an escort of several men in uniform and began his inspection of the guard of honour and the deputations from the Association of Knights of St. George, the Alliance of Army and Navy Officers, and the Council of the Union of Cossack Armies.

Among those who presented themselves to the Supreme Commander Listnitsky recognised the Don Ataman Kaledin and General Zaiyonchkovsky; the others were named by the officers around him.

'Kislyakov, Deputy Minister of Communications.'

'Rudnev, Mayor of Moscow.'

'Prince Trubetskoy, head of the diplomatic chancellery at G. H. Q.'

'Musin-Pushkin, member of the State Council.'

'Colonel Cayot, the French military attaché.'

'Prince Golitsyn.'

'Prince Mansyrev...' The names were uttered in tones of obsequious respect.

Listnitsky saw the mob of elegantly dressed ladies on the platform showering Kornilov with flowers as he approached. One pink blossom caught on his epaulette and hung there. Kornilov shook it off with an embarrassed, slightly hesitant gesture. A bearded veteran from the Urals began to stammer a speech of welcome on behalf of the twelve Cossack Armies. Before he could hear the rest, Listnitsky was crushed to the wall and nearly lost his sword-belt. After a speech by Rodichev, a member of the State Duma, Kornilov moved on with the crowd pressing round him. The officers linked arms to form a protective chain but they were forced apart. Dozens of hands stretched out to Kornilov. A stout dishevelled lady minced along at his side, trying to press her lips to the sleeve of his light-green uniform. At the exit a deafening cheer went up as Kornilov was hoisted shoulder high. Listnitsky thrust aside a dignified-looking gentleman and managed to grasp Kornilov's patent-leather boot as it floated past his eyes. Deftly changing his grip, he placed the leg on his shoulder and, scarcely aware of its weight, panting with excitement and trying only to maintain his balance and keep in step, allowed himself to be drawn on slowly by the crowd, deafened by the blast and blare of the brass band. At the door he hurriedly straightened the folds of his tunic that had been pulled out from under his belt in the crush. Down the steps they went and on to the square. In front was the crowd, the green blocks of troop formations, a Cossack squadron in mounted order. With his hand raised to the peak of his cap and blinking his moist eyes, he tried in vain to control his trembling lips. Vaguely he was aware of the clicking of cameras, the frantic excitement of the crowd, the officer cadets marching past, and the slim upright figure of the little general with his Mongoloid face taking the salute.

* * *

A day later Listnitsky left for Petrograd. He made himself comfortable with his greatcoat spread on an upper berth and lay smoking and thinking of Kornilov. 'The man escaped from a prison camp at the risk of his life— almost as though he knew he would be so indispensable to the Motherland. What a face! Carved out of rock— nothing superfluous or commonplace. And his character is the same. He probably has everything worked out already. When the right moment comes, he will lead us. It's strange that I don't even know what he is. A monarchist? Constitutional monarchy... If only we were all as sure of ourselves as he is.'

At about the same hour, in the corridors of the Bolshoi

Theatre in Moscow, during an interval between sessions of the Moscow State Conference, two generals, one slightly built with Mongoloid features, the other thick-set with a square close-cropped head, balding grizzled temples, and flat gristly ears, paced to and fro along a short strip of parquet and talked in low voices.

'Does that clause of the declaration provide for abolition of the soldiers' committees in military units?'

'Yes.'

'A united front, complete unanimity are absolutely essential. There can be no salvation unless the measures I have outlined are put into effect. The army is organically incapable of fighting. Such an army could not stand up to the smallest attack, let alone bring victory. Every unit has been corrupted by Bolshevik propaganda. And here, behind the lines? You see how the workers react to any attempt to find ways of bridling them? Strikes and demonstrations. The members of the Conference are obliged to come here on foot... It's a disgrace! Militarisation of the home front, punishment meted out with a firm hand, ruthless extermination of all Bolsheviks, the carriers of this marasmus—these are our immediate tasks. May I be assured of your continuing support, Alexei Maximovich?'

'I am with you unconditionally.'

'I was sure of it. Thank you. As you see, when firm and resolute action is needed, the government confines itself to half-measures and resounding phrases about "crushing with blood and iron any who, as in the July days, raise their hand against the people's power". No, we are accustomed to act first and speak afterwards. They do the opposite. Well, the time will come when they will reap the consequences of their policy of half-measures. But I have no wish to participate in this dishonest game! I have always been in favour of fighting in the open. I have no use for blather.'

The little general stopped and plucked at the metal button on his companion's tunic, stuttering slightly in his agitation.

'They have taken off the muzzle and now they themselves are scared of their own revolutionary democracy. They ask for reliable troops to be brought up to the capital, and yet at the same time they pander to this democracy and hesitate to take any real measures. One step forward, one step back. Only by the complete consolidation of our forces, by the strongest moral pressure can we squeeze any concessions out of the government. And if this fails—we shall see! I shall not hesitate to lay bare the front. Let the Germans bring them to their senses!'

'I've spoken to Dutov. The Cossacks will give you full support, Lavr Georgievich. All we have to do now is settle the question of our future co-operation.'

'After the session I shall be waiting for you and the others in my office. What is the mood on the Don?'

The thick-set general pressed his rectangular gleamingly smooth chin to his chest and looked up from under lowered brows. The corners of his lips quivered beneath the broad moustache as he spoke.

'I no longer have the same faith in the Cossack... In any case it's difficult to say what the mood is now. There must be a compromise. The Cossacks have got to sacrifice something in order to keep the support of the outsiders. We are taking certain steps in that direction, but success cannot be guaranteed. I'm afraid the break may occur where the interests of the Cossacks and the outsiders clash... The land—that's what they're all thinking about, on both sides.'

'We must have some reliable Cossack units ready to safeguard ourselves against any internal accidents. When I get back to headquarters, I'll talk to Lukomsky and we'll probably find some way of transferring a few regiments from the front to the Don.'

'I should be very grateful.'

'So today we shall settle the question of our future co-operation. I fervently believe in the success of our plans, but fortune is treacherous, General... If, in spite of everything, it should turn its back on me, may I count on finding a refuge with you on the Don?'

'Not only a refuge, but protection. From time immemorial the Cossacks have been famous for their hospitality.' Kaledin smiled for the first time during the whole conversation, softening the gloomy weariness of his sombre gaze.

One hour later Kaledin, Ataman of the Don, read out to a hushed audience the historic Declaration of the Twelve Cossack Armies. Across the Don, the Kuban, the Terek, the Ural, the Ussuri, throughout all the Cossack lands, from border to border, from one district to another, the threads of a vast conspiracy were being woven into a black web.

XV

About a verst from the ruins of a small township that had been razed by artillery fire during the June fighting the zigzags of trenches wound their way whimsically past a wood. The sector closest to the trees was occupied by a Cossack special squadron.

Behind it, beyond the green thickets of alder and young birch lay a rusty peat bog where there were still signs of the digging that had been done before the war; red hips glowed merrily on the bushes. Further to the right, behind a headland of forest ran a shell-battered highway, a reminder of all the roads the Cossacks had yet to ride. The forest was fringed with stunted, bullet-snipped weeds, the hunched shapes of charred tree-stumps, and a brownish yellow parapet, from which the wrinkles of other trenches spread far out across the bare fields. Behind the line, even the bog with its ripple of old workings, even the wrecked highway had about them a smell of life, of abandoned work, but the land at the forest's edge presented a joyless and bitter picture to the eye of man.

That day Ivan Alexeyevich Kotlyarov, the former engineman at Mokhov's mill, went off to the neighbouring town, where the squadron's support unit was stationed, and did not return until evening. As he made his way to his own dug-out he met Zakhar Korolyov. Zakhar came at him, waving his arms wildly and allowing his sabre to catch on the sand-bagged embrasures. Ivan stepped aside to let him pass, but Zakhar snatched at the button of his tunic and whispered to him, showing the unhealthy yellowish whites of his eyes.

'Have you heard? The infantry on the right's withdrawing! Mebbe they're leaving the front?'

Zakhar's matted beard looked like a stream of molten iron that had suddenly ceased to flow, his eyes stared with a hungry wretched eagerness.

'Leaving the front? How?'

'How, I don't know, but they're clearing out.'

'Mebbe they're being relieved? Let's go and ask the troop officer.'

Zakhar turned and headed for the troop officer's dug-out, his feet sliding about on the slimy, wet ground.

An hour later the squadron was relieved by infantry and marched off to town. The following morning they collected their horses from the stablemen and proceeded by forced marches into the rear.

A fine drizzle was falling. The birches hung their heads mournfully. As the road plunged into the forest, the horses, catching the scent of moisture and the poignantly sharp and sorrowful smell of last year's leaves, snorted and stepped out at a brisker pace. The wet berries of the spurge laurel hung like pink beads from the bushes, the foaming blossoms of maiden's clover shone irresistibly white. The wind shook down the round, heavy drops from the trees on to the passing horsemen, and their caps and greatcoats were soon covered with black spots, as though they had been sprayed with buckshot. Melting puffs of tobacco smoke floated up over the columns.

'They get us up and march us off the devil knows where.'

'Ain't you had enough of the trenches?'

'Where are they sending us anyway?'

'Some other sector, I suppose.'

'Don't look like it.'

'Well, let's have a smoke and forget our troubles!'

'I've got mine in my saddle-bags...'

'Will you allow us to strike up a song, Major?'

'Did he say he could?.. Go on, Arkhip, strike up!'

Someone near the head of the column cleared his throat and began:

> *Cossack rider, Cossack rider, riding home to rest,*
> *Stripes on his shoulders, crosses on his chest.*

The sodden voices drawled the song half-heartedly and fell silent. Zakhar Korolyov, who was in the same rank as Ivan, stood up in his stirrups and bawled derisively, 'Heh, you blind old men! Is that the way to sing? You ought to go begging outside a church. You croakers...'

'Sing up yourself then!'

'His neck's too short, there's no room for a voice.'

'Funk it now, would you, after all your bragging?'

Korolyov gripped the black mass of his lice-infested beard in his fist, closed his eyes for a minute, swung his reins wildly, and tossed out the first words:

> *Rejoice, rejoice, Don Cossacks brave...*

As though awakened by the resounding cry, the squadron bellowed out:

In your honour and your glory!

The song went up over the road and the wet forest.

> *Show us for every friend to see*
> *How well we shoot the enemy!*
> *Shoot well and in battle firmly stand,*
> *Obey one order and only one.*
> *For as the officers, our fathers, command,*
> *So shall we conquer with sabre, lance and gun!*

Happy to have got out of that 'wolves' graveyard', they sang for the rest of the way. By evening they had entrained and were heading for Pskov. Only after passing through three stations did they learn that their squadron, along with other units of the 3rd Cavalry Corps, was on its way to Petrograd to suppress the disorders that had broken out there. After that the talk died down and a drowsy stillness hung over the red vans.

'Out of the frying pan into the fire!' a lanky Cossack named Borshchev voiced the thought that was in most minds.

At the first stop Ivan Kotlyarov—chairman of the squadron committee since February—went to see the squadron commander.

'The Cossacks are worried, Major.'

The commander fixed his eyes on the dimple in Ivan's chin and said, smiling, 'I'm worried myself, my dear fellow.'

'Where're they sending us?'

'To Petrograd.'

'To put down disorders?'

'What did you think—to encourage them?'

'We don't want to do either.'

'It so happens that no one is asking us what we want.'

'The Cossacks...'

'What about "the Cossacks"?' the squadron commander interrupted, angrily now. 'I know myself what the Cossacks think. D'you imagine I like this task? Take this and read it out to the squadron. At the next station I'll talk to the Cossacks myself.'

The commander held out a folded telegram, then turned away and with a frown of disgust started chewing some fat-speckled bully beef.

Ivan returned to his troop, carrying the telegram like a hot coal in his hand.

507

'Call in the Cossacks from the other vans.'

As the train moved off, more and more Cossacks crowded into the van. Soon there were about thirty.

'The commander's had a telegram. I've just read it.'

'Well, what does it say? Let's hear it!'

'Come on, read it out!'

'Is it about peace?'

'Quiet!'

Amid a murky silence Ivan read aloud the proclamation of the Supreme Commander-in-Chief Kornilov. Then the sheet with its message in cablese was passed from one sweaty hand to another.

I, the Supreme Commander-in-Chief Kornilov, declare before the whole nation that my duty as a soldier, my devotion as a citizen of free Russia and my unbounded love for the Motherland have compelled me in these grave minutes of the country's existence to ignore the order of the Provisional Government and retain the supreme command of the Army and Navy. Supported in this decision by all the commanders-in-chief of the fronts, I declare before the whole Russian nation that I prefer death to removal from my post as Supreme Commander-in-Chief. A true son of the Russian people always dies at his post and sacrifices for the Motherland his dearest possession—his own life.

In these truly terrible minutes of the country's existence, when the approaches to both capitals have been virtually laid bare to the victorious advance of the triumphant enemy, the Provisional Government forgets the paramount question of the country's existence as a sovereign state and harasses the nation with illusory fears of a counter-revolution, which by its inability to govern, its weakness in authority, and its vacillation, it is rapidly bringing about.

It would be unfitting for me, a blood son of my people, who, in the full view of all, has devoted his whole life to their service, to refuse to stand guard over the great freedoms of his people's great future. But today that future lies in weak, inert hands. By means of bribery and treachery the arrogant enemy rules the affairs of our country, as if it were his own, and threatens not only the freedom but the very existence of the Russian nation. Open your eyes, Russian people, and look into the bottomless pit into which our Motherland is falling!

Avoiding all upheavals, preventing any shedding of Russian blood, any internal strife, and forgetting all grievances and insults, I appeal before the whole people to the Provisional Government and say: come to me at General Headquarters, where your freedom and security will be protected by my word of honour, and join me in working out and building a system of national defence which, by safeguarding freedom, would lead the Russian nation to the great future that a powerful and free people deserves.

General Kornilov

At the next station the train's departure was delayed. The waiting Cossacks gathered round the vans, discussing Kornilov's telegram and a telegram from Kerensky, which had just been read out by the squadron commander, and which denounced Kornilov as a traitor and counter-revolutionary. The Cossacks were confused. The squadron commander and his troop officers were at a loss.

'My head's in a real muddle,' Martin Shamil complained. 'Darned if I know which of 'em is in the wrong!'

'They've quarrelled amongst 'emselves and the troops get the kicks.'

'It's their fat that's fretting the high-ups!'

'They all want to be top dog.'

'When the masters fall out the Cossacks get the clout.'

'Everything's going haywire. We're in a real mess!'

A bunch of Cossacks came up to Ivan.

'Go to the commander and find out what's to be done.'

They went in a crowd. The officers were in conference in his carriage when Ivan entered.

'Commander, the Cossacks want to know what we ought to do now.'

'I'll be out in a minute.'

The squadron gathered round the rear van and waited. The commander made his way into their midst and raised his hand.

'We are subordinate not to Kerensky but to the Supreme Commander-in-Chief and our own immediate command. Isn't that right? So we must unquestioningly obey the orders of our command and proceed to Petrograd. In the last resort we can go as far as the station of Dno and find out what the situation is from the commander of the First Don Cossack Division—it should be clear by the time we get there. I ask you, Cossacks, not to worry. We're living in troubled times.'

The squadron commander went on at great length about the soldier's duty, the Motherland and the revolution, trying to calm the Cossacks and replying evasively to their questions. He achieved his aim. While he was talking, a locomotive was coupled to the train (without the men's knowledge two officers of the squadron had forced the station-master at gunpoint to speed up departure) and the Cossacks drifted back to their vans.

It took the train the best part of twenty-four hours to reach Dno. During the night it again had to wait while trains carrying Ussuri Cossacks and the Daghestan Regiment went through. The train was shunted into a siding, and the vans of the Dagestan Regiment rushed past with their lights glittering in the opal darkness, taking with them a murmur of guttural voices, the moan of a *zurna*, and unfamiliar songs.

The squadron got moving again at midnight. The low-powered locomotive stood for a long time by the water tower, the glow from its firebox lighting the ground. The driver leaned out of his window smoking a cigarette, as if he were waiting for something. One of the Cossacks in the van nearest the engine poked his head out and shouted, 'Hi there, Gavrila, get going, or we'll start shooting!'

The driver spat out his cigarette, silently watched the curve of its flight, then cleared his throat and said, 'You can't shoot everyone,' and stepped back from the window.

A few minutes later the engine gave a jerk, buffers clanked, and there was a clatter of hooves as the horses were knocked off their balance. The train floated past the water-tower, past a few lighted windows and the dark shapes of the birch-groves along the line. Most of the Cossacks turned in after feeding their horses and only a few stood smoking by the half-open doors, glancing up at the majestic sky and thinking their own thoughts.

Ivan was lying beside Korolyov, looking up through the half-open doorway at the shifting haze of stars. During the past day he had thought things over and firmly decided to do all he could to prevent the squadron's further progress towards Petrograd; now he was pondering how best to win the Cossacks over to his decision, how to influence them.

Even before Kornilov's proclamation he had been clearly aware that the general's road was not for the Cossacks, and he also had a hunch that it wouldn't do for them to defend Kerensky either. He mulled it over and decided: Yes, I'll have to stop the squadron from reaching Petrograd, and if there has to be a clash with someone, it'll have to be with Kornilov, though not in support of Kerensky, not for his government, but for the one that will come after him. Ivan was more than convinced that after Kerensky would come the government they really wanted, their own government. In summer he had been in Petrograd at the military section of the Executive Committee. He had been sent by his squadron for advice on the conflict that had arisen with the squadron commander, and after seeing the work of the Executive Committee and talking to some of the Bolsheviks there, he had thought, 'When that frame gets some of our workers' flesh on it, then it'll be a real power! Die, if you have to, Ivan, but hold on to it, like a baby holds on to its mother's breast!'

That night, as he lay on his horse blanket, he remembered often and with great love, a kind of love he had never known before, the man under whose guidance he had taken his first groping steps along the hard road he was to follow. Thinking of what he should say to the Cossacks on the morrow, he also remembered Stokman's words about the Cossacks and kept repeating them, as if he were driving home a nail. 'The Cossacks are conservative to the marrow. When you try to convince a Cossack of the truth of the Bolshevik ideas, don't forget that fact, and go about it cautiously, thoughtfully, adapting to the circumstances as you go along. At first they'll be just as prejudiced towards you as you and Mishka Koshevoi were towards me, but don't let that worry you. Keep on hammering away—we're bound to win in the end.'

Ivan had surmised that when it came to persuading the Cossacks not to follow Kornilov he would run into some objections, but in the morning, when in his own van he cautiously suggested that they ought to demand the squadron's return to the front and not go on to Petrograd to fight their own people, the other Cossacks readily agreed. Zakhar Korolyov and a Cossack from Chernyshevskaya stanitsa named Turilin were Ivan's closest assistants. All day they made their way from van to van, talking to the Cossacks, and that evening, when the train slowed down at a wayside station, Sergeant Pshenichnikov, of the Third Troop, jumped aboard Ivan's van.

'The squadron gets out at the very next stop!' he shouted to Ivan. 'What kind of committee chairman are you if you don't know what the Cossacks want? We've had enough of being made fools of! We're not going any further!.. The officers are out to trap us and we haven't heard so much as a squeak out of you. Is that what we elected you for? Well, what are you grinning at?'

'So you've woken up at last,' Ivan replied, smiling.

At the next stop he was the first out of the van. Accompanied by Turilin, he went to the station-master's office.

'Don't send our train any further. We're getting off here.'

'How's that?' the station-master asked in confusion. 'I have instructions...'

'Stuff it!' Turilin interrupted him grimly.

They sought out the station committee, explained to the chairman, a thick-set sandy-haired telegraphist, what it was all about, and a few minutes later the driver willingly shunted the train into a siding.

The Cossacks hurriedly let down the ramps and started bringing out their horses. Ivan stood by the engine, his long legs planted wide apart, wiping the sweat from his smiling swarthy face. The squadron commander ran up to him white-cheeked.

'What are you doing? Don't you know that...'

'Yes, I know!' Ivan cut in. 'And don't shout, Major!' Pale-faced and with nostrils twitching, he said clearly, 'You've done your shouting, mate! Now it's balls to you. And that's how it's going to stay!'

'The Supreme Commander Kornilov...' the major began, turning purple, but Ivan looked down at his battered boots that had sunk deep into the soft sand, waved his hand with a kind of relief, and advised, 'Hang him round your neck instead of a cross—we don't need him!'

The major turned on his heel and ran back to his carriage.

An hour later the squadron without a single officer but in full fighting order left the station and rode southwest. Ivan, who had taken command, and his right-hand man, the stocky Turilin, were at the head of the column, next to the machine-gunners.

Finding their way with some difficulty by the map they had taken from the former commander, the squadron reached the village of Goreloye and halted for the night. By common consent it was decided to head for the front and, if there was any attempt to stop them, to fight.

Having hobbled their horses and mounted guard, the Cossacks turned in. No fires were lighted. Most of the men seemed depressed. They bedded down without the usual talk and jokes, hiding their thoughts one from another.

'What will happen if they change their minds and give

themselves up?' Ivan wondered with some alarm as he tried to get comfortable under his greatcoat.

As though he had been listening to Ivan's thoughts, Turilin came over to him.

'You asleep, Ivan?'

'Not yet.'

Turilin squatted beside him and with his cigarette glowing in the darkness said in a whisper, 'The Cossacks are upset... They've kicked over the traces and now they're scared. We've got ourselves into a sticky spot. A bit too sticky, don't you think?'

'We'll see how things go,' Ivan replied calmly. 'You're not scared, are you?'

Turilin scratched the back of his head under his cap and smiled wryly.

'To tell you the truth, I am a bit. I wasn't to begin with, but now I've got the wind up.'

'So you're not so tough when it comes to facing the music.'

'Well, he's pretty strong, you know, Ivan.'

They were silent for a time. The lights went out in the village. From the wide reaches of willow-covered marshland came the cry of a wild duck.

'That's a big one calling,' Turilin murmured thoughtfully, and fell silent again.

A gentle nocturnal stillness was grazing on the meadow. The grass was bowed with dew. A light breeze carried the mingled scents of marsh herb, rotting rushes, boggy soil and dew-soaked grass to the Cossack camp. Now and then came the thwack of a horse's hobbling thong, a spluttering snort and the heavy thump and breathing of the horse as it rolled about. Then again a sleepy stillness, and far away, the barely audible throaty cry of a drake and the answer, a little nearer, of a duck. The rapid whirring of invisible wings in the darkness. Night. Silence. The misty dampness of the meadows. In the west, at the foot of the sky, a rising deep-violet dough of clouds. And right across the middle, over the ancient land of Pskov, burnt into the sky as an eternal reminder—the broad track of glowing embers known as the Tatar Way.

The squadron set out again at dawn. They rode through the village of Goreloye watched by the women and little children who were driving the cows out to pasture, and climbed a hill stained brick-red by the dawn. Turilin looked round and nudged Ivan's stirrup with his foot.

'Look behind you, there's someone riding after us.'

Three horsemen, swathed in a pink cambric dust, had left the village and were pursuing them at a gallop.

'Squadron, halt!' Ivan commanded.

Swift as ever, the Cossacks formed up in a grey square. With about half a verst to go, their pursuers slowed to a trot. One of them, a Cossack officer, pulled out a handkerchief and waved it above his head. They were watched intently by the Cossacks. The officer, who was wearing field uniform, rode out in front. The two others, in long Circassian coats, kept their distance.

'What's your business?' Ivan asked, riding forward to meet them.

'We wish to talk,' the officer replied, saluting. 'Which of you took command of the squadron?'

'I did.'

'I am authorised by the First Don Cossack Division, and these are representatives of the Native Division.' The officer indicated the highlanders with his eyes, drew his reins tight and stroked the glistening neck of his foaming horse. 'If you are willing to talk, order the squadron to dismount. I have a message to be delivered orally from the divisional commander, Major General Grekov.'

Cossacks and envoys dismounted. The envoys strode in among the Cossack ranks and the squadron fell back a little, forming a tight circle.

The first to speak was the Cossack officer.

'Cossacks! We have come to persuade you to change your minds and avert the grave consequences of your action. Yesterday divisional headquarters learned that you had at someone's criminal instigation taken it upon yourselves to leave the train. Today headquarters has sent us with instructions that you are to return immediately to the station of Dno. Yesterday the troops of the Native Division and other cavalry units occupied Petrograd—the message came through by telegraph today. Our vanguard has entered the capital, occupied all government offices, the banks, the telegraph and telephone exchanges, and all other key points. The Provisional Government has fled and is considered to be deposed. Take thought, Cossacks! You are heading for destruction! If you refuse to obey the divisional commander's instructions, armed force will be used against you. Your conduct is regarded as treason, as disobedience on the field of battle. Only by unquestioning submission can you avoid bloodshed among brothers.'

514

As soon as he had sighted the envoys Ivan, knowing the mood of the Cossacks, had realised that negotiations cold not be avoided. Refusal to talk would have led to opposite results. After a moment's thought he had given the order to dismount and with a wink at Turilin pushed his way through the crowd until he was close to the envoys. While the officer was talking, he watched the Cossacks' lowered heads and frowning faces; some of them were whispering to each other. Zakhar Korolyov was smiling wryly and his beard had welded itself to his chest like a cooling flood of molten iron; Borshchev was toying with his whip and looking to one side; Pshenichnikov was staring open-mouthed at the officer; Martin Shamil was rubbing his cheeks with a dirty hand and blinking; behind him loomed Bagrov's stolid face, Krasnikov, a machine-gunner, had narrowed his eyes expectantly; Turilin was breathing hard; the freckled Obnizov had pushed his cap on to the back of his head and was working his head from side to side like a bullock under a yoke; the whole of the second troop had bowed their heads as if in prayer; the crowd stood silent and bunched together, breathing heavily with agitation; ripples of dismay passed over their faces.

Ivan realised that the critical moment had come; another few minutes and this smooth-talking officer would be able to do what he liked with them. At all costs he had got to dispel the impression produced by the officer's words and shake the decision which, though unexpressed, was already forming in the Cossacks' minds. He raised his hand and scanned the crowd with dilated, strangely whitened eyes.

'Brothers! Wait a bit!' he cried, and turned to the officer. 'Have you got that telegram with you?'

'What telegram?' the officer looked at him in surprise.

'The one about Petrograd being occupied.'

'The telegram? No. What has that to do with the matter?'

'Aha! He hasn't got it!' the squadron heaved a single sigh of relief.

Many lifted their heads and looked hopefully at Ivan. Raising his husky voice, he shouted with a fierce and mocking confidence that captured attention.

'You haven't got it, you say? And you think we'll take your word? Want to catch us with that stuff, do you?'

'It's a trick!' a hollow gasp ran through the squadron.

'The telegram wasn't addressed to me, Cossacks!'

515

the officer's hands went persuasively to his chest.

But no one was listening to him. Sensing that the squadron's sympathies were again on his side, Ivan went to work like a diamond on glass.

'And even if you had it with you, we wouldn't take your road! We don't want to fight our own folk. We won't go against the people! You want to set us against them? Well, you won't! There's not so many fools about nowadays! We don't want to prop up the power of the generals. So get that straight!'

The Cossacks all started talking at once. The crowd surged forward and the shouts spilled over.

'That's the way to talk!'

'Bang on!'

'That's right!'

'Send 'em packing.'

'Fine match-makers, eh!'

'What about the three Cossack regiments in Petrograd right now? They don't seem to be in a hurry to go against the people.'

'Here listen, Ivan! Kick 'em out! Give 'em their marching orders!'

Ivan glanced at the envoys. The Cossack officer had pursed his lips and was waiting patiently; behind him, shoulder to shoulder, stood the highlanders—a stalwart young Ingush officer, arms folded on his splendid Circassian coat, slanting almond eyes glinting under the round black fur hat, and an elderly red-haired Ossetian, standing casually at ease with one hand on the hilt of his curved sword, watching the Cossacks quizzically. Ivan was about to end the discussion when he was forestalled by the Cossack officer; after a whispered consultation with the Ingush he shouted harshly.

'Don Cossacks! Let the representative of the Native Division speak!'

Without waiting for anyone's consent, the Ingush stepped forward softly in his heelless boots and entered the circle, nervously straightening his narrow metal-trimmed belt.

'Cossack brothers! Why is all this big noise?' he began in a guttural Caucasian accent. 'We must speak without bitterness. You don't want General Kornilov? You want war? All right! We'll give you war. It is nothing! Nothing at all! We will crush you today. Two highland regiments are behind us. Pah! What to shout about? Why big noise?' At first he spoke with apparent calm, but his voice rose passionately and words from his own language mingled with his guttural broken Russian. 'You led astray by that Cossack. He is Bolshevik, and you follow him! Pah! Can't I see? Arrest him! Disarm him!'

He pointed boldly at Ivan as he darted about in the cramped circle, gesticulating fiercely; a deep brown flush flooding his pale face. His fellow officer, the elderly red-headed Ossetian, maintained an icy composure; the Cossack officer toyed with his frayed sword-knot. Again the Cossacks fell silent, and confusion spread through their ranks. Ivan kept his eyes fixed on the Ingush officer, on the white snarl of his teeth, on the slanting grey trickle of sweat across his left temple, and reflected bitterly that he had let slip the moment when he could have cut short the negotiations and marched the Cossacks away. The situation was saved by Turilin. He sprang into the middle of the circle, waved his arms wildly, tore open the buttoned collar of his shirt and burst out hoarsely, his face twitching and foam breaking from his mouth.

'The creeping snakes!.. Devils!.. Swine!.. They're treating you like tarts! And you stand there lapping it up! These officers are palming off their troubles on you!.. What are you doing? Just what are you doing?! You ought to be cutting them down and you stand there listening?.. Slash their heads off, have their blood. While you're nattering here, we'll be surrounded and mown down with machine-guns. You won't hold many meetings with a machine-gun at your head! They're pulling the wool over your eyes until their troops catch up... Call yourselves Cossacks! You're a lot of old women!'

'To horse!..' Ivan thundered at the top of his voice.

His shout burst over the crowd like a shrapnel shell. The Cossacks dashed for their mounts and within minutes the squadron had formed into troop columns.

'Now listen! Cossacks!' the Cossack officer darted from one to another.

Ivan jerked his rifle off his shoulder, planted his thick-knuckled finger on the trigger, curbed his horse roughly as it reared, and shouted, 'We've finished talking! Next time we talk, it'll be with this!' And he shook the rifle expressively.

The Cossacks rode out on to the road troop by troop. Looking back, they saw the envoys mount their horses and go into a huddle. The Ingush, his eyes narrowed to slits, was arguing fiercely, arm raised, the silk cuff of his Circassian coat gleaming a snowy white.

517

As Ivan looked back for the last time and saw that dazzlingly white strip of silk he had a vision of the wind-whipped surging breast of the Don with its green foam-capped waves and the white wing of a fisher gull skimming the crests.

XVI

By August 29th it was clear to Kornilov from the telegrams he was receiving from Krymov that the attempt to seize power by force of arms had failed.

At two in the afternoon a dispatch officer from Krymov arrived at G. H. Q. Kornilov discussed the situation with him at great length, then summoned Romanovsky and, crumpling a sheet of paper nervously in his hands, said, 'Utter collapse! Our trump card is beaten... Krymov will not be able to bring the corps up to Petrograd in time and the moment will be lost. What seemed to be so easily attainable is encountering a thousand obstacles... The scales are weighted against us... Look at the pattern of troop movements!' he showed Romanovsky a map detailing the latest positions of the trains carrying Krymov's cavalry corps and the Native Division towards Petrograd; a shudder zigzagged across his energetic face, now crumpled from lack of sleep. 'It's those damned railwaymen that are tripping us up. They don't realise what the consequences will be. If we succeed, I'll have one in ten of them hanged on the spot. Read this report from Krymov.'

While Romanovsky read, stroking his bloated, oily face with a large hand, Kornilov wrote rapidly.

To Army Ataman, Alexei Maximovich Kaledin, Novocherkassk.

The gist of your telegram to the Provisional Government has been brought to my knowledge. Their patience exhausted in a fruitless struggle with scoundrels and traitors, the glorious Cossacks, foreseeing the inevitable destruction of the Motherland, will defend with arms in hand the life and freedom of a country that has grown and expanded thanks to their toil and blood. Our relations will remain restricted for a time. I beg you to act in consort with me, as your patriotism and Cossack honour dictate. 658. 29. 8. 17.

General *Kornilov*

'Send this telegram at once,' he told Romanovsky as soon as he had finished writing.

'Do you want me to send Prince Bagration a second telegram with instruction to continue the journey in marching order?'

'Yes, do.'

Romanovsky paused, then said thoughtfully, 'In my view, Lavr Georgievich, we have no grounds for pessimism as yet. You are inaccurate in your anticipation of events.'

Kornilov thrust out his hand nervously to snatch at a tiny mauve butterfly that had been fluttering above his head. His fingers clenched and his face wore a slightly tense, expectant expression. The butterfly, buffeted by the disturbed air, glided away towards the window. Kornilov managed to catch it and threw himself back in his chair with a sigh of relief.

Romanovsky waited for a reply to his comment, but Kornilov responded with a pensive and sombre smile.

'I had a dream last night,' he said. 'I dreamed I was a brigade commander in an infantry division and conducting an offensive in the Carpathians. I arrived at some farm or other with my staff and an elderly Ruthenian, very well dressed, came out to greet us. He offered me some milk to drink, then took off his white felt hat and said in perfect German, 'Drink it up, general! This milk has exceptional curative properties.'' I drank and felt no surprise that this Ruthenian should be patting me familiarly on the shoulder. Then we went on through the mountains and it no longer seemed like the Carpathians, but somewhere in Afghanistan. We were climbing a goat track... Yes, it was most certainly a goat track. Stones and brown gravel broke away from under our feet, and beneath us there was a splendid southern landscape, bathed in white sunlight...'

A slight draught stirred the papers on the desk and flowed out through the open windows. Kornilov's misty abstracted gaze roamed beyond the Dnieper, over the undulating hills streaked with the coppery yellow of meadows.

Romanovsky followed his gaze and, with a discreet sigh, turned his eyes to the glazed, mica-like surface of the windless Dnieper, to the hazy fields delicately softened by approaching autumn.

XVII

The units of the 3rd Cavalry Corps and the Native Division that Kornilov had flung against Petrograd were on the move over a vast area covered by eight railways. Revel, Vezenberg, Narva, Yamburg, Gatchina, Somrino, Vyritsa, Chudovo, Gdov, Novgorod, Dno, Pskov, Luga and all the other intervening stations and sidings were choked with trains that were moving slowly or not moving at all. The regiments were beyond the moral control of the senior command and the scattered squadrons had lost contact with each other. The confusion was made worse by the attempt to deploy the corps and the Native Division attached to it as an army while on the march; this involved the transfer and reassembly of scattered units and a general regrouping, which led to further muddle, to meaningless, often uncoordinated instructions, and forced the already strained atmosphere to a fresh pitch of intensity.

Encountering spontaneous resistance from railwaymen and officials and overcoming the obstacles that were placed in their path, the trains carrying Kornilov's army trickled slowly towards Petrograd, jamming up at junctions, then thinning out again.

Half-starved Cossacks from the Don, Ussuri and the Amur, from Orenburg and Nerchinsk, and Ingushis, Circassians, Kabardinians, Ossetians and Daghestanis from the Caucasus were cooped up with their half-starved horses in the box-like red vans. At the stations the trains stood for hours waiting to be sent on, and the men poured out of the vans and swarmed like locusts over the platforms and tracks, gobbling up anything edible that had been left behind by the trains in front, stealing quietly from the local populace and ransacking the food stores.

The yellow and red trouser stripes of the Cossacks, the dashing tunics of Dragoons, the long coats of the Caucasians... Never had the lack-lustre northern landscapes seen such a rich array of colours.

On August 29th the 3rd Brigade of the Native Division commanded by Prince Gagarin made contact with the enemy near Pavlovsk. Confronted by torn-up track, the Ingush and Circassian regiments at the head of the division detrained and proceeded in marching order in the direction of Tsarskoye Selo; Ingush patrols penetrated as far as the station of Somrino. The regiments advanced slowly, pressing back the opposing Guards and waiting for the other units of the division to come up. But most of these were still held up at Dno, and some had not even reached that station.

The commander of the Native Division, Prince Bagration, made his headquarters at an estate not far from the station, waiting for the rest of his units to concentrate and not daring to march on Vyritsa.

On the 28th he had received from the headquarters of the Northern Front a copy of the following telegram:

I request Commander of Third Corps and commanders of First Don, Ussuri and Caucasian Native divisions to pass on order of Supreme C.-in-C. that if, owning to any unforeseen circumstances, trains should encounter difficulties on the way, Supreme C.-in-C. orders divisions to proceed in column of route. 27 August 1917, No. 6411. *Romanovsky.*

At about nine in the morning Bagration telegraphed Kornilov that at 6.40 a. m. he had received through Colonel Bagratuni, Chief of Staff of the Petrograd Military District, an order from Kerensky to turn all the divisions back, and that the divisions' trains were being held up on the line between Gachka and Oredezh because the railway, acting on the orders of the Provisional Government, had refused to let them pass. But despite the instruction he had received from Kornilov, which read:

To Prince Bagration. Continue along the railway. If this proves impossible, proceed in march order as far as Luga, where you are to place yourself entirely at the disposal of General Krymov,

Bagration still hesitated to take to the roads and ordered his staff to entrain.

The regiment in which Yevgeny Listnitsky had once served, together with the other regiments composing the First Don Cossack Division was being moved up to Petrograd along the Revel—Vezenberg—Narva line. At 5 p. m. on the 28th a train carrying two squadrons of the regiment arrived in Narva. There the train commander learned that it could proceed no further that night because the track had been damaged. A unit of the railway battalion had been sent to repair it in all haste; if this were accomplished by morning, the train would be allowed to proceed. There was nothing for it but to agree and, muttering curses, the train commander climbed back into this carriage, passed on the news to the other officers and sat down to drink tea.

The night was overcast. A raw, penetrating wind was blowing from the sea. The Cossacks gathered on the tracks and in the vans, talking in low tones, while the horses, disturbed by the blast of locomotive whistles, stamped restlessly on the wooden floors. At the rear of the train a young Cossack voice began to sing, complaining in the darkness to no one knew whom:

> *Farewell, stanitsa, town o'mine,*
> *Farewell, my native village dear!*
> *Farewell, my lassie, young and kind,*
> *My little steppeland flower!*
> *Once I lay from dusk to dawn*
> *Upon my darling's loving arm,*
> *But now from dusk to dawn I stand*
> *With a rifle in my hand...*

A man appeared from behind the grey mass of the warehouses. He stood listening to the song for a moment, surveyed the tracks, punctuated with yellow commas of light, and made his way confidently towards the train. His footsteps sounded softly on the wooden sleepers and died away when he stepped off on to the hard-packed sandy soil. As he passed the rear van he was hailed by the Cossack who had been standing at the door, singing.

'Who's there?'

'Who d'you want then?' came the unwilling answer. 'What brings you snooping round here at night? We shoot thieves. Looking for something to nick, are you?'

Without replying the man walked on to the middle section of the train and, thrusting his head through the gap between the half-open doors, asked, 'What squadron?'

'Convicts!' someone laughed in the darkness.

'No, seriously—which is it?'

'The second.'

'Where's the Fourth Troop then?'

'Sixth van from the front of the train.'

Three Cossacks were smoking by the sixth van. One was squatting on his haunches, the other two were standing beside him. They watched in silence as the man approached.

'Good evening, Cossacks!'

'Praise the Lord,' one of them replied, peering at the newcomer's face.

'Is Nikita Dugin still around? Is he here?'

'Here I am,' the man who had been squatting responded in a light tenor voice and stood up, crushing his cigarette under his heel. 'I don't recognise you. Where d'ye spring from?' He thrust his bearded face forward, peering at the stranger, who wore a greatcoat and crumpled soldier's cap, and suddenly gave a grunt of astonishment. 'Ilya! Bunchuk! Where did the devil fish you up, old chum?'

He gripped Bunchuk's hairy hand in his own rough fist and, leaning forward, said quietly, 'These are our lads, you needn't worry about them. How d'ye come to be here? Come on, out with it!'

Bunchuk shook hands with the other Cossacks and replied in a strained voice that had no more ring in it than cast iron.

'I've come from Petrograd. It was a job finding you. There's work to be done. We must have a talk. I'm real glad to see you alive and well, mate.'

He smiled and his teeth showed white in the grey rectangle of his big broad-browed face, and his eyes gleamed with a restrained warmth and cheerfulness.

'Have a talk?' Dugin's tenor voice responded tunefully. 'So you don't look down on our company, even though you're an officer. Thanks for that, Ilya, Christ save you. We could do with a kind word and a cuddle now and again.' There was a note of good-humoured, ungrudging laughter in his voice.

Bunchuk returned the joke in the same tone.

'All right, you old cadger! Still playing around, eh! Though your beard's nearly down to your knees!'

'We can shave our beards any time, but you tell us what's going on in Petrograd? Have the mutinies started?'

'Let's go inside,' Bunchuk suggested. They climbed into the van. Dugin prodded the sleeping men with the toe of his boot, saying quietly, 'Get up, lads! There's a man we need come to see us. Look lively, boys, rouse yourselves!'

The Cossacks got up, clearing their throats. Bunchuk seated himself on a saddle and someone's big hands smelling of tobacco and horse-sweat felt his face gently in the darkness; a deep voice, thick as cart-grease, asked, 'Bunchuk?'

'Right. Is that you, Chikamasov?'

'Ay, it's me. Hullo, mate!'

'Hullo to you.'

'I'll just slip out and call the lads from the Third Troop.'

'All right! Off you go!'

The Third Troop came almost to a man, leaving only two of their number to mind the horses. The Cossacks crowded round Bunchuk, offering him their crusty hands, peering into his big gloomy face by the light of a lantern, and whether they called him 'Bunchuk' or 'Ilya 'Mitrich', or simply 'Ilyusha', there was equal warmth and friendliness in all the voices.

The van grew stuffy. Reflections of light danced on the boarded walls and weird shadows swayed and swelled as the lantern smoked greasily like the lamp under an ikon.

Bunchuk was given a seat in the light. The men in front squatted and the rest stood round in a tight circle. Dugin cleared his throat and spoke up in his tenor voice.

'We got your letter, Ilya 'Mitrich, not so long ago, but we'd like to hear it all from you and to have you advise us what to do in future. As you know, they're moving us up to the capital. What can we do about it?'

'You see, it's like this, 'Mitrich,' said a Cossack standing by the door, the same Cossack, with an ear-ring in the wrinkled lobe of his ear, that Listnitsky had once offended by refusing to let him boil up some water on a trench shield. 'All kinds of agitators come round telling us, don't you go to Petrograd, there's no reason for us to fight amongst ourselves, and all that kind o' thing. We listen to 'em all, but we don't trust 'em much. They're strangers. Mebbe they want to trap us in some way, put us in the cart—who knows? If we disobey, Kornilov will set his Circassians on us and there'll be more bloodshed. But you here, you're one of us, a Cossack, we've got more trust in you and we're real grateful for the letters you've been sending us from Petrograd, and for the newspapers... As a matter of fact, we were a bit hard up for paper for fags, and when we got them newspapers...'

'What are you babbling about, you mutt?' another Cossack interrupted indignantly. 'You can't read, so you think we're all as ignorant as you are? Talking as if we just used the newspapers for making fags! But we read 'em from top to bottom first, Ilya 'Mitrich, that we did!'

'A fine thing to say, you croaking devil!'

' "For fags"—listen to him!'

'He's as dumb as they make 'em!'

'Now, lads! I didn't mean it like that,' the Cossack with the ear-ring tried to justify himself. 'O'course, we read the papers first...'

'You did?'

'It so happens I never had any book learning... What I mean is we read 'em together like, then had 'em for fags.'

Bunchuk sat on the saddle, smiling quietly and watching the Cossacks; then, finding it awkward to speak sitting down, he stood up and, turning his back to the lantern, began slowly, uncertainly.

'There's nothing for you to do in Petrograd. There haven't been any mutinies. D'you know why they're sending you there? To overthrow the Provisional Government—that's why! And who's sending you there? The tsarist general Kornilov. Why does he want to bring down Kerensky? So that he himself can take over. Watch out, Cossacks! They may take the wooden yoke off your necks, but if they put another one on you, it'll be made of steel! Of the two evils you must choose the lesser. Isn't that so? So decide for yourselves. Under the tsar they knocked you about and used you to grab the spoils of war. They're still grabbing under Kerensky, but at least they don't knock you about. It's just a bit better under Kerensky, but it'll be a lot better when the Bolsheviks come to power. The Bolsheviks don't want war. If they had power, there'd be peace right away. I'm not in favour of Kerensky—he's the devil's brother, they're all tarred with the same brush!' Bunchuk smiled and wiping the sweat from his brow with his sleeve, went on, 'But I call on you not to shed the blood of the workers. If Kornilov takes over, Russia will be knee-deep in the workers' blood, and under him it'll be harder to seize power and hand it over to the working people.'

'Wait a bit, Ilya 'Mitrich!' a stocky Cossack, as thickset as Bunchuk himself, stepped out from the back rows; he cleared his throat, rubbed his long hands, which were like the rain-washed roots of an old oak, and looking at Bunchuk with smiling light-green eyes, as sticky as young leaves, asked, 'You've mentioned this yoke now... What about the Bolsheviks when they grab power, what kind of yoke will they put on us?'

'What, will you put a yoke on your own necks?'

'How d'ye mean—on our own necks?'

'Well, under the Bolsheviks, who will get the power? You will, if you're elected. Or Dugin, or this man here. It'll be an elected government, a soviet.* Understand?'

---

*The Russian *Soviet* means 'council'. From the earliest days of the revolution 'Soviet power' has meant government by councils. —*Tr.*

'But who'll be at the top?'

'Again it depends on who's elected. If they elect you, you'll be at the top.'

'Oh, yeah? Sure you're not kidding, 'Mitrich?'

The Cossacks all began laughing and talking at once. Even the sentry at the door left his post for a minute and joined in.

'What do they say about the land?'

'Are they going to take it away from us?'

'Will they stop the war? Mebbe they're only promising, so we'll vote for 'em.'

'Come on, be honest about it all!'

'We're right in the dark.'

'It's dangerous to believe strangers. There's a lot of lies flying around.'

'Yesterday there was a sailor feller round here, crying for Kerensky. So we grabbed him by the hair and threw him out.'

' "You're counter-revolutionaries," he shouts. Just a nut, he was!'

'We don't know what them long words mean.'

Bunchuk swivelled round, watching the Cossacks closely, testing their mood, waiting for them to settle down. His former uncertainty as to the success of his enterprise had gone. He had sensed the Cossacks' mood and now he was sure that, whatever happened, he would be able to hold back the train at Narva. The day before, when he had gone to the Petrograd District Party Committee to offer himself as an agitator for work among the units of the First Don Cossack Division that were approaching Petrograd, he had been confident of success, but on arriving at Narva his confidence had dwindled. He knew that a different kind of language was needed for talking to Cossacks, and he had been afraid he would not find it. For nine months now he had been back among the workers, again absorbed in their life. When he spoke he was used to being understood by the merest hint, but here, with his own countrymen, he would need a different, half-forgotten language, the language of the black earth, a lizard-like agility, a great power of persuasion, so as not merely to singe, but to burn out and destroy the fear of showing disobedience that had built up over the centuries, to break down prejudice, to make the Cossacks feel that they were in the right, and to lead them.

At first, when he began speaking, he himself heard the stumbling uncertainty, the affectedness in his own voice, as though he were listening from the side to his insipid phrases. He had been horrified by the feebleness of his arguments and had racked his brains for some massive, rock-like words with which to make a breakthrough. But instead, with an indescribable bitterness he had felt the light-weight phrases flying off his lips like soap-bubbles and the emasculated, slippery thoughts growing muddled in his head. He had stood there in a hot sweat, breathing heavily and even as he spoke the thought was boring into his brain. 'Here I am, entrusted with this big job and I'm making a mess of it... I can't put two words together... What's come over me! Anyone else in my place would have argued a thousand times better... Oh hell, what a hopeless failure I am!'

The Cossack with the green sticky eyes who had asked about the yoke had wrenched him out of his stupor; the talk that followed had allowed Bunchuk to pull himself together. An unusual flood of energy had welled up in him and to his own surprise, a rich choice of vivid, well-sharpened, incisive words presented itself. Outwardly calm but aflame within, he dealt fiercely and weightily with the sly questions, taking control of the discussion like a rider who has mastered a foaming untrained horse.

'Come on, then. Tell us what's wrong with the Constituent Assembly?'

'It was the Germans brought your Lenin here, wasn't it? Where did he spring from then? From a willow-tree?'

'Did you come here of your own free will, 'Mitrich, or did they send you?'

'Who's going to get the Don Cossacks' lands?'

'Did we have such a bad life under the tsar?'

'The Mensheviks are also for the people, aren't they?'

'Our Cossack Army Council is a people's government—what do we need Soviets for?'

It was after midnight when they broke up. They decided to hold a meeting of both squadrons the next morning. Bunchuk stayed the night in the van, and Chikamasov offered to share his bunk with him. As he crossed himself before going to bed, he warned Bunchuk.

'Mebbe you're not worried about bedding down with us Ilya 'Mitrich, but you'll have to excuse us... We've got plenty of lice, chum. So don't be offended if you pick some up. With all this worry, we've let 'em breed real big—it's terrible! Each one's the size of a prize calf.' After a pause, he asked quietly, 'Ilya 'Mitrich, what people does Lenin come from? I mean, where was he born, where did he grow up?'

'Lenin? He's a Russian.'

'Ho?!'

'But it's true, he is a Russian.'

'No, chum! I guess you don't know much about him,' Chikamasov boomed with a slight air of superiority. 'You know what breed he is? Ours. He comes from the Don Cossacks, born in the Sal district, Velikoknyazheskaya stanitsa—get me? He served as a gunner, they say. And he's got the face for it, just like a Cossack from the lower Don: great broad cheekbones, and those eyes of his.'

'Where did you hear that?'

'The Cossacks talk about it amongst themselves, I've heard 'em.'

'No, Chikamasov! He's a Russian, born in Simbirsk Province.'

'I don't believe it. And for why? Very simple! Pugachov was a Cossack, wasn't he? And Stepan Razin? And Yermak? So there you are! All the men who roused the poor folk against the tsars, they were all Cossacks. And you say he's from Simbirsk Province. Why, it's almost an insult, 'Mitrich, to hear such a thing.'

Smiling, Bunchuk asked, 'So they say he's a Cossack?'

'And he is, only he isn't declaring himself just now. As soon as I take a look at that face, I'll know right away what he is.' Chikamasov lighted a cigarette and, breathing the pungent fumes of common tobacco in Bunchuk's face, coughed thoughtfully. 'It makes me wonder though, and we nearly came to blows about it. If this Lenin is one of us Cossacks, a gunner, where could he have got hold of all that learning? They say as how at the beginning of the war he was taken prisoner by the Germans and studied there, then went through all the sciences, but as soon as he started getting their workers to rebel and scoring points off their learned men, they got scared to death. "Off you go where you came from, big head," they says, "and Christ be with you, or else you'll get us into such a mess we'll never sort things out!" And they packed him off to Russia because they were afraid he'd stir up their workers. Oho! He's a molar he is, chum!' Chikamasov uttered the last phrase almost boastfully, and laughed happily in the darkness. 'You haven't ever seen him, 'Mitrich, have you? No? That's a pity. They say he's got a right big head.' He cleared his throat and let out a reddish stream of smoke through one large nostril and, as he finished the cigarette, went on, 'The women ought to bear more of that kind. He'll settle the hash of more than one tsar...' And he sighed, 'No, 'Mitrich, it's no good arguing with me. This Ilyich, he's a Cossack... Why make a mystery of it! They don't grow 'em like that in Simbirsk Province, not on your life!'

Bunchuk said nothing and lay for a long time smiling, without closing his eyes.

Sleep was long in coming. He was indeed soon attacked by lice that crawled under his shirt and spread a fiery tormenting itch; Chikamasov lay sighing and scratching beside him, and a snorting, restless horse also kept sleep away. Just as he was dropping off, the horses suddenly started fighting and there was a stamping of hooves and fierce whinnying.

'Play about, would ye, devil!.. Whoa! Dang ye!' Dugin's sleepy tenor protested as he jumped up and hit the nearest horse with something heavy.

Afflicted by the lice, Bunchuk heaved about and, realising bitterly that he was still wide awake, started thinking of the morrow's meeting. He tried to foresee what resistance the officers would offer, and smiled grimly to himself. They'll probably turn tail, if the Cossacks all protest together, but you can't always tell with them. I'll have a word with the garrison committee just in case. Involuntarily he recalled an episode from the war, an attack in October 1915, and after that his memory, as though gratified at having been directed on to a familiar well-worn path, persistently and gloatingly threw up scraps of reminiscence: the faces, the grotesque attitudes of dead Russian and German soldiers, a babble of voices, colourless, time-faded fragments of scenery he had once seen, unexpressed thoughts that had stuck in his mind, the inward, barely recognisable echoes of artillery fire, the familiar chatter of a machine-gun, a rousing tune, the pale outline of the mouth of a woman he had once loved, so beautiful it almost hurt, then again those fragments of the war—the dead, the crumbling mounds of the common graves...

Bunchuk raised himself restlessly on his elbow and said aloud, or perhaps only thought, 'I'll have these memories with me till my dying day. And so will everyone else who comes through alive. You've mutilated our life, made a mockery of it! Curse you! Curse you! Even your death won't make up for your guilt!'

He also remembered twelve-year-old Lusha, the daughter

of a Petrograd metal-worker, who had been killed in the war. He had been a friend of Bunchuk's and they had worked together in Tula. One evening he had been walking down the boulevard and there she was—that gawky underfed slip of a girl—sitting on a bench, her thin legs boldly parted, a cigarette between her lips. The eyes in her faded face were tired and there was bitterness at the corners of her painted lips that were already drooping with a premature knowledge. 'Don't you recognise me, Uncle Ilya?' she asked hoarsely, with the practised smile of her profession, then stood up and in a childishly helpless and heartbreaking way burst into tears, leaning her head on Bunchuk's elbow.

Now, lying on his bed, he almost choked with a hatred that attacked him like poison gas; the colour drained from his face and he moaned and gritted his teeth. For a long time he lay rubbing his chest, lips trembling. The hatred was like a lump of hot slag. It constricted his throat and caused a pain in the left side of his chest, under the heart.

He did not fall asleep until morning. At daybreak, sallow-faced and even more sombre than usual, he went to the railwaymen's committee and reached an understanding that they would not let the Cossack train leave Narva. An hour later he went off in search of the members of the garrison committee. It was after seven when he returned to the train. He walked back, feeling the mild coolness of the morning in every fibre of his body, rejoicing vaguely at the probable success of his mission, at the sun that had climbed over the rusty roof of a warehouse, and at the lilting tone of a woman's voice in the distance. Before dawn the roofs had rung with a brief violent downpour. The sandy soil between the tracks was wrinkled with dozens of tiny channels; it smelled faintly of rain and its surface still retained the marks left by the raindrops, like a face pitted by small-pox.

An officer in mud-splashed top-boots came walking towards Bunchuk along the side of the train. Bunchuk recognised him as Major Kalmykov and slowed his pace expectantly. When they met Kalmykov halted with a cold glint in his dark slanting eyes.

'Cornet Bunchuk? So you're still at large? Sorry, but I won't shake hands.'

He compressed his lips and thrust his hands into the pockets of his greatcoat.

'I had no intention of offering you my hand. You

spoke too soon,' Bunchuk replied derisively.

'What are you doing here? Saving your skin? Or have you come from Petrograd? From our friend Kerensky?'

'What is this—an interrogation?'

'Legitimate curiosity about the fate of a fellow officer who deserted his post.'

Bunchuk held back a sneer and shrugged.

'I can reassure you on that point. I didn't come from Kerensky.'

'But aren't you now touchingly united in the face of the approaching danger? What are you anyway? No shoulder straps, a soldier's greatcoat...' Nostrils twitching, Kalmykov surveyed Bunchuk's hunched figure with contemptuous pity. 'A political bagman? Is that it?' And without waiting for a reply he turned on his heel and strode away.

Dugin was waiting for Bunchuk outside his van.

'Where've you been? The meeting has started already!'

'Already?'

'Yes. Our squadron commander Major Kalmykov was away and now he's back. He came in from Petrograd on an engine and called a meeting of the Cossacks. He's just gone there to talk 'em round.'

Bunchuk waited only to ask how long Kalmykov had been away in Petrograd. According to Dugin, he had been absent for nearly a month.

'One of the stranglers of the revolution that Kornilov sent to Petrograd on the pretext of studying bombing. Must be a staunch Kornilov man,' Bunchuk thought vaguely as he walked with Dugin to the meeting.

As they rounded a warehouse they were confronted by a stockade of grey-green Cossack tunics and greatcoats. Standing on a barrel in their midst, surrounded by officers, Kalmykov was declaiming fiercely.

'...carry the war to a victorious conclusion! We will justify the trust that has been placed in us! I will now read a telegram from General Kornilov to the Cossacks.'

A little too hurriedly he pulled a crumpled paper from the side pocket of his tunic and exchanged whispered remarks with the train commander.

Bunchuk and Dugin came up and mingled with the Cossacks.

' "Dear Cossack friends!" ' Kalmykov read out expressively and with real feeling. ' "Was it not the bones of your ancestors that laid the foundation of the growing Russian State? Was it not through your mighty valour, your feats of arms, your sacrifices and heroism that great Russia became strong? You, the free sons of the quiet Don, the stalwarts of the Kuban, the foaming Terek, the soaring eagles of the Ural, Orenburg, Astrakhan, Semirechye and Siberian steppes and mountains, and of distant Transbaikalia, the Amur and the Ussuri, have always stood guard over the honour and glory of our banners, and the Russian land is steeped in legends of the exploits of your fathers and grandfathers. The hour has struck for us to come to the aid of the Motherland. I accuse the Provisional Government of vacillation, of being unfit and unable to rule, of allowing the Germans to run rampant in our country, as was shown by the explosion in Kazan, where nearly a million shells were detonated and 12,000 machine-guns destroyed. What is more, I accuse certain members of the government of direct betrayal of the Motherland and submit the following proofs. When I was at a cabinet meeting in the Winter Palace on August 3rd I was warned by Kerensky and Savinkov not to speak freely because there were unreliable people in the cabinet. It must be clear that such a government is leading the country to destruction, that such a government is not to be trusted, and that under its rule there can be no salvation for unfortunate Russia. Therefore, when the Provisional Government, to please my enemies, demanded my resignation from the post of Supreme Commander-in-Chief, I, true to my Cossack honour and conscience, felt compelled to reject that demand, preferring death on the field of battle to shame and betrayal of my country. Cossacks, knights of the Russian land! You promised to join with me in saving the Motherland when I should find it necessary. That hour has struck—the Motherland is in peril! I will not submit to the Provisional Government's instructions and for the salvation of a free Russia I shall oppose it and oppose its irresponsible advisers who are betraying the Motherland. Cossacks, stand up for the honour and glory of valiant Cossackdom and, in so doing, save the Motherland and the freedom won by the revolution. Be disciplined and carry out my orders! Follow me! 28 August 1917. Supreme Commander-in-Chief General Kornilov." '

Kalmykov paused and then, as he rolled up the paper, shouted, 'The agents of the Bolsheviks and Kerensky are trying to prevent the movement of our troops along the railways. Orders have been received from the Supreme Commander-in-Chief that if it should prove impossible to proceed by rail, we must take to horse and march on Petrograd. We shall set out today. Prepare to detrain!'

Bunchuk elbowed his way into the crowd and, without going up to the officers, shouted in the strident tones of a street orator:

'Comrade Cossacks! I have been sent to you by the Petrograd workers and soldiers. You are being led into a war against your own brothers, a war to crush the revolution. If you want to go against the people, if you want to restore the monarchy and go on with the war until you're all dead or crippled, follow that lead!.. But the Petrograd workers and soldiers hope that you will not be Cains. They send you ardent fraternal greetings and want to see you not as enemies but as allies...'

He was not allowed to finish. A storm of shouting broke loose. The uproar seemed to sweep Kalmykov off the barrel. With his head thrust forward he strode up to Bunchuk and with only a few paces to go swung round on his heel.

'Cossacks! Last year Cornet Bunchuk deserted from the front, and you know it. Are we going to listen to this coward and traitor?'

The commander of the Sixth Squadron, Lieutenant-Colonel Sukin, drowned Kalmykov's voice with his booming bass.

'Arrest him, the scoundrel! While we were shedding our blood he was skulking in the rear! Hold him!'

'We won't do that in a hurry!'

'Let him have his say!'

'Why stop another man's mouth! Let him explain what line he's taking.'

'Arrest him!'

'We don't need no deserters!'

'Speak up, Bunchuk!'

''Mitrich! Cut 'em down to the stump!'

'Down with 'em!'

'Shut up, you shit-bag!'

'Go on, Bunchuk! Give it to 'em! Right in the midriff!'

A tall Cossack with no cap on his head, a member of the regimental revolutionary committee, sprang on to the barrel. With blazing fervour he urged the Cossacks not to support General Kornilov, the strangler of the revolution, spoke of the disasters that a war against the people would bring, and ended his speech by addressing Bunchuk.

'You needn't think we look down on you, comrade, like the officers do. We're glad to see you and welcome you as a representative of the people, and we also respect you for not clamping down on the Cossacks while you was an officer, but for being like a brother to them. We never heard a rough word from you, and don't think that we, uneducated folk, don't understand decent treatment—even cattle understand a kind word, let alone a man. We have great respect for you and ask you to tell the Petrograd workers and soldiers that we won't raise a hand against them!'

It was like a clang of cymbals; the roar of approval reached its highest pitch and slowly subsided.

Kalmykov sprang on to the barrel again, leaning over till his trim figure seemed about to break. Deathly pale, almost choking, he spoke of the glory and honour of the ancient Don, of the Cossacks' historic mission, of the blood that had been shed by officers and Cossacks together.

He was succeeded by a thick-set tow-headed Cossack. His vicious speech against Bunchuk was interrupted and the speaker was dragged down. Chikamasov jumped on to the barrel. He swung both arms down as though splitting a log, and barked, 'We won't go! We won't get out of the train! In the telegram it says the Cossacks promised to help Kornilov, but did anyone ever ask us about it? We never promised him anything! The officers from the Council of the Cossack Union promised! Grekov did the tail-wagging, so let him do the helping!'

More and more speakers came forward. Bunchuk stood with his massive head thrust forward, a dark, earthy flush on his face, the swollen veins in his neck and temples pulsating feverishly. The atmosphere was so electrified that only a little thing was needed, some thoughtless action, for the tension to break out in bloodshed.

The soldiers of the garrison came up in a crowd from the station and the officers left the meeting.

After half an hour Dugin ran up to Bunchuk, panting. ''Mitrich, what shall we do?.. Kalmykov's up to something. They're unloading the machine-guns now, they've sent a mounted messenger off somewhere.'

'Let's go! Bring along twenty Cossacks! And quick about it!'

By the train commander's carriage Kalmykov and three other officers were loading machine-guns on to horses. Bunchuk was the first to approach. He looked round at the Cossacks, thrust his hand into his greatcoat pocket and pulled out a new carefully cleaned officer's revolver.

'Kalmykov, you're under arrest! Hands up!'

Kalmykov sprang away from the horse he had been loading, ducked sideways and reached for his holster, but before he could draw the revolver, a bullet whined over his head; simultaneously Bunchuk repeated in a husky ominous voice, 'Hands up!'

The hammer of his revolver rose slowly, exposing the tip of the striker. Kalmykov watched it with narrowed eyes and with an effort raised his hands, snapping his fingers.

The officers reluctantly surrendered their arms.

'Must we give up our swords too?' a young cornet machine-gunner asked politely.

'Yes.'

The Cossacks unloaded the horses and carried the machine-guns into a van.

'Put these under guard,' Bunchuk told Dugin. 'Chika-masov will arrest the others and bring them here. D'you hear, Chikamasov? And we'll take Kalmykov to the garrison revolutionary committee. Major Kalmykov, kindly get moving.'

'Neat work!' one of the officers exclaimed admiringly, as he jumped into the carriage and watched Bunchuk and Dugin marching their prisoner away.

'This is a disgrace, gentlemen! We behaved like children! None of us had the gumption to shoot down that scoundrel! We should have acted the moment he pointed his revolver at Kalmykov and that would have finished it!' Lieutenant-Colonel Sukin glared at the officers as he fumbled to take a cigarette from his case.

'But there was a whole platoon of them, they'd have mowed us down,' the cornet machine-gunner responded sheepishly.

The officers smoked in silence and exchanged glances. They were stunned by the speed of what had happened.

For a time Kalmykov strode along biting the tip of his black moustache and saying nothing. His left cheek was glowing as if it had been slapped. Local people whom they passed stopped and stared in astonishment, whispering to one another. The overcast evening sky over Narva was fading. Fallen leaves from the birch-trees lay between the tracks, like red-gold ingots dropped by August in its retreat. Jackdaws were flapping around the green dome of the church. Somewhere beyond the station, beyond the dusky fields night had already fallen and its cool breath was in the air, but from Narva to Pskov and on to Luga a few ragged clouds, undercoated with the white lead of evening, were still advancing across the roadless expanse of the heavens, while night crossed an invisible borderline and closed in on the twilight.

Near the station Kalmykov swung round sharply and spat in Bunchuk's face.

'Scoundrel!'

Bunchuk ducked away from the spit and his brows shot up. His left hand gripped his right to stop it going into the pocket.

'Keep moving!' he said with an effort.

Kalmykov walked on swearing foully, mouthing filthy clots of words generated by the mortal anguish, fear, desperation and pain of life at the front.

'You're a traitor! A treacherous swine! You'll pay for this!' he shouted, stopping frequently and turning to Bunchuk.

'Keep moving! Please...' Bunchuk urged him.

And Kalmykov, clenching his fists, would jerk forward like an overriden horse. They reached the water-tower. Gritting his teeth, Kalmykov shouted, 'You're not a party but a gang of the vilest dregs of society! Who is your leader! The German General Staff! Bolsheviks they call themselves! Pah! Bastards! Your party, this riff-raff sells itself like a whore. Swine! Dolts!.. You've sold your country!.. I'd have you all strung up on one scaffold... Yes! The time will come!.. That Lenin of yours—didn't he sell Russia for thirty German marks?! He's grabbed his million and cleared out... The crook!..'

'Get up against that wall!' Bunchuk gasped out the words with a stutter.

Dugin started back in fright.

'Ilya! Wait! What are you doing? Stop!'

Bunchuk, his face distorted with fury, sprang at Kalmykov and hit him hard on the temple. Stamping on the cap that had fallen from Kalmykov's head, he dragged him to the brick wall of the water-tower.

'Stand there!'

'What d'you think you're doing!? You!.. Don't you dare! How dare you strike me!' Kalmykov growled, resisting.

When his back thudded against the wall of the water-tower he straightened up and understood.

'So you want to kill me?'

Bunchuk tugged at the revolver. Its hammer had caught in the lining of his pocket.

Kalmykov stepped forward, rapidly buttoning up his greatcoat.

'Shoot then, you bastard! Shoot! I'll show you how Russian officers can die... Even in the face of de—'

The bullet entered his mouth. A hoarse echo flew up in rising stages behind the water-tower. Kalmykov stumbled in his second stride, flung his left arm round his head and fell. His body arched as he spat out blood-blackened teeth on to his chest and his tongue clicked sweetly. Hardly had his back flattened against the damp gravel when Bunchuk fired again. Kalmykov jerked over on to his side, huddled his head away like a bird falling asleep, and gave a brief sob.

Bunchuk walked away. At the first corner Dugin caught up with him.

"Ilya... How could you, Ilya?.. Why did you do that?'

Bunchuk gripped Dugin's shoulders, looked at him with steely eyes and said in a strangely calm deflated voice:

'It's them or us! There's no middle way. No prisoners. Blood for blood. It's them or us ... war to the death... Understand? People like Kalmykov have got to be destroyed, crushed like snakes. And people who slobber with pity over his kind ought to be shot too. Understand? What are you slobbering for? Get a grip on yourself! Be fierce! If Kalmykov had it in his power, he'd have shot us down without so much as taking the cigarette out of his mouth, and you—you cry-baby!'

Dugin's head shook, his teeth chattered and his big feet in their rusty-brown boots seemed to have got into an absurd tangle.

They walked down the deserted lane in silence. Bunchuk looked back occasionally. Funereally black clouds foamed low overhead in the darkness and scudded eastward. A waning moon, washed clean by the rain of the day before, looked down through a tiny ragged gap in the August sky like the squinting green eye of a corpse. At the next crossroads a soldier and a woman with a white shawl draped over her shoulders were standing together. The soldier took the woman in his arms and held her tight, whispering something, but she thrust her hands against his chest, drew her head back, and protested breathlessly, 'I don't believe you! I don't believe you!' and broke into suppressed youthful laughter.

On August 31st General Krymov, who had been summoned to Petrograd by Kerensky, shot himself there.

Delegations and commanders from various units of Krymov's army streamed to the Winter Palace to confess and ask for pardon. The very men who had but recently been about to make war on the Provisional Government now bowed and scraped before Kerensky, assuring him of their devoted loyalty.

Though morally shattered, Krymov's army still writhed in its death throes; its units rolled on towards Petrograd by their own momentum, but to no purpose because the Kornilov *putsch* was petering out; the burst of reaction that had flared like Bengal light was fading and the republic's temporary ruler, his puffy cheeks noticeably leaner, was already addressing cabinet meetings with a Napoleonic quiver of his leather-encased calves and speaking of 'complete political stabilisation'.

The day before Krymov's suicide General Alexeyev had been appointed Supreme Commander-in-Chief. The punctilious Alexeyev, fully realising the embarrassing ambiguity of his position, at first flatly refused the appointment, but then accepted it solely out of a desire to make things easier for Kornilov and those who had been in some way involved in the anti-government revolt.

While still on the road to General Headquarters in Mogilyov, he telephoned through and tried to discover Kornilov's attitude to his appointment and arrival. The tedious discussion lasted with interruptions until late into the night.

That day Kornilov had been in conference with the members of the staff and his closest associates. Most of those present spoke in favour of continuing the struggle against the Provisional Government.

'May we hear your opinion, Alexander Sergeyevich?' Kornilov said to Lukomsky, who had kept silent throughout the conference.

In restrained but resolute terms Lukomsky spoke against any further civil strife.

'Then we must surrender?' Kornilov asked, interrupting him abruptly.

Lukomsky shrugged.

'The conclusions are obvious.'

The discussion dragged on for another half an hour. Kornilov said nothing, evidently maintaining his self-control with an enormous effort of will. When he had dismissed the conference he summoned Lukomsky.

'You are right, Alexander Sergeyevich!' He cracked the joints of his fingers and, staring into the distance with eyes that looked as if they had been sprinkled with ash, said wearily, 'Further resistance would be both foolish and criminal.'

He drummed on the desk with his fingers and seemed to listen to something—perhaps the mice-like scuffling of his own thoughts—then he asked, 'When will Alexeyev get here?'

'Tomorrow.'

Alexeyev arrived on September 1st. That evening, on the orders of the Provisional Government he arrested Kornilov, Lukomsky and Romanovsky. Before sending them to the Hotel Metropole, where they were to be kept under guard, Alexeyev spoke confidentially with Kornilov for about twenty minutes, then left his room, profoundly shaken and scarcely able to control his feelings. When Romanovsky tried to gain admission to Kornilov, he was stopped by his wife.

'I'm sorry, but Lavr Georgievich asked me not to let anyone in.'

Romanovsky ran his eyes over his distraught face and withdrew, blinking emotionally, almost black at the cheekbones.

In Berdichev the next day General Denikin, the Commander-in-Chief of the South-Western Front, and General Markov, his Chief of Staff, General Vannovsky, and General Erdeli, commander of the Special Army, were also arrested.

In the Bykhov high school for young ladies, where they were confined, the Kornilov movement came to an inglorious end, crushed under the wheel of history. But its end signalled the beginning of a new movement. For where else but here did there germinate the plans for the future civil war and full-scale attack on the revolution?

XIX

Early one morning in the last days of October Major Listnitsky received instructions from the commander of the regiment to march his squadron on foot into Palace Square.

Listnitsky passed on the order to the sergeant-major and dressed hurriedly.

The other officers rose yawning and cursing quietly.
'What's this all about?'
'It's the Bolsheviks!'
'Who's taken my ammunition, gentlemen?'
'Where're we supposed to be going?'
'Can't you hear the shooting?'
'What the devil! That's not shooting! You're suffering from aural hallucinations, man!'

When the officers came out into the yard, the squadron was forming up in troop columns. Listnitsky marched the Cossacks out of the yard at a rapid pace. The Nevsky was empty. Occasional shots were to be heard. An armoured car was driving about Palace Square and officer cadets were on patrol. The streets preserved a barren stillness. At the gates of the Winter Palace the Cossacks were met by a patrol of officer cadets and Cossack officers of the Fourth Squadron. One of them, the squadron commander, called Listnitsky aside.

'Have you got the whole squadron with you?'
'Yes. Why do you ask?'
'The Second, Fifth and Sixth refused to come, but the machine-gun platoon is with us. How are your Cossacks?'

Listnistky waved his hand desparagingly.

'Hopeless. What about the First and Fourth regiments?'
'They're not here. They won't come out. You know that a Bolshevik attack is expected today? The devil knows what's happening!' and he sighed wistfully. 'I'd be glad to get away to the Don, out of all this mess.'

Listnitsky marched the squadron into the palace yard. The Cossacks piled their arms and strolled about the spacious courtyard, which was like a parade ground. The officers assembled in the far lodge, smoking and chatting.

An hour later a regiment of officer cadets and the women's battalion arrived. The cadets took up their positions in the entrance hall of the palace and mounted their machine-guns. The women shock-troopers gathered in the yard and the Cossacks lounged up to them, making crude fun. Sergeant Arzhanov gave one of them, a stumpy creature in a tight greatcoat, a slap on the backside.

'You ought to be having babies, auntie, and here you are, on the men's beat.'

'Have 'em yourself!' the surly deep-voiced 'auntie' snapped back at him.

'Ah, my lovies! Come to join us?' Tyukovnov, an Old Believer and a woman-chaser, kept it up.

'A good hiding, that's what they need, the hussies.'

'Fighting fannies!'

'Why don't you stay at home! What brought you here!'

'Double-barrelled bits, peacetime pattern!'

'In front she's a soldier, but from behind she's either a priest, or the devil knows what... Makes you want to puke!'

'Hey you, shock-trooperess! Pull your bum in or I'll take my butt to it!'

The Cossacks guffawed cheerfully as they teased the women. But by midday their cheerfulness had evaporated. The women soldiers had formed up into platoons and were carrying thick balks of pinewood across the yard to barricade the gates. A burly woman with a mannish figure and the medal of St. George on her snug-fitting greatcoat was directing operations. The armoured car drove round the square more often; some cadets carried crates of cartridges and machine-gun belts into the palace.

'Well, Cossacks. We'd better watch out!'

'Looks as if we're going to fight?'

'What did you think? They'd brought you here to paw the soldier-girls?'

The Bukanovskaya and Slashchevskaya Cossacks had gathered around Lagutin and were discussing something among themselves. The officers had disappeared. The yard was deserted save for the Cossacks and the women soldiers. Several abandoned machine-guns stood near the gates, their shields gleaming wetly.

By evening the damp turned to frost. The Cossacks became restless.

'What's the idea? Bringing us here and keeping us outdoors without any grub!'

'We'd better find Listnitsky.'

'You can whistle for him! He's in the palace and the cadets won't let the likes of us in there.'

'Someone'll have to be sent for the kitchen. Let 'em bring us some grub.'

Two Cossacks were detailed to go and fetch the field kitchen.

'Go without your rifles or they'll take 'em off you,' Lagutin advised.

They waited another two hours, but neither the kitchen nor the detail appeared. Later they learned that the kitchen had been turned back as soon as it left barracks by the men of the Semyonov Regiment. Just before dusk the women's battalion that had gathered

541

round the gate took up their positions behind the balks of timber and started shooting across the square. The Cossacks merely stood about, smoking and grumbling. Lagutin assembled the squadron by the palace wall and with apprehensive glances at the windows started talking.

'Now, listen to me, Cossacks! There's no point in our staying here. We've got to get away, or else we'll be in trouble. They'll start shelling the palace. What's that got to do with us? There's not a sign of the officers. Why should we get ourselves killed? Let's go home, there's no point in hanging about here, propping up the walls! What the hell do we want with the Provisional Government anyway! How about it, Cossacks?'

'The Bolsheviks will mow us down with their machine-guns as soon as we put our noses outside.'

'They'll have our guts!'

'Why should they?'

'It'll be too late to sort that out!'

'No, we'd better stay put.'

'It's nothing to do with us.'

'I don't know about anyone else, but our troop's leaving!'

'So are we!'

'Send someone out to talk to the Bolshies! We won't harm 'em if they don't harm us.'

The Cossacks of the First and Fourth squadrons came up and the question was soon decided. Three Cossacks, one from each squadron, left the yard and an hour later returned in the company of three sailors. The sailors vaulted over the timbers piled in the gateway and strode across the yard with a deliberate swagger. They came up to the Cossacks with a friendly greeting. One of the sailors, a handsome young fellow with a black moustache, his pea-jacket unbuttoned and wide open, pushed his way into the midst of the Cossacks.

'Comrade Cossacks! We, representatives of the revolutionary Baltic Fleet, have come to propose that you leave the Winter Palace. Why should you defend a bourgeois government that's alien to you? Let the cadets, the pampered sons of the bourgeoisie, defend it. Not a single soldier has stood up in defence of the Provisional Government, and your brothers—the First and Fourth regiments—have come over to us. Anyone who wants to join us—move over to the left!'

'Hold on a minute, mate!' a stalwart sergeant of the

First Squadron said, stepping forward. 'We'd be glad to go with you, but what about if the Bolsheviks just mow us down?'

'Comrades! In the name of the Petrograd Military-Revolutionary Committee we promise you complete safety. No one will harm you.'

Another sailor, stocky and with small-pox scars on his face, took his place at the side of the black-moustached sailor. Slowly twisting his thick, bull-like neck, he surveyed the Cossacks and thumped the massive chest that bulged from under his tight sailor's shirt.

'We'll be your escort! You needn't have any doubts about us, mates. We're no enemies of yours, nor are the Petrograd proletarians. Your enemies are that lot over there...' He thrust his thumb in the direction of the palace and showed a row of close-set teeth in a smile.

The Cossacks hesitated, the women soldiers came over and listened, looked at the Cossacks and went away again to the gate.

'Hey you, women! Won't you come with us?' a big bearded Cossack called out to them.

There was no answer.

'Take your rifles and get moving!' Lagutin said resolutely.

The Cossacks grabbed their rifles willingly and formed up.

'What about the machine-guns?' a Cossack machine-gunner asked the black-moustached sailor.

'Take 'em. No point in giving 'em away to the cadets.'

Just before the Cossacks left, all the officers appeared. They stood in a bunch, staring at the sailors. The squadrons formed up and marched off with the machine-gun platoon in front, dragging its guns. The small wheels squeaked and clattered over the wet paving stones. The sailor in the pea-jacket marched beside the leading troop of the First Squadron. A tall fair-haired Cossack of Fedoseyevskaya stanitsa was gripping his sleeve and pouring out his feelings apologetically.

'D'you think we wanted to go against the people, matey? We landed up here through ignorance. We'd never have come if we'd known!' And he shook his thick forelock in disgust. 'Take my word for it, we wouldn't! God's truth!'

The Fourth Squadron was bringing up the rear. At the gate, where the whole women's battalion had gathered, there was a moment's delay. A burly Cossack climbed on to the timber barricade and wagged a black long-nailed finger persuasively and ominously at them.

'Now, listen here, you rifle women! We're going away now and you, because of your women's foolishness, are staying. Now let's have no nonsense about this! If you start shooting us in the back, we'll turn round and cut you all up into little bits. See what I mean? So, just you remember that. And goodbye for now.'

He jumped down from the barricade and ran to catch up with his troop, glancing back over his shoulder.

The Cossacks had almost reached the middle of the square when one of them looked round and said excitedly, 'Look, lads! There's an officer running after us!'

Many turned their heads without stopping and looked back. A tall officer was running across the square, gripping the hilt of his sword to steady it.

He waved his hand.

'That's Atarshchikov, of the Third Squadron.'

'What's he like?'

'Tall and he's got a mole on one eye.'

'So he wants to go with us.'

'He's a fine lad.'

Atarshchikov was rapidly overtaking the squadron. They could see a smile quivering on his face. The Cossacks waved and laughed.

'Hurry up, Lieutenant!'

'Put a spurt on!'

A single dry crack sounded from the palace gate. Atarshchikov flung his arms wide, reeled and fell over on his back; he lay kicking feebly and trying to rise. As if at a word of command, the squadrons turned to face the palace. The machine-gunners crouched over their guns. Ammunition belts rustled. But there was not a soul to be seen by the gates or on the wooden barricades. The crowd of women soldiers and officers that had been there a minute before had vanished. The squadrons formed up again hurriedly and marched on at a quicker pace. Two Cossacks in the rear troop returned from the spot where Atarshchikov had fallen and shouted loud enough for the whole squadron to hear, 'Got him under the left shoulder. He's had it!'

The thud of marching feet resounded clearly and steadily. The sailor in the pea-jacket took command.

'Left wheel—forward!'

The squadrons wheeled and left the square. The hushed, hunch-backed palace watched them go in silence.

XX

Autumn was still warm. Now and then it rained. The anaemic sun seldom showed itself over the little town of Bykhov. In October the birds started migrating. Even at night the bitterly disturbing call of the cranes rang out over the cool, dark earth. The migrating flocks were fleeing in haste from the approaching frosts, from the northern winds that chilled them in the upper reaches of the sky.

The prisoners, arrested in connection with the Kornilov affair, had been awaiting trial for six weeks. Their life in captivity at Bykhov had become settled and acquired its own established, if somewhat unusual routine. After breakfast the generals went out for walks; on their return they read their mail and received the relatives and friends who came to see them. After dinner and a nap, they worked in their rooms alone and in the evening usually gathered in Kornilov's room where they chatted and conferred late into the night.

The high school for young ladies that served as their prison was not uncomfortable.

The building was guarded externally by men of the St. George Battalion, and internally by Tekins. But although these guards may have somewhat restricted the freedom of their charges, they offered the substantial advantage of being organised in such a way that the prisoners could at any moment, if they wished, easily and safely escape. Throughout their confinement in the Bykhov prison they kept up unrestricted communication with the outside world and exerted pressure on bourgeois opinion by demanding a speedy investigation and trial. Meanwhile they covered up traces of the revolt, put out feelers to test the mood of the officers and, as a last resort, made preparations for escape.

Kornilov, anxious to keep his devoted Tekins at his side, got in touch with Kaledin, who, on his insistence, urgently dispatched several wagon-loads of grain to the Tekins' starving families in Turkestan. To help the families of his officers who had taken part in the mutiny, Kornilov wrote strong letters to some of the big bankers of Moscow and Petrograd, who promptly contributed tens of thousands of rubles for fear of becoming the object of embarrassing revelations. Right up to November Kornilov was in constant correspondence with Kaledin. In a long letter sent in the middle of October he inquired about the situation on the Don and how the Cossacks would react to his arrival in the area. Kaledin's answer was positive.

The October upheaval shook the ground under the feet of the Bykhov prisoners. The next day messengers were sent out in all directions, and a week later an echo of someone's concern for the fate of the prisoners came in the shape of a letter from Kaledin to General Dukhonin, now the Commander-in-Chief, in which Kaledin offered to accept responsibility for Kornilov and the other arrested generals. A similar offer came from the Council of the Union of Cossack Armies and the Main Committee of the Army and Naval Officers' Alliance. Dukhonin hesitated.

On November 1st, Kornilov sent him a letter. Dukhonin's marginal notes on that letter are a vivid testimony to the helplessness of General Headquarters, which by that time had virtually lost all authority over the army and was living out its last days in a state of prostration.

Your Excellency, Nikolai Nikolayevich,

Fate has placed you in a position to change the course of events that have brought the country to the verge of catastrophe, mainly owing to the vacillation and connivance of the senior commanding officers. For you the moment is approaching when a man must either stake everything in a bold action or resign; unless he wants to become responsible for the country's destruction and the shame of the army's final collapse.

Judging by the incomplete and fragmentary information available to me, the position is grave but not yet hopeless. But such it will become if you allow General Headquarters to be taken over by the Bolsheviks or voluntarily acknowledge their power.

The St. George Battalion, half of which is already under the influence of propaganda, and the weakened Tekin Regiment are by no means sufficient. Foreseeing the further course of events, I am of the opinion that you should without delay take steps to ensure the security of General Headquarters and provide favourable conditions for organising further struggle against the approaching anarchy.

The measures I propose are as follows:

1. The immediate transfer to Mogilyov of one of the Czech regiments and the Polish Uhlan Regiment.

DUKHONIN'S MARGINAL NOTE: *G.H.Q. thinks they are not completely reliable. These units were among the first to make peace with the Bolsheviks.*

2. Occupation of Orsha, Smolensk, Zhlobin and Gomel by units of the Polish Corps, strenghtened with artillery from the Cossack frontline batteries.

MARGINAL NOTE. *The second Kuban Division and a brigade of Astrakhan Cossacks have been concentrated for the capture of Orsha and Smolensk. Undesirable to move the regiment of the First Polish Division from Bykhov for the sake of the prisoners' safety. The units of the First Polish Division are badly weakened and cannot therefore be regarded as a real force. The corps stands firmly by the idea of not interfering in Russia's internal affairs.*

3. Concentration of all units of the Czechoslovak Corps and the Kornilov Regiment on the Orsha-Mogilyov-Zhlobin line under the pretext of moving them to Petrograd and Moscow, and also one or two of the most reliable Cossack divisions.

MARGINAL NOTE. *The Cossacks are irreconcilably opposed to fighting the Bolsheviks.*

4. Concentration of all British and Belgian armoured vehicles in the same area, their crews being entirely replaced by officers.

5. Concentration in Mogilyov and at some other point in the vicinity of supplies of rifles, ammunition, machine-guns, automatic weapons and hand-grenades for distribution among the officers and volunteers who are sure to assemble in the area.

MARGINAL NOTE. *This could give rise to excesses.*

6. Establishing of close contact and precise terms of agreement with the atamans of the Don, Terek and Kuban Armies and the Polish and Czechoslovak committees. The Cossacks have spoken definitely in favour of the restoration of order; for the Poles and Czechs the restoration of order in Russia is a question of their own existence.

* * *

Every day brought fresh alarms. In Bykhov anxiety was growing. Cars carrying Kornilov supporters who wanted Dukhonin to free the prisoners raced to and fro between Mogilyov and Bykhov. The Cossack Council even resorted to veiled threats.

Overwhelmed by the gravity of impending events, and

only now realising the tremendous responsibility he had placed on his own shoulders by assuming supreme command, Dukhonin vacillated. On November 18th he gave instructions for the prisoners to be moved to the Don, but at once countermanded the order.

The next morning a mud-bespattered car drove up to the main entrance of the Bykhov high school-prison. The driver opened the door with obsequious alacrity, and an elderly but trim officer stepped out. He presented the commander of the guard with papers in the name of Colonel Kusonsky of the General Staff.

'I'm from General Headquarters. I have a personal message for the arrested General Kornilov. Where can I see the commandant?'

The commandant, Lieutenant-Colonel Ergardt of the Tekins, instantly escorted the newcomer to Kornilov's quarters. Kusonsky introduced himself and reported in an emphatic, slightly affected manner:

'In four hours from now Krylenko will come to Mogilyov, which will be surrendered by General Headquarters without resistance. My orders from General Dukhonin are to tell you that all prisoners must leave Bykhov at once.'

Kornilov questioned Kusonsky about the situation in Mogilyov and summoned Lieutenant-Colonel Ergardt. Pressing heavily on the edge of the table with the fingers of his left hand, he said, 'Release the generals at once. The Tekins must be ready to march by midnight. I shall go with the regiment.'

Every pair of bellows in the makeshift forge sighed, wheezed and panted, the hot coals glowed red, the hammers rang, the horses whinnied fiercely in their stalls. The Tekins shoed their mounts on all four feet, mended their harness, cleaned their rifles and made ready.

During the day the generals left their prison one by one. And at the wolfish hour of midnight, when the little provincial town had put out its lights and was sleeping soundly, the mounted men, three abreast, rode out of the yard of the Bykhov high school. Their burnished figures stood out in sharp relief against the backdrop of the steely sky. Like black birds with ruffled feathers, the riders sat hunched in their saddles with their tall lambswool hats pulled forward over their eyes and their swarthy faces swathed in the long scarves of their hoods. In the middle of the regimental column, beside Colonel Kugelgen, the commander of the regiment, the slightly stooped figure of Kornilov swayed on a tall, lean horse. He frowned in the cold wind that roamed the Bykhov side-streets and with eyes narrowed to slits looked up at the frosty star-strewn sky.

The gentle clatter of freshly shod hooves swept along the streets and died away on the outskirts.

XXI

The regiment had been retreating for nearly two days. Slowly, fighting all the way, but retreating. The supply units of the Russian and Romanian armies struggled along the raised dirt roads, while the combined Austro-German units launched a deep enveloping movement in an attempt to cut off their retreat.

By evening it became known that the 12th Cossack Regiment and the neighbouring Romanian Brigade were threatened with encirclement. At sundown the enemy drove the Romanians out of the village of Khovineski and advanced to Ridge 480 bordering on the Golshsky Pass.

During the night the 12th Regiment, reinforced with a battery of mountain artillery, received orders to take up positions on the lower slopes of the Golshsky Valley. The regiment set up outposts and prepared for a head-on encounter.

That night Mishka Koshevoi and another man from his village, the stolid, chunky Alexei Beshnyak, were stationed at a listening post. They lay in hiding in a small ravine near a crumbling disused well, breathing the rarefield frosty air. Sometimes a late flock of wild geese swept across the ragged cloudy sky, signalling the way with cautious cries. Koshevoi remembered with annoyance that he was not allowed to smoke and began to mutter.

'This is a queer life, Alexei!.. People are just groping about like blind men. They come together and break away again. Sometimes they trample on each other. When you've been living like this for a while, so near to death, you begin to wonder what all the bullshit's about. If you ask me, there's nothing more terrible in the world than what's inside a man. You'll never be able to light up all the dark corners there... Here I am, lying beside you, but I don't know what you're thinking, and I'll never know, and I don't know what kind of life you've got behind you, and you don't know anything about me...

Mebbe I'm thinking of killing you and you offer me a share of your bread because you don't suspect anything... People don't even know much about themselves. I was in hospital in summer. There was a soldier in the next bed; from Moscow he was. And he was always asking and trying to find out how the Cossacks lived, the why and wherefore of it. They think there's nothing to a Cossack but his whip, they think the Cossack's a savage, with an empty bottle instead of a heart. But we're men just the same as them; we're as fond of the women and making love to the girls, we cry over our own troubles and aren't very glad to see others in luck... What about you, Alexei? I've got real hungry for life, boy. When I think how many lovely bits there are in the world, it makes me ache! I think to myself, I'll never be able to have 'em all and I feel like howling! I've got so fond of the women these days I'd love every one of 'em till it hurt... I'd mount her any way as long as she was pretty... But it's a fine kind of life they've thought up for us—they stick one woman on you and you're supposed to rub along with her till your dying day. As if you'd never get fed up with her? And on top of that they expect you to fight in wars, and how...'

'You haven't been cut up enough, you goddam stud bull!' Beshnyak grumbled without malice.

Koshevoi rolled over on his back and fell silent, staring up at the empty heavens and smiling dreamily, as he fondled the chilled forbiddingly indifferent earth with caressing hands.

An hour before their relief they were surprised by the Germans. Beshnyak managed to fire once before he doubled up, grinding his teeth in mortal agony as a German knife-edged bayonet ripped his intestines, pierced the bladder and sunk quivering into his spine. Koshevoi was stunned by a blow from a rifle butt. A burly trooper carried him half a verst on his back. Mishka came to with a feeling that he was choking in his own blood; he drew a deep breath, screwed up all his strength and without much difficulty wrenched himself off the German's back. A volley of shots followed him, but night and the bushes came to his rescue.

When the Russian and Romanian units had pulled out of the trap that had threatened to close on them, and the retreat had halted, the 12th Regiment was taken out of the line and moved back several versts and somewhat to the left of its sector. The regiment was then ordered to mount outposts along the roads, prevent deserters slipping through, by force if necessary, and bring them back under guard to divisional headquarters.

Koshevoi was one of the first to be detailed. He and three other Cossacks left the village in the morning and in accordance with the sergeant-major's instructions stationed themselves on the edge of a maize field, not far from the road. The road skirted a wood and disappeared among gentle slopes interspersed with patches of plough-land. The Cossacks took it in turns to keep watch. In the afternoon they spotted a group of about ten soldiers heading in their direction, obviously with the intention of making their way round a small village that nestled under the brow of the hill. On reaching the wood, they stopped, lighted cigarettes and seemed to discuss some-thing, then set off again, taking a sharp turn to the left.

'Shall I give 'em a shout?' Koshevoi asked the others, rising from a clump of maize scrub.

'Shoot in the air!'

'Hey, you there! Halt!'

The soldiers who were still some distance from the Cossacks heard the shout, stopped for a minute, then with seeming reluctance moved on again.

'H-a-a-lt!' one of the Cossacks shouted, emptying his magazine into the air in a rapid succession of shots.

With their rifles at the ready the Cossacks set off at a run and caught up with the slowly trudging soldiers.

'Why the hell don't you stop? What unit are you? Where're you going? Show us your papers!' Sergeant Kolychev, the commander of the outpost, shouted as he ran up.

The soldiers stopped. Three of them casually slipped their rifles off their shoulders.

The last man bent down to tie on a flapping boot sole with a length of telephone wire. They were all unbeliev-ably tattered and dirty. The skirts of their greatcoats were bristling with burrs. Evidently they had spent the night in the undergrowth. Two of them were wearing summer caps, the others, dirty grey lambswool hats with the flaps down and the strings hanging loose. The man bringing up the rear, a tall soldier with an old-mannish stoop, evidently their leader, shouted in an angry nasal voice, his wasted cheeks shaking, 'What's that to you? Are we bothering you? What are you pestering us for?'

'Show us your papers!' the sergeant interrupted, with a show of sternness.

A blue-eyed soldier with a face as red as freshly fired

brick, pulled a bottle-shaped grenade from under his belt, brandished it under the sergeant's nose and, glancing round at his comrades, burst into a furious tirade.

'Here's our papers, mate! Right here! And it's valid the whole year round! Look out for your life or I'll let you have it and no one will ever pick up the pieces. Get me? D'you get me, eh? D'you get me?..'

'Now then, no nonsense,' the sergeant pushed him in the chest, frowning. 'Don't play about and don't try to scare us. We've had enough scaring. You're deserters, so you'd better turn about and go with us to head-quarters. They're taking characters like you in charge.'

The soldiers exchanged glances and those that had not done so already slung their rifles off their shoulders. One of them, with a dark moustache and thin, emaciated face, a miner by the look of him, darted desperate eyes from Koshevoi to the other Cossacks and whispered, 'And what if we use our bayonets on you! Now then, stand aside! Keep away! By God, I'll put a bullet through the first one to come near me!'

The blue-eyed soldier brandished the grenade over his head; the tall stooped one, their leader, scratched the sergeant's greatcoat with the rusty tip of his bayonet; the one who looked like a miner swore and swung his rifle butt at Mishka Koshevoi. Mishka's finger quivered on the trigger of his rifle and the butt jerked under his elbow; one of the Cossacks grabbed a little soldier by the lapels of his greatcoat and dragged him along at arm's length, glancing round apprehensively at the others in fear of a blow from behind.

The withered leaves rustled on the maize stalks. The foothills of the mountains gleamed blue in the distance beyond the undulating valley. Reddish-brown cows were grazing on the pastures near the village. The wind stirred up a frosty dust round the wood. The October day was sleepy and tranquil; a blessed peacefulness hung over the sparsely sunlit countryside. But here, not far from the road, men were stamping about in senseless anger, ready to stain with their blood the rich, rain-softened seminal soil.

Tempers subsided a little after a while and the foot soldiers and Cossacks began to talk more peaceably.

'It's only three days since we were in the line. We weren't hanging around in the rear. And you run away, you ought to be ashamed! You're leaving your own comrades in the lurch! Who'll hold the front? You're a fine lot, you are! Why, I had a mate of mine bayoneted right beside me when we were at our post together, and you say we've never had a taste of war. You have the kind of taste we've had!' Koshevoi protested bitterly.

'What's all the arguing about?' one of the Cossacks interrupted him. "Off to headquarters with 'em and no nonsense!'

'Clear out of the road, Cossacks! Or we'll start shooting, by God, we will!' the soldier who looked like a miner urged.

The sergeant spread his arms despairingly.

'We can't do it, mate! If you shoot us, you still won't get away; our squadron's stationed up there in the village.'

The tall stooped soldier went over from threats to persuasion and was soon pleading humbly. In the end he rummaged nervously in his dirty knapsack, took out a bottle in plaited straw and with a wheedling wink at Koshevoi whispered, 'We'll give you, Cossack lads, a bit of money as well ... here's some German vodka ... and we'll find something else... Let us go, for Christ's sake... We've got kiddies back home ... you know what it's like yourselves... We've had as much as we can stand... How much longer?.. God almighty!.. Won't you let us go?' He dived into the leg of his boot, pulled out a tobacco pouch, shook out of it two crumpled Kerensky notes, and tried to press them into Koshevoi's hands. 'Take it! By God... Don't worry... We'll get by without!.. Money don't matter... We can manage without it... Take it! We'll find some more for you...'

Hot with shame, Koshevoi turned away from him, putting his hands behind his back and shaking his head. Blood surged into his face and he almost wept. It was what happened to Beshnyak made me sore like this, he thought.

'But why should I be? I'm against the war myself and I'm keeping these men back. What right have I to do it? My God, so that's what I've come to! That's the kind of cur I am!'

He went over to the sergeant, took him aside and, avoiding his eyes, said, 'Why not let 'em go? What d'you think, Kolychev? Come on, for God's sake!'

Also with shifty eyes, as though he were doing something shameful, the sergeant said, 'Let 'em go then... What the hell?.. We'll be taking the same road ourselves... What's the use of pretending!'

He turned to the soldiers and shouted indignantly,

'You bastards! We've been talking to you like decent folk, with proper respect, and you shove money at us? Haven't we got enough of our own?' And going purple in the face, 'Put your purses away or I'll march you off to headquarters!'

The Cossacks walked away. Glancing at the distant deserted streets of the village, Koshevoi shouted after the departing soldiers, 'Hi, you plodders! Don't wander out into the open! There's a wood over there. Stay in it for the day and go on at night! Otherwise you'll run into another outpost! And they'll nab you!'

The soldiers looked round, huddled together undecidedly and then, like wolves, trailed away one behind the other, in a dirty grey line into a hollow raggedly fringed with aspens.

* * *

In the early days of November conflicting rumours about the overthrow of the government in Petrograd began to reach the Cossacks. The staff orderlies, usually better informed than anyone else, maintained that the Provisional Government had fled to America, but that Kerensky had been caught by sailors, who had shaved his head, tarred him like a whore, and marched him round Petrograd for two days.

Later, when it was officially announced that the Provisional Government had been overthrown and power had passed into the hands of the workers and peasants, the Cossacks became guardedly quiet. Many were glad, expecting an end to the war, but anxiety was aroused by scraps of rumour that the 3rd Cavalry Corps under Kerensky and General Krasnov were advancing on Petrograd, while Kaledin had managed to assemble Cossack regiments on the Don and was pressing up from the south.

The front crumbled. In October the men had slipped away in scattered, unorganised groups, but by the end of November whole companies, battalions and regiments were withdrawing from their positions; some of them travelled light but the majority took over the regimental property, ransacked the stores, shot some of their officers, gathered more plunder on the road, and rolled in an unfettered, rebellious flood towards their homelands.

In the circumstances the 12th Regiment's task of

detaining deserters lost all meaning and the regiment—
after it had again been sent into the line in a vain attempt
to fill the holes and gaps left by the withdrawing infantry—abandoned its positions, marched to the nearest
station, entrained with all the regimental property,
machine-guns, stocks of ammunition, and horses, and
set off into a Russia that was seething with internal
strife...

On their way to the Don the regiment's trains passed
through the Ukraine. Not far from Znamenka Bolsheviks
attempted to disarm it. The negotiations lasted half an
hour. Koshevoi and five other Cossacks, chairmen of
the squadron revolutionary committees, asked to be
allowed to pass through with their weapons.

'What d'you need weapons for?' the members of the
station Soviet wanted to know.

'To smash our own bourgeois and generals! To knock
out Kaledin!' Koshevoi answered for them all.

'They're our weapons, the Army's, we won't give 'em
up!' the other Cossacks protested.

The trains were allowed to go through. At Kremenchug
another attempt was made to disarm them. They were
allowed to pass only when the Cossack machine-gunners
mounted their guns at the doors of the vans and trained
them on the station and one of the squadrons took up
positions for attack along the embankment. Near Yekaterinoslav, however, even a skirmish with a Red Guard
detachment proved of no avail. The regiment was partially disarmed, losing its machine-guns, over a hundred
boxes of ammunition, its telephones, and several spools
of wire. When asked to arrest their officers, the Cossacks
refused. In the course of the journey they had lost only
one officer, the regimental adjutant Chirkovsky, whom
the Cossacks themselves had sentenced to death; the
sentence was carried out by Uryupin and a Red Guard
sailor.

Late in the afternoon of December 17th at the station
of Sinelnikovo the Cossacks dragged the adjutant out of
the train.

'Is this the one that informed against the Cossacks?'
the gap-toothed sailor of the Black Sea Fleet, armed with
a Mauser pistol and a Japanese rifle, asked cheerfully.

'You think we don't know him? No, there's no mistake
here, he's the one!' Uryupin responded, panting.

The adjutant, a young captain, looked around huntedly, smoothed down his hair with a sweating hand and felt

neither the cold that burned his face nor the pain from a blow of a rifle butt. Uryupin and the sailor led him away from the van.

'It's devils like him that make men rebel. That's what started this revolution, through the likes of him... Now then, m'darling, don't shake so much or you'll fall apart,' Uryupin whispered, then took off his cap and crossed himself. 'Hold tight now, Captain!'

'Are you ready?' the sailor toyed with his pistol and flashed a wild white-toothed grin at Uryupin.

'Ready!'

Uryupin crossed himself again, glanced out of the corner of his eye at the sailor taking his stance, raising his pistol and closing one eye to take aim, and then with a grim smile fired first.

At Chaplin the regiment became involved in fighting that had broken out between anarchists and Ukrainians. It lost three Cossacks and only just managed to break through, having with great difficulty cleared the line of the trains carrying an infantry division.

Three days later the regiment's first train unloaded at Millerovo station.

The other trains had been held up at Lugansk.

At half its strength (the rest had ridden off home straight from the station) the regiment arrived at the village of Kargin. The next day they sold off their booty, the horses captured from the Austrians at the front, and shared out the regiment's cash funds and equipment.

Koshevoi and the other Cossacks from Tatarsky set out for home in the evening. They rode away up a hill. Below them the village of Kargin, the finest on the Upper Don, lay spread out above the whitish ice-bound curve of the River Chir. Little balls of smoke were popping out of the chimney of the steam mill; the square was black with people, the church bells were ringing for evensong. Beyond Kargin Hill the willow crowns of the village of Klimov were just visible, and beyond them, beyond the wormwood blue of the snowy horizon a smoky sunset spread its glittering purple radiance across half the sky.

The eighteen horsemen passed a burial mound topped with three bare crab-apple trees and broke into a brisk trot, heading north-east. A frosty night lurked furtively beyond the next ridge of hills. Muffling themselves in their hoods, the Cossacks sometimes broke into a gallop. The iron-shod hooves rang out clearly, almost painfully and the hard beaten track flowed away to the south behind them; on either side an icy crust of snow, shrunken and settled after the recent thaw, clung to the tall withered grass, and gleamed like chalk-white fire in the moonlight.

The Cossacks urged on their horses silently. The road flowed away southward. The woods of Dubovenky Ravine receded in the east. The delicately woven tracks of hares showed up alongside the galloping hooves. The Milky Way hung over the steppe like an ornamented Cossack belt girdling the sky.

PART FIVE

I

Late in the autumn of 1917 the Cossacks started coming home from the front. Khristonya, looking much older, returned with three other Cossacks who had served with him in the 52nd Regiment. Anikei, as hairless as ever, and gunners Ivan Tomilin and Horseshoe Yakov with a complete discharge were followed by Martin Shamil, Ivan Alexeyevich Kotlyarov, Zakhar Korolyov, and the tall ungainly Borshchev; in December Mitka Korshunov turned up unexpectedly, to be followed a week later by a whole party of Cossacks who had been serving in the 12th Regiment: Mishka Koshevoi, Prokhor Zykov, Old Kashulin's son Andrei Kashulin, Yepifan Maksayev and Yegor Sinilin.

The Kalmyk-looking Fedot Bodovskov, who had got separated from his regiment, arrived on a splendid tawny mount that he had captured from an Austrian officer. He had come all the way from Voronezh and for long afterwards told the story of his ride through the revolution-roused villages of Voronezh Province and his escapes from under the noses of the Red Guard detachments thanks to the speed of his horse.

Then, from Kamenskaya came Merkulov, Petro Melekhov and Nikolai Koshevoi, who had quitted the Bolshevised 27th Regiment. They brought the news that Grigory Melekhov, who had been serving in the 2nd Reserve Regiment, had gone over to the Bolsheviks and stayed in

Kamenskaya. The reckless Maxim Gryaznov, a former horse thief, had also stayed on with the 27th Regiment, attracted to the Bolsheviks by the novelty of these troubled times and the opportunities for a free-and-easy life. It was said of Maxim that he had acquired a horse whose unbelievable ugliness was matched by its equally unbelievable mettle; Maxim's horse was said to have a band of natural silver fur all along its back; though by no means tall, it was very long and its main colour was that of a red bull. Little was said about Grigory. People preferred not to talk, realising that his road had parted from that of the other men of his village and there was no telling when they would come together again.

The homes to which the Cossacks returned as masters or long-awaited guests swelled with joy. But this joy only stressed all the more ruthlessly the nagging, ever-present sorrow of those who had lost their dear ones for ever. Many of the Cossacks were missing, scattered across the fields of Galicia, Bukovina, East Prussia, the Carpathians and Romania and their bodies had rotted away to the funereal music of the guns. And now the high mounds of the common graves were overgrown with weeds, settled by rain, and canopied in drifting snow. And no matter how often the bare-headed Cossack women might run out into the lanes and gaze from under their hands, they would never see their loved ones again! No matter how many tears might flow from those swollen and faded eyes, never would the sorrow be washed away! No matter how they might howl on days of remembrance, the east wind would never carry their cries to Galicia and East Prussia, to the sunken mounds of the common graves!

As grass overgrows a grave, so does time overgrow pain. As the wind wafts away the traces of those who are gone forever, so does time waft away the bitter agony and memories of those who have waited for their dear ones and will wait in vain, because human life is short and not for long are we destined to tread this earth.

Prokhor Shamil's wife beat her head on the hard ground and gnawed the earthen floor after seeing her dead husband's brother, Martin Shamil, fondling his pregnant wife, taking the children on his lap and giving them their presents. The woman crawled and writhed on the ground while, huddled beside her like a flock of sheep, her own children wailed and stared at their mother with eyes drowned in fear.

Yes, rend your last shirt, dear woman! Tear the hair

that your joyless, grinding life has made thin. Bite your bleeding lips, wring your work-scarred hands and beat your head on the threshold of your empty house! It has no master, you have no husband and your children, no father, and remember that no one will care for you or your orphaned children, no one will protect you from back-breaking work and poverty, no one will clasp your head to his chest at night when you fall down, crushed by your weariness, and no one will say to you, as he used to say, 'Never mind, love! We'll manage somehow!' You will never have another husband because you are withered and wasted by work, want and the children; your half-naked, snivelling offspring will never have a father; and you yourself will pant under the strain as you plough and harrow, reap and cart the heavy sheaves of wheat until one day you feel something snap inside you, and then you will writhe with pain under your rags and bleed till there is no blood left.

As she sorted through her son's old underclothes, Alexei Beshnyak's mother sniffed at them and wept bitter sparing tears, but only his last shirt, the one Mishka Koshevoi had brought back, retained the faint odour of her son's sweat and the old woman buried her face in it, muttered pitifully and patterned the government-stamped calico with tears.

The families of Manytskov, Afonka Ozerov, Yevlanty Kalinin, Likhovidov, Yermakov and other Cossacks were all left fatherless.

Only for Stepan Astakhov no tears were shed—there was no one to shed them. His shuttered house stood empty, half derelict and dreary even on a summer's day. Aksinya was still living at Yagodnoye and little was heard of her in the village, which she seldom visited, feeling no desire to know what was going on there.

The Cossacks of the Upper Don came home in batches, according to what village they were from. By the end of December nearly all the frontline men had returned to the villages around Vyoshenskaya.

Day and night the horsemen passed through Tatarsky in groups of between ten and forty on their way to the left bank of the Don.

'Where from, soldiers?' the old men would ask, coming out of their yards.

'Chornaya Rechka', 'Zimovny', 'Dubrovka', 'Reshetovsky', 'Dudarevka', 'Gorokhovka', 'Alimovka', came the answers.

'Fed up with fighting, eh?' the old men would inquire slyly.

Some of the frontline men, the dutiful ones, would smile.

'Enough, fathers! We're fed up with it.'

'We've been through the mill and now we're heading for home.'

But the ones who were fierce and bitter swore and sent the old men about their business.

'Go and have a bellyful of it, you old croaker.'

'What are you fishing for? What d'ye want of us?'

'There's too many of you busybodies around here.'

By the end of winter the first seeds of the civil war began to sprout round Novocherkassk, but the villages and stanitsas of the Upper Don were as silent as the grave. The hidden strife came to the surface only at home, in the families. The old men could not get on with the men from the front.

Of the war that was brewing around the capital city of the Don Army Region nothing was known but rumours. Understanding little about the political trends that had emerged, people waited and listened for some hint of how events would develop.

Until January life in Tatarsky was also quiet. The Cossacks who had returned from the front rested and enjoyed themselves with their wives, ate their fill, and never suspected that far worse troubles and hardships than they had ever experienced in the past war lay in wait for them at their own thresholds.

II

In January 1917, in reward for distinguished service, Grigory Melekhov had been promoted to the rank of cornet and given the command of a troop in the 2nd Reserve Regiment.

In September, after recovering from pneumonia, he had been granted leave. He had spent about six weeks at home, recuperated after his illness, and, having been passed fit by the district medical commission, had returned to his regiment. After the October revolution he was put in command of a squadron. The deep change of heart that he experienced under the influence of the events that were going on around him and, in some measure, his acquaintance with one of the officers of the

561

regiment—Lieutenant Yefim Izvarin—could be said to date from this period.

Grigory got to know Izvarin on the first day after his return from leave and was later in constant contact with him on and off duty, and gradually, without noticing it himself, fell under his influence.

Yefim Izvarin was the son of a well-to-do Cossack of Gundorovskaya stanitsa. He had been educated at the cadet college in Novocherkassk and, on graduation, had gone to the front to join the 10th Don Cossack Regiment. He had served in it for about a year and been decorated, as he liked to say, 'with an officers' Cross of St. George on my chest and fourteen grenade splinters in all the proper and improper places', after which he had been transferred to the 2nd Reserve Regiment to complete his rather brief career in the army.

A man of outstanding ability and undoubted talent, educated well beyond the standards usually attained by Cossack officers, Izvarin was a dedicated champion of Cossack autonomy. The February revolution had roused him and given him scope for his abilities. Having made contact with the Cossack autonomist circles, he skilfully agitated in favour of complete autonomy for the Don Army Region and restoration of the kind of government that had existed on the Don before the total subordination of the Cossacks to the tsarist autocracy. He had a splendid knowledge of history, was full of enthusiasm, yet clear-sighted and sober in intellect, and able to paint a captivating picture of the future free and unrestricted life on his native Don, when it would be ruled by a Cossack Council, when not a single Russian would remain in the region and the Cossacks, with their state frontiers well guarded, would be able to talk to the Ukraine and Greater Russia as equals, with no doffing of caps, and carry on trade and commerce with them. Izvarin turned the heads of the simple Cossacks and their half-educated officers. And Grigory, too, fell under his sway. At first they had some heated arguments, but the unread Grigory was defenceless against an opponent of Izvarin's calibre and was easily routed in their verbal battles. They usually argued in a corner of the barrack room, and it was always Izvarin who won the sympathies of the listeners. His beguiling arguments and the picture he drew of the independent life that could be won in the future had a deep appeal for the greater part of the well-to-do Cossacks of the Lower Don.

'But how can we get on without Russia when there's nothing in our country but wheat?' Grigory would ask.

Izvarin would patiently explain.

'I'm not thinking of the Don as a single independent and isolated region. On the basis of federation, that is to say, association, we shall live together with the Kuban, the Terek and the mountaineers of the Caucasus. The Caucasus is rich in minerals; there we'll find everything.'

'What about coal?'

'The Donets coalfields are only a stone's throw away.'

'But they belong to Russia!'

'Who they belong to and whose territory they are on is a question that is open to argument. But even if the Donets Basin goes to Russia, we shall lose very little. Our federative union will be based not on industry. Our country is characteristically agrarian. So we shall buy enough coal from Russia to satisfy the needs of our relatively small industry. And not only coal. There're plenty of other things we shall have to buy from Russia: timber, metal, manufactured goods, and so on; and in return we shall supply them with high-grade wheat and oil.'

'But what'll we gain by separating?'

'A lot. In the first place we'll get rid of political tutelage, restore the institutions that were destroyed by the Russian tsars, and expel all the outsiders who have settled here. Inside ten years, by importing machinery we'll develop our economy to such an extent that we'll be ten times richer. This land is ours. It's soaked in the blood of our ancestors, fertilised by their bones, but ever since we were subjugated by Russia, for four hundred years we've been defending her interests and never given a thought to ourselves. We have outlets to the sea. We shall have a very powerful army, always ready for action, and neither the Ukraine nor Russia herself will dare to encroach on our independence!'

Of medium height, well built and broad-shouldered, Izvarin was a typical Cossack: yellowish curly hair, the colour of ripening oats, brown face, white sloping forehead, untouched by the sun, only the cheeks tanned, with a line just above the whitish eyebrows. He spoke in a high well-modulated tenor voice. When talking he had a habit of jagging his left eyebrow and twitching his small hooked nose in a peculiar way, as if he were always sniffing at something. His energetic walk, the self-confidence in his bearing and the candid glance of his brown eyes distinguished him from the other officers of the regiment. The Cossacks treated him with obvious respect, perhaps even more than they showed for the commander of the regiment.

He and Grigory had long talks together and, sensing that the firm ground of yesterday was again shifting under his feet, Grigory experienced feelings similar to those he had experienced in Moscow when talking to Garanzha in the Snegiryov Eye Hospital. Comparing the two men's words, he tried to grasp the truth but it evaded him. Yet unconsciously he began to accept the new faith and revise ideas firmly embedded in his mind.

Soon after the October upheaval the following conversation took place between him and Izvarin.

In the grip of contradictions, Grigory asked a cautious question about the Bolsheviks.

'Tell me this, Yefim Ivanich. What about the Bolsheviks? Have they got things right or not?'

Jerking up his eyebrow and wrinkling his nose humorously, Izvarin gave a chuckle.

'Got things right? Ha-ha... You're like a newborn babe, my dear fellow... The Bolsheviks have their programme, their prospects and aspirations. The Bolsheviks are right from their point of view, and we are right from ours. D'you know what the Bolshevik Party is actually called? No? But surely you should know that? The Russian Social-Democratic *Labour* Party! Understand? Labour! At the moment they are flirting with the peasants and Cossacks, but the main thing with them is the working class. They'll bring liberation to the working class and a new, perhaps even worse, oppression to the peasantry. In real life it never works out that everyone gets an equal share. If the Bolsheviks get the upper hand, it'll be good for the workers and bad for the rest of us. If the monarchy returns, it'll be good for the land-owners and the like, and bad for the rest. We don't want either. What we need is our *own* form of government, and above all to be rid of all political guardians, whether it's Kornilov, Kerensky or Lenin. We'll manage on our own lands without these figure-heads—God spare us from our friends and we'll deal with our enemies ourselves.'

'But most of the Cossacks feel drawn towards the Bolsheviks... D'you know that?'

'Grisha, old chum, try to grasp the main thing. *Now* the Cossacks and the peasants are going the same way as the Bolsheviks. Do you know why?'

'Why?'

'Because...' Izvarin wriggled his nose until it was almost round, and laughed. 'Because the Bolsheviks are for peace, for immediate peace, and the Cossacks have got war right up to here!'

He gave himself a ringing slap on his taut brown neck and, straightening his raised eyebrow, cried, 'That's why the Cossacks have a smell of Bolshevism about them and are keeping in step with the Bolsheviks. But!.. But as soon as the war's over and the Bolsheviks reach out to grab the Cossacks' land, the roads of the Cossacks and the Bolsheviks will part! That's proven and historically inevitable. Between the existing structure of Cossack life and socialism—the ultimate form of the Bolshevist revolution—there is an impassable abyss.'

'What I say is,' Grigory mumbled, 'that I don't understand a thing... I can't make head or tail of it... I'm as lost as if I'd been caught out in the steppe in a snowstorm.'

'You won't get out of it as easily as that! Life will make you sort things out. It'll force you to take sides.'

This conversation took place in the last days of October. And in November Grigory chanced to meet another Cossack who was to play a by no means unimportant role in the history of the revolution on the Don. The man he met was Fyodor Podtyolkov and after some oscillation the former truth again tipped the balance in his mind.

That day an icy rain had been falling since noon. Towards evening the sky cleared and Grigory decided to visit a man of his own stanitsa, Junior Cornet Drozdov, of the 28th Regiment. A quarter of an hour later he was wiping his boots on the mat and knocking at the door of Drozdov's lodgings. In the room with its array of feeble rubber-plants and shabby furniture there was another man besides Drozdov. On an officer's camp-bed with his back to the window sat a burly, thick-set Cossack with shoulder straps that showed him to be a sergeant-major of a Guards battery. He was leaning forward with his legs in their black woollen trousers wide apart and his broad ginger-haired hands resting on broad round knees. His tunic fitted tightly at the waist, wrinkled under the arms and almost burst on his massive bulging chest. As the door creaked, he turned his short, full-blooded neck, looked coldly at Grigory and buried the cool light of his eyes under the slightly puffy lids in their narrow sockets.

'Let me introduce you, Grisha. This is—Podtyolkov,

from Ust-Khopyorskaya, almost a neighbour of ours.'

Grigory and Podtyolkov shook hands in silence. Grigory sat down with a smile at his host.

'I've dirtied your floor, I'm afraid!'

'Never mind. The landlady will wipe it up. Have some tea?'

Drozdov, a stunted little man, as agile as a monkey, flicked the samovar with a nicotine-stained finger and concluded regretfully, 'You'll have to drink it cold.'

'I don't want any. Don't bother.'

Grigory offered Podtyolkov his cigarette case. The cigarettes were tightly packed and Podtyolkov's thick red fingers fumbled with them in vain. Purple with embarrassment, he said vexedly, 'Just can't get hold of it... Come out, darn you!'

At last he managed to extract a cigarette from the case and looked up at Grigory with eyes half closed in a smile that made them seem even narrower. Grigory liked his easy manner, and asked, 'What village are you from?'

'I was born in Krutovsky,' Podtyolkov replied willingly. 'That's where I grew up, but later I lived in Ust-Kalinovskaya. You'll know Krutovsky. You must have heard of it, I reckon? It's right alongside Yelanskaya. D'you know Pleshakovsky village? Well, beyond that there's Matveyevsky, and just a bit farther on there's Tyukovnovsky village, and then you come to the place where I was born: Upper and Lower Krutovsky.'

He spoke freely, without any formality and once even allowed his heavy hand to fall on Grigory's shoulder as if they were already friends. His big clean-shaven slightly pock-marked face was graced with a carefully trained moustache; his hair had been wetted and combed down with a twist round the small ears and a few curls escaping on the left side. He would have made a pleasant impression but for the big upturned nose and the eyes. At first glance there was nothing unusual about them but, when he looked closer, Grigory almost felt their leaden heaviness. Very small, like buckshot, they gleamed out of the narrow slits, as if from loop-holes, boring into one spot with heavy persistence and forcing down any glance that was directed at them.

Grigory watched him curiously and noticed one characteristic feature: Podtyolkov hardly ever blinked. While talking, he would level his sombre gaze at his companion, occasionally shifting it from one object to another, and his short sun-scorched lashes were all the time half-lowered and motionless. Only once or twice did he drop his puffy lids and suddenly jerk them up again to take aim with his buckshot eyes, ranging over everything around him.

'It's funny how it's worked out, lads!' Grigory began, addressing his host and Podtyolkov. 'We'll be leading a new kind of life when the war's over. The Ukraine will be ruled by its Rada, and we'll have our Army Council.'

'Ataman Kaledin, you mean,' Podtyolkov corrected him quietly.

'What's the difference?'

'No difference really,' Podtyolkov agreed.

'Yes, we've said goodbye to Mother Russia now,' Grigory went on with his retelling of Izvarin's speeches, curious to know what the response would be from his host and this burly gunner from the Guards. 'We'll have our own government, our own order of things. We'll get all the Ukrainians off our Cossack land and set up posts along the borders and they'd better not come near! We'll live as our great grandfathers did in the old days. I think the revolution's doing us a good turn. What d'you think, Drozdov?'

His host fidgeted and smiled.

'Of course, it'll be better! The muzhiks have been muscling in on us, they won't let us live our own life. And why the hell do we have to have these vice-atamans? They're all Germans anyway—von Taube, von Grabbe and suchlike! They've been parcelling out the land to these staff officers... Now at least we'll be able to breathe freely.'

'But will Russia put up with that?' Podtyolkov asked quietly, addressing no one in particular.

'She'll have to,' Grigory assured them.

'And it'll be the same thing all over again... The same broth as before, but a bit thinner.'

'How d'you mean?'

'Just that.' Podtyolkov deftly swivelled his buckshot eyes and threw a heavy direct glance at Grigory. 'The atamans will spurn the people, the working folk, just the same as before. You'll have to stand to attention before his nibs while he slings you one on the kisser. Ay ... a fine life that'll be... Better hang a stone round your neck and jump into the river!'

Grigory stood up. As he paced about the cramped room he brushed several times against Podtyolkov's massive knees, then he stopped in front of him and asked,

'How should it be then?'

'Go through with it to the end.'

'What end?'

'Once you've started, you've got to plough your furrow to the finish. Once you've got rid of the tsar and the counter-revolution, you've got to see to it that power goes to the people. And all that other stuff is just fairy-tales for the kids. In the old days the tsars squeezed us and now there'll be plenty of others to do the squeezing; make us dance they will!'

'What do we need then, in your view, Podtyolkov?'

And again those heavy buckshot eyes ranged about, as if seeking freedom of movement in the cramped room.

'A people's government—elected. If you let a general get his hands on you, you'll be at war in no time, and that's not what we want. What we want is for that kind of government to be set up everywhere, all over the world, so the people won't be oppressed, won't be wiped out in wars! What'll it be like otherwise? You can turn your old torn trousers inside out but there'll still be the same holes in 'em.' Podtyolkov gave his knees a resounding slap and smiled fiercely, uncovering innumerable small close-set teeth. 'We'd better steer clear of the old ways or they'll put us in a harness that'll feel a lot worse than the tsars'.'

Snatching at the air as if trying to catch some elusive object, Grigory forced out a question.

'Do we give up our land? Share it out, a slice for everyone?'

'No... Why should we?' Podtyolkov looked embarrassed, even confused. 'We won't give up the land. We'll divide it up amongst ourselves, amongst the Cossacks, and we'll take the landowners' estates away from them. But we can't give any to the peasants. They're a coat and we're only the sleeve. If we start sharing with them, they'll strip us bare.'

'Who will govern us then?'

'We'll govern ourselves,' Podtyolkov livened up. 'We'll take over power and that'll be the government. If they only loosen the saddle-girths a bit, we'll soon throw the Kaledins off our backs!'

Grigory stood at the steamy window and stared out at the street, at the children playing some fanciful game, at the wet roofs of the houses opposite, at the pale-grey branches of the bare poplars in the garden, and lost track of what Drozdov and Podtyolkov were arguing about; he was desperately trying to master the confusion in his head, to think something out, to make up his mind.

For about ten minutes he stood, silently tracing patterns on the windowpane. Outside, above the roof of a squat little house, a wintry, faded sun was burning out in the evening sky; its wet purple orb seemed to be balanced on the rusty ridge of the roof and about to roll away down one side or the other. Gritty leaves knocked off by the rain scurried along from the municipal park and a rising wind charged in from the Ukraine, from Lugansk, and went whooping over the stanitsa with Haidamak fury.

III

Novocherkassk had become the centre of gravity for all those who had fled from the Bolshevik revolution. The top generals, once masters of the destiny of the defunct Russian army, trickled down into the lower reaches of the Don, hoping for the support of the Don reactionaries and planning to use this springboard for an offensive against the Russia of the Soviets.

On November 2nd, General Alexeyev arrived in Novocherkassk accompanied by Major Shapron. After talks with Kaledin, Alexeyev set about organising volunteer detachments. The backbone of the future Volunteer Army was composed of officers, cadets, shock-troopers of the February revolution, students and *déclassé* elements from the army rank-and-file who had fled from the north, along with the most active counter-revolutionaries among the Cossacks and those who were simply in search of adventure and higher pay, even in Kerensky notes.

Generals Denikin, Lukomsky, Markov and Erdeli arrived in the last days of November. By this time Alexeyev's detachments mustered more than a thousand bayonets.

Kornilov arrived in Novocherkassk on December 6th, after losing his éscort of Tekins on the road and making his way to the borders of the Don country in disguise.

Kaledin, who by this time had succeeded in recalling to the Don nearly all the Cossack regiments that had served on the Romanian and Austro-German fronts, deployed them along the Novocherkassk—Chertkovo—Rostov—Tikhoretskaya railway. But the Cossacks, wearied by three years of war and returning from the front in a revolutionary mood, showed no great desire to fight the Bolsheviks. Most of the regiments could field barely a third of their normal strength. The most fully manned—the 27th, 44th and 2nd Reserve—were quartered in Kamenskaya. The Ataman's Life Guards and the Cossack Life Guards had also been sent there from Petrograd. The 58th, 52nd, 43rd, 28th, 12th, 29th, 35th, 10th, 39th, 23rd, 8th and 14th regiments, and the 6th, 32nd, 28th, 12th and 13th batteries were quartered in Chertkovo, Millerovo, Likhaya, Glubokaya, Zverevo, and also the mining district. The regiments from the Khopyor and Ust-Medveditsa districts detrained at Filonovo, Uryupinskaya, and Sebryakovo, took up their quarters there for a time, and gradually dispersed.

The home fires called irresistibly and there was no force on earth that could have restrained the Cossacks in their spontaneous desire to return to them. Of all the Don regiments only the 1st, 4th and 14th had been in Petrograd, and they had not stayed there for long.

Kaledin tried to disband some of the particularly unreliable units or to isolate them by surrounding them with formations that were to be trusted.

At the end of November, when he made his first attempt to throw the former frontline units against revolutionary Rostov, the Cossacks went as far as Aksaisk, then refused to take the offensive and turned back.

A widely organised drive to round up the 'remnant' detachments yielded results. On November 27th Kaledin was in a position to operate with reliable volunteer units and could borrow forces from Alexeyev, who had by this time mustered several battalions.

On December 2nd Rostov was captured and occupied by volunteer units and with Kornilov's arrival became the organising centre for the Volunteer Army. Kaledin was left to his own devices. He scattered his Cossack units along the borders of the region and advanced towards Tsaritsyn and the border of the Saratov Province, but for all important and urgent tasks used only officer-partisan detachments; these were the only units that the tottering, enfeebled military authority could rely on for everyday purposes.

Freshly recruited detachments were sent to put down the Donets miners. Major Chernetsov went to work in the Makeyevka district, where units of the regular 58th Cossack Regiment were stationed. In Novocherkassk detachments were hastily mustered by Semiletov and

Grekov and there were various other bands of volunteers; in the north, in the Khopyor district officers and partisans formed the so-called Stenka Razin Detachment. But columns of Red Guards were already closing in on the region from three sides. The forces for a massive attack were gathering in Kharkov and Voronezh. Storm-clouds hung low over the Don, growing thicker and blacker, and the winds from the Ukraine already carried the rumble of gunfire from the first clashes. Grim days were in store for the region. A time of blight was coming.

IV

Yellowish-white clouds, as full-breasted as the barks of old, were floating gently over Novocherkassk. A curly grey karakul hung motionlessly in the blue heights, right over the gleaming dome of the cathedral, and its long tail sloped away in silvery pink waves towards the stanitsa of Krivyanskaya.

The rising sun was not bright but the windows of the ataman's palace burned fiercely with its reflected rays. The iron roofs of the houses were glistening, and the damp from the rain of the day before still clung to the bronze figure of Yermak, who stood with arm extended, holding out the crown of Siberia to the north.

A troop of dismounted Cossacks was marching up the Epiphany Hill. The sun was playing on their fixed bayonets. The fine-drawn silence of the morning, broken only by an occasional pedestrian or the clatter of a cab, was scarcely stirred by the Cossacks' light, steady tread.

Ilya Bunchuk had arrived in Novocherkassk that morning by the Moscow train. He was the last to leave the carriage and walked along the platform straightening his shabby autumn overcoat and feeling generally ill at ease in civilian clothes.

A gendarme and two very young girls were strolling about the platform, laughing. Bunchuk set out for the town, carrying his cheap battered suitcase under his arm. He met scarcely a soul on the way to the outskirts. Half an hour later, after crossing the town by a diagonal route, he halted outside a small, dilapidated house. It was a pitiful sight. Under the weight of time's heavy hand the roof had fallen in and the walls had subsided; the shutters were sagging and the windows looked paralytically misshapen. Bunchuk opened the gate, running his eyes anxiously over the house and the cramped little yard, and hurried up to the porch.

In the narrow corridor half the space was taken up by a chest heaped with all kinds of odds and ends. In the darkness Bunchuk struck his knee on the corner of it but, scarcely feeling the pain, flung open the door. The low-ceilinged front room was empty. He walked through into the second and, still finding no one, stood still on the threshold. The unforgettably familiar smell of this house made his head swim. His eyes took in all the furnishings at once: the heavy ikons in the corner of the front room, the bed, the small table, the tarnished mirror hanging above it, the photographs, the few rickety bent-wood chairs, the sewing machine, the samovar stained with age and use on the wooden couch. With his heart suddenly beating wildly, breathing through his mouth as if suffocated, Bunchuk turned and, dropping his case, looked round the kitchen; the bulging fuchsine-stained stove was still a friendly green; the old piebald cat was looking out from behind the blue cotton curtain; there was a look of intelligent, almost human curiosity in its eyes; evidently visitors were rare. A pile of unwashed dishes stood on the table and on the chair beside it lay a ball of wool and glittering knitting needles holding an unfinished sock at four corners.

In eight years nothing had changed. It was as though he had left only yesterday. He ran out on to the porch. An old woman, bowed by all she had suffered and lived through, emerged from the door of a shed in the corner of the yard. Mother!.. It can't be? Is it really her?.. Lips trembling, Bunchuk rushed up to her, tearing off his cap and crushing it in his hand.

'Who is it you want? Who d'you want to see?' the old woman asked in alarm, putting her hand to her faded brows and standing very still.

'Mother!..' Bunchuk burst out huskily. 'Don't you recognise me?'

He stumbled forward and saw his mother sway as if his shout had struck her like a blow. She tried to run, or so it seemed, but her strength failed her and she lurched towards him as though fighting a strong wind. Bunchuk picked her up as she was falling and kissed her small wrinkled face and eyes that were clouded with fright and incredulous joy, and himself blinked helplessly and rapidly.

'Ilya, dear!.. Ilya, my own boy... My son! And I never recognised you... Gracious me, where did you spring from?' she whispered, trying to straighten her back and stand firm on her weakened legs.

They went into the house. And only then, after those first minutes of emotion, did Bunchuk again feel uncomfortable in the borrowed overcoat. It was too tight, he felt cramped under the arms, afraid to move. With a sense of relief he threw it off and sat down at the table.

'I never thought I'd see you again alive!.. How many years is it since we saw each other. My dearest! How could I have known you, when you've grown like this and aged so!'

'And how are you, Mum?' Bunchuk asked smiling.

She tried to tell him as she fussed about laying the table and putting charcoal in the samovar, smearing tears and charcoal dust over her wet cheeks. Often she ran up to her son, to stroke his hands and press her trembling body to his shoulder. She heated some water and washed his head herself, then found a set of clean underclothes, yellow with age, at the bottom of the chest, fed her dear guest well and sat till midnight, not taking her eyes off him, questioning him and shaking her head sorrowfully.

The nearby bell-tower had struck two when Bunchuk went to bed. He fell asleep at once and, forgetting the present, dreamed that he, a small unruly pupil of the local trade school, had gone to bed after running about all day and was just floating off to sleep when his mother put her head round the kitchen door and asked sternly, 'Ilyusha, have you done your homework for tomorrow?' He slept with a tense joyful smile on his face.

Several times before dawn his mother came over to him, straightened the bedclothes and pillow, kissed his big forehead and the lock of light-brown hair that had fallen across it, and silently withdrew.

Bunchuk left after only one day. In the morning a comrade in a soldier's greatcoat and brand-new field-service cap came to the house and told him something in a half-whisper. Bunchuk hurriedly packed his suitcase, throwing in the underclothes his mother had washed, and with a frown of discomfort pulled on his overcoat. He started saying goodbye to his mother but broke off hurriedly, promising to be back in a month.

'Where are you going, Ilyusha?'

'To Rostov, Mother, to Rostov. I'll soon be back... And don't be sad, Mother!' he tried to cheer her.

She hastily removed the small crucifix she was wearing and, kissing him and making the sign of the cross, hung it around his neck. She tried to tuck the cord under his collar, but her fingers were clumsy and icy cold.

'Wear it, Ilyusha. It's the cross of Saint Nicholas of Myra. May the good saint defend you and keep you safe, may he shield and protect you... My only son...' she whispered pressing her fevered lips to the cross.

As she hugged her son, she gave way; the corners of her lips quivered and drooped bitterly. One warm drop, then another fell like spring rain on Bunchuk's hairy hand. He freed himself from his mother's arms and ran out frowning on to the porch.

* * *

Rostov station was packed like a cattle-pen. The floor was ankle-deep in cigarette butts and the husks of sun-flower seeds. On the station square soldiers of the local garrison were selling off uniforms, tobacco and stolen goods. The kind of cosmopolitan crowd one sees in most southern seaport towns drifted along amid constant hubbub.

'As-s-molovskiye cigarettes, buy 'em loose!' a boy cigarette-vendor was shouting.

'You can have it cheap, citizen-sir,' an oriental-looking individual of suspicious appearance whispered conspira-torially in Bunchuk's ear and winked at the bulging hem of his greatcoat.

'Sunflower seeds, roasted and fried! Here they are!' the girls and women hawking their wares at the entrance trilled in various voices.

Six Black Sea sailors pushed their way through the crowd, talking loudly and laughing. They were in walk-ing-out dress with ribbons, gilt buttons, and mud-splashed bell bottoms. People stepped back respectfully to let them pass.

Bunchuk bored his way slowly through the crowd.

'Call that gold?! Like hell! Samovar gold, that's what it is... D'you think I can't see?' a puny little army tele-graphist commented scornfully.

'See what?' the seller boomed back indignantly, waving a suspiciously massive gold chain. 'It's gold all right! If you want to know I got it off a justice of the peace... Well, go to the devil, you ragamuffin! Want a hallmark, do you? Sure you don't want one of these?'

'The navy won't stand for that... That's sheer non-sense!' a voice said close by.

'Why won't it?'

'It's what these newspapers say...'

'Bring it here, lad!'

'We voted for list No 5*... Who else?'

'Hominy! Very tasty hominy! Tell us how much you want now!'

'He promised there'd be trains. We're supposed to be leaving tomorrow.'

Bunchuk found the Party committee building and climbed the stairs to the first floor. A Red Guard with a Japanese rifle, its knife-edged bayonet fixed, barred his path.

'Who d'you want to see, comrade?'

'Comrade Abramson. Is he here?'

'Third room on the left.'

A shortish man with a big nose and hair as black as a beetle, who kept the fingers of his left hand tucked under the lapel of his frock coat while he gestured methodically with his right, was taking an elderly railwayman to task.

'That won't do at all! That's not organisation! With such methods of agitation you will achieve the opposite results.'

The railwayman, judging by his confused, guilty expression, wanted to say something in his defence, but the man with the beetle-black head wouldn't let him open his mouth. Evidently irritated to the last degree, he continued his tirade, ignoring the other man's glance and his attempts to speak.

'Mitchenko must be dismissed at once! We can't look on indifferently at what's happening among you. Verkhotsky will answer before a revolutionary court! Has he been arrested? He has? I shall insist on his being shot!' he ended harshly and turned his flushed face towards Bunchuk; before he had quite recovered his self-control he asked, 'And what do you want?'

'Are you Abramson?'

'Yes.'

Bunchuk presented his papers and a letter from a highly placed comrade in Petrograd and sat down on the window-ledge.

Abramson read the letter attentively and gave a sombre smile (he was embarrassed by his own outburst).

---

* List No 5 was the list of Bolshevik candidates for the elections to the Constituent Assembly.

'Wait a little. I'll talk to you in a moment.'

He dismissed the perspiring railwayman and left the room. A minute or two later he returned with a tall shaven-headed man in military uniform with a blue sabre scar along his lower jaw and the bearing of a regular soldier.

'This is a member of our Military-Revolutionary Committee. Let me introduce you. You are Comrade... I'm sorry I've forgotten your name...'

'Bunchuk.'

'Comrade Bunchuk... You are a trained machine-gunner, I believe?'

'Yes.'

'That's just what we need!' the military man smiled.

The smile tinted his scar pink along its whole length, from the corner of the ear to the tip of his chin.

'Can you train some of our Red Guard workers as a machine-gun platoon? As quickly as possible?'

'I can try. It's a question of time.'

'How much time do you need? A week or two? Three?' the military man asked, leaning towards Bunchuk with an open expectant smile.

'A few days.'

'Splendid.'

Abramson rubbed his forehead and said with a percept-ible note of irritation in his voice, 'The garrison units are badly demoralised. They are of no real value. Here, Comrade Bunchuk—and it's the same everywhere, I imagine—we have to rely mainly on the workers. The sailors are all right, but the soldiers... So, you see, that's why we would like to have our own machine-gunners.' He tugged at the blue ringlets of his beard and asked anxiously, 'How are you provided for? Never mind, we'll fix you up. Have you had any dinner today? No, of course, not!'

'You must have been hungry a good many times yourself, chum, to be able to tell a man who's eaten from one who hasn't at first glance. And how much grief and horror did you see before you got that white streak in your hair?' Bunchuk thought affectionately as he noticed the small dazzling white patch amid Abramson's beetle-black hair. And while walking with his escort to Abramson's lodgings, Bunchuk kept thinking about him. 'That's a man for you, that's a Bolshevik! He's got that fierce drive in him, but he's kept his kindness, his human-ity. He doesn't hesitate to slap the death sentence on some saboteur called Verkhotsky and at the same time he can take care of a comrade and look after him.'

Still basking in the warmth of his meeting with Abramson, he walked to a house at the end of Taganrog Street, presented Abramson's note to the landlady, had a rest in a little room littered with books, ate his dinner and lay down on the bed. He was asleep as soon as he closed his eyes.

V

For four days Bunchuk kept at it from morning to night, training the workers the Party committee had sent him. There were sixteen of them. They were men of various trades, age and nationality. Two dockers, Khvylychko, a Ukrainian from Poltava, and Mikhalidi, a russified Greek, Stepanov, a compositor, eight metal-workers, Zelenkov, a face-worker from the Paramonov mine, Gevorkyants, a puny little Armenian baker, Johann Rebinder, a skilled mechanic of German extraction and two workers from the railway depot. A seventeenth warrant was brought by a woman in a soldier's wadded jacket and boots that were too big for her.

As he took the envelope she had brought Bunchuk asked, not guessing the reason for her arrival, 'Can you call at headquarters on your way back?'

She smiled, tried to tuck away the thick lock of hair that had fallen from under her kerchief and said shyly, 'I've been sent to you for training...' and overcoming her momentary confusion, ended abruptly, 'as a machine-gunner.'

Bunchuk flushed heavily.

'What's got into them up there—are they crazy? Do they think I'm forming a women's battalion?.. I'm sorry, but this is no job for a woman. It's rough work. A man's strength is needed... What's the idea?.. No, I can't accept you!'

He opened the envelope frowning and ran his eyes over the warrant, which stated rather drily that Party member Anna Pogudko had been sent to him for training, then read Abramson's covering note several times.

Dear Comrade Bunchuk,

I am sending you a very good comrade, Anna Pogudko. We have yielded to her ardent entreaties and, in sending

577

her to you, we hope you will make a fine machine-gunner of her. I know this girl well. I warmly recommend her and have only one request. She is a valuable worker but hot-headed, rather excitable (youthful feelings still running high), so restrain her from any reckless actions, look after her.

Your hard core, your cement is undoubtedly the eight metal-workers; I would draw your attention specially to Comrade Bogovoy. He's a very able comrade and devoted to the revolution. Your machine-gun detachment is international. That's a good thing, it'll be all the more efficient as a fighting unit.

Speed up the training. We have had word that Kaledin is about to march against us.

With comradely greetings,
S. Abramson

Bunchuk looked at the girl standing in front of him (they were in the basement of a house in Moscow Street, where the training took place). The dim light softened and blurred her features.

'Well, all right then,' he said gruffly. 'If it's at your own request... And Abramson has put in a word for you... You'd better stay.'

* * *

The heavy-jowled 'Maxim' was hemmed in on all sides by trainees leaning on each other's backs to watch how quickly it came apart in Bunchuk's skilled hands. Bunchuk would reassemble it with deliberate slowness, explaining the design and function of each part, how the gun should be handled, the rules of sighting and aiming, the degree of derivation in the trajectory and the maximum range that could be achieved. He taught them how to avoid being hit during enemy shelling and, lying down himself behind the blistered grey-painted gun-shield, explained how to choose a vantage point and where to keep the ammunition boxes.

Everyone learned easily except Gevorkyants the baker. Nothing would come right for him. No matter how many times Bunchuk showed him how to strip the gun, he just couldn't remember and was reduced to muttering confusion.

'Why doesn't it fit? Ah, of course, it's my fault... That ought to go here. But it still doesn't fit!' he would exclaim desperately. 'Why?'

'Here's why!' Bogovoy, a brown-faced man with blue powder-scars on his forehead and cheeks, teased him. 'It doesn't fit because you're slow on the uptake, that's why. This is how to do it!' And he confidently slid the part into the right place. 'I've had an interest in military matters since I was a kid,' he went on, pointing at the blue scars on his face while the others laughed. 'I made a cannon and it blew up. It was nasty for me then, but now I'm showing ability.'

He did indeed pick up the skills of machine-gunnery easier and quicker than any of the others. Gevorkyants was the only slowcoach and his tearful exasperated voice was often heard, 'Wrong again! But why? I don't know!'

'What a donkey, what a donkey! There can't be another one like him in the whole of Nakhichevan!' the fierce-tempered Mikhalidi would burst out indignantly.

'Unusually dull-witted,' the restrained Rebinder would agree.

'It's a bit harder than making bread rings!' Khvylychko snorted, and they all chuckled without malice.

Only Stepanov protested irritably, 'You ought to show the comrade how to do it, not make fun of him!'

He was supported by Krutogorov, a big elderly worker from the depot, with prominent eyes and long arms. There was something of the unfrocked priest about him.

'The job won't get done while you, cacklers, stand there laughing! Comrade Bunchuk, keep your master craftsmen in order or send 'em to the devil! The revolution's in danger and all they can do is titter! Call yourselves Party members! More like a lot of animals!' he boomed in his deep voice, and shook a fist like a sledgehammer.

Anna Pogudko studied everything with keen curiosity. She latched on to Bunchuk, often tugging at the sleeve of his ill-fitting overcoat and there was no keeping her away from the machine-gun.

'What if the water gets frozen in the cooling chamber? How much deviation is there when the wind's strong? And what's this, Comrade Bunchuk?' she besieged him with questions while her big dark eyes with their warm vibrant brightness stared up at him expectantly.

579

He felt somehow ill at ease in her presence and, as if in retaliation for this embarrassment, was particularly demanding of her and deliberately cold in his manner, but something exciting and unusual stirred within him when each morning at seven sharp she came into the basement with her hands tucked into the sleeves of her green wadded jacket and the soles of her big soldiers' boots clumping on the basement floor. She was a little shorter than he and had the taut fullness of figure that is natural in all healthy working girls. With her rather round shoulders, she would perhaps have been quite unattractive but for the big intense eyes that suffused her whole being with a wild beauty.

In the four days since they had first met he had not even had a proper look at her. There was little light in the basement and he lacked both the time and the effrontery to peer at her face. On the fifth day in the evening they left the basement together. She was in front and on the last step she turned to ask him a question and Bunchuk gasped inwardly as he saw her in the evening light. She straightened her hair with her usual gesture and waited for his reply, tilting her head slightly and glancing at him sideways. But Bunchuk had not heard the question; he climbed the steps slowly in the grip of sensation that was both sweet and painful.

He always experienced this poignant feeling when something big was about to happen to him. He had known it in the first moment of an attack, before emotion was dulled, and when he had heard Lenin's slightly guttural speech and been fired by the reasoning power of a leader and genius, and when admiring an exceptional sunset or embarking on some dangerous course of action. And this same feeling came to him now as he looked at the girl's dusky pink cheeks, at the June azure in the whites of her eyes, and the bottomless depth of the black irises. A slight tension (it was awkward to adjust her hair without taking off her headscarf) sent a quiver through her nostrils that were tinged pink by the setting sun. The lines of her mouth were brave but at the same time childishly tender. A faint fluff darkened her slightly raised upper lip, setting off the delicate whiteness of her skin.

Bunchuk ducked as if to avoid a blow and said with humorous inspiration, 'Anna Pogudko... Machine-gunner No 2, you're as beautiful as someone's happiness!'

'Nonsense!' she said confidently and smiled. 'Nonsense, Comrade Bunchuk!.. I asked you what time we've got to be at the range?'

The smile made her simpler, more accessible, nearer to the earth. Bunchuk halted beside her; staring dazedly at the end of the street, where the sun had got stuck and was flooding everything in its purple spate, he replied quietly, 'At the range? Tomorrow. Where are you going? Where do you live?'

She named a street on the outskirts. They set off together. At a crossroads they were overtaken by Bogovoy.

'Bunchuk! Where do we meet tomorrow?'

Bunchuk explained that they were to assemble on the other side of Quiet Grove. Krutogorov and Khvylychko would bring the machine-gun there by cab. The time of assembly was eight in the morning. Bogovoy walked two blocks with them and took his leave. Bunchuk and Anna went on for a few minutes in silence, then with a sideways glance at him she asked, 'Are you a Cossack?'

'Yes.'

'You used to be an officer?'

'Me? A fine officer I made!'

'Where are you from?'

'Novocherkassk.'

'Have you been in Rostov long?'

'A few days.'

'And before that?'

'I was in Petrograd.'

'How long have you been in the Party?'

'Since 1913.'

'Where does your family live?'

'In Novocherkassk.' And at that he raised his hand pleadingly, 'Hold on a bit. Let me ask you something. Are you from Rostov?'

'No, I was born down Yekaterinoslav way, but lately I've been living here.'

'Now I'll ask you the questions... Are you Ukrainian?'

She hesitated for a second, then answered firmly, 'No.'

'Jewish?'

'Yes. Why? Does my accent give me away?'

'No.'

'Then how did you guess I am Jewish?'

Shortening his stride to get in step, he replied, 'Your ear, the shape of your ear, and your eyes. Your nationality doesn't stand out much apart from that...' He thought for a moment and added, 'It's good we've got you with us.'

'Why?' she asked.

'Well, you see. The Jews have a reputation for preferring to give orders but never going under fire themselves, and I know that a lot of the workers believe it—I'm a worker myself,' he added in passing. 'It's a mistaken notion, and here you are, giving brilliant proof of how mistaken it is. Are you educated?'

'Yes, I finished high school last year. What education have you? I asked because you don't sound like a worker from the way you talk.'

'I've done a lot of reading.'

They walked on slowly. She deliberately took a roundabout route through the side-streets and, after telling him briefly about herself, went on questioning him about the Kornilov revolt, about the mood of the Petrograd workers, and about the October uprising.

Rifle shots crackled damply somewhere near the embankment and a machine-gun suddenly cut the silence.

Anna could not resist asking, 'What system is that?'

'Lewis.'

'How much of the belt has been fired off?'

Bunchuk did not reply. He was admiring the orange searchlight beam, sprinkled with emerald frost, that was reaching up from an anchored trawler to the zenith of the burnt-out evening sky.

After walking for about three hours through the deserted city, they parted at the gate of the house where Anna lived.

Bunchuk returned home glowing with inner satisfaction. 'She's a good comrade, an intelligent girl! What a good talk we had together. It's warmed my heart. I've got too rough lately. You need some friendly conversation with other people or you can get as hard as a soldier's dried crust,' he thought, deceiving himself and knowing that he was deceiving himself.

Abramson, who had just come back from a meeting of the Military-Revolutionary Committee, asked about the training of the machine-gunners, and, in passing, about Anna Pogudko.

'How's she getting on? If she isn't suitable we can give her other work, send you someone else.'

'No, don't do that!' Bunchuk responded in alarm. 'She's a very capable girl!'

He felt an almost irresistible desire to talk about her and restrained himself only with a great effort of will.

VI

At noon on November 25th Kaledin's troops were drawn up around Rostov. The attack began. The thin skirmish line of Alexeyev's officers' detachment advanced along the railway, fanning out on both sides of the embankment. On the right flank the grey moving figures of the officer cadets were thicker. The volunteers of General Popov's detachment flowed round a shallow ravine on the left flank. Some of them, no more than grey specks in the distance, jumped into the ravine, clambered up the other side, paused to regain their formation, and came on again.

Alarm spread through the Red Guard line on the outskirts of the suburb of Nakhichevan. The workers, many of whom had never handled a rifle before, got nervous and crawled about, from one position to another, dirtying their black overcoats in the autumn mud; others raised their heads to watch the distant diminished figures of the Whites.

Bunchuk was in the line, kneeling by his machine-gun with field-glasses raised to his eyes. The day before, he had changed his clumsy overcoat for an army greatcoat and was his usual calm self again.

The defenders opened fire before the order was given. The tense silence had been too much for them. At the first shot Bunchuk swore, and springing up to his full height, shouted, 'Cease fire!'

His shout was drowned in a flurry of shots and he gave an impatient wave of his hand; trying to make his voice heard above the sound of the firing, he ordered Bogovoy to open fire too. Bogovoy crouched over the breach with a smiling but grey face and locked his fingers round the handles. The familiar chatter burst on Bunchuk's ears. For a minute he tried to make out if there had been any hits among the enemy as they dropped flat, then he jumped up and ran along the line towards the other machine-guns.

'Fire!'

'Here we go then!.. Whoopee!' Khvylychko roared, looking up with a scared but happy face.

The men on the third machine-gun were not very reliable. Bunchuk ran towards them and, when he had gone half way, crouched down and looked through his field-glasses. Through the misty lenses he could make out grey lumps stirring on the ground. The next moment a well-timed volley came from that direction. Bunchuk dropped down and, while lying flat, spotted that the third machine-gun was badly aimed.

'Lower! You, devils!' he shouted, weaving his way along the line.

Bullets whistled deadly close over his head. General Alexeyev's men were shooting with the cool precision of a practice squad.

The machine-gun stood with its muzzle in the air and its crew flat on the ground. The Greek Mikhalidi was aiming absurdly high and firing off all his ammunition without a stop; the scared, green-faced Stepanov was clucking helplessly beside him; behind them a railway-man, a friend of Krutogorov's, was squirming about with his back humped like a tortoise.

Bunchuk pushed Mikhalidi aside, aimed carefully and the gun chattered steadily in his hands. The results were soon seen. The cadets that were running from cover to cover up a hillock scattered and withdrew, leaving one of their number behind on the bare loamy summit.

Bunchuk returned to his own gun. A pale-faced Bogo-voy (the powder scars on his face were an even deeper blue) was lying on his side, spitting curses and bandaging a flesh wound in his leg.

'Shoot, blast you!' a ginger-headed Red Guard bellowed, rising to his knees close by. 'Shoot! Can't you see, they're attacking!'

The officers' detachment was doubling along the embankment as if on the parade ground.

Rebinder took over from Bogovoy and fired skilfully, economically and without haste.

But from the left flank Gevorkyants came leaping like a hare, dropping flat at every bullet that flew over him. He reached Bunchuk and groaned, 'It's gone wrong. It won't shoot!'

Bunchuk darted along the zigzag line, scarcely taking cover.

From a distance he could see Anna kneeling beside the gun, staring at the advancing enemy with her hand to her eyes and pushing aside a falling lock of hair.

'Keep down!' Bunchuk yelled, black in the face with fear for her. 'Down, I tell you!'

She glanced in his direction and remained in the same kneeling position. A curse as heavy as stone rose to his lips. He ran up to her and forced her to the ground.

Krutogorov was behind the shield, grunting with exertion.

'It's jammed! I can't make it work!' he told Bunchuk in a trembling whisper and, as his eyes sought Gevorkyants, he let out a choking shout, 'He's run away! Your antediluvian monster has run away... Got me proper worked up with his moaning, he has! He won't let me get on with the job!'

Gevorkyants came wriggling up, like a snake. There was dried mud on his unshaven chin. Krutogorov twisted his sweating bull-like neck and looked at him for a second, then let out a shout that drowned the sound of the firing.

'What have you done with the belts?.. You dug-up fossil!.. Bunchuk! Take him away from me or I'll destroy him!'

Bunchuk struggled with the gun. A bullet pinged off the shield and he snatched his hand away, as if from hot metal.

When the gun was in order again, he fired it himself and forced the fearlessly advancing Alexeyev men to the ground, then crawled away, looking for cover.

The enemy lines came nearer. Through the field-glasses he could see the Volunteers advancing with their rifles slung over one shoulder, scarcely pausing to take cover. Their fire had become more deadly. Already the rifles and ammunition of three men in the Red Guard line had been taken over by their comrades—the dead need no weapons. Before Anna and Bunchuk's eyes a youngster in the line was hit. For a long time he writhed and gasped, his legs kicking wildly, until finally he raised himself a little on his outspread arms, grunted, pressed his face into the ground and breathed his last. Bunchuk glanced sideways at Anna. Horror was welling in the girl's great dilated eyes. She was staring unblinkingly at the legs of the dead lad in their ragged puttees, oblivious of Krutogorov, who was shouting into her ear, 'Give me a belt!.. Come on! A belt! Give me that belt, girl!'

Kaledin's men were pushing back the Red Guard line with a deep outflanking movement. The Red Guards' black overcoats and army greatcoats could be seen retreating along the streets of Nakhichevan. The far machine-gun on the right flank fell into the hands of the Whites. The Greek Mikhalidi was shot point-blank by a senior cadet, his number two was bayonetted like a training dummy, and only the compositor Stepanov managed to escape.

The retreat ended when the first shells came over from the trawlers.

'Forward in line! Follow me!' shouted Bunchuk's acquaintance on the Revolutionary Committee, running out in front.

The Red Guards' line rose unevenly to attack. Three of them, almost side by side, passed Bunchuk, who was croaching at the ready with Anna, Gevorkyants and Krutogorov beside him. One was smoking, another kept slapping the breach of his rifle against his knee, while a third was studying the muddied hem of his overcoat. There was a guilty smile on his face and at the tips of his moustache, as though he were not going to his death but coming home from a drink-up with his mates and examining his mud-stained coat to decide what measure of punishment he could expect from his quarrelsome wife.

'There they are!' Krutogorov shouted, pointing towards a distant fence and grey human figures scurrying along behind it.

'Help me!' Bunchuk lugged the machine-gun round.

The boisterous chatter of the gun made Anna stop her ears. When she looked up, there was less movement behind the fence, but a minute later steady firing began and bullets swept overhead, boring invisible holes in the murky canvas of the sky.

The machine-gun bursts resounded like drum-beats and the ammunition belts snaked through the breach with a dry rattle. Single shots cracked juicily. The shells fired by the Black Sea sailors from the trawlers passed overhead with an oppressive grinding roar and whine. Anna saw one of the Red Guards, a tall man in a lambskin cap with a moustache trimmed in the English fashion, greeting and involuntarily bowing to each shell as it flew over.

'Give it to 'em, Semyon!' he was shouting. 'Pile into 'em, thick and fast!'

The shells were indeed falling thick and fast. The sailors had got the range and were combining their fire. Isolated, slowly retiring groups of Kaledin's men were sprayed with round after round of shrapnel. One high-explosive shell burst in the middle of the retreating enemy line, flinging up bodies in the brown pillar of the explosion. As the smoke cleared over the crater, Anna threw down the field-glasses, and with a gasp pressed her muddy fingers to her eyes. In the magnifying circles of the lenses she had seen the tornado of the explosion and the destruction it had wrought. A choking spasm seized her throat.

'What is it?' Bunchuk cried, bending over her.

She gritted her teeth and a film spread over her dilated pupils.

'I can't...'

'Be brave! Anna, do you hear? You mustn't give way like this!' he thundered in her ear.

On the right flank some of the enemy infantry were gathering in a ravine at the foot of a low hill. Bunchuk spotted them, ran to a more convenient position with his machine-gun and trained it on the hill and the ravine.

Rat-a-tat... Rata-tat-tat! Rebinder's gun fired short uneven bursts.

About twenty paces away a hoarse angry voice was shouting for a stretcher, 'Aren't there any stretchers? We need one here!'

'At your targets, take aim...' the voice of a platoon commander from the regulars sang out. 'Platoon, fire!'

Towards evening the first whirling snowflakes began to fall on the sombre earth. After an hour the wet sticky snow had sprinkled the field and the black clay-stained heaps of the dead, who lay slumped wherever the contending lines had trampled in their advance and retreat.

Kaledin's forces withdrew.

During that murky night with its white glimmerings of young snow Bunchuk remained at a machine-gun post on the outskirts. Krutogorov had muffled his head in a splendid horsecloth he had found somewhere and was eating some wet stringy meat, spitting and cursing under his breath. Gevorkyants was there, too, at the gate of the yard, warming his numbed blue fingers over a cigarette, while Bunchuk sat on a zinc ammunition case with the skirt of his greatcoat wrapped round the shivering Anna, trying to prise her hands away from her eyes and occasionally kissing them. Unusual tender words came hesitantly from his lips.

'What's the matter now?.. You were so strong... Anya, get a grip on yourself!.. Anya!.. Anya, love... Come on, chum!.. You'll get used to it... If you're too proud to go away, try to be different. You mustn't look at the dead... Pass on! Don't give rein to your thoughts, curb them. There, you see, despite all you said, the woman in you is getting the upper hand.'

Anna was silent. Her hands smelled of the autumn earth and woman's warmth.

Snow flurries wrapped the sky in a dim, caressing curtain. A heavy drowsiness numbed the yard, the nearby field and the hushed, expectant city.

VII

The battle continued in and around Rostov for six days.

Fighting raged in the streets and at crossroads. Twice the Red Guards surrendered the station and twice they drove the enemy out again. In all the six days not a single prisoner was taken by one side or the other.

Towards evening on November 26th, as Bunchuk was walking with Anna past a goods yard, he saw two Red Guards shoot an officer they had captured. To Anna, who had turned away, he said with a challenge in his voice, 'That's a wise thing to do! They must be killed, exterminated without mercy! They won't show any mercy towards us, and we don't need it. It's no good pitying them. The earth has got to be cleansed of this filth! There's no room for sentiment when the revolution's at stake. They're doing the right thing, those workers!'

On the third day he fell ill. For another day and night he kept going, aware of a steadily mounting nausea and a weakness in every part of his body, while his head felt unbearably heavy and was filled with an iron clangour.

The battered Red Guard detachments withdrew from the city at dawn on December 2nd. Supported by Anna and Krutogorov, Bunchuk stumbled along behind a wagon carrying the machine-gun and the wounded. It was an enormous effort to move his limp, helpless body; he dragged his iron-stiff legs along as if in a dream. Anna's appealing anxious glance glimmered in the distance and her words seemed to reach him from afar.

'Get on the wagon, Ilya. Don't you hear me? Don't you understand, Ilya dear? Please, Ilya, you're ill!'

But Bunchuk had no idea of what she was saying or the fact that he had been captured and overpowered by typhus. Voices, strange or oddly familiar, fluttered round his consciousness without penetrating it. Somewhere at a great distance Anna's dark eyes burned with frantic anxiety, Krutogorov's beard swayed and billowed into monstrous shapes.

Bunchuk clutched his head and pressed his big hands

to his burning, purple face. He felt as if blood were seeping from his eyes, and the whole world, boundless, unstable, separated from him by an invisible curtain, was rearing up and leaping from under his feet. His fevered imagination fashioned strange unbelievable fantasies. Often he stopped and struggled with Krutogorov, who was trying to lift him on to the wagon.

'No, I don't want to! Wait! Who are you?.. Where's Anna?.. Give me a lump of earth... Those scum must be destroyed. Turn the machine-gun on them! At my command! No, wait! It's too hot!..' he croaked, snatching his hand away from Anna's.

They got him on to the wagon by force. For another minute or two he was aware of a pungent mixture of smells, saw some frenetic lighting effects and struggled fearfully to bring back consciousness, straining himself to breaking-point. But it was no use. A black soundless void closed over him. Only somewhere very high above a bluish opal patch burned iridescently, crisscrossed by loops and zigzags of scarlet lightning.

VIII

Thatch-yellowed icicles were falling from the roofs and breaking with a glassy tinkle. The thawing village had blossomed with puddles and patches of bare ground; half-moulted cows were roaming the streets, sniffing at the fences. The sparrows set up a springlike chirping as they busied themselves among the heaps of brushwood piled in the yards. Out on the square Martin Shamil was chasing a well-fed chestnut stallion that had bolted from its stable. With its matted tail high and uncombed mane flying, it would gallop round the square, scattering the melting snow in its wake, then stop by the churchyard wall to sniff at the bricks; it would allow its master to come near, squint with a violet eye at the bridle in his hands, then again stretch its back in a mad gallop.

January was treating the earth to some warm cloudy days. The Cossacks were watching the Don and expecting an early flooding. On the day in question Miron Grigorievich Korshunov stood for a long time in his back yard, staring at the snow-swollen meadow and the icy dove-grey green of the Don and thought, 'It looks as if it'll give us a bath as it did last year. After all the snow we've had. The earth must be feeling the weight of it—it can't breathe!'

His son Mitka, wearing only his army tunic, was cleaning out the cattle shed. His white lambskin cap clung to the back of his head by a miracle and his straight sweat-dampened hair had tumbled over his forehead. Mitka swept it aside with the back of a dirty hand that stank of cow dung. Frozen cattle droppings were lying in a heap at the gate of the yard and a fluffy-coated goat was trampling on them. The sheep were huddled against the fence. A ewe that had outgrown its mother was trying to suck her and the mother was butting it away; a ring-horned black wether was scratching its back against a plough.

Beside the barn with its yellow clay-washed door sprawled a tawny-browed dog with a heavy ruff. Some bag-nets were hanging on the wall and Grandad Grishaka was standing looking at them, evidently thinking about the coming spring and the work of mending them.

Miron walked over to the threshing floor and cast a calculating eye at what remained of a rick. He was about to rake up some millet straw that had been pulled loose by the goats when strange voices reached his ears. He tossed the rake on to the rick and went back into the yard.

Mitka was lounging with his feet apart, twirling a cigarette in one hand and with two fingers of the other holding a pouch richly embroidered by his sweetheart. Khritsonya and Ivan Kotlyarov were standing beside him. Khristonya had fished a greasy bit of cigarette paper out of the lining of his blue guardsman's cap. Ivan was leaning against the wattle gate of the yard with his coat open, feeling in the pockets of his wadded army trousers. There was a look of annoyance on his smoothly shaven face with its dark dimpled chin. Evidently he had forgotten something.

'Good morning to you, Miron Grigorievich!' Khristonya greeted Korshunov.

'Praise the Lord, soldiers!'

'Come and have a smoke with us.'

'Christ save you. I've only just had one.'

Miron shook hands with the young men, took off his red-topped fur cap, smoothed down his stiff straw-coloured hair, and smiled.

'What good news brings you here, Guardsmen?'

Khristonya looked down at him from his great height and did not answer at once. He took a long time wetting the strip of paper, licking it with his big rough ox-like tongue, and only when he had made the cigarette did he reply in his deep voice, 'There's something we want to see Dmitry about.'

Grandad Grishaka came shuffling past, holding the hoops of the bag-nets at arm's length. Ivan and Khristonya raised their caps to say good-morning. Old Grishaka carried the nets over to the porch and came back.

'What are you, fine warriors, doing sitting at home? Snug and warm beside your wives, are you?' he observed.

'Well, why not?' Khristonya responded.

'Enough of that, Khristonya, my lad! You mean to say you don't know?'

'God's truth, I don't!' Khristonya declared. 'By the holy cross, I don't, Grandad!'

'A man's just been here from Voronezh, a merchant. Some acquaintance of Sergei Platonovich Mokhov, or mebbe some relative of his—I don't know. Well, anyway, he says there're foreign troops at Chertkovo—these Bolshaks, as they're called. Will you stay at home while Russia makes war on us? And you, you ragamuffin... Mitka, d'ye hear me? Have ye nothing to say? What are ye thinking of?'

'We're not thinking of anything,' Ivan said with a smile.

'That's the whole trouble—that ye don't think!' Grishaka fumed. 'You'll be caught, the lot of you, like partridges under a net! The muzhiks will come down on you and bloody your noses for you...'

Miron smiled restrainedly; Khristonya passed his hand over his unshaven chin with an audible rustle; Ivan smoked and looked at Mitka. A host of tiny sparks had crowded into Mitka's vertical pupils and it was hard to say whether those green eyes of his were smiling, or smouldering with insatiable malice.

Ivan and Khristonya chatted for a while, then took their leave and called Mitka over to the gate.

'Why didn't you come to the meeting yesterday?' Ivan asked sternly.

'Didn't have time.'

'But you had time to go to the Melekhovs?'

Mitka nodded his cap on to his forehead and said with concealed anger, 'I didn't come and that's all there is to it. What is it you want to talk about?'

'All the village frontline men were there, except Petro Melekhov. You know what it's about... We decided to send delegates from the village to Kamenskaya. There'll be a congress of frontline men there on the 10th of

February. We cast lots and Khristonya here, me and you were drawn to go.'

'I won't go,' Mitka said decidedly.

'What's the idea?' Khristonya frowned and took hold of a button on Mitka's tunic. 'Are you breaking away from your own pals? Don't they suit you now?'

'He's in with Petro Melekhov...' Ivan touched the sleeve of Khristonya's greatcoat and his face paled noticeably as he said, 'Well, let's go then. We're wasting our time here... Are you sure you won't go, Dmitry?'

'No... I've said no and I mean it.'

'Well, goodbye to you then,' Khristonya said, tilting his head to one side.

'Good luck to you!'

Mitka held out a hot hand without looking at him, then walked away to the house.

'The bastard!' Ivan muttered under his breath, and his nostrils quivered. 'Bastard!' he repeated louder, staring at Mitka's broad back.

They called in on their way home to tell some of the frontline men of Korshunov's refusal, and to say that tomorrow the two of them would be going off to the congress without him.

At dawn on January 8th, Khristonya and Ivan rode out of the village. They were driven by Horseshoe, who had volunteered his services. With two sturdy horses harnessed to the sledge they passed quickly through the village and trotted away up the hill. But the thaw had made the road bare and sticky in places and the sledge jerked along with the horses tugging and straining at the traces.

The Cossacks got out and walked. Horseshoe Yakov, flushed by the morning frost, strode along, crunching the brittle ice under his boots. His whole face was aglow, except for the oval scar, always a deathly blue.

Khristonya kept to the settled porous snow along the side of the road and grew out of breath as he climbed the hill; he was still feeling the effects of the German poison gas he had breathed into his lungs at Dubno in 1916.

On the hill the wind was roaming freely and it was colder. The Cossacks tramped on in silence. Ivan muffled his face in the collar of his sheepskin. The distant woods came nearer and the road through them climbed to a ridge dotted with ancient mounds. In the woods the wind murmured like a stream. Scaly patches of rust patterned the trunks of the antlered oaks with greenish gold. Somewhere far away a magpie was chattering. It flew up over the road, tail askew, was caught by the wind and wheeled swiftly, showing its piebald plumage.

Horseshoe, who had been silent since leaving the village, turned to Ivan and said clearly (he must have been preparing the phrase in his mind for some time), 'When you're at this congress, try to see that there'll be no war. You won't find anyone who wants it.'

'That's clear enough,' Khristonya agreed, glancing enviously at the magpie's free flight and mentally comparing the thoughtlessly-happy life of a bird with that of men.

They reached Kamenskaya towards evening on January 10th. Crowds of Cossacks were making their way to the centre of the big stanitsa. There was excitement in the air. Ivan and Khristonya found Grigory Melekhov's lodgings and learned that he was not at home. The landlady, a buxom fair-browed woman, said that her lodger had gone to the congress.

'Where is this congress being held?' Khristonya asked.

'At the district administration, I expect, or at the post office,' the landlady replied and shut the door in Khristonya's face.

When they got there, the congress was in full swing. A large room with many windows was packed with delegates. Cossacks crowded the staircase, the corridors and the adjoining rooms.

'Keep behind me,' Khristonya grunted, using his elbows.

Ivan followed him along the narrow passage he had ploughed. When he had almost reached the door of the conference room Khristonya was stopped by a Cossack whose accent suggested he was from the Lower Don.

'Go easy with your pushing, you great lump,' he said sarcastically.

'Let me through!'

'You can stand here. Don't you see there's no room!'

'Let me through, mosquito, or I'll swat you!' Khristonya threatened and effortlessly shifted the stunted little Cossack out of his way.

'There's a bear for you!'

'A real Guardsman, eh!'

'He'd be all right for towing a four-inch gun!'

'Moved him nicely, didn't he!'

The tightly packed Cossacks grinned admiringly and eyed the towering Khristonya with involuntary respect.

They found Grigory squatting on his heels at the back of the hall, smoking and talking to a Cossack delegate from the 35th Regiment. At the sight of the men from his own village, his drooping burnished moustache twitched into a smile.

'Well... What wind brings you here? Hullo, Ivan Alexeyevich! Glad to see you, Uncle Khristonya! Big as ever!'

'Not so strong as I'm big, I reckon,' Khristonya chuckled, taking Grigory's hand in his own massive fist.

'How are our folk out there?'

'Praise the Lord. They sent you greetings. Your father said you should come and see him.'

'How's Petro?'

'Petro...' Ivan smiled awkwardly. 'Petro won't have anything to do with the likes of us.'

'I know. And what about Natalya? The children? Did you happen to see them?'

'They're all fit and sent their love. It's your dad who's sore...'

Khristonya turned his head to scan the Cossacks presiding on the platform. Even from the back he could see them better than anyone else. Taking advantage of a short break in the proceedings, Grigory went on with his questions. In telling him about the village and its news Ivan gave a brief account of the meeting of frontline men that had sent him and Khristonya to the congress. He was about to ask what was going on in Kamenskaya, when one of the presidium announced abruptly, 'Now a delegate from the mine-workers will speak—Syrtsov. Please, to listen attentively and keep proper order.'

A thick-lipped man of average height pushed back his light-brown hair and began to speak. The bee-like hum of voices broke off at once.

From the first words of the man's fiery impassioned speech Grigory and the others felt the power of his conviction. He spoke of the treacherous policy pursued by Kaledin, who was inciting the Cossacks to fight the working class and peasantry of Russia, of the common interests of Cossacks and workers, of the aims the Bolsheviks hoped to achieve in their struggle against the Cossack counter-revolution.

'We hold out the hand of fraternity to the working Cossacks and hope that in the struggle against the White Guard bands we will find staunch allies in the frontliners. While we were fighting the tsar's war, the workers and the Cossacks shed their blood together, and in the war against the dregs of the bourgeoisie that Kaledin is sheltering we must also be together—and together we will be! Shoulder to shoulder we will go into action against those who have been enslaving the working people for centuries!' he concluded in a trumpet-like voice.

'Good for him, the son-of-a-bitch!' Khristonya whispered admiringly and squeezed Grigory's elbow so hard that he winced.

Ivan was listening with his mouth slightly open, blinking with the effort of concentration.

'That's right! Ay, that's it!' he was muttering.

After the delegate a very tall miner rose to speak, swaying like an ash-tree in the wind. He straightened his lanky frame, surveyed the multitude of eyes, and waited for the hubbub to die down. He had the tough, wiry look of a tow-rope and there was a greenish glow about him, as if he had been treated with vitriol. His face was speckled with the coal-dust that had lodged forever in the pores of his skin and there was the same coal-like glitter in his faded eyes, which had lost their colour from the eternal gloom and blackness of his life underground. He shook his short hair and, lifting both clenched fists at once, drove his words home as though wielding a miner's pick.

'Who brought in the death penalty for soldiers at the front? Kornilov! Who's joined up with Kaledin to strangle us? The same Kornilov!' He began to speak more quickly, 'Cossacks! Brothers! Brothers! Brothers!' His words came in a staccato torrent. 'Whose side will you take? Kaledin wants us to drink ourselves senseless on our brothers' blood! But we won't do it! They won't get it their way! We'll smash 'em, smash 'em to bits! We'll throw these hydras into the sea!'

'He's right, the son-of-a-bitch!' Khristonya grinned from ear to ear, and spreading his arms, burst out, 'That's right!.. Give it to 'em!'

'Shut up, Khristonya! You'll be chucked out!' Ivan cautioned him in alarm.

Lagutin—that same Bukanovskaya Cossack, now the First Chairman of the Cossack section of the Second All-Russia Central Executive Committee—spoke with clumsy but telling phrases that stung the Cossacks to the quick. Podtyolkov, who was presiding, also spoke. He was followed by Shchadenko, a handsome man, with his moustache clipped in the English style.

'Who's that?' Khristonya asked Grigory, pointing with a rake-like arm.

'Shchadenko. Bolshevik commander.'

'And that one?'

'Mandelstam.'

'Where's he from?'

'Moscow.'

'And who are those over there?' Khristonya pointed to the group of delegates from the Voronezh congress.

'Can't you keep quiet for a bit, Khristonya!'

'By the good Lord, but I want to know!.. Tell me now—the one that's sitting next to Podtyolkov, the lanky one—who's he?'

'Krivoshlykov. He's from Yelanskaya, Gorbatov village. And the two behind him are ours—Semyon Kudinov and Donetskov.'

'Just one more little question then... That feller over there... No, not him! The one at the end, with the big forelock!'

'Yeliseyev... I don't know what stanitsa he's from. And that must be Doroshev next to him.'

Khristonya, satisfied at last, listened to the next speaker with his former unflagging attention and came in ahead of a hundred other voices with his resounding 'That's right!'

After Stekhin, a Cossack Bolshevik, had spoken, the assembly was addressed by a delegate of the 44th Regiment. He took a long time forcing out his rough agonised phrases. He would say a word, as if trying to brand the air, then lapse into a snuffling silence. But the Cossacks listened sympathetically, occasionally interrupting with shouts of approval. Evidently what he was saying struck a vital chord somewhere.

'Brothers! Our congress has got to ... deal with this serious matter ... so the people won't feel ... hard done by ... and it will all end ... good and peaceful!' he stammered. 'What I'm saying is ... we've got to avoid a bloody war. We were at it in the trenches for three and a half years and ... if we've got to do some more fighting on top of that ... what I says is ... the Cossacks won't stand for it...'

'That's right!'

'True enough!'

'We don't want war!'

'We've got to get an agreement both with the Bolsheviks and with the Army Council!'

'Peaceable like... No mucking about!'

Podtyolkov thumped on the table with his fists, and the uproar ceased. Fingering a broom-like beard, the delegate of the 44th Regiment plodded on.

'What we've got to do is... send deputies from this congress ... to Novocherkassk and ... ask the Volunteers and the various partisans ... peaceable like ... to go away. And there's no need ... for the Bolsheviks to be on our land either... We'll deal with the enemies of the working people ourselves... We don't need help from anyone yet, and when we do—we'll ask for it.'

'It wouldn't work!'

'He's right!'

'Hold on there! What's so right about it? What if they catch us on the hop? Try asking for help then. You'll have missed the boat.'

'We've got to set up our own government!'

'The hen's clucking out front but the egg's still up her... God forgive me! There are some stupid people around!'

After the delegate of the 44th Regiment, Lagutin made a fervent appeal. He was loudly interrupted. Somebody proposed a break of ten minutes, but as soon as silence was restored Podtyolkov hurled at the simmering crowd, 'Cossack brothers! While we're talking here, the enemies of the working people are not sleeping. We want to please everyone, but that's not what Kaledin wants. We've just intercepted his order that everyone taking part in this congress is to be arrested. Right now we're going to read out that order.'

A wave of alarm ran through the crowd of delegates after Kaledin's order for the arrest of the congress delegates had been read out. The uproar beat anything that had ever been heard at any village meeting.

'We'd better do something instead of talking!'

'Quiet! Sh-sh-sh!'

'Why be quiet? Lam into 'em!'

'Lobov! Lobov!.. Give 'em a piece of your mind!'

'Wait a mo'!'

'Kaledin—he's no fool!'

Grigory had been listening in silence and watching the swaying heads and hands of the delegates, but in the end even he rose on tiptoe and exploded, 'Belt up, you devils! What's this—the market place? Let Podtyolkov have his say!'

Ivan was locked in argument with one of the delegates of the 8th Regiment.

Khristonya was countering an attack by a man of his own regiment.

'This is where you've got to be on your guard!' he roared. 'What's this cat-lap you're giving me?.. You're daft, lad! I'm sorry for you, old pal! But our tail's a bit too thin for steering ourselves!'

The hubbub died down like a flagging wind on heaving waves of wheat, and the barely established hush was pierced by Krivoshlykov's girlishly high-pitched voice.

'Down with Kaledin! Long live the Cossack Military-Revolutionary Committee!'

The crowd roared. Thunderous shouts of approval wove themselves into a heavy rope that lashed the ears. Krivoshlykov stood with his hand raised. The fingers were trembling like leaves. As soon as the deafening roar subsided, Krivoshlykov shouted again, in the same ringing, high-pitched voice that the beater uses during a wolf round-up.

'I propose we elect from our number here a Cossack Military-Revolutionary Committee! It will be instructed to wage the struggle against Kaledin and organise...'

'Ah-ah-ah-ah!' a shell-burst of shouts brought plaster down from the ceiling.

The election of members of the Revolutionary Committee began. An insignificant number of Cossacks led by the delegate from the 44th Regiment and others continued to insist on a peaceful settlement of the conflict with the Cossack Army Government, but the majority would not support them. The Cossacks were incensed by the news of Kaledin's order for their arrest and insisted on hitting back at Novocherkassk.

While the voting was still going on, Grigory was summoned urgently to regimental headquarters. Before leaving he said to Khristonya and Ivan, 'Come to my place as soon as it's over. I'd like to know who is elected.'

It was night when Ivan appeared.

'Podtyolkov chairman, Krivoshlykov secretary!' he announced from the doorway.

'And the members?'

'Ivan Lagutin and Golovachov are in. So are Minayev, Kudinov and some others.'

'Where's Khristonya?' Grigory asked.

'He's gone off with the Cossacks to arrest the Kamenskaya authorities. He's red-hot. If you spat on him, he'd sizzle. He's a terror!'

Khristonya returned at dawn. He pulled off his boots, snuffling and muttering under his breath. Grigory lighted the lamp and noticed a trickle of blood on his tired face and a bullet scratch just above the forehead.

'Who did that to you?.. Shall I dress it? Here, wait

a minute, I'll find a bandage.' He sprang out of bed in search of lint and bandage.

'It'll heal,' Khristonya grunted. 'That was the army commandant, snicked me with his revolver. We come to his front door like guests, and he starts shooting. He wounded another Cossack too. I was going to pluck the soul out of him to see what an officer's soul is like, but the other Cossacks wouldn't let me. Otherwise I'd have had his guts, that I would! I'd have hurt him!'

IX

The next day, the 10th Don Cossack Regiment arrived in Kamenskaya with orders from Kaledin to arrest everyone who had taken part in the congress and to disarm the most revolutionary Cossack units.

The regiment detrained just when a meeting was being held at the station. The huge seething crowd of Cossacks was giving the speaker, a Latvian, a mixed reception.

The regiment detrained and joined in the meeting. Half of them were smart, magnificently built guardsmen, from the prosperous Lower Don stanitsa of Gundorovskaya. They mingled with the Cossacks of other regiments, and their mood changed abruptly. The regimental commander's order to carry out Kaledin's instructions was ignored. The intense agitation that the Bolsheviks' supporters immediately launched among them threw them into a turmoil.

Meanwhile Kamenskaya was in a frontline fever of activity. Hurriedly formed detachments of Cossacks were being packed into trains and sent off to occupy railway stations or reinforce those that had already been occupied along the Zverevo—Likhaya line. New unit commanders were being elected. The Cossacks opposed to war were leaving quietly. Belated delegates to the congress were still arriving. There was a stir and bustle in the streets that the little town had never known before.

On January 13th a delegation from the White Don Government arrived in Kamenskaya for negotiations. It was composed of Ageyev, the chairman of the Cossack Army Council, and Council members Svetozarov, Ulanov, Karev, Bazhelov and Lieutenant-Colonel Kushnaryov.

They were met at the station by a dense crowd. A party of Ataman's Life Guards escorted them to the Post and Telegraph Office, where they had a meeting with the

Military-Revolutionary Committee that lasted all night.

Of the seventeen members of the Committee who were present Podtyolkov was the first to speak. He gave a sharp reply to a speech by Ageyev, who accused the Military-Revolutionary Committee of betraying the Don and being in collusion with the Bolsheviks. He was supported by Krivoshlykov and Lagutin. Then came a speech by Lieutenant-Colonel Kushnaryov, who was frequently interrupted by shouts from the Cossacks crowding in the corridor. In the name of the revolutionary Cossacks a machine-gunner demanded the arrest of the delegation.

The meeting produced no results. At about two in the morning, when it became clear that no agreement could be reached, Karev, a member of the Army Council, proposed that a delegation from the Military-Revolutionary Committee should go to Novocherkassk to negotiate a final solution on questions of power. This proposal was accepted.

The Don Government delegation left for Novocherkassk and was followed shortly afterwards by delegates of the Military-Revolutionary Committee led by Podtyolkov. By general consent the delegates were Podtyolkov, Kudinov, Krivoshlykov, Lagutin, Skachkov, Golovachov and Minayev. The arrested officers of the Ataman Regiment remained in Kamenskaya as hostages.

X

Flying snowflakes flickered past the carriage windows. Wind-hardened snowdrifts loomed above sagging half-broken fences, their tops whimsically patterned with the marks of bird's feet. Stations, telegraph poles, the endless frightening monotony of the snowbound steppe streamed away to the north.

Podtyolkov, wearing a new leather jacket, was sitting by the window. Opposite him with his elbow on the little table and staring out of the window sat Krivoshlykov, slim and narrow-shouldered as a boy. In his youthfully clear eyes there was anxiety and expectation. Lagutin was combing his scanty chestnut beard. Minayev, a burly Cossack, was warming his hands on the hot-water pipes and fidgeting in his seat.

Golovachov and Skachkov were lying on the upper berths, chatting quietly.

The carriage was rather smoky and cold. None of the delegates on their way to Novocherkassk felt very sure of themselves. The conversation flagged and gave way to a

sour tedious silence. When they had passed Likhaya, Podtyolkov expressed the thought that was in everyone's mind:

'Nothing will come of it. We won't get an agreement.'

'Ay, it's a wasted journey,' Lagutin agreed.

Once again there was a long silence. Podtyolkov
worked his wrist rhythmically as if he were threading
a shuttle through the meshes of a net. Now and then he
glanced at his leather jacket, admiring its soft sheen.

As they were nearing Novocherkassk, Minayev, who
had been studying the winding course of the Don on the
map, told the other Cossacks quietly, 'In the old days
when the men in the Ataman's Regiment had done their
service, they'd be sent off home by train with all their kit
and horses. And near Voronezh, where the line crosses
the Don for the first time, the engine-driver would slow
down, go as slow as he possibly could, because he knew
what would happen. And as soon as the train started
crossing the bridge—Lord alive! What a hullaballoo the
Cossacks would make. They just went mad. "It's the
Don! Our Don! The quiet Don! Our father and provider!
Hurrah!" and they'd start throwing all kinds of things out
of the window straight into the water—caps, old greatcoats, trousers, pillow cases, shirts, all kinds of odds and
ends. These were their gifts to the Don on their return
from the army. And those blue guardsmen's caps would
go floating away like swans or flowers on the water...
It's an old custom.'

The train slowed down and stopped. The Cossacks
stood up and, as Krivoshlykov buckled the belt over his
greatcoat, he smiled wryly.

'Well, here we are—home, sweet home!'

'Where's the traditional bread and salt!' Skachkov
attempted a joke.

A tall debonair major entered without knocking. He
surveyed the delegates with probing hostile eyes and said
in a deliberately abrupt tone, 'I have orders to escort you.
Will you, Bolshevik gentlemen, kindly leave the train as
quickly as possible. I can't answer for the crowd or—
your safety.'

Longer than on any of the others his gaze rested on
Podtyolkov, or rather on his officer's jacket, then with
open hostility he commanded, 'Leave the train—at once!'

'Here they are, the scoundrels, the betrayers of the
Cossacks!' an officer with a long moustache shouted from
the crowded platform.

Podtyolkov paled and shot a slightly confused glance

at Krivoshlykov. The latter smiled as he followed Pod-tyolkov on to the platform and whispered, ' "Approval not in praises sweet we hear but in the vicious howls of spite..." Remember that, Fyodor?'

And though he had not heard the end of the quotation Podtyolkov managed a smile.

They set off accompanied by a strong escort of officers. All the way to the door of the Regional Government building they were harassed by a frenzied mob, athirst for a lynching.

Insults and abuse were hurled at them not only by officers and cadets but also by some Cossacks, well dressed women and students.

'How can you allow such carrying on!' Lagutin turned indignantly to one of the escorting officers.

'Thank God you're still alive... If I had my way, I'd deal with you, you lout ... you, scum!'

He was restrained by a reproachful glance from another officer, somewhat younger.

'It's a nice mess we're in!' Skachkov whispered to Golovachov when he had the chance.

'It's like being marched to the gallows.'

The Don Regional Government's assembly hall was already overcrowded. While the delegates took their seats on one side of the table, as instructed by an organising lieutenant, the members of the government arrived.

Kaledin with his slight stoop and firm wolf-like stride came in accompanied by Mitrofan Bogayevsky. He drew back his chair and sat down, placed his field-service cap with its white officer's cockade calmly on the table, smoothed his hair and, buttoning the large side-pocket of his tunic with the fingers of his left hand, leaned sideways to catch a remark of Bogayevsky's. Every movement was charged with solid unhurried confidence, with a mature strength; he had the manner of a man in whom years of authority had developed a special bearing, a way of carrying his head, a special walk. He had much in common with Podtyolkov. On the other hand, Bogayevsky, overshadowed by the imposing Kaledin, looked less impressive and more worried about the forthcoming negotiations.

Bogayevsky's lips moved vaguely beneath the light-brown curtain of his moustache and his sharp slanting eyes glittered from under his pince-nez. His nervousness showed in the way he kept straightening his collar, feeling his energetic chin, and twitching the bushy eyebrows that spread like wings across his broad forehead.

The members of the Cossack Army Government took their seats on both sides of Kaledin. Some of them—Karev, Svetozarov, Ulanov and Ageyev—had been in Kamenskaya. Yelatontsev, Melnikov, Bosset, Shoshnikov and Polyakov seated themselves a little further away.

Podtyolkov heard Bogayevsky mutter a remark to Kaledin.

Kaledin glanced narrowly at Podtyolkov, who was sitting opposite him, and said, 'I think we can begin.'

Podtyolkov smiled and in a clear voice announced the aims of the delegation's visit. Krivoshlykov held out the prepared text of the Military-Revolutionary Committee's ultimatum, but Kaledin brushed it aside with a white hand and said firmly, 'There's no need for each member of the government to see this document separately. That would be a waste of time. Kindly read out your ultimatum. Then we can discuss it.'

'Read it,' Podtyolkov told Krivoshlykov.

His manner was dignified but, like all the members of the delegation, he obviously did not feel quite sure of himself. Krivoshlykov stood up. His girlishly melodious but at the same time subdued voice resounded through the packed hall.

' "All power over army units of the Don Army Region in the conduct of military operations shall as of this day, 10 January 1918, be transferred from the Army Ataman to the Don Cossack Military-Revolutionary Committee.

' "All detachments operating against the revolutionary forces shall be recalled as of 15 January and disarmed. Likewise the Volunteer units, the cadet training schools and the corporals' schools. All members of these organisations who do not reside on the Don shall be sent out of the Don Region to their places of residence.

' "*Note*. Weapons, equipment and uniforms shall be handed in to the Commissar of the Military-Revolutionary Committee, who will issue passes to leave Novocherkassk.

' "The city of Novocherkassk shall be occupied by Cossack regiments chosen by the Military-Revolutionary Committee. The credentials of the members of the Army Council are declared invalid as of 15 January.

' "All police stationed by the Army Government are to be recalled from the mines and factories of the Don Region.

' "It shall be publicly announced throughout the Don Region, in all its stanitsas and villages, that the Army Government has voluntarily resigned in order to avoid bloodshed, and that power has immediately been transferred to the Regional Cossack Military-Revolutionary Committee and shall be exercised by this Committee until a permanent working people's government for the whole population be formed in the region." '

Hardly had Krivoshlykov's voice died away, when Kaledin asked loudly, 'What units gave you the authority to present this ultimatum?'

Podtyolkov exchanged glances with Krivoshlykov and began counting, as if to himself.

'The Ataman's Life Guard Regiment, the Cossack Life Guards, the 6th Battery, the 44th Regiment, the 32nd Battery, the 14th Special Squadron...' As he counted he pressed down the fingers of his left hand; whispering and a malicious titter ran through the hall. Podtyolkov frowned, planted his ginger-haired hands on the table and raised his voice, 'The 28th Regiment, the 28th Battery, the 12th Battery, the 12th Regiment...'

'The 29th Regiment,' Lagutin prompted him quietly.

'...the 29th Regiment,' Podtyolkov went on, more confidently now and louder, 'the 13th Battery, the Kamenskaya garrison, the 10th Regiment, the 8th Regiment, the 14th Regiment.'

After a few brief exchanges Kaledin leaned forward across the table, levelled his eyes at Podtyolkov and asked, 'Do you recognise the authority of the Council of People's Commissars?'

Podtyolkov drank a glass of water, replaced the jug on its plate, wiped his moustache and replied evasively, 'Only the whole people can decide that.'

Fearing that Podtyolkov in his simplicity might say too much, Krivoshlykov intervened.

'The Cossacks will not tolerate any body that includes representatives of the Party of People's Freedom.* We are Cossacks and we must have our own, Cossack government.'

'How are we to interpret that remark, when we know that the Council is controlled by people like Bronstein and Nakhamkis?**'

---

*Party of People's Freedom—Constitutional Democrats, opposed to the revolution.
**Bronstein, Lev Davydovich (1879-1940), real name of Leon Trotsky, then Commissar for War.
   Nakhamkis (pseudonym Steklov), Yuri Mikhailovich (1873-1941), of Jewish nationality, was a member of the Executive Committee of the Petrograd Council of People's Commissars, having joined the party in 1903. —Tr.

'Russia trusts them and so shall we!'

'Will you maintain relations with them?'

'Yes!'

Podtyolkov gave a grunt of approval and added, 'We're not concerned with individuals, we're concerned with an idea.'

One of the members of the Army Government asked innocently, 'But is the Council of People's Commissars working for the good of the people?'

Podtyolkov's probing eyes swung in his direction. With a smile he reached again for the water jug, filled a glass and drank thirstily, as though trying to douse a blazing inner fire.

Kaledin drummed on the table with his fingers and asked searching questions.

'What have you in common with the Bolsheviks?'

'We want to introduce Cossack self-government here in the Don Region.'

'Yes, but as you probably know the Army Council will assemble on February 4th. A new council will be elected. Will you agree to joint control?'

'No!' Podtyolkov raised his drooping lids and answered firmly. 'If you're in the minority, we'll dictate our will to you.'

'But that will be coercion!'

Yes.'

Mitrofan Bogayevsky, who had been watching Podtyolkov, switched his gaze to Krivoshlykov and asked, 'Do you recognise the Army Council?'

'Well, in so far as...' Podtyolkov shrugged his massive shoulders. 'The Regional Military-Revolutionary Committee will hold a congress of people's representatives. It will work under the control of all the military units. If the congress doesn't satisfy us, we won't recognise it.'

'But who will be the judge?' Kaledin raised his eyebrows.

'The people!' Podtyolkov tossed his head proudly and leaned back in his carved wooden chair, making his leather jacket creak.

After a brief interval Kaledin spoke. The hubbub in the hall died away and the low autumnally muted tones of the ataman's voice sounded clearly in the ensuing hush.

'The government cannot resign at the demand of the Regional Military-Revolutionary Committee. The present government was elected by the whole population of the

Don and only the population as a whole, not individual units, can demand our resignation. Under the influence of the criminal agitation carried on by the Bolsheviks, who want to impose their order of things on the region, you demand that power be transferred to you. You are a blind instrument in the hands of the Bolsheviks. You are obeying the will of Germany's hirelings and do not realise the tremendous responsibility you are taking upon yourselves for Cossacks everywhere. I advise you to reconsider the matter because you will bring untold disaster upon your homeland by entering into conflict with a government that expresses the will of the whole population. I am not clinging to power. The Grand Army Council will assemble and it will decide the fate of the country but until it assembles I must remain at my post. For the last time I advise you to reconsider.'

Speeches were then made by members of the government, Cossack and non-Cossack. The Socialist-Revolutionary Bosset delivered a long speech embroidered with flattering exhortations.

A shout from Lagutin interrupted him.

'Our demand is that you hand over power to the Military-Revolutionary Committee! What are we waiting for? If the Army Government stands for a peaceful settlement...'

Bogayevsky smiled. 'Then what?'

'It must be publicly announced that power has been handed over to the Revolutionary Committee. We can't wait more than a fortnight until your Council assembles! The people are angry enough as it is.'

Karev mumbled at great length and Svetozarov tried to find an unattainable compromise.

Podtyolkov listened to them impatiently. Glancing at the faces of his own men, he noticed that Lagutin was pale and frowning, Krivoshlykov had his eyes fixed on the table and Golovachov was bursting to speak. Krivoshlykov held back until the right moment, then whispered quietly, 'Now, let 'em have it!'

It was as though Podtyolkov had been waiting for this. He pushed back his chair and began to speak awkwardly, stuttering in his excitement, trying to find big, overwhelmingly persuasive words.

'You've got it all wrong! If people believed in the Army Government, I'd gladly give up our demands... But the people don't believe! It's not us, it's you that are starting a civil war! Why are you sheltering all these runaway generals on Cossack soil? That's why the Bolsheviks are making war on our quiet Don! I won't give in to you. I won't allow it! Only over my dead body! We'll show you up with facts! I don't believe the Army Government could save the Don! What measures are being taken against the units that don't want to obey you?.. Aha, that's got you! Why are you sending your partisans against the miners? By doing that you're starting up trouble all around! And tell me this. Who'll vouch that the Army Government will prevent civil war?.. You haven't got a leg to stand on. The people and the frontline Cossacks are behind us!'

A rustle of laughter passed through the hall; indignant remarks were thrown at Podtyolkov. He turned on the scoffers, his face flushed, and shouted, no longer trying to hide his pent-up fury, 'You're laughing now, but you'll be crying afterwards!' and facing Kaledin, he bored into him with those buckshot eyes of his. 'We demand that you hand over power to us, the representatives of the working people, and get rid of all the bourgeoisie and the Volunteer Army... And this government has got to go too!'

Kaledin bowed his head wearily.

'I have no intention of leaving Novocherkassk.'

After a brief interval the proceedings resumed with a fiery speech by Melnikov.

'The Red Guard detachments are heading for the Don to destroy the Cossacks! They've ruined Russia with their mad schemes and they want to do the same here! There has never been a case in history of a country being ruled wisely and for the good of the people by a bunch of pretenders and impostors. Russia will awake and drive out these false Dmitries! You have been blinded by the madness of others and want to snatch power from us and open the gates to the Bolsheviks! But we won't let you!'

'Hand over power to the Revolutionary Committee, and the Bolsheviks will stop their offensive,' Podtyolkov countered.

Kaledin gave the floor to a member of the public, Captain Shein. He had risen from the ranks and held all four crosses of the Order of St. George. He straightened the folds of his tunic, as if for an inspection, and went off at a gallop.

'What's the use of listening to 'em, Cossacks!' he shouted in a high-pitched commanding voice, chopping the air with his arm as if wielding a sabre. 'Our way is not the Bolsheviks' way! Only traitors to the Don and the Cossacks can talk about handing over power to the Soviets and call the Cossacks to join up with the Bolsheviks!' And pointing straight at Podtyolkov, he leaned forward and shouted in his face, 'Surely you don't think the Don will follow you, Podtyolkov, a half-educated, illiterate fellow like you? The only followers you'll get will be a gang of uprooted Cossacks who've gone on the rampage! But even they will wake up, lad—and hang you for it!'

All over the hall heads swayed like sunflowers in the wind and there was a howl of approval. Shein sat down. A tall officer in a short gathered sheepskin with lieutenant-colonel's insignia on his shoulder straps gave him a hearty slap on the back. Other officers gathered round him. A woman's voice cried hysterically, 'Thank you, Shein! Thank you!'

'Bravo, Major Shein! Bravissimo!' a cocky young student's bass crowed from the gallery, promoting him on the spot.

The cheer-leaders and professional orators of the Don Government went on and on with their attempts to shake the members of the Kamenskaya Revolutionary Committee. The air grew blue and heavy with tobacco smoke. The sun had nearly run its daily course. Fir-like patterns of frost appeared on the windows. Those sitting on the windowsills heard the church-bells ringing for evensong and the muffled whistles of railway engines through the rising wind.

It was too much for Lagutin. Interrupting one of the government speakers, he addressed Kaledin.

'It's time to end this! Come to a decision!'

He was quietly rebuffed by Bogayevsky.

'Don't get excited, Lagutin! Here, drink some water. Excitement is bad for family men and people with high blood pressure. Speakers should not be interrupted. This isn't one of your Soviets.'

Lagutin answered in kind, but everyone's attention switched to Kaledin. He was playing the political game as confidently as before and still running up against the simple homespun armour of Podtyolkov's replies.

'You said that if we hand over power to you, the Bolsheviks will halt their advance towards the Don. But that is only your opinion. We cannot tell how the Bolsheviks will act if they reach the Don.'

'The Committee is convinced the Bolsheviks will confirm what I've said. Try it. Give us power, clear the Don of the Volunteers, pay off your partisans, and you'll see. The Bolsheviks will stop the war!'

A few minutes passed, and then Kaledin rose. His answer had been prepared beforehand, and Chernetsov had already received orders to concentrate his forces for an attack on Likhaya Station. But still playing for time, Kaledin closed the proceedings with a further delaying move.

'The Don Government will discuss the Revolutionary Committee's proposal and an answer will be given in writing by 10 o'clock tomorrow morning.'

XI

The answer that the Don Government handed to the delegates of the Military-Revolutionary Committee the next day read as follows:

The Government of the Don Cossack Army has discussed the demands of the Cossack Military-Revolutionary Committee presented by the Committee's deputation on behalf of the Ataman's Life Guards, the Cossack Life Guards, the 44th, 28th and 29th regiments, units of the 10th, 27th, 23rd, 8th and 2nd reserve and 43rd regiments, the 14th Separate Squadron, the 6th Guards Squadron, the 32nd, 28th, 12th and 13th batteries, the 2nd Infantry Battalion, and the Kamenskaya garrison, and hereby declares that this Government represents the whole Cossack population of the region. As a government elected by the population, it has no right to resign until a new Army Council is convened.

The Army Government of the Don Cossack Army has deemed it necessary to dissolve the former Council and to hold elections of deputies both from the stanitsas and from the army units. The new Council, freely elected (with complete freedom to canvass) by the entire Cossack population on the basis of direct, equal and secret ballot, will convene in the city of Novocherkassk on February 4th, 1918, at the same time as a congress of the entire non-Cossack population. Only the Council, a legal institution restored by the Revolution and representing the Cossack population of the region, has the right to remove the Cossack Army Government from office and elect a new one. This Council will at the same time debate the question of the control of army units and whether there should or should not be volunteer units to defend the government's authority. As for the formation and activities of the Volunteer Army, the present coalition government has already taken the decision to place the Volunteer Army under the control of the Government with the participation of the Regional Military Committee.

With regard to the question of withdrawing from the mining area the police that are alleged to have been stationed there by the Cossack Army Government, the Government declares that this question will be referred to the Council on February 4th.

The Government declares that only the local population can take part in ordering local life and, therefore, in accordance with the will of the Council, it considers it necessary to oppose by every means at its disposal the penetration into the region by armed Bolshevik detachments seeking to impose their order on the region. The population, and only the population, must arrange its own way of life.

The Government does not desire civil war. It is endeavouring by every means to arrive at a peaceful solution. For this reason it proposes that the Military-Revolutionary Committee should take part in a joint deputation to be sent to the Bolshevik forces.

The Government holds that if no alien forces enter the region there will be no civil war, for the Government is only defending the Don territory, is undertaking no offensive action, does not seek to impose its will on the rest of Russia and, accordingly, does not desire that any alien body should impose its will upon the Don country.

The Government guarantees complete freedom for the elections in the stanitsas and army units, and every citizen will be free to canvass as he wishes and to uphold his point of view at the forthcoming elections to the Cossack Army Council.

In all divisions commissions of representatives from the units must be appointed to investigate the needs of the Cossacks.

The Cossack Army Government recommends all units that have sent their deputies to the Military-Revolutionary Committee to return to the normal task of defending the territory of the Don.

The Cossack Army Government considers it inconceivable that its own units should act against the Government and thus initiate intestine war on the quiet Don.

The Military-Revolutionary Committee must be disbanded by the units that elected it and all units must instead send their representatives to the existing Regional Military Committee, which represents all military units in the region.

The Cossack Army Government demands that all persons arrested by the Military-Revolutionary Committee be immediately released. In order that normal life may be restored in the region the administration must be allowed to return to its duties.

Since it represents only an insignificant number of Cossack units, the Military-Revolutionary Committee has no right to make demands on behalf of all units, let alone all Cossacks.

The Cossack Army Government considers it absolutely impermissible that the Committee should have relations with the Council of People's Commissars and receive financial support from it, for this would be tantamount to spreading the influence of the Council of People's Commissars to the Don Region, whereas the Don Cossack Army Council and the Congress of the non-Cossack population have declared the power of the Soviets to be unacceptable, as have the Ukraine, Siberia, and all the Cossack Armies without exception.

> Chairman of the Cossack Army Government,
> Assistant to the Field Ataman of the Cossack
> Army *M. Bogayevsky*,
> Commanders of the Don Cossack Army
> *Yelatontsev, Polyakov, Melnikov*

As members of the Kamenskaya Revolutionary Committee, Lagutin and Skachkov joined the delegation sent to Taganrog by the Cossack Army Government to negotiate with the Bolsheviks. Podtyolkov and the others were temporarily detained in Novocherkassk, while Chernetsov with a few hundred bayonets, a heavy battery mounted on railway trucks and two light guns captured the stations of Likhaya and Zverevo in a daring raid and, leaving a covering force there consisting of one company and two guns, led his main forces against Kamenskaya. Having broken the resistance of the revolutionary Cossack units at the small station of Severny Donets, he captured Kamenskaya on January 17th. But within a few hours, news was received that Sablin's Red Guard detachments had knocked Chernetsov's covering force out of Zverevo and Likhaya. Chernetsov swung round. With a swift head-on attack he shattered the 3rd Moscow Detachment, gave the Kharkov Detachment a thorough trouncing and threw the panic-stricken Red Guards back to their initial positions.

When the situation in Likhaya had been restored Chernetsov seized the initiative and returned to Kamenskaya. On January 19th he received reinforcements from Novocherkassk and the next day decided to advance on Glubokaya.

At a council of war it was decided to take Glubokaya by an outflanking movement, as suggested by Lieutenant Linkov. Chernetsov hesitated to attack along the railway for fear of encountering stubborn resistance from the units of the Kamenskaya Revolutionary Committee and the Red Guard detachments sent up from Chertkovo.

The outflanking movement began that night, led by Chernetsov himself.

The column reached Glubokaya just before dawn, changed formation smartly and spread out in line. Chernetsov gave his final instructions, dismounted and, while stretching his legs, hissed an order to the commander of one of the companies, 'Don't stand on ceremony, Major. You understand?'

His boots crunched on the ice-encrusted snow; he tilted his grey Astrakhan busby to one side and rubbed a pink ear with his glove. Lack of sleep had left dark-blue rings under his defiant light-coloured eyes. His lips were pinched with cold and there was a fluff of frost on his short-clipped moustache.

When he had warmed himself he leaped into the saddle, straightened the folds of his sheepskin-lined officer's coat, took the reins and with a firm and confident smile urged on his reddish white-browed Don stallion.

'Let us begin!'

XII

Just before the congress of frontline Cossacks in Kamenskaya Captain Izvarin deserted from his regiment. The previous day he had visited Grigory and hinted vaguely at the step he was about to take.

'I find it difficult to serve in the regiment in the present situation. The Cossacks are torn between two extremes—the Bolsheviks and the old monarchist system. No one wants to support Kaledin, partly because he's parading his demand for parity like a child with a new toy. What we want is a firm, strong-willed person who will put the non-Cossacks in their proper place. But my view is that it's better to support Kaledin at the moment, otherwise we shall lose the game altogether.' He paused and lit a cigarette, then asked, 'You, I gather, have adopted the Red faith?'

'Almost,' Grigory admitted.

'Sincerely? Or like Golubov—to make yourself popular with the Cossacks?'

'I don't need popularity. I'm looking for a way out.'

'You've come to a dead-end, not a way out.'

'We'll see...'

'I'm afraid that we shall meet again as enemies, Grigory.'

'Friends don't recognise each other if they meet in battle, Yefim Ivanych,' Grigory replied with a smile.

They sat talking for a while, then Izvarin left, and by morning he had disappeared without a trace.

On the day of the congress a Cossack Guardsman from Lebyazhy, in Vyoshenskaya stanitsa, called in to see Grigory. Grigory was cleaning and oiling his revolver. The Guardsman sat and chatted for a while and, before taking his leave, told him the news that was the real reason for his visit. He knew that Grigory's woman had been taken from him by Listnitsky, a former officer of the Ataman's regiment, and after seeing him at the station, had come to warn Grigory.

'I saw a pal of yours at the station today.'

'What pal?'

'Listnitsky. Remember him?'

'When did you see him?' Grigory asked quickly.

'About an hour ago.'

Grigory sat down. The old pain had clamped on to his heart with the grip of a wolfhound. He no longer felt the same furious hatred of his enemy but he knew that if they met now, in this situation of incipient civil war, blood would flow between them. The unexpected news of Listnitsky made him realise that time had not healed the old wound; a mere word could make it bleed. And how sweet it would be to take revenge on the man who had stripped his life of all its blossom and, instead of the full-blooded joy he had once known, left him with only a gnawing hungry yearning, a flower faded before its time.

He waited for a moment while the faint flush drained from his face, then asked, 'Was he on his way here, do you know?'

'I don't reckon so. Must have been heading for Novo-cherkassk.'

'Ah, I see.'

The Guardsman talked for a while about the congress and the regimental news, and then left. In the days that followed Grigory tried in vain to quell the smouldering inward pain. It was no use. He went about in a daze, recalling Aksinya far more often than before, with molten bitterness in his mouth and a stony weight on his heart. He tried to think of Natalya and the children but that joy had been frayed and tarnished by time. His heart

613

still lived with Aksinya and he still felt the same powerful undertow of her love.

When Chernetsov struck, they had to retreat hastily from Kamenskaya. The ill-assorted detachments assembled by the Don Revolutionary Committee and the semi-disbanded Cossack squadrons crowded into trains or went off in marching order, leaving behind everything that could not be carried. The lack of organisation was badly felt. There was no firm hand to marshal and deploy what were, in fact, quite considerable forces.

One of the elected commanders who had come to the fore in the past few days was a Lieutenant-Colonel Golubov. He had taken over the command of the most combative, 27th Cossack Regiment, and had at once, albeit with a touch of cruelty, knocked them into shape. The Cossacks obeyed him implicitly because he provided what the regiment was lacking, the ability to lead, to bring the men together and tell them what to do. A stout, plump-cheeked officer with insolent eyes, he was often to be seen at the station, brandishing his sword and shouting at the Cossacks who were not prompt enough with the loading.

'What's the matter with you? Think this is a game of hide-and-seek? Damn and blast you! Get on with the loading! In the name of the revolution I order you to obey on the spot! What! Who's a demagogue? I'll have you shot, you scoundrel! Silence! The saboteurs and undercover counter-revolutionaries will find no comrade in me!'

And the Cossacks submitted. Out of long habit many actually found this style to their liking—the past was still with them. In the old days the more an officer bullied them, the better commander he was in the eyes of the Cossacks. Of men like Golubov they would say, 'He'll flay the hide off you for a fault but fix you a new one when you're in his favour!'

The Don Revolutionary Committee units fell back and flooded into Glubokaya. Golubov virtually took command of all forces. In less than two days he marshalled the scattered units and made Glubokaya secure. On his insistence Grigory Melekhov took command of a force composed of two squadrons of the 2nd Reserve Regiment and one squadron of Ataman's Guards.

At dusk on January 20th Grigory left his quarters to check the guardsmen's outposts and bumped into Podtyolkov at the gate.

'Is that you, Melekhov?'

'Yes.'

'Where are you making for?'

'I want to have a look at the outposts. How long have you been back from Novocherkassk? How was it?'

Podtyolkov frowned.

'It's no good talking peace with the sworn enemies of the people. Did you see the trick they played on us? Negotiations—while they were egging on Chernetsov. What a snake Kaledin turned out to be?! Well, I'm in a hurry, I've got to get to headquarters.'

And with a hasty goodbye he strode off to the centre.

Even before being elected chairman of the Revolutionary Committee he had changed noticeably in his attitude to Grigory and his other Cossack acquaintances. A chilly note of superiority and even arrogance could be felt in his voice. Power had gone to the head of a man who by nature was unaffected and straightforward.

Grigory turned up his greatcoat collar and walked on at a quicker pace. It promised to be a frosty night. The wind was blowing from the Kirghiz steppes. The sky was clearing. There was ice on the ground and the snow crunched loosely underfoot. The moon climbed the sky slowly and lopsidedly, like a cripple climbing a ladder. Beyond the houses the steppe seemed to smoke in the violet-blue twilight. It was the hour before night when outlines, shapes, colours, distances dissolve, when daylight is still struggling in the toils of night and everything seems unreal and impermanent, as in a fairy-tale; at this hour even smells lose their pungence and acquire special subdued shades of their own.

After making the rounds, Grigory returned to his quarters. The master of the house, a railway clerk with a gap-toothed foxy face, got the samovar going and sat down at the table.

'Are you going to attack?'

'We don't know.'

'Or d'you mean to wait for them to hit at you?'

'We'll see.'

'And quite right too. You haven't got anything to attack with, I suppose, so of course it's better to wait. You'll have a better chance in defence. I went through the German war as a sapper, so I know a thing or two about tactical strategy... You haven't got much muscle behind you.'

'We've got enough,' Grigory tried to evade a discussion that was becoming tedious.

But his host persisted with his questions and hung about round the table, feeling under his cloth waistcoat to scratch his belly, which was as skinny as that of a dried Azov roach.

'Got much artillery? Any big guns, eh?'

'You say you've served in the army but you don't know the regulations!' Grigory said with cold fury and a look that made the man stagger. 'Don't you know the regulations? What right have you to ask me about the numbers of our troops and our plans? In a minute I'll be having you up for interrogation...'

'But your Hon... g... g... good s... sir!' his host stammered and gulped, and the gaps between his teeth showed up blackly on his pale face. 'It ... It ... was just ... foolishness! Forgive me!'

Over tea Grigory happened to look up at him and noticed his eyes blink as if at a flash of lightning. With the eyelashes raised they looked quite different—affectionate, almost adoring. The man's family—a wife and two grown-up daughters—spoke in whispers. Grigory left his second cup unfinished and went to his room.

Soon another six Cossacks, from the 4th Squadron of the 2nd Reserve Regiment, who were lodging at the same house, came in. They talked and laughed loudly while they were having their tea. Grigory caught snatches of their conversation as he fell asleep. Most of the talking was done by a voice that Grigory recognised as belonging to troop commander Bakhmachev, a Cossack of Luganskaya stanitsa; the others offered only occasional remarks.

'I saw it myself. Three miners from the Gorlovka district arrived from Mine No. 11. We've got this organisation, they says, and what we need is some weapons. Won't you share with us? And Podtyolkov—I heard him myself!'—the narrator's voice rose in reply to someone's inaudible comment, 'he says, "You'd better go and see Comrade Sablin, comrades. We haven't got anything." Haven't got anything! How could he say that? I know for a fact there were rifles to spare. But it wasn't that... The idea of the muzhiks sticking their oar in made him jealous like.'

'And quite right too!' another voice put in. 'If you give 'em weapons, they may fight and they may not. But when it comes to the land, they'll be wanting their share all right.'

'We know their kind!' a third voice grunted.

Bakhmachev tapped his glass thoughtfully with his spoon, then began to tap in time with his words as he said, 'No, this kind of thing won't do. The Bolsheviks are ready to meet us half-way for the sake of the whole people and we—what kind of Bolsheviks are we! All we want is to get rid of Kaledin, but then we'll get tough...'

'But can't you see!' a wobbly, almost boyish voice exclaimed persuasively. 'Can't you see we've got nothing to give! There's only about five acres of usable land per family and the rest is sandy loam, ravines, grazing. What have we got to give away?'

'They won't take any off *you*, but there're some people have got a right lot of land.'

'What about the Army's land?'

'Thank ye humbly, sir! Have we got to give away our own and beg from another?.. That's a fine idea!'

'We'll need the Army lands ourselves.'

'Of course, we will.'

'That's greed, that is!'

'No, it isn't!'

'We might have to find some land for our Upper Don Cossacks. We all know what their land's like—nothing but yellowsand.'

'That's just it!'

'There'll be no coat unless we can cut the cloth ourselves!'

'We won't sort this out without a drink or two.'

'Ah, lads, some fellers broke into a wine cellar the other day. And one of 'em himself drowned in the stuff.'

'I could do with a drink just now. Something to warm the cockles, eh.'

Through his drowsiness Grigory heard the Cossacks making up their beds on the floor, yawning and scratching, and rambling on about the land and the changes that were in the offing.

Just before dawn a shot rang out under the windows. The Cossacks scrambled up. Grigory fumbled to get his arms into the sleeves of his tunic and ran out, pulling on his boots and grabbing his greatcoat. In the street shots were going off all over the place. A cart went rattling by. Someone shouted wildly at the door, 'To arms!.. To arms!..'

Chernetsov's attack lines had driven back the outposts and entered Glubokaya. Horsemen were galloping about in the grey, murky darkness. Infantrymen thudded along in their heavy boots. A machine-gun was being mounted at a crossroads. About thirty Cossacks spread out in line. Another squad doubled across a side-street. There was a rattle of rifle-bolts sending cartridges into breaches. In the next block a commanding voice was giving orders.

'Third squadron, look lively there! Who's that breaking ranks?.. Atten—shun! Machine-gunners to the right flank! Are you ready? Squ-a-adron!..'

An artillery troop thundered past, horses going at full gallop, drivers brandishing their whips. The clatter of ammunition crates, the rumble of wheels and clank of gun-carriages mingled with the mounting roar of gunfire from the outskirts. Suddenly all the machine-guns in the vicinity spoke at once. At the next corner a field kitchen that had been galloping no one knew where caught its wheel on a tethering post and overturned.

'You blind devil!.. Couldn't you see, blast you?!' A panic-stricken voice was yelling.

Grigory assembled his squadron with some difficulty and led it at a canter to the edge of the stanitsa. Droves of retreating Cossacks came towards them.

'Where're you off to?' Grigory grabbed the first man by the barrel of his rifle.

'Lemme go!' the man shouted. 'Let go, you swine! Who're you grabbing? Can't you see we're retreating?'

'We're outnumbered!'

'They're attacking like crazy...'

'Where can we go now? Do we make for Millerovo?' panting voices spoke up on all sides.

Near a long shed on the outskirts Grigory tried to deploy his squadron, but a fresh crowd of fleeing troops swept them aside. The men of Grigory's squadron mingled with the runaways and galloped back into the streets.

'Stop!.. Hold your ground! Don't run away! I'll shoot!' Grigory bellowed, shaking with fury.

No one listened to him. A stream of maching-gun fire swept down the street; the Cossacks dropped to the ground, crawled away to the walls and slipped into the side-streets.

'You won't stop 'em now, Melekhov!' troop commander Bakhmachev shouted giving him a sharp look as he ran past.

Grigory followed him, gritting his teeth and brandishing his rifle.

The panic ended in a disorderly retreat from Glubokaya. Nearly all stores and equipment were left behind.

Not until daybreak could the squadrons be mustered and thrown into a counter-attack.

A purple-faced sweating Golubov with his coat flapping open ran along the advancing lines of his 27th Regiment and shouted in his rasping metallic voice, 'Keep moving!.. Don't lie down!.. Forward, forward!'

The 14th Battery drove out to its positions. The gun-trails were unhitched and the senior officer climbed on an ammunition crate to scan the field through binoculars.

The action began at between five and six in the morning. Dense lines of Cossacks and Red Guards from Petrov's Voronezh detachment moved into position, fringing the snowy field with a black border of running figures.

A chill wind was blowing from the east. The bleeding crest of the dawn appeared under a dark windswept cloud.

Grigory left half the Guards squadron to cover the 14th Battery and led the rest in the attack.

The first, ranging shell landed well in front of Chernetsov's line, unfurling a tattered orange-blue flag of fire. A second shot went off with a juicy smack. The ranging proceeded one gun at a time, with a departing howl from each shell. For a second there would be a tense hush, intensified by the volleys of rifle fire, then came the distant crump of the shell-burst. After the line had been straddled, the shells began falling thickly near the target. Eyes half closed against the wind, Grigory thought with satisfaction, 'They've got the range!'

The squadrons of the 44th were advancing on the right flank. Golubov led his regiment in the centre. Grigory was on his left. Beyond him the left flank was covered by Red Guard detachments. Grigory's squadrons were given three machine-guns. Their commander, a stocky Red Guard with a sombre face and broad, very hairy hands, directed the firing skilfully, paralysing the enemy's attacking manoeuvres. He was always near the machine-gun attached to the guardsmen's line. With him there was a sturdy woman Red Guard in an army greatcoat. As he walked along the line Grigory thought fiercely: "The man must be woman crazy! Can't even leave his girl-friend behind when he's in the line. We'll do a lot of fighting with the likes of him! Why didn't he bring his kids along, and a feather-bed as well!' The commander of the machine-gun platoon came up to him, straightening the string of his revolver across his chest.

'Are you in command of this detachment?'

'Yes, I am.'

'I'll give covering fire on the sector of the Guards half-squadron. You can see that's where we're held up.'

'Get on with it then,' Grigory said and turned at the sound of a shout from the machine-gun that had stopped firing.

A burly bearded machine-gunner was shouting fiercely, 'Bunchuk!.. We'll melt the gun!.. We can't keep this up!'

The woman in the greatcoat had dropped on her knees beside him. Her dark eyes burning under the fluffy woollen shawl reminded Grigory of Aksinya and for a second he eyed her longingly and held his breath.

At noon an orderly rode up to Grigory with a note from Golubov. The message was scrawled on a sheet torn from a field notebook.

In the name of the Don Revolutionary Committee I order you to withdraw the two squadrons under your command from their positions and proceed at a canter to turn the enemy's right flank. Your direction should be towards the sector that can be seen from here, a little to the left of the windmill, along the ravine... Keep under cover (a few illegible words) ... Attack on the flank as soon as we make a resolute push.

Golubov

Grigory withdrew the squadrons, got them mounted and rode back, trying to deceive the enemy as to the direction he was taking.

They made a detour of twenty versts. It was heavy going for the horses. The ravine they were using for their outflanking movement was snowed up. In places the drifts came up to the horses' bellies. As he listened to the bursts of gunfire Grigory glanced worriedly at the watch he had taken off a dead German officer in Romania. He was afraid of being late. Though he had checked his direction by compass, he had nevertheless veered slightly to the left. They climbed a long slope into open country. The horses were steaming and wet under the groin. Grigory gave the order to dismount and climbed to the nearest vantage point. The horses remained below in the ravine with the minders. Other Cossacks followed Grigory up the slope. He glanced back and saw more than a hundred men spread out over the snowy side of the ravine and felt stronger and more confident. Like most men in battle he was strongly influenced by the herd instinct. When the battlefield came into view, Grigory realised that he was at least half an hour late, having failed to make allowance for the difficult terrain.

In a bold strategic manoeuvre Golubov had almost cut off Chernetsov's path of retreat. With covering forces on both flanks he was now attacking the half-encircled enemy in a frontal assault. Artillery volleys were thundering amid a constant rattle of rifle fire that sounded like buckshot being poured onto a frying pan; the crumpled lines of Chernetsov's troops were being raked by shrapnel from a rain of shells.

'Into line!'

Grigory attacked with his squadrons from the flank. They started as if on parade, without taking cover, but a skilled Chernetsov machine-gunner used his Maxim so effectively that the line gladly dropped flat, having lost three men.

Some time after two o'clock in the afternoon a bullet chose Grigory as the object of its affection. The small red-hot lump of lead in its nickel sheath burned through the fleshy tissue of his leg just above the knee. Grigory gritted his teeth as he felt its hot impact and the familiar nausea from loss of blood. He crawled out of the line and in the heat of the moment struggled to his feet, shaking his head to overcome the dizziness. The pain in his leg was made worse because the bullet was still there. It had been almost spent when it found its mark and after penetrating the greatcoat, trousers and skin, had buried itself in a bunch of muscles and begun to cool. Immobilised by the hot surging pain, Grigory lay down again, remembering the 12th Regiment's attack in the Transylvanian Mountains in Romania, when he had been wounded in the arm. The scene rose vividly before his eyes—Curly Uryupin, Mishka Koshevoi's face distorted with anger, Yemelyan Groshev, running down the mountain-side, dragging the wounded lieutenant.

Grigory's righthand man Pavel Lyubishkin, an officer, took over command of the squadrons. On his orders two Cossacks helped Grigory back to the spot where the horses were being minded. As they held his stirrup they offered sympathetic advice.

'Better bandage it up.'

'Got a bandage?'

Grigory was already in the saddle, but after a moment's thought he dismounted, lowered his trousers and, wincing as a great shudder gripped his sweating back, belly and legs, hastily bandaged the small inflamed and bleeding wound, which looked as if it had been made with a pen-knife.

Accompanied by his orderly, he rode back by the same roundabout route to the place where the counter-attack had begun. As he stared at the churned-up snow and the familiar features of the ravine along which he had led his squadrons a few hours before, he began to feel sleepy. What was happening on the hill already seemed far away and of little importance.

Meanwhile the rifle fire on the hill had become hasty and ragged. The enemy's heavy battery had opened up thunderously to assist the defenders and intermittently chattering machine-guns seemed to be drawing an invisible dotted line under the results of the battle.

Grigory kept to the ravine for about three versts, but it was hard work for the horses.

'Let's get out into the open,' Grigory grunted as he rode up the snowy bank.

The dark forms of the dead dotted the distant field, like rooks. A riderless horse, dwarfed by the distance, was galloping along the knife-edge of the horizon.

Grigory saw Chernetsov's main force, now reduced to shattered remnants, break off the engagement and fall back into Glubokaya. He threw his bay into a gallop. Scattered groups of Cossacks came into view in the distance. Grigory rode up to the nearest of them and spotted Golubov. He was leaning back in his saddle. His half-length coat with its yellowed astrakhan trimming was unbuttoned, his cap tilted back, exposing his sweating forehead. Twirling his sergeant-major's pointed moustache, Golubov shouted hoarsely, 'Good work, Mele-khov! But you're wounded, I see? Damn nuisance! Is the bone all right?' And without waiting for an answer, he smiled broadly. 'We've beaten 'em! Knocked the stuffing out of 'em! That's one detachment the officers will never put together again!'

Grigory asked for a smoke. Cossacks and Red Guards were approaching from all sides. A mounted Cossack came cantering towards them from a dark crowd that had loomed up ahead.

'We've captured forty of 'em, Golubov!' he shouted while still at a distance. 'Forty officers and Chernetsov himself!'

'Not really!' Golubov swung round anxiously in his

saddle and galloped off, using his whip ruthlessly on his tall white-stockinged horse.

Grigory rested for a while, then trotted after him.

The bunch of captured officers was hemmed in on all sides by an escort of about thirty Cossacks of the 44th Regiment and one squadron of the 27th. Chernetsov was out in front. When trying to escape, he had thrown off his coat and was now striding along in only a light leather jacket. His left shoulder strap had been torn off. A fresh scratch showed bloodily under his left eye. He was walking at a quick steady pace. His rakishly angled lamb-skin busby gave him a carefree, dashing appearance. There was not a shadow of fear on his rosy-cheeked face. Evidently he had not shaved for several days and the light-brown stubble gave a golden tint to his cheeks and chin. His quick stern eyes surveyed the Cossacks who ran up to look at him and a bitter furrow of hatred showed darkly between his brows. Without pausing in his stride he struck a match and lighted a cigarette, gripping it in the corner of his firm pink lips.

Most of the officers were young men; only a few were touched with a frosty grey. One of them, with a leg wound, was lagging behind, and a little Cossack with a large head and small-pox scars was jabbing him in the back with his rifle butt. A tall debonair major was walking almost level with Chernetsov. Two others, a cornet and a lieutenant, were walking along arm in arm, smiling; behind them was a broad-shouldered curly-headed cadet, hatless. Another officer was wearing a soldier's greatcoat draped over his shoulders with the insignia of his rank firmly sewn on to the shoulders. Another, also hatless, had pulled his red-lined officer's hood down to his dark femininely beautiful eyes; the scarves of the hood were flying back over his shoulders in the wind.

Golubov was riding along behind them. He dropped back a little and shouted to the Cossacks, 'Now, listen to me, all of you! You will be answerable for the safety of these prisoners with all the severity of revolutionary war! They must be brought to headquarters unharmed!'

He called over one of the mounted Cossacks and without dismounting scribbled a note, folded it and gave it to the Cossack.

'Off you go! Give this to Podtyolkov!'

Then he turned to Grigory and asked, 'Are you going that way too, Melekhov?'

In response to Grigory's nod he rode up level with him and said, 'Tell Podtyolkov that I'll go bail for Chernetsov! D'you understand?.. Yes, tell him that. Off you go!'

Grigory rode on ahead of the bunch of prisoners and reached the Revolutionary Committee's headquarters, which had been set up in a field near a village. Podtyolkov was pacing about beside a big Ukrainian machine-gun cart with ice-encrusted wheels and a gun under a green cover. His staff, the messengers, a few officers and some Cossack orderlies were standing about near by. Minayev was there too. Like Podtyolkov, he had only just returned from the line and was sitting on the box of the cart, biting off pieces of frozen white bread and munching them noisily.

'Podtyolkov!' Grigory rode off to one side. 'They'll soon be bringing in the prisoners. Have you read Golubov's note?'

Podtyolkov cracked his whip fiercely and, lowering his blood-shot eyes, shouted, 'I don't give a damn for Golubov!.. There're plenty of things he wants! Let him go bail for Chernetsov, that bandit and counter-revolutionary? No, I won't!.. Shoot 'em all and have done with it!'

'Golubov said he would go bail for him.'

'I won't let him!.. You heard! I won't let him! And that's all there is to it! Chernetsov is going to be tried by a revolutionary court and punished on the spot. As a lesson to others... Do you know,' he went on more calmly, throwing a keen glance at the approaching bunch of prisoners, 'do you know how much bloodshed he's caused? Oceans!.. How many miners did he butcher?' And as his fury surged up again, he rolled his eyes fiercely, 'No bail for him!'

'You needn't shout!' Grigory raised his voice too; he was shaking inwardly, as though infected by Podtyolkov's frenzy. 'There's a lot of you judges around here! Why don't you go out there!' with quivering nostrils he pointed back to the battlefield. 'There's plenty of you here wanting to settle accounts with prisoners!'

Podtyolkov walked away, crushing his whip in his hands. From a distance he shouted, 'I was there! Don't think I was keeping out of it on the machine-gun cart. And you, Melekhov, had better keep quiet!.. Understand?.. Who're you talking to? Eh?.. Keep your officer's ways to yourself! This will be a trial by a Revolutionary Committee, not just any...'

Grigory rode his horse towards him and sprang out of the saddle, forgetting his wound. The pain flung him flat on his back and he felt hot blood spurting from the wound. He scrambled to his feet without help, limped to the machine-gun cart and leaned against the rear spring.

The prisoners arrived. Some of the escorting infantry mingled with the orderlies and Cossacks who had been guarding headquarters. The Cossacks had not yet cooled down after the fighting and their eyes blazed fiercely as they flung remarks to each other about the details and outcome of the battle.

Dragging his feet heavily through the loosely packed snow, Podtyolkov walked up to the prisoners. Chernetsov, who was standing in front, looked at him with his defiant, light-coloured eyes contemptuously narrowed; he stood jauntily with his weight on his right leg, keeping a horseshoe of white teeth clamped to the inside of his pink lower lip. Podtyolkov came right up to him. He was trembling. His unblinking eyes raked the rutted snow, then rose, clashed with Chernetsov's fearless contemptuous gaze and broke it with the sheer weight of his hatred.

'So we've caught you—you bastard!' Podtyolkov said in a low voice that seethed with anger, and took a step back; a jagged smile split his face like a sabre stroke.

'Betrayer of the Cossacks! Scoundrel! Traitor!' Chernetsov twanged the words through clenched teeth.

Podtyolkov jerked his head sideways, as though to avoid a slap on the face; his cheeks darkened and he gulped air through his gaping mouth.

The rest happened with astonishing speed. Chernetsov, pale, snarling, leaning forward with his fists pressed to his chest, strode towards Podtyolkov. Indistinct words mingled with obscene curses spurted from his trembling lips. Only the slowly retreating Podtyolkov heard what he said. 'You—, you know what's coming to you, don't you?' Chernetsov's voice rose suddenly.

These words were heard by the captured officers, the escort and the headquarters staff.

Podtyolkov gave a stifled cry and snatched at the hilt of his sword.

There was a sudden hush. The crunch of the snow was clearly audible as Minayev, Krivoshlykov and several others dashed towards Podtyolkov. But he was too quick for them. Crouching and swinging his whole body to the right, he tore his sabre from its sheath and, springing forward, brought it down with terrible force on Chernetsov's head.

Grigory saw Chernetsov shudder and raise his left hand to ward off the blow; he saw the hand, severed at the wrist, break off and the blade descend soundlessly on the head. First the cap fell, then, like an ear of wheat cut at the stem, Chernetsov dropped slowly, his mouth grotesquely distorted and eyes tightly closed as if against an agonizing flash of lightning.

Podtyolkov slashed again, then drew back with a sudden age and heaviness in his stride, wiping the blood-streaked blade of his sabre.

. He lumbered over to the machine-gun cart, then turned to the escort and shouted in an exhausted voice that rose to a howl, 'Cut 'em down, blast the ... lot! All of 'em! We take no prisoners! Kill them! Death to them all!'

Shots rang out feverishly. The officers huddled together, then scattered. The red-hooded lieutenant with the beautiful feminine eyes ran clutching his head in his hands. A bullet made him jump high, as if to clear a hurdle. He fell and did not rise again. The tall debonair major was attacked by two men. He snatched at their blades and blood streamed from his slashed hands on to his sleeves; he screamed like a child and fell on his knees, then on his back, rolling his head in the snow; only his bloodshot eyes and the black screaming mouth were visible. The flying blades slashed the face, the black mouth, but he went on screaming in a voice whittled by pain and horror. A Cossack in a greatcoat with a torn back belt straddled him and despatched him with a shot. The curly-headed cadet nearly broke through the escort line but was caught and killed with a blow on the back of the head by a Cossack guardsman. The same guardsman sent a bullet between the shoulder blades of the lieutenant, who was running with his greatcoat spread out in the wind like wings. The lieutenant sank on to his haunches, clawed at his chest and went on clawing till he died. A grey-haired captain was killed on the spot; before he breathed his last he dug a deep pit in the snow with his kicking feet and would have gone on kicking, like a spirited horse at the tethering post, if the Cossacks had not taken pity and ended his agony.

The moment the massacre began Grigory flung himself away from the cart and with his bloodshot eyes fixed on Podtyolkov limped rapidly towards him. Minayev grabbed him from behind, wrenched his revolver away, and, staring at him dull-eyed, asked breathlessly, 'And what did you think?'

XIII

The blindingly bright snow crest of the hill, glazed by the sun and drenched in the blue of the cloudless sky, glistened and sparkled like sugar. Beneath it the settlement of Olkhovy Rog spread its patchwork quilt. To the left lay the blue curve of the Svinyukha, to the right the misty blobs of Cossack villages and German colonies and, further on, beyond the bend in the river, the lighter blue of Ternovskaya. Beyond the settlement to the east rose the crouching shape of a smaller hill, its slopes scored with gullies and topped by a line of telegraph poles leading away in the direction of Kashary.

It was an unusually clear and frosty day. The sun rested on irridescent pillars of light. The wind had veered to the north and was hissing low across the steppe. But the snowy expanses were bright and only in the east, on the very edge of the horizon, was the steppe veiled in a smoky lilac haze.

Pantelei, who was driving Grigory home from Millerovo, decided not to stop in Olkhovy Rog but to push on and spend the night in Kashary. He had come out in response to a telegram from his son and arrived in Millerovo by evening on January 28th. Grigory had been waiting for him at an inn. They had left the next morning and by eleven o'clock Olkhovy Rog was behind them.

After being wounded at Glubokaya, Grigory had spent a week in the field hospital at Millerovo, allowing his leg time to heal over, then decided to go home. The men of his village had brought him his horse and Grigory set out on his journey with mixed feelings of regret and joy. Regret because he was leaving his unit at the height of the struggle for power on the Don, and joy at the mere thought of seeing his home and family again; he concealed from himself his desire to see Aksinya, but the thought of her was also in the back of his mind.

There was a touch of estrangement in his meeting with his father. Petro had filled the old man's head with stories and he now kept a surly watchful eye on Grigory; in his brief sidelong glances there was disapproval and anxiety.

During the evening at Millerovo he had questioned Grigory at length about the events that had flared up around them, and was evidently not satisfied with his son's answers. He munched his greying beard, stared at his leather-soled felt boots, and sniffed expressively. He seemed to be in no mood for argument but he flared up in defence of Kaledin and in the heat of the moment snapped at Grigory in his old style and even stamped his lame leg.

'Don't you argue with me! Kaledin himself came to our village last autumn! There was a meeting on the square. He got up on a table and talked to the old men. Prophesied like the Bible, he did, that the muzhiks would come and there would be war and that if we kept shilly-shallying they'd grab everything and take over the whole region. Even then he knew there was going to be a war. What are you, young bastards, thinking about? Or doesn't he know as much as you? An educated general like him, who's been in command of an army, and you reckon he knows less than your lot? It's uneducated windbags like you that have set themselves up in Kamenskaya and are stirring up the people. Your Podtyolkov—what is he? A sergeant-major?.. Oho! The same rank as me. Well, well!.. The things we've lived to see... What next!'

Grigory argued half-heartedly. He had known where his father stood even before he saw him. And now he was up against something new: he could neither forget nor forgive the way Chernetsov had died and the shooting without trial of the other White officers.

It was easy going for the horses with the light sledge. Grigory's horse trotted along behind with its saddle on and hitched to the sledge by a tethering rope. Settlements and villages that he had known since childhood unfolded on either side of the road—Kashary, Popovka, Kamenka, Lower Yablonovsky, Grachov, Yasenovka. All the way home Grigory thought disconnectedly and vaguely about the recent events, trying to make out at least a few landmarks for the future, but his thoughts got no farther than the idea of rest and recovery at home. I'll just have a bit of a rest at home and get my leg better, and then we'll see, he thought, shelving the whole matter. Things will work out one way or another.

He was also oppressed by war weariness. He longed to turn away from this hostile and incomprehensible world with its seething hatred. All that he had experienced up to now had been muddled and contradictory. It was hard to find the right path; the ground heaved like a bog under his feet, the path divided and he couldn't be sure which branch to take. He had felt drawn towards the Bolsheviks, so he had gone along with them and taken others with him, but then had come second thoughts and he had cooled. Perhaps Izvarin had been right after all? Then whose side should he take? Who could he turn to for a handful of certainty? Grigory thought of such things vaguely as he lay back in the sledge. But when he pictured himself preparing the harrows and wagons for the spring and weaving mangers out of willow branches, and then, after the soil had dried, driving out into the steppe, getting a grip on the plough handles with hands that yearned for work, and following the plough, feeling its living thrust and kick; when he imagined himself breathing in the sweet scents of the young grass and crumbling black earth, earth that had not yet lost the faint aroma of melted snow, he felt happier at heart. He wanted to clean out the cattle sheds, toss the hay, breathe the fading scents of clover and quitch and the heady smell of dung. He longed for peace, for stillness, and there was a shy joy in his stern eyes as he gazed around him, at the horses, at his father's sturdy back in its snug-fitting sheepskin. The smell of the sheepskin, the homely appearance of the ungroomed horses, a cock crowing in one of the settlements—everything reminded him of the old life he had half forgotten. With all that was going on around him, life here, in this backwater seemed to him as sweet and overpowering as young wine.

They reached the village on the second day, towards evening. From the crest of the hill Grigory looked across the Don. There were the backwaters of the far bank all sabled with rushes; there was the withered poplar. But the sledge road across the river was in a different place. The village, the familiar patchwork stitched with streets and lanes, the church, the square... The blood rushed to Grigory's head as his eyes rested on his own home. Memories flooded over him. The well-sweep poised above the yard seemed to beckon with its grey willow-wood arm.

'Aren't your eyes stinging?' Pantelei smiled as he looked round at his son, and Grigory confessed frankly and without dissembling, 'Yes, they are—that they are!'

'That's the homeland for you!' his father observed with a sigh of satisfaction.

He drove on towards the centre of the village. The

horses quickened their pace down the hill and the sledge slithered from side to side. Grigory guessed his father's intention but asked all the same, 'Why're you driving into the village? Head for home.'

Pantelei turned round and winked at his son, smirking into his frost-rimed beard.

'I saw my sons off to the war as plain Cossacks and they've risen to the rank of officer. D'you think I'm not proud to drive my son through the village? Let 'em look and envy us. It's a balm to my heart, lad.'

As they drove down the main street he quietly urged on the horses and, leaning sideways, used his tasseled whip playfully. The horses, sensing that home was near, stepped out spiritedly, as though they had not left a hundred and forty versts behind them. Passing Cossacks bowed their heads. Women shaded their eyes and looked out of the houses and the yards. A flock of chickens ran squawking across the street, like tumbleweed. Everything was just as it should be. They drove across the square. Grigory's stallion squinted at a mare tethered to Mokhov's fence, gave a lusty neigh and held its head high. The end of the village, the roof of Astakhov's house came into view. But at the first crossroads a mishap occurred. A young pig hesitated as it was running across the street, was caught under the horses' hooves and rolled away, crushed and squealing, trying to lift its broken back.

'What the ... the devil sent you here!' Pantelei swore furiously, managing to get in a whack at the crippled pig as he went past.

As luck would have it, the animal belonged to Anyutka, the widow of Afonka Ozerov, a real crosspatch of a woman with a very sharp tongue. She was out in her yard in a trice, pulling on her shawl and spouting a stream of such choice abuse that Pantelei reined in the horses and turned back.

'Be quiet, you foolish woman! What are you shouting for? We'll pay for your mangy animal!'

'Wretch!.. Fiend!.. Mangy yourself, you lame old dog!.. I'll have you up before the ataman!..' she screamed, waving her arms. 'I'll learn you to crush the only animal a widow has!'

That got under Pantelei's skin and, turning purple, he shouted, 'You hussy!'

'Rotten Turk!' Anyutka responded promptly.

'Bitch, born of a hundred devils!' Pantelei raised his voice even higher.

But Anyutka had never been at a loss for words.

'Furriner! Old bugger! Thief! Pinched someone else's harrow! Running after grass-widows!..' she reeled off her charges like a chattering magpie.

'I'll take my whip to you, you bitch!.. Shut that trap of yours!'

But then Anyutka let fly with something that made even Pantelei, who had seen and heard a good deal in his tie, blush with embarrassment and break out in a muck sweat.

'Get going! Why bother with her?' Grigory blurted out angrily, noticing that the street was beginning to fill with onlookers who had an attentive ear for this casual exchange of views between old Melekhov and the honest widow.

'What a tongue, eh! Long as a horse's rein!' Pantelei spat in disgust and whipped up the horses as if he meant to crush Anyutka herself.

At the next crossroads he turned and looked back, not without some apprehension.

'Spitting and swearing like that!.. I wish you'd burst your sides, you fat harpy!' he said with relish. 'I ought to have trampled on you as well as your pig! Get caught on that trollop's tongue and she'd shrivel you up!'

The Melekhov's blue shutters flashed by. Petro, hatless, his tunic unbelted, came out to open the gates. A white kerchief and Dunyashka's laughing face with its dark shining eyes showed up on the porch.

As he kissed his brother, Petro glanced quickly into his eyes.

'Are you well?'

'I was wounded.'

'Where?'

'At Glubokaya.'

'You wanted something better to do! You should've come home long ago.'

He gave Grigory a hearty shake and passed him on to Dunyashka. Grigory hugged his sister's mature shapely shoulders, kissed her on the lips and eyes, and stepped back in wonder.

'Why, Dunyashka—what the devil!.. You've grown up to be a fine girl! And I thought she'd be a plain little wench!'

'Now, now, brother!' Dunyashka evaded his attempt to pinch her and slipped away with a dazzling white-toothed smile just like Grigory's.

As Ilyinichna came out carrying the children, Natalya ran past her. She had blossomed with a wild beauty. Her gleaming black hair, combed back into a heavy knot, set off her happily flushed face. She clung to Grigory, touching his moustache and cheeks several times haphazardly with her lips and, snatching her son from Ilyinichna's arms, held him out to Grigory.

'Look what a son you've got!' she said in a voice ringing with pride and happiness.

'Let me look at *my* son!' Ilyinichna protested, pushing her aside.

She pulled Grigory's head down and kissed him on the forehead, passed her rough hand swiftly over his face and burst into tears of joy.

'And what about your daughter, Grisha!.. Take her too!'

Natalya planted a little girl swaddled in a shawl on Grigory's other arm and he simply didn't know where to look—at his wife, his mother or the children. The frowning sombre-eyed little boy was perfectly cast in the Melekhov mould: the same slanting dark eyes and vigorous sweep of the brows, the same prominent bluish whites of the eyes, and olive-brown skin. He thrust his grubby little fist into his mouth and, leaning back, stared at his father with stubborn aloofness. Of his daughter Grigory could see only the small, attentive and equally dark eyes, for the rest of her face was hidden under the shawl.

'Here, you'd better take them, Natalya,' Grigory smiled guiltily, out of the corner of his mouth. 'I shan't be able to get through the door.'

Darya was standing in the middle of the kitchen, patting her hair into place... She swaggered smilingly up to Grigory, closed her laughing eyes and pressed her warm, moist lips to his.

'Oh, how you reek of tobacco!' And her pencilled eyebrows rose coquettishly.

'Now let me have another look at you! My darling boy!'

Grigory smiled and his heart tingled with agitation as he pressed up against his mother's shoulder.

Out in the yard Pantelei unharnessed the horses and limped round the sledge, his red sash and red-topped hat showing up in the evening light. Petro had already taken Grigory's horse to the stables, and as he carried the saddle into the porch turned to say something to Dunyashka, who was lifting a barrel of kerosene off the sledge.

Grigory took off his outdoor clothes, hung his sheep-skin and greatcoat on the back of the bed, and combed his hair. Then he sat down on a bench and called his son.

'Come to me, Mishatka. What's wrong? Don't you recognise me?'

Without taking his fist out of his mouth the little boy sidled up to the table and stopped timidly, watched lovingly and proudly from the stove by his mother. She whispered something in the little girl's ear, put her down and gave her a gentle push.

'Go on!'

Grigory swept them both up in his arms and perched them on his knees.

'Don't you recognise me, my little hazel nuts? Don't you know your own Daddy either, Polyushka?'

'You're not my Daddy,' the boy whispered (he felt bolder in his sister's company).

'Who am I then?'

'You're a strange Cossack.'

'There's a voice for you!' Grigory chuckled. 'And where's your Daddy then?'

'He's in the army,' the little girl (she was the livelier of the two) piped up with conviction.

'That's the way, my little ones! Give it to him! Let him know his own home better. He thinks he can go flitting around for a whole year and expect you to know him at once,' Ilyinichna intervened with mock severity and smiled in response to Grigory's smile. 'Why, your own wife will soon give you up. We were thinking of finding her another husband.'

'What's all this, Natalya? Eh?' Grigory questioned his wife jokingly.

She blushed and, overcoming her shyness of the family, went up to him, sat by his side, gazing at him with boundlessly happy eyes, and caressed his lean brown fingers with her hot rough hand.

'Darya, lay the table!'

'He's got a wife of his own,' Darya countered laughing-ly and stepped over to the stove with her usual light swinging stride. She was still as slim and smart as ever. Her shapely legs were clad in close-fitting violet wool stockings and the neat leather slippers fitted as if carved to the shape of her foot; her gathered raspberry-coloured skirt was taken in tightly at the waist and her embroi-dered apron gleamed immaculately white. Grigory turned his eyes to his wife and noticed a distinct change in her appearance. She had dressed herself up for his arrival. A blue sateen blouse with narrow sleeves and lace cuffs clung to her fine figure and swelled over her big soft breasts; the dark blue skirt with its embroidered and gathered hem was flared at the bottom and tight at the top. Out of the corner of his eye Grigory surveyed her firm shapely legs, her excitingly taut stomach under the waisted skirt, and her broad buttocks, like a well-fed filly's, and thought to himself, 'You can always tell a Cossack woman. The dress to show you everything and it's up to you whether you look or not. But with the muzhiks' women you can't tell the front from the back. They look as if they're walking about in sacks.'

Ilyinichna intercepted his glance and said with deliberate boastfulness, 'That's how our officers' wives dress! They could knock spots off the town ladies!'

'What are you saying, Mother!' Darya interrupted her. 'How can we compare with the townsfolk! Here am I with a broken ear-ring and it wasn't worth a farthing anyway!' she concluded bitterly.

Grigory rested his hand on his wife's broad, working woman's back and thought for the first time, 'She's a fine-looking woman. It hits you in the eye. How did she manage all this time without me. I bet the Cossacks were after her and she may have taken a fancy to one of 'em herself. What if she did have a fling?' The unexpected thought made him wince, and he felt inwardly sullied. He stared into her pink face, bright and fresh with cucumber pomade. Natalya flushed under his searching gaze and, when she had overcome her embarrassment, whispered, 'Why do you look at me like that? Have you been missing me?'

'Of course, I have!'

Grigory drove away his unwelcome thoughts, but a barely understood feeling of hostility towards his wife had stirred in him.

Pantelei came in, clearing his throat, prayed before the ikon, and grunted, 'Well, once again, you're all well, I hope!'

'Praise be, Father... Are you frozen? We've been waiting for you. The soup's all ready and piping hot,' Ilyinichna hurried to and fro, clattering the spoons on to the table.

Pantelei untied his red scarf and stamped his frozen felt boots. Having pulled off his sheepskin, he clawed the icicles out of his beard and moustache and sat down beside Grigory.

'Ay, I was frozen, but I got warmed up in the village... We ran over Anyutka's pig.'

'Which Anyutka?' Darya asked with lively interest, and stopped slicing the tall white loaf.

'Ozerova's. The way she led off at me, the rotten bitch! I was this and that, I was a thief and I'd stolen someone's harrow. What harrow? Damned if I know what she was on about!'

The old man enumerated all the names Anyutka had called him and failed to mention only her charge of philandering. Grigory gave a dry little laugh as he sat down at table and, wishing to justify himself in his son's eyes, Pantelei concluded furiously, 'She came out with such a pack o' lies I wonder it didn't choke her! I wanted to go back and give her a taste of the whip, but Grigory was there and it'd have been a bit awkward.'

Petro opened the door and Dunyashka led in a chestnut-coloured calf with a white blaze on its forehead.

'Come Shrovetide, we'll be eating pancakes with whipped cream!' Petro cried gaily, giving the calf a shove with his foot.

After the meal Grigory untied his bag and started giving out presents to the family.

'This is for you, Mother...' he said, holding out a warm shawl.

Ilyinichna accepted the gift, frowning and blushing like a girl, then she put it on and swung her shoulders in front of the mirror so dashingly that Pantelei burst out indignantly, 'Look at her, the old crow, showing off in front of the mirror! Bah!'

'And this is for you, Father,' Grigory said, displaying a new Cossack peaked cap with a high top and fiery red band.

'The Lord be praised! I was in a bad way for a cap! There haven't been any in the shops for the past year... Don't know how I got through the summer. But I was ashamed to go to church in the old thing. It was only fit for a scarecrow and I had to wear it,' he grumbled, glancing over his shoulder as if he were afraid of having his son's gift snatched away from him.

He was about to go and try it on in front of the glass, but Ilyinichna had her eye on him. The old man caught her glance and with a quick turn limped over to the samovar, where he was able to catch a crooked reflection of himself as he tried on the cap, tilting it at a rakish angle.

'What are you up to, old stick?' Ilyinichna pitched into him.

But Pantelei brazened his way out of it.

'Good Lord, woman! How stupid you are! This is a samovar, not a mirror, isn't it? There's a difference, you know.'

Grigory gave his wife a skirt-length of woollen cloth and shared out a pound of honey-flavoured sweet-breads among the children; for Darya there were silver ear-rings with little stones in them; for Dunyashka a blouse, and for Petro, some cigarettes and a pound of tobacco.

While the women were chattering and looking at their presents, Pantelei strode about the kitchen like the King of Spades, puffing out his chest.

'There's a Cossack for ye! A Cossack of the Life Guards Regiment! Won prizes he did! Took the first prize at the imperial review! A saddle and a full set of equipment! Well now!'

Petro sat munching a wheaten whisker and admiring his father. Grigory chuckled into his moustache. They all lighted up and Pantelei with an apprehensive glance at the windows said, 'Before all the relatives and neighbours start coming round—tell Petro what's happening out there.'

Grigory cut the air with his hand.

'They're fighting.'

'Where're the Bolsheviks right now?' Petro asked, settling himself more comfortably.

'Coming up on three sides—from Tikhoretskaya, from Taganrog and from Voronezh.'

'Well, and what does your Revolutionary Committee think about that? Why's it letting them on to our land? Khristonya and Ivan came here and told us a lot of yarns, but I don't believe 'em. Sounds fishy.'

'The Revolutionary Committee can't do anything. The Cossacks are making for home.'

'Is that why it leans towards the Soviets?'

'Of course, that's why.'

Petro was silent for a moment, then lit another cigarette and gave his brother a candid look.

'What side are you on?'

'I'm for Soviet power.'

'You're a fool then!' Pantelei exploded. 'Petro, can't you tell him!'

Petro smiled and clapped Grigory on the shoulder.

'He's as fiery as a horse that's not been broken in. Can anyone tell him anything, Dad?'

'I don't need anyone to tell me!' Grigory blazed. 'I'm

not blind myself... What do our men who were at the front say?'

'Why listen to them! Or don't you know that blockhead Khristonya by now? What understanding could he have of things? The people have lost their way, all of 'em, they don't know where to turn... It's enough to make you weep!' Petro bit his moustache. 'You'll see what'll happen by the spring. There'll be no getting them together... Yes, we played at being Bolsheviks when we were at the front, but now it's time we came to our senses. "We don't want anything that belongs to anybody else and don't you take what's ours!"—that's what the Cossacks must say to anyone who comes barging in on us. And in Kamenskaya you made a dirty deal. You got too pally with the Bolsheviks and now they're laying down the law.'

'Think it over, Grishka. You've got some sense in your head. You know that Cossacks are Cossacks and always will be. We can't let stinking Russia rule us. And you know what the non-Cossacks are saying now! They want all the land shared out so much per head. How d'ye like that?'

'We'll give land to the non-Cossacks, the ones who've been living in the Don region from way back.'

'They'll get nothing! They can whistle for it!' Pantelei made a fig with his big rough-nailed thumb and waved it round Grigory's hooked nose.

The sound of tramping feet came from the porch and the frozen steps creaked and groaned. Anikei, Khristonya and Ivan Tomilin, wearing an absurdly tall hareskin hat, marched in.

'Hullo there, soldier! Pantelei Prokofievich, what about standing us a drink, eh!' Khristonya boomed.

The calf, which had been dozing by the warm stove, at his shout moved in alarm, then scrambled up sliding and slipping on its shaky legs and staring at the newcomers with its round agate eyes, and probably from fright let loose a fine jet on the floor. Dunyashka checked its desire with a gentle slap on the back, wiped the floor and put an old pot under the animal.

'You've frightened the calf, you great bawler!' Ilyinichna exclaimed crossly.

Grigory shook hands with the Cossacks and invited them to sit down. Soon some more men from their end of the village arrived. While they were talking, the tobacco smoke grew so thick that the lamp began to flicker and the calf started coughing.

'Drat you!' Ilyinichna scolded as she turned the guests
out at midnight. 'Go out in the yard and puff away,
you chimney-pots! Go along, do! Our soldier hasn't even
had time for a rest after his journey. Off you go and God
be with you!'

XIV

The next morning Grigory awoke later than anyone
else. He was roused by a chirping of sparrows from under
the eaves and around the windows that was as loud as in
spring. A golden shower of sunbeams glowed dustily
through the chinks in the shutters. The church bells were
ringing for service. Grigory remembered that it was Sunday. There was no sign of Natalya but the featherbed
still retained the warmth of her body. Evidently it was
not long since she had risen.

'Natalya!' Grigory called.

Dunyashka entered the room.

'What is it, brother?'

'Open the windows and call Natalya. What's she doing?'

'Helping Mother with the cooking. She'll come in a
minute.'

Natalya came in, peering in the darkness.

'So you're awake?'

Her hands smelled of fresh dough. Grigory took her
in his arms and lay back, laughing as he remembered
the night.

'You overslept, eh?'

'Uh-huh! What night...' She smiled and lay her head
blushingly on Grigory's hairy chest.

Then she helped him to put a fresh bandage on his
wound, took his best trousers out of the chest and asked,
'Will you wear your tunic with the crosses on it?'

'Oh, not that one!' Grigory dismissed the idea in
alarm.

But Natalya was not to be put off.

'Do wear it! Father will be pleased. You didn't get
them for nothing, did you? Why should they be left
lying in the chest all the time?'

Grigory yielded to her pleadings. He got up, borrowed
Petro's razor, shaved and washed his face and neck.

'What about the back of your neck?' Petro asked.

'Oh, hell, I forgot!'

'Sit down and I'll do it for you.'

The cold shaving brush made his skin tingle. In the glass Grigory saw Petro stick his tongue boyishly out of the side of his mouth as he set to work with the razor.

'Your neck's got thinner, you're like an ox after ploughing,' he said with a smile.

'No one gets fat on army grub.'

Grigory put on his tunic with its cornet's shoulder straps and dense array of crosses and, when he looked in the heat-misted mirror, scarcely recognised the tall, lean Gypsy-dark officer that stared back at him.

'You look like a colonel!' Petro declared delightedly, admiring his brother without envy.

Despite himself, Grigory could not help feeling pleasantly flattered. He went into the kitchen and was greeted with Darya's admiring gaze. Dunyashka gasped aloud.

'Oh, aren't we grand!'

Ilyinichna once again gave way to tears. As she wiped them with her dirty apron she answered Dunyashka's teasing.

'You have a few like these, you little chatterer! At least I've got two sons and they've both made their way in the world!'

Natalya couldn't take her misty adoring eyes off her husband.

Grigory draped his greatcoat over his shoulders and went out on to the porch, but his wounded leg checked him at the steps. I won't manage without a stick, he thought, holding on to the rail.

They had taken the bullet out at Millerovo and a brown scab had formed over the wound, tightening the skin and preventing him from bending his leg freely.

The cat was basking on the coping round the house. There was a puddle under the porch, where the snow had melted in the sunshine. Grigory inspected the yard with pleasure and attention. The post with the cart-wheel nailed atop of it was still there by the porch. Grigory remembered that wheel from the days of his childhood. It was there for the women, so that they could put out their pots of milk on it for the night without leaving the porch, and during the day they dried the dishes and left the earthenware pots there to bake in the sun. There had also been a few changes that leapt to the eye. The door of the barn had been given a wash of yellow clay to replace the old faded paint and the shed had been thatched with rye straw that had not yet had time to turn brown;

the stack of poles seemed to have shrunk; some of them must have been used to repair the fences. A hump of bluish-grey ashes had risen over the outdoor cellar and a rooster, as black as a crow, was perched on it with one chilled foot raised and a dozen motley hens that had been left for breeding pecking about round him. The farm implements were sheltered from the winter weather under the overhang of the shed; the frames of the wagons showed up like bare ribs and the metal of the reaper blazed in the sunlight filtering through a crack in the roof. The geese were sitting on a warm bed of dung near the stables, and the tufty-headed Dutch gander squinted arrogantly at Grigory as he limped by.

Grigory completed his inspection and returned to the house.

The kitchen was filled with the sweet aroma of melting butter and baking bread. Dunyashka was washing some soused apples in a brightly patterned dish. They caught Grigory's eye at once.

'Have you got any salted watermelons?' he asked.

'Go and get him one from the cellar, Natalya!' his mother responded.

Pantelei came home from church. He broke the consecrated host into nine pieces, one for each member of the family, and handed them out at the table. They all sat down to breakfast. Petro, who had also smartened himself up and even greased his moustache, sat down beside Grigory. Darya perched herself facing them on the edge of a stool. As a shaft of sunlight fell full on her pink face, which she had been trying to whiten with a mixture of dripping and saltpetre, she screwed up her eyes and lowered the gleaming black arches of her brows discontentedly. Natalya fed the children on pumpkin pie, now and then sending a smiling glance at Grigory. Ilyinichna took her place by the stove.

As always on Sundays and feast-days, it was a big, filling meal. Cabbage-and-mutton broth was followed by noodles, then came boiled mutton and chicken, a lambs-foot jelly, fried potatoes, millet porridge with butter, stewed fruit, pancakes and baked cream, and salted watermelon. Loaded with food, Grigory rose with an effort, crossed himself drunkenly before the ikon, and lay down on the bed to get his breath back. Pantelei was still busy with his porridge; he patted it down firmly with his spoon, made a hole (known as the 'well'), filled it with amber butter, and then set to work spooning the butter-soaked porridge into his mouth. Petro, who was very fond of children, was feeding Mishatka and now and then playfully daubed the boy's cheeks and nose with soured milk.

'Don't play about, Uncle!'

'What have I done?'

'Why are you smearing me?'

'Am I?'

'I'll tell Mummy!'

'What about?'

Mishatka's sombre Melekhov eyes glittered angrily and tears of resentment quivered on his lashes; wiping his nose with his fist, he gave up trying to persuade his uncle in a nice way and cried.

'Don't smear me!.. Stupid!.. Silly fool!'

Petro roared with laughter and again served his nephew, putting one spoonful in his mouth and another on his nose.

'You're like a little boy yourself... What a way to carry on!' Ilyinichna grumbled.

Dunyashka sat down beside Grigory and told him, 'Petro's just crazy, he's always up to something. The other day he went out into the yard with Mishatka and the boy wanted to do something, so he asks, "Uncle, can I do it by the porch?" "Oh, no," says Petro. "Keep away from there." So Mishatka runs a bit further away. "Here?" "Oh no! Off you go to the barn." And from the barn he takes him to the stables, and from the stables to the threshing floor. And he kept him running about till he did it in his trousers... How Natalya scolded!'

'Let me feed myself!' Mishatka's voice rang out like a harness bell.

But Petro twitched his moustache humorously and shook his head.

'Oh no, my lad! I'm going to feed you.'

'I want to feed myself!'

'They feed themselves in the pigsty. You've seen 'em, haven't you? Granny gives them the swill.'

Grigory listened with a smile, making himself a cigarette. His father came over to him.

'I'm thinking of going over to Vyoshenskaya today.'

'What for?'

Pantelei belched heavily from the stewed fruit and stroked his beard.

'There's something I want to see the saddler about. He's been mending two of our horse-collars.'

'Will you manage it in a day?'

'Why not? I'll be back this evening.'

After a rest he harnessed their old mare, which had gone blind that year, to a flat sledge and set off. He took the meadow road and in two hours arrived in Vyoshenskaya. He called at the post-office and the general store, collected the collars, then dropped in to see an old friend and kinsman of his who lived near the new church. His hospitable host made him sit down to dinner.

'Have you been at the post-office?' he asked, pouring something into a glass.

'I have,' Pantelei replied, keeping a vigilant and wondering eye on the decanter and sniffing the air like a hound scenting its quarry.

'Did you hear anything new?'

'No, nothing new, I reckon. Why?'

'Kaledin has passed on.'

'You don't say so?!'

Pantelei turned quite green, forgot about the suspicious-looking decanter and its strange aroma, and fell back in his chair.

His host blinked grimly and went on, 'The message just came through by telegraph that he'd shot himself in Novocherkassk. And he was the only worthwhile general in the whole region. He'd got all the honours, been in command of an army. And what a heart the man had! He wouldn't have let the Cossacks down!'

'Just a minute, kinsman! What's going to happen now?' Pantelei asked confusedly, pushing his glass aside.

'God knows. There are bad times coming. A man wouldn't have put a bullet through his head, if life was good.'

'What made him do it?'

His kinsman, a tough old fellow, made an angry sweep with his hand.

'The frontline men had turned agin him and let the Bolsheviks into the region. That's why he left us. Will there ever be another like him? Who'll defend us now? In Kamenskaya there's some sort of Revcom been set up, with Cossack frontline men in it... And you've heard what they're doing here, haven't you? They've sent us an order to get rid of the atamans and elect these Revcoms. So, of course, the muzhiks are getting real uppity! All these carpenter fellers and blacksmiths, all these grabbers of one kind or another—swarms of 'em in Vyoshenskaya, like gnats over a meadow!'

Pantelei sat in silence with his grizzled head sunk on his chest, and when he raised it, his eyes were stern and unrelenting.

'What's that you've got in the decanter?'

'Just a drop o' spirits. My nephew brought it from the Caucasus.'

'Well, kinsman, let's drink to Kaledin, our late ataman. May his soul rest in the kingdom of heaven!'

They drank. The host's daughter, a tall freckled girl, brought in some snacks. At first Pantelei kept glancing through the window at the mare standing despondently in front of her master's sledge, but his kinsman reassured him.

'Don't worry about the mare. I'll tell 'em to water and feed her.'

And what with the heated discussion and the contents of the decanter Pantelei soon forgot about the horse and everything else under the sun. He rambled on about Grigory, wrangling with his tipsy host, and, though it was a long argument, he could never remember afterwads what it had been about. He came in the evening to himself and, resisting all urgings to stay the night, decided to leave at once. His host's son harnessed up the mare and his host helped him on to the sledge, then decided to ride part of the way with him. So he rolled on to the sledge and they lay in each other's arms. The sledge caught on the gate as they drove out and then caught on all the other obstacles along the road until they drove out on to the meadow. At this point the host burst into tears and quite voluntarily fell off the sledge. He pulled himself up, swearing, on to all fours, but could not get to his feet. Pantelei whipped the mare into a trot and failed to notice his host crawling in the snow, burying his nose in it, roaring happily with laughter and begging hoarsely, 'Oh, don't tickle... Don't tickle me, please!'

After several flicks of the whip the mare broke into a fast but blindly uncertain trot. Soon her master, overcome by a tipsy drowsiness, slumped sideways and fell silent. The reins slipped out of his hands and the mare, helpless and unguided, slowed to a gentle walk. At the first fork in the road she lost her way and headed for the village of Little Gromchonok. A few minutes later she lost that road too and headed off across open fields. Hindered by the deep snow on the edge of some woods, she laboured down into a dell. The sledge caught on a bush and she stopped. The jerk woke the old man for a second. He raised his head and shouted hoarsely, 'Now then, you devil!..' then lay back again.

The mare made her way round the woods, successfully negotiated the slope down to the Don and, sensing the smell of dung smoke carried by the east wind, headed towards the village of Semyonovskaya.

About half a verst from the village there was a deep hole in the left bank of the Don, where the thaw water ran off in spring. All winter the streams rising from the loamy bank kept the ice from forming properly. A warm pool spread out from the bank in a broad green arc, and the sledgeroad across the Don gave it a wide berth. In spring, when the flood waters flowed plenteously back into the Don, it became a roaring whirlpool, whose swirling currents washed away the riverbed; and all summer long the carp sheltered at a great depth among the sunken trees that had been swept into the river by the floods.

It was towards the left side of this hole that Melekhov's mare turned her blind footsteps. She had only about forty paces to go when Pantelei stirred and opened his eyes. Yellowish green stars, like unripe cherries, were looking down from the black sky. It's night-time, Pantelei thought vaguely, and tugged fiercely at the reins.

'Hi-yup! I'll give it to ye, ye old bugger!'

The mare broke into a trot. The smell of the nearby water caught her nostrils. She pricked up her ears and squinted at her master with a blind astonished eye. At the sound of the lapping waves she gave a wild snort, turned aside and tried to draw back. The ice, eaten away underneath, crumbled softly under her feet and the snowy edge broke off. The mare let out a mortally frightened snort and strained backwards with her hind legs, but the forelegs were already in the water and the mushy ice was breaking up under her milling hind feet. The ice gave way with a groan and a splash. As the pool engulfed her, the mare gave a last kick with her hind leg and touched the shaft. At that moment Pantelei noticed something wrong, jumped out of the sledge and rolled backwards. He saw the sledge drawn on by the mare's weight stand up on end with its runners glinting in the starlight and then slide into the black-green depths. Water mixed with ice closed over it in a seething wave that nearly reached him. Pantelei crawled backwards at astonishing speed and, only when he was standing firmly on his feet, did he let out a frantic shout, 'Help! Help, good people! We're drowning!..'

His tipsiness fell from him as if cut away by an axe. He ran up to the gap in the ice. The freshly broken edge was glittering. The wind and current were chasing bits of ice in a broad circle round the pool. The green waves whirled and hissed but all around there was dead silence. A few yellow sparks of light gleamed from the distant village. The stars burned and quivered in the velvet sky like freshly winnowed grain. A ground wind sprang up and swished the ice, sweeping a floury dust into the black maw of the pool. The water was giving off a light vapour, and the black depths looked as grim and inviting as ever.

It dawned on Pantelei that it was no use shouting now. He stared around, realised where he had got to in his drunken unguided journey, and began to shake with anger at himself and at what had happened. The whip that he had been holding when he jumped off the sledge was still in his hand. Swearing aloud, he lashed his back with it time and again, but it didn't hurt through the thick sheepskin coat and there seemed to be no sense in taking the coat off just for that. He tugged a handful of hair out of his beard and, having reckoned up in his head the cost of the mare, the sledge, the collars and his purchases, uttered a stream of furious curses and stepped a little closer to the ice-strewn edge of the pool.

'Ye blind devil!..' he moaned in a trembling voice, addressing the lost mare. 'Ye rotten bitch! Ye drowned yourself and wanted to drown me as well! Where was the foul fiend leading ye?! All the devils in hell will harness you up, but they won't have anything to drive you with!.. So here's the whip as well!' And with a wild swing he flung the cherry-wood whip into the middle of the pool.

It plopped into the water, stood upright for a moment, and vanished into the depths.

XV

After the mauling that the Cossack revolutionary forces had been given by Kaledin's forces, the Don Military-Revolutionary Committee, compelled to shift its headquarters to Millerovo, hastened to clarify its political stand. To Antonov-Ovseyenko, who at that time was in direct command of operations against Kaledin and the counter-revolutionary Ukrainian Parliament, the Don Revolutionary Committee despatched the following declaration:

19 January 1918. From Lugansk, No 449, 18:20 hrs. Kharkov. To Commissar Antonov.

The Cossack Military-Revolutionary Committee requests you to forward the following resolution of the Don Region to the Council of People's Commissars in Petrograd.

On the basis of the decision taken by the frontline congress in Kamenskaya the Cossack Military-Revolutionary Committee resolves:

1. To recognise the central state power of the Russian Soviet Republic, the Central Executive Committee of the Congress of Soviets of Cossacks', Peasants', Soldiers' and Workers' Deputies, and the Council of People's Commissars elected by it.

2. To set up a regional government for the Don Region on the basis of the congress of Soviets of Cossacks', Peasants' and Workers' Deputies.

Note. The land question in the Don Region shall be decided by the afore-mentioned regional congress.

> Per pro Chairman, Warrant Officer *Krivoshlykov*
>
> Secretary *Doroshev*
>
> Members: Warrant Officer *Strelyanov, Kopalei, Krivushev, Chernousov, Yeronin*

After this declaration was received, Antonov-Ovseyenko moved Red Guard detachments in to help the Revolutionary Committee's forces and it was with their support that Chernetsov's punitive detachment was defeated and the situation restored. The initiative passed to the Revolutionary Committee. After the capture of Zverevo and Likhaya, Sablin's and Petrov's Red Guard detachments, reinforced by the Revolutionary Committee's Cossack units, developed the offensive and pushed the enemy back to Novocherkassk.

On the right flank, in the Taganrog sector, Sivers was defeated at Neklinovka by Colonel Kutepov's Volunteer detachment and forced back to Amvrosievka with the loss of one heavy gun, twenty machine-guns and an armoured car. But in Taganrog on the day of Sivers's defeat and withdrawal, a rebellion broke out at the Baltic Works there. The workers drove the officer Cadets out of the city. Sivers recovered, took the offensive and forced the Volunteers towards Taganrog.

The tide of success was clearly running in favour of the Soviet forces. They were closing in from three sides on the Volunteer Army and the remnants of Kaledin's 'rag-bag' detachments. On January 28th Kornilov sent Kaledin a telegram informing him that the Volunteer Army was abandoning Rostov and withdrawing to the Kuban Region.

At nine in the morning on the 29th an emergency session of the Don Government was held in the ataman's palace. Kaledin was the last to arrive. He sat down heavily at the table and pulled some papers towards him. His cheeks were sallow from lack of sleep and dark blue shadows had appeared under his sombre faded eyes; it was as though some process of decay had yellowed his drawn face. Slowly he read the telegram from Kornilov and the reports from the commanders of the units facing the onslaught of the Red Guards to the north of Novocherkassk. After carefully smoothing down the pile of telegrams with his broad white hand he said dully, without raising his puffy, blue-tinged eyelids, 'The Volunteer Army is withdrawing. We have only one hundred and forty-seven bayonets to defend the region and Novocherkassk.'

A nervous tick took possession of his left eyelid and was joined by a spasm from one corner of his tightly compressed lips. He raised his voice and went on, 'Our position is hopeless. The local population, far from supporting us, is actually hostile. We have no forces and resistance is useless. I want no unnecessary bloodshed, no unnecessary loss of life. I propose that we resign and place authority in other hands. I resign my powers as Ataman of the Cossack Army.'

Mitrofan Bogayevsky sat staring at the wide windows, adjusted his pince-nez and, without turning his head, said, 'I also resign.'

'The whole government will resign, of course. But then the question arises—to whom do we hand over power?'

'The City Duma,' Kaledin answered curtly.

'That will have to be stated officially,' Karev, a member of the government, said hesitantly.

There was an awkward silence. The opaque light of the cloudy January morning clung to the steamed-up windows. The city lay in a drowsy silence under its veil of mist and frost. None of the ordinary pulsations of city life were to be heard. The rumble of gunfire (echoes of the fighting near the station of Sulin) paralysed all movement and hung over the city like a muttered threat.

The crows flying back and forth outside uttered their

647

curt clear cries. They circled over the white bell-tower as over a piece of carrion. The snow on the Cathedral Square was lilac fresh, marked only by the footprints of an occasional pedestrian or the dark threads left by a passing sledge.

Bogayevsky broke the frigid silence by proposing that they should draft an official statement transferring power to the City Duma.

'We ought to hold a joint meeting for the actual transference of power.'

'What time would be best?'

'Later on, about four o'clock.'

As though overjoyed that the fettering silence had been broken, the members of the government began to discuss how and when power should be handed over. Kaledin sat quietly tapping the table with his convex fingernails. His eyes had the dull, opaque gleam of mica. Utter weariness, revulsion and overstrain made his glance heavy and repellent.

A member of the government got into a long and tedious argument with a colleague. Kaledin interrupted him with quiet fury.

'Gentlemen, less talk! Time won't wait! It's all this chatter that has ruined Russia. I propose a recess of half an hour. Discuss what you want to discuss and then— we must have done with this.'

He withdrew to his own quarters. The members of the government broke up into groups and talked quietly. Someone said that Kaledin was not looking well. Bogayevsky, who was standing at the window, heard the half-whispered remark, 'For a man like Alexei Maximovich suicide is the only possible way out.'

Bogayevsky gave a start and strode quickly to Kaledin's quarters. Soon he returned with the ataman.

It was decided that they should meet with the City Duma at four o'clock for the official act of relinquishing power. Kaledin rose. The others rose with him. As he said goodbye to one of the older members of the government, Kaledin kept his eye on Yanov, who was whispering something to Karev.

'What is it?' he asked.

Yanov came up to him, rather embarrassed.

'The non-Cossack members of the government would like to be paid their travelling allowance.'

Kaledin frowned.

'I have no money... This is intolerable!' he snapped.

They began to disperse. Bogayevsky, who had over-heard this exchange, called Yanov aside.

'Come up to my room. Tell Svetozarov to wait in the hall.'

They followed Kaledin as he hurried out, shoulders sagging. In his own room Bogayevsky handed Yanov a wad of banknotes.

'Here's fourteen thousand. Give it out.'

Svetozarov, who had been waiting for Yanov in the hall, accepted the money, thanked him and walked towards the door. As Yanov was taking his coat from the doorman he heard a noise on the staircase and looked round. Kaledin's aide-de-camp Moldavsky was bounding down the stairs two at a time.

'Get a doctor! Hurry!!'

Yanov threw down his coat and ran up to him. The duty adjutant and the orderlies in the hall gathered round Moldavsky.

'What's happened?' Yanov shouted, turning pale.

'Alexei Maximovich has shot himself!' Moldavsky flung himself on to the banisters and sobbed.

Bogayevsky appeared. His lips were trembling as if from intense cold. He could only stammer.

'What is it? What?'

They ran up the stairs in a bunch, racing each other. The noise of their running feet made a resonant clatter. Bogayevsky ran with his mouth open, gasping for air. He was the first to reach the door. He flung it open and pushed through the anteroom into the office. The door from the office into a smaller room beyond was wide open. From it there came a faint bluish wisp of acrid-smelling gunsmoke.

'Oh-oh-oh! Alyosha!.. Dearest...' Kaledin's wife was crying out in a choked unrecognisable voice.

Bogayevsky tore at the collar of his shirt as if suffocated and ran into the room. Karev was standing hunched at the window, gripping the tarnished gilt handle. Under his frockcoat his shoulder blades were heaving violently; long slow shudders shook his body. The muffled animal-like howling of a grown man nearly destroyed Bogayevsky altogether.

Kaledin was lying on an officer's camp-bed, legs out-stretched, arms folded on his chest. His head was turned slightly sideways to the wall; the white pillow-case framed the damp bluish forehead and the cheek pressed into it. The eyes were sleepily half-closed, the corners of the stern mouth twisted as if in suffering. His wife was writhing at his feet in a paroxysm of grief. Her crazed, choking cries were cuttingly sharp. On the bed lay a Colt revolver. A thin merry stream of blackish-red blood was running down the shirt.

A high-necked tunic was hanging neatly over the back of a chair and a wrist-watch lay on the bed-table.

Bogayevsky swayed, dropped to his knees and pressed his ear to the warm, soft chest. It had the strong vinegary smell of male sweat. Kaledin's heart had stopped. Bogayevsky listened desperately—his hearing was his life at that moment—but he could hear only the steady ticking of the watch on the table, the choking voice of the dead ataman's wife, and through the window, the strident foreboding cry of the crows.

XVI

Anna's dark eyes glistening with tears and smiling were the first thing Bunchuk saw when he opened his eyes.

He had been in a state of delirium for three weeks. For three weeks he had wandered in another, intangible and fantastic world. He recovered consciousness in the evening of December 24th. For a long time he stared at Anna with grave misted eyes, trying to recall everything that was associated with her. He succeeded only in part; his memory was stiff and unyielding and still kept much hidden in its depths.

'Water...' his own voice reached him again, as it had done before, from afar, and it sounded so odd that Bunchuk smiled.

Anna darted up to him, all aglow with the smile she had tried to hold in check.

'Drink from my hand.' She gently pushed away the limp hand that Bunchuk held out for the mug.

Trembling with the effort of raising his head, he drank and fell back wearily on the pillow. His eyes wandered sideways and he tried to say something, but was too weak and dozed off.

And again, just as when he had first awoken, he saw Anna's anxious eyes fixed upon him, then the saffron glow of the lamp, and the white circle that it cast on the bare boards of the ceiling.

'Come to me, Anna.'

She came up and took his hand. He responded with a slight pressure.

'How are you feeling?'

'My tongue doesn't belong to me, nor does my head, nor my legs, and the rest feels about two hundred years old,' he said, uttering each word carefully. And after a slight pause he asked, 'Is it typhus?'

'Yes.'

His eyes roamed round the room and he said faintly, 'Where are we?'

She understood the question and smiled.

'In Tsaritsyn.'

'But you... How is it you are here?'

'I stayed with you.' And as though to justify herself or to evade his unspoken thought, she hastened to add, 'You couldn't be left with strangers. Abramson and the comrades from the bureau asked me to look after you... So, you see, I quite unexpectedly had to take care of you.'

He thanked her with a glance and a weak movement of his hand.

'Krutogorov?'

'He's gone off to Lugansk through Voronezh.'

'Gevorkyants?'

'He ... he died of typhus.'

'Oh!..'

They fell silent, as though in homage to the dead man.

'I was afraid for you. You were very ill,' she said softly.

'What about Bogovoy?'

'I've lost touch with all of them. Some went off to Kamenskaya. But isn't it bad for you to talk? Wouldn't you like some milk?'

Bunchuk shook his head; in the same tongue-tied fashion he went on with his questions.

'Abramson?'

'He left for Voronezh a week ago.'

A careless movement made his head swim and blood rushed painfully to his eyes. Feeling her cool hand on his forehead, he opened his eyes again. There was one question that tormented him. While he had been unconscious, who had kept him clean? Anna? A faint flush coloured his cheeks.

He asked, 'Did you look after me all by yourself?'

'Yes.'

He turned away to the wall and whispered, 'They ought to be ashamed—the scoundrels! Leaving me on your hands.'

The typhus had affected his hearing, making him

slightly deaf. The doctor sent by the Tsaritsyn Party Committee told Anna that treatment could begin only after the patient had fully recovered. Bunchuk was slow in returning to health. His appetite was enormous, but Anna kept strictly to the prescribed diet and on this point they often quarrelled.

'Give me some more milk,' Bunchuk would ask.

'You mustn't have any more.'

'Please, give me some more! Are you trying to starve me?'

'Ilya, you know I'm not allowed to overfeed you.'

He would lapse into an injured silence, turn away, sighing resentfully, and refused to talk. Though tortured by pity, she would not give in. After a while he would turn over and with a sullen expression that made him all the more pitiable beg imploringly, 'Can't I have some salted cabbage? Please, Anna dear! Just to please me... How can it be bad for me? That's all doctors' tales!'

Faced with her blunt refusals, he would sometimes insult her.

'You have no right to ill-treat me like this! I'll call the landlady and ask her myself! You're a disgusting heartless woman!.. I'm beginning to hate you. Yes, hate you!'

'So that's my reward for all I've been through nursing you,' Anna could not help retorting.

'I didn't ask you to stay with me! It's not fair to reproach me with that! You're taking advantage of me. Still, never mind... Don't give me anything! Let me starve to death... It'll be no great loss!'

Her lips trembled but she said nothing, bearing it all patiently for his sake.

Only once, after a particularly sharp exchange, when she had refused him another helping of pies, did her resolution fail. Bunchuk turned away and her heart contracted as she noticed a gleam of tears in his eyes.

'But you're just a child!' she exclaimed.

She ran to the kitchen and came back with a plate full of pies.

'Here, eat as much as you like, Ilyusha, dear! Don't be cross! Here's a nice crisp one!' and with trembling hands she offered him a pie.

Torn between hunger and shame, Bunchuk tried to refuse, then gave in; wiping his tears, he sat up and took the pie. A guilty smile crept over his gaunt face, now almost covered in a soft curly beard, and his eyes begged forgiveness.

'I'm worse than a child... Didn't you see—I nearly cried.'

She looked at his strangely thin neck, at the sunken fleshless chest showing through the open collar of his shirt, at his bony hands and, moved by a love and pity deeper than she had ever experienced before, put her lips to his yellow forehead in a kiss of simple affection.

It was two weeks before he could move about the room without help. At first his withered legs gave way under him and he had to learn to walk again.

'Look, Anna, I'm walking!' he would cry as he tried to take a few quick strides on his own, but the weight of his body was too much for him and the floor slid from under his feet.

He would cling to the first support that came to hand, grinning like an old man, the skin on his transparent cheeks creased and taut. Laughter, cracked and senile, would break from his lips and, exhausted by the effort, he would fall helplessly on to the bed.

Their lodgings were not far from the wharves. From their window they could see the vast snowy expanse of the Volga, the grey arc of the forest beyond, and the soft wavy outlines of distant fields. Anna would spend long hours at the window, thinking about the fantastic change that had come over her life. Bunchuk's illness had strangely drawn them together.

But even before this, in Rostov, after their first meetings she had realised with an inward shiver that she was firmly, forever attached to him. And in what an untimely, ominous year, in the nineteenth spring of such a short young life, had her feeling for Bunchuk awakened. Plain and outwardly unattractive though he was, her heart had chosen him and the fighting had tightened the bond; and now she had snatched him from death, nursed him back to health...

When they first arrived in Tsaritsyn after a long and arduous journey, the misery and disappointment of it all had driven her to tears. It was her first glimpse of the crude side of living with the man she loved. She gritted her teeth as she changed his linen, combed the lice out of his fevered head, turned over the heavy inert body and, trembling with revulsion, glanced furtively at the gaunt masculine body, at the envelope in which that precious life barely flickered. Everything reared up and rebelled within her, but she did not allow the outward filth to stain her closely guarded inner feeling. Under its imperative command she learned to fight down pain and repugnance. And when she had won, there was only compassion and love that welled up from the very depths.

One day Bunchuk said to her, 'You must find me repulsive after all this, don't you?'

'It was a test.'

'What of? Endurance?'

'No, my feeling for you.'

Bunchuk turned away and for a long time could not control his tremling lips. They spoke no more of that subject. Words would have been superfluous.

After Bunchuk's recovery their friendly relationship was not marred by a single quarrel. He seemed to be trying to make up for everything she had gone through for his sake. He was exceptionally attentive, anticipated her every wish, but he was not importunate; he did it all with the gentleness that was buried deep in his nature, and she appreciated that. His eyes, when he looked at her, were still hard, yet different—humbled and infinitely devoted.

In the middle of January they left Tsaritsyn for Voronezh. As she watched the city receding into the distance, Anna rested her hand on Bunchuk's shoulder and said, as if to complete what had passed between them before, 'We came together in extraordinary circumstances... Perhaps it shouldn't have happened... That's my mind speaking, of course, not my heart. And d'you know why I say it shouldn't? Look...' She pointed at the snow-covered steppe encircling the railway like a gigantic silver ruble. 'Out there everything is seething. We've got to make the biggest effort we can, but emotion, it seems to me, weakens resolve. We ought to have met either before or later.'

'No, I don't agree!' Bunchuk smiled and held her close. 'You and I will be one person and, far from weakening our resolve, it will strengthen it. Look: it's easy to break on twig, but it's more difficult if two are woven together.'

'That's not a very good example, Ilya.'

'It'll do ... but talking like this won't get us anywhere.'

'Yes, and besides I'm not really so sorry that we...' she broke off in confusion, '...are together, or at least half way towards it. After all, the personal side can't stifle our will to fight...'

'...and win, damn it!' Bunchuk added, squeezing her small, militantly clenched fist in his hand.

The fact that they had still not been physically intimate

endowed their relationship with an adolescent, exalted tenderness. They were not burdened by the desire to cross the final boundary of intimacy. In her own way Anna rejoiced in this and, thinking of it, she asked, 'Our relationship is not a bit like the usual kind, is it? Our landlady in Tsaritsyn, and everyone else, took us to be man and wife, didn't they? Apart from anything else, it's good in that it goes beyond the set middle-class notion of things. In battle we've grown to love each other and managed to keep our feeling unsullied by anything low or bestial...'

'Romanticism!' Bunchuk said with a half smile.

'What did you say?' she asked.

Bunchuk stroked her head without replying.

Anna stared misty-eyed at the snowy expanse, at the faint outlines of villages floating past in the distance, at the violet ridges of woodland and the fissures of the ravines. She began to speak hurriedly; the deep cello-like timbre of her voice was soft and musical.

'And besides, how vile and pitiful any thought of building one's own individual little happiness seems at a time like this. What would it amount to compared with the boundless human happiness that suffering humanity is achieving by revolution? Isn't that true? You've got to dissolve, melt into that effort for liberation, you've got to ... to merge with the collectivity and forget about yourself as something individual and apart.' Quietly, like a child in its sleep, she smiled with the corners of her brave tender mouth; the smile left a shadow hovering on the upper lip. 'You know, Ilya, I think of life in the future as a very distant, beautiful music. Like something you sometimes hear in a dream... Do you ever hear music in dreams? It's not just one fine thread of melody, but a mighty, coordinated anthem, with growing harmonies. Everyone loves beauty. I love it in all, even its smallest manifestations... And won't life be beautiful when there's socialism? No wars, no poverty, no oppression, no national barriers! What an awful mess people have made on earth... How much human grief has been caused!..' She turned swiftly to Bunchuk and felt for his hands. 'Tell me now: wouldn't it be sweet to die for that? Tell me! Wouldn't it? What else would one believe in if not that? What is there to live for?.. I think that if I die in battle...' She pressed Bunchuk's hand to her chest, so that he felt the muffled beating of her heart, and, looking up at him with a dark, intense gaze, whispered, 'And if death is not instantaneous, the last thing I shall hear will be that triumphant, staggeringly beautiful anthem of the future.'

Bunchuk listened with his head bowed. He had been fired by her young, passionate fervour and, through the steady rumble of the wheels, the creaking of the carriage, and the hum of the rails, he fancied he could hear a faint but powerful melody. With a thrill of excitement sending shivers up his spine, he walked to the outer door and kicked it open. A whistling wind, steam, fine prickly snow dust and the ceaseless roar of the engine burst into the corridor.

XVII

Bunchuk and Anna arrived in Voronezh on January 16th, in the evening. They spent two days there and, on learning that the Don Military-Revolutionary Committee and the units loyal to it had moved to Millerovo after being forced out of Kamenskaya by Kaledin's forces, they left for Millerovo.

The town was packed and nervous. Bunchuk stayed only a few hours there and left by the next train for Glubokaya. The following day he took over a machine-gun platoon and the next morning was in action against Chernetsov's detachment.

After Chernetsov's defeat, Anna and Bunchuk unexpectedly had to part. Anna arrived from headquarters in the morning, looking excited and rather sad.

'Abramson's here. He wants to see you. And there's another piece of news—I'm going away.'

'Where to?' Bunchuk asked in surprise.

'Abramson, myself and some of the other comrades are going to Lugansk to agitate there.'

'So you're deserting the detachment?' Bunchuk said rather coldly.

She laughed and pressed her flushed face to his.

'Confess that you're sorry not because I'm deserting the detachment but because I'm deserting you? But it's only for a time. I'm sure I'll be more use where I'm being sent than as your assistant. Agitation is more in my line than machine-guns...' she threw him a laughing glance, 'even though I was trained by such an experienced commander as Bunchuk.'

Abramson soon arrived. He was as active and energetic

as ever, with the same gleaming white patch in his beetle-black hair. He was sincerely glad to see Bunchuk.

'Back on your feet again? Fine! We're taking Anna along with us.' He gave a knowing wink. 'You don't object, do you? No objections, eh? Well, very good! The reason I ask that question is because you probably got chummy in Tsaritsyn.'

'I don't deny I'll be sorry to part with her,' Bunchuk said with a gloomy smile.

'Sorry?! Well, that's something... Anna, did you hear that?!' He paced about the room, dug out a dusty volume of Garin-Mikhailovsky from behind the chest, then was suddenly in a hurry to go.

'How much longer will you be, Anna?'

'Go on ahead. I'll catch you up,' she called from behind the partition.

She came out after changing her underclothes. She was wearing an army tunic with a leather belt and pockets that bulged slightly over her breasts, and the same black skirt, darned in places but immaculately clean. Her recently washed hair fluffed out of the heavy knot. She put on her greatcoat and, as she buckled the belt, asked (her recent liveliness had disappeared and her voice was dull and beseeching), 'Will you be taking part in the attack today?'

'Of course, I will! You don't expect me to sit twiddling my thumbs, do you?'

'Please, be careful! For my sake! You will be, won't you? I'm leaving you an extra pair of woollen socks. Don't catch cold and try not to get your feet wet. I'll write to you from Lugansk.'

Her eyes seemed to have faded all of a sudden; as they said goodbye, she confessed, 'See how it hurts me to leave you. At first, when Abramson suggested going to Lugansk, I was keen, but now I feel it will be so empty there without you. It only goes to show that there's no room for feelings these days; they tie you. Well, anyway, goodbye!'

It was a cool farewell but Bunchuk took it as it was meant: she was afraid of whittling down her resolve.

He went out to see her off. Anna walked away, holding herself unnaturally straight and not looking back. He wanted to call out to her but when they parted he had noticed the moist intensity in her sidelong, misty glance; mastering himself, he shouted with affected cheerfulness.

'Hope to see you in Rostov! Good luck, Anna!'

She looked round, then quickened her pace.

When she had left, Bunchuk felt the sudden crushing grip of loneliness. He went back into the room but dashed out of it like a man scorched by flames. Every object that had been in her hands—the forgotten handkerchief, the field bag, the copper mug—reminded him of her presence, retained her smell.

He wandered about till evening, disturbed as never before, feeling as if he had lost a limb and could not get used to his new condition. He stared vaguely at the faces of the Red Army men and Cossacks he passed, recognising some and being recognised by many.

Eventually he was stopped by a Cossack who had served with him in the German war. The man dragged him off to his lodgings to play cards. The Red Guards from Petrov's detachment and some recently arrived sailors led by Mokrousov were hard at it in a game of pontoon. Swathed in clouds of tobacco smoke, they slapped their cards on the table and rustled their Kerensky notes, shouting and swearing without restraint. Bunchuk felt a longing for fresh air and left as soon as he could.

He had the good excuse that within an hour he was to take part in an attack.

XVIII

After Kaledin's death Novocherkassk stanitsa handed over power to the Campaign Ataman General Nazarov. On January 29th he was elected Vice Ataman of the Don Cossack Army by delegates of the Army Council. Only a handful of delegates were present, most of them from the southern districts, bordering on the Lower Don. The Council became known as the Little Council, and with its support Nazarov announced that all Cossacks from the age of 18 to 50 were to be mobilised. But the Cossacks were slow to take up arms, despite threats and the despatch of armed detachments to the stanitsas to see that mobilisation was carried out.

The day the Little Council began its work, General Krasnoshchokov's 6th Don Cossack Regiment, commanded by Colonel Tatsin, marched into Novocherkassk from the Romanian front. All the way from Yekaterinoslav it had been fighting the encircling Bolshevik forces. Although hard pressed at Pyatikhatka, Matveyev-Kurgan and many other places, it arrived almost at full strength, with all its officers.

The regiment was given a heroes' welcome. After a thanksgiving service in the Cathedral Square, Nazarov expressed his gratitude to the Cossacks for maintaining discipline and appearing in such fine order, fully armed and ready to defend the Don.

Soon afterwards the regiment was sent to the frontline near Sulin, and two days later the grim news reached Novocherkassk that under the influence of Bolshevik agitators the regiment had abandoned its positions and refused to defend the Don Army Government.

The Council made little progress in its work. Everyone felt that the outcome of the struggle with the Bolsheviks was a foregone conclusion. During sessions Nazarov, such an energetic and enthusiastic general, sat with his hand to his brow, as though lost in painful meditation.

The last hopes were crumbling like rotten wood. The Bolshevik noose was tightening round the neck of the region. The rumble of gunfire could be heard at Tikhoretskaya. There were rumours that Red troops under Cornet Avtonomov, the local Bolshevik commander, were marching on Rostov from Tsaritsyn.

Lenin had ordered the Southern Front to take Rostov by 23rd February.*

On the morning of the 22nd Major Chernov's detachment, hard pressed by Sivers and with its rearguard under fire from the Cossacks of Gnilovskaya stanitsa, withdrew into Rostov.

Only a narrow escape route was left and Kornilov, realising that it was not safe to stay in Rostov, ordered his forces to withdraw to the stanitsa of Olginskaya. All day the workers in the Temernik district sniped at the station and the officers' patrols. Towards evening a dense column of Kornilov troops set out from Rostov. It stretched its length across the Don like a fat black adder, twisting and crawling in the direction of Aksai. The depleted companies pounded heavily over the soggy snow. An occasional gymnasium greatcoat with light-coloured buttons or the greenish coat of a modern-school student was to be seen among them, but most of the column wore officers' and soldiers' greatcoats. The platoons were commanded by colonels and majors and manned by cadets and officers, ranking from ensign to

---

*Dates in New Style from here on. —*Ed.*

colonel. Behind the long baggage train came a straggling crowd of refugees—elderly respectable folk in city overcoats and galoshes. The women struggled along beside the wagons, sinking into the deep snow and wobbling on their high heels.

In one of the companies of Kornilov's regiment marched Major Yevgeny Listnitsky. His nearest companions were Major Starobelsky, a smart-looking officer of the line, Lieutenant Bochagov of the Suvorov Grenadiers, and Lieutenant-Colonel Lovichev, an aged and toothless field commander, bristling all over with grizzled reddish hair, like an old fox.

Dusk was falling and it was getting frosty. A damp salty wind was blowing from the mouth of the Don. Listnitsky tramped along through the mush of snow with his usual firm tread, peering closely at anyone who overtook the company. Major Nezhentsev, the regimental commander, and Colonel Kutepov, formerly commander of the Preobrazhensky Guards Regiment, strode past along the side of the road. Kutepov had unbuttoned his coat and pushed his cap on to the back of his head.

'Commander!' Lieutenant-Colonel Lovichev called out to Nezhentsev, deftly changing his grip on his rifle.

Kutepov turned his big bull-like face with its widely set eyes and square clipped beard; and Nezhentsev glanced over his shoulder in response to the shout.

'Order the first company to march faster! We'll soon be frozen stiff at this pace. Our feet are wet already.'

'Disgraceful!' the noisy, loud-voiced Starobelsky trumpeted.

Nezhentsev walked on without answering. He had been arguing with Kutepov about something. A little later the company was overtaken by General Alexeyev. The coachman was driving the sleek black horses hard and snow was flying in all directions from under their hooves. Alexeyev with a bristling white moustache and white eyebrows, his face red from the wind, had pulled his army cap right down over his ears and was leaning back sideways in the light carriage, holding the collar of his coat up with his left hand. The sight of his familiar face roused smiles among the officers.

Yellow puddles appeared on the churned-up road. It was heavy going. Feet slithered and the damp penetrated even the strongest boots. As he tramped along, Listnitsky listened to the talk ahead of him. An officer with a deep baritone, wearing a fur jacket and an ordinary Cossack sheepskin hat, was saying, 'Did you see that, Lieutenant? Rodzyanko, the Chairman of the State Duma, an old man, and he has to walk!'

'Russia is going to her Golgotha.'

Someone coughed and spat phlegm, then tried to make an ironic remark.

'Yes, Golgotha it is, except that the stony road is snowy and wet and perishingly cold.'

'Does anyone know where we are going to spend the night, gentlemen?'

'In Yekaterinodar.'

'We were on a march like this once in Prussia...'

'How will the Kuban greet us, I wonder?.. What?.. Of course, it'll be different there.'

'Have you anything to smoke?' Lieutenant Golovachov asked Listnitsky.

He pulled off a rough mitten, took a cigarette, thanked Listnitsky, then blew his nose soldier-fashion and wiped his fingers on his greatcoat.

'Acquiring democratic manners, are you, Lieutenant?' Lieutenant-Colonel Lovichev asked with a thin smile.

'What else can one do? Or have you a dozen handkerchiefs in reserve?'

Lovichev made no reply. Small greenish icicles were hanging from his reddish grizzled moustache. From time to time he snuffled and frowned as the cold penetrated his unlined greatcoat.

'The flower of Russia,' Listnitsky reflected with a sharp sense of pity as he watched the column straggling along the road.

Several horsemen galloped past. One of them was Kornilov, riding a tall Don stallion. His light-green half-length coat with slanting pockets and his tall white lambswool busby stood out above the marching ranks of the column for a long time, and the officers' battalions sent a long echoing cheer in his wake.

'I could bear it all if it wasn't for my family...' Lovichev gave an old man's cough and looked sideways at Listnitsky, as though seeking sympathy. 'My family is stranded in Smolensk...' he went on. 'My wife and my daughter, still only a girl. Seventeen last Christmas... How about that, Major?'

'Indeed...'

'Are you a family man too? From Novocherkassk?'

'No, I'm from Donets District. My father is still there.'

'I have no idea what's happening to them... How

661

can they manage without me,' Lovichev continued.

He was irritably interrupted by Starobelsky.

'We all have families who've been left behind. I don't know why you're making such a fuss, Colonel? Some people—really! Here we are, scarcely out of Rostov and...'

'Starobelsky! Pyotr Petrovich! Weren't you in action near Taganrog?' someone shouted to him from a few ranks back.

Starobelsky turned and his irritated face broke into a gloomy smile.

'Ah, Vladimir Georgievich, how did you get into our platoon? Got a transfer? Did you fall out with someone? Uh-huh, I see... You asked about Taganrog? Yes, I was there—what about it? Quite true—he was killed.'

As he listened half-heartedly to the conversation, Listnitsky recalled his departure from Yagodnoye, his father, Aksinya. A sudden surge of longing came near to choking him. He plodded on, staring at the swaying rifle barrels with their fixed bayonets, at the heads in tall sheepskin hats, peaked caps and cowls, bobbing up and down in the rhythm of the march, and thought, 'Every one of these five thousand ostracised individuals is charged with the same hatred and boundless fury as I am. We've been thrown out of Russia by these swine, and they think they'll trample on us here. But we'll see. Kornilov will yet lead us to Moscow!'

At that moment he recalled Kornilov's arrival in Moscow and gladly gave himself up to memories of that day.

A battery was bringing up the rear of the company. He heard the snorting of the horses, the clank of the gun carriages, and even caught the smell of horse sweat. Recognising its exciting tang at once, he turned his head; the driver of the leading team, a young ensign, was looking at him and smiling as if at an old acquaintance.

* * *

By March 11th the Volunteer Army was concentrated in the area of Olginskaya. Kornilov had called a halt to await the arrival of General Popov, the Campaign Ataman of the Don Cossack Army, who had had marched out of Novocherkassk into the Don steppes with a force of 1,600 sabres, 5 artillery pieces and 40 machine-guns.

On the morning of the 13th, Popov rode into Olginskaya, accompanied by his chief of staff Colonel Sidorin and a bodyguard of Cossack officers.

He reined in his horse outside the house taken over by Kornilov and holding on to the pommel, lifted his leg heavily over the saddle. His orderly, a young Cossack with a black forelock, swarthy face and the beady eyes of a lapwing, ran forward to help him. Popov threw him the reins and strode in a dignified manner towards the porch. Sidorin and the other officers dismounted and followed him. The orderlies led the horses through the gate into the yard. While one of them, an elderly stiff-legged Cossack, was putting on the nose-bags, the other, the one with the black forelock and lapwing's eyes, struck up an acquaintance with the kitchen maid. In response to his jest the maid, a rosy-cheeked wench in a coquettishly tied kerchief and galoshes that she was wearing on her bare feet, laughed and ran past him, sliding and splashing through a puddle, into the shed.

The dignified, elderly Popov entered the house. In the hall he gave his coat to the orderly who promptly appeared, hung his whip on the hat-rack, and blew his nose loudly and at great length. The orderly escorted him and Sidorin, who was smoothing down his hair, to the drawing-room.

The generals summoned to the conference had all assembled. Kornilov was sitting at the table with his elbows on a map spread out before him; on his right hand sat the white-haired Alexeyev, trim, erect and freshly shaven. Denikin, his prickly clever eyes glittering, was saying something to Romanovsky. Lukomsky, who bore a faint resemblance to Denikin, was pacing slowly about the room, plucking at his short beard. Markov was standing by the window, watching the Cossack orderlies attending to the horses and joking with the kitchen maid.

The newcomers greeted the assembled generals and went up to the table. Alexeyev asked a few unimportant questions about their journey and the evacuation of Novocherkassk. Kutepov and several other line officers whom Kornilov had invited to the conference came in.

Kornilov stared hard at Popov, who had taken his seat with calm assurance, and asked, 'Tell me, General, what is the strength of your detachment?'

'Fifteen hundred sabres, a battery, forty machine-guns and their crews.'

'You are aware of the circumstances that compelled the Volunteer Army to withdraw from Rostov. Yesterday we held a council of war. The decision was taken to

663

march to the Kuban in the direction of Yekaterinodar, where Volunteer detachments are already in action. We shall take the following route...' Kornilov drew an unsharpened pencil across the map and spoke more hurriedly. 'On the way we shall recruit the Kuban Cossacks and break up the small unorganised and inefficient Red Guard detachments that try to impede our progress.' He caught Popov's frowning averted glance and concluded, 'We invite you to attach your force to the Volunteer Army and march with us to Yekaterinodar. It is not in our interests to dissipate our forces.'

'I can't do that!' Popov announced bluntly and decisively. Alexeyev leaned slightly towards him.

'Why not, if I may ask?'

'Because I can't leave the territory of the Don Region and go marching off to the Kuban. With the Don to cover us in the north we can bide our time in the stud-farm district. The thaw will be here any day now and there's little likelihood of the enemy engaging in active operations against us. It'll be impossible to bring artillery or even cavalry across the Don. From the stud-farm district, which is extremely well provided with fodder and grain, we shall be able to develop partisan warfare in any direction we choose.'

With a weighty assurance Popov advanced arguments that disposed of Kornilov's proposals. He paused for a moment to take breath and, seeing that Kornilov wished to say something, stubbornly shook his head.

'No, kindly allow me to finish... Apart from this, there is one extremely important factor and we who are in command must take it into account. That factor is the mood of our Cossacks.' He held out a fleshy white hand with a gold ring grooved into the forefinger, and went on, raising his voice a little and surveying all present. 'If we were to turn towards the Kuban there would be the danger of the detachment's falling apart. The Cossacks may refuse to go with us. We must not forget that the hard core of my detachment is made up of Cossacks and they are not so reliable morally as—well, let us say, your units. They have no breadth of view. They'll refuse to go and that's all there is to it. And I can't risk losing the whole detachment,' he concluded sharply, and again would not allow Kornilov to interrupt. 'Forgive me, I have told you our decision and I assure you that we are quite unable to change it. It is not in our interests, of course, to scatter our forces, but there is one way out of the situation. I believe that on the basis of the ideas I have put forward it would be wiser for the Volunteer Army to march not to the Kuban—I am rather worried about the mood of the Kuban Cossacks at present—but to join the Don detachment and head for the Don-side steppes. There it will have a respite and time to recover its strength, and in spring it will be reinforced with fresh volunteers from Russia...'

'No!' Kornilov exclaimed, although he himself had only the day before favoured a turn towards the steppes of the Don and had stubbornly contested the opposite view held by Alexeyev. 'There would be no point in our heading for the stud-farm district. There are about six thousand of us.'

'If it's a matter of food supplies, I can assure you, Your Excellency, you could wish for nothing better than the stud-farm district. And there you will be able to get horses from the private stud owners and remount part of your army. You will have a fresh chance of conducting a war of manoeuvre in open country. You must have cavalry and the Volunteer Army is not very well off in that respect.'

Kornilov looked at Alexeyev, to whom he had been particularly deferential that day. Probably he was in doubt about the choice of direction and was seeking support in the other man's authority. Alexeyev was listened to with great attention. Accustomed to making clear-cut decisions, the old general expressed himself briefly in favour of marching to the Kuban and Yekaterinodar.

'That direction gives us the best chance of breaking through the Bolshevik encirclement and linking up with the detachment operating near Yekaterinodar,' he concluded.

'But suppose that proves impossible?' Lukomsky asked cautiously.

Alexeyev munched his lips and drew his hand across the map.

'Even in the event of failure, we shall still have the possibility of reaching the Caucasian Mountains and disbanding the army.'

He was supported by Romanovsky, and Markov added a few impulsive remarks. There seemed to be nothing to oppose to Alexeyev's weighty arguments, but Lukomsky spoke and restored the balance.

'I support General Popov's proposal,' he said, choosing

his words carefully. 'The march to the Kuban will entail great difficulties that cannot be assessed now. Above all, we shall have to cross two railways...'

All eyes followed the course of his finger across the map. Lukomsky continued forcefully, 'The Bolsheviks will not fail to give us a proper welcome. They will bring up armoured trains. We have heavy baggage and lots of wounded that we can't leave behind. All this will overburden the army and slow down its progress. And another thing I don't understand is what makes us so sure that the Kuban Cossacks are friendly towards us? If the Don Cossacks, who were supposed to be feeling oppressed by the Bolshevik authorities, are anything to go by, we should be extremely cautious about such rumours and treat them with a big dose of healthy scepticism. The Cossacks of the Kuban are infected with the same Bolshevik trachoma from the former Russian army... They may be hostile to us. In conclusion, I must repeat my view that we should march to the east, into the steppes, and threaten the Bolsheviks from there, when we have built up our forces.'

Supported by the majority of his generals, Kornilov decided to take a route slightly to the west of Velikoknyazheskaya, replenish his non-combatant units with any horses he could collect on the way, and then turn towards the Kuban. He closed the conference, exchanged a few words with Popov and with a cold goodbye retired to his own room, accompanied by Alexeyev.

Sidorin, the chief of staff of the Don detachment, walked out on to the porch with his spurs clanking and shouted lustily for the horses.

A young Cossack lieutenant with a fair moustache picked his way among the puddles, steadying his sword, halted by the porch, and asked in a whisper, 'How was it, Colonel?'

'Not bad!' Sidorin replied with quiet elation in his voice. 'Our man refused to go to the Kuban. We're leaving now. Ready, Izvarin?'

'Yes, they're bringing the horses.'

The orderlies rode out leading the other mounts. The one with the black forelock and lapwing's eyes was winking to his companion.

'Nice bit of stuff, eh?' he asked with a chuckle.

The older one checked a grin.

'Nice as a mangy horse.'

'D'you think she'd be willing?'

'Drop it, you fool! We're in the middle of Lent.'

Izvarin, who had once served with Grigory Melekhov, sprang on to his ungainly, white-muzzled horse and shouted to the orderlies, 'Ride out into the street!'

Popov and Sidorin walked down from the porch, saying goodbye to someone from Kornilov's staff. One of the orderlies held the horse and helped the general's foot to find the stirrup. Popov, waving a homely Cossack lash, whipped his mount into a smart trot. The orderlies, Sidorin and the other officers trotted after him, rising slightly in their stirrups and leaning forward.

After two days' march the Volunteer Army reached Mechetinskaya, and there Kornilov received fresh information about the stud-farm district. The information was negative. Kornilov assembled the commanders of his fighting units and told them of his decision to march to the Kuban.

An officer was dispatched to Popov with a second invitation to join up with the Volunteers. The officer delivered the message and caught up with the army in the area of Staro-Ivanovskoye. Popov's reply was the same—a polite and cold refusal. He wrote that his decision could not be changed and that for the time being he would remain in the Sal district.

XIX

Bunchuk was with Golubov's detachment when it began a wide encircling movement to capture Novocherkassk. On February 23rd they left Shakhtnaya, passed through the stanitsa of Razdorskaya and by nightfall were in Melikhovskaya, which they left at dawn on the following day.

Golubov forced the pace. His stocky figure showed up constantly at the head of the column with his whip falling impatiently on the horse's crupper. That night they passed through Bessergenevskaya, gave the horses a brief rest, and once again the riders moved off through the grey starless night with the icy crust of the steppe-land track crunching under their horses' hooves.

Not far from Krivyanskaya they lost their way and did not reach the stanitsa till dawn was breaking. There was no one about, save an old Cossack breaking the ice in a trough by a well. Golubov rode up to him and the detachment halted.

'Good-day to you, old man.'

The Cossack slowly raised his mittened hand to his sheepskin hat and replied with a dour 'Good morning.'

'Well, grandad, have your Cossacks gone off to Novocherkassk? Was there a mobilisation here?'

The old man hurriedly picked up his axe and walked away to his gate without replying.

'Get moving!' Golubov shouted, and rode away swearing.

That day the Little Army Council, which was still sitting in Novocherkassk, had intended to evacuate to the stanitsa of Konstantinovskaya. General Popov, the newly appointed Campaign Ataman of the Don Cossack Army, had already withdrawn his forces from the town, taking the Army funds with him. With morning came the news that Golubov had left Melikhovskaya and was advancing in the direction of Bessergenevskaya. The Council sent out Major Sivolobov to negotiate with the Red commander on the terms for the surrender of Novocherkassk. But no sooner had he left than Golubov's cavalry, meeting no resistance, burst into the town from another direction. Golubov himself, surrounded by Cossacks, galloped up to the Council building on a foaming horse. A few bystanders were gathered round the porch and an orderly was waiting for Nazarov with a saddled horse.

Bunchuk sprang off his horse and unloaded a light machine-gun. He and Golubov with a crowd of Cossacks on their heels ran into the building. As the door of the large assembly hall crashed open, the heads of the delegates turned, revealing a white sea of faces.

'Stand up!' Golubov shouted tensely, as if at a review of troops and, stumbling in his haste, strode up to the presidium table with Cossacks all round him.

There was a clatter of chairs as the members of the Council responded to his imperious command. Only Nazarov remained seated.

'How dare you interrupt a meeting of the Council?' his voice rang out angrily.

'You're under arrest! Silence!' Turning purple, Golubov darted up to Nazarov and ripped the shoulder-straps off his general's double-breasted tunic. His voice rose to a hoarse yelp. 'Stand up, I tell you! Arrest him!.. Now then, you! Yes, I'm talking to you! You brass-hat!'

While Bunchuk mounted the machine-gun in the doorway, the members of the Council huddled together like sheep. The Cossacks tramped out, dragging Nazarov,

Voloshinov, the chalk-faced President of the Council, and several others.

Golubov followed them with his sword clattering, his face a blotchy reddish-brown. A member of the Council clutched his sleeve.

'Colonel, my dear sir, where shall we go?'

Another thrust a darting, elusive head over Golubov's shoulder. 'Are we free?'

'Go to the devil!' Golubov roared, waving them aside and, as he reached Bunchuk, turned on the Council members and stamped his foot. 'Go and— yourselves! I've no time for you! D'you hear!'

His hoarse, weathered voice sent booming echoes through the hall.

Bunchuk spent the night at his mother's house and the next day, on learning that Sivers had captured Rostov, asked Golubov's permission to leave and set out for the city on horseback.

For two days he worked for Sivers, who knew him from the days when he had been editor of the Bolshevik paper *Trench Truth*. In his spare time he made inquiries at the Revolutionary Committee, but there was no news of Abramson or Anna. At Sivers's headquarters a revolutionary tribunal had been organised that was handing out summary justice to captured White Guards. Bunchuk worked on it for a day, taking part in raids and roundups, and the next day without much hope called again at the Revolutionary Committee. As he was mounting the stairs he heard the familiar sound of Anna's voice. The blood rushed to his heart and he slowed his pace as he entered the inner room from which the sound of voices and Anna's laughter had come.

The room, which had once been the commandant's office, was wreathed with tobacco smoke. At a small, ladies' writing-desk a man in a greatcoat with no buttons and the earflaps of his army hat hanging loose was writing something. He was surrounded by soldiers and civilians in sheepskins and overcoats, who stood in bunches, smoking and talking. Anna was by the window and had her back to the door. Abramson was sitting on the window-ledge with his fingers locked round one knee. Beside him stood a tall Red Guard of Lettish appearance with his head cocked to one side. He was holding his cigarette affectedly, with the little finger raised, and telling the others about something that appeared to be amusing. Anna was leaning back and laughing heartily, Abramson's face was creased in a smile and others nearby had stopped talking to listen, and were also smiling. The Red Guard's big face, every line of his rough-hewn features, revealed a sharp and rather fierce intelligence.

Bunchuk placed his hand on Anna's shoulder.

'Hullo, Anna!'

She looked round. Colour flooded into her face and spread down her neck to her collarbones, forcing tears into her eyes.

'Where did you spring from? Abramson, look! He's turned up as good as new, and you were worried about him,' she stammered without looking up and, unable to overcome her embarrassment, walked away to the door.

Bunchuk squeezed Abramson's hot hand, exchanged a few phrases and, feeling a foolish and boundlessly happy smile on his face, ignored Abramson's next question (he had not even understood what it was about) and walked over to Anna. She had recovered by now and took revenge for her confusion by being rather pert.

'Well, hullo again. How are you? Quite well? When did you get here? You're from Novocherkassk? Were you in Golubov's detachment? I see... Well, and what now?'

Bunchuk replied to her questions, keeping his heavy unwavering eyes on her. Her answering glance sagged and slipped sideways.

'Let's go outside for a minute,' she suggested.

Abramson called to them.

'Will you be back soon? There's something I want to talk to you about, Comrade Bunchuk. We have a job for you.'

'I'll be back in an hour.'

In the street Anna looked straight into Bunchuk's eyes with gentle affection and made an angry little gesture.

'Oh, Ilya, Ilya! What a fool I made of myself! Like a little girl! First it was surprise and second it was because of our ambiguous relationship. After all, what are we? An idyllic young man and his bride-to-be? One day while we were in Lugansk Abramson asked me if I was living with you. I denied it but he's terribly observant and must have noticed what was so obvious. He left it at that, but I could see from his eyes that he didn't believe me.'

'Tell me about yourself. How are you? What have you been doing?'

'Oh, we made things hum there! We got together a detachment of two hundred and eleven bayonets. We were doing organisational and political work... But how can

I tell you in a few words? I still can't get over your appearing out of the blue like this. Where are you... Where do you ... spend the night?' she asked, changing the subject.

'In town ... at a comrade's house.'

Bunchuk felt embarrassed at having told her a lie; he had spent the past few nights in the headquarters building.

'You must move in with us today. Do you remember where I live? You saw me home once.'

'I'll find it. But—won't I be in the way? How about your family?'

'You won't be in anybody's way and don't talk like that.'

That evening Bunchuk collected all his belongings in one big army pack and went to the little side-street on the outskirts where Anna lived. On the threshold of a small brick-built annexe in a courtyard he was met by an old woman. Her face was vaguely reminiscent of Anna's; there was the same bluish-black gleam in the eyes, the same high-bridged nose, but the skin was wrinkled and flaccid and the sunken mouth spoke frighteningly of age.

'Are you Bunchuk?' she asked.

'Yes.'

'Come in, please. My daughter has told me about you.'

She led Bunchuk into a small room and showed him where to put his things, then pointed around with an arthritically crooked finger.

'This is where you will live. This is your bed, sir.'

She spoke with a noticeable Jewish accent. Besides her in the house there was a teen-age girl, rather delicate-looking and with the same deep-set eyes as Anna.

Anna soon arrived, bringing noise and bustle into the house.

'Has anybody called? Did Bunchuk come?'

The mother answered in her native tongue and Anna came to his door with firm light steps.

'May I come in?'

'Of course.'

Bunchuk rose from his chair and stepped towards her.

'Well? Are you comfortable?'

She surveyed him with a laughing satisfied air.

'Have you had anything to eat? Let's go into the other room.'

She took him by the sleeve of his tunic and led him into the first room.

671

'This is my comrade, Mother.' And with a smile, 'So you mustn't ill-treat him.'

'But how could I?.. He's our guest.'

During the night shots kept going off all over the city like the popping of the ripe pods of locust-trees. Occasionally a machine gun chattered. But gradually the sounds grew less, and night, the majestic black night of February, swaddled the streets in stillness. Bunchuk and Anna sat together in his austere neat room.

'My sister and I used to have this room,' Anna told him. 'It's very plain, isn't it—like a nun's room. No cheap pictures, no photographs, none of the things that befitted my status as a high-school girl.'

'What did you live on?' Bunchuk asked in the course of the conversation.

And not without a touch of inward pride Anna answered, 'I worked at the Asmolovskaya factory and gave lessons.'

'And now?'

'Mother does dress-making. The two of them don't need very much.'

Bunchuk related the details of the capture of Novocherkassk and the fighting at Zverevo and Kamenskaya. Anna gave him her impressions of the work in Lugansk and Taganrog.

At eleven, as soon as her mother put out the light, Anna left him.

XX

In March Bunchuk was sent to serve on the Tribunal of the Don Revolutionary Committee. The tall dull-eyed chairman, his face haggard from overwork and sleepless nights, took him aside to the window and said, stroking his wrist-watch (he was late for a meeting), 'What year did you join the Party?.. Ah, that's good. Well, you're going to be our commandant. Last night we sent our previous commandant to the heavenly headquarters for taking bribes. He was a downright sadist, a proper swine— we don't need that kind. This is dirty work, but you've still got to keep intact your sense of responsibility to the Party and you must—mind you get me right now...' he added forcefully, 'keep your humanity. We are physically destroying the counter-revolutionaries because it's a necessity, but we mustn't make a circus of it. Get me? Good, then go and take over.'

At midnight Bunchuk and a squad of sixteen Red Guards drove out of town with five condemned men and shot them. Two of the condemned were Cossacks of Gnilovskaya stanitsa, the others were citizens of Rostov.

Nearly every night at midnight they made similar expeditions. Hasty graves were dug with some of the Red Guards working side by side with the condemned. Then Bunchuk would form up his squad and utter words that had the dull finality of cast iron.

'At the enemies of the revolution...' And throwing up his revolver, 'Fire!'

In one week his face grew gaunt and black, as if he had been buried under ground. His eyes hollowed out, and the nervously twitching lids failed to hide their anguished brightness. Anna saw him only at night. She was working in the Revolutionary Committee and came home late, but she would always wait up until the familiar urgent rapping on the window announced his arrival.

Once, when Bunchuk returned as usual after midnight, Anna opened the door and asked, 'Do you want any supper?'

Bunchuk made no reply. He swayed drunkenly, walked through into his own room and flung himself on the bed, just as he was, in his greatcoat, boots and hat. Anna came up and looked into his face; his eyes were screwed up, there was a sparkle of saliva on his clenched teeth, and his hair, thinned by typhus, lay in a damp lock on his forehead.

She sat down on the bed beside him, pity and pain clawing at her heart, and asked in a whisper, 'Is it that bad, Ilya?'

He squeezed her hand, ground his teeth and turned away to the wall. He fell asleep like that, without speaking, but in his sleep he muttered barely audible, pitiful words and struggled as if he were being held down. She noticed with a shudder of instinctive fear that he was sleeping with his eyes only half closed and the eyeballs had rolled so that only the yellowish whites gleamed from under the inflamed lids.

'Leave that place!' she begged him in the morning. 'You'd better go to the front. You look like nothing on earth, Ilya! This job will kill you.'

'Shut up!' he shouted, his eyes white with frenzy.

'Don't shout. Have I offended you?'

Bunchuk suddenly faded, as though the shout had splashed out all the pent-up frenzy in his heart. Staring wearily at his upturned palms, he said, 'Destroying human filth is a dirty business. Being in command of a firing squad, you see, is bad for body and mind... And by—' For the first time in Anna's presence he swore obscenely. 'The only people who will do dirty work are fools and brutes or fanatics. Isn't that so? We all want to walk in a flowering garden but—damn it all!—before you plant out the flowerbeds and the trees, you've got to get rid of the filth! You've got to manure the ground! You've got to get your hands dirty!' he raised his voice, although Anna had turned away and was silent. 'The filth has got to be cleared away and people don't like doing that!' By this time he was shouting and thumping the table with his fist and blinking his bloodshot eyes.

Anna's mother glanced into the room, and he forced himself to speak quietly.

'I won't leave this work! Here I feel tangibly that I'm doing something useful! I'm raking away the filth! I'm manuring the earth to make it richer! More fertile! One day there'll be happy people on it... Perhaps one of them will be my son, the son I haven't got...' He broke into a grating laugh. 'How many of them I've shot, those swine, those ticks... A tick is an insect that eats its way into the body... I've killed a dozen with these hands...' Bunchuk held out his clenched hairy hands with finger-nails like the claws of a kite, then dropped them on to his knees and whispered, 'But to hell with it all! A man's no good if he just smoulders and smokes, he's got to burn... But it's true, I am tired... I'll stick it just a bit longer, then go off to the front... You're right...'

Anna had listened to him in silence and now she said, 'Go to the front or take up some other work... You must, Ilya, or you'll go off your head.'

Bunchuk turned away from her and drummed on the window.

'No, I'm tough... You needn't think that anybody's made of iron. We're all made of the same stuff... In real life there isn't a man who doesn't know fear in battle, there's no one who can kill people without feeling ... without getting morally scratched. But it's not the ones with officers' epaulettes I'm sorry for... They know what they're doing as well as we do. But last night there were three Cossacks among the nine I had to shoot ... ordinary working men... I started to untie one of them...' Bunchuk's voice sank and became muffled, as if he were going further and further away. 'I happened to touch his hand and it was as hard and rough as a boot sole... All calloused... And the palm was scarred and ... kind of lumpy... Well, I must be going,' he broke off and surreptitiously rubbed his throat, which felt as if a horsehair lasso had been tightened round it.

He pulled on his boots, drank a glass of milk and left. Anna followed him into the corridor. She stood holding his heavy hand in hers, then pressed it to her burning cheek and ran out into the yard.

* * *

Time shook off the short days of winter. The weather grew warmer. Spring was coming up from the Azov Sea and knocking at the gates of the Don. At the end of March the Ukrainian Red Guard detachments, hard pressed by Haidamak nationalist forces and Germans, began to arrive in Rostov. Murder, looting and unauthorised requisitioning spread through the city. Some of the most demoralised detachments had to be disarmed by the Revolutionary Committee. This was not achieved without skirmishes and shooting. Around Novocherkassk the Cossacks were stirring. In March, the contradictions between Cossacks and non-Cossack 'outsiders' began to swell like the buds on the poplar-trees. Uprisings broke out here and there and counter-revolutionary plots were uncovered. But Rostov was leading a fast full-blooded life. In the evenings crowds of soldiers, sailors and workers thronged the main boulevard, airing their views, nibbling sunflower seeds, spitting the husks into the flowing gutters, and amusing themselves with the women. Just as they had always done, people worked, ate, drank, slept, died, gave birth, loved, hated, breathed the salty sea breeze, and lived in the grip of great and petty passions. Days big with menace brooded over Rostov. The air was laden with the scent of the thawing black earth and the blood of imminent battles.

On one such pleasant sun-drenched day Bunchuk came home earlier than usual and was surprised to find Anna there.

'You usually come in so late. Why are you early today?'

'I don't feel well.'

She followed him into his room. Bunchuk took off his coat and with a tremulously joyful smile said, 'Anna, from today I shan't be working for the tribunal any more.'

'Really? Where are they sending you?'

'The Revolutionary Committee. I spoke to Krivoshlykov today. He's promised to send me out into one of the districts.'

They had supper together. Bunchuk went to bed but he was too excited to sleep. He smoked and tossed about on his hard mattress, sighing happily. He was glad and thankful to be leaving the tribunal because he felt that he had reached breaking-point. He was finishing his fourth cigarette when he heard the door creak faintly. Looking up, he saw Anna. Barefoot and in only her night-shirt, she slipped into the room and came softly up to the bed. Through a chink in the shutters the shadowy green light of the moon fell on the oval of her bare shoulder. She bent over him and placed her warm hand on his lips.

'Move over. Don't speak...'

She lay down at his side, her legs were hot and trembling at the knees; impatiently she pushed back a lock of hair as heavy as a bunch of grapes, and with her eyes flashing a smoky blue fire whispered in a forced, almost rough voice. 'If not today, then tomorrow I may lose you... I want to love you with all my strength!' And she shuddered at her own resolve. 'Be quick!'

Bunchuk kissed her taut cool breasts and fondled her pliant body and with a great shame that swept over his mind like a wave, felt that he was impotent.

His head shook and his cheeks burned with shame. Anna freed herself and pushed him away angrily. With disgust and aversion she asked in a choking, scornful whisper, 'Are you... Are you impotent? Or are you ill?.. Oh, how disgusting!.. Leave me alone!'

Bunchuk squeezed her fingers so hard that they cracked faintly, stared into her dilated darkly hostile eyes and stammered between the jerky paralytic movements of his head, 'Why? Why scorn me like this? Yes, I've burned myself out!.. I can't even do that now... No, I'm not ill... Try to understand! I'm drained...'

With a hoarse moan he sprang out of bed, lit a cigarette, and stood with sagging shoulders at the window as if he had been thrashed.

Anna rose, embraced him in silence and kissed him calmly on the forehead, like a mother.

And a week later, when what should have happened did happen, she confessed, hiding her flushed face under his arm, 'I thought you'd spent it all before... I didn't realise it was the work that had taken it out of you.'

And for long afterwards Bunchuk felt not only the caresses of his beloved but also the overflowing warmth of a mother's care.

He was not sent out to the provinces. On Podtyolkov's insistence he stayed in Rostov. The Don Revolutionary Committee was seething with preparations for the regional congress of Soviets, for fresh clashes with the counter-revolution that was astir all along the Don.

XXI

The frogs were clamouring among the riverside willows. The sun had taken itself off behind the hill, and the cool of evening was spreading through the village of Setrakov. Huge slanting shadows from the houses fell across the dry road. A drove of horses from the steppe trotted by in a cloud of dust. Cossack women came in from the common, driving their cows with switches and calling out their news to one another. In the sidelanes the Cossack children, bare-footed and already sunburnt, were playing leap-frog. The old men were sitting in dignified fashion on the copings round the houses.

The village had done its sowing. There were only a few strips still waiting to be scattered with millet and sunflower seed.

By one of the last houses in the village three Cossacks were seated on a pile of felled oaks. The owner of the house, a pock-marked artilleryman, was relating an incident from the German war. His companions, an old man from next door and his son-in-law, a young curly-headed Cossack lad, were listening in silence. His wife, a tall fine-looking woman, came down from the porch. The sleeves of her pink blouse were turned up, exposing her brown shapely arms. She was carrying a pail; with the free swinging stride that distinguishes the Cossack woman she walked to the cowshed. Her hair was falling from under her spotlessly white kerchief (she had just been making up the stove in readiness for tomorrow's cooking), and the plain leather shoes on her bare feet flopped loosely as they pressed the young green shoots that were sprouting all over the yard.

Presently the ringing patter of milk flowing into the pail reached the ears of the Cossacks seated on the oaks.

The housewife finished milking and returned to the house with a full pail, leaning over a little and keeping her arm bent like a swan's neck.

'Syoma, why don't you go and look for the calf!' she called from the steps.

'Where's Mityashka then?' her husband answered.

'Plagued if I know. He's run off somewhere.'

The man rose unhurriedly and walked to the corner. The old man and his son-in-law also got up to go, but their host called to them from the corner.

'Hi, look here, Dorofei Gavrilich! Just look at that!'

The old man and his son-in-law went over to him and he pointed out into the steppe. A great purple ball of dust was rolling along the highway, and in its midst were ranks of infantry, wagons and cavalry.

'It must be an army?' the old man screwed up his eyes in astonishment and put his hand to his white brows.

'Who might they be?' his host asked in alarm.

His wife came out of the gate with a jacket draped over her shoulders. She stared across the steppe and gasped.

'What are all those people? Lord a'mercy, how many there are!'

'I don't like the look of 'em.'

The old man shuffled his feet for a moment, then walked to his own yard and shouted to his son-in-law, 'Come along home. Don't stand staring!'

The women and children ran to the end of the lane, the men followed in bunches. The column was marching along the highway, about a verst from the village, and now the hum of voices, the neighing of horses and the creak of wheels reached the yards faintly on the wind.

'They aren't Cossacks... Not our folk,' the woman said to her husband.

He shrugged.

'Of course, they aren't. I hope they're not Germans! Nay, they're Russians... See that red rag they're carrying! Ah, so that's it.'

A tall Cossack guardsman came up to them. He apparently had a fever; his face was a sandy yellow, as if he had been down with jaundice, and he was wearing a winter coat and felt boots. He raised his shaggy sheepskin hat.

'See that flag?.. They are Bolsheviks.'

'Ay, that's what they are.'

Several riders broke away from the column and galloped towards the village. The Cossacks exchanged glances and silently dispersed, the girls and little children scattered like peas. In five minutes the lane was dead. The horsemen rode into it in a bunch and, spurring their mounts, galloped to the pile of felled oaks where the Cossacks had been sitting only a quarter of an hour before. The owner was standing at his gate. The leading rider, evidently senior in rank, on a chestnut horse, wearing a Kuban Cossack hat and a huge red silk ribbon on his strapped and belted field tunic rode up to the gate.

'Good-day, master! Open your gate.'

The pock-marks on the artilleryman's face whitened. He took off his cap.

'And who may you be?'

'Open the gate!' the soldier in the Kuban hat shouted.

The chestnut, squinting fiercely and chasing the bit in its foaming mouth, pawed the fence with its forefoot. The Cossack opened the side-gate and one by one the horsemen rode into the yard.

The man in the Kuban hat dismounted smartly and strode quickly up to the porch on his bandy legs. While the others were dismounting, he sat down on the porch, took out his cigarette-case and offered it to the master of the house. It was refused.

'Don't you smoke?'

'No, thanks.'

'You aren't Old Believers here by any chance?'

'No, Orthodox... And who are you?' the Cossack repeated dourly.

'Us? Red Guards of the Second Socialist Army.'

The others led their horses up to the porch and tethered them to the rails. One great hulking fellow with a forelock matted like a horse's mane strode to the sheeppen, kicking his sabre as he walked. He flung open the gate as if he owned the place, ducked under the crossbar and, seizing a big heavy-tailed ram by the horns, dragged it out into the yard.

'Petrichenko, give us a hand!' he shouted in a cracked falsetto.

A little soldier in a skimpy Austrian greatcoat ran up to him. The Cossack farmer stroked his beard and looked round as if he were not in his own but someone else's yard. He said nothing and only when the ram with its throat cut by a sabre lay kicking its thin legs in the air did he cough and walk up on to his porch.

The soldier in the Kuban hat and two others, one a Chinese, the other Russian, followed him into the house.

'Don't take offence, Cossack!' the man from the Kuban said cheerfully as he crossed the threshold. 'We'll pay you good money!'

He slapped his trouser pocket, let out a guffaw and suddenly stopped laughing as his eyes rested on the mistress of the house, who stood by the stove, tight-lipped and staring at him with frightened eyes.

He turned to the Chinese and, glancing round guardedly, said, 'Walky-walky with this man here.' He pointed to the owner. 'Walky-walky with him and he'll give us some hay for the horses... Yes, and you go and give it to him. Get me? We pay good money! The Red Guards don't go in for looting. Get moving, Cossack, get moving!' A steely note sounded in his voice.

Escorted by the Chinese and his companion, the Cossack left the house. Hardly had he gone down the steps when he heard his wife scream. He ran back into the porch and wrenched the door. The flimsy latch jumped out of its socket. The man from the Kuban had seized the woman's smooth bare arm above the elbow and was dragging her into the semi-darkness of a side room. She was resisting and pushing him away. He tried to get his arms round her and carry her, but at that moment the door burst open, and the Cossack strode between them, shielding his wife. His voice was boggily soft.

'You came into my house as a guest... Why're you laying hands on my woman? Eh?.. Leave her alone! I'm not afraid of your weapons! Take what you want, rob, steal, but keep your dirty hands off my wife! You won't touch her but over my dead body... And you, Nyurka...' he turned to his wife with twitching nostrils, 'you'd better get out of here and go to Uncle Dorofei's. This is no place for you!'

The man from the Kuban straightened the holster straps over his tunic and leered.

'You're very touchy, Cossack... Can't I even have my joke... I'm the biggest joker in the company, didn't you know?.. I was only kidding. I'll just have her on a bit, I thought, and she got cross... Haven't you given out the hay? What, no hay? How about the neighbours—they got any?'

He walked out whistling and swinging his whip. Soon the whole detachment, counting some eight hundred sabres and bayonets in all, about a third of whom were Chinese, Latvians and other foreigners, marched up to the village and camped for the night outside it. Evidently the commander could not trust his motley band of undisciplined soldiers and preferred to spend the night outside the village.

The Tiraspol Detachment of the Second Socialist Army, harassed by Ukrainian nationalist forces and the Germans who were marching across the Ukraine, had fought its way through to the Don, detrained at the station of Sheptukhovka and, finding Germans ahead of it, had turned north and was marching through the districts of the Migulinskaya stanitsa in the direction of Voronezh. Demoralised by the criminal elements that had flocked to the detachment, the Red Guards left a trail of excesses behind them. On April 16th, having camped for the night outside the village of Setrakov, they defied the orders and threats of their commanders and invaded the village, killing sheep, raping two Cossack girls on the outskirts, and starting a gun fight on the square, during which one of their own men was wounded. The sentries got drunk: every wagon of the baggage train was carrying a stock of alcohol. Meanwhile under cover of darkness three mounted Cossacks rode out to raise the alarm in the surrounding villages.

During the night the Cossacks, frontline men and veterans, armed themselves and saddled up their horses. Led by the officers who had taken refuge in the villages, or even sergeants-major, they closed in on Setrakov and the Red Guard detachment, and lay in wait in ravines and behind hilltops. Half-squadrons rode out from Migulinskaya, Kolodezny and Bogomolov. The men of the Upper Chir, the Napol, the Kalinovka, the Yeja and the Kolodez were up in arms.

The Pleiades burned out, the glossy black fur of night moulted and grew thin, and at dawn the yelling Cossack cavalry charged down on the Red Guards from all sides. A machine-gun chattered for a moment and broke off, wild shooting flared up and died away, and then the sabres began their silent work.

In an hour it was all over. The detachment was wiped out. More than two hundred men were sabred or shot, and about five hundred taken prisoner. Two four-gun batteries, twenty-six machine-guns, a thousand rifles, and a large stock of equipment fell into the hands of the Cossacks.

The next day the red pennants of galloping messengers blossomed on every track and highroad. The villages and stanitsas were in an uproar. Soviets were overthrown and atamans hastily elected in their place. Squadrons from as far away as Vyoshenskaya and Kazanskaya set out belatedly for the scene of events.

Towards the end of April the stanitsas of the Upper Don broke away from the Donets District and formed their own district, calling it the Upper Don. The populous stanitsa of Vyoshenskaya, second in size and the number of villages attached to it only to Mikhailovskaya, was chosen as the district centre. The new stanitsas of Shumilinskaya, Karginskaya and Bokovskaya were formed. And the Upper Don District, now comprising twelve stanitsas and one Ukrainian volost, began to live a life of its own. From the former Donets District it had taken Kazanskaya, Migulinskaya, Shumilinskaya, Vyoshenskaya, Yelanskaya, Karginskaya, Bokovskaya and Ponomaryovskaya volost; from the Ust-Medveditsa District, Ust-Khopyorskaya and Krasnokutskaya; and from the Khopyor District, Bukanovskaya, Slashchevskaya and Fedoseyevskaya. As their District Ataman the Cossacks unanimously elected a Cossack of Yelanskaya stanitsa, one Zakhar Akimovich Alferov, a general who had graduated from the military academy. Alferov was said to have made his way up from being a lowly Cossack officer only thanks to his energetic and intelligent wife; she had dragged her dull-witted spouse out of his rut and never let him rest until, after three failures, he had passed the Academy entrance examination.

But if Alferov was spoken of at all in those days it was only in passing. There were other matters to occupy men's minds.

XXII

The flood waters had only just begun to abate. Down on the leas the brown silty earth was bare and the fences round the vegetable patches were banked with driftage— the withered rushes, branches, dead leaves, and windfallen trees that the Don had carried away when it burst its banks. The riverside willows were noticeably greener and catkins were dangling from their branches. The buds on the poplars were about to open and the young branches of the willow bushes round the yards where the flood was still high hung low over the water, their yellow fluffy buds diving like unfledged ducklings among the waves and dancing in the wind.

At daybreak flocks of duck and wild geese swam up to the vegetable patches in search of food. The brazen-throated loons screamed in the backwaters. And even at noon the white-bellied teal could be seen bobbing on the waves of the wind-ruffled Don.

Migrating birds were in abundance that year. The Cossacks rowing out to their nets when the waters were stained by the wine-red dawns, often saw swans resting in some sheltered inlet. But beyond all belief was the news brought back one day by Khristonya and Old Matvei Kashulin. They had been out to the state forest to choose a pair of young oaks for their domestic needs and, while making their way through the thickets, had surprised a wild goat and its kid. The skinny yellowish-brown goat sprang out of a gully overgrown with thistle and thorn bushes, stared for a few seconds at the woodmen, stamping its thin chiselled legs, while its tiny offspring pressed timidly to its side, and at the sound of Khristonya's astonished gasp sprang away through the young oaks so swiftly that the Cossacks saw nothing more than a glimpse of the shining grey-blue hollows of its hooves and its stumpy camel-coloured tail.

'What kind of creature was that?' Matvei Kashulin asked, dropping his axe.

With inexplicable elation Khristonya bellowed for the whole bewitchedly silent forest to hear, 'A goat! A mountain goat, bless her soul, by all the—! We saw ones like that in the Carpathians!'

'So it was the war chased her out here into the steppe, the poor thing?'

Khristonya had no choice but to agree.

'Must have been. And did you see the kid, Grandad! Well, I'll be damned... What a fine little brat it was! Like a baby, that's for sure!'

All the way home they talked about this unprecedented addition to the region's wild life. And in the end Old Matvei began to have his doubts.

'But was it a goat?'

'It was. God's truth, it was a goat and nothing else!'

'But mebbe... If it was a goat, why didn't it have any horns?'

'What d'you need horns for?'

'I don't need 'em. What I'm asking is, if it was a creature of the goat tribe, why wasn't it the proper shape? Have you ever seen a goat without horns? No, you haven't. Mebbe it was a wild sheep or something.'

683

'Your mind's gone wool-gathering, Grandad Matvei, that's for sure!' Khristonya took offence. 'Go to the Melekhovs and have a look. Their Grigory's got a whip made of a goat's leg. Will you recognise that, I wonder?'

So Old Kashulin had to go to see the Melekhovs that day. The handle of Grigory's whip was indeed skilfully covered with the skin of a goat's leg, and the tiny hoof was still intact and rimmed no less skilfully with a small copper shoe.

In the sixth week of Lent Mishka Koshevoi rowed out early one morning to inspect his nets near the forest. He left the house at dawn. The earth had shrunk in the morning frost and the mud had stiffened under a thin coating of ice. Mishka in his wadded jacket, wearing leather shoes, with his trousers tucked into white socks walked along with his cap on the back of his head, breathing in the winy morning air and the vapid smell of thaw damp. He was carrying a long oar on his shoulder. Having unhitched the boat, he paddled away swiftly, standing up in the stern and putting his weight on the oar.

He soon checked the nets, took the fish out of the last one and lowered it again, adjusted the stays, paddled quietly away and decided to have a smoke. The dawn was just breaking. In the east the lower edge of the twilit greenish sky looked as though it had been sprinkled with blood. The blood was spreading out along the horizon and turning a rusty gold. Mishka watched the unhurried flight of a loon and lit his cigarette. The smoke drifted away, melting and clinging to the bushes. When he had inspected the catch of his three nets—three small sterlet, an eight-pounder carp and a heap of small fish—he thought to himself, 'I'll have to sell it. Cross-eyed Luke-rya will take it. I'll change it for some of her dried pears, and Mother will stew them for us one day.'

Still smoking, he paddled towards the pier. By the fences where he usually tied up his boat a man was sitting.

'Who could that be?' Mishka wondered, pulling harder and steering deftly with the oar.

The man squatting by the fence was Knave.

He was smoking a huge cigarette made of newspaper.

His sharp polecat's eyes were gleaming sleepily and there was a shadow of stubble on his chin.

'What brings you here?' Mishka shouted.

His shout rolled across the water like a big soft ball.

'Row in.'

'Want some fish?'

'What the hell for?'

Knave coughed harshly, spat out a volley of phlegm, and rose reluctantly. His greatcoat was too big for him and hung like a robe on a scarecrow. The drooping top of his peaked cap came down over the pointed gristle of his grimy ears. He had only recently appeared in the village, with the dubious reputation of having been a Red Guard. The Cossacks had wanted to know where he had been since demobilisation, but Knave had answered evasively and avoided any dangerous discussion. To Ivan Kotlyarov and Mishka Koshevoi he had confessed that he had spent four months in a Red Guard detachment in the Ukraine, had been captured by the Haidamaks, escaped, joined up with Sivers, campaigned with him in and around Rostov, then awarded himself leave for recovery and repair.

Knave took off his cap, and with a look over his shoulder, smoothed his bristly hair, walked down to the boat and hissed, 'Things are bad ... very bad... Leave the fishing! Fishing won't get us anywhere!'

'What's the news? Out with it!'

Mishka squeezed Knave's bony fingers in his slimy, fishy-smelling hand and smiled warmly. They had been friends for a long time.

'There was a massacre of Red Guards in Migulinskaya yesterday. It's started, mate. The fur's flying!'

'What Red Guards? What were they doing in Migulinskaya?'

'They were marching through and the Cossacks cleaned 'em up... A whole batch of prisoners has been driven to Karginskaya! And a court martial's handing out sentences there already. Today general mobilisation will be announced here. They'll be ringing the bell any minute now.'

Koshevoi hitched up the boat, tipped his fish into a sack, and set off with long strides, using the oar as a stick. Knave trotted along like a foal beside him and sometimes ran ahead, pulling the skirts of his greatcoat round him, swinging his arms.

'Ivan told me. He just took over from me at the mill. The mill's been working all night, so much grain has been brought in. And he got it from the boss himself. An officer rode in from Vyoshenskaya to see Sergei Platonovich.'

'What do we do now?' A shadow of confusion spread

over Mishka's face, which in the years of war had both matured and faded. He glanced sideways at Knave and repeated, 'What do we do now?'

'We'll have to get out of the village.'

'Where to?'

'Kamenskaya.'

'But the Cossacks are there.'

'A bit to the left.'

'Where then?'

'Oblivy.'

'How can we get through?'

'You'll get through if you want to. And if you don't, you can bloody well stay behind!' Knave snapped suddenly. ' "What do we do now? Where do we go?" How am I to know? When you're in a tight spot, you'll find your own way out! Smell your way out!'

'Hold your horses or they'll run away with you! What does Ivan say?'

'Your Ivan takes a lot of moving...'

'Don't shout... There's a woman looking at you...'

They both glanced apprehensively at a young woman, Avdeich the Braggart's daughter-in-law, who was driving the cows out of their yard. At the first crossroads Mishka suddenly turned back.

'Where're you off to?' Knave exclaimed.

Without looking round Koshevoi muttered, 'I'm going to take the nets in.'

'What for?'

'It'd be a pity to lose 'em.'

'So we're going?' Knave burst out joyfully.

Mishka waved his oar and said from a distance, 'Go to Ivan's. I'll take in the nets and be along right away.'

Ivan had already sent word round his circle of Cossacks. His son had been to the Melekhovs' and brought back Grigory. Khristonya had come himself, sensing that trouble was in the offing. Soon Koshevoi returned and the discussion began. They all spoke at once, expecting to hear the alarm bell ring at any moment.

'We've got to get cracking! We must be out of here today!' Knave urged excitedly.

'Can't you give us a reason, though? Why should we go?' Khristonya asked.

'A reason? When they start mobilisation, d'you think you'll wriggle out of it?'

'I just won't go, that's all.'

'They'll make you.'

'Oh no, they won't. I'm not a bullock on a halter.'

Ivan sent his cross-eyed wife out of the house and grunted angrily, 'They'll make you all right. Knave's talking sense. Only where do we go? That's the snag.'

'I've told him that already,' Mishka Koshevoi sighed.

'Why tell me? What do I care? I'll go alone! I don't want any wobblers! You with your "Why this, why that?" You'll know all right when you've been nabbed and had a spell in gaol for Bolshevism!.. What did you think? In times like these... Any bloody thing can happen!'

Grigory Melekhov, who had pulled a nail out of the wall and had been toying with it intently, with a kind of quiet fury, interrupted Knave coldly.

'Stop this cackle! You're in a different position. There's nothing to hold you, you can just up sticks and go. But we've got to think this thing out. I've got a wife and two kids... And I've seen a lot more action than you!' A sudden glint of anger appeared in his dark eyes and, baring his firm fang-like teeth, he shouted, 'You can gab as much as you like... You're just Knave and that's what you'll always be! You've got nothing to your name but the shirt on your back...'

'What are you snarling for! Showing us your officer's ways! You needn't bawl at me! I don't give a damn for you!' Knave shouted.

His hedgehog-like face was pale with anger, and his fierce little eyes darted to and fro in their narrowed slits; even the smoky stubble on his chin seemed to twitch.

Grigory had merely been venting on him the anger he felt at having his peace disturbed by the news he had heard from Ivan of the Red Guards incursion into the district. Knave's retort detonated his latent fury. He jumped up as if he had been stung, planted himself in front of Knave, where he sat fidgeting on his stool, and, barely restraining the hand that longed to strike, said, 'Shut up, you squirt! You rotten snot! You runt! Who're you to give orders? Get out then! Who's stopping you! Take your stink out of here! And keep your trap shut or I'll give you something to remember me by...'

'Drop that, Grigory! That's not the way!' Koshevoi intervened jerking Grigory's fist away from Knave's wrinkled face.

'It's about time you gave up your Cossack bullying... Aren't you ashamed?.. You ought to be, Melekhov! Downright ashamed!'

Knave stood up, coughed awkwardly, and walked to the door. At the threshold, unable to restrain himself, he turned and snapped at the spitefully smiling Grigory, 'And you were in the Red Guards... You gendarme pig!.. We rubbed out plenty of the likes of you!'

Grigory could not restrain himself either. He hustled Knave out into the porch, treading on the heels of his worn army boots, and threatened, 'Get out! Or I'll tear your legs off!'

'There's no need for all this! You're like a couple of kids!'

Ivan shook his head disapprovingly and gave Grigory a look of disgust.

Koshevoi bit his lip in silence, evidently holding back some bitter comment.

'He shouldn't take so much on himself! Why did he start chucking his weight about?' Grigory tried to justify himself not without some embarrassment; a sympathetic look from Khristonya brought a simple boyish smile to his face. 'I nearly beat him up!.. But there's hardly anything there to beat. One slap and you'd squash him.'

'Well, what d'you say? We've got to decide something.'

Ivan hummed and hawed under Koshevoi's intent glance and gave a hesitant reply.

'Well, Mikhail?.. Grigory here—he's right in a way. How can we drop everything and clear out? We've got our families to think about... Now wait a bit!' he went on hurriedly, noticing Mishka's impatient movement. 'Maybe it'll all blow over. Who can tell? Now they've smashed one lot at Setrakov, the rest will keep out... We'll just sit tight for a bit, and see. I've got a wife and child too, by the way. Our clothes are all worn out, we're short of flour ... how can we just pack up and go? What will they be left with?'

Mishka's eyebrow twitched irritably. He thrust his glance into the earthen floor.

'So you're not going?'

'I think we'd better wait a bit. It'll never be too late to go. What about you, Grigory? And you, Khristonya?'

'I reckon ... we should bide our time.'

On receiving this unexpected support from Ivan and Khristonya, Grigory livened up.

'Of course, that's just what I was saying. That's why I quarrelled with Knave. It's not like cutting down a vine. A couple of strokes and you're done. We've got to think. Think it over, that's what I say...'

Dong-dong-dong-dong! The sound of the tocsin burst from the bell-tower, filling the square, streets and lanes; the clangour rolled over the smooth brown expanse of flood waters, over the damp chalky headlands, broke up in the forest into lentil-like fragments, and died away in a whimper. Then again it rang out, urgent and incessant. Dong-dong-dong-dong!

'There it goes, they're calling us now!' Khristonya blinked. 'I'll be off in my boat. Over to the other side and into the forest. Let 'em try and find me!'

'Well, what's it to be?' Koshevoi rose heavily, like an old man.

'We won't go just now,' Grigory answered for himself and the others.

Koshevoi's eyebrow twitched again and he swept his heavy golden-curled forelock back from his forehead.

'Fare ye well then... It seems our ways must part!'

Ivan smiled apologetically.

'You're young, Mishka, and hot-headed... You think they won't come together again? Yes, they will! Have hope!'

Koshevoi said goodbye and left. He crossed the yard and slipped through to the neighbour's threshing-floor. Knave was crouching there by a ditch. He must have known that Mishka would come this way. He stood up to meet him.

'Well?'

'They won't come.'

'I knew that. They're yellow... And Grigory... He's a bastard, your friend is! That's a sour devil if ever there was one! He insulted me, the swine! Just because he's stronger... If I'd had a rifle with me, I'd have killed him,' he concluded with something like a sob in his voice.

As Mishka strode along beside him he glanced at Knave's prickly, bristling head and thought, 'And he would too, the polecat.'

They walked quickly, every clang of the bell driving them on like the lash of a whip.

'Come home with me, we'll get some grub and be on our way! On foot. I'll leave my horse behind. Are you taking anything?'

'Mine's all on my back already,' Knave sneered. 'I never got me any mansions or estates... There's half a month's wages I haven't collected though. Well, let old pot-belly Sergei Platonovich get rich on it. He'll dance with joy because I didn't draw my pay.'

23—1106

The bell stopped ringing. The drowsy morning stillness remained undisturbed. Chickens were scratching in the ashes by the road, calves roamed along the fences, already fat on the young green shoots. Mishka looked back. Cossacks were hurrying towards the square for the meeting. Some of them came out of their \yards, buttoning up their uniform coats and tunics. A horseman scorched across the square. By the school a crowd had gathered, the women's kerchiefs and skirts showing up whitely, the men's backs a solid mass of black.

A woman carrying empty pails stopped in their path and, not wishing to offend tradition, said crossly, 'Come on then or I'll have to cross your path!'

Mishka wished her a good morning and, darting a smile at him from under softly curving brows, she asked, 'All the Cossacks are going to the meeting, but you're headed the other way? Why aren't you going, Mikhail?'

'I've work to do at home.'

They reached the lane. The roof of Mishka's little house and the nesting box for starlings with its dangling cherry-stick perch swinging in the wind came into view. On the hill beyond, the windmill was turning feebly, a loose strip of canvas flapping from one of its sails, the steep tin roof rattling.

The sun was not bright, but warm. A fresh breeze was blowing from the Don. At the corner, in the yard belonging to Arkhip Bogatiryov, a craggy old fellow with Old Believer principles, who had once served in a Guards battery, some women were claying and whitewashing the large round-shaped house in readiness for Easter. One of them was puddling clay and dung. She was tramping round the pit, holding her skirt high with her fingertips and laboriously dragging her plump white legs out of the mire. Her calves still bore the red marks of the garters which she had pulled up above the knee, and which were now biting into her thighs.

She was very fond of her appearance and, although the sun was still low on the horizon, her face was swathed in a kerchief. Her companions, two young women, Arkhip's daughters-in-law, were perched high on ladders under the eaves of the smartly thatched roof, and were busy whitewashing. Their sleeves were rolled up to the elbows, the bast brushes were swishing to and fro, and splashes of whitewash were falling on their faces despite the kerchiefs they had pulled down to the eyes. They were singing together in well attuned voices. Maria, the elder daughter-in-law, a widow, who had been openly chasing Koshevoi, was a freckled but good-looking woman. She led the song in a low, almost masculine voice, whose strength and richness were renowned throughout the village.

...Ah, there's no one suffers more...

The others took it up and the three voices skilfully span the innocently mournful lament:

> *Than my darling at the war.*
> *A gunner-boy is he*
> *But he only thinks of me...*

Mishka and Knave walked along by the fence, listening to the song, which was overlaid now and then by the lusty neighing of horses in the meadow.

> *Then a letter came for me*
> *To say my love was dead.*
> *Oh, he's dead, my darling's dead,*
> *And lies beneath a tree.*

Maria glanced round at Mishka with her warm grey eyes gleaming from under her kerchief, her whitewash-stained face brightening in a smile, and she went on in that deep-toned loving voice:

> *His curls, his light-brown curls,*
> *By the wind are blown about.*
> *And his eyes, his dark-brown eyes,*
> *A black crow has pecked them out.*

Mishka gave her one of the affectionate smiles he always had for women, and to Pelageya, the one who was puddling the clay, said, 'Pick 'em up now! I can't see all of you over the fence.'

Pelageya frowned.

'You could if you wanted to.'

As she stood on the ladder with a hand on her hip, Maria looked round and drawled softly, 'Where've you been, lovey?'

'Fishing.'

'Don't go far away and we'll have a tumble in the barn.'

'What about your father-in-law, you shameless hussy!'

Maria clicked her tongue and with a laugh swung her whitewash brush at Mishka. The white drops sprinkled over his cap and jacket.

'Couldn't you lend us Knave at least? He could help us to do the house!' the younger girl called after them, with a flash of her sugar-white teeth.

Maria said something in an undertone and the women burst out laughing.

'The randy bitch!' Knave frowned and quickened his pace, but a gentle, languorous smile spread over Mishka's face and he corrected him.

'Not randy, she just likes a good time. And I'll have to leave her behind, the darling. Well, "Fare thee well, my love!"' he murmured in the words of the song, and turned in at the gate of his yard.

XXIII

After Koshevoi's departure the other Cossacks sat for a time without speaking. The bell was still clanging wildly over the village, making the narrow windows of the little cottage vibrate. A dim morning shadow stretched across the yard from the shed. The young grass was grizzled with dew. Even through the window the blue sky beckoned with azure depths. Ivan glanced at Khristonya's shaggy drooping head.

'Mebbe it won't go any further? After the pasting they got from the Migulinskaya men, they won't want to try again...'

'Not likely!' Grigory writhed impatiently. 'Now they've started, they'll keep it up. Well, shall we go to the meeting?'

Ivan reached for his cap; fighting his own doubts, he asked, 'Well, lads, maybe we are stuck in the mud? Mikhail's a hot-head, but he knows what he's doing. He's made us look small.'

No one replied. They trooped out in silence and headed for the square.

Ivan strode along, staring thoughtfully at the ground. His conscience was troubling him. Truth was on the side of Knave and Koshevoi; all of them should have got out right away instead of hanging about in the village. The excuses he had made for himself were flimsy, and a mockingly reasonable voice from within crushed them as a horse's hoof crushes the ice on a puddle. The only firm decision Ivan could reach was that in the first skirmish he would desert to the Bolsheviks. The decision formed in his mind as they were walking to the meeting, but he told neither Grigory nor Khristonya about it, realising vaguely that their feelings differed from his own and, somewhere in the back of his mind, fearing them. The three men had stood together in rejecting Knave's proposal on family grounds, but each of them had known that the excuse was not valid and could provide no justification. Now separately, each in his own way, they felt embarrassed, as though they had done something vile and shameful. They walked on without speaking. As they were passing Mokhov's house, Ivan could bear the hateful silence no longer and, in a fit of self-accusation, said, 'You can't get away from it. We were Bolsheviks when we came home from the front, and now we're running for cover! Let others fight for us while we cling to the women's skirts.'

'I've done my share of fighting,' Grigory muttered, turning away.

'But look at them... Acting like a bunch of bandits, and we're supposed to join 'em? What kind of Red Guards are they? Raping women, stealing other people's property. We've got to stop and see where we're going. The blind man always trips up at the corners.'

'Did you see all this, Khristonya?' Ivan asked fiercely.

'It's what people say.'

'Ah, what people say...'

'Well, no more now... Someone might hear.'

The square had blossomed with Cossack caps and trouser stripes; here and there a black sheepskin busby was to be seen. The whole village had assembled, save the women. It was all old men and Cossacks of frontline age and younger. In front, leaning on their sticks, were the oldest of all,—honorary judges, members of the parish council, school patrons, and the churchwarden. Grigory looked round in search of his father's silvery grey beard. His father and father-in-law, Miron Korshunov, were standing together. In front of them, in his grey dress uniform and all his regalia stood Grandad Grishaka, propping himself up on a knobbly stick. Next to Korshunov stood Avdeich the Braggart, Matvei Kashulin, Arkhip Bogatiryov and shopkeeper Atyopin, also sporting a Cossack cap; then came a semi-circle of familiar faces— the bearded Yegor Sinilin, Horseshoe Yakov, Andrei Kashulin, Nikolai Koshevoi, the lanky Borshchev, Anikei,

Martin Shamil, the bony miller Gromov, Yakov Koloveidin, Merkulov, Fedot Bodovskov, Ivan Tomilin, Yepifan
Maksayev, Zakhar Korolyov, and the Braggart's son
Antip, a little snub-nosed Cossack. While crossing the
square, Grigory had spotted his brother, Petro, with the
orange and black ribbons of his George Crosses pinned to
his shirt, exchanging banter with one-armed Alexei Shamil. The green eyes of Mitka Korshunov showed up to
the left. Mitka was taking a light from Prokhor Zykov's
cigarette. Prokhor was helping him by puffing hard,
goggling his calf-like eyes and pursing his lips. Behind
them was a crowd of younger Cossacks. In the middle
of the circle, at a rickety table that had sunk its four legs
deep into the still damp soil, sat the chairman of the
village Revolutionary Committee Nazar and beside him,
one hand resting on the table, stood a lieutenant unknown to Grigory in a field-service cap with the small
oval cockade of the old Russian army, a tunic with its
shoulder straps intact, and tight khaki breeches. The
chairman of the Revolutionary Committee was speaking
to him diffidently, and he was bending forward to
listen, tilting a large protruding ear towards the chairman's beard. The square was buzzing quietly like a
beehive. There was much chatting and joking, but all
faces were tense. Someone, unable to bear the suspense
any longer, shouted in a young voice, 'Come on, let's get
on with it! What are you waiting for? We're nearly all
here!'

The officer straightened up, took off his cap and began
speaking in an easy, relaxed manner, as if to his own
family.

'Elders, and you, brother Cossacks of the frontline!
You've heard about what happened in the village of
Setrakov?'

'Who is he? Where does he come from?' Khristonya's
voice boomed.

'Vyoshenskaya stanitsa, Chornaya Rechka, I think.
His name's Soldatov,' someone answered.

'A few days ago,' the lieutenant continued, 'a detachment of Red Guards marched into Setrakov. They had
been driven back from the railway when the Germans
occupied the Ukraine and approached the borders of the
Don Army Region. Having lost the railway, they struck
out across Migulinskaya country. When they entered the
village, they started pillaging the Cossacks' property,
raping the women, making illegal arrests, and so on.

Word was sent to the surrounding villages, who took up arms and attacked the marauders. Half the Red detachment was destroyed and the other half taken prisoner. The Migulinskaya men captured some very valuable equipment. Now both the Migulinskaya and Kazanskaya stanitsas have thrown off the yoke of the Bolshevik power. Old and young, the Cossacks have risen in defence of the quiet Don. In Vyoshenskaya the Revolutionary Committee has been broken up and an ataman elected in its place, and the same thing has happened in most of the villages.'

At this point in the lieutenant's speech a restrained murmur rose among the old men. The chairman writhed on his chair, like a trapped wolf.

'Everywhere detachments have been formed. And you, too, must form a detachment out of frontline men to protect the stanitsa from a fresh onslaught of these barbaric bandit hordes. We must restore our own form of government! Red power is not what we need—it brings only depravity, not freedom! We cannot allow the muzhiks to dishonour our wives and sisters, to defile our Orthodox Christian faith, to desecrate our holy places of worship, to rob us of our property, of what is ours by right. Isn't that so, elders?'

The square gave a loud grunt of agreement. The lieutenant started reading out a mimeographed appeal. The chairman slipped away from his table, forgetting his papers. The crowd listened without breathing a word, save for a few mutterings from the frontline men at the back.

As soon as the officer began to read, Grigory left the crowd and made for home, walking unhurriedly across the square towards the corner of Father Vissarion's house. Miron noticed his departure and nudged Pantelei.

'Your younger one's taken himself off!'

Pantelei limped out of the crowd and called in a voice, both beseeching and imperative, 'Grigory!'

Grigory turned and stopped, but did not look round.

'Come back, son!'

'Why're you leaving? Back you come!' other voices clamoured and all faces turned towards Grigory.

'And they made him an officer!'

'Don't snub us!'

'He was with their lot!'

'He's drunk plenty of Cossack blood!'

'Red belly!'

The shouts reached Grigory. He listened gritting his teeth, evidently fighting a battle with himself; another minute, perhaps, and he would have walked away without a backward glance.

His father and Petro breathed with relief when Grigory seemed to wobble and then walked back to the crowd with his eyes lowered.

The old men went to work with a will. In next to no time Miron Korshunov was elected ataman. The freckles on Miron's white face turned grey as he stepped forward into the middle of the circle and with an embarrassed air accepted the symbol of office, a bronze-headed ataman's staff, from his predecessor. He had never been ataman before. Whenever the choice had fallen on him, he had refused, pleading that he had not deserved such an honour and lacked the education for it. But the old men greeted his nomination with clamorous urgings.

'Take the staff! Don't try to back out, man!'

'You're the best farmer in the village.'

'You won't throw away the village property!'

'Mind you don't drink the villagers' shares like Semyon did!'

'This one wouldn't do that!'

'At least, he'll be able to pay the fine, if he does!'

'We'll fleece him like a lamb!'

The sudden election and the whole atmosphere of impending battle was so unusual that Miron consented without much persuasion. And the election itself was different from what it used to be. In the old days the stanitsa ataman would arrive, the spokesmen, one for every ten households, would be summoned, and they would cast their votes for the candidates, but now the procedure was simple, 'All those who are for Korshunov, kindly, step to the right.' The crowd surged to the right leaving only the cobbler Zinoviy, who had a grudge against Korshunov, standing on the same spot, solitary as a burnt tree-stump in a meadow.

Before Miron could wipe the sweat from his brow, the staff was thrust into his hands and voices were roaring all over the square near and far,

'You owe us a drink on that!'

'You've swept the board!'

'Come on, stand us a pailful!'

'Up with him! Carry him shoulder high!'

But the lieutenant interrupted the shouting and skilfully steered the meeting to the consideration of practical matters. He reminded them that a commander for the detachment would have to be elected too. Probably he had heard about Grigory in Vyoshenskaya and, in praising him, praised the whole village.

'You ought to have an officer as your commander! You'll do better an action and have fewer losses. There are plenty of heroes in your village—enough and to spare! I can't impose my will on you, Cossacks, but for my part I would recommend Cornet Melekhov.'

'Which one?'

'We've got two of 'em.'

The officer ran his eyes over the crowd and settled on Grigory's bowed head, which could just be seen at the back. His face broke into a smile and he shouted, 'Grigory Melekhov!.. What d'you say, Cossacks?'

'Good for him!'

'We'll be only too glad!'

'Grigory Panteleyevich, damn his guts!'

'Out in the middle! Out you come!'

'The elders want to have a look at you!'

Propelled from behind, a purple-faced Grigory stepped out into the middle of the circle and stood looking round like a hunted animal.

'Lead our sons!' Matvei Kashulin thumped his stick on the ground and swept his arm across his chest in the sign of the cross. 'Take charge of 'em and lead 'em so that they'll be safe as geese with a good gander. Just as the gander guards his tribe and defends them agin man and beast, so must you guard ours! Earn yourself another four crosses, God grant you strength!'

'Pantelei Prokofievich, what a son you've got!'

'He's got a fine head on his shoulders! Real sharp he is, the rapscallion!'

'You lame devil, you'll stand us a gallon for this.'

'Haw! Haw! Haw!.. We'll celebrate!'

'Elders! Quiet there! Shall we enlist two or three age-groups without calling for volunteers? You can't be sure with volunteers.'

'Take three age-groups! Three years!'

'Five!'

'Better have volunteers!'

'Volunteer yourself then! What the devil's stopping you?'

While the lieutenant was discussing something with the new ataman, four old men from the top end of the village came up to him. One of them, a puny, toothless old fellow, who went by the nickname of 'Wrinkle', was known to have spent a lifetime in litigation. He went to court so often that his white mare, the only horse on his farm, knew the road there herself. It was enough for her drunken master to fall on to the wagon and chirp in his high-pitched voice, 'To the court!' and she would set off in the right direction... Pulling off his tattered cap, Wrinkle came up to the lieutenant. The other old men, one of whom, Gerasim Boldyrev, was a good farmer and much respected in the village, halted near by. Wrinkle, who apart from his other merits, had exceptional gifts of oratory, was the first to appeal to the lieutenant.

'Your Honour!'

'What is it, elders?' The lieutenant bowed politely and brought his big fleshy ear closer to the old man.

'Your Honour, you can't be very well informed like about our man here that you've given us as commander. We, old men, protest agin this decision of yours, and we're competent to do so. We reject him!'

'Reject him? But why?'

'Because we can't trust him when he himself was in the Red Guards and was one of their commanders and came back only two months ago because he was wounded.'

The lieutenant flushed pink. His ears seemed to swell with the inrush of blood.

'But that's impossible! I'd heard nothing of the kind. No one ever told me anything about this.'

'It's true, he was with the Bolsheviks,' Gerasim Boldyrev confirmed sternly. 'We don't trust him!'

'Get rid of him! Ye know what the young Cossacks are saying? He'll betray us in the first battle, they say!'

'Elders!' the lieutenant cried, rising on tiptoe; he addressed himself to the old men, cunningly avoiding the frontliners. 'Elders! We have just elected Grigory Melekhov as detachment commander, but there seem to be some objections. I've just been told that during the winter he was in the Red Guards. Can you trust him with your sons and grandsons? And you, brother frontline men, will you follow such a commander with an easy mind?'

The Cossacks stood in stunned silence. The outburst, when it came, was an incomprehensible jumble of shouts and exclamations. Only when the hubbub had subsided did old bushy-browed Bogatiryov step forward. He took off his hat and surveyed the assembled Cossacks.

'What I think with my foolish head is that we won't

give Grigory Panteleyevich this post. He has gone astray, we've heard all about it. First, let him earn our trust and atone for his guilt, and after that we'll see. He's a good fighter, that we know... But no one can see the sun when it's covered in mist. And we can't see his merits—our eyes are misted by his service with the Bolsheviks!'

'Reduce him to the ranks!' young Andrei Kashulin blazed.

'Let's have Petro Melekhov as commander then!'

'Grigory can go with the herd!'

'A fine commander he'd have made!'

'Don't have me then! What the hell do I care!' Grigory shouted from the back, reddening from the strain he was under. Cutting the air with his hand, he repeated, 'I wouldn't take it on myself! I'll be damned if I want the job!' He plunged his hands into the deep pockets of his trousers and with shoulders hunched stalked away towards home.

Shouts followed him.

'Now then! Not so much of that!'

'Stinkhorn! Sticking his nose in the air!'

'Ho! Ho!'

'That's the Turkish blood in him!'

'He won't take that quietly. He wouldn't even take it from the officers in the trenches, let alone here.'

'Come back!'

'Haw! Haw! Haw!'

'Grab him!'

'Hold him!'

'Boo!'

'What are you sucking up to him for? He needs dealing with, he does!'

It was some time before they calmed down. In the heat of argument someone pushed someone and someone else drew blood from somebody's nose; one of the young men unexpectedly earned a black eye. When peace had been restored, they set about electing the commander of their detachment. Petro Melekhov was chosen and turned almost scarlet with pride. But at this point the lieutenant ran into unforeseen trouble, like a spirited horse facing a fence that was a little too high for him. The time came for the volunteers to sign up, but there were no volunteers. The frontline men, who had showed no particular enthusiasm for the proceedings, hummed and hawed and offered various jocular excuses.

'Why don't you put your name down, Anikei?'

To which Anikei muttered, 'I'm a bit too young. Haven't grown any whiskers yet.'

'Keep your jokes to yourself! Are you trying to make fun of us?' old Kashulin howled into his ear.

Anikei waved him aside like a troublesome mosquito. 'Go and put your own Andrei down.'

'I have already!'

'Prokhor Zykov!' came a shout from the table.

'Here!'

'Shall we put you down?'

'I dunno...'

'Your name's down!'

Mitka Korshunov walked up to the table with a serious look on his face and commanded abruptly, 'Put me down!'

'Well, is there anyone else who feels like it?.. Fedot Bodovskov—what about you?'

'I've got a rupture,' Fedot muttered almost inaudibly, modestly lowering his squinting Kalmyk eyes.

The frontline men guffawed and held their sides while the jokers let themselves go.

'Take your old woman with you! If your lump comes out, she'll push it back.'

'Haw! Haw! Haw!' the men at the back roared and coughed, teeth gleaming and eyes butter-bright with laughter.

And from the other side a new jest fluttered across like a tom-tit.

'We'll take you as cook! If you make us a rotten borshch, we'll fill ye up with it till your rupture comes out t'other end!'

'He won't be able to run too fast—he'll do all right for retreating.'

The old men stormed indignantly.

'Enough o'that! Very funny, aren't they!'

'This is a fine time to show your foolishness!'

'Shame on you, lads!' one of the old men tried to remonstrate. 'What about God! Eh? What about Him! He won't forgive you. While men are getting killed out there, you... What about God?'

'Tomilin, Ivan,' the lieutenant turned round with a searching look.

'I'm an artilleryman,' Tomilin responded.

'Shall we put you down? We need artillerymen.'

'All right then, put me down.'

Zakhar Korolyov, Anikei and several others started

teasing the gunner.

'We'll make you a wooden pop-gun!'

'You can load it with pumpkins and use spuds for buckshot!'

Amid the jokes and laughter sixty Cossacks were enlisted. The last to volunteer was Khristonya. He came up to the table and said firmly, after a little pause, 'Stick me down too, then! Only I'm telling you beforehand, I won't fight.'

'Then why put your name down?' the lieutenant asked irritably.

'I'll have a look, officer. I just want to have a look.'

'Put him down,' the lieutenant said with a shrug.

It was nearly noon before the meeting broke up, having decided that the Cossacks should march out the next day in support of the Migulinskaya men.

The following morning out of the sixty volunteers only forty assembled on the square. Petro, dashingly attired in a greatcoat and top boots, surveyed his Cossacks. Many had blue shoulder straps freshly sewn to their uniforms with the numbers of their old regiments on them; others preferred to have none. The saddles bulged with bags and bundles containing food, spare underwear, and cartridges saved from the front. Not everyone had a rifle, but most had cold steel.

Women, girls, children and old men had gathered on the square to see them off. Caracoling on his restive horse, Petro formed up his half squadron, surveyed the motley array of mounts and riders, some in greatcoats, some in tunics, some in tarpaulin raincoats, and gave the order to march. The little force climbed the hill at a walk, heads turning to look back sombrely at the village, and someone in the rear rank fired a shot. At the summit Petro pulled on his gloves, stroked his wheaten-coloured moustache, turned his horse so that it danced sideways, and, smiling and holding on his cap with his left hand, shouted, 'Squadron. At the canter, forward!'

The Cossacks rose in their stirrups, waved their whips and broke into a canter. The wind blowing in their faces and tousling the horses' manes and tails, promised rain. The talk and jokes began. Khristonya's mighty black stallion stumbled. Its master swore and used his lash; the horse arched its neck and broke out of line at a gallop.

The Cossacks' cheerful mood lasted all the way to Karginskaya. They were sure there was no fighting to be done, and that the Migulinskaya affair had been nothing but a chance Bolshevik incursion into Cossack territory.

XXIV

They rode into Karginskaya just before evening. There were no frontline men in the stanitsa—they had all left for Migulinskaya. Petro dismounted his detachment on the square, outside merchant Levochkin's shop, and went to the stanitsa ataman's house. He was met by a brown-faced officer of magnificent physique. His long loosely fitting shirt had no shoulder straps and was girdled with a Caucasian belt, his wide Cossack trousers were tucked into white woollen socks. A pipe hung from the corner of his thin lips. His brown twinkling eyes looked out cannily from under lowered brows. He stood on the porch, smoking and watching Petro as he approached. His whole massive figure, the bulging iron-hard banks of chest and arm muscle that showed up under his shirt suggested a man of no ordinary strength.

'Are you the stanitsa ataman?'

The officer puffed a cloud of smoke from under his drooping moustache and answered in a deep baritone, 'Yes, I'm the stanitsa ataman. With whom have I the honour to speak?'

Petro gave his name. The ataman shook hands and inclined his head.

'Likhovidov, Fyodor Dmitrievich.'

Fyodor Likhovidov, a Cossack of Gusyno-Likhovidov-sky village, was no ordinary person. After finishing his education at a cadet college, he had disappeared for some years, then suddenly reappeared in the village with permission from the highest authority to recruit volunteers from among the Cossacks who had completed their active service. In the region of what was now Karginskaya stanitsa he had mustered a squadron of daredevils and led them off into Persia, where he and his men had served as the Shah's personal bodyguard for a year. During the Persian revolution he, like the Shah, had been forced to flee and, having lost most of his detachment on the way, had as suddenly as before turned up again in Karginskaya with some of his Cossacks, three Arab thoroughbreds from the Shah's stables, and a rich haul of booty—precious rugs, rare ornaments, and silks of the finest hues. He made merry for a month, scattered a good many Persian gold coins here and there, galloped about the village on a snow-white exquisitely graceful horse that carried its head like a swan, rode it up the steps of Levochkin's shop, made his purchases and paid for them without dismounting, and rode out through the door at the other end. Then once again Likhovidov disappeared as suddenly as he had appeared. And with him went his inseparable companion and messenger Pantelyushka, a Cossack of his village and a fine dancer, the horses, and everything that he had brought from Persia also disappeared.

Six months later Likhovidov showed up in Albania. From the Albanian town of Durazzo his acquaintances in Karginskaya started receiving blue-skied picture postcards of the Albanian mountains with strange postmarks. From there he went on to Italy, explored the Balkans, visited Romania and Western Europe, and even got as far as Spain. The name of Fyodor Likhovidov carried an aura of mystery. All kinds of rumours and conjectures about him circulated around the villages. It was known that he was in close contact with monarchist circles, that he had connections with certain important personages in Petersburg, and that he was thought highly of by the Alliance of the Russian People, but as to the nature of the missions he performed abroad no one had any knowledge whatever.

On his return from abroad Fyodor Likhovidov settled in Penza, at the residence of the Governor General. His acquaintances in Karginskaya once saw a photograph that caused much shaking of heads and astonished clicking of tongues. 'Well, I'll be!..' 'Fyodor Dmitrievich is going up in the world!' 'The people he has to do with, eh?' The photograph showed Likhovidov with a smile on his swarthy hook-nosed Serbian face, giving his arm to the governor's wife as she stepped into a landau. The governor himself was smiling affectionately at him as if he were one of the family, while in the background a broad-backed coachman, arms outstretched, held back the straining horses, that were ready to plunge into a head-long gallop. Likhovidov had one hand raised gallantly to his shaggy sheepskin busby, while the other cupped the elbow of the governor's wife.

After several years' absence, Likhovidov surfaced at the end of 1917 in Karginskaya and established himself there, apparently for good. He brought with him a wife, either Ukrainian or Polish, and a child, took up residence in a modest four-roomed house on the square, and spent the winter hatching certain mysterious plans. All winter (and it was an unusually cold winter for the Don) the windows of his house to the general amazement of the

Cossacks remained wide open—he was toughening himself and his family.

In the spring of 1918, after the Setrakov affair, he was elected ataman. And this was the moment when Fyodor Likhovidov's limitless abilities showed themselves to the full. The stanitsa fell into such ruthless hands that after a week even the old men were shaking their heads. So tight was his hold on the Cossacks that at village meetings after one of his speeches (and he spoke well, for nature had endowed him with mind as well as muscle) the old men would bellow like a herd of prize bulls, 'Good luck to you, Your Honour!' 'Our humblest respects to you!' 'How very true!'

The new ataman ruled with a rod of iron. No sooner came the news of the fighting at Setrakov than all the frontline men in the stanitsa set out for the village. The non-Cossacks (who accounted for a third of the inhabitants) were at first disinclined to go and some of the frontline men with strong Bolshevik sympathies had also showed signs of baulking, but Likhovidov insisted on a meeting and the elders signed a decree that he had drafted for them, deporting all 'muzhiks' who refused to take part in the defence of the Don. And the next day dozens of wagons crammed with soldiers playing accordions and singing, set out in the direction of Napolov and the settlement of Chernetskaya. Out of the non-Cossacks, only a few young soldiers led by Vasily Storozhenko, who had served in the First Machine-gun Regiment, deserted to the Red Guards.

Even from the way Petro walked the ataman could tell that he was an officer who had risen from the ranks. He did not invite him into the house and addressed him with good-natured familiarity.

'No, there's nothing for you to do in Migulinskaya, my dear fellow, they managed without you. I had a telegram yesterday evening. Go home and wait for orders. And give your Cossacks a good shaking-up! A big village like yours and only forty fighting men?! Give 'em a good clouting, the scoundrels! It's their own skins that are at stake! Well, good-day to you and good luck!'

His plain leather shoes scraped the floor as he turned away and carried his powerful body into the house with unexpected ease. Petro went back to the Cossacks on the square and was showered with questions.

'Well? What's going on?'

'Do we head for Migulin?'

Making no attempt to hide his joy, Petro replied with a chuckle, 'Home we go! They managed without us.'

The grinning Cossacks walked to the horses they had tethered to the fence. Khristonya sighed as if a great weight had fallen from his shoulders and slapped Tomilin on the back.

'So home we go, gunner!'

'The women will have been missing us!'

'Well, let's get going.'

Having decided to set off at once without stopping for the night, they rode out of the stanitsa in a disorderly bunch. They had approached Karginskaya unwillingly, seldom even breaking into a trot, but now they rode their horses hard. Sometimes they flew along at a gallop, and the earth that had grown hard from lack of rain muttered dully under their hooves. From somewhere beyond the distant ridges along the Don came gentle shimmers of lightning.

They reached home at midnight. As they rode down the hill Anikei fired his Austrian rifle and a volley of shots announced their return. The dogs all over the village answered with frenzied barking and, scenting the home fires, someone's horse gave a long rasping neigh. In the village they all took their separate ways.

As he said goodbye to Petro, Martin Shamil gave a grunt of relief.

'Well, we've done our fighting. So much the better!'

Petro smiled in the darkness and headed for his yard.

Pantelei came out to tend the horse. When he had unsaddled it and led it into the stable, he and Petro entered the house together.

'So you've given up your campaign?'

'Uh-huh.'

'Well, thank the Lord for that! May it be the last we hear of it!'

A sleepily warm Darya rose and made supper for her husband. Grigory came out of the front room half dressed and, scratching his black-haired chest, winked mockingly at his brother.

'What, beaten them already?'

'I'm beating what's left of the borshch.'

'Well, that's not so bad. We'll soon deal with the borshch, specially if I come and lend you a hand.'

24–1106

Not a word was heard about war right up to Easter, but on Easter Saturday a messenger galloped in from Vyoshenskaya, left his foam-flecked horse at the Korshunovs' gate and with his sabre clattering on the steps ran up on to the porch.

'What's the news,' Miron asked, meeting him on the threshold.

'I want the ataman. Is it you?'

'Yes.'

'Muster your Cossacks at once. Podtyolkov and his Red Guards are marching through Nagolinsky district. Here's the order.' And along with the letter he pulled out the sweat-dampened lining of his cap.

At the sound of voices Old Grishaka appeared on the scene, fastening a pair of spectacles to his nose; Mitka ran in from the yard. The three read the district ataman's order together. The messenger stood leaning against the rail and smearing the streaks of sweat and dust over his wind-scorched face.

On the first day of Easter the Cossacks, after breaking their fast, rode out of the village. General Alferov's order was stern and threatened loss of Cossack status, so the force that marched against Podtyolkov numbered not forty, but one hundred and eight, including several of the old men who were eager for a brush with the Reds. Beaky old Matvei Kashulin rode with his son. Avdeich the Braggart was in the front ranks, sporting a good-for-nothing little mare, and all through the march kept the Cossacks amused with his unbelievable tales; and there was also old Maksayev and a few other greybeards... The young rode because they had to, the old at their own zealous wish.

Grigory Melekhov had pulled the hood of his raincoat over his cap and was riding in the last rank. A fine drizzle was falling from the overcast sky and heavy stormclouds were rolling across the bright green steppe. High up, under the banked clouds, an eagle was hovering. With occasional sweeps of its outspread wings it caught the wind and, borne up by a rising current, flew away to the east, heeling over with a dull glint of brown plumage as it disappeared into the distance.

The steppe was a glistening green, save for the patches of last year's wormwood, the purple saxifrage, and the gleaming bluish-grey mounds standing guard on the ridge of the horizon.

As they rode down the hill into Karginskaya the Cossacks met a Cossack lad who was driving some bullocks out to pasture. He was walking along waving his whip, his bare feet slithering in the mud. At the sight of the horsemen he stopped to stare at them and their mud-bespattered horses with tied-up tails.

'Where're you from?' Ivan Tomilin asked.

'Karginskaya,' the lad answered brightly, smiling from under the jacket he had draped over his head.

'Have your Cossacks gone away?'

'Yes. They've gone to chase out the Red Guards. Would you have some tobacco for a fag? Would you, uncle?'

'Want some baccy, do you?' Grigory reined in his horse.

The Cossack lad came up to him. His rolled-up trousers were wet and the stripes were glistening scarlet. He stared boldly into Grigory's face as he took his pouch out of his pocket, and spoke in a nimble tenor voice.

'Down there, a bit further on, you'll see the dead 'uns. Yesterday our Cossacks were driving some Red prisoners to Vyoshenskaya and they killed them right there... I was minding the cattle, uncle, near that sandy mound, and I saw them being cut down. Terrible it was! As soon as the sabres started slashing, how they screamed and ran... I went and had a look afterwards: mostly Chinese they were. One of them had his shoulder cut right off but he was still breathing, very quick like, and you could see his heart beating under the blood. And his liver was all blue... It was terrible!' he repeated, marvelling to himself that the Cossacks were not frightened by his story, or at least so it seemed to him as he watched the cold indifferent faces of Grigory, Khristonya and Tomilin.

When he had lighted his cigarette, he stroked the wet neck of Grigory's horse and with a 'thank 'ee' ran off after the oxen.

Near the road, in a shallow ravine washed out by the spring floods, lay the mutilated bodies of the Red Guards, lightly sprinkled with sandy loam. A dark-blue leaden face with blood-encrusted lips or a blackened leg in a blue wadded trouser showed up here and there.

'They couldn't even bury 'em properly... The rotten swine!' Khristonya muttered and, suddenly lashing his horse, overtook Grigory and galloped away down the hill.

'Well, now we've seen blood on the Don land too,' Tomilin said with his cheek twitching in a crooked grin.

24*

XXV

It was an extraordinary morning. At nine the heat was already quite noticeable, and at noon a wind came romping in from the south, clouds skimmed across the sky, and in the suburbs the air grew heady with the smell of sticky young poplar leaves and of brickwork and earth baking in the sun.

The day before, Bunchuk and Anna with a mixed detachment from the Don Council of People's Commissars had been at the station, disarming an anarchist detachment that had mutinied; only yesterday Bunchuk's face had looked old and deeply lined; but today the south wind seemed to have dispelled his worries and he was busy on the porch with an oil stove in quite a domesticated fashion, glancing suspiciously now and then at Anna, whose lips were curved in a sceptical smile.

Before breakfast he had unwisely boasted of having once had quite a talent for cooking cutlets in Galician sauce.

'You don't mean it?' Anna had asked doubtfully.

'Yes, I do.'

'Where did you learn that?'

'What does that matter? During the war, a Polish woman taught me.'

'Go and make some then. I'm not so sure you can.'

And here he was at the stove, his brow furrowed again. There was so much hidden mischief in Anna's smile that he just couldn't stand it. He shook the burnt potatoes in the frying pan and frowned.

'Of course, if you keep breathing down my neck and making fun, how can you expect me to produce anything. Besides, what sort of cooking stove is this? It's a blast furnace, if you want to know!'

Anna drawled her reply almost dreamily.

'Why didn't you become a chéf? What wonderful dishes you would have made... How masterfully you would have run the kitchen with its intoxicating odours of onion and bay leaf. Really now, why didn't you take up the culinary art? So many mysteries, so much that has not yet been studied.'

'Oh, come off it!'

Anna toyed with a strand of her hair, winding it round her finger, and looked up laughingly at Bunchuk.

'I'm going to tell the boys today that you're only a self-styled machine-gunner and used to be chief chéf in the kitchen of some Royal Highness or other.'

Bunchuk was sincerely disappointed with the evil-smelling and horrible-tasting concoction he produced instead of his Galician sauce.

Anna ate it heroically and even found words of modest praise.

'Not bad... Quite a nice sauce... Rather bitter though.'

'So it's not so bad after all?' Bunchuk exclaimed more cheerfully, his spirit reviving. 'You know, if you could add a bit of grated horse-radish, then it'd be great...' And he clicked his tongue with relish, failing to notice the look of courageous self-denial on Anna's compressed lips.

Towards the end of their breakfast Anna seemed to droop. She chewed apathetically, lost in thought, and took a long time answering Bunchuk's casual questions. Afterwards she went out and stood by the garden fence, bathed in sunlight and toying absent-mindedly with a wisp of straw she was holding in her teeth.

Bunchuk pressed her head to his shoulder, drinking in the exciting smell of her tousled hair and asked, 'Why are you like this? What's the matter?'

She looked steadily at him, only occasionally dropping her lashes, then unfastened one button of his shirt, fastened it, and again unfastened it.

'Are you going into town?' And without waiting for an answer she went on through bitterly clenched teeth, 'I'll soon be out of action, Ilya...'

'Why?'

She shrugged and watched the shifting patterns of sunlight under a poplar. Leaning forward on the low fence, she said with unexpected bitterness, 'I've been waiting. I didn't believe it. But now I know—in seven or seven and a half months from now I shall be a mother.'

The salty wind from the sea stirred the leaves of the poplar and flicked Anna's hair over her face. She made no attempt to push it back. Her dilated pupils darkened. Bunchuk waited, silently stroking her hand. But as though nursing some secret grudge, she did not respond to his tenderness and walked dejectedly back to the house.

Bunchuk followed her into their room and closed the door. Unable to overcome his impatience, he asked, 'What do we do now?'

'Nothing,' she replied indifferently.

Their silence was a torture. Bunchuk groped for words, painfully aware of the confusion in his thoughts.

'Have it, Anna. By that time we'll have finished with the counter-revolution. What's so bad about having children?' Instinctively he sensed this promised a way out and, smiling awkwardly, he added hurriedly, 'You must have it, Anna! Have a real broth of a boy, plump and bonny. I'll be a peaceable mechanic, and just think what a fine life we'll have! In about three years' time you'll get a nice layer of fat on you and I'll grow a pot-belly, we'll buy ourselves a little house... And, of course, we'll have a geranium on the windowsill and a canary in a cage. On holidays we'll invite people round or we'll go out visiting to other worthies like ourselves. You'll bake Sunday pies and cry your eyes out if the pastry's a failure. We'll have savings in the bank...'

Anna, who had listened at first with a reluctant and cheerless smile, finally gave a little snort.

'That's a fine ideal!'

'Don't you like it?'

'It's not bad.'

'The trouble is there's nothing good in it!'

They went into town together. Rostov, democratised beyond recognition, was teeming with soldiers, workers and poorly dressed office employees. A verdigris sea of shirts, a gleaming array of leather jackets, a black sprinkling of frock coats and here and there a woman's dress embroidering the drab background with white. In the general mass of impoverished petty bourgeois and workers an official's wife in a shabby overcoat, hurrying about her domestic errands, would scarcely have been noticed.

Wind-torn proclamations and orders flapped on the fences. The unswept streets smelled of horse dung and overheated stone.

For some reason Anna was struck by the change in the city's appearance.

'Just look, Ilya, how democratic the city's become. Not a single top-hat to be seen, or a waistcoat either. It's all the colour of stone.'

'A city's a chameleon. If the Whites get here, you know how it will change colour?' Bunchuk said, smiling at some thought of his own and watching a high school student crossing the road in a flapping greatcoat with its buttons cut off and a dark mark on his cap band, where the badge had once been.

An old Chinaman with a wrinkled skin like lemon peel was dancing in a circle on the corner of Sadovaya and Taganrog streets. Beads of sweat stood out on his face.

A sailor was watching his feet with owlish half-tipsy eyes, spitting sunflower husks and making a squeaking sound with his shiny galoshes.

Bunchuk and Anna walked in silence as far as an apartment block that had once belonged to Paramonov, then parted without a word and rather coldly...

That evening, when Podtyolkov interrupted a meeting of the Don Executive Committee to assemble a detachment and lead it in a counterattack against the Novocherkassk Cossacks who were marching on the city, they met again in the same column.

'Go home,' Bunchuk begged quietly, touching Anna's hand.

But she pursed her lips stubbornly.

'Anna, go back!'

This brief encounter in the suburbs was interrupted by an elderly woman who came running out of a lodge gate. She threw soft pieces of a fresh loaf into the passing ranks and, waving her free left hand, shouted bitterly, 'Give it to 'em, the scum! Chernetsov—that aristocratic bastard—killed my husband! How many miners' families have the Cossacks orphaned... Give it to 'em good and hard!.. Pay 'em back for our tears!..'

A soldier with a big balding forehead caught a piece of bread as he passed and swore at her.

'What are you yelling for, you old nosebag! Shut up or one fine day your neighbours will give you away to the Cossacks.'

'Isn't that a symbol of our bond with the working class?' Anna smiled as she noticed Bunchuk looking at her.

'Take cover!' someone at the head of the column shouted.

By now they had left the suburb behind. The fighting started. Short of ammunition, the Cossacks, mounted and on foot, attacked half-heartedly.

But Podtyolkov, striding up and down the line, boomed encouragement.

'Don't grudge your gunpowder, boys! We've got enough for all the contras!'

And ammunition was not spared; volley after volley burst through the stillness and the echoes clucked away somewhere behind the smoky chimney of a brickyard.

Bunchuk licked the bitter-tasting sweat from his lips.

'Shall we mount it here?' a crewman asked.

'That's right.'

'Shall I load it?'

'Yes, come on!'

Bunchuk hurriedly dug a shallow emplacement for the gun and mounted it. His assistant fitted the belt.

XXVI

One of Bunchuk's crew was Maxim Gryaznov, a Cossack from Tatarsky village. Since losing his horse in a skirmish with Kutepov's detachment he had taken to drink and cards. When his horse—that same ox-coloured one with a silver stripe down its back—had been shot from under him, Maxim had taken off the saddle and carried it all of four versts and then, realising that he wouldn't get away alive from the hotly pursuing Whites, had ripped off the richly ornamented breast-band, and with it and the bridle had deserted the field of battle. He had turned up again in Rostov, soon lost at pontoon the silver-mounted sabre that he had taken from a Cossack major he had cut down, gambled away the rest of the harness and even his trousers and kid-leather boots, and reported all but naked to Bunchuk's platoon. Bunchuk found him some clothes and made him welcome. And Maxim might have mended his ways, but in the fighting that soon began round Rostov a bullet opened his head like a meat can. One of Maxim's blue eyes fell out on to his shirt and the blood spurted from the gashed cranium. And it was as if Cossack Gryaznov of Vyoshenskaya stanitsa, once a horse-thief and more recently a hopeless drunkard, had never been.

Bunchuk watched Maxim's death throes for a moment and carefully wiped the gun barrel clean of the blood that had gushed from Maxim's broken head.

The signal for retreat was given and Bunchuk dragged the machine-gun clear, while Maxim lay cooling on the hot ground with his brown back bared to the sun and his shirt pulled up over his head (where he had clawed it in his death agony).

The Red Guard platoon, entirely made up of men who had returned from the Turkish front, dug in at the first crossroads. A soldier with a half-rotted sheepskin cap pushed back off his balding forehead helped Bunchuk to mount the machine-gun, the others built a makeshift barricade across the street.

'Come up and see us sometime!' a bearded fellow

shouted with a grin, scanning the arc of the horizon beyond the nearby hill.

'We'll give 'em a pasting from here!'

'That's right, break it up, Samara!' someone called to a burly lad, who was ripping planks out of a fence.

'There they are! They're coming!' cried the soldier with the balding forehead, who had climbed on to the roof of a vodka store.

Anna dropped down beside Bunchuk. The Red Guards crowded behind the makeshift barricade.

At that moment about nine Red Guards came running like partridges down the side-street on the right, and as they rounded the corner one of them shouted, 'They're just behind us. Run for it!'

The crossroads instantly became silent and deserted. A minute later a mounted Cossack with a white ribbon on his cap and a carbine pressed to his side burst into the square in a cloud of dust. He reined in his horse so hard that it fell back on its hind legs. Bunchuk got in a shot from his revolver and the Cossack dashed away, flattening himself on his horse's neck. The men round the machine-gun hesitated uncertainly, two of them ran along the fence and crouched by the gate.

They were obviously wavering and about to run. The tense silence and dismayed looks offered no promise of steadiness.

Of what happened next only one moment remained vivid in Bunchuk's memory. Anna with her kerchief and hair all awry, unrecognisable in the excitement that had drained her face white, sprang up, rifle in hand, looked round and, pointing at the house beyond which the Cossack had disappeared, shouted in a wobbling voice that was as unrecognisable as her face, 'Follow me!'— and broke into an unsteady, stumbling run.

Bunchuk half rose. An inaudible cry twisted his mouth. He snatched a rifle from the man next to him and with his legs trembling uncontrollably ran panting after Anna, going black in the face from the great and futile effort to shout, call her, turn her back. He could hear the breathing of a few men pounding up behind him and with every fibre of his being he felt that something terrible, irreparable, utterly monstrous was about to happen. In that one moment he knew already that her action could not carry the others along, that it was senseless, irrational, doomed.

At the corner he ran full tilt into the charging

713

Cossacks. They fired a scattered volley. Bullets whistled round him. A pitiful cry came from Anna, like the yelp of a wounded hare. And there she was, sinking to the ground with one arm outstretched and mad-looking eyes. He did not see the Cossacks turn back, did not see those of the platoon who had been near his machine-gun chasing them, inspired by Anna's forward dash. He had eyes only for her as she lay struggling at his feet. Unable to feel the touch of his own hands, he turned her over to pick her up, carry her somewhere, and then he noticed the bloody stain in her left side and the strips of her blue blouse hanging limply round the wound, and realised that the wound was from an explosive bullet, that it meant death for Anna, and saw death in her clouded eyes.

Someone thrust him aside. Anna was carried into the nearest yard and put down in the shade of an outhouse.

The soldier with the balding forehead pushed swabs of cotton wool into the wound and threw them away as they became sodden and black with blood. Bunchuk recovered his self-control, unbuttoned Anna's blouse, tore up his vest and, as he pressed the strips of cloth to the wound, saw the blood bubbling, saw Anna's face turn a bluish white and her black mouth quiver in agony. She gasped for breath, but the air her lungs panted for passed only through her mouth and the wound. Bunchuk cut open her slip and without shame bared her mortally sweating body. Somehow they managed to plug the wound. A few minutes later Anna recovered consciousness. Her sunken eyes glanced up at him from the dark contused circles and were shadowed by the quivering lashes.

'Water! I'm so hot!' she cried and tossed about weeping. 'I want to live! Ilya-a-a! Darling... A-a-ah!'

Bunchuk pressed his swollen lips to her blazing cheeks and poured water on to her chest. It filled the hollows of her collar-bones and dried instantly. She was in a mortal fever. The water was no use. She struggled and tried to break out of his arms.

'I'm so hot!.. I'm on fire!'

As her strength ebbed, she cooled a little and said audibly, 'Oh, Ilya, why? You see how simple it all is... Silly you!.. It's terribly simple really... Ilya... Dearest, try to tell mother... You know...' She half closed her eyes as if in laughter and, trying to overcome her pain and terror, broke into a choking whisper. 'First you feel... just the impact and the burn... Now everything's burning... I feel I'm going to die...' And she frowned as she saw the bitter denying sweep of his hand. 'Don't pretend! My lungs are full of blood... Oh, I can hardly breathe!..'

In moments of respite she spoke volubly, as though trying to throw off everything that weighed upon her mind. With infinite horror Bunchuk noticed that her face was growing lighter, becoming transparent, and yellow at the temples. His glance shifted to the hands lying lifeless at her sides and he noticed that the fingernails were a pinkish blue, like a ripening plum.

'Water... On my chest... It's so hot!'

Bunchuk dashed to the house for water and on his way back no longer heard Anna's gasping cries from the shed. The setting sun shone on her mouth in its last convulsion, on the still warm wax copy of her hand pressed to the wound. Slowly, squeezing her shoulders, he lifted her and for a minute stared at her tapered nose with the tiny darkened freckles at the bridge, and caught the last frigid gleam of the eyes under the black branching brows. Her head fell back helplessly, lower and lower, and in a blue vein on the thin girlish neck a pulse counted her last heartbeats.

Bunchuk pressed his lips to a black half-closed eyelid and called, 'Anna! Friend!' then he stood up, swung round on his heel and walked away, holding himself unnaturally straight and keeping his arms stiffly to his sides.

Like a blind man he walked into a gate-post, gave a choking cry and, imagining he could hear her call, crawled on all fours, faster and faster, his face almost touching the ground. Incoherent mutterings broke from his frothing lips. He crawled along the fence like a wounded animal, with laborious haste; from a shed three Red Guards who had remained in the yard watched him wide-eyed. They exchanged glances, shocked by so repulsive and naked a manifestation of human grief.

XXVII

In the days that followed he lived as if in the delirium of typhus. He went about and did things, he ate and slept, but it was all a kind of stupefied half-awakeness. With wild swollen eyes he gazed uncomprehendingly at the world spread out around him and failed to recognise people he knew well, staring as if he were drunk or had only just recovered from a long and exhausting illness.

Since the day of Anna's death his feelings had temporarily atrophied; he wanted nothing and could think of nothing.

'Eat something, Bunchuk!' his comrades urged him, and he ate, working his jaws lazily and staring dully at one spot.

They watched him and talked of sending him to hospital.

'Are you ill?' one of the machine-gunners asked him the next day.

'No.'

'What's up then? Missing her?'

'No.'

'Well, let's have a smoke. You can't bring her back now, mate. It's no good wasting steam on that.'

When it was time to sleep, they told him, 'Go to bed, Ilya, get some sleep.'

And he went.

He remained in this state of temporary withdrawal from the world of reality for four days. On the fifth, Krivoshlykov met him in the street and took him by the sleeve.

'Ah, so here you are, I've been looking for you.' Not knowing what had happened, he gave him a friendly slap on the shoulder and smiled anxiously. 'What's the matter? You're not drunk, are you? Have you heard of the expedition that's being sent out to the northern districts? A commission of five has been elected. Fyodor's leading it. The northern Cossacks are our only hope. Otherwise we'll be cornered here. Things look bad! Will you go? We need agitators. Well, will you go?'

'Yes,' Bunchuk replied curtly.

'Good. We'll be leaving tomorrow. Go and see Grandad Orlov. He's our astrologer.'

Still in a state of complete mental prostration, Bunchuk got ready to leave, and on the next day, May 1st, rode out with the expedition.

By this time an obviously threatening situation had developed for the Don Soviet Government. The German occupation forces were advancing from the Ukraine and the whole of the Lower Don was in the grip of counter-revolutionary insurrection.

General Popov was ranging across the stud-farm lands and threatening Novocherkassk. The regional Congress of Soviets, held in Rostov from the 10th to 13th of April, was constantly interrupted because the insurgents from

Novocherkassk were marching towards Rostov and had occupied some of the nearby townships. Only in the north, in the Khopyor and Ust-Medveditsa districts were the fires of revolution still smouldering, and it was to their warmth that Podtyolkov and others who had lost all hope of support from the Lower Don Cossacks, were involuntarily drawn. The mobilisation had failed and Podtyolkov, recently elected chairman of the Don Council of People's Commissars, had, on Lagutin's initiative, decided to go north to mobilise three or four regiments of frontline men and hurl them at the Germans and the Lower Don counter-revolution.

An emergency mobilisation commission of five men, headed by Podtyolkov, had been set up. On April 29th they drew from the treasury ten million rubles in gold and old regime notes to finance the mobilisation, hastily assembled a detachment, mainly from the Cossacks of the former Kamenskaya garrison, to guard the cash-box, got together several Cossack agitators and on May Day, already under fire from German aircraft, the expedition set out northwards in the direction of Kamenskaya.

The railway was choked with Red Guard forces retreating from the Ukraine. Cossack insurgents were blowing up bridges and derailing trains. Every day German aeroplanes appeared over the Novocherkassk—Kamenskaya line, hovered like vultures, then swooped with short bursts of machine-gun fire, and the Red Guards came tumbling out of their trains; volley after volley was fired and the smell of slag at the stations mingled with the acrid stench of war and destruction. The planes soared to unbelievable heights, but the marksmen went on emptying their rifles, and anyone near the trains walked ankle-deep in spent cartridges, which covered the sand as golden oak leaves cover a ravine in November.

There was destruction everywhere. Charred, gutted vans and carriages were scattered along the embankments. The insulators on the telegraph poles gleamed white among tangles of slashed wires. Many houses had been destroyed and the fences looked as if they had been hit by a hurricane.

The expedition spent five days trying to get through to Millerovo. On the morning of May 6th Podtyolkov assembled the members of the commission in his carriage.

'We can't go on like this! Let's dump all our stuff and march.'

'What?' Lagutin exclaimed. 'While we're slogging all

717

the way to Ust-Medveditsa, the Whites will ride over us.'

'It's a long way,' Mrykhin said doubtfully.

Krivoshlykov, who had only just caught up with the expedition, sat silently, muffling himself in his greatcoat with its faded red buttonhole tabs. He had malaria. His ears were ringing from the quinine he had taken, and his head was burning and stuffed with pain. He sat hunched on a sack of sugar, taking no part in the discussion and looking angrily, with fevered eyes at Zinka, Podtyolkov's 'sweetheart', the big-breasted blonde he had been taking around with him on the pretext of her being a nurse. Zinka responded to the slender Krivoshlykov's antipathy in kind; lounging with her plump legs up on a box of tea, she chewed at a cigarette with her small vixenish teeth and grinned impudently. They had disliked each other intensely since the day they met. Krivoshlykov had been waiting for the chance to take Podtyolkov to task and get rid of the creature.

'Krivoshlykov, have you lost your tongue?' Podtyolkov asked drily, without looking up from his map.

'What is it?'

'Don't you hear what we're talking about? We've got to march or they'll catch up with us and we'll be finished. What d'you think? You're the learned man among us. Why don't you say something?'

'We could march,' Krivoshlykov began slowly, but suddenly his teeth snapped like a wolf's and he started shaking in a paroxysm of fever. 'We could do that, if we hadn't got so much baggage. You've got more women with you than you can carry. What the hell! I propose we get rid of the lot.'

'Aw, drop that, Mikhail,' Podtyolkov remonstrated, looking embarrassed.

'I won't drop it!' Krivoshlykov forced out through chattering teeth, while Lagutin listened with a quiet smile of encouragement. 'This is no time to cart women around!'

Zinka jumped to her feet, blue eyes smouldering.

'I'm not riding in your cart, you dithering dummy! Stop shaking, can't you!'

'Now then, that's enough!'

'You think a lot of yourself, you drip! Bloody officer!'

'Stop that!' Podtyolkov shouted in a parade-ground voice and shook his fist at Zinka. 'You pipe down! Or I'll throw you out of here by the hair!'

Zinka subsided, nostrils quivering with indignation. Podtyolkov rounded furiously on Lagutin.

'What are you grinning at like a tart! Give me a proper reason why we can't march across country!'

He carried the map of the region to the door and unfolded it. Mrykhin held the corners. The map fluttered and rustled in the wind from the cloudy west and tried to tear itself out of their hands.

'Here, this is how we'll go!' With a smoker's finger Podtyolkov traced a diagonal line across the map. 'See the scale? A hundred and fifty versts, two hundred at the outside. What about it?'

'That's true, damn it!' Lagutin agreed.

'What d'you say, Mikhail?'

Krivoshlykov shrugged irritably.

'I've no objections.'

'I'll go and tell the Cossacks to detrain right away. No point in wasting time.'

Mrykhin looked round expectantly and, encountering no opposition, jumped out of the carriage.

On that sombre rainy morning the train in which Podtyolkov's expedition was travelling had halted not far from Belaya Kalitva. Bunchuk was lying on a seat, covered from head to foot with his greatcoat. The Cossacks in the van were brewing up tea, laughing and cracking jokes at one another.

Vanka Boldyrev, a Migulinskaya Cossack and a great leg-puller, was making fun of one of the machine-gunners.

'What province are you from, Ignat?' his hoarse tobacco-charred voice croaked.

'Tambov,' the docile Ignat replied in his soft bass.

'And you come from Morshansk, I reckon?'

'No, Shatsk.'

'Ah!.. Shatsk—they're a tough lot there. They don't mind fighting anyone as long as it's seven against one. Wasn't it in your village they tried to cut a calve's throat with a cucumber?'

'Go on with you!'

'Oh no, I forgot, that was a different case. In your village they caulked the church with pancakes, then wanted to roll it downhill on some peas. That was it, wasn't it?'

The kettle boiled and Ignat was spared Boldyrev's jokes for a while. But as soon as they sat down to breakfast, he started all over again.

'Ignat, why aren't you eating your meat? Don't you like it?'

'It's all right.'

'Here, take the pig's fanny. It's yummy!'

There was a burst of laughter. Someone choked and broke into racking coughs. There was a scuffle and clatter of boots and a minute later Ignat's vexed breathless tones were heard.

'Eat it yourself, you devil! Who're you shoving your fanny at?'

'It's not mine, it's the pig's.'

'Well, it's unclean anyway!'

And Boldyrev's calm husky voice drawled, 'Unclean? Are you crazy? It had the Easter blessing. You'd better admit you don't eat pork.'

Boldyrev's fellow villager, a handsome Cossack with light brown hair, a holder of all four crosses of St. George, cautioned him.

'Give over, Ivan! You'll run into trouble with this feller. He'll eat the fanny, then we'll have him squeaking for a hog. And where will you get one?'

Bunchuk lay with his eyes closed, oblivious of the talk. He was still reliving the recent past with a pain that seemed to have grown even more intense. Against the blurred screen of his closed eyes he saw the snow-covered steppe with the brown ridges of a distant forest on the horizon; he could almost feel the cold wind and Anna's presence beside him, her dark eyes, the brave and yet tender lines of her sweet mouth, the tiny freckles at the bridge of her nose, the thoughtful line across her brow... The words that came from her lips inaudible, were drowned by other voices, other laughter, but from the gleam in her eyes and the quivering of her lashes he guessed what she was saying. But then there arose a different Anna, her face a bluish yellow, with streaks of tears on her cheeks, a tapered nose and tortured lips.

He bent to kiss the black hollows of her eyes. He groaned and pressed his hand over his mouth to stifle his sobs. Anna never left him for a moment. Her image neither faded nor tarnished with time. Her face, figure, walk, gestures, expressions, the sweep of her brows, they all came together to recreate the whole, the living Anna. He recalled her talk, her sentimentally romantic effusions, all that he had lived through with her. And the vividness of his recall multiplied his suffering tenfold.

He made no attempt to analyse his condition and gave himself up irrationally, like an animal, to his misery, seeking no antidote. Strong and hard though he was, he withered with grief, like a tree attacked by maggots from within.

He was roused when the order came to detrain. He got up, collected his things indifferently and stepped out of the van, then helped with the unloading. Just as indifferently he climbed on to a wagon and rode away on it.

It was drizzling. The stunted grass along the roadside gleamed wetly.

Steppe. The wind sweeping freely over ridges and ravines. Scattered villages, settlements. Behind them the smoke of locomotives, the red cubes of station buildings. More than forty wagons, hired in Belaya Kalitva, were strung out along the road. The black rain-soaked earth made it heavy going for the horses. Mud clung to the wheels and wound on to them like black wads of cotton wool. Both ahead and behind there were crowds of the local miners fleeing eastwards from Cossack violence, taking with them their families and scant belongings.

At the junction of Grachi they were overtaken by the badly mauled detachments of the Red commanders Romanovsky and Shchadenko. The men's faces were an earthy grey, exhausted by the fighting, lack of sleep and constant hardship. Shchadenko came up to Podtyolkov. His handsome face with its clipped English moustache and thin prominent nose was haggard. As Bunchuk walked past he heard Shchadenko say with a fierce weariness in his voice, 'What are you trying to tell me? D'you think I don't know my lads? We're in a tight spot and on top of it all there's the Germans, blast 'em! How can you get a force together now?'

After this exchange Podtyolkov, frowning and disconcerted, ran to catch up with his wagon and started talking agitatedly to Krivoshlykov, who had half risen at his approach. Bunchuk saw Krivoshlykov cut the air with his hand and fire off a few phrases in reply. Podtyolkov looked more cheerful and jumped on to the wagon. Its side gave a crack as it took the gunner's fifteen stone; the driver brought his whip down on the horses' backs and mud spattered on all sides.

'Get a move on!' Podtyolkov cried, screwing up his eyes and throwing his leather jacket open to the wind.

XXVIII

For several days the expedition had been pushing on into the Donets district in an effort to reach Krasnokutskaya. The population of the Ukrainian settlements had everywhere given them a cordial welcome, willingly selling them food and fodder for the horses and offering them shelter, but as soon as the question arose of hiring horses to take them as far as Krasnokutskaya, the Ukrainians began to scratch their heads and, after some humming and hawing, flatly refused.

'We're offering you good money. Why're you giving us the cold shoulder?' Podtyolkov asked one of the Ukrainians.

'Well, man, I value my life more than money.'

'It's not your life I want, I want your horses.'

'I can't do it.'

'Why can't you?'

'You're going into Cossack country, aren't you?'

'And what of it?'

'Something bad might happen. D'you think I don't care for my animals? What'll I do, if they kill my horses? No, man, let me be, I won't go!'

Anxiety grew as they approached Krasnokutskaya. They sensed a change in the attitude of the local people. The friendly hospitality they had encountered in the first settlements gave way to open hostility and suspicion. Food was sold reluctantly, questions left unanswered. The expedition's wagons were no longer surrounded, as they had been at first, by a colourful throng of young Ukrainians. Sombre looks followed them from the windows and people hurried out of their path.

'Are you Christians here or heathens?' the Cossacks in the expedition asked indignantly. 'What are all the dirty looks for?'

And in one of the settlements of the Nagolino district Vanka Boldyrev was so incensed by the cold reception that he threw his hat on the ground and, looking over his shoulder in case any of the senior men were around, shouted hoarsely, 'What are you—men or devils? Can't you speak, blast you? We're shedding our blood for your rights, and you just look through us! That's a fine kind of morality—you ought to be ashamed! We're all equal now, comrades—Cossack or Ukrainian, it's all the same, so you've no call to muck us about. Come on, out with those eggs and chickens. We're paying for everything in old money!'

Half a dozen Ukrainians who had listened to Boldyrev's outburst stood despondently, like horses harnessed to a plough.

Not a word was said in response to his fiery speech.

'Tufties you were and Tufties you'll always be, curse your guts! May you all rot in hell, you devils! There's not a plague bad enough for you, you pot-bellied bourgeois!' Boldyrev threw his tattered hat on the ground again and turned purple with scorn. 'Skinflints! It'd be no good asking you for snow in winter!'

'You needn't growl!' was all the Ukrainians would say to him, and went their separate ways.

In the same settlement one of the Red Guard Cossacks was questioned by an elderly Ukrainian woman.

'Be it true ye're going to rob everyone and kill all our men?'

Without batting an eyelid the Cossack replied, 'Sure it's true. Not all, of course, but all the old ones.'

'Oh, lordy, lordy! What d'ye need them for?'

'We eat 'em with our gruel. The mutton's not very sweet these days, but when you put an old grandad in the pot, you get a fine stew...'

'Ye wouldn't be joking, would ye now?'

'He's pulling your leg, missus! Talking a lot of stupid rot!' Mrykhin interrupted.

And when they were alone, he gave the jester a fierce reprimand.

'Know who to joke with and how to joke! You'll be getting a punch on the jaw from Podtyolkov for that kind of talk! Why stir up trouble? She'll go spreading it around that we really chop up the old folk.'

Podtyolkov started cutting short their rests and stopovers. Burning with anxiety, he pressed on. The day before they entered Krasnokutskaya stanitsa he had a long talk with Lagutin and confided his thoughts.

'We'd better not go very far, Ivan. We'll get down to business as soon as we reach Ust-Khopyorskaya! We'll make a call for recruits and offer them a hundred each, but only as long as they bring their own horses and equipment. No need to throw public money away. And from Ust-Khopyorskaya we'll strike north, through your Bukanovskaya, Slashchevskaya, Fedoseyevskaya, Kumylzhenskaya, Glazunovskaya, Skurishenskaya. By the time we get to Mikhailovka we'll have a division! Won't we?'

'We will, if it's all quiet up there.'

'You think there's trouble up there too?'

'How can you tell?' Lagutin stroked his wispy beard, and said in a thin, uncertain voice, 'We're a bit late... I'm afraid we won't get there in time, Fedya. The officers are at work up there. We ought to hurry.'

'We're hurrying as it is. And don't be afraid! We're not allowed to be afraid.' A stern look came into Podtyolkov's eyes. 'We're leading an expedition, how can we be afraid? We'll be in time! We'll break through! In a couple of weeks from now I'll be thrashing the Whites and the Germans! They'll think all the devils in hell are after 'em when we strike from the Don land!' He paused to pull greedily at his cigarette, then confided the thought that was in the back of his mind. 'If we're too late, it'll be all up with us—and with Soviet power on the Don. We just can't be late! If the officers' revolt gets there before us, it's the end!'

Towards evening on the next day the expedition entered the territory of Krasnokutskaya stanitsa. A little way from the village of Alexeyevsky, Podtyolkov, who was riding with Lagutin and Krivoshlykov in one of the leading wagons, saw a herd grazing in the steppe.

'Let's question the herdsman,' he suggested to Lagutin.

'Yes, go and see what he says,' Krivoshlykov agreed.

Lagutin and Podtyolkov jumped off the wagon and strode towards the herd. The sun-scorched pasture was a glittering brown. The grass was stunted and hoof-marked, and only near the road were there a few yellow clusters of winter-cress and sturdy foxtail rustling its bearded tops. Crushing a sprig of old wormwood in his hand and breathing in the bitter scent, Podtyolkov walked up to the herdsman.

'Hullo there, Father!'

'Praise be.'

'Grazing the herd?'

'Yes.'

The old man lowered at them from under his bushy grey brows and fingered his knob-ended staff.

'Well, how're you getting on?' Podtyolkov began with the usual question.

'We manage, with God's help.'

'What's the news around here?'

'I've heard nothing. And who might you be?'

'Soldiers, going home.'

'Where're you from?'

'Ust-Khopyor.'

'That Podtyolkov isn't with you, is he?'

'Yes, he is.'

The herdsman looked frightened and turned pale. 'What's the matter, Grandad?'

'Well, lads, they say you're going to kill off all the Orthodox folk.'

'Nonsense! Who's spreading such rumours?'

'The ataman said so at a meeting the day before yesterday. Either he'd heard the rumour or got an official paper to say Podtyolkov was on his way here with the Kalmyks to cut us all to bits.'

'So you've got atamans again?' Lagutin glanced at Podtyolkov, who was biting a stalk of grass with his big yellow teeth.

'We elected him the other day. They've closed down the Soviet.'

Lagutin was about to ask another question but a huge white-browed bull suddenly mounted one of the cows and crushed her to the ground.

'He'll break her back, the devil!' the herdsman gasped and with unexpected agility for a man of his age ran towards the herd, shouting, 'It's Nastya's cow!.. He'll break her!.. What are you up to! Heh, Baldy!'

Podtyolkov strode back to the cart, swinging his arms. Lagutin, ever a good farmer, stood looking worriedly at the frail young cow clamped to the ground under the bull's weight and could not help thinking at that moment, 'Yes, he will break her. I reckon he has already, the devil!'

Only when he had assured himself that the cow had survived with her backbone in one piece did he turn and head for the wagons. 'What are we going to do? Surely they haven't got the atamans back all along the Don?' he asked himself. But his attention was again diverted by the superb thoroughbred bull standing by the roadside. Now it was sniffing at a big broad-beamed black cow and nuzzling her with its bulging forehead. Its great dewlap came down to its knees, its long solidly powerful body was taut as a bow-string. Its shortish legs were planted like pillars in the soft ground. And as he reluctantly admired the thoroughbred and let his eyes roam fondly over its glossy dapple-red coat, Lagutin sighed and out of a swarm of anxious thoughts fixed on one, 'We could do with a bull like that back home. Ours are a bit on the small side.' The thought came to him in a flash and stuck. But as he approached the machine-gun cart and looked

at the glum faces of the other Cossacks, he started thinking of the route they would now have to take.

* * *

Worn out by his malaria, Krivoshlykov, the dreamer
and poet, said to Podtyolkov, 'We're racing the counter-
revolutionary wave, trying to keep ahead of it, but it's
sweeping right over us. We'll never beat it now. It's
moving too fast, like surf on a flat beach.'

Of all the members of the commission, only Podtyol-
kov, it seemed, realised the full gravity of the situation.
He sat leaning forward, constantly shouting to the driver,
'Get a move on!'

Some of the men in the rear wagons began to sing,
then fell silent. An occasional shout or burst of laughter
sounded above the creak of the wagon wheels.

The information received from the herdsman was confirmed. Further along the road they met a former frontline Cossack, who was driving to the village of Svechnikov
with his wife. He was wearing shoulder-straps and a
cockade on his cap. After questioning him, Podtyolkov
looked even blacker.

They passed through Alexeyevsky village and it began
to spot with rain. The sky darkened. Only in the east did
a slit in the clouds reveal a scarp of deep-blue sky flooded
with slanting sunlight.

As they drove down a slope into the Ukrainian settlement of Rubashkin they saw people running out of it on
the other side, followed by several wagons going at full
gallop.

'They're running away. They're afraid of us,' Lagutin
said with a look of dismay at the others.

Podtyolkov shouted, 'Get 'em back! Give 'em a shout,
devil take you!'

The Cossacks jumped up on their wagons and waved
furiously. Someone let out a long halloo. 'Heh, where're
you going? Wait!'

The expedition's wagons drove into the settlement at
a rapid trot. Only the wind stirred on the broad deserted
street. In one of the yards a lamenting old Ukrainian woman was tossing pillows into a wagon. Her husband, barefooted and hatless, was holding the horses.

In Rubashkin they learned that the man Podtyolkov
had sent ahead to find billets for the night had been

taken prisoner by a Cossack patrol and carried off. Evidently the main force was not far away. After a brief conference they decided to turn back. Podtyolkov, who had at first insisted on pushing on, wavered.

Krivoshlykov was shivering in a renewed attack of malaria and took no part.

'Shall we try to go on?' Podtyolkov asked Bunchuk, who was also present.

Bunchuk shrugged indifferently. It was all the same to him as long as they kept moving, as long as he could get away from the grief that pursued him relentlessly. Podtyolkov paced up and down by the machine-gun cart and talked of the advantages of making for Ust-Medveditsa, but he was curtly interrupted by one of the Cossack agitators.

'You're mad! Where're you leading us? Into the arms of the counter-revolution? No more of that nonsense, mate! We're going back! We don't want to get killed! What's that, eh? Look, over there!' He pointed to the hill beyond the settlement.

They all turned to look. The figures of three horsemen stood out clearly on the crest of the hill.

'That's one of their patrols!' Lagutin exclaimed.

'And there's another!'

More horsemen appeared on the hill. They bunched together and broke up, disappeared below the skyline, then reappeared. The expedition returned through Alexeyevsky village, where the local people, evidently warned by the Cossacks, ran away or hid themselves at the sight of their wagons.

Dusk fell. A cold persistent drizzle set in. Soaked and shivering, the men walked beside the wagons, keeping their rifles at the ready. The road ahead wound its way down a slope into a hollow and wound its way up again. Cossack patrols appeared on the skyline and disappeared. They were shadowing the expedition, screwing the nervous tension to an even higher pitch.

Where the hollow was cut by a ravine Podtyolkov sprang down from his wagon and shouted to the others to be on the alert. He slipped the safety catch off his cavalry carbine and walked on beside the wagon. A blue pond of flood water came into view behind a dam. The muddy edge of the pond was patterned by the hoofmarks of cattle. The crumbling top of the dam was overgrown with tall grass and bindweed. Stunted sedge grew by the water and the sharp-pointed sabre grass hissed in the rain.

Podtyolkov had expected a Cossack ambush at this spot, but the patrol he sent on ahead discovered no one.

'Don't expect them now, Fyodor,' Krivoshlykov whispered, calling him over to the wagon. 'They won't attack now. They'll come at night.'

'That's what I think too.'

XXIX

The clouds gathered in the west and it grew dark. From somewhere very far away, beyond the Don, came a flash of lightning. The shimmering orange light quivered like the wing of a wounded bird. On the other side the sunset glowed palidly under the black blanket of cloud. Like a bowl filled with silence, the steppe still harboured in its folds the last sad glimmerings of day. There was something autumnal about that May evening. Even the grass, which had not yet flowered, gave off an indefinable odour of decay.

Podtyolkov noticed the many faint fragrances of the wet grass as he strode along. Now and then he would stop and knock the mud off his heels, then straighten his big body and trudge on wearily, his flapping leather jacket creaking in the wet.

They reached the village of Kalashnikov well after nightfall. The Cossack troops left their wagons and roamed through the village in search of shelter for the night. Podtyolkov, still worried, ordered sentries to be posted, but the men responded unwillingly. Three refused to go on duty.

'Let them be tried by a court of their own comrades! And shot for disobeying orders!' Krivoshlykov burst out angrily.

Worn out by the constant tension, Podtyolkov let his arm drop in a bitter gesture.

'The road's knocked all the spirit out of 'em. They won't put up a fight. We're finished, Mikhail!'

Lagutin got a few men together and set up posts round the village.

'Don't go to sleep, lads! Otherwise they'll get us!' Podtyolkov urged the Cossacks he knew best, as he made the rounds of their billets.

He sat all night at a table with his chin resting in his hands, sighing huskily. Just before dawn he dozed off for a moment and let his massive head sink on to the table, but almost at once Robert Fraschenbruder came in from next door, and they started preparing for the march. It was light when Podtyolkov opened the door. He was met in the porch by the mistress of the house, who had been milking the cow.

'There're horsemen on the hill,' she said matter-of-factly.

'Where?'

'Out there.'

Podtyolkov darted out into the yard. On the higher ground, beyond the white pall of mist that hung over the village and the willow groves, several groups of Cossacks could be seen. They were trotting or cantering towards the village from all sides.

Podtyolkov's men soon began to assemble in the yard where his machine-gun cart was standing.

Vasily Miroshnikov, a sturdy Migulinskaya Cossack with a bushy forelock, came in from one of the outposts and called his commander aside. Eyes on the ground, he said, 'Well, Comrade Podtyolkov, we've just seen some delegates from their lot,' he waved in the direction of the hill, 'and they told us to tell you to lay down your arms and surrender. Otherwise they're going to attack.'

'You!.. You, bastard!.. What are you trying to tell me?' Podtyolkov seized Miroshnikov by the lapels of his greatcoat, flung him aside and ran to the machine-gun cart. Snatching up his rifle by the barrel he shouted to his Cossacks, 'Surrender?.. Talk to counter-revolutionaries? That's who we're fighting! Follow me! Action stations!'

They tumbled out of the yard and ran to the edge of the village. As they approached the last of the houses Podtyolkov was overtaken by Mrykhin, a member of the commission.

'This is going too far, Podtyolkov! Are we to fight our own brothers? Shed their blood? Surely we can settle it peaceably!'

Seeing that only a few of his men had followed him and realising that he would inevitably be defeated if there was a clash, Podtyolkov silently took the bolt out of his rifle, threw it away and, pulling off his cap, waved it resignedly.

'As you were, lads! Back to the village.'

They walked back and the whole expedition assembled in three adjoining yards. A force of some forty mounted Cossacks had ridden down from the high ground. Some of them entered the village.

At the invitation of the village elders Podtyolkov went to the outskirts to discuss the terms of surrender. The enemy's main forces remained in position, surrounding the village. As he walked along the cattle track Podtyolkov was overtaken and halted by Bunchuk.

'Are we going to surrender?'

'They've got the whip hand... What's the use... What else can we do?'

'D'you want to get killed?' Bunchuk's face twisted in a violent tremor.

Ignoring the old men who were escorting Podtyolkov, he shouted in a hoarse toneless voice, 'Tell them we won't give up our arms! You're no leader for us now! Who've you consulted? Who agreed to let you go and betray us?' Then he turned away sharply and, brandishing his revolver, walked back into the village.

On his return he tried to persuade the others to fight their way through to the railway, but the majority were obviously in a mood for reconciliation. Some turned away from Bunchuk, others were openly hostile.

'Fight 'em yourself, mate. You won't get us to fight our own brothers!'

'We'd trust ourselves to them even unarmed.'

'It's Holy Week, and you expect us to shed blood?'

Bunchuk strode to his wagon, which was standing near a barn, threw his greatcoat under it and lay down, still gripping the ribbed butt of his revolver. His first impulse had been to escape but the idea of slipping away, of desertion was hateful to him and, giving up the thought, he waited resignedly for Podtyolkov's return.

Podtyolkov did not reappear until about three hours later. A huge crowd of Cossacks from other districts followed him into the village. Some were mounted, others were leading their horses. Those who were simply on foot pressed round Podtyolkov and Captain Spiridonov, who had formerly served in the same battery as Podtyolkov and was now in command of the force that had been assembled to round up his expedition. Podtyolkov was holding his head high and walking very straight and carefully, as if he had taken too much to drink. Spiridonov was saying something to him, smiling maliciously. Behind him rode a Cossack clasping the rough-hewn pole of a large white flag.

The streets and yards where the expedition's wagons stood were soon thronged with the newcomers. A lively hubbub broke out at once. Some of the newcomers were former regimental comrades of the Cossacks in the expedition. Joyful exclamations and laughter rang out.

'So it's you, chum. How did you land up here?'

'Hullo there, Prokhor!'

'Praise be.'

'And we nearly got into a fight with you. Remember how we chased the Austrians at Lvov?'

'Cousin Danilo! Christ is risen!'

'Verily he is!' came the reply, followed by the traditional smacking kiss, and the two Cossacks stood smoothing their moustaches and smiling as they slapped each other's shoulders.

The talk nearby was on a different note.

'We haven't had the chance to break our fast yet.'

'But you're Bolsheviks, what fast would you have been keeping?'

'We may be Bolsheviks but we still believe in God.'

'Ho! Ho! That's stretching it!'

'God's truth!'

'Where's your cross?'

'Here!' and a burly broad-faced Red Guard Cossack unbuttoned his tunic and fished out the tarnished bronze cross that hung on his brown hairy chest.

The old men with pitchforks and axes, who had also been with the detachment for catching the 'rebel Podtyolkov', exchanged wondering glances.

'They told us you'd denied your Christian faith.'

'They say you've sold yourselves to Satan.'

'We had word that you were robbing the churches and killing off all the priests.'

'That's a lot of cock!' the broad-cheeked Red Guard declared confidently. 'They've been giving you all that bosh. Why, before we left Rostov I went to church and took the sacrament.'

'Well, bless me!' a gnarled old man carrying a lance with its shaft cut short clapped his hands joyfully.

The hubbub spread through the yards and down the street. But after half an hour a group of Cossacks led by a sergeant-major from Bokovskaya stanitsa came along the street, pushing their way through the crowd.

'All those from Podtyolkov's detachment, fall in to have their names taken!' they shouted.

Captain Spiridonov in khaki tunic with khaki-coloured shoulder-straps took off his officer's cap with its sugary-white officer's cockade, and, swinging round, shouted, 'Everyone from Podtyolkov's detachment, move over to the fence on the left! Everyone else to the right! We, your frontline brothers, together with your delegation, have decided you must hand in all your weapons because the local people are afraid of you when you're armed. So pile your rifles and other weapons on your wagons and we'll guard them together. We'll send your detachment to Krasnokutskaya and at the Soviet there you'll get all your weapons back.'

A stir of alarm passed through the Red Guard Cossacks. Shouting broke out in one of the yards. Korotkov, a Cossack from Kumshatskaya stanitsa, raised the cry, 'No surrender of weapons!'

A low threatening murmur spread along the street and through the crowded yards.

The Cossacks of the pursuit force surged to the right and the Red Guards were left standing in scattered groups in the middle of the street. Krivoshlykov, his greatcoat draped over his shoulders, looked round huntedly. Lagutin curled his lip. Voices were raised in protest.

Bunchuk, who had firmly resolved not to give up his weapons, ran up to Podtyolkov carrying his rifle.

'We won't surrender our weapons! D'you hear?!'

'It's too late now,' Podtyolkov muttered, crumpling the expedition roll nervously.

The roll fell into the hands of Spiridonov. He glanced through it and asked, 'It says you have a hundred and twenty-eight men. Where are the rest?'

'They dropped out on the way.'

'Ah, so that's it. Well, order them to give up their arms.'

Podtyolkov was the first to take off his revolver holster; as he handed it over he muttered almost inaudibly, 'The sabre and rifle are in the wagon.'

The disarming began. The Red Guards handed in their weapons unwillingly, tossing revolvers over fences or hiding them as they scattered through the yards.

'We shall search anyone who doesn't surrender his weapons!' Spiridonov shouted, grinning cheerfully.

Some of the Red Guards led by Bunchuk refused to surrender their rifles; they were disarmed by force.

Much commotion was caused by a machine-gunner, who galloped out of the village taking the breachlock of his machine-gun with him. Some of the others slipped away in the confusion. Spiridonov at once detailed an escort, surrounded those who had remained with Podtyolkov, searched them all and tried to call the roll. The prisoners responded reluctantly; some answered back.

'What's all the checking for? We're all here.'

'Take us to Krasnokutskaya!'

'Comrades! Pack it up!'

When he had sealed the cash-box and sent it off to Karginskaya under a strong escort, Spiridonov formed up the prisoners and changed both his tone and manner.

'Double file! By the left! Quick march! Silence!'

A growl of protest passed through the Red Guard ranks. They stepped off raggedly and soon broke up into a straggling crowd.

Podtyolkov, who in the end had urged his men to give up their arms, must still have been hoping that something would save the situation. But as soon as the prisoners were outside the village the escorting Cossacks started harassing them and riding into those on the flanks. An old Cossack with a fiery red beard and an age-blackened ring in his ear struck Bunchuk with his whip for no reason at all. The lash raised a weal across Bunchuk's cheek. Bunchuk turned clenching his fists, but a second even fiercer blow made him dart in among the crowd. His involuntary reaction was prompted by the instinct of survival and as the bodies of his comrades closed tightly round him, for the first time since Anna's death his lips twisted in a nervous smile and he marvelled at the thought of how tenaciously the desire to live persists in every human being.

The escort began beating up their prisoners. The old men, their brutality roused by the sight of defenceless enemies, rode them down and leaned out of the saddle to lash or batter them with the flat of their swords. Those who were being hit involuntarily tried to take refuge in the crowd; scuffles and shouting broke out.

A tall smart-looking Red Guard from the Lower Don shook his fists and cried, 'Kill us now if you're going to kill us! Why are you taunting us!'

'What about your promise?' Krivoshlykov's voice rang out.

The old men calmed down a little. In reply to one of the prisoners, who asked where they were being taken, one of the escort, a young frontline man, who evidently had Bolshevik sympathies, whispered, 'The order was that you were to go to the village of Ponomaryov. Don't get scared, lads. We won't do you any harm!'

They reached the village.

Spiridonov and two Cossacks posted themselves at the door of a little shop and questioned the prisoners as they filed inside.

'Christian name? Surname? Place of birth?' He wrote down the answers in a dog-eared field notebook.

It came to Bunchuk's turn.

'Surname?' Spiridonov put the point of his pencil to the paper and, glancing at the Red Guard's sullen broad-browed face, saw the lips quivering to spit and dodged hastily. 'Get inside, you cur! You can die without a name!'

Inspired by Bunchuk's example, a Tambov man refused to answer. A third prisoner also preferred to die nameless and stepped silently across the threshold.

Spiridonov locked the door himself and posted sentries.

While the food and weapons taken from the expedition's wagons were being shared out near the shop, a hastily organised court-martial composed of representatives of the villages that had taken part in the capture of Podtyolkov was being held in one of the neighbouring houses.

The president of the court was Vasily Popov, a stocky fair-browed Cossack major, born in the stanitsa of Bokovskaya. He was sitting at a table under a mirror draped with embroidered towels, his elbows planted far apart, his cap tilted on to the back of his head. His oily benevolently stern eyes roved searchingly over the faces of the Cossack members of the court. The subject under discussion was the measure of punishment to be meted out.

'What shall we do with them, gentlemen?' Popov repeated his question.

He leaned over and whispered something to Captain Senin, who was sitting beside him. Senin nodded hastily. Popov's eyes narrowed, the cheerful gleam faded from the corners, and a different pair of eyes, glitteringly cold and hard, showed under the sparse lashes.

'What shall we do with these traitors to their native land, who came to plunder our homes and destroy the Cossacks?'

One of the elders, an Old Believer named Fevralev from Migulinskaya, jumped up like jack-in-a-box.

'Shoot the lot!' He shook his head like one possessed and, staring round with squinting, fanatical eyes, almost choking in his own saliva, shouted, 'No mercy for them, the judases! Kill all the yids among them! Kill them! Crucify them! Burn them to death!'

His scanty beard wagged and his gingerish grey hair fluttered wildly. He sat down panting and wet-lipped, his face a brownish-brick colour.

'What about exiling them?' Dyachenko, another member of the court, proposed hesitantly.

'Shoot them!'

'Put 'em to death!'

'That's what I say too!'

'Execute them all in public!'

'Clear our soil of this vermin!'

'Death to them!'

'Of course, they ought to be shot! What else!' Spiridonov exclaimed indignantly.

With every shout Major Popov's mouth drooped at the corners, becoming coarser and losing the recent complacent benevolence of a man well satisfied with himself and the world. Soon it was set in hard, crooked lines.

'To be shot!.. Write that down!' he ordered the clerk of the court, looking over his shoulder.

'What about Podtyolkov and Krivoshlykov? Are they to be shot as well? That's too good for them!' said an ancient thick-set Cossack sitting by the window, who up to now had been occupied with turning down the wick of the spluttering oil lamp.

'As the ringleaders, they shall be hanged!' Popov replied curtly and repeated what he had said to the clerk. 'Now write, "Decree. We, the undersigned..."'

The clerk, whose name was also Popov (he was a distant relative of the major's) bowed his blond, neatly combed head over the table and scratched with his pen.

'We must be running out of oil,' someone sighed regretfully.

The lamp flickered and the wick smoked. The silence was broken only by the buzzing of a fly trapped in a spider's web on the ceiling, the scraping of the pen on the paper, and the heavy, asthmatic breathing of one of the members of the court.

DECREE

April 27 (May 10), 1918

We, the undersigned, elected representatives of the following villages of Karginskaya, Bokovskaya and Krasnokutskaya stanitsas

Vasilevsky	Stepan Maksayev
Bokovsky	Nikolai Kruzhilin
Fomin	Fyodor Kumov

Upper Yablonovsky	Alexander Kukhtin
Lower Dulensky	Lev Sinev
Ilyinsky	Semyon Volotskov
Konkovsky	Mikhail Popov
Upper Dulensky	Yakov Rodin
Savostyanov	Alex. Frolov
Milyutinskaya stanitsa	Maxim Fevralev
Nikolayev	Mikhail Groshev
Krasnokutskaya stanitsa	Ilya Yelankin
Ponomaryov	Ivan Dyachenko
Yevlantyev	Nikolai Krivov
Malakhov	Luka Yemelyanov
Novo-Zemtsev	Matvei Konovalov
Popov	Mikhail Popov
Astakhov	Vasily Shchegolkov
Orlov	Fyodor Chekunov
Klimo-Fyodorovsky	Fyodor Chukarin

President of the Court *V. S. Popov*

HEREBY DECREE

(1) That the despoilers and betrayers of the toiling people, listed below, numbering eighty in all, be put to death by shooting, with the exception of two—Podtyolkov and Krivoshlykov—who, as the leaders of this group, shall be hanged.

(2) That the Cossack Anton Kalitventsov from Mikhailovsky village be acquitted for lack of evidence.

(3) That Konstantin Melnikov, Gavril Melnikov, Vasily Melnikov, Aksyonov and Vershinin, who fled from Podtyolkov's detachment and were arrested in the stanitsa of Krasnokutskaya, be punished in accordance with Article One of this decree (put to death).

(4) That this decree be carried out tomorrow, April 28 (May 11), at 6 a. m.

(5) That Captain Senin be put in charge of the prisoners and that by 11 p. m. today two Cossacks from each village armed with rifles be placed at his command; the members of the court shall bear the responsibility for any failure to carry out this order; the sentence shall be carried out by five Cossacks from each village, who shall be sent to the place of execution.

Signed *V. S. Popov,*
President of the Military Department
A. F. Popov, Clerk

LIST
of members of Podtyolkov's detachment condemned to death by court-martial 27 April (O. S.) 1918

No	Stanitsa	Name and Surname	Sentence
1	Ust-Khopyorskaya	Fyodor Podtyolkov	Hanged
2	Yelanskaya	Mikhail Krivoshlykov	Hanged
3	Kazanskaya	Avraam Kakurin	Shot
4	Bukanovskaya	Ivan Lagutin	"
5	Nizhegorodskaya prov.	Alexei Iv. Orlov	"
6	Nizhegorodskaya	Yefin Mikh. Vakhtel	"
7	Ust-Bystryanskaya	Grigory Fetisov	"
8	Migulinskaya	Gavril Tkachov	"
9	Migulinskaya	Pavel Agafonov	"
10	Mikhailovskaya	Alexander Bubnov	"
11	Luganskaya	Kalinin	"
12	Migulinskaya	Konstantin Mrykhin	"
13	Migulinskaya	Andrei Konovalov	"
14	Poltavskaya prov.	Konstantin Kirtsa	"
15	Kotovskaya	Pavel Poznyakov	"
16	Migulinskaya	Ivan Boldyrev	"
17	Migulinskaya	Timofei Kolychev	"
18	Filim.-Chelb.	Dmitry Volodarov	"
19	Chernyshevskaya	Georgy Karpushin	"
20	Filim.-Chelb.	Ilya Kalmykov	"
21	Migulinskaya	Savely Rybnikov	"
22	Migulinskaya	Polikarp Gurov	"
23	Migulinskaya	Ignat Zemlyakov	"
24	Migulinskaya	Ivan Kravtsov	"
25	Rostov	Nikifor Frolovsky	"
26	Rostov	Alexander Konovalov	"
27	Migulinskaya	Pyotr Vikhlyantsev	"
28	Kletskaya	Ivan Zotov	"
29	Migulinskaya	Yevdokim Babkin	"
30	Mikhailovskaya	Pyotr Svintsov	"
31	Dobrynskaya	Illarion Chelobitchikov	"
32	Kazanskaya	Klimenty Dronov	"
33	Ilovlinskaya	Ivan Avilov	"
34	Kazanskaya	Matvei Sakmatov	"
35	Lower Kurmoyarskaya	Georgy Pupkov	"
36	Ternovskaya	Mikhail Fevralev	"
37	Khersonskaya prov.	Vasily Panteleimonov	"
38	Kazanskaya	Porfiry Lyubukhin	"

39	Kletskaya	Dmitry Shamov	Shot
40	Filonovskaya	Safon Sharonov	"
41	Migulinskaya	Ivan Gubarev	"
42	Migulinskaya	Fyodor Abakumov	"
43	Luganskaya	Kuzma Gorshkov	"
44	Gundorovskaya	Ivan Izvarin	"
45	Gundorovskaya	Miron Kalinovtsev	"
46	Mikhailovskaya	Ivan Farafonov	"
47	Kotovskaya	Sergei Gorbunov	"
48	Lower Chirskaya	Pyotr Alayev	"
49	Migulinskaya	Prokopy Orlov	"
50	Luganskaya	Nikita Shein	"
51	Senior Mechanic R.P.T.K.	Alexander Yasensky	"
52	Rostov	Mikhail Polyakov	"
53	Razdorskaya	Dmitry Rogachov	"
54	Rostov	Robert Fraschenbruder	"
55	Rostov	Ivan Silender	"
56	Samarskaya prov.	Konstantin Yefimov	"
57	Chernyshevskaya	Mikhail Ovchinnikov	"
58	Samarskaya prov.	Ivan Pikalov	"
59	Ilovlinskaya	Mikhail Koretskov	"
60	Kumshatskaya	Ivan Korotkov	"
61	Rostov	Pyotr Biryukov	"
62	Razdorskaya	Ivan Kabakov	"
63	Lukovskaya	Tikhon Molitvinov	"
64	Migulinskaya	Andrei Shvetsov	"
65	Migulinskaya	Stepan Anikin	"
66	Kremenskaya	Kuzma Dychkin	"
67	Baklanovskaya	Pyotr Kabanov	"
68	Mikhailovskaya	Sergei Selivanov	"
69	Rostov	Artyom Ivanchenko	"
70	Migulinskaya	Nikolai Konovalov	"
71	Mikhailovskaya	Dmitry Konovalov	"
72	Krasnokutskaya	Pyotr Lysikov	"
73	Migulinskaya	Vasily Miroshnikov	"
74	Migulinskaya	Ivan Volokhov	"
75	Migulinskaya	Yakov Gordeyev	"

Three others refused to disclose their identity.

The clerk finished copying out the list, put a mis-shapen colon at the bottom of the decree, and handed his pen to the nearest member of the court, 'Sign your name!'

Konovalov, the representative of Novo-Zemtsev village, in his best tunic of grey German cloth with red lapels,

leaned forward over the table, smiling sheepishly. His thick, calloused, burnished-black fingers gripped the schoolboyishly nibbled pen stiffly.

'I'm not much of a hand at writing,' he said, carefully tracing the letter K.

The next to sign was Rodin, who frowned and perspired with the effort of penmanship. Another man set about the task with a preliminary shake of the pen, then signed and withdrew the tongue that had curled out of his mouth in the process. Popov wrote his name, underlined it with a flourish, and stood up wiping his damp face with a handkerchief.

'The list must be appended,' he said with a yawn.

'Kaledin will thank us in the other world for this,' Senin said with a youthful smile as he watched the clerk blotting the damp sheets on the whitewashed wall.

For some reason no one responded to the jest. They walked out in silence.

'Lord Jesus...' someone muttered with a sigh in the darkness of the porch.

XXX

During that night of milky yellow starlight hardly any of the prisoners cooped up in the little shop could sleep. The scraps of talk quickly petered out. Anxiety and the lack of air were suffocating.

In the evening one of the Red Guards had asked to be let out.

'Open up, comrade! I want to go outside. It's a call of nature!'

He stood with his undershirt hanging out over his trousers, tousled and barefooted, pressing his darkening face to the keyhole.

'Open the door, comrade!'

'A wolf is your comrade,' one of the guards responded at length.

'Open up, brother!' the suppliant tried a new form of address.

The sentry put down his rifle, listened to the swish of wings of some wild duck flying over for the night's foraging and, when he had got his cigarette going, pressed his lips to the keyhole.

'Do it in your pants, chum. They won't rot in one night and, come morning, they'll let you into the heavenly kingdom even in wet ones.'

'We're done for!' the Red Guard said despairingly, and turned away from the door.

They sat with their shoulders touching. In one corner Podtyolkov emptied his pockets and tore up a pile of banknotes, muttering and swearing violently. When he had finished with the money he took his boots off and touched Krivoshlykov on the shoulder.

'Well, they've tricked us, that's clear! Tricked us, blast their guts!.. Ah, it's a pity, Mikhailo! When I was a kid I used to go out shooting with my father's gun in the woods on the other side of the Don. And it was like being in a great green tent. You'd come to a pool and there'd be ducks sitting there. Sometimes I'd miss and I'd be so riled I'd want to howl. And it's like that now—I missed my chance! If we'd left Rostov three days earlier, we wouldn't be facing death here now. We'd have turned their whole counter-revolution upside down!'

Krivoshlykov gave a tortured smile in the darkness.

'To hell with 'em, let them kill us! I don't feel scared of death yet... "Of all my fears the sum is we'll meet as strangers in the world to come..." We won't know each other when we meet over there, Fedya... That's the terrible thing!'

Lagutin was telling someone about his home village and how his grandfather used to tease him and call him 'wedge head' because he had such a long head, and what a whipping the old man had given him when he caught him on someone else's melon patch.

The rambling threads of conversation were easily broken that night.

Bunchuk had found a place just by the door and was hungrily breathing in the faint draught that came through the crack. As he looked back over his past life he suddenly recalled his mother, but the thought was like a hot stab of pain and he drove it away, taking refuge in memories of Anna, of their last days together... This brought him the relief of happy resignation. He was not in the least frightened by thoughts of death. He felt no shiver down the spine or gnawing dismay at the idea that his life was about to be taken. He prepared himself for death as for some dreary repose after a hard and bitter journey which had left his body so tired and aching that nothing could rouse him.

The men around him were talking both cheerfully and sadly about women, about love, about the joys, great or small, that it had woven into each man's heart.

They spoke of their families, their dear ones... They spoke of harvest. The wheat was coming up well, already it could hide a rook. They pined for vodka and freedom and had some hard words for Podtyolkov. But at last sleep covered many of them with its black wing and, exhausted both physically and morally, they fell asleep, lying, sitting, standing.

At daybreak someone, either awake or sleeping, broke into a violent sobbing. It is frightening when big, rough men, who have not known the salty taste of tears since childhood, begin to weep, and the drowsy stillness was shattered at once by half a dozen voices.

'Shut up, you bastard!'

'Old woman!'

'I'll tear your throat out if you don't stop!'

'The family man shedding a tear!'

'Some people here are trying to sleep—where's your conscience?!'

The man who had given way to tears snuffled and fell silent.

Stillness was restored. Cigarettes glowed in various corners but no one talked. The place smelled of male sweat, of confined healthy bodies, of cigarette smoke, and the fresh effervescence of the dew that had fallen during the night.

A cock bugled awakening day. Footsteps were heard, and the clank of iron.

'Who goes there?' one of the sentries called softly.

Someone coughed and a young, ready voice answered from a distance, 'Friends. We're going to dig the grave for Podtyolkov's lot.'

There was a general stirring in the shop.

XXXI

The Tatarsky detachment commanded by Cornet Petro Melekhov arrived in Ponomaryov at dawn on May 11th.

The village was full of Cossacks from the Chir. Some were taking their horses down to the stream, others were making their way in bunches to the outskirts of the village. Petro halted his detachment in the square and ordered them to dismount. Several men came up to them.

'Where're you from, Cossacks?' one of them asked.

741

'From Tatarsky.'

'You're a bit too late... They've caught Podtyolkov without your help.'

'Where are they then? Have they sent 'em off somewhere?'

'Over there...' The Cossack waved towards the sloping roof of the little shop, and broke into a laugh. 'Cooped up like chickens.'

Khristonya, Grigory Melekhov and a few others came closer.

'Where would they be going to send 'em?' Khristonya inquired.

'To kingdom come.'

'What's that?.. What's this yarn?' Grigory seized the man by the lapel of his greatcoat.

'Tell a better one, Your Honour!' the Cossack replied challengingly and gently freed himself from Grigory's clutching fingers. 'Look over there, they've got a swing ready for 'em.' And he pointed to the gallows that had been erected between two stunted willow-trees.

'Tether the horses in the yards,' Petro commanded.

* * *

Dark clouds draped the sky. Rain pattered down. A dense crowd of Cossacks and their women had gathered on the edge of the village. The local people, informed that the execution was to take place at six in the morning, attended willingly, as though it were some rare, entertaining spectacle. The Cossack women were festively attired, some had their children with them. The crowd gathered on the common, jostling round the gallows and the long pit about fifteen feet deep nearby. The children danced about on the damp clay thrown up on one side of it; the men greeted each other and entered into lively discussion about the forthcoming execution; the women whispered sorrowfully.

Major Popov arrived looking sleepy and serious. He chewed at his cigarette, baring a sound row of teeth, and gave orders to the guard platoon.

'Keep the crowd away from that pit! Tell Spiridonov to bring up the first batch!' He checked the time and stood watching the onlookers, hustled by sentries, back away from the place of execution, and then gather round it in a tight colourful semicircle.

Spiridonov and a squad of Cossacks marched quickly to the shop. On the way he met Petro Melekhov.

'Any volunteers from your village?'

'Volunteers for what?'

'To carry out the sentence.'

'No, there aren't and there won't be any!' Petro answered sharply, stepping round the officer and walking on.

But some volunteers came forward. Mitka Korshunov swaggered up to Petro, brushing aside the straight hair that had fallen from under his cap and showing the glittering rushy green of his half-closed eyes.

'I'll have a shot... Why'd you say no? I'm willing.' He lowered his eyes in a smile. 'Give me some bullets. I've only got one clip.'

Mitka, Andrei Kashulin, his palid face viciously tense, and the Kalmykish-looking Fedot Bodovskov, volunteered for the firing squad.

A whisper, then a restrained murmur rippled through the huge jostling crowd when the first batch of condemned men surrounded by the escort left the shop.

Podtyolkov was in front, barefooted, in his loose black woollen breeches, his leather jacket unbuttoned and wide open. He planted his big white feet confidently in the mud, slipped and lifted his left hand a little to keep his balance. Krivoshlykov, deathly pale, staggered along beside him, scarcely able to walk. His eyes were unnaturally dry and bright, his mouth was twitching. He tugged at the greatcoat draped over his shoulders and jerked his shoulders as though shivering with cold. These two had for some reason not been stripped, but the rest were in only their underclothes. Lagutin picked his way along beside the heavily striding Bunchuk. They were both barefooted. A rent in Lagutin's pants revealed a yellowish calf covered with a fine down of hair. He looked embarrassed, holding the torn edges together, and his lips were trembling. Bunchuk was staring over the heads of the Cossack escort into the grey cloud-swaddled distance. His cold sober eyes were blinking nervously and his big hand had crept under the open collar of his shirt to stroke the dense hair on his chest. He seemed to be waiting for something impossible and joyous to happen... Some of the others kept a semblance of indifference on their faces. The grey-haired Bolshevik Orlov swung his arm challengingly and spat at the feet of the guards, but two or three had such desperate misery in their eyes, such

743

infinite horror on their contorted faces that even the Cossack escort turned away to avoid their glance.

They were walking fast. Podtyolkov supported Krivoshlykov as his feet slid from under him. The sea of white kerchiefs and blue-and-red Cossack caps drew nearer. Podtyolkov glowered at it and uttered a loud obscene oath, then suddenly noticed Lagutin looking at him.

'What's up?'

'You've gone grey in the past few days... Proper dappled you are at the temples!'

'It's enough to make anyone turn grey,' Podtyolkov heaved a sigh and, wiping the sweat from his narrow forehead, repeated, 'Such pleasures would turn anyone grey. Even a wolf goes grey in captivity and I'm a human being.'

No more was said. The crowd was all round them. The yellow clay-strewn ditch that was to be their grave showed up on the right.

'Halt!' Spiridonov commanded.

And then Podtyolkov stepped forward and let his eyes roam wearily over the foremost ranks of the assembled villagers, where the beards were mostly grey or grizzled. The ex-frontline men were keeping to the back, stung by conscience. Podtyolkov spoke huskily but clearly, his drooping moustache twitching slightly.

'Elders! Allow me and Krivoshlykov to watch our comrades go to their death. You can hang us afterwards. Right now we'd like to be able to watch our friends and comrades and help the ones who are weak in spirit.'

It grew so quiet that the rain could be heard pattering on his cap.

Major Popov, somewhere at the back, showed his yellowed, nicotine-stained teeth in a grin; he had no objections. The old men replied in a discordant chorus.

'We'll let ye!'

'Let 'em stand by!'

'March 'em back from the grave.'

The crowd parted and formed a lane for Krivoshlykov and Podtyolkov to pass along. They stood at a short distance, hemmed in on all sides, scanned by hundreds of eyes, and watched the Cossack guards unskilfully forming up the Red Guards with their backs to the grave. Podtyolkov could see well, but Krivoshlykov had to stand on tip-toe and stretch his thin unshaven neck.

Bunchuk was on the far left. His shoulders were slightly hunched and he breathed heavily, keeping his eyes fixed on the ground. Next to him stood Lagutin, leaning over to pull the hem of his vest over his torn trouser leg. The third was Ignat, the man from Tambov, and next to him was Vanka Boldyrev, who had changed beyond recognition and looked at least twenty years older. Podtyolkov tried to make out the fifth man and with difficulty recognised Matvei Sakmatov, a Cossack from Kazanskaya stanitsa, who had shared all their troubles and joys ever since the days in Kamenskaya. Two more men stepped up to the grave and turned their back to it. Petro Lysikov laughed in arrogant defiance, shouted obscene abuse, and brandished his dirty clenched fist at the subdued crowd. His companion, Koretskov, kept silent. The last man was carried forward. He tried to hang back and dragged his lifeless legs on the ground, clutching at the Cossacks who were pulling him, turning his tear-stained face this way and that, and trying to break free.

'Let me go, brothers! Let me go, for God's sake! Brothers! Good lads! What are you doing? I won four crosses in the German war!.. I've got children!.. Oh God, I've done nothing wrong!.. What are you doing this for?..'

A burly guardsman thrust a knee into his chest and flung him towards the grave. Only then did Podtyolkov with a thrill of horror recognise the man as one of the most fearless of his Red Guards, a Migulinskaya Cossack called to the colours in 1910, a handsome fair-moustached man, holder of all four crosses of St. George. They picked him up, but he at once fell to the ground and crawled up to the Cossacks, pressing his parched lips to the boots that kicked him in the face; his voice came in terrible strangled gasps.

'Don't kill me! Have mercy!.. I've got three children!.. A little girl... Good lads, brothers!..'

He flung his arms round a guardsman's knees, but the man shook himself free and kicked him on the ear with an iron-tipped heel. Blood spurted from the other ear and flowed down on to the white collar of his shirt.

'Stand him up!' Spiridonov shouted furiously.

Somehow they pulled him to his feet and ran back. The volunteers in the opposite rank raised their rifles. The crowd gasped and froze into silence. A woman gave a scream of horror...

Bunchuk felt a great urge to look again at the grey haze of the sky, at this sorrowful earth where he had lived and struggled for twenty-nine years. He raised his eyes and saw the line of Cossacks drawn up at a distance of fifteen paces; one of them, a big man with narrowed greenish eyes and a forelock that had fallen from under the peak of his cap on to his narrow white forehead, was leaning forward with tightly pressed lips and aiming straight at his—Bunchuk's—chest. Just before the shot Bunchuk's ear-drums were slashed by a scream as a young freckled woman darted out of the crowd and ran away into the village, clasping her child to her breast with one hand and covering its eyes with the other.

After the straggling volley, when the eight had fallen and lay sprawled by the graveside, the men in the firing squad ran up to them.

Seeing that the Red Guard he had shot was still writhing and gnawing at his shoulder, Mitka fired again.

'Look at that devil,' he whispered to Andrei Kashulin. 'He chewed his shoulder up but died silent, like a wolf.'

Ten more condemned men were driven with rifle butts to the edge of the pit.

After the second volley the women began to cry out loud and ran out of the crowd in confusion, pulling their children along. The men also began to drift away. The abominable scene of destruction, the screams and groans of the dying, the howls of those who were awaiting their turn, the whole loathsome and shocking spectacle drove people away. Only the ex-frontline men, who were hardened to the sight of death, and the more rabid of the veterans remained.

Fresh batches of barefooted half-naked Red Guards were brought forward, the volunteers were relieved, volleys crashed out and were followed by dry single shots as the wounded were despatched. In the intervals between shootings the layers of the dead were hastily sprinkled with earth.

Podtyolkov and Krivoshlykov went to those who were awaiting their turn and tried to comfort them, but words no longer had any meaning—the men whose lives were about to be snapped off like leaf-stems were possessed by other feelings.

As Grigory Melekhov pushed his way through the scattered crowd on his way back to the village he came face to face with Podtyolkov. Podtyolkov stepped back frowning.

'So you're here too, Melekhov?'

A bluish pallor flooded Grigory's cheeks and he halted. 'Yes. As you see...'

'I do see...' Podtyolkov slanted a smile at him, then stared into his pale face with a sudden blaze of hatred. 'So you're shooting your brothers? You've changed sides?.. That's the kind of man you are.' He stepped up close to Grigory and whispered, 'Serving two masters? The highest bidder, eh? What a man!..'

Grigory seized his sleeve and asked chokingly, 'Don't you remember the battle at Glubokaya?.. The officers were shot on your orders. Weren't they? And now it's come back at you! So don't moan! You're not the only one who can crack other men's skulls! You're finished, chairman of the Don Council of People's Commissars! You sold the Cossacks to the yids, you bastard! Got that? Or d'you want to hear some more?'

Khristonya put his arm round the raving Grigory and led him away.

'Let's go back to our horses, chum. Let's get moving. This is no place for us. Lordy! Lordy! What's come over people these days!'

They walked away but stopped at the sound of Podtyolkov's voice. Hemmed in by ex-frontline men and old men, he was shouting in a voice that surged high with passion.

'You're ignorant ... blind! You're like blind men! The officers have tricked you, forced you to kill your own blood brothers! You think if you kill us, it'll end there? It won't! Today you've got the upper hand, but tomorrow they'll be shooting you! Soviet power will be established all over Russia. Mark my words! You're wrong to shed this blood! Wrong and foolish!'

'We'll deal with the others too!' an old fellow snapped, darting forward.

'You can't shoot everyone, Grandad!' Podtyolkov said with a smile. 'You can't hang all Russia on the gallows. Look after your own head. You'll come out of your fuddle one day, but it'll be too late!'

'Don't threaten us!'

'I'm not threatening. I'm showing you the way.'

'You're blind yourself, Podtyolkov! Moscow's blindfolded you!'

Grigory turned away and almost ran to the yard where his tethered horse, made restive by the shooting, was stamping impatiently. Grigory and Khristonya tightened their saddle girths and rode away over the hill without looking back.

But in Ponomaryov more puffs of smoke rose as the shooting continued, as Cossack killed Cossack.

The pit was full to overflowing. Earth was heaped on it and stamped down. Two officers in black face-masks seized Podtyolkov and Krivoshlykov and led them to the gallows.

Podtyolkov lifted his head proudly and bravely, climbed on to the stool, unbuttoned his collar and, without twitching a muscle, slipped the well-soaped noose on to his brown neck. Krivoshlykov was brought forward, one of the officers helped him on to the stool, and put on the noose.

'Allow me to say my last words before death,' Podtyolkov requested.

'Speak then!'

'Go ahead!' the ex-frontline men shouted.

Podtyolkov pointed to the now much sparser crowd.

'Look how few of you there are left who want to see our death. Conscience can kill! We fought for the toilers, for their interests against that scum, the generals. We were ready to give our lives! And now we are to die at your hands! But we have no curses for you... You have been bitterly deceived! A revolutionary government will be established and you'll realise who was right. You have flung the best sons of the quiet Don into this pit...'

The hubbub rose to such a pitch that Podtyolkov's voice could scarcely be heard. One of the officers took advantage of this and deftly kicked the stool from under his feet. Podtyolkov's massive body twisted and dropped suddenly, but his feet touched the ground. The noose tightened round his throat, choking him and making him stretch upwards. He rose on his bare toes, kicking the damp earth, gulped in air and, looking round at the crowd with eyes staring from their sockets, said quietly, 'So you haven't learned how to hang yet... If I had to do it, your feet wouldn't touch the ground, Spiridonov...'

He foamed at the mouth. The masked officers and the Cossacks near at hand hesitantly lifted the helpless heavy body back on to the stool.

Krivoshlykov was not allowed to finish his speech. The stool flew from under his feet and clattered against a spade that someone had left lying on the ground. His lean muscular body swung for a long time, contracting until the knees almost reached the chin, then stretching out again in a shuddering convulsion... He was still alive, still moving his black lolling tongue when the stool under Podtyolkov was kicked away again. Once more the body plunged heavily, a seam burst on the shoulder of the leather jacket, and again the tips of his toes touched the ground. The crowd gasped. Some of the Cossacks turned away, crossing themselves. So great was the confusion that for a minute everyone stood as though bewitched, staring fearfully at Podtyolkov's darkening, contorted face.

But he was speechless, throttled by the noose. He only rolled his streaming eyes and, twisting his mouth, tried to relieve his suffering by an agonised and terrible stretching upward.

Someone at last found the answer and began to dig hurriedly with a spade, cutting the sods from under Podtyolkov's feet. With every stroke the body hung straighter, the neck lengthened and the slightly curly head was forced back. The rope could scarcely hold the fifteen-stone weight; creaking at the cross-bar it swung gently and, obedient to its rhythm, Podtyolkov swung and turned in all directions, as if to show the murderers his purple-black face and chest flooded with hot streams of spit and tears.

XXXII

It was only on the second night after the alarm that Mishka Koshevoi and Knave left Karginskaya. Mist was foaming across the steppe, swirling in the ravines, creeping into the hollows and licking at the steeper slopes. It fringed the mounds and lighted them from below. The quails were piping in the young grass. And far above, amid the heavens, the moon floated like a full-blown lily in a pond full of sedges and sabre grass.

They walked until dawn. The canopy of stars faded. The dew fell. And just as they topped the ridge some three versts from Lower Yablonovskaya they were overtaken by Cossacks. Six horsemen had been tracking them. Mishka and Knave tried to run, but the grass was short and the moon bright. They were caught and turned back. They walked for about two hundred paces in silence, then a shot rang out. Knave staggered and went stumbling, like a horse frightened by its own shadow, then lay down rather than fell in a greyish-blue clump of wormwood.

Mishka walked on for about five minutes, ears ringing, body dissolving into air, feet dragging along the dry ground.

Finally, he asked, 'Why don't you shoot, you bastards? What are you keeping me on edge for?'

'Keep going. And don't talk!' one of the Cossacks said gently. 'We killed the muzhik, but spared you. You served in the Twelfth against the Germans, didn't you?'

'Yes.'

'You'll live to serve in the Twelfth again. You're still

young. You've strayed a bit, but never mind. We'll cure you!'

Mishka was 'cured' three days later by a court-martial in Karginskaya. In those days the courts had only two punishments: shooting and the rod. Those condemned to be shot were taken to the outskirts at night, but those for whom there was hope of correction were publicly birched on the square.

First thing on Sunday morning, as soon as the bench was placed in the middle of the square, a crowd began to gather. People filled the square, climbing onto stalls, piles of boards, house-tops and the roofs of shops. The first to be thrashed was Alexandrov, the son of the priest of Grachov. The young man was reputed to be a rabid Bolshevik and might well have been shot, but his father was a good priest, respected by all, so the court decided to give the priest's son a score of the best. They took off his trousers and stretched him out on the bench. A Cossack sat on his feet (his hands had been tied under the bench) and two others with bunches of willow rods took their stand on either side. When they had finished, Alexandrov stood up, dusted himself, picked up his trousers and bowed to all four sides. He was so glad not to have been shot that he had to express his gratitude.

'Thank you, esteemed elders!'

'Keep it to sit on, if you like it!' someone replied.

And such a roar of laughter went up over the square that even the prisoners sitting in a shed nearby smiled.

Mishka was also given his twenty strokes. But the disgrace stung more than any pain, for the whole stanitsa—young and old—was looking on. Mishka picked up his trousers and, almost weeping, said to the Cossack who had thrashed him, 'It's all wrong!'

'What is?'

'I thought with my head, but my arse had to answer. I've been shamed for life!'

'Never mind, shame won't hurt you,' the Cossack remonstrated, and as a consolation to his victim said, 'You're a tough nut, lad; I gave you a couple of real hard ones, wanted to make you cry. But no, I saw I wouldn't get a sound out of this one. One fellow we thrashed the other day made a mess all over himself. Weak in the guts, he was.'

The next day, in accordance with the sentence, Mishka was sent off to the front.

Two days later Knave was buried. Two Cossacks from Yablonovskaya, sent by the village ataman to dig the